Accidental Engagement Series- Billionaire Romance Series

THE ENTIRE ACCIDENTAL ENGAGEMENT SERIES

By Bridget Taylor

© 2021

TABLE OF CONTENTS

FREE BONUS CONTENT

Thanks for purchasing Books 1-5 of Bridget Taylor's new series "The Accidental Engagement Series". <u>BEFORE YOU START READING THIS COLLECTION</u> I strongly recommend you sign up to my mailing list below. There is BONUS FREE CONTENT that compliments this book that you can ONLY get from my mailing list.

Just go to https://bit.ly/aebonuscontent to Sign Up to Get Notified of New Releases, Giveaways and Free Bonus Content

MAKE SURE YOU SIGN UP TO Bridget Taylor's VIP list FOR free below. YOU WILL GET LOTS OF

COOL STUFF FOR FREE AND GET NOTIFIED OF ALL THE NEW AND EARLY RELEASES!

Just go to https://bit.ly/aebonuscontent to sign up

*EXCLUSIVE UPDATES

*FREE BOOKS

*NEW REALEASE ANNOUCEMENTS BEFORE ANYONE ELSE GETS THEM

*DISCOUNTS

*GIVEAWAYS

*FREE BONUS CHAPTERS AND CONTENT

FOR NOTIFACTIONS OF MY *NEW RELEASES*:

The Sign-Up Page Will Look Like This:

Join Bridget Taylor's Exclusive Mailing List for FREE BONUS CONTENT and Discount Coupons

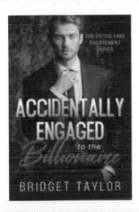

✷ Click below to receive free bonus content, discount coupons, take part in giveaways and get notified of Bridget Taylor's new releases.

✷ A new series is about to be launched. You will be one of the first to be notified with a discount coupon.

CLICK HERE TO SIGN UP

AUDIO BOOK

Make sure you get a copy of the audio book of The Accidental Engagement Series Books 1-5. You're going to want to listen to it as well as read it :-). It's a great compliment to reading and enhances the experience. I strongly recommend you listen as well as read. Especially, if this is something you haven't tried yet. Give it a try. You will LOVE it!

If you have an Audible Membership, go to https://bit.ly/aeboxedsetkindleb ookaudioboxedsetpromo to get The Accidental Engagement Series Books 1-5 Audible Version

For those of you that do not already have one , you can try it for one month for FREE and you can continue after that with a small monthly fee if you wish. You can cancel at anytime. :-)

Just go to https://bit.ly/aebookonekindlebookaudiobook1promo to Try Audible for One Month for FREE and Read the Accidental Engagement Series Books 1-5

The Accidental Engagement

Series Book One

Description

Charles Bentley was always due to inherit his late father's fortune, and he loved to boast about it. He was the typical son of privilege with more money than sense and an appetite for partying that was rarely satisfied - although he did try his hardest. But there's one thing standing in his way of this fortune; a stipulation that states he must marry before his thirty-fifth birthday. With no plans of settling down, but every intention of getting the money, a plan forms in his head.

Jane Miller's world is turned on its head when Charles asks her to marry him. She doesn't know the man, and what she's seen of him so far, she's not sure that there's much to like. But he's willing to pay off *all* of her college debt, and that's an offer that Jane just can't bear to refuse. With his own family determined to see him fail, and Jane fighting her own morals to help him, will they succeed? Or will the secrets of the rich come back to haunt them?

CHAPTER 1

Before you start reading book one on the next page please make you get notified for the release of next series. Go to **https://bit.ly/aebonuscontent** to sign up to get notified of Bridget Taylor's new series coming out and to receive free bonus content and take part in giveaways. If you like this series you will love the next one :-).

Join Bridget Taylor's Exclusive Mailing List for
FREE BONUS CONTENT and Discount Coupons

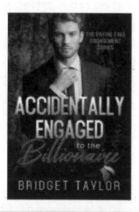

☆ Click below to receive free bonus content, discount coupons, take part in giveaways and get notified of Bridget Taylor's new releases.

☆ A new series is about to be launched. You will be one of the first to be notified with a discount coupon.

CLICK HERE TO SIGN UP

Just go to https://bit.ly/aebonuscontent to follow Bridget Taylor

START OF CHAPTER ONE

Charles woke up with the feeling that someone had tied an elastic band around his head. He groaned and rolled over in his bed as he heard the all too familiar sound of company around him.

"Good morning." A female voice spoke up from next to him. She sounded far too cheerful and clearly wasn't feeling anywhere nearly as rotten as he was. Charles could only respond by groaning as he shut his eyes again.

It was a routine that he knew well; the dance of the morning after. There were different options that now lay ahead of him, different tactics that he was going to have to use to get out of the situation he'd found himself in yet again. The first step was to pretend to go back to sleep, he'd give it another half hour before he'd move onto the second step if the woman still persisted to wait. It worked sometimes, but many of the women who would share a bed with him the night before always seemed so keen to talk about it the next morning. He'd never understood that.

If she was still there after another half hour, Charles would stir long enough to explain that he had a busy day of meetings ahead of him. Some women, the smarter ones, would take the hint and leave promptly. However, there were still the dozy ones who would hang around until he was fully awake.

By that point, Charles was normally thoroughly annoyed by the situation and would call his housekeeper. He knew how much Anna hated dealing with it, he could see it in the way that her face would drop at the mention of the code word, but he always thought that it was better for her to deal with it than him.

His head was hurting much more than usual that morning, but Charles hadn't thought he'd drunk more than usual. He could remember the point in the night when things had taken a turn, it was when he'd bought everyone shots, and many people had wanted to buy him one back to return the favor.

Charles grimaced with his face sunk into his pillow as he faced away from the girl clinging to his back like a small animal. He thought about the many 'friends' he'd made last night, but he'd known deep down that many of them were just trying to siphon free drinks off of him.

His ears were still ringing from the loud music, and the sour taste on his lips told Charles all he needed to know about whether he'd been sick last night...or perhaps it had been earlier that morning. He knew that there was no point in concerning himself with the details, the fog that had settled over the events of last night wasn't likely to lift any time soon.

"The other girl left a while ago, but I thought I'd stick around." The female voice came again.

Charles hoped that his heavy breathing would be enough to convey the idea that he was now fast asleep and not listening to her chatter about the party. However, he was confused that he'd brought two girls home. It wasn't completely out of the question that he would do such a thing, but he was more disappointed that he didn't fully remember it.

Another half-hour passed, and Charles let out a heavy sigh as he realized that he was going to have to move to step two.

"How are you feeling?" The girl asked, as he finally turned around to look at her.

She was pretty, but of course, that was why he'd picked her. She was his typical type; blonde, skinny, slightly tanned, and not much going on upstairs apparently.

"Pretty rough." Charles grunted out his response as he pushed on his arms until he was in a sitting position against the headboard.

The position gave him a chance to survey his domain, and as he'd expected, it was a wreck. The bed was perhaps the only thing that gave the room some kind of order; the blinds were disheveled and looked like they would have to be replaced, clothing littered the floor like the aftermath of some kind of battle, and the room itself smelled like it needed to be aired out.

Charles turned up his nose as he knew that Anna wouldn't be happy to see this, she never was. His only hope was that step two would work and he wouldn't have to summon his poor housekeeper to help him.

"I've got a busy day ahead of me." Charles said, as he stretched and started to rise from the bed. He was hoping that his movements would prompt the girl to do the same, but she remained laid out on the bed.

"A man like you in meetings?" She asked with a laugh.

Charles frowned as he looked at her and tried to remember her name, he was sure that it began with an A.

"Yeah, you don't get rich by just lying around." He shrugged off her question. "And you certainly don't stay rich by doing that either."

She laughed at his comments, and he could feel her eyes on him as he moved to grab a fresh pair of boxers. He wasn't in a laughing mood, and being up on his feet made him slightly dizzy. Nausea was creeping up on him, but he pushed it down in an attempt to regain some stability in his body.

His boxers were on as a knocking sound came from one of the large wooden double doors. His bedroom had impressively high ceilings, and Charles knew that the doors were unnecessarily heavy as a result of their height and thickness. He quickly opened the door for his housekeeper in a feeble attempt to look apologetic as she walked into the room.

Charles thought that he heard Anna curse under her breath as she shook her head and looked around at the state of the room. The girl in his bed covered herself with the duvet as Charles lowered his voice.

"Thank you, Anna, if you could please take out the trash and clean the room, that would be perfect."

He wished that he hadn't looked up to see the glare that Anna was directing at him, although he knew that he definitely deserved it. Charles pushed his floppy hair out of his eyes and flashed her an innocent smile before moving out of the room as quickly as he could.

A bloody mary for his headache awaited him on the terrace, along with a selection of pastries. Charles couldn't help but smirk to himself as he took a seat and stared out over the acres of land that belonged to his family's fortune. The house was impressive in its size, but it was nothing compared to the amount of land that they owned around it - not to mention the other properties that were also in the fortune.

He could hear a slight commotion behind him as Anna walked the girl out of his house. Charles stared straight ahead and didn't dare move as he heard her protests.

"Oh come on, I was with him last night, he knows me! Charles! Charles!" Her voice was getting louder. "Charles, it's me, Lacy! Can't I at least stay a little longer?"

So that was her name, he thought to himself. Charles couldn't help but chuckle as he took another sip of his cocktail, he'd been incredibly far off in thinking that her name started with an A. He then thought of the other girl that Lacy had mentioned, *maybe her name started with an A.*

The ruckus died down and ended with the slamming of a door from downstairs. Charles liked that the terrace looked out over the rear of the large house; he didn't want to know who was coming and going, that wasn't his job.

The sound of footsteps behind him alerted him that he was no longer alone and in his own world on the terrace. However, Charles winced at the idea of talking to Anna about what had happened.

"She's gone, I put her in a taxi and she's gone home." Anna spoke in a matter-of-fact tone.

"Thank you, Anna. I'm sorry that you had to deal with her, but she just wouldn't leave."

"It's fine, Sir." Anna said. "I'm used to it."

The heavy sigh that followed her remark caused Charles to grimace as he thought about how much she must hate her job.

"Right, well thank you for the breakfast." He nodded to the array on the small table in front of them.

"My pleasure, Sir."

Charles waited a moment for her footsteps to fade before breathing out in relief. He knew that she didn't agree with many of the things that he did in his life, but he also had absolutely no plan to change his ways.

"Anna." He called out to her. There was still one thing on his mind. "Was there another woman who left earlier than...L...L-"

"Lacy, Sir." Anna finished for him as she stood in the doorway. "And yes, there was, she left quite early thankfully for you."

"All right, thank you for clarifying." Charles said, as he turned around to nod at her. Anna opened her mouth to say something, but Charles got there first. "I don't want to hear it."

"But you know that this can't continue." Anna fired back.

"I just said that I don't want to hear it."

His housekeeper had always been very vocal in her opinions about how he lived his life, but she was still the only one willing to stay in the job and clean up his messes.

"I'm only saying it because...you know what's coming up." Her voice lowered slightly.

"Anna, I really don't want to have this discussion again."

"Well, you're going to have to have it right now with your cousin, because he's waiting down in the drawing room." Anna fired back at him.

"James is here?" Charles jumped up at the realization. "Get my robe, I'll be down in a moment!"

"I'm your housekeeper, not your assistant."

CHAPTER 2

"James," Charles put on his best smile as he walked down the grand staircase to see his cousin. "You're looking well."

"Ah." James nodded to him as he turned to see Charles approaching. "And you're looking...almost dressed."

"I'm sorry about this." Charles chuckled and tried to brush it off. "A bit of a late one last night."

The velour robe was covering his modesty from his uptight cousin, but he was very much aware of how haggard he must have looked.

"I wouldn't expect anything less." James' response was rather dry. Charles ignored his tone and led him through into one of the many parlors of the house.

It was an old mansion, the kind that old men owned, which made sense since the deeds of it were still in Charles' father's name. He grimaced at the thought of what he would have to do to get it changed to his name.

"You're looking well." Charles said again as the two of them sat down in the plush seats. "Anna, can you have the kitchen prepare us some tea and coffee? Would you like anything stronger, cousin?"

James simply shook his head as he glanced around the room. "I'm not staying too long." James explained as he finally stared at his cousin. "I just wanted to come and talk to you about your birthday arrangements, since you haven't been returning my calls on the matter."

"That's because I've been organizing my own birthday celebrations," Charles waved off the comments.

"I'm not talking about the party, I'm talking about the implications that we both know turning thirty-five will have." James' tone was much more serious as he spoke.

Charles pursed his lips and stared at his cousin with narrowed eyes. "I know what it means, and I know that I'll figure out a way to get around it." He said rather nonchalantly.

"You can't get out of a stipulation like this one, that's the point of it; you have to do what the document says in order to get your inheritance."

Charles thought about this for a while and stared up at the ceiling. It was decorated with gold leaf details and intricate paintings that had been completed by artists that his father had hired.

"I still plan to follow through on what the documents state I should do." Charles said with a curt nod.

"You're going to be married before your thirty-fifth birthday?" James scoffed as he spoke. "And where are you going to find a wife? Do you know how close your birthday is?"

Charles was only becoming more irritated by the conversation as he let his cousin have his taunts. His father's stipulation about marrying before he was thirty-five otherwise he would lose his inheritance was one that had always angered Charles. However, when it had first been proposed, there were many years that stood between him and this problem. Now, there was only a matter of weeks.

"I'll find someone to marry." Charles said, making it sound as casual as though he was looking for someone to work for him.

"And what if you don't? You know that there are plenty of Bentleys around these parts that are willing to step in and take all of this fortune from you. You might find that you're not the sole heir to all of this for long."

"Is that a threat?" Charles asked.

"Only a warning. You know me, I couldn't care less about this family drama, but there are some that are waiting for you to slip up even slightly so that they can pounce."

Charles knew exactly who he was talking about; his uncle and his father's lawyer had been conspiring against him ever since his father had put the stipulation about marriage into the contract. He pursed his lips into a fine line and tried not to think about how irritating the situation was.

"What do you think I should do then?" Charles asked, as he held up his hands.

"You should find someone to marry, and quick." James spoke with a smirk of amusement on his face.

Knowing that his cousin was getting some form of amusement from the fact that he was struggling only irritated Charles further. "I'll find someone." He nodded, prompting only more laughter from James. "Thank you for having such strong trust in my capabilities."

"I'm sorry, but you do realize how ridiculous this is? You're going to have to find a woman to marry in a matter of weeks, do you really think that it will be for love at such short notice?" James asked, as he sat forward in his seat.

Anna's return to the room with a tray of tea and coffee halted their conversation, giving Charles time to think about the question he'd been asked. "I don't need to marry for love if that's not what I want." He shrugged it off once his housekeeper had made a swift exit.

"That's preposterous, everyone wants to marry for love." James said and shook his head.

"I don't feel that it will benefit me in any way, and so I don't feel that I want it at the moment. The marriage will be for the purpose of securing my inheritance."

"With a gold digging woman at your side?"

17

Charles paused before responding. "If that's what it takes."

"For god's sake, Charles, you need to start taking this seriously or they're going to find a way to rob you of what your father wants you to have."

Charles stared out one of the many floor to ceiling windows in the parlor. He was growing bored of the conversation and his headache was persisting despite his previous medicinal attempts.

"I know you don't want to hear this right now, but there will be consequences to your actions, regardless of whether or not you're used to that. I gather that you're not." James said. His words were followed by a heavy sigh as he shook his head and turned to see what Charles was looking at. "Even now, you're acting like a child."

"I'll figure it out." Charles muttered.

"Sure you will." James said. "And I'll be right here to tell you that I told you so when it all goes wrong."

Charles was done talking about it, he wasn't going to resolve the issue while they spoke, and so he saw no reason to continue to talk about it. The conversation finally started to fizzle out as James clearly realized that he was fighting a losing battle.

"All right." He sighed and pushed up from his plush chair. "I'll leave you, but you're going to have to do better than just trying to handle it."

"I'll handle it." Charles responded in a monotonous tone.

He heard his cousin sigh before he exited the room. Charles continued to stare out of the window that overlooked the grounds to the rear of the property. They stretched on for so long that Charles realized for the first time that he didn't really have a proper grasp on how far they extended to. He started to wonder if he could run away through the thick woods that lined his manicured lawn. If it really did stretch on forever, could he not just leave?

"Shall I send in your next appointment for the day?" Anna asked from the doorway after a while.

Charles jolted slightly at her presence; he'd thought he was alone and didn't like the idea of her seeing him so vulnerable, although he was sure that she had seen him in much worse states.

"You know, when I told that girl this morning that I had a really busy day, I was only making it up." Charles said with a groan. "Can you cancel all of my meetings for the day?"

He didn't even bother turning around to receive the glare that Anna was no doubt giving him.

"Of course, Sir." She said finally. Her tone of voice sounded incredibly weary, and Charles took a moment to feel slightly sorry for the woman.

*****

Charles was fully recovered by the evening from his previous night's endeavors, although he ignored the random waves of nausea that would overcome him. He knew that he shouldn't be so lazy with his days, but as he grew older, it was getting harder for him to recover from such taxing nights on his body.

"Can you tell the cook that I'll order in tonight." Charles said, as he waved off Anna.

"Of course, Sir." Anna nodded to him. It was a phrase that she used all the time with him, and Charles realized that when she said it, she was probably imagining that she was saying something less diplomatic to him.

Charles was craving pizza and not the kind that his cook would create in the woodfire oven. He was craving the kind that was greasy and filled with nothing good. He didn't have to wait long, for soon enough the pizza delivery guy was rasping on the expense door knockers outside.

"I'll get it." Charles called before Anna could even come down the stairs.

He didn't mind being waited on most of the time, but after a full day of doing nothing, he felt almost obliged to do the bare minimum of answering his own door. What he hadn't been expecting was the woman on the other side of it.

CHAPTER 3

"I didn't know that they let pretty girls like you be delivery drivers." The man on the other side of the grand door spoke in a silky tone.

Jane wanted to roll her eyes, but she remembered that she was supposed to deliver not just the pizza, but a 'customer experience to be remembered.' The house was large, and the grounds around it were even larger. Jane had ridden on her moped for a good ten minutes to just get down the main driveway. She wasn't supposed to be working so late, but when she saw that order go through, she knew the address straight away and knew that it would mean a big tip was in order.

"Here's your pizza, Sir." Jane said. She ignored his previous remark as she quickly handed out the pizza that was piping hot in her hands.

The man behind the door might have been attractive if he didn't look so haggard. However, there was mischief in his eyes that slightly unnerved her. Jane wanted nothing more than to get off of the grand porch and away from the man before her.

"What's your name?" He asked, as Jane moved to step back.

"It's Jane, and I really should be going. I hope you enjoy your..."

"But I haven't even tipped you yet." He persisted.

Jane was in half a mind to forget about the money completely and just leave, however, her feet remained rooted to the spot.

"Please, come in for just a second, Jane." The man opened the door a little wider. Jane peered in to see that the grandeur from the outside continued on into the interior of the building too. The wooden carvings and pillars were complimented by expensive-looking stone, a mix of old and new that was

21

incredibly stylish. She hovered for two seconds as she pondered on whether it was a good idea or not.

Jane wasn't dumb, she'd seen the horror movies and knew that this was exactly the kind of situation that could lead to her getting locked in a basement. Yet when she peered inside, she could see a woman who looked like a member of staff, and she could hear noises coming from a kitchen somewhere. She took a step forward and stood just inside of the doorway as the man in front of her moved back.

"I'm Charles, by the way." He continued to speak. "Charles Bentley."

The name sounded familiar, but it was an incredibly affluent area, and Jane was sure that there were many rich men with very similar sounding names.

"So what do you do, Jane? Aside from being a delivery driver." Charles asked.

Jane didn't want to engage in too much conversation, and she hoped that by looking down at her scuffed trainers she would give off the impression that she wasn't interested.

"I'm a college student." She kept it vague. "I just deliver takeouts to pay my bills."

"I see." Charles nodded, as he flicked through a rather thick-looking wallet. "And what if I told you that I could pay for your entire college tuition in exchange for one thing?"

Jane blinked as she stared at the man who was now leaning casually against a piece of stone that looked like it cost more than her whole tuition. She couldn't believe that she had heard him just say those words.

"Is this some kind of practical joke?" Jane spoke up.

Charles was wearing a velour robe and radiated an arrogant tone that completely put her off him. She had heard of arrangements like this before between rich men and younger women, however, she'd never considered it as an option for herself.

"I'm not joking." He said with a shrug and a small smirk.

Jane narrowed her eyes as she glanced around the expensive house. Everything within the place just oozed a grandeur that was so far out of her reach. Jane felt like an imposter, but then again, she knew that her tuition was probably nothing to him, it was a small cost for whatever he wanted from her.

Jane sometimes worked twelve-hour shifts just to cover her bare minimum bills, and even then she still struggled. The prospect of someone coming into her life and erasing that stress from it was more of a fever dream than any kind of reality.

"What would I have to do in exchange?" She asked with narrowed eyes. Jane tried to keep her voice neutral in an attempt to avoid letting him know that she was leaning more toward the idea.

"Just one thing." Charles shrugged nonchalantly. "Marry me."

"What?" Jane gasped at him.

"In name only!" He quickly responded.

"I...I..." Jane wasn't sure what she'd been expecting, but it certainly wasn't that. "I don't know what to say..."

"Well, when the time comes, I'm sure that all you'll have to say is 'I do.'" Charles said with a small chuckle.

"I can't tell if you're being serious or not." Jane narrowed her eyes and peered at him in confusion.

"Oh I'm being very serious." Charles said.

"I'm...I don't get it...why?" Jane couldn't shake the confusion from the situation.

"I have my reasons, but I don't feel they need to be disclosed. At least, not until you've agreed to this."

"I still don't understand. I have to marry you and then you'll pay off all my college tuition?" It sounded even less sane when Jane said it out loud.

"Yes, would that be all right? I'm going to have a contract drawn up between us, but we'll be married in name only." Charles reiterated. "That means that you can do what you want, be with who you want. I don't expect you to sleep with me as I don't expect to sleep with you. As I said, it would be in name only."

Jane was suddenly reminded of why she didn't tolerate rich people; they thought that they could have anything and everything that they wanted in some way or another. She scowled at the man in front of her and shook her head. He was preying on the fact that she needed the money.

Jane ignored the fact that she would have to marry the man and thought about how much her life would change if she was to get that kind of money to pay off her tuition.

"If that's not enough, I'll give you more money."

"You can't just buy people, you know." Jane fired back at him.

"I think I can." His tone was suddenly very cutting as he stood up a little straighter.

"I'm not intimidated by you." Jane held her ground.

"I'm not trying to be intimidating, I'm trying to help you."

"Help me?" She scoffed.

"Look, you're clearly the one that needs me." Charles said and held up his hands.

Jane wasn't sure how he'd come to that conclusion since he clearly needed her for something, he just wasn't going to disclose that something with her. "I don't need anyone, never have." Jane shrugged it off.

24

She was growing tired of how arrogant the man in front of her was. Charles was trying to use his power and money to get what he wanted; she was nothing more than an innocent just trying to get by in life, the last thing that she wanted was to help him in any way.

"Well, it sure sounds like you could use my money, if not me." Charles persisted. "Come on, Jane. In name only you will be my wife, but in every other aspect of your life, you're free to do what you want."

Jane stared down at the immaculate floors around her as she considered his offer once again. She was terrified of passing up such a large sum of money; it felt like she had won the lottery in some twisted way and she was now considering not taking it. Jane tried to imagine what her sister Helena would do in the situation or how she would react if Jane took him up on this. She couldn't imagine that she would be too happy to learn that her sister had married an older man all in the name of money.

"And you promise that I'll have my own freedoms to do what I want?" Jane asked slowly. She knew that it sounded as though she was already convinced.

"Of course, you'll get to read over the contract before you sign it." Charles nodded to her.

Jane hated that she could see the hints of a new smirk on his face. She was playing into his hands and she didn't like it one bit. "I'll do it." Jane said with a sigh after another hesitation.

"Really?" Charles' eyes were wide.

"Don't say it like that or I'll change my mind." Jane glared at him again. She didn't like him, but she knew that she wouldn't have to like him to have him pay for her college tuition.

"Fine, thank you very much for being so agreeable." Charles smiled, as he spoke. "I'll make sure that you don't regret this."

"All right." Jane nodded, as she glanced around the house that she was sure she'd be seeing an awful lot more of. "I can't believe I'm doing this." She spoke under her breath, masking it with a heavy sigh.

"Here's my number, and I believe that I already have yours from the delivery site?" Charles asked, as he handed her a small card.

Jane took it and quickly placed it in her pocket as she nodded to him.

"I'll call you to arrange everything, but if you have any other questions, please feel free to give me a call."

Jane held her breath as she blocked out all thoughts of doubt that she was suddenly having about the situation. She pushed away from her anxiety when she thought about how she was going to break the news to her sister, but that was another matter entirely.

"Oh, and one more thing." Charles called to her as Jane turned back towards the doorway. She winced at the idea of there being more than he hadn't told her. "Your tip for the pizza."

Jane glanced at the two notes in his outstretched hand. Two hundred dollars.

She felt her stomach churn in conflict; a mixture of excitement and dread coursed through her as she realized the benefits this would bring to her, as well as the danger of dealing with someone who had more money than sense.

"Thanks." Jane let out a shaky breath as she took the money from him. That action alone felt as though she had just done her first business deal with Charles Bentley, and Jane was positive that it wouldn't be the last.

CHAPTER 4

Jane swallowed thickly as she made her way back to the small apartment that she shared with her sister. The rooms were cramped with peeling paint on the walls and ceilings, and the dingy apartment block was cursed with the perpetual stench of damp. It was a stark slap of reality after the grandeur that Jane had just endured.

This was where she belonged, but the promise of a better life was now firmly in her hands, she just had to go against all of her morals to get to it. Jane grimaced at the thought, although she was sure that Helena, her older sister, would eventually understand.

Jane glanced around their dimly lit apartment with an upturned nose. She had always known that it wasn't the nicest looking place, however, being in the mansion that Charles called his home only made everything look a little worse.

Helena wasn't home yet, but Jane knew that if her shift involved closing, her sister wouldn't be home until dawn. Living in such unglamorous accommodation meant that unglamorous jobs weren't off the table either. Her older sister worked behind a bar in a strip club around the corner, just on the cusp of the dodgy end of town. Jane remembered the time that she had tried to work there with her sister, she knew that they would make an all right amount of income if she did so. But Helena wouldn't let her. She'd told her sister that there were just some things that she didn't want her to see.

Jane was only two years younger than her sister, but at the age of thirty, she liked to think that she could handle herself. She'd gone back to college with the intention of having a better life afterward, however, until recently it had seemed that she was just going to be paying off the debt for the rest of her life. She wanted to get her degree so that she could help people who were living beneath the poverty line as she had once done with her sister, although they were only just above it now. Her non-profit was supposed to be a good thing, and she knew that if she had as much money as Charles Bentley, she wouldn't hesitate to help others.

*****

Jane followed the routine that happened almost every other day; Helena would arrive home just after six in the morning, Jane would have a meager cooked breakfast ready for them both after sleeping for a few hours, Jane would go off to work as Helena would go to bed. They worked like a well-oiled machine. Although it was less oil and more stress, caffeine, and desperation for money.

Her sister's footsteps on the stairs were heavy, but the sound of the door creaking open grated on Jane even more than she had anticipated. Jane winced as Helena walked into the apartment without saying a word. They saw one another often enough that pleasantries felt like too much effort when they were both exhausted. However, Jane was feeling particularly anxious about the conversation ahead of her. She knew that her sister wanted to protect her at all costs, but what she'd done was something that Helena couldn't save her from.

"Good morning." Jane smiled at her, causing Helena to frown.

"What did you do? And why does my breakfast smell so good?" Her older sister frowned and moved closer to her.

"It always smells like this, but I thought I'd add some bacon this morning." Jane knew as soon as she said it, that it was too much. She was acting as though this was all completely normal, but she was still terrified inside.

"You're up to something." Helena narrowed her eyes as she sat down on one of the rickety stools in their kitchen area.

28

Helena had similar dark hair like Jane, although hers were often worn in tight curls and pushed back off her face. Jane always found her sister's work uniform amusing, the skimpy outfit was yet another reminder of why she didn't like the rich. They fell for the fantasy that businesses like the strip club that Helena worked at were selling them, and it worked.

"I got some good tips last night." Helena remarked.

"That's good to hear." Jane smiled over at her sister as she started to plate up the breakfast.

"No trouble?"

"There's never a night without trouble." Her sister chuckled. "Just some guys who'd had too much to drink. They always get so much more handsy after too many shots."

Helena's comments made Jane's skin crawl as she tried not to think about the things that her sister had to deal with.

"What about you? Any trouble with deliveries?"

Helena's question made her want to laugh. To say that she'd had trouble was a gross understatement in describing the night that she'd had.

"Something like that." Jane muttered.

"What was that?" Her sister looked up from the plate that Jane had just served her with a sudden frown.

"It's a really long story, are you sure you want to talk about it now? It can wait until later I suppose." Jane tried to shrug it off.

"Nope, we're doing this now. I knew something was going on." Helena said, as she pushed her plate to the side.

"But your good breakfast is going to go cold." Jane tried one last attempt at deterring her sister.

"Speak."

Jane sighed in frustration. "Fine, but you're not going to like this."

"Well then, you better say it."

"I had to deliver a pizza last night that was out of town, you know on the East Side. The houses over there are incredible, and I only did it because I knew that it would lead to a good tip." Jane paused, as she thought about the two hundred dollars that she still had to declare to her sister.

"Go on."

"Well, the house belonged to...Charles Bentley and he-"

"You know how I feel about the Bentley's." Helena snapped. Her tone was suddenly filled with such venom that Jane had to bite her lip to stop herself from speaking for a moment.

"He offered me a deal, and it was too good to refuse." Jane explained in what she hoped was an innocent tone.

"Don't tell me that you're making deals with the Bentleys now." Helena said with an exacerbated sigh.

"See, I told you that it could wait for later, let's talk about it after you've rested and-"

"What was the deal?" Her sister looked up at her.

"He's going to pay for my entire college tuition." Jane decided to start off with the positive of the situation in an attempt to lessen the blow of the condition attached to it. "But I have to marry him in return."

"What!"

"In name only!" Jane quickly stood up to defend herself.

Helena's eyes were wide and both of her hands were resting flat on the table. Jane was terrified of how her sister was going to react properly when the news had fully sunk in, as it was obvious that for the time being she was in a deep level of shock.

"You're going to marry Charles Bentley?" Helena's voice was surprisingly quiet.

"In name only." Jane said again.

"That's still more than it should be." Her sister fired back.

"Think about it though, he's willing to pay for things. We won't have to struggle like this again, I've found us an out." Jane tried to defend her actions.

"By marrying a rich man! I thought that we always said we'd stay true to ourselves, no matter what."

"I know, but I don't think I could have gone to work today knowing that I had passed on the chance to turn my life around." Jane admitted. "You won't have to work at the strip club anymore, you can go and do something that makes you happy."

"While I watch my sister fall into unhappiness at the price of trusting a Bentley. That doesn't sound like my idea of paradise, Jane."

"I'm sorry, I know that I should have spoken to you first, but I-"

"But you know that I would have told you not to do it." Helena finished the sentence for her.

"He put me on the spot!"

"And you let him buy you!"

Jane had nothing to respond to her sister's harsh words. She knew deep down that Helena was right, but she wished more than anything that she could deny it. "I'm sorry, but I promise this will make life better in the end. I don't care what the cost is for me, I'll marry the guy, but I won't have any debt and that's all that matters." Jane stood her ground.

"You've really let him convince you into this, haven't you?" Helena asked with a sigh.

"I have to do this, Helena."

"God, I would have even let you work with me behind the bar over this." Her sister scoffed. "You know how ridiculous this sounds?"

"I do." Jane nodded.

"And you know what people will think and what they'll say behind your back?"

"I'm hoping that news won't get around about it, to be honest." Jane said.

"Don't be so naive, you can't afford to be naive in the world of the rich. In fact, you can't afford much in the world of the rich because it isn't your place."

Her words stung, but they were honest. Jane knew that she was playing in a game where she had no right to even be a pawn, yet she was playing regardless.

"It's going to be all right. It's a temporary measure to get us enough money to live comfortably." Jane said.

She was keeping her voice deliberately steady and didn't let it waver as she stared at her sister. There was no way that Helena could talk her out of it since Jane had already agreed to it, but she knew that she was still going to try.

"I don't care about that, think about your pride for god's sake. You clearly have none if you're willing to let a man like him pay for you to live." Helena shook her head as she spoke.

"All I can see is that this will be a good thing, it will help us. You might be used to this, but I'm not. I can't live like this anymore, not when there are people out there like Charles who can help us."

The silence that followed her words felt too loud. Jane winced at how harsh she sounded toward her sister. She hadn't intended to sound so cutting with her words, but she was sick of Helena thinking that she was better than her and that she couldn't handle herself.

"You're going to feel like a fool for trusting a Bentley." Helena's voice was low.

"I guess only time will tell." Jane said with a shrug.

"I'm going to get some sleep." Helena muttered as she pushed her untouched breakfast to the side and got up from the table.

Jane felt a lump forming in her throat at how the situation had been left. She didn't want to fight with her sister, she was all Jane had left, but she knew that Helena wasn't going to come around easily on this particular subject. There was nothing left for her to do but head to work. Jane might have solved all of her financial woes, but her boss didn't know that yet.

CHAPTER 5

"Any news on the inheritance front?" James asked deliberately, much to Charles' annoyance. He sat on the back porch of his large house with a glass in hand, and he would much rather be having different conversations.

His cousin was accompanying him, along with one of his least favorite people in the world. Charles held a certain disdain for his aunt and uncle, however, that same feeling was also extended to his father's lawyer. Wyatt Tucker was a weedy man that couldn't be trusted with an ounce of anything. Charles knew that the lawyer disliked him just as much in return, and he was always scheming something that would trip him up. The stipulation to getting his father's inheritance was a particular point that Tucker liked to press on almost every time that he encountered Charles.

Charles waited for the lawyer to take a sip of his iced tea before responding to his cousin's question. "As a matter of fact, yes." Charles spoke confidently. "I'm engaged."

He pressed his lips into a fine line in an attempt to make his smirk of amusement less obvious. Tucker coughed slightly on his drink and squinted his eyes shut. Even James, who usually wasn't too interested in family diplomacy, looked startled by the revelation.

"What?" Tucker asked in a much louder voice than Charles had been expecting. "How?"

"Well, I asked a girl, and she said yes, and now we are getting m-"

"Don't be smart with me, boy!" The older man scolded him. "I mean, how did this happen? You've always been so against settling down."

"I know, but the stipulation states that I have to in order to get my father's inheritance." Charles said with a nonchalant shrug. He was quite enjoying being the one to deliver such shocking news to the two men before him.

"Who is this girl?" Tucker peered at him.

"She's nice, a little younger than me, doing well for herself." Charles kept it as brief as he could.

"Do we know the family? Is she well connected?"

Charles thought about what he knew of Jane; she was a delivery driver who was struggling her way through college, it didn't sound like she was well connected to him. He'd also found her rather uptight, and there was a look in her eyes that she'd given him a few times that he wasn't too fond of. He could practically feel the judgment coming off of her, and he could only imagine what she must have been thinking about him. However, he didn't care, she needed him just as much as he needed her, and that meant that he could ensure she'd go through with it.

"She's connected well enough, she's got this far in life successfully." Charles shrugged off his questions.

"And you...love this woman?" Tucker asked with narrowed eyes.

Charles didn't give off any outward sign that he was thrown by the question, he knew that it was bound to come up, but he hadn't expected Tucker of all people to be the one to ask. The dilemma of how to answer it was one that Charles had been thinking about in the days after his first encounter with Jane. It had already been three days since then, and Charles was sure that she was deliberately keeping her distance from him.

"I think love is a very subjective thing." Charles began as he stared out over the lawn. He could practically see the obvious eye-roll that Tucker was giving him. "But in the way that I understand it, yes I do."

35

He thought it was a very clever way to get around the question, but as he looked back at the two men, James had an amused smirk on his face, and Tucker held his head in his hands. "I don't know what you've done, but you have to go through with this stipulation the natural way. You can't get around this and you won't get around this, I'll see to it myself." Tucker said, as he rose from his seat and grabbed his jacket.

"Goodbye, Tucker. Always a pleasure." Charles said dryly, as he didn't look over his shoulder to watch the lawyer leave.

The silence that followed Tucker's exit was quite comforting. Charles felt relieved to not have to answer any more of his accusative questions. Being part of the Bentley family often felt like he was on trial, especially with the way that Tucker investigated affairs, and Charles was rather sick of it.

"Is it true? Or were you just winding him up?" James asked with a light chuckle as he sat down in Tucker's former seat.

"It's true." Charles nodded with a grin. "I've found somebody who's willing to marry me before my thirty-fifth birthday."

"And she's comfortable going through with this?" James was laughing, although Charles was sure that it was a laugh of disbelief.

"As far as I'm aware." Charles nodded.

"I don't believe it." James shook his head. "I knew that you'd find a way to get around this, but deep down, I hoped you'd just find someone to love and marry. I want you to be happy, Charles, I really do, but you have to be open to these things. How did you convince her anyway?"

"I'm paying off her student loans." He responded.

"Charles." James pinched the bridge of his nose as he spoke. "She's marrying you for the money?"

"No, I'm basically paying her to marry me in name only. I've already told her that she's free to do as she pleases, heck, she doesn't have to see me if she doesn't want to." Charles chuckled as he spoke. "I know that it might sound stupid, but it's the only way that I can see me getting through this stipulation."

"What if Tucker finds a way to get around it too?" James sounded a lot more serious now.

"How would he do that? I have to marry someone before I'm thirty-five, and that's what I still plan to do." Charles couldn't see how his plan could go wrong; he was doing everything that he was told to do, and there was nothing wrong with the circumstances around it as far as he knew.

"But if he does find a way, that inheritance goes straight to your Uncle Jack and Aunt Rosalyn."

"I won't let them get the chance." Charles shook his head.

"Is she pretty at least?" James asked.

"She is." He nodded. "Although, she's a delivery driver."

"Christ." James couldn't hold back his laughter. "You know that the rest of the family aren't going to like this?"

"I know." Said Charles. "But just because I don't want to marry another rich girl from another of the wealthy families in the area doesn't mean that they should be cruel."

"You've literally picked someone off the street and you're going to pay her to marry you." James said while laughing again. "They're going to use every part of this to get to you."

"If you're referring to Uncle Jack, I can handle him."

"And his snobby wife?"

"She can't say a word about my situation, she's a gold digger herself." Charles quickly fired back.

"I'd pay to see you say that to her face." James chuckled. "But seriously, you're going to have to make up some kind of story as to how the two of you met. It's not going to cut it if you say she turned up on your doorstep to deliver something to you."

"Well, I'll think about that closer to the time when I introduce her to everyone." Charles waved it off. "Anyway, I was thinking of going out tonight if you wanted to join me? A celebration of my triumph at finding someone."

"I don't think I should, besides, I can never keep up with you."

Charles knew that he could go very hard with his partying if he wanted to. He'd seen his cousin do the same for a few years, but James had recently calmed down a lot with his own partying. "You're killing me, James, just one or two drinks?" Charles suggested.

"All right fine, but that will be it." James said with a sigh. "I'm going to need it if you're going to announce to the family that you're engaged to a delivery driver."

Charles knew that his family could be very elitist in their ways. It often led to them donning descriptions such as being out of touch and rather harsh with people who were viewed as lower in class to them. It made them unlikeable, but Charles knew that this opinion of the Bentleys wasn't new information. It was something that had followed them for generations. He thought about how his family would react to Jane; she was pretty enough, and he was sure that with the right style advice, he could help make her look presentable for them. However, he wasn't sure that she was going to fit in when the time came to make polite conversation.

He pulled out his phone and found her contact almost immediately. Charles didn't like the idea of her judgmental eyes being on his once more, but he knew he was going to have to see her for the next few weeks. He waited for James to leave him on his own before dialing the number.

"Jane? Hi, it's Charles...Charles Bentley." He began and rose from his chair to speak to her.

"Hi Charles." She responded with a weary sigh.

"I was just wondering if you could come over tomorrow?" He didn't like the way that his voice sounded. It was as though he were back in high school and was nervous while talking to his crush for the first time. He scolded himself for being so ridiculous; he didn't feel that way for her, he was just tentative and didn't want to upset her in case it deterred her from going through with his plan.

"Uh...well I have work in the day and-"

"Great, so how much would you normally earn during those hours?" Charles asked, as he reached for one of his checkbooks.

"Uh...uh, I...what? Why?" Jane said from the other side of the line. He could hear the confusion and panic that had welded together in her voice.

"Because I'll give you the money for it tomorrow," Charles spoke, as though it were an obvious answer to her question.

"Oh...right, that's okay I really need to work and I can't give my boss such short notice so-"

"Okay, I'll double it?" He offered.

His words were followed by silence on the other end of the line as Jane hesitated. "W-what time did you want me to be there for?"

CHAPTER 6

Jane parked her moped on the gravel outside of the grand house as she gawked at it for the first time in full daylight. The mixture of modern and gothic worked so well and was complemented by the perfectly manicured grounds that extended out in every direction from the main house. She couldn't believe that the man who owned all of that was wanting to marry her, it still felt like some kind of stupid dream that Jane would have after eating something off for dinner. Once her bike was parked and secured - although Jane was sure that nobody would steal it - she walked hesitantly up the stairs to the grand doors. She remembered how in awe she had been of even the doors that night when she'd delivered his pizza. Jane laughed as she realized that she really hadn't had any idea of how much her life was about to change.

The knockers themselves were so large that she had to use two hands just to get a good enough grip around it to rasp it against the wood of the door.

"I'm here to see, Charles Bentley?" Jane spoke up as the housekeeper appeared in the doorway.

The woman gave her a good look up and down with small, beady eyes before turning to look over her shoulder.

"He is expecting me." Jane added as she realized that she was going to be faced with barriers like this throughout this experience.

Helena's words were echoing through her mind as she felt that this encounter only reinforced how much she wasn't supposed to be there. She was supposed to be delivering pizzas across town, but with the promise of more money, Charles Bentley was getting his way again.

"Mr. Bentley is still sleeping at the moment, but you can wait in the front parlor." The housekeeper spoke slowly.

Jane nodded quickly and stepped into the house, aware of the way that the housekeeper was still scanning her attire. She was dressed simply in jeans, sneakers, and a hoodie, nothing that would normally scream out of the ordinary. However, under that roof, she looked like a smear of dirt against a white wall.

The housekeeper led her through to one of the many rooms on the ground floor. Jane wasn't sure that she would get used to a house that large, it felt uncomfortably vast in size, and she couldn't understand why one man needed so much space.

Jane checked her watch again - doing the maths quickly in her head as it was twelve minutes fast but she never had enough money to fix it - she had arrived right at two o'clock. Charles had sounded rather urgent in his demands on the phone the day before, and she had assumed that it was an urgent matter since he was going to pay her double her daily wage.

She tried not to think about how her sister had looked at her when she told her that she wasn't going to work that morning, but instead she was going to the Bentley residence that afternoon.

"I'll go and urge him to get dressed." The housekeeper said, as she turned to leave the room. "Can I get you any refreshments while you wait?"

"Uh...no, I'm good, thanks." Jane shook her head as she spoke. She wasn't used to meetings being so formal like that. She thought about the odd occasion when she would get to go and visit her friends, it was never anything like the experience that she was having at that moment. The housekeeper nodded to her one more time before leaving her alone in the large room.

Jane stood up almost immediately as she started around the room to inspect the various items of interest and elaborate decorations. She was still trying her hardest to process the change in the environment that she was going through constantly; from this morning in their dingy apartment to now being in one of Charles Bentley's many parlors felt so wrong in so many ways. Jane wanted to tell someone about how insane this was and how beautiful she found the house, but she knew that there was no point in gushing to her sister about the grandeur that she was being paid to take in.

Jane walked over to the beautiful fireplace that dominated one half of the room. Intricate carvings had been made into the wood that Jane followed with her fingers as she took in the gold leaf details that accented the wood. The precious stone tiles around the wood looked like some kind of colored jade, and Jane was rather impressed with herself for being able to identify something like that.

Of course, she'd never been able to see something that expensive up close, and so it felt as though with each step that she took, she was experiencing something for the first time.

The plush couches in the room were stitched with a velour material and the cushions were accented with thick tassels of wool. A glass table stood in the center where the couches circled, although if one were to catch the light at a wrong angle, it became almost invisible to the eye.

Jane was careful as she skirted around the table and moved over to the windows. She was known for being clumsy, and the expression 'bull in a china shop' had never felt more apt.

Upon glancing out over the front lawn, Jane could see how much her moped stuck out as an anomaly over the otherwise perfect landscape. A white fountain sat in the center of the driveway, with a path pathed perfectly out of the gravel and encircling the water feature. The garage was around the corner and out of sight, but Jane could imagine the kinds of cars that a man like Charles must own.

She was still incredibly confused as to why he was sleeping at such a late hour of the day. But then again, Jane corrected herself as she realized that there wasn't much in the world that Charles Bentley had to worry about. She was perhaps one of the only things that were of his concern at that moment since he was about to marry someone who was a virtual stranger to him and she still didn't know why. Jane waited for another twenty minutes before she heard movement from out in the main hall of the house.

"Jane." Charles said, as he opened the large, painted doors and walked into the room. "Have my breakfast brought in here, Anna." He called back to his housekeeper. "I'm sorry to have kept you waiting."

"It's fine." Jane shrugged it off. She was slightly irritated to be kept waiting after thinking that it was an urgent matter, but then she remembered the money, and she knew that she had no grounds to be annoyed.

"It's not, I truly apologize. I'm normally much better with my time-keeping." He said, as the housekeeper appeared with a tray and set it down on the table. At his words, Anna couldn't help but scoff and she shook her head.

"Could you go and attend to the kitchens, Anna? The cook might need help with the washing up and I can pour my own tea, thank you." Charles spoke with a rather pointed look aimed in her direction.

"Of course, Sir." Anna muttered, as she left the room.

"Sorry about her, she's worked here for so long that she forgets her manners." Charles stated and waved it off.

Jane couldn't help but realize how old-fashioned the rich were. He was so proper in his ways and still used his manners when talking to the staff, which Jane hadn't expected from him at all. Although the rich were rude, they sure knew how to upkeep their manners while doing so.

Now that it was light outside, she could see his features clearly; Charles could be a good looking man if he kept himself a little better, his brown hair was growing into long curls on top of his head and the shadow of unkempt stubble persisted around his sharp jaw. He had piercing blue eyes that seemed to be able to understand situations very quickly, and only reinforced her previous perception of him that he was actually very sharp beneath his nonchalant persona.

"So what did you want to see me about?" Jane asked, as she sat opposite him and crossed one of her legs over the other.

"I wanted to talk to you about meeting my family." Charles said, as he looked up from setting his teapot down.

"Buy me dinner first." Jane said with a sarcastic chuckle.

"I know, I know." he held up his hands. "It's a weird situation to be in, and I understand that this is all going to be very strange for you. But I thought that we should at least spend some time together before we pull this off."

"May I ask why you want me to go through with this?" Jane asked with narrowed eyes. She was feeling particularly brave as she questioned him.

"Yes, well I suppose you should know since you've now agreed to it." He said with a sigh. She waited patiently as Charles stirred his tea rather slowly. Jane could tell that he was stalling, and she was starting to regret asking him such a question. "There's a stipulation in the way of me getting my inheritance from my father." He finally began as he blew on the tea. "I am the sole heir of his fortune you see, and so he wanted to make sure that I would do good with the fortune. The stipulation states that I must be married before my thirty-fifth birthday in order to have the inheritance that I deserve."

Jane looked slightly stunned at the revelation. She couldn't even imagine having a parent put such an obstacle in her way unless they knew that her behavior needed correcting.

However, when she looked at Charles, that was exactly what she saw; a grown man with a behavior issue due to his privilege.

"So all of this just because you want to inherit your father's fortune?" Jane spoke slowly as she finally understood his motivations for needing to marry her.

"Exactly." Charles nodded.

"And you just happened to ask the first person that you saw?" Jane couldn't help but smirk at how that sounded.

"Well, you weren't the *first* person that I saw, but you were the first person to say yes." He said with a shrug.

"I don't believe you."

"All right, it's something I've known about for quite a few years now, but I've never done anything about it." Charles sighed.

"And how old are you now?"

"Thirty-four, soon to be-"

"Thirty-five." Jane breathed out as she nodded. "Of course."

"Does it make a little more sense now?"

"It does, but I still think you should have tried a little harder to at least find someone that you would have liked to marry." Jane said.

"Well, I'm not ready for marriage. A serious marriage."

"You mean the kind where you remain faithful to the person you love?" Jane liked how her blatant words were making the wealthy man shift in his seat. His eyes narrowed for a moment as he thought about her comments.

"Look, I have my own reasons for not wanting to get married, and if it wasn't for this stipulation, then I wouldn't be getting married at all." He said.

"All right, is that all you wanted to discuss?" Jane was already sick of him and they weren't even married yet.

"No, I wanted to talk more about you meeting certain members of my family." Charles continued.

He sat up a little straighter and sipped at his tea as he spoke. Jane waited patiently for him to put the teacup down and resume what he was talking about.

"I was hoping that we would have a little more time before this, but they are anxious to meet you." He explained.

"I'm not sure that I'm able to say the same for my family...well, my sister." Jane responded.

"It's just the two of you?"

"As of recently, yes." Jane said, although she didn't elaborate. Her own family history wasn't something that she wanted to get into with someone like him.

"I'm sorry to hear that." Charles said in a mutter, although she didn't believe him. "In terms of my own family, it's just my uncle and aunt that I have to warn you about the most. Oh, and also my father's lawyer."

"What's so bad about them?" Jane asked with a frown.

"They are sharp-tongued, elitist people who are greedy and only think about themselves."

Jane had to refrain with all of her might from saying anything to do with the fact that this was the exact image that she had of how he was. She bit her lip and nodded slowly along with his words.

"They would rather see me struggling than thriving, I don't know what kind of family would do that." He said and shook his head.

"It's more common than you think." Jane's response was rather nonchalant.

"I don't know about you, but I won't let my family beat me on this. That's why everything has to run smoothly in terms of the engagement and the wedding. I can't have them thinking that this is all just a stunt to get the money, even though it is."

"So you want me to play along with your little charade as well as marry you?" Jane asked.

She was using any opportunity that she could to at least get a little more out of the situation for herself. Jane knew that if the roles were reversed, Charles would do the same. She knew that the way she was playing him was enough to make her older sister proud.

"All right, what do you want?"

"My sister works an awful job, and I want her to have the financial freedom so that she doesn't have to work that job anymore." Jane spoke plainly.

"Done, how much do you need?" Charles sighed, as he reached for a checkbook.

Jane had to blink a few times as she realized how easily these things were happening to her. It felt as though Charles had just fallen out of the sky as her own personal guardian angel, although he didn't always act like one.

"I...I'll need to talk to her, but I'll have a figure with you by the end of the week?"

"Of course, but you know, for you to receive all of the money for your tuition, you really do need to go through with this."

"I'm prepared for that." Jane nodded curtly.

"Good, then it's a pleasure doing business with you, Miss. Miller." Charles said with a small smile playing on his lips.

"So you had a heavy night last night?" Jane asked, as she quickly diverted the attention away from the subject of money.

"What makes you say that?" Charles frowned.

"Well, it's two o'clock in the afternoon and you're having breakfast." Jane said while gesturing to the tray in front of him. It was the first time that she was noticing the bloody mary on said tray, which only further backed up her point.

"We were...celebrating last night." He explained. "Celebrating that I'm going to have a lot of money to inherit when this is over."

"I think you mean that we are going to have a lot of money to inherit." Jane said with a small smile. "I'm joking." She chuckled after registering the slight look of panic on his face.

"We're definitely going to have a prenup signed before there's an 'I do' from either of us." Charles muttered. "We are having separate bank accounts still, but you have my word that I will keep up my side of the bargain. I have no reason to betray you if you help me, and you don't even have to take my name."

"I wasn't planning on it." Jane said dryly.

She was aware that he knew she didn't like him, it wasn't a fact that Jane was trying to hide. She didn't want him to be under any kind of illusion that she admired him in this situation. Of course, he had a lot of money, and his father's fortune was something to be admired. But Charles had done nothing for that fortune but party and pretend to be an adult all of his life while staff waited on his every need.

She didn't feel the need to tell him this, because it was all said in a singular look that she gave him. Jane did want to chuckle at the thought of taking his name though, she could imagine the look on Helena's face if she came home one night as Jane Bentley. They may not have fought about much, but that could have easily been a tipping point in their relationship.

"Back to my uncle." Charles said, as he sipped at the bloody mary. She could see the hint of a grimace as he tasted it, and Jane was almost positive at that stage that he was still hungover from whatever he'd been doing the night before.

"Oh yes, your dreaded uncle who sounds just like an older version of you." Jane nodded.

She wasn't sure where the courage had come from that prompted her to say that out loud, but she was past caring. Charles had made it clear that he was going to pay her if she stuck this through, however, he didn't say that she had to stick it through quietly.

"Right." He said after a long hesitation. "Uncle Jack can be rather good at...pressing on uncomfortable issues. For instance, if you have a troubled past, he does love to go poking his nose into business where it doesn't belong. He always thinks that family dinners are the perfect places to bring them up too."

Jane turned her nose up at the idea of having to sit around a grand table as more Bentleys were fed with silver spoons. Helena's words were nagging at her again. *You don't belong there.*

"He's really that bad?"

"He's the worst." Charles nodded. "And he doesn't want me to marry before my thirty-fifth birthday, so I fear he's already planning to disrupt it in some way. If I don't follow through with the stipulation, then all of the fortune goes to him."

Jane couldn't believe how greedy one family could be. She was amazed at how money could make some people turn on even their own blood.

"You said about a lawyer too?"

"Yes, Wyatt Tucker." Charles made a face as though he'd taken another sour sip of his bloody mary. "He's also the worst."

"Lawyers generally aren't the best, especially the most expensive ones." Jane agreed.

"Well, Tucker is much worse than you could even imagine. He also doesn't like me and will stop at nothing to make sure that I don't inherit that money."

"It sounds like this inheritance has created a lot of enemies for you." Jane remarked.

"It has, my own blood would rather see me turned out." Charles said. "I know that it sounds as though we're all guilty, but it is hard having family betray me like this."

"I'm sure." Jane was slightly mocking him, but he hadn't yet caught on.

There wasn't a single bone in her body that felt even a little sorry for Charles Bentley. She guessed that he was taking her for a fool if she really was going to fall for his pity party about his family betraying him.

"Anyway." Charles continued. "These are all characters that you're going to have to meet in due course. I'm sure that there will be a few dinners before the actual wedding, but we do need to have a formal dinner soon to announce our engagement."

"And the wedding itself, it's going to be a relatively small affair?" Jane asked hopefully. She didn't want a flashy wedding with members of the press covering it. The last thing that she wanted was her name in magazines or even just being associated with the Bentley name.

"No, it's going to be a small gathering here. It's in name only, remember? So there's no point spending money on a wedding that the bride and groom don't even want to attend."

Jane knew that he had a point, but the entire situation was still incredibly strange to her. She nodded and managed a small smile as she thought about meeting more people like Charles. Her stomach churned slightly.

CHAPTER 7

Charles dropped his smile as soon as Jane was led out of the room by Anna. He didn't like her, and she certainly didn't like him. He took his half-empty bloody mary glass with him as he walked through the labyrinth that was the house's ground floor until he made his way to the back of the house.

Curled up on one of the plush sofas and stinking of alcohol was the same man who had said twenty-four hours previously that he would only go out for one or two drinks.

"Good morning, sunshine." Charles said with an amused smile.

James only groaned in response.

"This is why I never say yes to going out with you." James sighed, as he managed to roll onto his back. It looked like it took him a lot of energy to do so, and Charles felt slightly bad for letting his cousin suffer in such a way.

"You missed the special guest." Charles said. He couldn't help the bitterness that seeped into his tone when he talked about her.

"Are you talking about the girls from last night or the one you're supposed to be marrying?" James may have looked as though he were on his deathbed, but he was still able to squeeze out a joke.

"It was Jane, and she wasn't as happy to see me as she seemed last time." Charles said, as he took a seat opposite James. "You know, I thought she could have at least been a little more polite towards me since I am going to get rid of all the debt she owes. Oh, and I've also agreed to pay for her sister's way in life too."

"You need to stop being so generous." James said.

Charles couldn't tell if his cousin was being sarcastic or not. However, he quickly shook it off and decided that it wasn't worth picking at.

"I told her about Uncle Jack and Tucker." He changed the subject.

"Did that scare her off?"

"No, but I don't think she fully understands how bad they can be." Charles sighed and rubbed a hand over his slightly clammy face.

"Oh." James laughed while his eyes closed. "She's going to be in for a shock at her first dinner then, when is that by the way?"

"This weekend, I'm pretty sure?"

Charles was suddenly filled with dread at the thought of having to prepare her again for what would surely be a hellish night. They were going to have to rehearse things like where they met, how they got together, where they've been on dates. There was so much information, not enough time, and not enough willingness to cooperate between them that the entire situation was already feeling impossible.

"I don't know if I can do this." Charles groaned, as he threw himself back until he was lying down on the sofa like James was.

"You're going to have to find a way to do it." James said honestly.

"And what if you're right? What if they pick it apart and my plan unravels?"

"You're only having hopeless thoughts because you feel like crap right now. Wait until you're better to plan it."

Charles nodded at his cousin's advice, although he wasn't sure how good it was. Time was running out and he was going to have a lot of big decisions to make rather quickly.

"But what if we really can't pull this off?"

"Shut up, Charles, you sound pathetic." James sighed, as he rolled over.

He could tell that his cousin's hangover was clearly much more violent than his own, and Charles knew that it would be foolish to push James to his limit.

*****

Jane was even more confused by the time that she arrived home. She wasn't sure what to make of her encounter with Charles in the light of day. All she could be sure about was that if she played her cards right, she could get a lot of money from the situation.

"So how was it?" Helena asked, as she glanced up from her seat on the couch. During her days, she normally would awaken in the late afternoon before getting ready for work in the evening. Jane couldn't even imagine what it must be like to completely change your routine around to fit a work schedule, although she was getting a taste of it now that she was having to go for meetings with Charles.

"It was all right, he just wanted to talk." Jane said with a shrug as she sat down next to her sister.

"Just talk?"

Jane's eyes widened as she realized what her sister was alluding to. She hated that it was even a question that was coming between them. "Just talking." Jane spoke again but in a much more cutting tone.

"All right, all right, forget I asked." Helena sighed in defeat.

"Do you really think that I would sleep with a man like that?" Jane asked in horror.

"Well, at the moment I really don't know what you're capable of!" Helena fired back.

"Oh come on, I'm doing something that we haven't been able to do before. Like I said the other morning, I've got us a way out of this life."

"At what cost?" Helena was quick with her words.

"That doesn't matter, the cost doesn't matter."

"It will." Helena nodded. "Because one day you'll look back on this and you'll wonder if it really was that great of an idea after all. I just don't want you to regret doing something so stupid and rash."

Jane was quiet for a while as she thought about her sister's words, they felt like they had another meaning behind them. Helena sounded as though she was in pain as she spoke, she sounded as though she was trying to hold back tears.

"I don't know what you mean, Helena. I...I don't regret it so far, and I don't think I'm going to any time soon. Besides, I spoke to Charles today about you too, and he said that he can help you financially so that you don't have to work in the strip club bar anymore-"

"No." Helena cut her off quickly. "I don't want a penny of that family's money."

"Why are you so against them? I don't understand it." Jane narrowed her eyes in frustration. All she wanted was to better understand her sister's resentment because it felt a lot deeper than just because they were rich and the Millers weren't.

"That's not a conversation that I want to have right now, all right?"

Jane knew that tone from years of experience, and she also knew that Helena meant what she said when she used it. She decided not to press the issue any further since there was clearly nothing good that would come from it.

"We're going to have to go to dinners with the other members of the family." Jane recalled from her earlier conversation with Charles.

"No."

"You're seriously going to make me go to them alone?" Jane asked in disbelief.

"It wasn't me that made this stupid pact in the first place, was it?" Helena said while shaking her head. "I'm not a part of this deal, and I'm not going to accept their hospitality. I don't want to go to dinners with the family, heck, I don't think I'll even show at the wedding."

"It's not going to be a real wedding, Helena." Jane snapped in a sharper tone than she had anticipated.

"Then there's no need for me to show up, is there?"

She hated when her sister was in that dismissive kind of mood. There was no reasoning with her, and Helena knew exactly what she was doing.

"If this really works and I can start up my non-profit with this family's help, then it could be really successful and-"

"And you're going to owe them a massive debt, don't you see?"

"I'm not going to owe them anything, I'm doing Charles a favor, and he's doing one for me. That's how this is working. He's paying off my debts so that I won't owe anyone anything."

Jane hated having to defend someone like Charles, but she also hated the way that the entire situation was making her fight with her sister. They'd had peace in their household for so long, their bond had never been stronger, and now it was back to the old times.

"You're going to end up as one of them, I can just see it." Helena spoke, as though it were an insult.

"I really don't want to argue about this." Jane said with a heavy sigh.

"Well then why did you sign your soul away to the devil?"

"Stop being so dramatic!"

"I'm the one being dramatic? You're the one marrying a guy so that you can go to college for free!" Helena had raised her voice to a level that made Jane wince, and their neighbor above stomp on the floor. Their action caused a thin trail of dust to float down from where the paint has flaked away so much that the ceiling boards were exposed.

"You work in a strip club, and I know that you give me that crap about working behind the bar, but I bet you do more for your money!"

Jane knew that she had crossed a line almost as soon as the words flew out of her mouth. She quickly clasped a hand to her mouth as her eyes widened. Helena was glaring at her with slightly glassy eyes as their neighbor above stomped on the floor once more.

Jane watched as her sister's nostrils flared, but she knew that there was no stopping Helena's anger once it had been ignited.

"I'm sorry, I didn't-"

"Get out."

Jane didn't have to be told twice. After grabbing her jacket and keys as quickly as she could, Jane burst out of the old apartment building and out into the fresh air of the evening. The sun was already setting, and she had no idea where to go.

Helena would be getting ready for work over the next couple of hours while simultaneously cooling off, but Jane had no plan to return to their apartment any time soon. She knew that she was going to need to do some serious groveling to give her an apology that was worth enough. Jane felt awful about how she had spoken to her sister, but she had much the same kind of angry streak within her, and Helena had pushed her too far.

Her blood was boiling as she thought about the verbal blows that her older sister had dealt her. Jane didn't like the way that Helena always tried to act better than her, but it had never come out as much as it had that evening. She grimaced as she thought about just how much this marriage was going to cut a divide through the bond she had with her sister.

"Charles? Hey, it's me...Jane." She spoke into her phone with a reluctant sigh.

"Hi, is everything all right?"

Jane could hear the reservations in his tone, but she chose to ignore it.

"Uh...well I've sort of had a fight with my sister and she's kicked me out for a few hours. I'm not expecting a knight in shining armor moment, but I sort of wouldn't like to be on the streets out here after dark. It's a little scary."

"I'll send a car over if you text me your location?" He spoke rather dismissively.

"Sure, thank you so much."

Jane hadn't known what she'd been expecting, but that response wasn't it. She glanced down at her attire and knew that this staple combination of jeans and a hoodie really wasn't going to cut it while she was with him. However, her current circumstances had dictated for her that there was no hope of going back to the apartment and changing.

As she waited for the car to arrive, Jane found herself trying to make light of the situation. If 'sending a car over' was the modern-day rich person equivalent of saving a damsel in distress, then Jane had decided that chivalry was well and truly dead. The dark car that did pull over on the side of the street left Jane with no doubts that it was for her to get into. It was a black Mercedes with completely tinted windows and a private number plate, it was perhaps the grandest private Uber she would ever get into.

Jane hadn't realized just how far she'd walked away from her apartment building by the time she'd decided to call Charles. However, the car ride took a lot less time than her journey from her apartment to his mansion last time. The chauffeur didn't say a word to her, although Jane could see the white gloves that he wore, as well as the blazer that all seemed incredibly unnecessary to her. She couldn't understand why the rich demanded that everything be so eloquent all of the time. Jane wondered if they did like to relax properly, where they didn't have to dress up and act so posh all of the time.

In answer to her thoughts, she was led through the house until she came across Charles sprawled out on a coach. "Good evening." He nodded to her.

Jane smiled weakly at him as she suddenly felt rather awkward and vulnerable by calling on his aid once more. She then felt her cheeks flush as she realized that there was somebody else in the room with them.

"Jane, this is my cousin James. He's a harmless extension of the family." Charles spoke with his usual nonchalance.

"Pleasure to meet you." The man sat upright in a chair by the fireplace nodding to her. He looked rather pale, and this was only further emphasized by his hair that was a few shades darker brown than Charles' hair. He had the same blue eyes that were apparently a Bentley feature, but Jane viewed it as simply another way that they were so different.

"So you're the famous Jane that my dear cousin has been telling me so much about." James spoke up with far too much interest for her liking.

"I'm not sure there's really that much to say." Jane said with a shrug.

"Nonsense, take a seat." He gestured to one of the many free seats around them.

Jane was hesitant, but she knew that she couldn't refuse anything after Charles had been so kind as to let her stay for a few hours.

"So you're from town?" James spoke up before the silence around them could become too long.

"Yes, although I'm not from this area." Jane laughed awkwardly as she spoke. "It's a little further west from here."

"I see." James said, as he pursed his lips together. Jane hoped that Charles had briefed him enough so that he understood what she meant by that. "So, how do you feel about this whole...situation?"

Jane was slightly taken aback by the question, and she glanced at Charles uneasily, yet he still looked as though he couldn't have cared any less. "Well, we're both benefiting from it, so if it all goes smoothly, it should be fine." Jane tried to sound confident, but she knew it was hopeless.

"Here's hoping." James said with a light chuckle. "It sure as hell is going to be interesting when you meet his uncle."

"Yes, I've heard that he's quite intimidating." Jane glanced between the two men.

"That may be a little bit of a gross understatement when it comes to how Uncle Jack is with outsiders...no offense." James said.

The man before her held himself in a very similar way to how Charles did, although there seemed to be something slightly more to him than his cousin. James was asking all the right questions and poking around in a way that she had expected from the other relatives that Charles had described. It made Jane slightly dread the thought of meeting the others.

"Well, it's nice to welcome you to the family, Jane." James spoke up again.

"Thank you, hopefully, it will all be fine." She nodded to him.

"Oh I'm hoping for both of your sakes that you're right." He said while nodding between Charles and Jane.

"So what happened between you and your sister?"

Jane froze as Charles spoke up. She hadn't been prepared for him to speak that much since he seemed so content in letting his cousin do all of the talking. Jane swallowed thickly and turned to him as she felt both of the Bentleys' inquisitive gaze fall onto her.

CHAPTER 8

"We just had a small argument." Jane tried her best to shrug it off.

"A small argument?" Charles asked with a frown. "So small that it meant you were kicked out of your own home for a few hours?"

Jane knew that there was no getting out of this one. She pondered over what would really be the worst outcome of just coming clean to him; it didn't seem like a bad idea, but she could never be too sure as to how they would take it.

"Well, I told her about all of...this, obviously." Jane started to explain herself. She didn't like the way that her voice wobbled, it made her feel weak and vulnerable, especially under their gazes. "Helena doesn't like to get help from too many people, she likes to make her own money."

"What does she do for a living?" James asked.

"She works in a...bar." Jane caught herself from saying the words *strip club*. She could imagine the kind of impression that the pair of them would get from her sister without even meeting her. Jane didn't want to completely tarnish her sister's reputation when she wasn't even there to defend herself.

"Interesting." James nodded. However, Jane felt as though the three of them knew that it really wasn't that interesting.

"So she was upset that you've taken up this offer?" Charles asked.

"Yes, and just that I have to spend time with you in order to prepare for it. She'll come around eventually, but today she just wasn't in a reasoning kind of mood I guess."

"Sounds like she's headstrong." James remarked.

"She's very headstrong. We had quite a rough time growing up, and Helena had to be the one to grow up rather quickly. I think it's always been that way with her." Jane tried to explain her sister in the vaguest possible way that she could get away with. "I want her to come here and meet you, but it really is going to have to be on her terms."

James chuckled at her words and shook his head, which caused Jane to frown as he sent Charles an amused look.

"That's not really how things work around here." Charles said with a sigh.

"He means that things work on our terms instead." James shrugged.

"Just because you're the ones with money?" Jane dared to say while cocking an eyebrow.

"Well...yes." James nodded with a growing smirk.

Jane huffed in annoyance at how they were acting with her, although she wasn't sure what she had expected. The two men in front of her were clad in the kinds of sweaters that her grandfather might have worn if he were alive. She frowned at how they were clearly so out of touch with the real world and how calm they seemed about that fact.

"Would you say that you're close with your sister?" James asked.

"We normally are, but when we fight, we fight pretty hard." Jane admitted to them.

"Sounds like any family," James said.

Jane thought about their family history and how it was far from what 'any family' had gone through. Their mother had only recently passed, and from what Jane remembered of her father, Helena told her that he was a waste of space. She was sure that was why Helena didn't trust men so easily, it all circled back to the man who had never been there for them.

"We are going to have the first dinner this weekend, by the way." Charles spoke as he sipped at an amber-colored drink. Jane took a wild guess that it was the kind of drink that burned on the way down his throat.

"This weekend?" Jane's eyes widened. "That's...that's rather soon, don't you think?"

"Well, time is ticking on for us to meet this deadline, and we're going to have to announce the engagement formally as soon as possible." Charles explained. "I'm also not getting any younger and would ideally like all of this sorted while I'm still on this side of thirty-five."

"All right, all right." She sighed. "I get it."

"Good, now we are going to have to do something about your wardrobe standards." Charles continued.

"There's nothing wrong with my wardrobe standards." Jane fired back with narrowed eyes.

"Maybe not for where you're from, but when you're dining a la carte with multiple courses, it won't do."

She wasn't sure if they were doing it on purpose, but Jane had never felt so attacked for something as simple as what she was wearing. She suddenly felt incredibly self-conscious about what she was wearing and how much it made her stand out in the grandeur of the room.

"All right, well what are you guys going to do about it?" Jane asked, as she tried to flatten out a crease that she saw in her pants.

"I suppose we'll have to go shopping before the dinner." Charles suggested.

"Good idea." His cousin agreed. "And what about your sister? Will she be attending the dinner?"

"It would be good if she did, better to have the two families mixing as early on as possible. I want the wedding day to be smooth and quick with no dramas."

"Are you implying that there will be dramas over dinner?" Jane frowned. "I swear your family are so dramatic over things that really don't matter."

"Aren't you the one who's been kicked out this evening?"

Jane glared at James as he seemed to be even more sharp-tongued than his cousin.

"Don't worry about him, he's too clever for his own good, but he doesn't ever mean it." Charles waved off the sudden tension in the room. "We'll get you some nice clothes to wear for these events, and while we do that, we can brief you on everything you need to know to survive a Bentley dinner party."

"I can't wait." Jane said with no enthusiasm in her voice.

Jane thought about being dressed up in the kinds of clothing that the two men were wearing. The concept of being grand, even just for a night, was one that excited her, and she couldn't deny that. She couldn't imagine Helena playing along, not even for a second. That was one of the ways that she was very different from her sister; she didn't like to stick out, while Helena would turn up in her worst outfit to simply make a point.

*****

Jane left after a few hours of hanging around the mansion. Charles had known that he couldn't really refuse her things like that, however, he was still irritated that she felt as though she could just show up.

"She seems a lot nicer than you gave her credit for." James said with a slight chuckle.

"She's so judgmental, can't you feel it?"

"You're just being paranoid."

"You're just trying to wind me up, aren't you?" Charles asked with a huff.

"It was nice of you to let her stay here for a while." James said.

"Yeah, well I can't exactly do anything to anger her, or she could call this whole thing off and then I'll be right back where I started."

"She seems all right, honestly Charles, you shouldn't give the girl such a hard time."

"But think about when she meets the others, she's going to be like a fish out of water and it's only going to reflect badly on me." Charles knew that he sounded like a stropping child, but he didn't care.

"Since when have you ever minded if things reflect badly on you?" James chuckled, as he asked the question. "I thought you lived your life without caring for such things."

"Yeah, well not on this matter." Charles grumbled.

"Look, there are still a few more days until the dinner, why don't you at least try and fix the relationship that you currently have with your future wife and-"

"Don't call her that." He groaned.

"What? She's going to be your wife in a matter of weeks whether you like it or not. Sure, you might not want to act like an actual couple, but on paper, she'll still be your wife."

"I liked you better when you were hungover and couldn't say too much." Charles said, as he stood up and walked over to the counter.

They had moved into the library, where his father's scotch collection was quickly diminishing with each day that Charles lived in the house. He couldn't wait for everything around him

65

to properly be his so that he didn't feel so guilty about using it all up.

"What do you think really happened between the two sisters?" James spoke up.

"What do you mean?"

Charles hadn't been too questioning on Jane's reasoning for being kicked out. He'd already experienced the smart mouth that she had on her when she got the courage to speak up, and so he didn't really see any cause for suspicion on the matter.

"Well, she said that they were arguing over this whole affair. It makes me want to meet her sister more, I want to see just how much she must hate people like us if she's willing to kick her own sister out to make a point."

"There are no people like us." Charles said in a mutter.

"Exactly." James said while nodding his head in his cousin's direction.

The two men spent the rest of the evening talking about more trivial matters to try and distract Charles from the heavy subject of his wife-to-be. However, it was constantly playing on the back of his mind as he grimaced at the thought of actually getting married.

"Can you promise me one thing?" Charles' words came out of the blue as they had no link to their previous conversation.

"What is it?"

"I really don't want the press to get wind of this. I know that they've been quiet with us for a long time, but I just know that my uncle and Tucker will play on this in order to try and get my plan to fall apart. Jane won't like it, and I can't risk it."

"This really is all you're able to think about at the moment, isn't it?" James remarked with a chuckle.

"I'm going to get married to a stranger who practically hates me all in an attempt to get my father's inheritance. If that's not the kind of issue that dominates your thoughts, then I envy how you function."

"All right." James held his hands up in defense. "I get it, but can we at least try not to speak of it for the rest of the night?"

"Fine." Charles huffed, as he leaned back in his seat and stared up at the carved ceiling.

CHAPTER 9

Jane was thankful that by the time the car dropped her outside of her apartment block, the time told her that Helena's shift had already started at the club. The apartment was empty as she stepped quietly inside and only dared to turn on the dim light after hesitating for a moment in the darkness. There was always the possibility that Helena had called in sick and could be sleeping, but Jane thought about how many times Helena had taken a sick day in her life.

When she actually thought about it, Jane was slightly disturbed by the fact that her sister had continued to go to work even when she was actually sick. The only time she'd taken a day off was after their mother had passed. Jane quickly banished the memory, deciding that it wasn't the time to focus on a time when she had been so broken.

It felt wrong to be in the apartment while knowing that her sister was still angry at her. However, Jane knew that she should at least try to get some sleep while she could. She was going to get up extra early to make Helena another breakfast that would couple her apology for her harsh words. Jane knew that Charles and James still wanted her sister to make an appearance at the dinners that they were going to host, however, that seemed like a far cry from ever being possible.

That night, Jane's dreams were plagued with images of the rich and the poor mingling in ways that made her realize why she shouldn't have ever agreed to such a thing. They were all laughing at her, and the shame of so many judgmental eyes on her was enough to make Jane shrink. The people were pompous and rude, they were fat with elegant foods and so out of touch with the world around them that they had created their own world.

Jane didn't like any of them, but as she turned to look at who sat at the head of the table, she decided that she hated her. It was herself. She was wearing expensive fabrics and her hair was styled in a way that didn't seem possible with just her two hands. Jane was sneering at people and passing judgment with an air that she just couldn't imagine herself ever carrying. She shuddered at the thought of ever being that person, and it only filled her with more doubt about her decision.

Jane was jolted awake and back to the stark reality of her bedroom that was no bigger than a storage cupboard. She groaned and rolled over at the blaring sound of her alarm. She was suddenly incredibly anxious about the next few hours that lay ahead of her; Helena was coming home, and she was going to have to face her. She thought about the alternatives that she had, although Jane was sure that the only plausible one would be becoming homeless since there was no way that she was going to rely on Charles for help again. Their apartment was so small that there was no avoiding it, she was going to have to speak to her sister and get the awkwardness out of the way.

Jane quickly started to use up the rest of the bacon that was in the fridge and boiled some eggs in a feeble attempt to make up for her harsh words. She hadn't even meant it, and even if her sister did strip for money, Jane knew that she couldn't say a word about it. She was marrying a stranger for money, and she knew that it was enough to make her eat her own words.

She swallowed the lump down that had formed in her throat as she heard her sister's footsteps getting closer. Helena walked through the door and stopped suddenly at the sight of her sister. Jane glanced up at her, and as the two of them made eye contact, she felt her heart drop.

Helena's lip was cut slightly and there was the beginning of a bruise forming on the skin around her right eye. The eye itself was slightly more closed than her other one, and the white of her eye was a sickening red color. Jane dropped the spatula out of her hand, not caring for the clattering sound that followed her action. Her heart hammered in her chest as she quickly rushed forward and pushed the door shut behind her sister.

"What happened?" Jane's voice was hoarse as she felt her throat closing up in terror.

"Just some trouble at work." Helena said, as she waved it off.

"This isn't just some trouble at work, Hel, this is assault." Jane said, as she quickly moved over to their faulty freezer. Luckily, there was still some ice at the bottom of it that she could use. "Here." Jane handed her the ice after she put a towel around it.

"Thanks." Helena said in a mutter as she winced but placed it on her eye.

"Are you going to tell me what really happened?" Jane was careful with her words. The last thing that she wanted was to create any more tension between the two of them.

"No, I don't think so." She muttered.

"All right, well I'll be here when you're ready." Jane sighed, as she quickly turned down the heat on the bacon. Her main priority at that moment was no longer breakfast, but her sister's injuries. "Are you hurt anywhere else?"

"No."

"Okay, do you want to go to the police or-"

"No." Helena said again. Jane continued to stare at her sister until she spoke up again. "I'm still mad at you, this doesn't change that."

Jane nodded and ran a hand through her dark hair.

"I didn't expect it to." Jane admitted. "I just want to make sure that you're alright."

"I'll be fine."

Jane didn't believe her sister for one moment as she spoke.

She left her to nurse her own injuries as it was clear that Helena was still not wanting to properly talk about what had happened. Jane wanted to apologize properly for what she'd said, but this certainly wasn't the correct moment to do so.

"Here you go." Jane muttered, as she placed the plate on the table in front of her sister. The sentiment was long gone, and now she was simply focused on making sure that Helena ate something after the shock had worn off.

"Thanks." Helena spoke with her eyes down. She put down the wet towel so that she could start to pick at her breakfast. "Where did you go last night?"

Jane didn't want to answer her question, she knew that Helena wouldn't approve and it would only drive the wedge further between them. However, her silence seemed to be the only kind of answer that Helena needed. Her eyes returned to her breakfast as she shook her head.

"Look, I didn't want to be out on the streets on my own after dark, especially not around here." Jane tried to defend herself.

"I didn't say anything." Helena said. She was being difficult, and they both knew that she was doing it deliberately.

"You didn't need to." Jane fired back. She regretted being so quick almost as soon as she spoke, there was no point in bickering, not when tensions were already so high between them.

"I wanted to apologize to you this morning, because what I said last night was out of line." Jane spoke up eventually. She couldn't stand the silence in the room, it felt far too awkward for two people who only had each other in the world. "I really am sorry, Helena, it was uncalled for. I was just angry, and that's not an excuse, there's no excuse for what I said."

"It's all right, I was angry too." She sighed eventually. "After how my night went, it really wasn't a big deal."

Jane breathed out a heavy sigh of relief as she felt her knees dip in strength slightly. She rolled her shoulders back in an attempt to release some of the stress that had gripped her body. "What happened?"

"Some guys got too wasted, so I refused to serve them. They were saying all sorts of insults to me and the bouncers kicked them out, but they waited for me until my shift was over," Helena explained. "I managed to get away before they could properly do any damage though."

Jane knew that her sister was the stronger one of the pair of them, however, she was still impressed that she'd been able to get out without letting them attack her more. "I'm sorry that you had to go through that." Jane spoke in a small voice.

"One of the bouncers could see that the situation was about to happen, he was having a smoke out the back as the men started to approach me. I called out to him for help, but he said that it wasn't on the property, so he couldn't do anything about it. I thought I could trust those guys to help me." Helena spoke bitterly.

"Well, a very wise person once told me that we can't trust anyone in this world, least of all men." Jane spoke with a small, comforting smile on her face. She was talking about Helena herself, and her sister nodded as she looked down at her lap for a moment.

"Thanks, Jane, I just can't believe that happened." Helena breathed out.

She could see her sister's eyes becoming glossy as her voice wobbled. The shock was finally giving way to emotion, and she quickly moved forward to engulf her sister in a tight hug as she cried on her shoulder.

Jane couldn't help but realize how much the tables had turned. It was normally her that was the one in need of comfort, and Helena who would be the big sister on hand to help her through whatever it was. Jane felt as though she could finally pay Helena pack for all of the times that she was there for her, and she held on tightly to her older sister.

"I'm sorry." Helena whispered, as she moved back and wiped her eyes quickly.

"You have nothing to apologize for." Jane said while shaking her head. "Please don't be sorry. I'm just so glad that you're alright."

"I'm quitting my job today." Helena said while breathing out.

"I don't blame you." Jane nodded.

She knew what was coming next, although she felt no sense of 'I told you so' toward her sister. The circumstances definitely weren't right for that kind of attitude. Instead, Jane felt a little more dislike toward the man that she was supposed to marry since they were both now going to be in his debt as Helena had said.

"I'll talk to him later on today." Jane spoke in a small voice.

She'd almost forgotten that she was going to have to go shopping and get some new clothes since hers apparently didn't cut it. That was yet another thing that she knew her sister would hate; if Jane were to come back dressed up as one of the rich, she wasn't sure how Helena would react to it.

"Don't mention this." Helena spoke clearly as she quickly looked up at her sister.

"Don't worry, I wouldn't even dream of it." Jane shook her head. She knew that being so vulnerable wasn't something that Helena was used to. She was resisting it because of her pride, but Jane knew deep down that her sister was likely glad to have some kind of help.

"I can't believe you're really going to do this." She breathed out.

"It's only so we can live a life where we're not having to put ourselves in dangerous situations in the name of money." Jane explained.

"Your way to stop us from getting into dangerous situations is by getting into yet another dangerous situation?" Helena asked.

Jane felt a chill run down her spine at her sister's words; the people that she was dealing with were dangerous, and she knew that she would be a fool to not see that.

CHAPTER 10

Jane arrived at the mall for the time that Charles had said to her before she'd left his house. She grimaced as she glanced around at the many shops that she normally avoided - they weren't in her usual price range. Being frugal was an art that both Jane and Helena had mastered many years ago. She knew how to treat herself from time to time, but she never went above her means. They would ration everything from food to clothes, and if she were to get a hole in an item of clothing, she would simply stitch it up. They had become resourceful after years of being so poor and living below the poverty line; Jane had homed in skills that she hadn't even known she'd be good at.

"Afternoon." Charles' voice spoke from behind her.

"Hi." Jane nodded to him. She felt incredibly guilty that she was out shopping with a billionaire while her sister was back in their small apartment. However, she had left her sleeping, and there wasn't much else that Jane could do while Helena slept to help out.

"Have you made up with your sister?" He asked, as he motioned for the two of them to start walking toward the first store.

"Yes, we're fine now." Jane said. She noted how wooden her voice sounded, but she couldn't help it. She wasn't going to say a word about how Helena had been attacked, she wasn't sure how Charles would react, but she was sure that it wouldn't be too animated and that would only anger her more. She knew that he cared little for her in the end, but there was a line where it stopped being rude and started being indecent. Jane didn't want to find that line.

"That's good to hear." Charles nodded. "Right, we need to find you a few outfits that will be considered acceptable to wear around my family."

"Have you people never heard of denim jeans?" Jane asked, as she stepped into the first store. Even the carpet was unnecessarily plush, and as soon as they entered, they were greeted by an entire fleet of staff members.

"Yes, we have." Charles nodded. "But jeans won't cut it for a dinner party like the ones that my family hosts."

"What will cut it?" Jane asked, as she glanced around at the various items of clothing that caught her eye.

Everything was formal inside of the store, even the area of designated 'casualwear' looked far too formal to be lounging around it. Jane dared to peak at the label of one of the nearby plain tops, however, there was no price on it. She pursed her lips into a line as she realized that she really was in another world at that moment; the kind of world where money wasn't a problem, it was a given.

"What about these?" Charles pointed to a long dress with a dramatic neckline.

"Very good, Sir, this is the new season that we've just brought into the store." The woman at his side spoke.

The staff were all dressed in black with slicked-back hair, even the women wore slicked back ponytails. They looked as though they could be part of some kind of intimidating mafia gang or perhaps a modern day tribe, in reality, they were just underpaid retail staff. They were working the same kind of job as the people that she saw in more affordable stores, however, they were having to upkeep their appearance.

"Great, we'll have one of those for her to try on. In the meantime, let's keep browsing?"

Jane felt like a child that was being dragged along to look at things that she didn't understand. For the most part, she could tell what the clothes were, however, there were a few things that she'd never thought to wear. Charles was pointing to a selection of capes that were meant to be worn over the top of dresses, and Jane realized just how out of her depth that she was.

"What about shoes, do you own anything that's not that pair of trainers?" Charles asked. His question caused her to flush as Jane realized that there were also multiple members of staff that were also waiting for her to answer the question.

"Nothing that will go with these dresses." Jane said in a mutter.

She didn't want to tell him the truth that those trainers really were one of two pairs of shoes that she owned. The others were holding on by a thread, and she couldn't wear them if it was going to rain due to the number of holes in their soles. She kept her head down as they walked across the store and over to the shoes. The assistant who was talking with Charles about what shoes came from which season was starting to state some of the prices, and Jane felt a chill run down her as she realized how expensive everything around her was. Some of the shoes cost as much as her rent; a figure that Jane couldn't ever imagine justifying on just one pair of shoes. Helena's voice was nagging in her mind again as she felt slightly guilty for pointing out anything in the store anymore.

"What do you think of these?" Charles asked, as Jane glanced up. He was holding a pair of modest heels in a shiny silver color, they looked good and not too difficult to walk in.

"I like them." Jane nodded to him as she managed a smile.

"All right, add them to the pile." Charles said with a chuckle as he gave them to the assistant.

Jane could tell that the staff around her were clearly pleased that he'd decided to come into their store. It seemed that he was going to spend more in one hour than the store would probably on a normal day or week.

"Great." The girl beamed, as she passed the shoes back to one of the other assistants.

Jane glanced over at the growing pile of clothing that he was going to no doubt make her try on. She didn't think that she had the worst body shape, but she hated the idea of so many eyes staring at her as she tried things on.

"Could you just give us a minute?" Charles asked while smiling brightly at the woman.

"Of course." She nodded and walked away.

Charles led her over to an area of the store where there was nobody to overhear their conversation. As soon as the woman was gone, his smile dropped as he stared at her. "What's your problem? I thought you would have enjoyed some shopping?" Charles asked. She hated how accusing he sounded.

"I'm sorry, I'm just not used to all of...this." Jane didn't know how to put it, and so she simply gestured to the room around her. "I don't shop in these kinds of places normally, I don't know what to do."

"Then just follow my lead. Stop thinking about the money, the money isn't important." He said with a scowl.

Jane wanted to leave there and then, but she knew that she didn't have a choice but to stay.

"I'm sorry, but where I come from, we can't afford this type of luxury. That's why I only have one good pair of sneakers, it's not because I choose to do so." Jane spoke back with more venom in her tone than she had been expecting.

Charles blinked at her and it was clear that he also hadn't been expecting it from her. "Well, you now do have a choice." He countered. "And you're going to like it."

Jane huffed as he turned back and instantly put on his polite smile that made her feel slightly nauseous. Everything was about appearances in this world, that was something that she had learned already, and she was anxious about having to play a part in that too.

"All right, shall we start trying things on?" Charles asked, as he gave her a rather pointed look. She knew that look and it told her not to test his patience, Jane swallowed and nodded slowly at his request.

"I'm sure that it will all fit great." Jane said rather quickly. "If this store really is as good as it says it is, then I have little doubt that all of the clothes in my size will fit."

Charles narrowed his eyes as he stared at her for a moment, and Jane knew that she'd overstepped. However, she decided to stand her ground. She was going to show him that he couldn't talk to her like that and think that she was just going to take it without making a scene of her own.

"All right, you heard the lady." Charles said with a chuckle. "We'll take them all."

Jane laughed along with him as she touched his arm gently. The lady smiled as she looked between them before nodding and turning back to the large pile of clothes in the corner of the room.

"They had all better fit like a glove." He spoke through gritted teeth.

Jane gave him a wide smile as she nodded and pretended that he had said something hilarious. From that moment on, she decided to stop letting the guilt get to her; if Charles was going to pay for everything, then she was going to milk it.

"I'll have these brought out to your car, Sir, so that you can finish your day of shopping in peace." The woman said as she pointed to the multiple large bags that were next to the counter.

"Thank you very much, and here's your tip for that."

Jane's eyes widened slightly as she saw the bills in his hand, however, she quickly stopped herself from reacting to it so much and tried to act natural. This was her world now too, and she was going to have to play her part.

"I see that you're starting to embrace all of this finally?" Charles questioned as they walked back out into the open space of the mall.

"Well, if you're paying." Jane said with a shrug. "And as you said, money doesn't matter." She pushed down the heavy stone of guilt that seemed to be growing inside of her as she spoke those words out loud. Jane didn't like the way that she suddenly could make herself sound so privileged without too much difficulty.

"Exactly the right kind of attitude to have around my family." Charles said with a chuckle. "They can be the absolute worst at times, and so sometimes the only way to combat it is if you act even more awful than them."

Jane wasn't sure about that kind of logic, but she certainly wasn't going to question him any more. The look that he'd given her when he'd pulled her to the side in the store had scared her more than she cared to admit. She glanced around before allowing Charles to lead her toward the next shop.

It seemed that he was clearly a well-known client in that mall because the staff would see him approaching their store, and Jane caught the looks that they would exchange between one another. If Charles Bentley was going to be shopping with them that day, then some of them were going to earn much larger tips than normal.

"Good afternoon, Mr. Bentley. Can we get you any refreshments while you shop?" The man spoke almost as soon as Charles and Jane had set foot in the store.

Jane hadn't even known that stores could offer food and drink, and the entire experience seemed slightly ridiculous as she glanced out of the store's borders to see that the food court was just downstairs.

"I think we're alright for the time being." Charles brushed it off.

Jane had thought that they would be done for the day, but it was clear that Charles had an appetite for shopping, and that wasn't something that he was going to let go of after going into just one store.

"All right, you're also going to need some more casual outfits for when we have lunches or when the men are playing golf. I hate to tell you this, but if you come along to those kinds of events, you'll be stuck with my Aunt Rosalyn."

"And if I want to play golf instead?" Jane asked with a frown.

"It's only for the men in the family, I'm afraid. You'll be having tea up on the terrace with Aunt Rosalyn, where she will no doubt be grilling you on every little detail."

"Great." Jane said dryly. "That sounds like just the event that I want to go to."

"I don't make the rules." Charles said with a sigh.

He picked out some more casual outfits for her, although none of them were made of denim. Jane felt as though she was going to have to learn to be a lot more traditional in her thinking since most of her outfits were also very traditional. She'd never been the kind of woman who wore skirts that often; they weren't practical with her job, and if she did go out in the evening, she just couldn't see the appeal. However, it seemed that all Charles had picked out for her were the damned things. Finally, she turned to see that there were some trouser options for being more casual, although she could tell that Charles was trying to deter her away from them.

"I think that skirt over there looks nice." He pointed to one a few rails away from the pants section.

"I think we've got enough skirts, darling." Jane smiled as she turned to look at him. "I want some trousers that I can at least be slightly more comfortable in."

"Fine." He sighed and stood back as she sorted through the ones that she liked.

"What's so bad about your Aunt?"

"She's married to my uncle, but she doesn't love him. She's bitter and vain, and she's only doing all of this for the money."

"Like me then?" Jane chuckled as she lowered her voice so that the staff wouldn't hear her.

"Not at all like you, I didn't say that you were bitter or vain." Charles shook his head.

"Was that...a compliment?" Jane mockingly acted completely shocked by his words. However, her remark only prompted him to roll his eyes as he turned away from her.

"All I meant is that she's a gold digger through and through. She doesn't have a good bone in her body, and she's helping my uncle in any way that she can to make sure that the inheritance goes to them instead."

"Do you think that you would like your uncle without the subject of the inheritance getting between you?"

Jane's question caused him to pause for a while as she held a pair of beige pants against her and stared in the mirror. Even for a casual outfit, they were much more formal than anything else that she owned, but this was the new Jane that she was going to have to invent. This was the Jane who married for money and didn't care about it. At least, that was what she told herself to convince her that she could do this.

"No, I don't think that my uncle has ever liked me that much, and I think the feeling is rather mutual." Charles admitted after a while.

"I'm sorry to hear that, I'm sure that family affairs could have all been a lot easier if you all got along." Jane said, as she placed the pants on yet another growing pile of clothing.

"Don't be sorry, we all get along when we have to get along. A prime example will be this weekend; you'll see what family diplomacy looks like and you'll get a first-hand experience of it too."

"I can't wait." Jane said sarcastically. She thought about having to tolerate multiple people who looked, talked, and acted like Charles in a room. It was an awful thought, one that turned her lips into a curled grimace.

After a while, Jane could feel herself growing tired of the repetitive shopping. She was sure that she didn't need as many outfits as Charles was willing to buy for her, and so she couldn't understand why he was persisting with visiting every store in sight.

"Don't you think we've got enough?" Jane asked, as she groaned at the sight of him heading into yet another shop.

"What's enough?" He frowned, although his expression quickly broke out into a triumphant grin at the sight of Jane rolling her eyes.

"We must have spent the equivalent of someone's yearly salary on clothes today and I still don't think there will ever be enough events for me to get to wear them all." Jane said, as she shook her head.

"What did I say before?" He asked with a heavy sigh.

Money doesn't matter, *but it does*, Jane thought to herself. *It really does and I feel sick at how much you've spent*, she wanted to say to him.

"I'm just not used to this." Jane groaned. "I'm also tired, and hungry, and I just feel that we've done enough shopping for one day."

Jane realized at that moment that for however long their marriage lasted, she was going to be the one to pull him back when he tried to overindulge. She'd already glimpsed his drinking habits and knew that it was just one of the many ways in which he liked to live an overindulgent lifestyle.

"All right, you're right I suppose. We have enough new clothes, now, do you want to put them in a closet at my place, or yours?"

Jane thought about the small rail that displayed how few items of clothing she actually owned, as well as making an obvious point of her lack of hanging space. She then tried to count in her head how many bags of shopping were waiting for them inside of his car, and Jane knew without even having to come to a figure that they would live in his house.

"It's probably easier for them to stay with you, I don't want to risk damaging them at my place." Jane said with a mere shrug.

"Where do you live, a zoo?" Charles chuckled.

"Something like that." She muttered in response.

Jane couldn't help but smile as she thought about the idea of bringing Charles over to the apartment one day. It would be a pretty funny sight to see him so out of his element for once so that the roles would be reversed. However, Jane imagined him meeting Helena for the first time in their apartment, and the amusement of the situation seemed to evaporate.

"All right, let's go."

CHAPTER 11

Jane stared at herself in the floor-to-ceiling length mirror in awe. She'd never had expensive clothes like this, and she couldn't help but admire the way that she looked in her favorite dress that they'd bought. The cream material hugged her figure perfectly, and the straps sat at the right angle on her shoulders as she twirled around. Her heels weren't too high thankfully, it seemed to be the one mercy of the elite that worked in her favor; too high of a heel and the outfit lost its class very quickly. Jane glanced at herself as she moved around in the dress, trying it out as the fabric flowed with her body.

"That is a very pretty look." Charles remarked, as he leaned on the thick wooden doorframe.

Jane jumped slightly at his sudden presence and pressed a hand to her chest where her racing heart was pounding. "You could have at least knocked." She grumbled. "I could have been indecent."

Charles shrugged off her comment and stepped further into the room. He glanced at the many clothes that she was yet to try on, but Jane was already growing tired of having her own fashion show. She was still unable to get over the fact that Charles' version of a closet was actually an independent room. It wasn't just a cupboard off of the bedroom, it housed couches and all sorts of other pieces of furniture that Jane hadn't even realized could go in a closet.

"You're going to wear this one for the first dinner?" He asked, as Jane was suddenly filled with doubt.

"Do you not think that's a good idea?" She frowned.

"I think it's definitely going to make an impression on the others." Charles said with a growing smirk.

She couldn't tell if that meant it was a good or bad thing, but Jane swallowed thickly and turned to look at herself in the mirror.

"With the right styling of your hair and makeup, I think this will be a really good first outfit." He spoke in a much more reassuring tone.

Jane faltered slightly as she remembered her dream and how she had looked in it; the girl who stared back at her in the mirror was coming dangerously close to looking like that too. She glanced back at Charles to see that he was still looking at her, although she couldn't quite place the look that was in his eyes. Jane hadn't seen it before and she was slightly worried that she may have done something wrong, or worse, that he was setting her up for failure of some kind.

"And you're sure that this won't be too much?" Jane asked, as she hugged her arms to her chest.

"No, not at all. It's perfect." Charles spoke in a mutter as he suddenly looked down. "I'll leave you to change and try on your other things." Before Jane could say another word, he quickly turned and strode out of the room. She was left to guess at why he had suddenly acted so strange around her.

By the time that she had finished trying on clothes and hanging them up in the large closet room, Jane felt exhausted and knew she should head back home to check on her sister. She hoped more than anything that Helena wouldn't go to work that night, she knew her sister said she would quit, but she hoped she would follow through on her word.

"Will you be able to come tomorrow?" Charles asked when she found him standing by one of the many ornate fireplaces on the ground floor.

"I should be able to, although my boss isn't going to like it." Jane said.

"You should quit then." Charles suggested.

Having him pay for her college debt was one thing, but to not have to work was properly like winning the lottery. Jane bit her lip at his words as she knew that he would never understand how it wasn't that easy. She was starting to question her own pride at the concept of quitting her job so that she could live off of the money that he was going to give her.

"But I want to work." Jane spoke back. "I want to do something."

"And you can, and I'm sure that you will in the future. But for the time being, you shouldn't waste a moment in preparing to meet my family, unless you want to be picked apart and served as dessert on Saturday night?"

"No, I don't want that." Jane spoke bitterly to him.

She didn't feel as though she had much of a choice in anything anymore.

"All right, well I'll see you here tomorrow at two?" Charles asked. He was still staring at the fireplace while speaking to her, it was as though he was hypnotized by the flames that licked against the protective grill.

"If you're going to be awake by then." Jane wasn't sure why she had bothered to make the dig at him, but she did feel slightly better for being able to say something like that. She was surprised that Charles didn't even so much turn around at her comment, and before the silence could become any more awkward, Jane turned and left.

*****

"How was your day?" James asked, as he walked into the house.

"Do you just live here now?" Charles ignored his question with a groan.

87

"No, but I thought I'd come and check on you since you can't be trusted to do basic things on your own." James shrugged, as he sat down opposite Charles.

"What's that supposed to even mean?"

"If it weren't for you housekeeper, do you really think that you would know how to live on your own?"

"I'd be just fine." Charles scowled at him. "Anyway, I don't need this right now, I've got enough on my mind."

"I told you the other day, stop thinking about this so much, it's going to work."

"I didn't mean that." Charles said, as he sat forward so that his elbows were resting on his knees.

"Then what's troubling you?" James said, although he quickly scoffed at his own words. "I feel that every day I spend here, I become less your cousin, and more your private therapist."

Charles ignored the comments and thought about what was really on his mind. "I took Jane shopping today."

"And how was that?"

"It was quite unpleasant, the woman has absolutely no fashion sense and no desire to shop either." Charles said with a huff of annoyance.

"I suppose she's never really had the money to do it." James offered, but Charles wasn't looking for excuses.

"I know, but I was paying for everything. I thought she would be like a kid in a candy store, but she looked like I was keeping her hostage or something." Charles said, as he saw the look that James was giving him. "Don't say a word."

"Fine." He said.

"But something happened when we got back here and she went upstairs to try on some of the dresses that we bought." Charles

88

said. He caught himself as he realized that he'd referred to the two of them as a 'we' for the first time, as though they were a real couple. "I went to see how she was getting on, and she was wearing this dress - I knew as soon as I saw it in the store that it would look great on anyone, but..."

"But what?" James frowned as he clearly wasn't seeing his point.

"But she just looked so...beautiful, I guess. Charles spoke with a frown. He was so confused and conflicted by the way that he'd reacted to seeing her. He watched as his cousin's expression melted away from one of confusion to one that was a sort of subtle amusement. Charles sighed heavily and wished that he'd never said anything.

"No, go on." James encouraged. "I'm intrigued, how did it make you feel? See, I'm sounding like a therapist again."

"I don't know what it is that I felt. All that happened was...well I just...froze."

"You froze because you saw a pretty girl." James stated as though it was the most obvious thing in the world.

"Yes, but I've been around her multiple times, it was the dress and the room around her...I don't know. Everything just seemed so...right."

"Do you like her?" James asked with a cautious tone in his voice.

"No." Charles stood up and walked back over to the fireplace as he took another sip of his scotch. The liquid burned down his throat as he searched for answers in the flames in front of him.

"That would be foolish to feel something for someone who is marrying me for my money." Charles shook his head. "I'd be no better than Uncle Jack."

James didn't say anything from behind him, and Charles found that he was suddenly craving his cousin's opinion. "Do you get my dilemma?"

"No, and I don't think you do either. I think you're just seeing an attractive girl that you can't have and you're sulking about it." James tried to reason with him by chuckling. "It's nothing but a small crush, you probably haven't had one in years because you can just go out and get any girl that you want. It's a lot more common than you think actually."

Charles thought about his cousin's words for a while. He pondered over whether this was true; if he really did feel that way for someone like her, would it pass?

"I've just never frozen up like that before." He admitted with a shrug. "You'll see what I mean on the weekend when she's in the dress. I just...I lost my nerve for a moment."

"Well you'd certainly better find it before the dinner party, or you're going to be fighting a losing battle from the beginning."

Charles knew that the dinner party would be a different story; he was going to have his game face on and be ready to put on a show if need be, he was going to do whatever it took to distract the others from the fact that Jane and he weren't engaged for love.

"I'm going to have to act as though we're a couple on Saturday, aren't I?" He groaned.

"Of course, or the entire game will be given away." James nodded.

"Do you think she'll play along?"

"She'll have to." He said.

"I still need to ask her if she's bringing her sister." Charles muttered more to himself than to James.

"Oh yes, because things were already going to be difficult enough trying to control one person and stop them from making a bad impression."

Chapter 12

"Helena?" Jane asked, as she quickly burst through the door of their apartment. She found her sister straight ahead of her on the couch. "How are you feeling? How are the injuries?" Jane quickly crouched in front of her to inspect her face.

The bruise had come up a lot more since she'd last seen her that morning, but it didn't look as bad as Jane had pictured it would in her mind. Some of the swelling was already coming down around her eye, and it wasn't nearly as bloodshot anymore.

"I feel a lot better, I think it looks a lot worse than I feel." Helena said with a shrug as she continued to watch the TV that was hardly used. Some months they didn't pay for the cable bill because nobody was ever in the apartment or had enough time to watch anything on it.

"That's good." Jane sighed in relief. "I've been worried about you all day."

"Did you go out with Charles?" She asked, as she turned to face her.

"I did, he took me to a mall and made me pick out some fancy clothes." Jane tried to brush it off as nothing. The last thing that she wanted to do was to focus on the day that she'd had when Helena's injuries were still so fresh.

"Did you get anything nice?"

"A few dresses." Again, Jane was quick to shrug it off.

"That must have been nice."

"Did you quit your job?" Jane asked.

"I did, I called my boss before and explained what happened. He was incredibly apologetic, but then he got angry when he realized that I was supposed to be working tonight." Helena explained as she sighed and glanced at the clock. "I could still make it in for my shift if I just-"

"No, you're not going anywhere." Jane shook her head and stopped her from getting up. "You're going to rest for the next few days, and you're not going to worry about anything."

"But what about-"

"Money is included in that bracket of anything." Jane quickly cut her off.

"You still don't have to do this."

Helena sounded as though she meant it, but Jane was sure that she knew as well as she did that she now really had no choice. With Charles encouraging Jane to quit her job, Helena had already left her job and the Bentley fortune being their only source of income, Jane was completely sure that she was now going to have to go through with this.

"I do, Helena, I really do." Jane sighed ,as she rose from her crouched position and dared to glance at what food they had in the fridge.

"I've decided that I'll come with you this weekend." Helena spoke up.

Jane had never seen her sister looking as vulnerable as she did at that moment, and it scared her slightly that Helena was saying such rash things all of a sudden.

"Are you sure?" Jane asked, as she blinked a couple of times.

"Yes, I'll be there for you." She nodded.

Jane smiled at her sister in thanks as she realized how much easier that was going to make her life.

"Thank you." Jane said. "But you're really not going to go anywhere if your black eye doesn't heal. That won't exactly make the best first impression on his family."

"I do see your point there." Helena said with a light chuckle. "It won't be good if I tell the story of how I got it either."

Jane couldn't help but laugh with her sister. She was glad that their conversation was able to lighten up the mood even slightly. It gave her some reassurance that things would be all right between them.

"Thank you though, I really do appreciate your support." Jane spoke in a much more serious tone.

"Don't worry about it, we need each other. Ever since mom...I don't think that I could go through this life without you, little sis." Helena admitted openly to her.

They had held one another together, and Jane realized that they really did need one another. She felt her heart almost bursting with love for her sister as she thought about having her at her side for when they met the rest of the Bentley family. With Helena next to her, Jane felt as though she could do anything.

"So what do you want for dinner?" Jane asked, as she glanced back at the fridge.

"What do we have?" Helena's question was followed by a cautious expression as she braced herself for whatever would be in their fridge.

"We could have some leftover bread with slightly blue cheese." Jane tried to make her voice sound as enthusiastic as possible as she spoke. "Or we could have some stale crackers with slightly blue cheese!"

"Do we have to have slightly blue cheese at all?" Helena winced.

"I hear it's what the rich eat." Jane said with a smirk of amusement.

"Yeah but their cheese is blue by choice; they don't grow the mold themselves." Helena chuckled.

*****

Saturday approached much quicker than Jane would have liked. She'd come to dread even the word 'dinner party' and everything that Charles promised it would entail. Over the past few days, she had been taught about the different courses that would be served as part of their meal, as well as the many different utensils to use for each course. Her brain was just about ready to explode when it came to what etiquette she should use and how she should talk or even just sit. Charles had commented on how she had terrible posture, although Jane hadn't thought it was that bad. She would go home in the evenings with a cheque in hand to cover their days of lost earnings from work, and then relay the information that she had been told to Helena. Her injuries hadn't been too bad, and so she recovered well enough from them that a little bit of concealer was all that she needed to cover up the speckled remnants of her bruising.

"All of my outfits are at Charles' place, we're going to head over there early and you can pick out a dress to wear too?" Jane explained to her older sister as Helena nodded.

She could tell that Helena was apprehensive about going outside. She'd only been on one very cautious walk around the block since the incident after she'd left work. Jane knew that her sister was absolutely terrified of running into the men who had waited outside of the club for her. Luckily, she was completely confident that they wouldn't be seeing men of their standing in the part of town that they were going out to.

"The car is waiting for us just outside of the apartment, so there's no need to worry about anything." Jane spoke with a reassuring smile. She felt as though she had embodied the role of big sister over the last couple of days, she'd had to be a lot stronger than normal to support Helena.

"Thank you." Helena said, as she caught her arm before Jane could leave through the door.

95

"What for?"

"For being there for me." She spoke in a small voice. Jane flashed her a small smile and squeezed her hand as she took it.

"You do the same for me all the time, it's the least that I could do."

Jane led the way as they walked out and got into the typical black car that was waiting for them. She could tell that Helena was already trying to hide how amazed she was at the luxury transport that Charles had arranged for them.

"He doesn't talk." She gestured to the chauffeur with a chuckle.

"This is already too much." Helena said in a mutter.

"Wait until you see the house." Jane sent her a concerned smile. She was scared that Helena was going to act out in some way when she saw just how grand the world of Charles Bentley was.

The ride was relatively quick, the chauffeur was good at his job and weaved through the traffic with ease. Jane was no longer surprised at how quickly the scenery around them could change from urban poverty to semi-rural grandeur. She watched as Helena's eyes were glued to the window; she was watching the many beautiful houses that rushed past in a blur.

"Even just these gates…" Helena said, as her voice trailed off. She was completely stunned by how grand it was and Jane remembered her first time driving through that neighborhood. "Is all of this just his driveway?"

Jane nodded slowly as the car continued down the singular road past the gates. It kept going for a while before the large brick walls of the mansion started to rise up in front of them. Helena wasn't able to hide the way that she was gawking at the property in front of them anymore. She gasped slightly and craned her neck to glance further through the tinted window.

"I told you that it was kind of crazy here." Jane said with a chuckle.

"Yeah but Jane, there's crazy and then there's this." Helena breathed out. "This is...this is like royalty."

"This is how billionaires live." She corrected her sister.

Jane wasn't sure what it was inside of her, but she was incredibly nervous for her sister to suddenly be introduced to this world that she'd started to grow more used to. There was still a pinch of doubt that was nagging in the back of her mind, it told her that she should have brought her sister here a lot earlier than the day of the dinner party.

"Are you sure that you're going to be up for this?" Jane asked, as she glanced hesitantly at her sister.

"I think so, but I feel as though I'm having dinner with the president or something." She admitted with a chuckle.

"I know that it's a lot to take in, but try to just act natural." Jane managed to mutter before the chauffeur was opening her door.

They were led up to the main entrance and straight through the house by Anna, the housekeeper. Jane could see the shock on Helena's face as she tried to take everything in at once, even down to the fact that only one man lived here with so many members of staff.

"Jane, I knew that he was rich, but I never expected this." She spoke in a low voice so that nobody else would hear their conversation.

"Mr. Bentley is just through there." Anna gestured to the library. Jane could feel herself wincing slightly as she remembered how grand the library was and how much it was going to freak out her sister.

"Thank you, Anna." Jane nodded to her.

"Ah, there you are." Charles said, as he rose from his chair.

"Charles, this is my sister, Helena." Jane smiled at him as she gestured to the awe-struck girl at her side.

"A pleasure to meet you." Charles smiled at her. However, Helena didn't return the smile and instead simply nodded. Jane felt her heart drop almost instantly. Charles' own smile faltered at the not-so-welcome introduction, but he quickly recovered as he turned back to her.

"Was the car ride okay?"

"It was fine thanks." Jane nodded to him. "Is this your getup for the evening?"

She gestured to the black tie suit that he was wearing; it was tailored almost too perfectly to his body and made him look much more handsome than when he wore the cricket sweaters every day.

"It is, and I'm assuming that you two ladies are going to get ready soon?" He raised an eyebrow as he spoke.

"Yes, Helena's going to borrow one of my dresses." She explained to him.

"One of *your* dresses hm?" Charles smiled in amusement. Jane found it rather strange how the man in front of her didn't intimidate her nearly as much now that she had her sister at her side. Helena was like a support bubble who was always there for her, and Jane felt a little stronger with her around.

"Yes, one of mine, now if you excuse us, we'll get ready and then we can make our final preparations for the evening." Jane spoke up.

Even she was shocked by how her voice came off. There was a certain edge to it that wasn't normally there, and with her shoulders back, and her back straight, she suddenly felt rather powerful in her position.

"Of course." Charles bowed his head as he let them go.

Jane turned to see her sister staring at her with a strange frown on her face. However, she didn't have time to question it, since they were both going to have to get ready. She led her sister out of the room and toward the grand staircase in the center of the main hall.

*****

Charles watched them go and narrowed his eyes. It seemed that Jane was finally on board with trying to convince his family that their engagement was legitimate, however, he wasn't so sure about her sister.

"How did that go?" James called, as Charles walked out onto the porch.

"You should have been there, it was quite entertaining." He responded, as he took out a cigarette to light.

"Is her sister like her much?" James asked while taking a cigarette too.

"She's similar in the fact that she seems quite strong-willed." Charles explained. "Although, we may have a problem with her tonight if she doesn't want to play along."

"I'll take on the role of keeping her in check if that helps." James offered. "You're going to have your hands full enough with making sure that yours and Jane's stories line up."

"Thank you." Charles nodded to him while breathing out. "That would be a big help to me."

James nodded in response as they both stared out over the back lawn. He tried to imagine how the evening would go, but it only filled Charles with dread as he wondered whether it would run as smoothly as he was hoping for.

"There was something else as well." Charles said.

"What is it?"

"Jane's sister looked as though she had some kind of bruise around her eye." He remarked and shook his head. "I couldn't be sure in the light of the library though."

99

"Jesus." James chuckled as he took a drag of his cigarette. "You really have invited the riff-raff in."

CHAPTER 13

"I don't think I can breathe in this." Helena muttered, as she tried to walk toward the mirror in one of the dresses.

"You do look really good in it though." Jane was trying to be supportive. She felt rather comfortable in her own dress as it wasn't the first time that she'd put it on. Charles had given her some more encouragement that she should wear it, and after seeing him in his expensive suit, it didn't feel like too much.

"But look at you, you look amazing!" Helena sighed.

Jane had managed to do her sister's makeup in a way that hid the remainder of the bruising on her face. Although it was almost completely gone anyway, she really didn't want to be answering questions about it.

"You do too." Jane fired back as she smiled at her. "Do you want to try on the blue one though?"

"Yes, if it will let me breathe while I'm wearing it." Helena muttered, as she grabbed the dress from her and quickly shuffled behind the screen.

"I'm feeling quite nervous about this, Helena." Jane sighed. "They're going to scrutinize everything about us."

"Then we're just going to have to remain strong and not cave under their questions. We've got nothing to feel ashamed about in terms of where we've come from, we've worked hard for every single damned day of our lives - that's more than any of them will be able to say."

Jane liked her sister's feisty attitude, but she really wasn't sure that it was going to hold up when she thought about the lion's den that they were going to be entering. She glanced at herself in the mirror and straightened her posture in the way that Charles had shown her. The woman who stared back at her didn't look much like the same woman who delivered takeaways for a living.

"What do you think of this one?"

What the other dress had lacked in giving her sister any confidence, the blue dress seemed to deliver in an abundance. The color complimented her pale blue eyes, and Jane was amazed at how well her sister scrubbed up.

"You look absolutely incredible." She breathed out.

"You're too kind." Helena chuckled. However, her smile faltered slightly and melted into an expression of shock as she turned to look at herself in the mirror.

"I'm just being honest." Jane shrugged.

Together, the two of them had never looked so good, and she was sure that they were going to make a good impression on their guests when they arrived.

"Oh god, I'm so scared." Jane admitted, as she closed her eyes for a moment.

"You've got nothing to be scared of, they're just people." Helena reassured her.

"They're not, Charles told me what they're like. They sound more like vultures than people." Jane felt uncomfortable while thinking about that analogy.

"Then we'll face them together." Helena said while looking incredibly determined.

"How are you ladies getting on-wow." Charles said, as he stopped in the doorway of the large closet.

"Again with the lack of knocking?" Jane groaned, as she scowled at him.

"I'm...sorry." He muttered and glanced down for a moment.

"What is it?" She frowned. He seemed much more on edge than usual and she didn't like how it unnerved her too.

"It's nothing." Charles shook his head as he straightened up. Even while she was wearing heels, he was still at least a head taller than her. "The guests will be here soon so we should start to get ready for them downstairs."

"Sure." Jane nodded, as she glanced over at Helena.

There was a look in her eyes that she couldn't quite read, and upon hearing Charles' footsteps fading behind her, Jane took the opportunity to warn her.

"Please don't act out." She said quickly.

"I won't." Helena looked slightly offended at her sister's request.

"Promise me?" Jane asked with a wince.

"I promise, alright?" Helena said. She was irritated by her sister, and that was never a good thing. "Now let's go and get this over with, shall we?"

*****

"They're on their way down." Charles muttered, as he quickly moved down the stairs to where James was waiting.

"How do they look?" He asked. James was dressed in a similar suit to Charles, and when he caught a look at their reflection, it looked as though they could have been brothers instead of cousins.

"They look amazing." Charles said in a low voice.

"You're going to have to keep it together, man." James chuckled.

However, Charles watched as the smile washed right off of his cousin's face at the sight of the two women coming down the stairs. There was no mistaking that they were sisters; they shared the same dark colored locks, although Helena's had been styled in a much more curled fashion, and their blue eyes were rather captivating. Charles couldn't help but feel that his gaze was stuck on Jane's, he knew that for the evening they were going to have to pretend to have feelings for one another, yet he still felt so conflicted. He coughed to clear his throat, but also to pull himself together as he stood a little taller and clasped his hands behind his back.

"Jane, you've already met my cousin here." Charles spoke, as they made it down to their level finally. "But Helena, this is my cousin."

"James Bentley." He said from his side and nodded politely to her.

"Nice to meet you." Helena spoke, but there was still a distinct lack of warmth in her voice.

Charles caught the look of panic that Jane sent his way at how her sister was already acting. He nudged James slightly as a signal to do something about the situation.

"Why don't we go and get a drink?" James gestured in the direction of the parlor at the front of the house.

"What is she doing?" Charles whispered harshly as Helena and James went ahead. Jane looked at him with slightly fearful eyes for a moment.

"I don't know, she told me that she would behave." Jane shook her head.

"She had better." He grumbled, as he turned and followed the other two.

Jane shifted her weight from one foot to the other for a few moments and she realized how hard her sister was finding it to act as though she liked the people that she was around.

"Just keep your mouth shut if you don't have to talk." James warned Helena as Jane walked into the room.

All three pairs of eyes were on her for a moment, and Jane felt as though she had walked into a conversation that she wasn't meant to have heard.

"Everything all right?" Jane asked, as she walked over to her sister once James moved away.

"It's fine, I promise I'll play nice." Helena brushed it off.

"You said that earlier, and I'm yet to see any evidence of that." Jane said.

"I'm sorry, I'm just finding this all very difficult. I don't think you fully understand the extent of why I don't like them, but you're in too deep now that I don't have a choice."

Jane didn't know what her sister was talking about, but the sound of knocking from behind her left her with no time to worry about Helena.

"Remember." Charles muttered as he took her arm. "We're a loved up couple who really love one another. We're so pleased to be getting married and we-"

"We want it done as soon as possible." Jane cut him off. "I've got this, I promise."

It was the first time that she was seeing panic spread over Charles' face, but there wasn't any time to make things right since she was going to have to pretend to be happy with him for the next few hours.

"Here we go." He muttered under his breath as Anna opened the door for their guests.

Jane wasn't sure what she had been expecting, but the first man to appear in the doorway was incredibly tall and thin. His eyes quickly surveyed the scene in front of him as though he were trying to scan the area for one person in particular. Jane noted that he has beady eyes, the kind that were dark and couldn't be trusted. Since he had shown up alone, Jane guessed that he was the lawyer that Charles had been talking so much about.

According to Charles, the lawyer hated him and wanted nothing more than to see the fortune go to his uncle. Jane was incredibly intrigued to see if Charles' descriptions of his guests were going to be accurate.

"Mr. Tucker." Charles beamed, as he moved forward to shake hands with the man. "How are you, please come in."

"Thank you, Charles." Tucker nodded to him although he kept his thin lips in a tight line. "It's good to see you again, and you must be…"

"Jane Miller." She spoke with a broad smile as she put her hand forward, expecting him to shake it.

"Pleasure to meet you, Miss Miller." Tucker's gaze was on her and Jane didn't like the way that she could feel the scrutiny through it. He was very tactful in how he examined her appearance, however, as he took her hand, Jane had to force her smile to stay put as he lifted it to his lips and kissed the top of it.

Jane managed to smile through the strange interaction before swiftly returning her arm to Charles'. She had never thought that she would be seeking comfort in this man, but he was already seeming like the lesser evil in the room compared to the lawyer.

"Drinks are being served in the parlor with some light canapes if that interests you?" Charles directed him through to where James and Helena were waiting in the other room. Jane couldn't help but wonder what they were talking about in there, although she was sure that James had a few things to say about her behavior.

"Thank you." Tucker nodded between them. He clasped his hands behind his back once one of the members of staff had taken his coat off of him and made his way through the house.

Jane gave Charles a look of relief once the man was out of sight, she couldn't believe that someone could be so calculating without even saying too many words to her.

"I feel as though that man just looked into my soul." She whispered to Charles as she tried to make light of the situation.

"I've always said that he is one of the devil's henchmen." Charles joked, as he shook his head.

"I see why." Jane nodded. So far, Charles hadn't been wrong in his descriptions it seemed.

"Oh no, we've got more incoming."

Jane straightened at his words as she turned to see that there were two more people coming through the wide open doors.

"Ah, if it isn't my good Uncle and his wife." Charles said with an exhale as he stepped forward to greet them.

The couple in front of Jane were much older than Charles and his cousin, and they both seemed to share the same sour expression as though it were simply how their faces rested.

"Uncle Jack, Aunt Rosalyn, this is Jane Miller." Charles spoke, as he gestured for her to step forward.

"It's lovely to meet you both." Jane said with a sweet smile. She didn't want to give them any reason to be rude toward her at first, killing them with kindness was going to be her way through the dinner. She could only hope that her sister was going to go for a similar approach.

"Evening." His uncle nodded to her.

Jane didn't hold out her hand as she had for the lawyer, she didn't want a repeat of the last encounter. She turned and smiled at the woman at the older man's side; it was clear that she was much younger than him, and as Jane continued to smile at her, Rosalyn's only response was to quickly look her up and down with her eyes. These were the top of the food chain that Charles had been telling her about; the worst of the worst, as he had put it. They were already acting like bullies and they had barely taken three steps through Charles' front door.

"Do you know if anyone else is joining us tonight, Uncle?" Charles asked.

"Well, unless you're going to resurrect my dear brother, I don't think so." His uncle muttered before chuckling to himself. He clearly thought that he was much funnier than the other people in the room did, and Jane felt rather uncomfortable as to whether she should laugh at such a thing.

Rosalyn merely rolled her eyes at her husband's words, she held onto his arm and glanced around the place with a look that showed she could do a better job of decorating. Jane had never met somebody who completely embodied the word 'snob' without talking. She was slightly glad to have only had to exchange a few words between them.

"Right, well then, let's go and have some drinks." Charles announced.

Jane quickly nodded to his suggestion as she realized very quickly that nobody in the room planned on getting through the event sober.

"So Charles, do tell us about this lovely young woman by your side." Tucker spoke up as they entered the room.

Jane had known that all eyes would be on them for the evening, but she hadn't anticipated just how tense the atmosphere around them would be.

"As I introduced you before, this is Jane, and we've been seeing one another for quite a while now." Charles explained with a content smile.

Jane smiled down at the ground as he spoke for her, she kept her arm locked with his and shuffled a little closer to him. As much as he irritated her for an entire multitude of reasons, she felt that there was no need to jeopardize their aim at that moment.

"Lovely." Tucker spoke with a faint smile ghosting on his lips. It didn't feel genuine at all.

If Jane had learned anything, it was that nothing in the world of the rich seemed real. Everything was paid for in advance to be artificial, even the veneered smiles around her.

"You've been together for a while now, isn't that so nice to hear." Tucker turned to Jack with another forced smile. "I wonder, has he told you about the many women who come in and out of here regularly?"

CHAPTER 14

Charles could feel Jane stiffening at his side in the wake of Tucker's words. She shouldn't be too upset since they had always said that this would be in name only, however, he did feel a slight shame at the lawyer's words. He wondered how Tucker had come to learn about what he did after dark, but that was the least of his concerns at that moment. Jane was supposed to be smitten with him, and Charles knew that she was going to have to think fast to get out of this.

"Yeah, we've had a very open relationship these last few months." Jane spoke rather nonchalantly. Charles held his glare directed toward Tucker as the room felt incredibly still around him. He was aware that for the other guests, this was nothing more than some pre-dinner entertainment. Charles just hadn't realized how ruthless the lawyer would be to get to him and stop him from marrying.

"I see." Tucker nodded.

"I suppose it's quite a modern concept, but we're both really similar in that way." Jane continued. "He likes to party, and I suppose I do too at times. But it's an agreement that we both understand and respect."

Charles hid his relief by clearing his throat slightly. He was impressed at how she'd acted so quickly, even though the story was a little ridiculous. His family was used to ridiculous things, and they'd definitely heard worse.

"Dinner is served." The cook called from the hallway as the guests rose from their seats.

Charles caught Jane throwing her sister a panicked look, Helena herself looked incredibly concerned by what had just happened.

"Don't worry about it." Charles whispered to her as they brought up the rear of the party.

"They're going to do and say everything they can to dismantle this."

Jane nodded her head as she walked slightly in front of him. He still couldn't quite get over how ravishing she looked in her dress, but he still had far too much on his mind to be thinking about such a thing.

Charles took a seat between Jane and Rosalyn, with Jack next to his wife, and Tucker next to Jane. The circular table allowed for everyone to get a good view of one another, something that Charles was sure his father had purposefully meant for when he'd installed the table into the house. Directly opposite himself and Jane were James and Helena, he could tell that Jane's sister was trying her hardest not to look around at the decor, but she was failing to be discreet. James gave her a gentle nudge, but this only elicited a glare from her.

Charles could tell that Helena was certainly the more headstrong of the two; even in the short time that he'd been around her, it was clear that she wasn't going to stand for people who tried to walk all over her. He glanced around the table and realized that they were in real danger of some kind of argument that evening. Charles felt as though he should be bracing himself instead of working up an appetite.

"The first course, if you please." The extra waiters that had been hired for the evening entered with delicate trays of food. Jane had been prepared for the small portions of food, but as he glanced around, Charles realized that Helena hadn't been briefed for such a thing.

He groaned internally as he wished that he had been better prepared and had cared a little more about how Jane's sister may ruin his night.

"This looks delicious, Charles." His uncle remarked, as he picked up his first fork of the evening. "Now tell me, when did the two of you meet?" He asked while gesturing with his fork between Charles and Jane.

For a moment, Charles wanted to imagine the looks that he would receive from his family if he were to explain to them the truth about how he and Jane had met. He thought about how his uncle's face would twist into one of shock and horror at being so bold with his words.

However, Charles wasn't sure that it would work in his favor since they would easily find a way around the stipulation if that was the case.

"Well, I just had a normal retail job in the center of town, Charles caught me on my lunch one day and we just hit it off." Jane said with a nonchalant shrug. She smiled up at him and was rather good at acting as though they were a couple.

Charles swallowed thickly as he followed along with the narrative. "What can I say?" He smirked as he stared between Tucker and his uncle Jack. "I'm just a hopeless romantic at heart."

He could see how their expressions changed as they clearly disagreed with what he was saying, however, Charles continued to smirk in amusement. They ate in silence for a while as each member of the party ate the food that was on their plate. The small amount of food meant that the interval from the heated conversation wasn't nearly as long as any of them wanted it to be.

*****

Jane could only watch as her sister looked to James for guidance in terms of table etiquette. It wasn't something that either of them had been taught, since they'd never been able to afford such affluence in their life. However, Jane had the advantage of the situation and could only watch as Helena looked completely clueless.

"What do you do for a living?" James muttered, as he tried to strike up a conversation between himself and Helena. Jack was talking with his wife in a muttered tone and Charles was having to defend himself against the nosy lawyer yet again. Jane tried to act as though she wasn't listening to what the pair were saying.

"I work behind the bar in a strip club."

Jane dropped her fork, causing it to clatter against the fine china plate in front of her.

"Sorry." Jane muttered, as she quickly recovered from the shock of hearing her sister speak so plainly.

James was looking at her with wide eyes as he shifted uncomfortably in his seat. Helena had a proud smirk on her face as she shrugged in her sister's direction. Jane had managed to shift the attention onto her with her clumsiness, and so she kept her head down to not catch anyone else's eyes. Charles was continuing to talk with Tucker, although Jane had mostly tuned out of their conversation. They were only one course into the dinner, and she was already wishing more than anything that she could leave and go back to the comfort of their small apartment.

"Wow, how did you get into that?" James asked while blinking.

"I needed money, it pays better than most bar jobs." Helena shrugged it off.

"Right." James nodded.

If the situation around them wasn't so serious, Jane wouldn't have been able to contain her laughter. But as it stood, she was terrified that someone else was going to overhear the conversation and all of the attention would be put onto them in a very negative way. She shuddered at the thought and tried not to think about what a dangerous game her sister was playing.

"Don't act like you're embarrassed." Helena persisted with a light chuckle.

James glanced up and over at Charles in a panic, but Charles was far too engaged discussing something completely different. She had never been surrounded by so many hot heads in all of her life. The courses just seemed to keep going. Jane had been told that there would be multiple small dishes, but she hadn't anticipated just how many that would be. She tried to keep her eyes down as she ate to avoid catching anyone's eyes. Jane was especially intimidated by Charles' aunt; the woman looked at her with such disgust that Jane was terrified by the option of conversation between them. The room was growing much warmer as the evening continued, but Jane still felt a slight chill running down her back whenever she dared to glance in the direction of Rosalyn.

"I'm just going to use the bathroom." Helena muttered, as she rose from the table. Jane noticed the slight looks that the other guests were giving each other. It seemed that even disclosing where you were going was an outrageous amount of information.

Jane waited a moment before excusing herself and following her sister into the bathroom around the corner.

"What are you doing?" Helena spoke harshly under her breath as her sister barged into the room with her.

"What am I doing?" Jane scoffed. "You promised to be good!"

"I'm just having some fun." Helena played it off.

"This isn't the place to be having it!" Jane fired back. "I can't believe that you would put this plan in jeopardy like that!"

"I don't want to pander to every question that they ask, let's just give them something to talk about." Helena was acting as though there wasn't a lot of pressure weighing on the situation.

"It's not about that!" Jane groaned in frustration as she looked at her sister in disbelief. "This is about us passing off as a happy couple long enough for the people out there to leave us alone. We just have to look like we blend into high society and they'll be out of our business as soon as possible."

"I don't think you realize what you've gotten yourself into. These aren't the kind of people that just give up easily, they're going to come for you in any way that they can for the rest of your life." Helena said while shaking her head. "These aren't the people that you mess with in the beginning, and you should know that these aren't the kind of people that you can beat."

Jane glared at her older sister as she realized that Helena had come to the Bentley mansion with an agenda of her own; to cause chaos.

"You've quit your job for this, I'm going to do the same, and then what? We have to make this work or we really have nothing, we'll be out on the streets by the end of the month."

"We can just sell all of your fancy clothes." Helena said nonchalantly.

"They're not mine to sell." Jane fired back. "Just please try a little harder."

"I make no promises." Helena responded. "And I really wasn't joking when I said that I needed to use the bathroom."

Jane let out one final groan of annoyance as she turned on her heels and exited the bathroom.

"What was going on in there?" James asked, as she found him waiting out in the corridor.

"Nothing, it's fine." Jane shook her head as she walked back towards the dining room.

"She's going to ruin this entire thing if she isn't careful, and then I won't be able to help you anymore." He warned her as he kept up with her quick pace.

"She's got her own agenda and I don't know what to do about it." Jane shook her head. "How much longer is this dinner going to be?"

"I'm not sure." James said while sucking in a breath. "She's already said some rather outrageous things, and I'm confident that Rosalyn heard some of them too."

"Oh god." Jane closed her eyes for a moment. "This can't be happening."

They arrived back at the table and instantly Jane cast her eyes downwards as she sat beside her 'husband-to-be.'

"Everything all right?" Charles asked in a whisper. Jane merely shrugged in response, she didn't want to lie to him, but she had no idea how to explain what was happening.

"So Jane, what did you say your sister did for a living?" Rosalyn spoke up with a rather triumphant look already on her face. Jane knew for a fact that she was yet to mention her sister's occupation. She gulped.

CHAPTER 15

"She used to work in a bar." Jane said in as calm of a voice as she could muster. She tried to stop herself from letting her voice waver, but it was proving impossible.

"I see." Rosalyn nodded. "Used to?"

"Yes, she recently quit due to having some trouble at work. You know what people can be like after a couple drinks." Jane held her nerve.

"You don't have to make it sound so cryptic." Helena chuckled as she reappeared in the doorway, causing her sister to freeze up. Jane shook her head slowly at Helena as all eyes were now on her. "Well, I worked behind the bar in a...gentleman's club, not a very nice one at that."

"Oh!" Rosalyn gasped, as she made the connection rather dramatically. She turned to her husband with wide eyes, although Jane could see that she was pleased by the news.

Jane dared to peek a glance at Charles next to her, and she knew that he was also very tense in his body language. "That doesn't sound too glamorous, dear."

"No, it really wasn't. Lot's of long nights and sleeping through your days." Helena continued. Jane wished for her to close her mouth more than anything.

"And how long did you do that for?" Rosalyn asked.

Judging by the look on his aunt's face, Jane knew that she was loving every moment of what was going on.

"A couple of years I suppose, you get to see a lot of familiar faces when you're in there as well. A lot of regulars." Helena said as she turned her gaze from Rosalyn to her husband.

James choked on his water slightly from next to her as everyone around the table made the connection of what she was insinuating.

Jane was in shock that her sister had the balls to say such a thing and throw around accusations like that. Although, she couldn't deny that she had enjoyed the way that the triumphant smirk had dropped straight off of Rosalyn's face.

"Ah, here's dessert!" Charles spoke with a heavy tone of relief as the chef walked into the tense room.

His uncle Jack was glaring at Jane's sister, and if looks could kill, then Helena would have already been six feet in the ground. Jane breathed out as the plates distracted everyone for a while, it allowed them a moment away from the wild accusations that had been used only moments before. Jane was constantly trying to catch her sister's eye, but it was to no avail. She grimaced as she glanced down at the final course, her appetite had long since disappeared. Helena's previous statement had rendered Jack and Rosalyn speechless, and Jane watched Tucker carefully. His eyes were darting around the table, and his expression was cold and calculating as he took in the people around him. He was clearly looking for a way to turn the tables back so that it was Helena who was the one feeling sheepish at the table. But Helena was wearing her past like a badge of honor, and that meant that nobody could use it to disarm her. Jane understood at that moment why she had done it, but she still felt as though she couldn't do the same since her position was slightly different in the family.

The table was silent as they tucked into the chocolate mouse, although Jane was having to force down each mouthful with a lot of effort. Charles was silent beside her, but she could imagine the kind of thoughts that he was having as to what had gone down.

Jane also noticed how pink Jack Bentley's cheeks had been since Helena had said the rather offensive comment about him being a regular at the strip club. She wondered if it was really true. Finally, the meal was over, and while Jane knew that the guests were likely to want to stay around while they had drinks and let their food settle, the intensity of the table was thankfully abolished.

"There are some refreshments in the parlor on the south side of the house." Charles announced as Tucker, his uncle, and aunt all rose from the table rather quickly. Jane did too since she knew that it was better to at least try and do some damage control while she could. She sent a glare in her sister's direction, but Helena simply responded by raising her glass slightly.

"I can show you around the grounds if you like?" James offered to Helena quietly while the others filed out of the room.

"In the dark?" Helena asked with a frown.

James muttered something that Jane didn't quite catch from her position across the room, but she saw the way that her sister rolled her eyes before complying with him.

"I mean, it could have gone a lot worse." Jane muttered to Charles as he shook his head and moved past her.

"I wouldn't say that we're out of the woods just yet." He spoke as he followed her into the room with their awaiting guests.

"Jane, do sit next to me." Rosalyn had a sickly sweet smile on her face as she spoke. Jane nodded slowly as she tried to imagine what kind of plan the woman had come up with to come out on top.

"Did you enjoy the food?" She asked politely.

"Yes, it was quite wonderful." Rosalyn said. "Although I don't think anything will ever beat our chef, Andy, he's like some kind of miracle worker in the kitchen. I suppose it's why my standards are always so high when it comes to dining elsewhere."

Rosalyn was the kind of person who always had to have the upper hand and be the most impressive in conversations. Jane didn't like that kind of quality, but she hoped her face wasn't showing that.

"So, your sister used to work in a gentleman's establishment as she said earlier." Rosalyn said, which Jane thought was rather bold of her to bring up once more. "And I assume that you were also working there at some point?"

"Excuse me?" Jane narrowed her eyes as she glanced over at the men who were sitting on the other side of the room. The three of them were having a separate conversation, and so there was nobody to save her from the woman's awful comments.

"Well, those kinds of things do run in the family. With one sister in the business, I'm just checking that the other-"

"I was never a stripper if that's what you were referring to?" Jane cut her off. She remembered Charles telling her to refrain from doing such a thing, but Rosalyn was infuriating.

"And you never worked behind the bar either?" She was acting unfazed by the conversation.

"No, I've worked as a delivery driver, and I've worked in other stores in town. I don't like working in service that much."

"And I suppose you've found an out to that?" Rosalyn said with a growing smile on her face.

"An out?"

"Charles." Rosalyn spoke up, earning the man's attention in the process. "He's your out, right?"

"He's not my anything, we're just seeing each other." Jane shrugged it off.

"It's all right, you can tell me these things. Think of it as girl to girl, these are the kind of chats that we can't have at the table." Rosalyn winked at her.

But Jane was no fool. She knew exactly what was going on and what Rosalyn was playing at. The woman was trying to coax her into revealing the fact that the marriage was for nothing other than convenience, but Jane wasn't going to give her the opportunity.

"I actually really am taken by him." Jane admitted it as though Rosalyn was one of the first people that she was confiding in this with. "I really like him, and I'm glad it's going so well. It's been a strange few months and it was very on and off in the beginning so-"

"Wait, I can't tell if you're actually serious about this." Rosalyn held up her hand.

"What do you mean?" Jane frowned innocently. She glanced over at Charles to see that he was now trying his hardest to pay attention to two conversations at the same time.

"Well, you don't actually expect me to believe that, do you?" Rosalyn asked with a chuckle as she shook her head. "I don't believe for a second that the two of you have this bond that you can't break."

Jane didn't know what to say to her comment, since the woman was trying to tell her how she felt.

"I like him, I don't know what you want me to say, there's no acting here." Jane chuckled.

"Well, if there ever is anything like that going on, just know that you can talk to me." Rosalyn spoke with another sickening smile on her face. Jane didn't believe for one moment that she was going to be able to help her or that she would keep conversations between them.

"I don't get what you mean." Jane narrowed her eyes.

She knew exactly what the older woman was referring to, but Jane just wanted to make her say it. She realized how harsh that sounded and grimaced at the fact that fitting in with the elite was becoming scarily easy for her.

"Well, I just mean that I didn't exactly marry old Jack over there for his charm and looks." Rosalyn spoke, as she shifted in her seat. Jane could tell that she'd managed to make her feel uncomfortable and saw that as a win.

"I see." Jane nodded. "Well, I very much am attracted to the man that I'm with." She said with a smile similar to the one on Rosalyn's face. The smile was slightly too wide, giving off a tone that made it seem incredibly fake.

"Well then, I'm happy for you both." She nodded, although Jane didn't believe her for a second.

"Everything all right over here?" Charles asked hesitantly as Jane smiled up at him and nodded.

"Oh yeah, all good over here." Jane said. "We were just having a little girl chat."

"All right, don't let me interrupt you then." Charles said with a frown as he glanced between the pair of them.

"He can be good when he wants to be, I suppose." Rosalyn spoke with a sigh as they watched him walk back over to the men.

"What's that supposed to mean?" Jane asked with narrowed eyes.

"Oh, you know, he doesn't exactly behave like a thirty-four-year-old man at times. What with all the partying, and drinking, and girls...just things that you expect men to grow out of."

Jane noted how Rosalyn hesitated after talking about Charles and the many people that she was sure he'd slept with. It didn't bother her because they weren't really together, and Jane started to pity any real girl that Charles tried to introduce to his family. She really wasn't going to make it past the first dinner party.

"What about your parents?" Rosalyn pressed.

Jane wished that she could abandon social decorum for just a moment so that she could groan out loud at the many questions she was having to answer.

"Well, my father left when we were quite young." Jane started.

"I'm sorry to hear that, families can be tough."

"Thanks, but he wasn't a nice man. He was actually quite awful, some of the things that I've been told he did. I was too young to properly remember, but I think Helena can remember the end of it." Jane felt the words coming to her easily since none of it was a lie. "And my mother passed away quite recently. She was supposed to have some big operation that would have saved her life, but she never got to have it."

"That is terrible, I'm so sorry to hear that she couldn't have it." Rosalyn said with what Jane guessed was her first genuine expression of the evening. "Life really isn't fair, especially for the good ones."

Jane didn't count Rosalyn as one of the good ones; she had done well for herself in picking a good husband with a lot of money; that seemed to be the only thing that the woman had accomplished in her life though.

"It's fine, I have my sister and we've gotten through everything together. I don't think I would have been able to do it without her, though." Jane said, as she glanced out the window to where she could see a torch out on the lawn.

CHAPTER 16

"You really had to make a big show in there, huh?" James asked as they walked across the freshly cut lawn. Helena was hugging her arms to her chest as she wished that she'd taken a jacket before leaving the house.

"You've been told to bring me out here?" She asked with a slight chuckle. James made a face that told her all she needed to know. "You guys are treating me like a dog, sending me outside when I get too loud."

"Yeah? Well then you should stop acting like a bitch if you don't want to be treated like one." James fired back quickly.

"Wow." Helena breathed out. She was slightly taken aback by how harsh his words had been, she hadn't been expecting it from him. Although he was a Bentley, she could tell that he was definitely one of the more timid members of the family. He was one of the only ones to display any kind of humility. "So that's what you really think of me?"

"You just caused such a scene in there. I'm sorry for calling you a bitch, but I really think you should have thought that through a little better."

"I thought it through to the best of my ability." Helena said quickly. "If I had told them that I worked in a bar, they would have tried to use it against me in some way. They would have tried to patronize me and that would have gotten under my skin. This way, it means that I had the upper hand."

"It was about defense tonight, not offense." James said.

Helena didn't care whatever games they were playing with his relatives, she didn't want any part of it. All she wanted to do was have a good evening and not be scrutinized for her life choices. It seemed that there were certain members at that table who weren't going to let her have that.

"You've got to admit though that it was pretty funny to see their faces." Helena said with a light chuckle. "Did you see how red Jack went? He must have cheated on her a lot if he had that reaction. No innocent man would react like that."

"All right, it was a little funny." James admitted. "But it was still incredibly foolish and rash. What if that was it for your sister and this whole engagement crap?"

"We would have found a way to continue on, we're good at that. We've survived our entire lives without any clear-cut path, without any family fortune to fall back on. I think we'll manage long after the Bentleys are out of our lives." Helena said as she glanced down at her shoes.

Her heels were sinking into the soft ground of the lawn, but she didn't care, they were shoes from the many that Charles had bought for her sister. She tried to hazard a guess as to how much they may have cost him, but she had no concept of how much it could be.

"So what do you think of the grounds?" James asked, as he tried to strike up a conversation with her.

"I thought this was all just to get me out of the house? We don't actually have to talk now that we're out here, you know?"

"All right, suit it yourself." James grumbled, as he shone the torch light that was coming from his phone ahead of them.

They continued walking around the perimeter of the lawn in silence. The house was lit up and looked like a painting as Helena turned towards it to admire it for a moment. She could have sworn that it was all a dream, that she was actually back in their tiny apartment and this was all just some fantasy that she had made up in her sleep-deprived state.

"Would you like my jacket? You look cold." James spoke up as he stood next to her.

Helena had been hugging her arms to her chest for the past few minutes and stood with her shoulders up by her ears whenever a slight breeze danced through the air. She was stubborn at the best of times, but she was also cold, and Helena wasn't sure how much longer she could deny that fact.

"But then you'll be cold." She frowned, as he started to take it off anyway.

"Just shut up and put it on."

Helena huffed and tugged the large blazer over her shoulders. Instantly, it provided warmth for her that caused her body to relax slightly. The material smelled of an expensive cologne that had mingled with the remnants of cigarette smoke, it was quite a unique smell, and one that she knew would linger on her after she gave him back his jacket.

"Thanks." She muttered as they continued walking back toward the house. "Do you think it will be socially acceptable for us to go home yet?"

"Let's just wait until the guests have gone and then we'll see." James said. "I don't think your sister is happy with you."

"She rarely is, or I rarely am with her. It's a fine balance between us, but she'll get over it."

"Don't expect to be invited back to any more of these events." James said with a slight chuckle.

"I'll see you at the wedding." Helena responded dryly.

"I can't wait to hear your speech." He chuckled and shook his head.

She thought that perhaps the Bentleys weren't all bad, but Helena still got the sense that James was looking at her like she was an outsider. It wasn't the nicest thought, and it made her slightly uncomfortable to think that the members of the family were probably looking at her and her sister as though they were charity cases. Helena may have played it down with James, but she was slightly worried at how her sister was going to react to the way she'd acted. She'd caught the glares that Jane had been sending her way, and she knew that Jane wasn't going to let this go too easily.

"Are we going to head back inside?" Helena asked, as they started to near the house.

"If you promise not to open your mouth again." James nodded and shot her an amused smile.

"My lips are sealed." Helena said with a smirk.

He rolled his eyes and shook her head but still led the way inside. She followed after him, although Helena was much less confident about how she would be received this time.

"Ah, there you both are, we were just leaving." Jack spoke, as he put on his coat in the main hallway. His wife appeared moments later, still looking as sour as when she had arrived. Rosalyn barely glanced in Helena's direction, which caused her to smirk slightly as she realized that she really did get to her.

The remainder of the dinner party came out of the parlor, with Charles and Jane at the rear. She was holding onto him as though the two of them were together and madly in love. What scared Helena the most was how natural it really did look between them. Jane was succeeding in avoiding her sister's glances, and Helena knew right at that moment that she was going to have a lot of groveling to do.

The polite goodbye and good nights were thrown around as the three guests exited the house. Helena decided to stay by the only person who was being some kind of ally toward her; James. She found it odd how she'd thought at the beginning of the night that she wouldn't be able to stand the man, but he was now looking like the only one who would talk to her.

Helena was used to being the bad guy in the situation, it had happened to her many times before and she wasn't feeling too bad about it.

"Well that could have gone a whole lot worse than it did." James tried to lighten the mood. However, Helena saw the fire that seemed to ignite in her sister's gaze as she finally turned to look at her.

*****

"How could you be so rash?" Jane asked, as she stepped toward her sister in the grand hall almost as soon as the door closed.

"What do you mean? I explained to you in the bathroom what I did and why I did it." Helena was quick to defend herself.

Now that the most judgmental people had left the building, Jane felt as though she could somewhat relax and actually talk to her sister properly.

"No, what you did out there put everything at risk." Jane fired back.

"Oh come on, I told you, I was just having a bit of fun. Charles found it funny, didn't you?"

Charles glared at her and shook his head in response, Helena decided to simply glare back at him.

"Look, I think that the two of you should just get some rest and you can talk about this in the morning/" James stepped in with his hands up as though he was skilled in de-escalating situations.

"I'm not going home with her." Jane said stubbornly. She didn't like the idea of being stuck in a car and having to listen to her sister trying to justify herself.

"What do you mean?" Helena chuckled. "You can't stay here, this isn't your home."

"You can stay for the night if you'd like to, Jane." Charles offered from behind her.

"There you go, I'm staying here."

"No, we're leaving, and we're leaving now. I'll call an Uber if I have to, I don't want to use any more of his money anyway."

"But you don't have any money!" Jane fired back at her.

"All right, that's enough." James said, as he continued to step between them.

"No, that's the truth." She continued. "We don't have any money, and that's why we're in this situation. I don't know what you think we're doing here, but we need this, Helena. So we can't do anything stupid like you did tonight."

"I already said sorry because I didn't think it would upset you this much, I just wanted to put that old man in his place." Helena said.

It was clear to everyone in the room that the older of the Miller sisters were fighting a losing battle. She stared between the three of them and narrowed her eyes. It felt like they were ganging up on her, and Helena hated when people did that.

"I never thought I'd see the day." She spoke with a laugh of disbelief in her voice. "You're really going to stay here tonight?"

"I am." Jane held her ground. "I don't want to argue with you anymore tonight."

"You're picking them over your own family." Helena argued anyway.

"Family is supposed to have your back, tonight you didn't have my back at all." Jane spoke quickly. "Now I'm done talking about this and I think you should leave."

Helena's face dropped as she realized just how upset her sister really was. The silence that followed Jane's words sunk in around her, and Helena shook off the other two pairs of eyes that were staring at her.

"Jane, I-"

"Just go, I don't want to talk to you right now."

CHAPTER 17

"Wow." Charles said with a chuckle as the door shut. "I thought that my family was messy."

"They are." Jane glared at him. "And now they've caused this between me and the only family that I have left."

"She did start it." Charles countered, as he let his housekeeper start with the clearing up operation in the wake of the dinner party.

"She only reacted because your elitist uncle and his wife provoked her." Jane defended her sister even though she was still seething inside. She understood why Helena had spoken up about her dodgy past, but she just wished that she'd thought it all through a little better.

"Will you talk to her tomorrow?" Charles asked, as Jane glanced between him and his cousin.

"I...I don't know yet. I'm too tired to properly think about it right now."

"All right, I can show you to your rooms if you'd like?" Charles asked, as he gestured up the stairs.

Jane tried to ignore the way that the word room had been plural, implying that she was going to have more than one room to herself. She didn't understand why she would need any more than just the one room, since she was sure that all she needed at that moment was a bed to sleep on. Jane was so used to the bare minimum that she would have happily slept on one of the couches in the library.

"It's just through here." Charles nodded, as he opened a door and turned on the light. Jane glanced around in awe at how large the room was, and it was all hers. She felt as though she were a princess that was about to be tempted into a room and locked up in a castle, but she didn't care.

The grandeur was more than she ever could have expected with windows longer than the width of her entire apartment on the other side of town. The curtains were the same staple velour material that all of the couches and chairs were made with downstairs, but the material looked to be incredibly thick. They draped all the way from the top of the room to the floor, and the impressive ceiling heights made her suddenly feel very small in the space.

"Thank you for this." She muttered, as she turned to see that Charles was still there and staring at her. She wasn't sure what it was that had changed within him that evening, but he was being much more tender with her than usual. It was something that she liked, although Jane couldn't put her finger on why he was being that way.

"I hope you don't fight with your sister for long." He admitted. "She might have said some things that were out of line tonight, but she's not a bad person, and she certainly didn't say anything that really jeopardized us in the end."

"She could have continued on if I hadn't told her to stop." Jane reasoned. "I was so sure that she was going to expose us as a sham."

"But she didn't, and that's all that matters." Charles was surprisingly calm about the whole thing.

Jane realized that perhaps she had overreacted a bit to the situation.

"I hope you're right about it not jeopardizing this, they could still think it over and come to their own conclusions."

"Don't worry about them, that's something for us to deal with at another time. For the time being, I suggest that you get some rest, we've had quite a stressful evening." Charles smiled at her.

"Good night." Jane nodded, as he left her alone, closing the door after him.

*****

"Well." James began, as Charles reappeared in the library and quickly moved to pour himself some scotch. "That was an eventful evening, to say the least."

"We always knew that something was bound to kick off." Charles admitted, as he offered a glass to his cousin.

"No thanks, I've had enough." James shook his head. "I know, but I thought that the drama would have come from the other side of the table in all honesty."

"I know, I think we may have been directing our efforts toward the wrong Miller sibling." Charles admitted.

"She was rather feisty, wasn't she?" James said with a light chuckle.

"I think that might be a bit of an understatement." He responded.

The two of them sat in silence for a while as they tried to decompress and think about what had happened that evening. Charles was convinced that Tucker was up to something, for the majority of the evening he'd been too quiet.

"What are you thinking?" James asked, as Charles turned to him.

"I was thinking about Tucker and how unnerving I found him this evening." He admitted.

"Unnerving?"

"He was just so much quieter than usual. He came in, made a few remarks, and then sat back and just watched everything unfold. Sure we spoke about various more mundane things one to one, but he was just...calculating the whole time."

"Do you think he saw through it?" James asked with a slight wince.

"I don't know." Charles shook his head slowly as he stared at the recently lit fireplace. "All I know is that we really can't be too careful. Tucker is definitely going to do some digging into their family history, and I know that neither of them are going to like that."

"This is exactly why we don't mix with people like them, Charles." James said.

"You do realize how you sound?" He asked while cocking an eyebrow.

"I don't care how I sound, to be honest, I'm just being truthful." James brushed off his judgment. "We wouldn't have this kind of drama if you had just found a pleasant young woman to marry from a family that had taught her respect and manners."

"I thought that Jane was very well behaved tonight." Charles defended her.

"You know what I mean, someone who just already knows everything and doesn't have to be told. Someone who just understands how this world works, they don't have to learn about it and break old habits to fit in."

"Is that what you think she's having to do?"

"That's what I know she's having to do. Jane did a good job tonight, but you could still tell that both of them were completely out of their depth. They had no idea what they were doing or how they were going to succeed in this situation."

"It was never about succeeding, just about keeping our heads above the water for as long as was needed."

The two of them stayed up for a while as Charles thought about the girl who was now staying in his mansion. Jane had done well to remain loyal to him and the cause, and it made him think that he could actually trust her moving forward. It was a step in the right direction, even if her sister wasn't quite the same kind of thing. He felt reassured by Jane's actions and knew that she was going to help him in any way that she could in the future. Charles thought about the weeks that lay ahead of them and how he was going to have to be tough with her if they were going to get through this.

*****

Jane awoke the next morning feeling slightly sick. She couldn't believe that she had been so angry with her sister like that. She remembered how Helena had looked when Jane announced that she wouldn't be going home with her. Helena had been heartbroken at the fact that Jane was starting to choose this life over family. That hadn't been her point at all though. Jane had only chosen to stay with Charles because she couldn't bear the thought of having to go home to their cramped apartment and still remain mad at her sister.

Jane sighed and rolled over in the giant bed that Charles had let her use. The bed stretched out in both directions for so long that she was sure she could get another couple of people comfortably in the thing. The ceilings above her seemed to stretch on for much longer than the average room, and everything just seemed a lot bigger in general. Jane couldn't help but smirk as she wondered if Charles was compensation for something. She held onto the small ounce of amusement that she could think of since it helped to break through the hopeless misery that she was feeling. Jane finally groaned as she started to roll out of the large bed and over to the en-suite that was attached to the large room. There was also another door that led off into another room, but Jane was yet to explore that avenue.

After washing and dressing into one of the casual outfits that she had picked out with Charles, Jane turned to look at herself in the mirror. The pants were still what she would have considered formal, and the shirt wasn't even what she would

135

call casual. However, she knew that it would fit Charles' idea of casualness, and if she was staying in his house for however long, she really didn't want to upset him in any way.

"Good morning." Jane muttered, as she made her way into the dining room to see James sitting there.

"Morning. He smiled up at her as he took in her appearance.

"No Charles yet?"

"He doesn't quite understand the concept of the morning." James shrugged off the question.

Jane sat down opposite him at the table as Anna walked in and saw that they were going to have to prepare even more breakfast now.

"So." James said, as he looked up from his plate. "You seem to be fitting in well."

"Do you think?" Jane asked with a slight frown.

"I do." He nodded. "Even down to your outfits now." He gestured to what she wore. "It's a big improvement from even just a few days ago. Tell me, what's changed?"

"I suppose there was just no point in fighting it." Jane explained with a simple shrug. "I'm going to have to go through with this, so I might as well just try and make it work."

"I wish your sister had that attitude." James chuckled. But he stopped laughing as he saw the way that Jane dipped her head down at the comment. "I apologize, I shouldn't have brought it up."

"It's all right, I bet she feels stupid today." Jane said. "She'd had a lot to drink, so I suppose we should have seen it coming."

"I get the feeling that she would have done all of that regardless of how much she'd had to drink." James smiled to himself.

"Rosalyn was trying to get to me after dinner last night." Jane spoke up. "She was trying to get under my skin and get me to reveal that it was all a sham to her. I don't know what made her think that I would trust her after the way that she had been treating all of us for the best part of the whole night."

"I know, she thinks she's being smart at times, she thinks she has the upper hand, but she doesn't. She's only in it for the money, everyone knows that, even Jack." James shrugged it off. "I like to say that it is perhaps the worst kept secret within our family."

"What would you say is the best-kept secret?" Jane asked out of curiosity.

"Well, it would lose its title if I were to tell you." James spoke with a cocked eyebrow. Jane couldn't help the small smile that rose across her lips at his comment.

She knew that a family as well off and old as theirs was bound to have its fair share of secrets and scandals. With nothing else to do but talk about things, Jane felt that she should at least try to get some out of the man.

"See, you fit in a lot better than you give credit for." James said.

"What do you mean?"

"Asking about secrets, that's the exact thing that we would do." He pointed out as though it were obvious. "Because as much as money is power, secrets also hold a lot of weight in these kinds of parts. They pretty much have their own currency."

Jane thought about what he said for a moment and felt a shudder run down her spine. It wasn't a comfortable thought and it certainly wasn't nice to think that she was going to be part of a family that could be so scandalous.

"And I suppose in a way, I'm now a big part of one of those secrets." Jane pointed out.

"Indeed you are. You're part of something that could potentially be the best kept scandal of our Bentley's generation."

She wasn't sure how to feel about that; she would always be known as the scandalous outcast who was only in the situation for money, Jane felt her cheeks flush as the housekeeper came back into the room. A large array of foods were brought out for her, but Jane wasn't feeling all too hungry after her talk with James. She decided to pick at a croissant as she was sure that he was far from finished with his rather philosophical talk.

"How long do you think I'm going to have to stay married to him?" Jane asked carefully.

She felt that the Bentley's eyes on her from across the table and continued to pick at her breakfast instead of meeting his gaze.

"Do you already have divorce on your mind?" James asked with a slight chuckle. There was a tone of uneasiness in his voice that Jane could tell was due to uncertainty on the subject.

"Well, I'm just being practical." Jane shrugged it off. "I don't want to have him thinking that this arrangement will be continuing for the rest of my life."

"I'm afraid that's a conversation that you're going to have to have with Charles." James said while holding up his hands. "That's not the kind of area that I'm familiar with."

"Of course, forget I said anything." Jane nodded, as she started to bite tentatively into the pastry. Her mouth felt very dry as she realized that by talking to James, the information about her uncertainties would no doubt get back to Charles. She still didn't feel as though she could be herself around them, and she felt as though everyone was either watching or listening - waiting for her to slip up.

CHAPTER 18

Helena woke up rather disappointed to see that she didn't have any messages from her sister about what had happened. She felt a lump forming in her throat as she realized just how Jane really was with her. She groaned and rolled over in her bed as she caught sight of the crumpled blue dress on the floor. She hated it. She hated the Bentleys, and she hated how they were back in their lives and ruining them in yet another way. Helena thought about what would happen if she told her sister what she knew. It was a long shot, but she knew that it would bring Jane back to her so that she could heal this rift. She knew that they both meant it when they said that they needed one another in life, Helena wasn't sure that she could go through any more without Jane.

She managed to get herself up, despite the slight headache that was tapping against her temple. Helena made a face at the way that the apartment looked in comparison to the grandeur that she had experienced last night. If it weren't for the dress on the floor in the corner of the room, Helena felt that she would have been able to convince herself that it was another dream.

She thought about the greedy people that had been around that table and just how bad news they were. Helena was a rather good judge of character, at least she'd like to think that, but she knew confidently that the majority of the people in the room last night hadn't been good.

She didn't like the thought of Jane waking up on her own in such a place, but then a thought entered her mind. Helena frowned as she pondered over whether or not it could be true; was Jane sleeping with Charles?

It wasn't something that seemed completely off of the cards, especially when Helena thought about how they had been so close the night before. She bit her lip and thought for a moment, the idea that their claws were in her sister too deep made her chest hurt. Her heart was aching for Jane and how she thought that she was doing the right thing for them both. Helena wished that the roles were reversed and that she could carry the burden for her, but that wasn't how life had dealt this hand. Helena ran a hand through her slightly greasy hair and groaned as she moved to get ready for the day. She tried to call Jane, but it went straight to voicemail.

*****

Jane had switched her phone off for the past couple of days. In a house like Charles' there didn't seem to be any need for one, and she didn't want to speak with her sister just yet.

Charles had been very kind in letting her stay for a few more nights, although Jane had promised to be gone by the weekend.

Jane thought about the prospect of going home to her sister and how angered Helena was going to be with her for ignoring her. It wasn't going to be pretty, but she knew that she couldn't avoid her sister forever.

"Have you spoken with your sister?" James asked, as they walked through the woodlands at the rear of the property.

"Not yet." Jane muttered and shook her head.

"She's probably worried about you."

If Jane was being honest with herself, then she was more worried about Helena. She knew that the apartment wasn't safe, nor was the area around it. The thought of her being there on her own wasn't at all comforting, but she was still too angry to go and see her.

"Perhaps even just a phone call to let her know that you're alright?"

"I'll think about it." Jane grumbled. She didn't want to talk about it, and she certainly didn't want to talk about it with

Charles' right-hand man. "Why are you always hanging around here?"

"I live just a few houses down on the same street." James explained. "Although, mine isn't quite as nice as this is."

"Do you know where these grounds end?" Jane asked with a slight chuckle. She wanted to move the conversation away from her family drama in any way that she could.

"I have no idea, much further than my own though, I'm sure."

"Are you married, James?" Jane asked to keep the conversation from reverting back to Helena.

"No, do I seem like the married kind?"

"I suppose not." She chuckled. "Do you have any kind of stipulation that you have to follow?"

"None at all, I'm a free man in this family. It's quite a nice feeling, although you do get bumped down the list of importance quite a lot."

"It's not all it's cut out to be, having all of the attention on you at dinner parties." Jane waved it off.

"You still did a good job." He said with a kind smile. "I'll be honest, I really did think that you were going to crumble under all of that pressure, but you held strong."

"Thanks, I think." Jane laughed at the rather back-handed compliment she had received from him.

"My pleasure." James smirked. "Do you think that you'll make up with your sister?"

"We fight a lot." Jane said as she clenched her jaw. She had noticed recently that James asked a lot of questions about Helena, although she wasn't sure why that was exactly. "All through out our lives, we have disagreed over things, but it all works out in the end. It always does."

"Do you ever wonder if things go too far sometimes?"

"Of course, I already know that I should have called to check that she's okay. But I haven't, and now it feels slightly too late."

"I don't think it's too late, and I'm surprised that she hasn't stopped by here to see if you're alright," James said.

"She's too stubborn, but so am I. It will be a bit of an impasse for a while, but we'll eventually make up again."

They walked on some more until the woods became too thick for a clear path through to be made for them.

"Why don't we head back?" James suggested as she nodded in response. "Oh, and Charles wanted to ask if you would like to go to golf with him tomorrow?"

"Golf?" Jane asked with a frown. She remembered when he had first briefed her on how it would work. She would be sat up on the terrace with Rosalyn, while the men below were having their fun on the range. Jane grimaced at the idea and she started to wonder how much of a choice she really had in the matter. "And Rosalyn will be there?"

"Unfortunately, yes." James nodded and pursed his lips. "She will, but I think that you're able to handle her better than you give yourself credit for."

"I'm going to have to go, aren't I?" Jane asked with a wince.

"Charles may have already accepted on your behalf." James spoke slowly as Jane felt her eyes close for a moment.

"So there really wasn't a choice that I had when you *asked* me if I wanted to go." Jane said with a sigh.

"You know what he's like, he wants this whole thing to be perfect and watertight. You're going to have to show your face at more than one dinner party if he wants to do that." James explained.

Jane nodded as she wondered what kind of get up Charles was going to make her wear for meeting with the devil herself on the terrace at the golf club.

"So you'll come?"

"James, you just said that I don't have a choice." Jane pointed out. "Yes, I'll come, but I feel like I'm going for a tea party with a wolf."

"Vulture." He corrected. "She's not the main predator as a wolf would be; she waits for things to either be killed by other animals or drop dead."

Jane actually quite liked the analogy since it did work perfectly for Rosalyn. She was a vulture through and through.

"And even though she has all that money, her nose still looks like a beak." Jane said with a chuckle.

"Harsh." James laughed and shook his head.

Jane knew that it wasn't nice to talk about people like that, but this wasn't the kind of world where nice got one very far. This was the kind of world where you had to do what you had to do in order to survive. Because despite the change in environment, the status that came with that, and all of the luxurious clothes and meals; Jane still felt as though she was only surviving.

*****

She rode in the passenger seat of Charles' flashy sports car the next day. Jane's knee was bobbing out of anxiety as Charles blared some kind of alternative music through the speakers.

"Just be pleasant with her, like you were at the dinner party but with slightly less sass."

"Is sass reserved for the evening events?" Jane asked with a snort.

However, as she turned to look at him, she realized that he really wasn't joking about that.

"The golf club has a lot of ears, and I don't want you getting into any more trouble by saying things that you aren't meant to."

Jane nodded along, but she had already had this talk with him over dinner the previous night. Jane still felt incredibly guilty for not contacting her sister. She had decided that as soon as she got through this event, she would finally go home and see her. That was if Helena was willing to see her after a couple of days away. She twiddled with the dainty ring that was on the correct finger of her left hand and bit her lip. It was a new edition, the first kind of inclination that two of them were engaged for. The ring displayed a simple diamond, although Jane was sure that it must have cost a lot of money to have made. Even the simple diamond looked to be costing more than what she would have made as a delivery driver over the course of an entire year.

"You've got this." Charles spoke from next to her.

He'd been a lot softer over the past week than ever before, and Jane realized that perhaps he was starting to become a lot more fond of her. It was a foolish thought, but she smiled at the idea of the two of them at least having a friendship while they pretended to be married. Jane knew that it would make everything a lot easier if they got along well.

"I know, it's just going to be a lot of talking, and I'm not sure that I'm ready for that." Jane sighed.

"You're going to do fine, just don't bring up your sister, and only talk about the engagement if she notices the ring."

They were simple instructions, but as they pulled into the golf course, Jane could feel her mind going into a kind of survival mode. She felt as though she was simply leaving one lion's den and replacing it with another.

CHAPTER 19

Charles got out of the car first and walked around to help Jane out of the passenger seat. He liked how well she was adjusting to things when it was just the two of them at the house, or even when James was over. He'd also reassured Charles by saying that Jane was doing a good job of it. He remembered when he'd first asked her the question and how horrified she'd looked. Charles had just told her that he could solve all of her financial woes, and Jane had looked at him as though he were nothing more than mud on her shoes. Although, Charles was sure that Jane didn't care so much about mud on her shoes as he did.

"Morning." He nodded to his uncle and James who were both waiting for him already.

"What time do you call this?" Jack asked with a chuckle as he pointed to his flashy watch.

"Charles time." Charles said with a shrug. He really didn't care to keep his uncle waiting, if there was anyone in the world who deserved to at least wait a bit for him, it was Jack.

"All right, shall we get to it?" Jack asked, as he held onto his bag of clubs with his gloved hand. "Ladies, I wish you both a nice time upstairs."

Charles glanced over at a terrified and rather stiff looking Jane, but he sent her a reassuring nod as she walked over to where Rosalyn was waiting. He watched as pleasantries were forced between the two women, Jane wobbled slightly in her heels as she leaned in to kiss both of the older woman's cheeks. Rosalyn was all about being polite, but also being classy. It was a complete contrast to her personality, but it was the appearance that she liked to show off - especially in public.

"Come on Charles, unless you'd rather have tea with the ladies upstairs?" Jack called, as the two men waited for him by their caddies.

*****

"You're looking well." Rosalyn remarked as the two of them sat down for tea on the terrace. Jane had quickly glanced at the woman's day dress and white cardigan, her heels were slightly higher than Janes' but Jane still felt uncomfortable in her outfit. She had gone for the more comfortable option of some loose fitting dark green pants and a white blouse. Rosalyn wore a bright pink shade of lipstick that really did nothing for her appearance, but Jane felt that she was being far too judgmental by that point.

"Thank you, so are you."

"You don't have to lie to me, dear." Rosalyn chuckled, as she looked out over the terrace. The golf course seemed somehow to be even more perfectly manicured than the grounds back at Charles' house. Jane wasn't sure how they had managed that, but she was looking at a place that had achieved such elegance in disciplining nature. "Tell me, have you ever been here before?"

"No, I've not." Jane shook her head as she took the question as an opportunity to look around the room.

There were other women dining, as well as some old men, but it seemed that the majority of the men were out on the course already.

"Do you play?"

"Oh no, of course not." Rosalyn said. "I leave that sort of thing to the men, I normally invite some of my friends and have them come here for tea while they play their golf."

"That sounds like a nice thing to do." Jane nodded, as she turned back toward the table.

She had to stop her expression from dropping slightly as Rosalyn clicked her fingers while holding her hand up by her shoulder. It was something that Jane had never understood; there were so many more humane ways of getting a server's attention, and clicking at them certainly wasn't one of them.

Jane felt that it just radiated the type of entitlement that wasn't pleasant or welcoming at all. She forced the smile to stay on her face as Rosalyn searched her expression for any sign of irritation. While the men might have been playing a very obvious game out on the course, Jane realized at that moment that she was playing a much more discreet one with Charles' aunt.

"I see there's a ring on your finger?" Rosalyn spoke with a gasp as she quickly took Jane's hand into her own to examine it.

Jane tried not to roll her eyes as she watched the older woman trying to work out in her head how much such a thing may have cost. That seemed to be all she was capable of talking about; fancy things and their price tags.

"Is it a promise ring?" Rosalyn asked in a slightly patronizing tone.

"Uh, no." Jane chuckled, as she took her hand back. She was putting on the slightly ditsy and clueless act again, but it seemed to be working. "It's actually an engagement ring."

"Oh my!" Rosalyn didn't seem to care for the other guests out on the terrace. She placed a hand on her chest as her mouth hung open. "Congratulations."

"Thank you." Jane smiled and looked down at her lap as she let her shoulders rise up. Playing the innocent was a lot easier than playing the bitch.

"But don't you think that it's a bit...soon?" She asked after she had taken a moment to pause and calm down.

"Soon?" Jane frowned. "I don't think it's too soon." She said while slowly shaking her head. "I mean, we've been dating on and off for a few months, we're both in our thirties and pretty happy with one another. I think it all feels very natural."

"I'm so happy for you." Rosalyn spoke with a little less enthusiasm in her voice than from before.

"Thank you." Jane said again. She wasn't going to give the woman any more information than what she asked.

"I'd heard rumblings along the grapevine that this might have been happening, but I never thought that it would be true!" Rosalyn explained.

Jane could only wonder at who would have leaked that information. Yet as she looked out over the terrace, she could see Tucker glancing up at them every so often. He was like a rat, from her point of view, and Jane realized that they were going to have to be incredibly careful with what they said around him.

"And your sister is aware of this?"

"She is." Jane nodded. It wasn't technically a lie, after all.

"And she's happy for you?"

"Yes, she's really happy." Jane said, although that was almost certainly a lie.

"Well, I'm happy to hear it." Rosalyn lifted up her dainty tea cup. "To the happy couple."

Jane copied her actions and clinked the delicate china ever so carefully together before taking a sip of the herbal tea that Rosalyn had ordered. It wasn't her favorite, but Jane was starting to get used to tolerating fancy things that were too expensive to not eat or drink.

"So have you thought about when the wedding will be? I'm sure that Charles will be wanting something high-key, and they do take months to plan."

"Actually, he only wants a small event for it." Jane said with a simple shrug. "He told me that he doesn't want all of the fuss with this, and he doesn't even want to tell the press."

"Really?" Rosalyn blinked in confusion. "But it would be the perfect way to propel this family back into the limelight after his father…"

"I don't think he wants the limelight back." Jane responded. "So I think that we'll be getting married in a few weeks."

"Weeks!" Rosalyn squealed. "They have family in Europe, you know? Do you think that weeks will give them enough time to organize flights and get here?"

"I'm assuming if they're as well off as Charles is that they won't have anything better to do." Jane said with a small smile playing on her lips.

"You can't be so naive if you're going to be marrying into this family, girl," Rosalyn sighed.

Jane hated how patronizing the woman was being with her, but she kept the fake smile plastered on her face regardless.

Jane hesitated slightly at her words and swallowed thickly. She glanced back over to where Charles was trying to spot them on the terrace as the other two men were talking.

"I thought your sister would have joined us today." Rosalyn remarked.

"She's got her own plans I think." Jane said in an attempt to deter conversation about Helena.

"Ah yes, it must be nice knowing that you're going to have a balance in terms of your family life."

"A balance?" Jane frowned.

149

"You know, two different classes to mingle with."

Jane didn't rise to the bait that Rosalyn had laid out for her. She pursed her lips and quickly decided to busy herself with sipping at her tea. There was no point in engaging with her pettiness, Jane knew that, but she was finding it increasingly difficult to bite her tongue.

"So where are you from originally?" Jane quickly switched up the subject before Rosalyn could press on any more of her pressure points.

"New Jersey," Rosalyn said with a smile.

"Oh, you don't have an accent."

"Do you really think that I would have been able to marry that man over there if I'd come in with a Jersey twang?" Rosalyn asked with a chuckle. "I don't think he would have even given me a sideways glance."

Jane knew that she was right; these people were elitist, even against accents that were deemed lower class. She nodded in response to this and turned back to look out at the amazing view that the golf course provided.

They talked for a little while longer, and Jane remained pleasant as she ate the small sandwiches and sipped at her tea. The entire affair felt incredibly labored and wasn't the kind of thing that Jane was going to be in any hurry to do again. She could see the men walking further and further into the distance until they rounded a corner and were sheltered out of sight by a cluster of trees. Jane realized that their pot of conversation was slowly starting to dry up since neither of them were truly there because they liked the other. Rosalyn was there to get whatever information she could out of Jane, but Jane wasn't going to bite and say whatever she could think of to fill the silences.

It felt very much like when she would fight with her sister; both of them were so stubborn that it was difficult to tell at times if they were ever going to make up again. Jane didn't like to think about Helena at that moment. She knew that she should be with her sister and trying to patch things up with her, instead, she was having high tea with a vulture.

*****

"So things are going well with your girl, then?" Jack asked, as they walked further around the course.

"Yes, things are starting to get quite serious too." Charles said, as he thought about the ring he'd given Jane for show.

It was starting to feel very real that he was actually going to be getting married before his birthday. Something that had once felt like an obstacle that he would manage to wiggle around now stood firmly in his way, and he knew that there was only one thing to do about it.

"Interesting." Jack nodded. "Do you think she's a keeper?"

Charles glanced at a concerned-looking James as they watched Jack line up his club with the ball. "I do actually." Charles spoke with his chest pushed out slightly. "I think she's really something special."

"How...convenient." He thought he heard his uncle mutter. But Charles wasn't in the mood to cause an argument, so he pretended that he didn't hear his response.

"I've actually asked for her hand in marriage." He declared, however, he waited for the right moment when his uncle was just about to swing.

The ball skittered off at the wrong angle and disappeared into the shrubbery on their left. Jack was clearly very tense upon hearing the news and turned back around to look at his nephew with wide eyes.

"That's incredible!"

"I know." Charles pretended to act as though it was the best news he'd had in a long time. "She said yes, and so we've already started planning it."

"Charles, my boy." Jack said after a moment of hesitation. "I know that it may seem like the right thing to do, and I can see how fond you've grown of her, but don't you think it's a bit…"

"A bit what, Uncle?" Charles asked, with a frown as the man walked closer to him.

"A bit soon." He said after spending some time settling on the right word.

"Soon?" Charles frowned, as he looked between them. "I don't think so, the two of us have been dating for a couple of months already. It's been rather on and off, but I'm finally ready to do it."

"You're telling me that the billionaire playboy Charles Bentley is going to settle down, and with someone like her?"

"What's that supposed to mean?" Charles narrowed his eyes as he took a daring step toward his uncle.

"Now let's not get too-"

"I mean that she's not exactly one of us, is she? No matter what kind of fancy dresses you put her in, she's still not one of us deep down." Jack cut off James' attempts to calm the situation down.

"That doesn't matter if you love someone." Charles spoke quickly. He could feel himself getting actually angry at what his uncle was saying, although he couldn't understand why. He was used to his uncle's comments like that, but he was starting to feel a certain duty within him to protect and defend Jane.

"And do you?"

"Do I what?" Charles spat at him.

"Love her, do you love her?" Jack's voice was raised.

He was aware that the caddies were probably loving the drama that was unfolding on their course at that moment, but Charles was thankful they were out of sight so that they wouldn't cause too much of a scene.

"I do." he declared.

"Then you're a fool because she's only with you for the money." Jack quickly responded.

"And why do you think your own wife is with you?"

"Come on now, let's not do this here." James cut in quickly as he stood between the two of them. He was shaking his head discreetly at Charles in a way to tell him to stop, but Charles was far too angry to want to hear it.

"Don't speak about my wife," Jack snapped.

"Then don't speak about my...fiance." Charles almost forgot the word for a moment.

"Tucker told me of this, but I thought you were just messing with him, I didn't think that you would actually find someone in time."

"In time for what?"

"Don't play dumb with me, boy! We both know about the stipulation, and we both know that you were always going to do whatever it took to get the inheritance!" Jack's voice echoed through the trees.

"That inheritance has always been rightfully mine to get, and I don't see why you're so hell bent on taking it from me. You don't deserve it, and I certainly won't let you take it."

"So you admit that this is all so you'll get the inheritance?"

Charles hesitated for a moment, and James shot him a look of panic.

"Not at all." Charles said while straightening up. "I love her, and I can't wait to marry her. The timing is just a good coincidence."

"Bullshit!" Jack screeched. His face had turned a blotchy pink color as he continued to shout.

"Don't lie to me!"

"I'm not lying, and I would appreciate it if you didn't try to pick apart every little thing in my life." Charles kept his voice steady and didn't dare raise it to the level that his uncle was using. He wanted to look like the logical and rational out of the two, and he knew that it was the only way he would win this fight.

Jack glared between the two of them before shoving his club into the hands of the nearest caddy and storming off. James and Charles were left to stand in a stunned silence at what had just unfolded before them.

"Nothing like a bit of golf with the family, huh?" James said, as he nudged him gently with his arm. Charles hadn't realized until that moment that he was breathing incredibly heavily as he tried to calm down from the confrontation.

"He's not going to let this go, is he?"

"If anything, Cousin, I believe that you may have just lit a fire underneath him. He's going to be more determined than ever to stop this marriage from being official."

Charles' expression morphed into a grimace as he knew that his cousin was correct. Jack would never stop until he had the inheritance money, even if it meant tearing his own family apart.

CHAPTER 20

Jane wasn't sure how many more modest sips of tea her body was going to be able to take. Her stomach was now turning at even the thought of having to consume another drop of the herbal liquid. However, the situation on the terrace had grown dire, and she had nothing else to do but sip at her cup while Rosalyn droned on about holidays and new purchases. They were all conversation topics that Jane couldn't really get too involved with since she was still so new to that world.

She thought about what would happen if she slipped into the conversation that she had been stitching up the holes in the same pair of jeans for the last year and a half. Jane was really starting to consider it as they saw the men making their way back toward the golf club.

But Jane could tell that something was wrong.

Jack was walking much quicker and he was further ahead than the other two men. Even from where she sat, she could see how red in the face the older man had become and just how much he was scowling.

"Ah, here they come." Rosalyn said, as she seemed to act as though she hadn't noticed the strange break in the group.

Jane wished that she could have been there for whatever had happened since Jack looked to be rather furious. It didn't take long for him to climb the stairs and walk inside of the club within moments, and the two women waited in silence for Jack to walk out onto the terrace.

"There you are, how was it?" Rosalyn asked, as she put a sweet smile back onto her face.

"We're leaving." Jack muttered.

Jane watched as the sour woman's face dropped in confusion as she glanced over his shoulder to see that James and Charles hadn't followed him out onto the terrace.

"Why?" Rosalyn asked. "I haven't finished my tea yet and Jane and I were just talking about-"

"We're leaving, I'll meet you in the car." He seethed, as Rosalyn glanced between Jane and her husband.

At that moment, Jane received a text from Charles telling her to meet him outside too.

"I should be going too, I think the other two are waiting downstairs."

She said a chaste goodbye to Rosalyn before quickly making her way through the club and down to the exit before they were on the move.

"What happened?" Jane asked, as she walked out into the parking lot to see Charles and James leaning against his sports car. They were both smoking and looked far too casual to be leaning against a vehicle that cost the same price as a small house.

"Jack was just a little upset to hear that we're engaged."

"Well, then I suppose we get on the road, *darling*, because he didn't look too happy to see me up on the terrace." Jane spoke, as she let her hands rest on her hips.

"She's right, you should probably go." James nodded, as he put his cigarette out with his sneakers. "I'll stay back and maybe try and talk to him if he's calmed down a little?"

"Thank you." Charles nodded to his cousin. "All right, let's go."

They didn't waste a second in getting into the ridiculously low down car after saying goodbye to James. Jane thought about

156

what she should do for the rest of the day, but she knew that there was only one thing that she should be doing.

"I'm going to go home this afternoon." She announced to him once they were on the road. "I think it's about time that I go and talk to Helena."

"Good idea, I'll have a driver bring you-"

"I'll call a cab." Jane quickly cut him off.

"All right." Charles nodded slowly but he was frowning.

They didn't speak any more on the subject, although Jane was curious as to when he would need her again. She bit her lip as she thought about how their arrangement was going to work. Being married to him in name only was going to be difficult to explain to other guys if she wanted to date. Jane had no doubt in her mind that Charles wouldn't be able to stay faithful to whoever he did end up marrying. She knew that it was definitely going to put a lot of guys off if she mentioned that she was technically still married while dating other people. Although, she was sure that some guys would for some reason be into it.

*****

Jane packed a few things when they got back to the house while she waited for her cab to arrive. She didn't know when she would next be at the Bentley mansion, and so she took it all in properly once more.

"The cab's outside." Charles called to her after a while. Jane quickly picked up her bag and started down the grand stairs that led to the main entrance hall.

"I'll call you when everything has calmed down between Helena and I?" Jane asked, as Charles shrugged.

"Sure thing." He nodded rather nonchalantly.

She felt as though she was interacting with the version of him that couldn't have cared less as to whether or not she called him. He was acting indifferent toward her again, and Jane found herself having to refrain from rolling her eyes.

The cab ride was quick, although the man was trying to talk to her about why she was getting a taxi back from such a posh house. Jane was starting to wish that she had taken Charles up on his offer to have the usual chauffeur drive her home. At least with him, there would have been no talking.

She sighed heavily as he finally pulled into the road that housed the dingy apartment building. It seemed that even the sky above was a little more grey and miserable on that side of town, and Jane was terrified to think about the confrontation that awaited her in those walls.

"Hey." She said rather hesitantly after climbing the stairs up to their floor. Her heart was hammering in her chest as she placed down her keys and bag.

Helena was sitting watching the TV with her legs curled up on the small sofa that they would normally share. She didn't even react to Jane's entrance, and she knew that they were going to have a rather heated discussion about her disappearing act.

"I'm home, are you all right?"

Upon her second phrasing, Helena finally turned around to glare at her sister. Her eye had completely healed and there was no remnant of the bruising on her face anywhere. Jane was at least relieved by that.

"Don't ever do that again." Helena said in a strangely calm voice.

"I won't, I promise." Jane sighed, as she sat on one of the chairs in the kitchen area of the room. "I'm sorry for not coming home sooner, but I was just so angry."

"I know." Helena nodded. "And I'm sorry for the way that I acted at that stupid dinner party. I know that it really could have screwed us over if I'd said anything else."

The two of them looked at each other in slight confusion. In the past when they had fought, there would be a lot more yelling and arguing about things that wouldn't have even been the main points of conflict.

"That was surprisingly easy." Jane said with furrowed brows.

"I was going to comment on how ridiculous you look in that outfit while in this neighborhood, but you didn't insult me first." Helena said in a mutter.

"Well, you don't look great, if that counts as an insult?" Jane offered.

Her sister really didn't look good; there were dark bags under her eyes, and her hair looked greasy as though she had just been sitting on the couch for the past few days.

"I haven't been out." Helena said with a weary sigh. "I've been sitting in this damned apartment with no money and no idea when you would be home. I didn't want to risk leaving in case you suddenly returned to find that I wasn't in."

"You could have just left a note or…"

"Or what? Called you? Yeah...oh wait, your phone has been off for the past few days." Helena's voice grew more and more snappy as she spoke. The argument was brewing, and they could both feel it. "So while I've been stuck in here, you've been gallivanting around and playing dress-up with the rich."

"You know it's not like that, I had to go to those events to make it look believable that Charles and I were a couple. Especially after how the dinner party went, we had to make it look as though I hadn't just been plucked out of thin air and presented to his family." Jane tried to reason with her.

"You still chose the Bentley's over family." Helena fired back.

"I didn't do anything of the sort!" Jane raised her voice as she stood off the chair. "You didn't give me a choice, I had to stay and do some damage control. I also didn't want to talk to you after that night, but I wasn't about to go and sleep on the streets."

"Oh yeah, because you've never had to do that before." Helena remarked. "Well, I hope that the California King Bed was worth it."

"As a matter of fact, it was!" Jane wasn't sure why she was bothering to argue with her at that point. "I've slept better these last few nights than ever before!"

"Well then why didn't you stay there?" Helena asked with narrowed eyes.

"Because they aren't my family, sure they may be by name in a few weeks, but you're my family. You're the only family that I have and I couldn't take not speaking to you for that long!"

"I think you waited too long to come back with that excuse." Helena muttered bitterly.

"Look, we've both apologized, now can't we just move on from this?"

"Not ye.," Helena said in a low voice. "Because you abandoned this family, just like Dad did, and just like the doctors did with Mom. I don't know why I was so shocked that you did in the end, but I suppose I'm just disappointed."

"No, you don't get to use that against me! I didn't do anything wrong, you were the one who was out of line that night!"

"Do you know why I hate that family so much?" Helena asked, but she had finally snapped. Jane winced slightly at how loud her voice had become. "Huh? Do you?"

"B-because they're rich and they think they're better than us, and-"

"No!" Helena laughed and shook her head. There was a bitter look in her eyes, and Jane had never seen her look so angered by a conversation. "You probably don't remember it, but I do, I do very clearly."

"Remember what?" Jane asked.

"Remember when the insurance company told us that they weren't going to pay for the operation that would have saved Mom's life." Helena's voice had quietened as she spoke. Tears were starting to glisten in her eyes.

"What has that got to do with the Bentley family?" Jane asked although she could feel nausea building up inside of her. She hated talking about their parents, especially their mom, it was a subject that broke her.

"Do you know where the Bentley's get their fortune from?" Helena asked, as Jane held onto the kitchen counter for some stability.

"What are you saying?"

"Sure they have their property portfolios, their golf courses, and all of the usual assets that keep the rich rich. But a large proportion of their wealth comes from interest."

"Interest in what?" Jane asked although she didn't want to know.

Helena looked at her for a moment as a single tear ran down her cheek.

"Interest in health insurance companies." She spoke in a whisper. "And do you know what company they have their highest stake in? It's so high that they're practically joint owners. The one that killed our own mother."

CHAPTER 21

Before she was fully processing what she was doing, Jane was running. She ran down the stairs of their apartment block and ran as fast as she could until she was bursting out of the main doors and heading straight for her moped. Her tears were blurring her vision and Jane cried as she thought about all of the ways in which she had been such a fool. She should have done some kind of research into the family, she should have found out so much earlier about where their money comes from. She couldn't believe that she had been such an idiot.

Jane wiped her eyes and quickly turned the key in the ignition. She had left her sister calling after her, but Jane knew that there was only one person that she had to see. She had to see him, she had to talk to him and let him know that he had done this. Jane knew that she and her sister needed money, but the revelation of information had told her all she needed to know about that family. She was cautious as she drove, as cautious as she could be while pushing the limits of how fast her moped could go. Jane even drove on the pavement at one point as she circled around traffic and weaved through cars as though she had a death wish. In a strange way, she liked the rush and the recklessness that the driving gave her. But soon enough, she was passing through the gates and zooming down his driveway like she was on the run.

Jane skidded to a halt and caused some of the gravel around her wheels to spray out as a result of how she angled her stop. She wasted no time in removing her helmet and marching up to the front doors.

"Good after...Jane?" Anna frowned, as she opened the door wider to see the distressed woman on her porch.

"Where is he?" She asked, as she pushed past the smaller woman.

"Well he's...he's in the study, but he said that he wasn't to be disturbed!" Anna called after her as Jane stormed through the ground floor rooms until she came across the closed doors of the study.

"Anna!" Charles snapped as he turned around. "I told you not to...Jane?"

"How dare you." She snapped at him as she pointed an accusing finger at him.

James was in the room, but his eyes were wide with shock as he glanced between them. Without saying a word, he quickly darted out of the room behind her.

"What's wrong? What happened?" Charles asked in a surprisingly soft voice. "Is it Jack? Or Tucker?"

"Stop thinking about your own damned family for one moment and listen to me." She snapped at him. "Your money, your family's money, tell me something about that. Do they have a large stake in health insurance companies?"

"I...yes...yes they do."

More tears fell as Charles nodded at her question. "I can't marry you." She whispered.

In an instant, his expression fell and his shoulders sagged slightly while his eyes widened.

"What? No, you don't mean that" He spoke quickly. "You have to, there's no going back on this now!"

"I can't do it, and I won't do it." She shook her head.

"What's changed?" He snapped.

"The fact that your family has funded the company who killed my mother!" Jane snapped back at him with as much venom and conviction in her voice as she could muster.

"I don't know what you're talking about!"

"I'm talking about the fact that our insurance company had refused to pay for my mother's operation, the one that would have saved her life. She would still be here today and Helena and I wouldn't be struggling through life as much! That company ruined our lives, they cast us out and gave us no support. All they did was take the last of our money." Jane explained. She could hear the bitterness in her tone, but she didn't care. "They had enough money to pay for that operation, and your family basically owns the company."

Charles was taken aback by her words, and he didn't say anything for a while. Jane knew that there was nothing to be said, there was nothing that he could say to defend himself or his family from this.

"Please, just reconsider on the marriage front, I-"

"See!" Jane laughed in disbelief as she ran a hand through her hair. "You don't even care about what I just told you. Your. Family. Ruined. Our. Lives. And still, all you care about is how you're going to get more money from this."

"No, Jane, that's not what I meant, if you just listen I'll-"

"You'll what?" She snapped back at him. "This isn't just another issue where you can write a cheque and all of your problems will go away for a while. You might be able to buy most of the people in your life, and you almost had me for a moment, but I won't take your money."

"You already have." He fired back. He was now glaring at her as he'd clearly realized that she wasn't going to tolerate him anymore.

"I know, and I feel sick to my stomach about that. But that's something that I'll have to live with, tell me, how do you live with yourself?" She got dangerously close to him as she spoke.

"Jane, our business with those companies, it's just business. We don't do any work with them we just-"

164

"You just give them money so that they can make financially good but morally bad decisions like the one that killed my mom." Jane finished his sentence for him. "She died a horrible, painful death because we didn't have enough money to cover the overheads that our insurance had previously promised to pay."

"I'm so sorry that happened to you but I-"

"Your people don't care about my kind of people." She spoke in a much lower voice. Her eyes were still glaring daggers at him as she shook her head. "That's all it's ever been."

"I'm sorry Jane." Charles said.

"See, you don't even have any way to defend yourself because you know that I'm right." She laughed again.

Jane had never felt so much rage before in her life, and she didn't know how to process it. Her body was shaking and there were tears constantly falling from her eyes. But she didn't care how she looked at that moment, all she cared about was how she was going to make sure that Charles never got his inheritance money.

"You're seriously not going to marry me?"

"I wouldn't even dream of it." Jane shook her head. "I can barely stand the sight of you now, and you still don't even look like you're sorry for what your family has done."

"I am, I just-"

"You just look angry that you're not going to get your own way."

"You'll still be in debt if you leave now." Charles tried to persuade her from a new angle. "You'll be poor, and you can go back to your small apartment and be poor with your sister. I suppose you'll both have to work at the strip club after this."

"Yeah? Well at least I won't have other people's blood on my hands because of where my money comes from." Jane fired back at him. "I'll have a clear conscience, Charles, and you won't be able to say the same."

"I'll just find someone else to marry, someone else who will take the money." He tried to shrug it off. However, Jane could still hear the panic in his voice.

"Go ahead." Jane nodded, as she quickly removed the ring from her finger. "Here, she'll need this I guess."

"I thought you would have needed to pawn that." He sneered at her.

It was starting to get rather nasty between them, and Jane wasn't sure how much longer she could listen to him. She couldn't stand the way that Charles was clearly angry, yet he still managed to look rather smug beneath it.

"As I said, I'm not using any more of your dirty money." She fired back at him.

"Don't think you're not replaceable, *darling*." Charles glared at her.

"Then good luck with the next one." Jane shouted over her shoulder as she turned to walk out of the house.

James was waiting outside of the door and jumped back as she burst through them. She sent him a glare, but she didn't care if he had heard that entire thing, she hoped he had and that he would maybe be the more reasonable one about it. Jane didn't waste any time in walking out of the house, ignoring the stunned look that Anna was giving her as she went. She got onto her moped and sped off before anyone could stop her. Her heart was racing, but she felt good for having let herself tell Charles exactly how she felt.

*****

Charles stood in silence for a while as he stared at a spot on the far wall of the study. He'd always thought that the wooden panels had made the room feel much smaller than others on the ground floor. He let his thoughts wander to random topics like that as he tried to banish all panic from his mind.

"Are you all right?" James asked, as he quickly entered the room and shut the doors behind him.

"Fine." Charles sighed. "I feel that I need a drink after that, though."

"I'll call Anna."

Once a drink had been sent for, Charles and James sat down on the couches. Both of them were in deep thought over what had just happened.

"Do you think she really meant it?" James asked, prompting Charles to look at the ring that she had thrown back at him.

"I don't know."

"Do you want me to talk to Helena, perhaps she can talk her around?" he offered.

"I don't know." He said again as he kept his eyes on the modest jewel.

When he picked it out, he thought that it would be best to not pick out anything that would be considered too flashy. Jane didn't like that sort of thing and he hadn't wanted to upset her. That now felt like a rather foolish thought to have had. Anna arrived in the room with a glass of scotch that contained two ice cubes.

"Thank you, Anna." Charles muttered absentmindedly.

"Is there anything else that I can get you, Sir?"

"Just make sure that nobody else disturbs us for the remainder of the day." Charles spoke but his eyes never left the ring.

"Of course, Sir."

CHAPTER 22

"I'm worried about you." James admitted, as Charles and he had moved to sit out on the terrace at the rear of the house.

"Why?"

"Why?" James scoffed. "Because it's been a few hours already and you've barely said a few words about what happened."

"I don't know what there is to say." Charles shrugged. "She was really upset, wasn't she?"

"I'm afraid so." James nodded. "Are you going to try and find someone else to marry?"

"No." Charles said with a slight chuckle as he looked down at his lap. "I'd just been angry when I said that." He explained with a simple sigh.

"I knew it." James chuckled with relief. "So we're going to have to start 'Operation win Jane back', aren't we?"

"We're in too deep with her." Charles admitted. "She's met the family, and I can't just be engaged to someone else by the time the next dinner party rolls around."

"Do you think we will be able to talk her around to still going through with the marriage?"

"I don't see how we're going to be able to." Charles sighed. "You heard what she said, her mother died and...it sort of is our fault. That's not the kind of offense that she's going to think is very forgivable."

"I know, but perhaps if we just sweeten the deal and-"

"James, thank you for trying to help the situation." Charles stared. "I really do appreciate your help and I'm thankful that you're here for me. But right now, this is all just feeling like too much. I know that you mean well, but we've got time until my birthday, and so I think we should just try to process what has happened."

That seemed to shut his cousin up for a while, and Charles was thankful for the silence as he stared out across his land and returned to his thoughts. Jane had been rather distressed when she'd left, and he was hoping that she had managed to get home without any trouble. He shuddered at the thought of her getting into an accident because she had been too upset to travel, and he couldn't imagine how much her sister would hate him after that.

"Hello?" James spoke as he answered his phone, cutting through the silence that had been so pleasant. He walked away from Charles, and his voice faded until it was barely audible.

"Yes, yes all right." James continued. He wasn't gone for too long and seemed rather eager to get off of the phone. "Yes, I'll er...I'll talk to him about all of that."

"Who was that?" Charles asked while sipping his scotch as his cousin sat back down.

"It was your uncle." James said with a sigh.

Charles wished that he hadn't asked.

"What does he want after earlier?"

"Well, firstly, he wants me to extend his apologies to you for how he acted at the golf course. He says that he wished it hadn't happened and hopes that perhaps we'll all be able to put it behind us soon."

"So that means that he wants something from me if he's trying to make amends." Charles muttered. He knew his uncle too well, and he knew that he never did anything nice without needing some kind of favor to follow it.

"Yes, well he was just calling because he wants to know when the wedding is. He and Rosalyn are going to be taking a vacation soon, and they don't want those dates to clash with the wedding that is totally still going ahead."

Charles froze for a moment as he thought about this. He was going to have to keep up the charade that he was still getting married to Jane no matter what was really going on between them. He didn't like the sound of that, and so he simply shook his head before holding it in his hands.

"It's all right, you'll find a way out of this like you always do." James tried to reassure his clearly distressed cousin.

"Why is this happening to me now? Why couldn't she have found out that information at a later date?" He asked with a groan.

"It's fine, we'll go and talk to her, and together we'll make sure that she doesn't wriggle her way out of this."

"What about lawyers?" Charles suggested. "We could have another lawyer look at the stipulation to see if there is any way around it. What if we just push it back a year? I'll get married by the time my next birthday rolls around."

"We can always try, but I'm not sure how well that will work."

"There must be something." Charles huffed in frustration.

"What should I tell Jack about when the wedding is? He asked me to call him back as soon as I talked to you." James explained.

"He's doing this on purpose." Charles growled. "I can't believe the man, he's so spiteful. He's not sorry at all for earlier, he's just trying to put me on the spot right now. It's working and he's not even here, how evil can one uncle be?"

"It'll be okay, let's just make up a date and work towards that still?"

"All right." Charles nodded and closed his eyes for a few moments. "Next month?"

"July." James nodded. "Always a good month to get married during. Your birthday is the thirty-first, so shall we say the wedding should be on the twenty-fifth? It gives us more time that way and it's well within the stipulation."

"Okay." Charles said. He wasn't able to think clearly and so he was glad that James was doing all of the workings out for him. "That will be good, we'll have a few more weeks to get everything sorted and to convince her."

"You're really going to have to put the time in and grovel, you know?"

"I know." He said. "But what else have I got to do?"

Charles decided from that moment that he was going to cut down on the drinking and partying so that he could focus on being his best self to convince Jane to marry him. He had never thought that he would be in this situation, especially since he had always been told that women would be lining up to be his wife. Yet the tables had turned, and he was now going to have to beg for it from one woman. He waited for James to speak with his uncle once more and breathed out a sigh of relief as he sat back down next to him.

"Do you think it worked?"

"He sounded convinced by it and he said that they would save the date." James said with a shrug.

"Oh god." Charles muttered as he felt the stress of it all starting to get to him already. He put his head in his hands and breathed heavily.

"It's going to be alright."

"You know, you keep saying that, but I don't see how it is going to be all right. We've just confirmed the date for my wedding, except there's going to be nobody walking down the aisle at this rate."

Charles held up the engagement ring to show James. He'd been holding onto it ever since she had thrown it back at him, it had felt like the ultimate insult to everything that he had offered her.

"God, they both quit their jobs for this too." Charles sighed. "What are they going to do for money? They're going to get awful jobs, aren't they?"

"They're resourceful women." James said with a shrug. "I'm sure that if they really put their heads together, they'll come up with something."

Charles grimaced at the thought of what they would have to do for money if they became truly desperate. It was only something else that he added to the list of things that he was feeling guilty about. He hated the fact that the two sisters were in a small apartment together and clearly suffering because they were too stubborn to accept his help. Charles could understand why they didn't want to take the money though, he knew that if it were the other way around, he would have acted the exact same.

CHAPTER 23

Helena sat in shock as she stared at the open door that her sister had stormed out of. It took her a few moments to collect herself before she could move and get up to close it. Jane hadn't said where she was going, but Helena knew exactly where she would go. She wondered if it had been to escape her, but she'd seen the look in Jane's eyes. It had been one of fury. She knew that there was no way Jane was going to Charles' with the intention of being nice to him, Helena just wasn't sure how far her sister was going to go.

Helena was still rather shaky on her feet and the fresh onslaught of tears in her eyes were blurring her vision. She hated the fact that the Bentleys were just showing up in their lives constantly and ruining everything. Helena thought about how awful it must have been for Jane and how she was feeling at that moment. She wished that she'd been able to stop her sister before she had run out of the door, but Jane was gone before she could properly process what was happening. She remembered when she had first learned about the family who were benefiting from the last of their money. The hate and anguish that she felt toward them was something that she couldn't put into words. But she had managed to live with it because it wasn't healthy to be that angry at people that she didn't even know. Yet when Jane had come home and told her about the agreement that she had struck up between herself and Charles Bentley, Helena had seen red again. All of the anger that she thought she'd got rid of had come right back.

She's tried to play along with their charade, but even being in his giant home with all of the pomp and fuss was too much. Helena still didn't regret the way that she had acted out at the Bentley's, she felt that it was the least she could do when she thought about how much they had ruined her family. Fresh tears were stinging in her eyes again as Helena tried to focus on anything else that wasn't the current drama that was taking up so much of their lives. She realized that if Jane wasn't going to marry Charles, then they were going to have to make some quick financial arrangements, and fast. Helena wondered if her old boss would take her back, but the memories of being attacked were still far too fresh for her to even consider working at that club again. Even just the thought of putting herself in that kind of danger again for the sake of a few bucks caused panic to rise within her.

Helena was supposed to be the strong one, she was supposed to be the one that got them out of the tight situations. Jane had tried her hand at that, and it was fair to say that it hadn't gone too well. That was why Helena stuck to the financial worries, she knew what she was doing and she did what she had to do so that they could pay rent and survive.

The hours started to blend together as she waited for her sister to return. Helena had thought that Jane wouldn't have been too long and that she would have just gone over to give him a piece of her mind. She had been expecting her sister to return so that they could cry together and help one another to stay strong, but Helena had been wrong. She started to doubt her sister's will and wondered if Charles had managed to bribe her with more money to stay. The thought caused her thoughts to darken as she wondered whether it was a good idea to call her or not. But when Helena thought about Jane riding around on her moped while upset, she was filled with worry at the idea of her sister being in an accident. That alone prompted her to pick up the phone and call her sister.

"Come on, Jane." She whispered upon hearing the phone ring. It was much more promising than when she had kept her phone off for a few days. Helena didn't want to imagine losing her for that long again.

She was realizing at that moment that she had significantly downplayed just how worried she'd been for Jane during the days when she left her. Helena had hoped she was safe, but she had no idea when she was next going to see her sister, and that thought terrified her.

"Jane, I don't know where you've gone, but please just call me when you get this. I'm starting to get really worried over here." She spoke up as the phone went to voicemail.

Helena waited a little while longer before calling again. Then again, and again. She kept calling until she knew that her phone network wouldn't allow it any longer. After a while, the phone stopped ringing and it just went to voicemail. That meant that Jane's phone was either dead, or she had deliberately turned it off to avoid her calls. Helena groaned in frustration as she didn't know what to do. She thought about calling the police and filing her as missing, but then she knew how stupid that would be if Jane was simply at Charles'.

She found it a rather humiliating thought; if she had just told her about their mother and Jane had continued to go through with the marriage anyway. But it just seemed so out of character for her, Jane had seemed so broken when she'd revealed the truth about the Bentley's ties with the insurance company. Helena really couldn't imagine her sister abandoning her, she really didn't think that she had it in her to do something like that.

Time was ticking on, and with each minute that passed, Helena could feel herself worrying more and more about where Jane was. It seemed that her mind was determined to come up with every awful scenario as to what could have happened to her, but Helena was still focused on being hopeful.

"All right, that's it." She sighed as she glanced at her phone. There was one other number that she knew she could call on to help her out. As much as it was going to pain her to talk to him, Helena had waited long enough, and she knew that she really didn't have a choice.

*****

James and Charles started planning what they were going to do that evening. After a few more glasses of scotch, Charles was much easier to please and relaxed about the situation a lot more. James was glad about that since the last thing that either of them needed to do was stress; it would only make the process of winning back Jane a lot more difficult, and the unnecessary worry wasn't going to get them anywhere.

"I'll work on her sister." James offered, as Charles nodded quickly.

"Yes, that's a good idea." Charles said. "If we can get through to Helena, then perhaps she can help us in convincing Jane to do this. We're probably going to have to pay them a lot more money though, like a substantial amount more."

"I know." James nodded and pursed his lips. "How much are you thinking?"

"I don't know, perhaps a couple million?"

"What!" James sat up straight in his seat. "We can't do that!"

"I can if I get this inheritance, and I'll put that in writing for them. All Jane needs to do is say 'I do' on the day...and maybe sign some paperwork, but you get what I mean." Charles said.

"Do you really think that will convince her?"

"It's got to! Who would turn down that kind of money?"

"She said that she didn't want your money." James reminded him.

"Everyone wants my money." Charles said while holding up his hand. "And it seems that everyone, aside from the one woman that I'm actually giving some of it to, wants to take it from me. So we need to make this work."

"We will, don't you worry about it." James brushed it off. "It's all going to go smoothly." His phone was buzzing on the sofa next to him and he frowned at who was calling him in the evening. The number wasn't known on his phone, but it looked like a local one.

"Hello?"

"James? Is that you?"

He knew that voice instantly, and it only caused his confusion to deepen as he excused himself and took the call into the hallway.

"Yeah, it's me." He said. "Is this Helena?"

"Yes." Her tone sounded incredibly cutting and he could tell that she wasn't in the mind frame for small talk. He thought about the way that Jane had been so angry earlier that day and wondered if he was in for a similar screaming match over the phone.

"Is everything alright?"

"No, where's my sister?"

He froze at her words. It wasn't what he'd been expecting at all. James checked the time and thought about the number of hours that had drifted away between the time that he had watched Jane drive off and up the driveway and what time it was at that moment.

"She's not here anymore." He stated. James could hear her sharp intake of breath from the other end of the line. He guessed that Helena had assumed she'd been at the house all day. "I thought she went home to you?"

"The last time that I saw her, I thought that she was heading out to Charles' house."

"Ah, well it seems that we were both wrong then." James muttered.

"This isn't funny, she hasn't come home and I really don't know where she is." He could hear the panic building in her voice.

"All right, all right, don't panic. I'll help you find her."

He glanced back over at the open door to the study, James thought about the last words he'd spoken to Charles. The process of convincing Jane to marry Charles wasn't going to be as easy as he had previously boasted if nobody knew where she had gone.

"Where was the last time that you saw her?" He asked into the phone as he tried to stop his own worry trickling into his voice.

"I...I was speaking to her after she arrived back here. We were talking about...family things, and-"

"I know, she came over here and screamed at Charles."

"She was rather upset, we both were actually." Helena's voice sharpened slightly. "I'm assuming that you heard what was said, but I don't want to get into that right now. I just want to know where she went."

"Well, when she was done telling Charles that she wasn't going to go through with the marriage, she rode off the property." James recalled. "I assumed that she was going home to you, but clearly I was wrong."

"Oh god, what are we going to do? She could be anywhere, she could be in real danger. This is serious!"

"All right, let's not panic just yet. We'll find her, okay?"

"How do you know that?"

"We're going to have to remain hopeful that she's only nearby. Now, she was very upset when she left here, can you think of anywhere that she might have gone to while in that kind of state?"

The line was silent for a while, but James was sure that he could hear sniffling. He felt bad for thinking of the wedding first and not the fact that Jane could be in serious danger. However, he also couldn't help but think about how angry Charles was going to be when he learned of what had happened.

"I...I really don't know. She normally just goes to work or comes home, there's never any time and-" Helena's voice was wobbling as she openly cried down the phone now. It seemed that whatever hard exterior she had been trying to put up the last time that they had met, it was completely crumbling now.

"Look, Helena, I'm going to send a car to come and get you, and then we'll figure it out from there. I don't think that you should be alone right now."

"No!" She called through the phone. "No, I'm staying right here. If she's going to go anywhere, it would be here, it's our home. She wouldn't go back to Charles' place, I just know it. She was so angry."

James glanced between the study door and the spot that he had been staring at on the wall opposite him while he tried to calm her down on the phone.

"Yeah, you're right I suppose." He sighed and shook his head. He knew that there was no point in agitating her, she was far too distressed to argue. "I'll come to you then? We'll make a start on looking together."

"I...alright." She breathed deeply as she spoke.

"Just don't go out alone, okay? It's dark outside and it's dangerous."

"Jane is out there somewhere." Her voice sounded so small and helpless.

"I know, I'll be fifteen minutes tops, can you text me the address?"

"Y-yes." Helena said.

"Okay, just hang on, I'll be there."

"Are you going to tell Charles?"

James thought about what the implications would be depending on how he answered the question. From the tone of her voice, it sounded like a warning to him that he shouldn't tell his cousin about what was going on. However, he knew that there would probably be worse implications on Charles' side if he didn't tell him.

"I have to, I'm sorry, but I really do. He has a right to know." James spoke apologetically.

"Alright, just get here or I'm going out by myself. Don't bring Charles." She added bitterly.

"I won't, don't worry. He's had too much to drink to be out tonight anyway." He said with a weary sigh.

"Of course he has." Helena huffed before hanging up.

James was left to his own thoughts in the hallway as he glanced back at the door and swallowed thickly. This was the kind of conversation that he wished he didn't have to be the one to have with him.

"Who was on the phone?" Charles asked, as James walked into the room. "You can sit back down, you don't have to go just yet." He added, as he saw the way that James was lingering in the doorway of the study.

"I know, but something has...come up." James knew that it sounded rather cagey in the way that he had said it.

"What do you mean?" Charles narrowed his eyes at him.

"I mean that we may have an issue regarding the whole plan to get Jane back on board with this deal." James said slowly.

"Who was on the phone?" Charles asked, as he sat up a lot straighter and all of the amusement left his face. "James?"

"It was her sister, Helena." He revealed. "She was calling to see if Jane was here."

"Why would she be here after her little stunt earlier?"

"According to Helena, Jane hasn't come home."

He watched as the color drained from Charles' face. He shook his head and turned to look into the fireplace.

"What do you mean she hasn't come home?"

"I mean just that, her sister doesn't know where she's gone. That means we were the last people to see Jane." James said.

It was a rather sickening realization, but it was one that made him feel somewhat responsible for finding her.

"But the wedding-"

"Her safety," James quickly cut in. "Let's talk about Jane's safety before we even start to think about the wedding."

"Right." Charles swallowed, as he was put in his place slightly. "Of course. Should we call the police?"

"I'm going over to see Helena right now, she's expecting me there imminently so I'm going to need to leave now. But if we don't find anything in the next few hours, then yes, we may have to call the police about this."

"Don't let Tucker or Jack hear about this." Charles muttered. "I'm coming with you."

"I don't think that's a good idea." James shook his head. "If there's anyone that she won't want to see right now, then it's you I'm afraid. Helena is sure to be just as upset by everything, so I think I should just go alone. Besides, Jane could turn up here again."

"Why would she do that after everything?" Charles asked with narrowed eyes.

"Because there's safety and security here." James responded. "Even if she doesn't want to admit it, they do need us...well, you. She might need help and this is the place that she will unwillingly come to. So I suggest that you stay here, and I'll stay in touch."

182

"Alright," Charles sighed, as he sat back. "But you have to promise that you'll go and find her for me. Show that we really do care about her."

It was one of the first times that James could see the genuine concern on his cousin's face, and he felt slightly bad for the way that he had been vilified. It wasn't Charles who had organized those deals with the health insurance companies after all, but his late father had. It was he who was really to blame if the Miller women did want to point fingers. James sighed as he knew that neither of them would be willing to reason with them on that subject though.

"We'll find her." James reassured his cousin. "And the wedding will go ahead. It just seems that we are just going to have a few more...complications in the way before that happens."

We hope you Enjoyed Book One of the Accidental Engagement Series. Now Continue Reading the Story by Reading the Book Two.

Make sure you signed up to Bridget Taylor's mailing to receive FREE BONUS CONTENT which compliment this book. Just go to https://bit.ly/aebonuscontent to Sign Up and Get Notified of New Releases.

THE ACCIDENTAL ENGAGEMENT

SERIES BOOK TWO

DESCRIPTION

Charles Bentley has been left with the task of planning a wedding on his own, while also fending off his uncle's attempts to find out that the marriage is a sham. He's under pressure and all he wants to know is where his wife-to-be has run off to. Jane didn't tell anyone where she went, but it was clear enough for all to know that she didn't want to be followed. While Charles struggles to hold the fort back home with his uncle, aunt, and his father's lawyer all breathing down his neck, it's up to Helena and James to find Jane.

Helena has made her stance perfectly clear on how she feels about James Bentley, but the sudden situation calls on them to spend a long amount of time together. They can't stand one another, and time stretches before them as they realize that they're going to have to find a way to stop arguing if they're going to get home without going insane. Through the bickering and arguments, will James and Helena find a middle ground that they can agree on? Or will this trip only draw them further apart?

CHAPTER 1

Before you start reading book two on the next page please make you get notified for the release of next series. Go to

https://bit.ly/aebonuscontent to sign up to get notified of Bridget Taylor's new series coming out and to receive free bonus content and take part in giveaways. If you like this series you will love the next one :-).

Just go to https://bit.ly/aebonuscontent to follow Bridget Taylor

START OF CHAPTER ONE

Charles stood on the rear terrace with a frown permanently etched onto his face. He couldn't believe that this was actually happening. It was four in the morning, and he wasn't sure that he would be able to sleep ever again. At least not until he had knowledge of Jane's whereabouts.

Charles was struggling to come to terms with the fact that the wedding really couldn't happen.

He shook his head in disbelief before going over to the table where his scotch was situated. The fiery liquid was almost daring him to finish it, as though it was some kind of competition that he knew that he would never win. He shuddered as he thought about having to tell either his uncle or Tucker about the fact that his bride had run off.

"Damnit." He muttered to himself and sighed heavily.

"Is there anything else you need, Sir?" Anna asked from the doorway.

"No, Anna." Charles said. "Just let me know if anyone is at the door."

She nodded slowly before disappearing into the house. Even Anna's tone was much softer than usual, it was laced with concern for the situation.

He'd been waiting to hear word from James and Helena, but there was still nothing. They had gone to Jane's apartment, and he could only assume that they'd had no luck with hearing from her. He was still in shock that she was really gone. It could be bad, it could have been some kind of accident, or she could have run off because of the circumstances that she was in.

Charles thought that things had been going rather well. Jane had been doing a good job of fitting in with his family, and he was pleased to see that she was playing her part well. The concept of having to tell them all that there would be no wedding just wasn't an option. He thought about the concept of not getting his father's inheritance; Charles knew that he would lose it all. He took a seat and reclined back, the world around him felt rather unimportant in comparison to his own problems. Charles pushed back his hair, uncaring for how unkempt it appeared. It had been a long day, and he wasn't in the mood to focus on his appearance.

Jane's words were still playing over in his mind; his father's company had been the people who hadn't paid her medical bills, they had technically had a hand in her mother's death. It left a rather sick feeling inside of him, knowing that their family, their wealth, had become so big that it had that much of an impact on other people's lives. Charles let out a puff of air. He could only hope that his cousin and Jane's sister would be able to find her. He waited patiently at the house, although he was a bag of nerves. There was still the slim possibility that Jane could come back to the house, and Charles wanted to be ready for that.

He would offer her more money as compensation, he'd give her some kind of life-long guarantee that would be too good to refuse. He was at the point where he really was willing to do whatever it took to get Jane back on board with his original plan. The idea of Helena and James out there together did amuse him; he could tell that the two of them weren't exactly fans of one another, but he wished that they would be able to get along while they searched for Jane. He was sure that she couldn't have gone far on a moped, although if they were looking in the wrong place, it would give her even more time to get away from town.

*****

Helena couldn't believe this was happening. Her knee bounced as she sat in the passenger seat of the sleek car that belonged to one James Bentley. The mood in the car was sullen as they drove away from the Bentley's stately home. Helena grimaced as panic set in; her sister was actually lost, and nobody knew where she was. It was the kind of nightmare that she had never wanted to live through.

Her heart was pounding, and she tried to focus on anything other than her worry. Helena thought about what she would do when she found her sister, she was planning on giving her a very hard time about the situation. She didn't want Jane to feel as though she was going to get off the hook for this too easily. Helena sighed as she stared out of the window, it felt rather hopeless trying to search for Jane in the dark.

"We'll find her, don't worry." James said.

"I know." She shrugged off his comment.

These were the last people that she wanted to speak with at that moment. Helena hated them, and she wasn't the kind of person who hated easily. She hated that they had caused the entire circumstances around them, right down to the fact that they had no money after their mother's death. All they had was debt and no money, and nothing that could help them. Helena couldn't believe that after everything, she was in a car with one of the very people that she claimed to not be able to stand.

"You know, we're going to be looking for her together. You don't have to be so closed off to me about it." He said, with a chuckle while glancing over at her.

Helena simply ignored his comment and stared straight ahead. If there was one thing that she wasn't in the mood for, it was being told what to do by a Bentley.

"I'm fine." Helena shrugged it off when she noticed that he was still waiting for a response from her.

"You don't seem fine, your sister is missing and-"

"I know." Helena snapped. She cut him off and she didn't regret it. "Just drive."

James quickly turned his attention back to the road, although Helena still caught the looks that he was giving her at times.

"Is there anywhere else that she might have gone?"

"I'm still thinking about that." Her tone was rather monotonous as she stared straight ahead. "Let's just check the apartment, and then we'll figure out where else to look."

Helena was worried that Jane had gone back to the apartment while she was at the Bentley mansion, and she knew that it wouldn't hurt to try. Jane still wasn't answering her phone, and she guessed that it was turned off since it didn't even ring anymore when Helena called it.

The drive felt much longer than normal. The dark was slightly disorientating, and for a while, Helena wasn't sure if James was even going the right way to her apartment. But familiarity quickly started to rise up around her in the form of apartment buildings and blocks that she had grown up around. They really were a stark contrast to the grandeur of the private streets where the Bentley's lived, and Helena started to wonder if James had ever even been to that side of town.

"It's just over here on the right." Helena pointed down a smaller road.

The car swung around and pulled up by the curb. She held her breath as she knew that James was going to be in for a rude awakening when he saw their apartment. Helena was in half a mind to tell him to wait in the car, but she also didn't want to make it into more of an issue than it needed to be. James was silent as they both got out, he was hesitant which was something that she hadn't expected from him. They quickly moved over to the entrance of the dingy-looking building, and Helena could see the disgust on his face almost immediately. It wasn't the kind of apartment block that had a nice lobby with a concierge waiting to smile at you at a desk as well as room service. This was the kind where you didn't want to be hanging around once it was dark, and you certainly didn't want to interact with too many people.

Helena had seen all sorts of things going on in the area and normally kept her head down. She entered the building quickly and quietly, deciding that the stairs would be a much better option than the faulty elevator. If her day could get any worse, it would be getting stuck in there with someone like James Bentley. She bit her lip as they ascended the concrete stairs. James still hadn't said a word about their living conditions, and she was starting to take offense from his silence.

*****

He wasn't sure what to say. He'd known that the women were poor, that they didn't have much to their name. But he just couldn't imagine two young women living in a place like that on their own. The entire aura of the building radiated a sense of danger and violence, it was the kind of place that any parent would hope their child would never grow up to live in. James was trying his best to keep a neutral expression on his face, but it was proving to be an impossible task. Helena was walking in front of him, but she would turn around to glance at him hesitantly every now and again.

He had been brought up with good manners, but at that moment, they were failing him miserably. He would have normally complimented someone on what a nice abode they had, but this was anything but nice. Paint peeled from the corridor walls, and the concrete beneath them was soiled with all sorts of things that he was in no hurry to figure out what they were. His nose turned at the smell of old urine, and the overhead putrid green lights of the fire escape did nothing to redeem the place he'd found himself in. It was the kind of place that he saw in a crime movie, the kind that someone might take a victim to hurt them. There was nothing warm or inviting

190

about the tall apartment block, and he was starting to breathe a lot heavier as they climbed the stairs.

"Would it not have been easier to take the elevator?" He called ahead, as Helena kept going up to the next floor.

"Trust me." She said with a weary sigh. "I don't think you'd want to risk it."

James wasn't sure what she meant by that, but he didn't ask any more questions. The more that he thought about it, the more he realized what a bad idea it would be to get into such a contraption in that building. He remembered the movies he'd seen and knew that they'd definitely made the right choice in going up the sketchy side stairs. Besides, he really didn't want to get stuck in an elevator with Helena.

Finally, she stopped outside of a front door that had clearly seen better days. James tried not to think anything too bad about what could lie on the other side of the door. This was their home, and he knew that it would be incredibly rude of him if he were to start disrespecting it. He forced a small smile onto his face as she opened the door and kicked at it to force it open.

The bottom of the door was littered with dents where the sisters had clearly needed to use a lot more force than first imagined to open it. The paint was also peeling and there was the ghost of a figure where their door number had once been. James didn't understand how people could live like this. It sent a wave of pity running through him for the two girls. He'd never known poverty like this, and he'd certainly never been so far into its clutches before. He knew that he was going to have to tread carefully.

CHAPTER 2

"Wow." He said, as he stared around the small space. The singular lightbulb was doing nothing to showcase off the apartment, its dull light illuminated the four walls that he thought would have stretched on much further. There were two doors on one of the walls and another one by the entrance; James knew that they were the two bedrooms and a bathroom.

The space before him was clearly very multifunctional. The flat smelled of whatever the women had eaten last, as well as something else. It was a mustiness that he had only ever come across before when venturing into the attic at his home. There was one small window in the room that looked out over the road, it wasn't exactly a scenic view to behold. James stepped further inside and turned around as he stared at the old kitchen. It looked as though it had been pasted there from a VHS video, and he wondered whether the outdated appliances were even working properly.

"Wow, it's..."

"You don't have to lie." Helena muttered, as she opened one of the doors and looked inside.

She then quickly moved over to the other and stared at the empty room that looked back at her. Nothing. Jane wasn't there.

"Is it time to start thinking about other possible places that she could be?" James asked, as Helena sat down slowly onto their small sofa. The material had been patched up in many places, but in others, there were still holes that showed off the white foam inside of it. James could also see some scratches that looked to have been made by a cat. This confused him since there weren't any other signs that there was a cat in the apartment.

"I think so." Helena said.

She turned to look up at him, and James quickly saw that her eyes were turning glassy as they filled with tears.

"Don't cry, I'm sure that we'll find her soon." He tried to reassure her. His words came out rather wooden, and he knew that he should probably try harder at helping her.

It was difficult because the two of them didn't exactly get on. James remembered the way that they had glared at one another throughout the family dinner. Helena knew exactly how to make him feel uncomfortable, and she was good at using that as a way to get to him. James felt his nostrils flare up as he remembered the smug look on her face when she would say something vulgar that would agitate him.

"Alright, so if she didn't come back here, and she's not with Charles, where else would she go? Are there any ex-boyfriends that she could have maybe gone to?"

"Definitely not." Helena shook her head quickly. "She wouldn't have gone there, even if he was the last person on Earth."

"Okay." James chuckled at the comment. However, he couldn't help but wonder what had happened in that situation. "Where else then?"

"There's only one other place that I can think of." Helena said with narrowed eyes. "It's quite far, and she can't get there on just a moped alone. At least, I don't think she could, but Jane might try to. It's an old family home where we grew up. It's nothing special, but it's out of town."

"Is it too much of a risk to go there?"

"I don't know where else she would go." Helena said while shrugging. "It's not like we have an abundance of family who would take us in. We're on our own."

James thought about this for a moment. The risk of going on a long journey when there was no guarantee that Jane was even there could result in a lot of disappointment. But if Helena was right, then they should leave right away.

*****

"James? Did you find her?" Charles asked, as he answered the phone. He jumped up from his chair on the terrace and swayed slightly. He blamed the scotch, but it could have easily been the way that he felt so exhausted.

"No...well, not exactly." His cousin's voice sounded hesitant from the other side of the phone.

"What's that supposed to mean? This isn't the time for being vague!"

"I know, I know, I'm sorry." James said with a heavy sigh. "I just think that you should hear the conflict that we're in at the moment."

"Alright, go ahead."

"So she's not at the apartment, and we've had a drive through the town. I can't see her anywhere and the only other place that Helena thinks her sister could have gone is out of town. It's an old family home or something." James spoke quickly.

Charles stood upright as he accepted the news. His eyes were narrowed and he tried to understand what would be going through Jane's head at that moment. It was clear that her plan was a temporary one; she couldn't stay at the family home forever, even if she felt that she could try. She would run out of money, she would have to come back. If not for her sister, for the life that she had built for herself on her dwindling funds. Charles shuddered at the idea of her being out there and not knowing what to do. While the wedding did worry him, so did her safety and wellbeing.

"Are you still there?"

"Yes, I'm here." He said after clearing his throat. "I just don't know what to do."

"Well, I think that you should stay there. Have someone outside of their building maybe, just in case Jane goes back to her apartment?"

"Who do you think I am? I don't have the kind of resources where I can just hire a man out of thin air and expect him to help us like that." Charles said.

"I'm sure you'll think of something. If there's anyone who does have the resources, it's you, Charles." James said through the phone.

He was starting to regret letting James be the one to be out there and calling the shots in terms of where they look. Charles didn't like the helpless position that he had found himself in. From the house, he didn't feel as though he could be too productive in terms of the situation, and that was beginning to bother him.

"Alright, and you're both going to drive to this family home that they mysteriously own? I thought they were...you know..."

"Poor?" James finished the sentence, but the word stung. He didn't like to think of himself as too judgmental, and Charles had always been brought up not to be too rude. "You should see their apartment, it's-"

"Alright, I suppose the two of you should be getting on the road soon, right?" Charles cut him off. He didn't want to hear about it.

Jane had told him about the part of town that she lived in before, and Charles had done enough research to know what to expect of a place like that. He didn't want to hear his cousin slandering their living situation.

"Sure, I'll talk to you when we have an update."

"Try not to kill each other." Charles added.

"Believe me, it's not going to be the most enjoyable car journey of my life." James sighed through the phone.

Charles chuckled at the thought of the two of them spending hours together in a confined space. In a way, he sort of wished that he could be a fly on the wall for the conversations that they were going to have.

James hung up the phone shortly after, and Charles yawned as he returned to his seat on the terrace. The scotch was working and dragging him closer to sleep, but the horizon was already starting to break into a light shade of blue. The thought of staying up to watch the sunrise had crossed his mind a couple of times, there weren't any clouds in the sky, and he could tell that it was going to be a beautiful morning to behold. However, the claws of sleep had dug into him and Charles was on the cusp of slumber.

Each moment that he spent sitting watching the lawn before him was another moment where his eyes got slightly heavier. He moved about in his chair and tried all sorts to stay awake, but it was proving to be no use. Charles let his neck roll as he closed his eyes, succumbing to the much-needed rest. The gentle morning breeze was doing nothing to aid in waking him up, but it only relaxed him further.

"Are you...Mr Bentley? Are you dead?"

He frowned at the voice that swam through his head. For a while, he forgot about where he was. He forgot about the stress of the situation that he was in and all the implications that were going to complicate his life in the near future. Charles groaned and slowly opened his eyes with a frown. He jolted slightly at the way that the realization hit him so hard of where he was.

"What?"

"Don't worry." Anna muttered, as she picked up the empty glass from the table at his side. His frown only deepened as he saw that the morning was now in full swing, with the sun already almost climbing over the height of the trees that bordered his rear lawn.

"What time is it?"

"Eight in the morning, Sir." Anna said, as she walked back over to the door.

"Has any-"

"I'm afraid not." She shook her head.

With that, she walked back inside of the house, leaving Charles alone with his thoughts. He knew that she didn't necessarily agree with a lot of the things that he did in his life, but he also didn't employ her to pass judgment. Charles groaned, still groggy from the strangely deep sleep that he'd fallen into for a couple of hours. His neck ached from the angle and his body was stiff as he slowly stood up. He felt like some kind of hinge that hadn't been bent or moved for many years.He could imagine his bones with cobwebs hanging from them as his movements to stand had shifted the thick layers of dust from them.

"Anna!" Charles called inside as he steadied himself and started for the door to the terrace. "Can you bring me a coffee?"

Charles hadn't thought that he'd drank that much the night before, but then he couldn't quite remember many times when his glass had been empty. Anna, or someone, had been refilling it for him, and so he wasn't inclined to blame the hangover on himself. He rubbed his slightly blurry eyes and tried to focus on what he had to do next in terms of finding Jane.

"Are you sure that nobody called?" Charles asked, as she reappeared with cleaning supplies in hand.

"I'm positive." She nodded. "Nobody called while you were asleep and nobody showed up."

"Alright, thank you." He sighed in frustration. "I just want to find her."

"We all do. But if they don't find her soon, don't you think that it would be wise to call the police?"

"Of course I do, but if the police get wind of this, then it won't be long before Tanner and my uncle finds out too." Charles said. His voice was still hoarse from the sleep he'd been disturbed from.

"Can you perhaps just for once think about something that isn't yourself?" Anna snapped at him.

Charles blinked at the sudden outburst, he hadn't been expecting it from her at all.

"I am, I'm extremely worried that she's not safe!" He fired back at her.

"Well, then you need to do more about it!"

"I can't right now, we're doing all we can. I'm having someone stake out their apartment to wait for her to come home." He explained in a much calmer voice.

The raised voices were doing nothing for his headache.

"You need to call the police by the end of the day." Anna persisted.

"And you need to remember your place." He snapped and walked past her.

Charles didn't wait for her to say anything else, he just listened to the way that she was cursing him under her breath. Anna had always been rather outspoken when it came to his lifestyle, but he could normally handle it. These weren't the circumstances where he felt as though he could handle it. Charles hadn't had much sleep, he was running on fumes, and he was also incredibly worried about Jane. There was so much going on in his thoughts that he held onto a door frame with one hand as he squeezed his eyes shut in an attempt to try and block out the fast thoughts swimming in his mind.

"We'll find her." He muttered to himself as he started down the stairs to see if there was anything he could have for breakfast.

CHAPTER 3

Helena and James had barely said a word since setting off for the house. She was sort of glad about it, but she was also slightly uneasy about the way that he was so accepting of what they had to do. After giving him the address and watching him type it into the sat-nav in his car, Helena sucked in a deep breath.

To spend so many hours in a car with James Bentley felt like it was going to be as bad as some kind of strange torture method. She scowled at the idea of making small talk with him and instead turned to look out of the window on her side. The quiet of the car felt suddenly very loud as they drove through the outskirts of the town.

It seemed to get even louder as they drove out onto the roads with less bustle and even fewer other cars. It was early in the morning, and sunrise was still some time off. Helena kept her mouth closed and even let her eyes close for a while, that was until a sudden swerving motion jolted her back to reality.

"What the hell was that?" She cried out, as James tried not to look too phased by what had happened. However, she could see that his eyes were still slightly wide and his arms were outstretched as though he were holding onto something that gave off an awful smell.

"It was nothing." He muttered.

"It was something!"

"I'm just tired, alright?" He sighed.

Helena shook her head in disbelief, she wanted to shout at him and scold him for the way that he was being so careless, but she was exhausted herself.

"We can't all have the luxury of falling asleep." He continued and shook his head.

"It's not like I didn't offer to drive." Helena muttered.

"As if you're going to drive this car." James chuckled.

"I'd drive it a lot better than you, tired or not." She fired back quickly. "Just...put the windows down or something, it's supposed to help wake you up."

"Maybe if you weren't giving me the cold shoulder, it would be a little easier to stay awake and not almost kill us."

Helena rolled her eyes, but she knew that he was technically right. If she stayed up and spoke to him, it would be a little more reassuring to her that he wasn't going to swerve off the road and get them into some kind of accident.

"Fine." She grumbled and twisted her body so that she was no longer facing away from him. "What do you want to talk about?"

"Don't put pressure on it like that." He said, and scrunched up his nose. "I just meant that we should talk like this and that it will help me stay awake."

"I know what you mean." She said, "I just think that talking like this is what's known as bickering to other people, and if we're going to do that, then I'm going back to sleep."

"If you go back to sleep, then I'll do the same thing." He quickly fired back at her.

"Then you'll kill us both!"

James merely shrugged in response, earning nothing but a scoff from Helena. She knew that he was doing it on purpose. She thought back to the dinner party that she had pretty much ruined with her words; he had been glaring at her all night and told her how inappropriate she had been, but Helena had continued on regardless. She still didn't fully regret the way that she had acted. It had all felt worth it to see the way that Rosalyn's face had dropped and her husband's had turned so pink that he looked almost sunburnt.

"Did you go to school around here?" James asked after a while.

His question cut through a tense silence that had settled between them both, although neither of them made any move to fall asleep - much to Helena's relief.

"Is that really what we're going to talk about?" She laughed.

"You got a better idea?"

Helena narrowed her eyes at him but she thought about his question for a moment. "I went to the state school down the road from where we live now, then I went to community college for a few years."

"Your sister is back in college?"

"She never went." Helena shook her head. "Things...happened in our personal lives, and it just made more sense to focus on that than our education at the time."

"Oh...right." James said, but he didn't pry any more into her life.

"What about you?" Helena spoke up. She couldn't wait to scoff at the disparity between them that she knew all too well was going to come up.

"Well...I went to a good school I guess." James said while trying to emulate the tone that Helena had used to talk about her education. He was trying to come across as though it wasn't that big of a deal, but he was failing miserably. "I then managed to get into Yale and studied there."

"Of course." She chuckled and sighed heavily.

"Look, I managed to get in because I'm actually intelligent. I got all of the necessary scores on all my tests, I got in like anyone else would have."

"I never said otherwise." Helena pointed out as she gave him a look.

She could tell that James knew instantly how he had been caught out by her. She hadn't even needed to say anything for him to start getting so defensive about the fact that he'd got into a school without using his father's money.

"You know." He spoke up after a while. "It is possible to get into an Ivy League school without any help financially from your parents."

Helena had to turn to stare out of the window to stop him from seeing the amused smile that moved across her features.

"I never said any differently, James." She said with a shrug.

"I know that." He quickly fired back. "But you did sort of imply it, and you can't deny that."

Helena rolled her eyes at his comment and thought about the many ways that they were so different from one another. Even down to what they were wearing in the car; Helena was still in her sweats from earlier and the same scuffed trainers that she always wore. Part of the sole was coming away from them and all she could do was hope that it didn't rain while they were out since the holes in her shoes only invited wet socks.

"So what do you actually do all day?" Helena asked out of curiosity.

"What do you mean?" He asked with a frown.

"Well, do you…you know, have a job?"

It sounded like a stupid question, but she had to remember that she was talking to a man who was part of a billion-dollar estate. She just couldn't fathom what she would do with her days if she didn't have to work and earn money.

"Well, not exactly." He said with narrowed eyes as he stared at the road ahead of him. "I…I do things though. I work on projects with my cousin and Jack, there are always issues to talk about. I go to important lunches and golfing sessions."

Helena nodded slowly as he listed off the many activities that he spoke about.

"I read and write sometimes, I've always enjoyed writing but I just never have the time to sit and…"

"You've just listed things off to me that I would do perhaps once a year if I was lucky to have the time. And you're telling me that you don't have the time to sit down and write?" Helena chuckled as she couldn't believe what she was hearing.

"I just mean that I'm always busy with social occasions or other things. Writing has always been quite far down my list of priorities."

"Why? If you really like it, surely you should make it more of a thing that you should do?"

James was thinking about her response for a while, but he didn't choose to say any more on the subject. Once again, the car was plunged into a thick silence.

Helena tried to think again about how she would fill her time if she was ever in that situation. She had come to accept that in this life, she would be poor. She had always been brought up with the mindset of being frugal, and she really couldn't see her ways changing any time soon. She found it quite a sad truth, but it was just something that she had come to accept.

"What kind of things do you like to read?" She asked again to break the silence.

James pondered for a while, which she found slightly odd since it should have been something that he could talk about easily.

"I read a lot of journals and financial papers." His answer wasn't what she had been expecting. "I mainly read a lot of nonfiction."

"What's wrong with fiction?" She asked with narrowed eyes.

"Stories are for children." He shrugged it off.

She noticed the slight look of disgust that he wore as he spoke about fiction. Helena frowned, she'd thought that was what he'd meant when he said that he enjoyed reading and writing.

"You can enjoy stories and be an adult, you know? Haven't you ever heard of the classics?"

"I don't see the point."

"I thought you were supposed to be educated."

"I'm aware of the arts." His response was quick and quite sharp. "I'm not appreciative of them though."

Helena decided not to press him any further on the subject. James was clearly in a touchy mood, and she put it down to his lack of sleep.

*****

By the time that the sun had risen high enough that the world around them was light again, Helena was incredibly excited by the prospect of getting out of the car to take a break. She wanted nothing more than to stretch her legs from the hours that she had spent curled up in the passenger seat.

"Can we stop soon?"

"Why?" James asked.

The car had been silent for quite a while, and Helena winced at the sudden volume of his voice.

"Well, I think we both need a break." She suggested.

"We have to catch up to your sister, we aren't exactly in the position for taking breaks."

"Oh, come on." She huffed. "You're telling me that you don't need to use the bathroom yet?"

Helena watched the way that James' face flinched slightly at her question. "So you *were* just being too stubborn."

"Shut up." He said, and shook his head.

"That was unnecessarily rude. I thought they taught you good manners at those boarding schools."

"Yeah, well that was a long time ago, and I've forgotten an awful lot of my manners." He said with a sniff.

There was something rather stiff in his response that caused her to narrow her eyes. Helena could see a lot of pain in his expression all of a sudden, and it only caused her to wonder more if he'd really had as good of a childhood as he had painted it.

She couldn't imagine what would have made it worse if he'd had all the money in the world. There were no obstacles that could get in his way from her point of view; if he wanted to go to a certain school, then his family had the funds to facilitate that. In fact, if he dreamed of doing or being anything, he could do it if he so wished. Helena tried to imagine a life with so few limits, and she knew in an instant that that version of herself would be one that she would hate too.

"We'll stop in a moment." He yielded eventually. She thought about commenting on the fact that she had so clearly won the battle, but Helena decided to save it for when she won the war.

CHAPTER 4

James got out of the car with a clenched jaw as they reached a small gas station. Out on the open road, there weren't too many places to stop safely, and so they had to keep going for another fifteen minutes before finding somewhere. There was just one problem; there were no toilets in the small building. There wasn't even an operator, the entire thing was controlled by a keypad. James wanted to call out in frustration since the land around them was rather flat and there weren't too many trees about.

"What are you going to do?"

The last thing that he wanted to do at that moment was to explain his frustrations to Helena. She had already gotten on his nerves so much that he didn't want to talk to her if he could help it. Small talk had been a really bad idea earlier in the car; she had lured him into a situation where he knew that he couldn't win against someone like her. They were always looking for pity or someone to agree with them on what a bad card they had been dealt in life. James always felt uncomfortable when such conversations arose, but when in a car like that, there was nowhere for him to escape to. He quickly made a mental note to perhaps not ask so many questions about her past.

"I don't know." He shrugged, as he finally answered her question.

"There are some trees over there." She gestured to behind him.

"I'm not a dog."

"No, but you're a grown-ass man who needs the toilet. I'm sure you've peed in worse places." Helena pointed out.

James was going to reply with something smart, but he quickly held his tongue and narrowed his eyes. He wasn't in the mood to argue when he already felt so drained. He knew that he was going to need food soon, or his mood was only going to worsen.

"All right, but don't peek, will you?"

"You think I want to see anything?" Helena said while giving him a look resembling a death stare.

"Whatever."

"I need to go too, but I'm going to go over here." Helena warned him.

"How are you...actually, I don't want to know." He muttered and turned toward the direction of the trees.

"If you even think about looking, I've got a can of pepper spray in my pocket." She called back to him as the two of them started to walk their separate ways.

"I wouldn't dream of it!" He called back to her while shaking his head in an exaggerated manner.

James couldn't believe that she would think he'd even want to see her like that, it was barbaric. Of course, he couldn't deny that his traveling companion was rather easy on the eyes, he didn't feel as though he could ever act on that. She was...different to him. They were from different worlds, and they clashed as though they were sworn enemies. James scowled as he waited for the cover of the trees before checking the coast was clear.

*****

"How's it going?" Charles asked through the phone as he started to walk back toward the car.

"It's going fine." James lied. "Although, I'm not sure how much longer I'm going to be able to stand this woman."

"You've just got to find Jane and then I'll make sure that the only other time that you see her is on the wedding day. Perhaps you'll see her at a few dinners here and there, but I'll make an effort to keep the two of you apart."

"Great." James breathed out. "I'm going to have to call her family soon as well, that's going to be exciting."

"Come on, she can't be that bad."

"She threatened to spray me with pepper spray." James said in a monotonous tone.

"Well, it could have been worse." Charles spoke while clearly trying to stop himself from laughing. "She could have actually done it."

"I don't know why I tolerate you either sometimes." James said with a scowl on your face.

"Oh come on, it's only a short road trip. You'll be back before you know it."

All James could think about was how with each mile that they traveled away from their home, it was another mile that they were going to have to do on the way back. Dread trickled into his gut as he thought about the idea that Jane might not be at the house when they get there. He didn't want to even entertain the thought of driving all the way back home with Helena in the car while they were still not done with their search.

"Please tell me that you're confident about Jane being at this house." Charles said through the phone.

"What do you mean? We're as confident as we can be at the moment, but I can't guarantee anything."

"Anna wants me to call the police. She said that I shouldn't be so easy going about all of this. Does it seem like I'm easy going? Because I'm actually freaking out, I don't know about you." Charles sounded rather breathless as he ranted.

"Look, I'm just as desperate as you are to see if Jane's at this house, I'm really hoping that she is so that we can all go home and just plan the wedding like we were going to."

There was silence from the other end of the line. James glanced up to see that Helena was also emerging from the trees where she had gone. He squinted and tried to make out what she was holding in her hand. The realization hit him in the form of his lips bending into a grimace; she was holding pepper spray.

"What took you so long, did you get pee shy?" She asked, with an amused smirk on her face. James shook his head and tried to ignore what she was saying to him.

"No, Charles phoned." He explained and pursed his lips.

"Has he heard anything about Jane? Has she showed up there instead?" She asked, with narrowed eyes.

"No, nothing like that, unfortunately." He said. "He was just wanting an update on our situation."

"Did you tell him how annoying you've been ever since we set off?"

"No."

"Did you tell him how you almost totaled the car by falling asleep at the wheel?" She raised an eyebrow as she spoke.

"That's just not true!" He fired back.

"Well, it could have easily happened." She said while holding her hands up in defense.

James rolled his eyes and brushed past her as he walked over to the car. All he wanted was for their little trip to be over and done with so that he could go back to his life and get on with it.

"So, we're going to get back on the road already?" Helena snapped in protest as she followed him.

"Look, I'm really not in the mood for this." He quickly said back. "I'll stop again soon if we find somewhere that sells food, but we really do need to get on the road."

"Aye, aye, captain." She muttered and climbed into the passenger seat. Helena stopped before she was fully in the car. "Can I drive?"

"No."

*****

Helena couldn't believe that she was still stuck in the car with him even hours after they had set off. She knew that it would be a long drive, but what she hadn't expected was for time to be against her. Every minute in that car felt like an age, and she wasn't feeling particularly patient. Her lips were pressed into a thin line, and her arms were folded across her chest as though she were a teenager who had been told she can't go and see her friends.

"What's up?" He asked eventually.

Helena could see that it pained him to ask such a thing, and it made her smile slightly.

"I'm just bored." She shrugged.

"Well, shall we-"

"I don't think we do well with this small talk stuff."

"I was going to say why don't we just listen to some music?"

Helena turned to the radio that had been neglected for the entirety of their trip so far. She felt almost stupid for having not taken advantage of it sooner.

"What sort of stuff do you usually listen to?" She asked, as she pressed the button on the screen that turned it on.

Instantly, the small screen displayed that his default station was *Classics FM*, Helena snorted and couldn't contain her laughter as she saw this. She had to wait for her laughter to die down before she could say anything.

"What is this?" She continued to laugh as the symphony filled the car.

"It's good music." James said in a rather defensive tone. "Look, I don't like listening to modern-day stuff, it's too…"

"Up tempo?"

"No."

"Catchy?"

"No."

"Actually enjoyable?"

"Will you just let me enjoy my music? Can't you just accept that not everyone has the same music taste?" James huffed wearily.

"Alright fine, but you need to accept that sometimes your taste resembles that of an old man's."

"And what do you listen to? The strip club top ten?" James fired back.

Helena didn't say anything for a moment, she simply shot him a glare that warned him not to say anything like that again.

"Oh come on, you were so proud of that the other night at the dinner party." He continued.

"Watch it, or I will pepper spray you and get out of this car." She snapped.

"You're really going to do that to me in a moving vehicle while we're traveling at seventy miles an hour?" He chuckled and shook his head. "I don't think so."

"Do you want to test me right now?" Helena asked, as she produced the small can from her pocket once again.

"Jesus! Are you crazy?" He said ,as he tried to move away from her. Of course, being confined to the small space within the car meant that neither of them could really move too far away.

"I don't want to talk about it." She reiterated.

James swallowed and nodded. However, he waited for her to put the can back in her pocket before his foot went back to the accelerator.

"Alright." He said quietly,

The car returned to the silence that had almost become a welcome relief for Helena. The last thing that she wanted was to be lectured about the shame of working in a gentleman's club by a rich white man. He was the kind of guy that would be a regular in her place, although perhaps he was a little on the young side to be a regular yet.

She thought about how many men came into their establishment and how many men had cheated on their partners while in the building where she worked. Helena often thought about it and tried to ignore the pang of guilt that ran through her. She did, after all, have a part to play in the breakdown of many relationships and marriages.

James didn't dare to say anything else for a while, which she was rather grateful for. Helena could still recognize some of the road signs and knew that they were quite far from the house still. It was going to be a long journey, and James wasn't making it any more bearable.

CHAPTER 5

Charles paced around after waking from a disturbed nap. He'd been a wreck all day as he waited for news from James, but it never came. The journey was taking them a lot longer than he had anticipated, and he'd thought that they would have arrived by now. He was just about to try and get some better sleep again when Anna came in.

It seemed that their previous outburst was just going to be swept under the rug as she acted as she usually wood.

"You have a visitor, Sir." She said slowly.

"Is it someone that can be sent away?"

"Your uncle, and Mr. Tucker." Anna said with a slight wince. Even she knew that this was going to be awful timing on their behalf.

"Alright, I suppose it will only raise more suspicions if I send them away." Charles muttered. Although his comment had been more aimed at himself as he tried to think through his limited options.

"I'll send them into the parlor to wait for you?"

"Please do." He nodded. "And send them some tea while they wait, preferably camomile. I don't want them agitated just yet."

Charles quickly glanced at his appearance in the vanity nearby to him. To say that he wasn't looking his best was a bit of an understatement; dark circles could have been mistaken for some kind of attempt at a smokey eye look with Jane's makeup, his hair was incredibly disheveled and he was still in his robe.

The only thing that he could fix out of those were his hair somewhat, and he quickly changed into a presentable pair of pants and shirt. Charles started to quickly consider his options in his mind as to what kind of excuse he could use for Jane's absence. It wouldn't be the first time that he was lying to either of the men that were now waiting for him downstairs, but it also wouldn't be the first time that any of them would try to pick apart his stories.

Charles groaned as he thought about the dance that he was about to do with two of the devil's henchmen. He took a deep breath and a quick shot of scotch from the cabinet by his bed, just to make sure that his nerves had been eradicated.

"Gentleman isn't this a nice surprise." Charles opened his arms in welcome as he entered the parlor to find Tucker and his uncle waiting for him.

"We've had this scheduled for some weeks." Tucker said with narrowed eyes.

"We did? I suppose we've had lunches and whatnot so frequently as of late that this one slipped my mind." Charles said in an attempt to quickly brush off the blunder.

He hadn't even thought to consult the calendar, he hadn't had any time. The last thing that he wanted to do was to give off any kind of impression that something was wrong.

"Is everything all right?" His uncle asked.

Busted already, he thought to himself.

"I'm fine, why?" He fired the question back at the older man.

"I don't know, you just look a little…tired."

In the world of business meetings and diplomacy, Charles knew the move that his uncle had just made. It was a play where he could make another man feel inferior within themselves before they've even given much of themselves away. It was a clever tactic right before a big business pitch, a way to put off a competitor and stop them from succeeding because they have doubts in themselves.

But Charles had no such doubts. He knew he looked awful, and he was going to own it. The one thing that he wasn't going to do under any circumstance was to admit the truth of what had happened with Jane to either of them.

"Is it unusual for me to look tired?" Charles asked with a light laugh. "I mean, I'm no stranger to a few late nights."

"I can't argue with you there." His Uncle Jack held up his hands in defeat.

There was silence among them for a moment as Charles forgot his manners.

"Anna." He then decided to call out to her. "Would you have lunch ready within thirty minutes or so?"

"Of course, Sir."

She quickly scurried off with the request, and Charles turned back to the two vultures that were waiting on the edges of their seats for him to make a mistake.

"No Jane today? I thought she would be able to join us for some lunch." Jack remarked.

"No, she's gone with her sister to Europe." He said, as he brushed it off.

"What?" Jack's eyes were incredibly wide at this news.

"Yes, it was all rather sudden." Charles nodded, as he reached for a cup of herbal tea. He tried to ignore the way that his hand was shaking; it was a mixture of poor sleep, too much alcohol, and stress, but he tried to ignore it the best that he could. "She wanted to go out because she'd traced some of her family back and found some long lost grandparents in...Austria I think she said. So they've gone out there for a few days."

"Wow." Tucker blinked. "That's a long way to go for a few days, I'm assuming that you...funded this?"

Charles knew what he was getting at, that Jane was only with him for the money. But Charles didn't care about winning that battle on that day. All he cared about was getting them off of his back about where she was.

"Of course I did." Charles nodded. "Would you not want your wife-to-be to find some family of her own that are still alive and good before her wedding day?"

"Oh, so they may make an appearance at the wedding?"

"We're not sure yet, it depends on if they want to I suppose." He shrugged.

Tucker's eyes were narrowed. He was pulling the face that he made when he was deeply calculating things. Charles shifted in his seat slightly, it always made him feel uncomfortable as he wondered what the older man was thinking about.

The lawyer had never liked him and Charles was always that one at the butt end of his schemes, even if they were the kind that planned to ruin him. But he was determined to stay strong in the face of such a threat. The last thing that Charles wanted was for them to find out about the large web of lies and for them to start untangling them.

"That must be very exciting for her to find out that there are more of them out there." Jack remarked as he sipped at his tea.

"I know, I sort of wish that our family wasn't quite so well-documented. It would leave at least some mystery for us to unravel and find out about." Charles said with genuine curiosity.

"Well, that's what happens when your family does well for themselves. People are a lot more inclined to document your achievements."

Charles knew that the word his uncle was searching for was privilege, but he didn't dare to aggravate the situation yet. He had no cause to do so, and putting his uncle on the defensive so early would only make him even more tired than he already was.

"I helped her to do the tracing and it was pretty simple once we had found a match for their family name." Charles continued on.

He made sure to maintain a nonchalant tone when he spoke so that there wasn't anything that could give him away as trying too hard or even seeming nervous.

"When will she be back?"

Charles hesitated, "I think by the weekend."

There were a number of days that stretched forward before the weekend would be upon them. He was terrified of giving James and Helena a deadline in case they weren't back by them, but Charles couldn't see how it would take them that many days to find her unless something went very wrong.

"Ah, we should organize another lunch some time around then." Jack said with a large smile on his face. "I want to hear all about her trip to Europe."

Charles could see the look on his uncle's face. It was one that he'd noticed before, and he knew exactly what it meant. His uncle was daring him to see if it really would be true, he was testing out the limits of Charles's lie and waiting for it to somehow crumple in on itself. Charles knew that if Jane was back by the weekend, they were going to have to have a lot of difficult conversations as well as a thorough briefing on her fictional trip to Europe.

For all Charles knew, she could be on a plane to Europe at that very moment. Although he thought that it would be very unlikely, he wasn't sure that he was willing to rule anything out in case he was wrong in his assumptions.

"That would be great." He said eventually and nodded quickly. "I'm sure she'd love to tell you all about it. I could invite her sister, Helena, as well, she's on the trip with her. I think it's going to give them some good time to strengthen their sibling bond."

"Was it ever that weak?" Jack asked.

"Well, it was...strained at times. I think they get a bit on top of one another at times while they've been living together." Charles shrugged.

He knew that he was just blabbing, but he was content that he was at least blabbing well. He wasn't sure what other questions they were going to throw in his direction, but he was confident that he would be able to answer them with ease.

"I see. It sounds good that they're going to be off together and doing something that will bring them closer." His Uncle said politely.

They all took sips of their teas to fill the silence that followed his words. Jack was glancing over at the lawyer who hadn't said anything for a while. His silence unnerved Charles. It could only mean one thing; that he was thinking. He didn't like the idea of Tanner scheming right in front of him, it made him feel vulnerable, and there was nothing else that Charles hated more.

"I was wondering when we'll golf together again." Charles said.

He remembered how awfully the golfing had gone last time, with Jack's outburst still fresh on people's lips. Charles couldn't help but smirk slightly at the way that he had so innocently managed to bring it back into the conversation. He could see the way that his uncle had turned a particular shade of pink that matched the couch cushions they were sitting on. Charles tried to look rather innocent as though he didn't fully understand the implications of his words, but he wasn't fooling anyone with his look.

"I'll have to check my schedule." Jack ended up muttering to himself as he took another sip of his chamomile tea.

Charles took the small victory in the form of a curt nod. He tried not to be too smug about it, but that was a rather difficult task when facing two men who were always waiting for him to trip. They continued talking about the politics of their world. Jack was worried about some men at the golf club who had tried parking in his space in the parking lot. If one were to hear such talk, it wouldn't have sounded like a lot, and they were acting as though it would be the end of the world if someone was to park in their spot.

Charles nodded along and listened as though he was going to contribute to the conversation, but he had no intention of doing so. Instead, he took the break in attention being on him to relax and try to rid his body of the tension that had been building up inside of him. He'd been so concerned that they would find him out and pick apart his far-fetched story that Jane was Europe. Just as he thought he was in the clear, both of them turned back to him and were staring inquisitively. He thought for a moment that he had missed a question that had been aimed at him, but Charles thought back on the conversation and realized that nothing like that had occurred.

"I believe we should head through for lunch now." He said, as he started to rise from his chair. He wasn't sure what the sudden attention being placed back on him was about, but he worked quickly to deflect it.

Charles couldn't stand the thought of having to continue to defend himself against these men over lunch when he had barely managed to get out of having a cup of tea with them unscathed.

CHAPTER 6

Helena stared out of the window, her thoughts were wandering as she got lost in the blur of trees and shrubbery. They were well and truly out in the country now, and there weren't too many signs of civilization for a while.

"So what's the story of this house?" James spoke up.

They had managed to go a total of twenty minutes in silence. Helena had counted on purpose because their interactions felt to her like a thunderstorm. She would always count as a child the interlude between thunder and lightning, and whenever there was a silent period between herself and James, that was exactly what she was anticipating would come. His voice, like a rumble of thunder, wasn't exactly a sound that she welcomed.

"It was our parent's house." She explained. "It's not really worth that much, I'm not even sure that you could legally call it a house because of the state it's in."

"Why hasn't someone even bought it up to redo it?" James asked with a frown.

"It's a long story, but it's also such a remote place that nobody really goes over to that part." Helena tried not to give too many details. "It's not the kind of place that many people would want to live, let alone to fix up a place. It's owned by the bank now, so if Jane is there, she's technically trespassing."

"I'm sorry to hear that, it mustn't be easy for your family home to have fallen into ruin like that." James said.

"You know, that may have just been the most genuine thing you've ever said to me." She said with a chuckle.

"Oh come on now, don't ruin the moment." James said with an exaggerated whine.

"We weren't having a moment."

"If you say so."

Helena shook her head, she didn't want his pity, all she wanted was his help in finding her sister. She wondered if Jane really would go back there, it was such a far off place to get to and she just couldn't understand the logic in it. She could understand why her sister was so angry at the Bentleys. They were all the same emotions that Helena had had herself when she'd first made the connection. But what did upset her was the fact that Jane hadn't come to her for help or comfort on the matter. Instead, she had chosen to run and deal with it all on her own.

She had thought that if her sister had learned one thing in this life, it was that she really couldn't deal with these things on her own.

"And you say that you aren't working at the strip club anymore?" James piped up again. It felt as though the storm between them was getting closer since their intervals of silence were getting shorter.

"No, I no longer work there." She said through gritted teeth. The memory of the attack was still so fresh in her mind, but she didn't bring it up.

"What made you quit?"

She refrained from snapping at him since she didn't want to be the one to start the fresh conflict between them this time.

"Your cousin's money." She said with a nonchalant shrug.

Helena was looking to see if her answer would drag out some kind of reaction from him. Since she could imagine if she was on the other side of this conversation, Helena knew that she wouldn't be too happy at the thought of people using her family for money.

"Would you still be doing that without my cousin's money then?" James asked with a clenched jaw.

"I don't know. I've been trying to get out of it for a while now, it's not a healthy way to make a living. Anyone can see that. It's dangerous and very long hours, but we've always needed the money."

"And now you're just going to take it off my cousin?"

"It's not like he hasn't got enough of it." Helena said, as she shrugged her shoulders.

"But it's also not like he's supporting a charity, he's just paying two women to live their lives."

"Hey, I'm not a charity case." Helena couldn't help but snap finally.

"There she is." James smirked, as he glanced in her direction slightly with his eyes.

"You're just doing this for fun? You think that you're going to get a rise out of me?" Helena scoffed. For a moment, she couldn't believe him, but then she thought about James and how he had been throughout the trip. She realized that she really could believe that he was doing this to her.

"I was only joking." James said with a twisted chuckle. "I don't really care if you get money from my cousin."

"Whatever." She said with a scowl as she turned back toward the window.

"Look, why don't we just try and get on for a while? Surely it can't be that hard for the two of us to at least have one conversation where we don't end up arguing?"

"You were literally the one just trying to get a rise out of me." Helena frowned. "You can't say one thing and then ask to do another."

"Alright, I'm sorry, let's start over." James sighed. "Remember after the dinner party when we went for that walk? I'm pretty sure that we managed to have a few good conversations then where there wasn't so much bickering."

"That was different." Helena muttered. She knew that she was being difficult, but she didn't care. James deserved to see how much he annoyed her, and she wasn't about to hold back.

"How was that any different to this?"

"Because my sister wasn't missing and I wasn't completely worried about that." Helena said back. "I just want to find her, I don't want to talk to you so much anymore, especially if you're just going to comment and criticize my life."

"That's not at all what I've been doing, and this certainly hasn't just been one sided." He said with a frown.

"Whatever."

"You're only saying that because I won." James said while smirking.

"Won what? This stupid argument that we're having? Do you really have to be so immature about this?" She raised her voice as she spoke, but Helena wasn't about to back down.

"You really think that I'm the immature one here?"

"We're not doing this right now, can't we just go back to silence?"

Helena had been wrong about the silence being worse; she would have welcomed the ambiance of just listening to trees whirl past her window accompanied by the dull purr of the engine. It would have been much better than having to tolerate James' voice.

"You can't just decide that you're not going to talk to me when we've got to spend so long in a car together." James said.

"I can, and I just did."

"And you're calling me the immature one?" He said again with a chuckle.

"Are you kidding me?" She shouted at him as she sat up in her seat and turned to him.

A sudden thumping sound stopped their argument dead in its tracks. The car tilted to the left slightly, causing Helena to grip onto his arm as shock ran through her body. She wasn't sure what it was going to mean for their safety, but all previous animosity for one another had briefly been forgotten. She shrieked slightly as James managed to steer the car off of the road and into the hard shoulder lane. The change of road texture from the smooth surface to a gravel crunch caused her to wince, and she found herself glancing around to make sure that they weren't going to crash. The thumping continued on the left side as they finally slowed to stop, where the noise ceased completely.

"And you thought that I couldn't be your knight in shining armor." James chuckled slowly as Helena continued to breathe heavily. She wasn't sure what had happened, but she was absolutely terrified of what it would mean for the two of them and their journey to get Jane.

"What happened?"

"Flat tire, I suspect, but I can't be sure. Let's hope that's all it is." He said, as he tried to move.

A sudden awkwardness settled over them both as they came to the mutual realization that Helena still had hold of his arm. She swallowed thickly before gingerly letting go of him, ignoring the smirk of triumph on his face as she quickly moved to get out of her seat.

"Yep." He said, as they both stared down at the burst rubber. "That is what you'd call a blown tire."

"Thanks for that, Sherlock." She said with a scoff and shook her head.

"Oh come on, I said it was before we even got out here!" He said in protest.

"I don't care, we're going to need to fix this and get back on the road."

They still hadn't stopped for some food, and Helena was incredibly hungry. This was really the last thing that she needed as the day wore on. It was already the afternoon, and she wanted to try and get to the house before dark, although she was starting to doubt that this would happen.

"I'll call a mechanic, I'm sure that we can have someone out here in an hour or so."

"We haven't got that kind of time." She quickly fired back at him.

"Then what do you want to do, change it yourself?"

"As a matter of fact, I do." Helena said while putting her hands on her hips.

"You're actually insane if you think that I'm going to let you go anywhere near that car." James said with a chuckle. "I'm not going to let you."

"Oh come on." She said while pointing at the car. "We need to get on the move, and I know how to change a car's tire. You've just got to trust me."

"You really think that I'd do that?" He laughed in disbelief.

"We don't have another option."

"We call a mechanic."

Helena glared at him. "We don't have time."

*****

James shook his head. He couldn't believe that he was actually agreeing to this. He didn't mean to sound so harsh when he'd said it to her, but he really couldn't imagine that she would be any good at changing a tire. He was also very cautious of his car since it was much more expensive than whatever car she had previously worked on.

"Are you sure about this?"

"I wouldn't have offered it if I wasn't." Helena shook her head. "And I don't appreciate the amount of doubt that you have in me."

He narrowed his eyes; they barely knew each other at the end of the day, and he wasn't sure what she was capable of. There was still a rather strong chance that Helena was just lying to him and that she really had no idea how to change a tire.

"Just be careful, do you know how expensive this car is?"

"I don't want to think about that." She muttered. "But I'll hazard a guess, it probably costs more than I would make in about three years, right?"

James found himself stunned into silence. He hadn't realized the impact that his question could have had on her and felt his cheeks heat up instantly. With a heavy reluctance, James stepped back and sucked in a breath as Helena positioned the jack and spare tire near to the busted one. He shook his head as he watched her work. He knew that the gentlemanly thing to do would be to offer his hand at this, but he'd never changed a tire before and didn't want to have to prove that fact.

He didn't understand how Helena was so resourceful when it came to something like that. She'd told him that she'd pretty much worked every day of her adult life, and so he couldn't see how fixing cars could have been a hobby that she pursued. Yet sure enough, she was only a couple of minutes with the task. He looked on in disbelief as she rolled the old tire over to the other side of the road.

"See there." She pointed to a small cut in the rubber. "That's the original puncture. Whatever it was that we hit, we hit it at a speed that blew the rubber open from the pressure."

She was pointing to the small hole and talking about it as though she were a scientist that had discovered a new element. James paused for a moment as he admired just how passionate she was about this. It caused him to reflect for a moment as he tried to think about something that he was just as passionate about. He grimaced when nothing surfaced easily in his mind.

"Alright, are we ready to go?"

"Do you trust my work in the end then?" She asked with a small smirk.

"We'll have to see how it fares on the road," James tried to shrug it off. However, he would have been lying to her if he'd said that he wasn't impressed.

"Try not to drive over anything else sharp."

He was slightly stunned as he watched her stride over to the passenger side of the car. Helena had managed to prove herself as incredibly useful after all.

"Where did you learn to do that?" He asked her after climbing back into the car.

"It's just one of those things that you pick up over the years, you know, being poor and all."

James was slightly thrown off by the way that she could speak about her substandard quality of life like that.

"You don't like it, do you?"

"Don't like what?" He frowned as he looked at her.

"You don't like it when I speak like that." She elaborated. "You don't like when I talk about being poor."

"I mean, it's not that. It's just a little uncomfortable to hear about." He admitted softly.

"It's not that bad, you know. You get to learn all sorts of skills that you would probably pay someone to do when you're rich. I'm one hell of a seamstress, you know?"

"I can imagine." He chuckled.

"So do you see? I can be useful after all."

"I suppose you can be." He said with a sigh as he started up the engine again.

James was still slightly hesitant as they started to roll the car forward. He was waiting for the sudden jerk on the left-hand side of the car that would alert them both to the fact that she hadn't put the new tire on properly. But it never came. James started to drive quicker and increased their speed as he started to put more trust in his traveling companion.

CHAPTER 7

Charles felt as though he could collapse as the door to the large house finally closed. His uncle and Tucker were gone, and he could relax again. The lunch felt as though it had dragged on for hours, and Charles had at one point thought that they had him. He was just so thankful that they were gone and he didn't have to keep up such an appearance any longer. His head was persisting to pound with fresh aches, and his body felt ready for a night of deep and long sleep.

"Do you think they were convinced enough?" Anna asked from behind him.

"I really hope so." He sighed. "I just want to know where she is."

"May I say something that is...out of term?"

"You normally do anyway without asking." He remarked.

Anna bowed her head for a moment as a small smile played on her lips out of amusement. However, it was gone by the time that she had straightened up.

"I wanted to know if James or Helena have gotten back to you while you've had lunch?"

"I...I don't think so."

"Do you think that it's time to call the police?"

"No." Charles responded quickly to her question. "Not yet, no."

"Of course, Sir." She said, although there was the hint of a glare in her expression.

He watched his housekeeper go before groaning at the sound of his phone buzzing. James would be calling him only to tell him that they had either found Jane or that they had found trouble.

"James?"

"Hey, we've uh...we've got into a little trouble over here." He started.

Charles closed his eyes slowly and tried not to let his knees give in. It was exactly what he didn't need to hear at that moment. He thought about how good it would have been to rejoice in the fact that Jane had been found, but Charles knew that he was going to have to wait a little longer to hear that news.

"What's happened?" Charles asked after taking a deep breath.

"Well, I may have blown a tire." He said slowly. "But we're back on the road, it just slowed us down for a bit. I just wanted to keep you in the-"

"Did you take the Jag to drive?" Charles asked, as he pinched his nose.

"I...may have." James's voice was clearly hesitant.

"I want you to bring back Helena and Jane in one piece, but I'd also like to extend that request to the very limited edition car that is now in your possession."

There was a pause from the other end of the line. "Of course." James said eventually.

"Let me know when you arrive at the house."

"Roger that." James said.

He seemed to be in strangely high spirits, which caused Charles to frown. However, he didn't want to question it since he could hear that James was driving, and that meant that he would have him on speakerphone.

*****

231

"So." Helena said, with narrowed eyes as soon as the phone hung up. "This car isn't yours?"

"Not technically." James seemed rather reluctant to say.

"Does it belong to your cousin?"

"I don't see why this amuses you so much?" James said in a tone of clear annoyance.

"Oh it's nothing." Helena said with a knowing smile on her lips. She then pretended to cough as the words "charity case" slipped out too.

"What was that?"

"Absolutely nothing." Helena said with a chuckle. She was sure that he'd heard her, and she turned to see that he was shaking his head as he stared at the road ahead of him. "When you said that this car was really expensive, you meant it, huh?"

"I wasn't going to say anything, but I don't think it's worth only three years of what you would earn." He muttered.

"Probably what I'd earn over a lifetime."

Helena pursed her lips at that depressing thought. She felt almost wrong for sitting in it, and if it wasn't for her sister's disappearance she would hate herself for even entertaining the idea of a car costing so much money.They were silent for a while as the hours started to blend into one another. The reality that they were going to make it before dark was slowly starting to settle in, but Helena wasn't sure she was willing to accept it yet.

Every now and again, she would glance over at James to make sure that he was awake, but she knew that he would want to stop soon. He hadn't been to sleep yet, and so she knew that he was going to start struggling soon if he wasn't already.

"What are you thinking?" She asked, as she saw the way that his eyes suddenly narrowed.

Her sudden voice made him jump slightly in his seat, but James was quick to recover. He coughed and slowly looked over at her as he shook his head.

"I was ugh...I was just thinking about the fact that I'm incredibly tired."

"You look it."

Her comment only earned a glare from him.

"I know that, I feel like I've been hit by a bus. You've been lucky, you've managed to get some sleep in the passenger seat." He started to grumble.

"I did offer to drive." Helena defended herself.

"You know how expensive this car is." He said with a scoff. "You're not going to sit anywhere near the driver's seat."

Helena huffed at the way that he was being so stubborn.

"So the only other option is that we find a motel for the night?" She said with a slight wince.

"We're not going to make it any time soon, are we?"

"I don't think so." Helena breathed out as she spoke. It was a very depressing thought, and she knew that it was time they both faced the reality of it.

"So we stop for the night?" James sighed.

"I haven't seen any signs for any motels coming up." Helena said, as she stared out the window.

"I'm sure that one will turn up soon."

"I hope you're right."

Sure enough, they only had to wait a little longer for a motel sign to appear along the side of the road. The evening sun was slowly starting to set, and Helena felt rather reluctant as she watched him pull into the turning.

"We don't know if there'll be another motel within driving distance down here." He reasoned, as though she had said something to say otherwise. "I think it's best that we stop here."

"Alright." She muttered and looked down at her lap.

Helena felt far too worried to properly try and comprehend what was going on. All she wanted was her sister back, and the thought of delaying that for the next few hours while they slept just didn't sit right with her.

"Look, I've been driving all day with no sleep, I'm exhausted."

Helena continued to nod as she stared out of the window. The building was much smaller than she had expected and the rooms gave off the kind of vibe that told her this could be dangerous. But Helena remembered that she had already lived in a dangerous place for a long time, and she wasn't too scared of it. James, however, looked ready to turn the engine back on and drive off.

"Are you sure about this?" She teased ,as he rolled his eyes.

"I don't think I've ever put my sleep before my safety."

"Well, there's a first for everything. Come on, you're going to be so grateful to put your head down on a pillow."

The bags under his eyes had only gotten worse, and James looked rather pale all of a sudden. Helena knew that feeling well; it was the same way she felt in the morning after a shift that had felt as though it was much longer than she had anticipated. She didn't envy him, and she wasn't running on much sleep herself. The motel would do them good, she decided, and they would need to refuel soon too.

"Just the one room?" The woman at the front desk asked while glancing between them.

"Yes, but two beds." James spoke up before Helena could even open her mouth.

She narrowed her eyes at him but kept her thoughts to herself. At times, she couldn't believe that he could be quite such an ass towards her.

"All right, here's your room key."

The woman went about her usual speech of when food times were, what time they had to be out by. It was the usual kind of stuff, but Helena was so tired that she was barely listening to a word that she was saying. She thought for a moment that she would rely on James to listen to her, but she then remembered what a bad idea that would be.

They quickly left the building and circled around until they found the balcony that led to their room. The paint was peeling off of the walls, and there were strange noises coming from some of the rooms that they passed. Helena still felt rather nervous about this, but the prospect of sleeping on a mattress instead of in a car was far outweighing any kind of fear that rose inside of her.

"Here we go." James muttered ,as he saw that they were standing outside of the right room.

"Are you sure this is the right one?"

"Don't even try to start something like that right now." James mumbled. It took Helena a minute to realize that he was talking to her since his words had been so quiet.

She closed her mouth and followed behind him as he walked into the room slowly. It was rather similar to her apartment in a lot of ways, and that thought acted as a slight comfort, although Helena was still rather cautious of the place.

"Two beds, huh?"

"Did you really want to share a bed with me?" James asked with a scoff.

Helena could think of much worse companions to have in a bed, but she kept those thoughts to herself. The last thing that she wanted to do was boost his ego in any way possible.

"What time did she say that dinner was at?"

"I don't care, I'm going to sleep." He mumbled and quickly moved the bed apart. In an instant, he'd created a border between them, and Helena was thankful as she sat down on her side of the bed that it would mean no accidental cuddling during the night.

"All right, we'll get breakfast then." She said.

Helena could feel the emptiness in her stomach was starting to rise, and she grimaced at the idea of not being able to eat until the morning. Her body was tired, there was no denying that, but part of the reason it was tired was due to the lack of food in it.

She thought about protesting against him and asking if she could have some food, but as she turned around, Helena couldn't help but smile at the sight of James with his eyes closed.

Sleep seemed to consume him and clearly welcomed him with open arms. She noted that he looked a lot younger and calmer in sleep, a lot more innocent than before.

"Good night." She whispered to him before climbing under the covers herself.

*****

Daylight streamed into the motel room from the early hours of dawn. Helena groaned as she was forced to face the sudden and rather extreme ray of light from her pillow. She shook her head and tried to get rid of it as she turned over and tried to get back to sleep, but her rumbling stomach made that almost impossible.

Finally, after what felt like an age of trying to continue her sleep, Helena threw the covers back and gave up. She padded across the floor with her bare feet and headed into the bathroom. The awful yellow light inside of the small room made her miss the natural light of the sunrise that she had just been woken up by.

Helena quickly splashed some water on her face and shook her head in an attempt to wake up some more. She started to wish that one of them had paid attention to what the woman had said in regard to meal times.

Helena walked over to the door and decided to stand out on the communal balcony since it was empty. The sun was splitting through the sky in a beautiful myriad of orange, pink, and red hues. It truly would have been a sight to behold if Helena had felt as though they had the time to marvel over such a thing. Instead, she could only grimace as she thought about what kind of conditions her sister was waking up to.

Their family home could have been no more than a shell by that point, and she wasn't sure that Jane had fully thought through the consequences of trying to stay in such a place. There was also always the option that there were squatters or gangs using that house to lay low for a while. The thought that Jane had only gone and gotten herself into more trouble wasn't exactly a comforting one. Helena could hear movement in the room behind her, James was clearly awake.

"There you are." He breathed out in relief as he slightly opened the door.

"What do you mean?" She narrowed her eyes.

"I thought you'd left me." He muttered.

Helena wasn't in the mood to deal with his dramatics, and so she merely scoffed and turned back to appreciate the sunrise.

"Can we get some food?"

"I thought you'd never ask." She responded dryly.

He was muttering something behind her, and she was sure that it would be some kind of smart response, but she didn't want to hear it. All Helena wanted was something for breakfast. They walked over to the diner that was open and smelled delicious. Helena felt as though she could devour anything that they would dare to put in front of her, but she waited patiently as they were shown to a table and told about the menu.

"You still look tired." James muttered once the waitress was gone.

"And you sure know how to talk to a lady." She responded dryly.

"I never said that you were a lady, only tired." James said, as he looked up at her.

"Well, you don't exactly look well rested either."

"That's because I've had springs digging into my back all night."

Helena realized that James must have been used to lying on a cloud when it came to sleeping. She couldn't help the amused smirk that twitched the corners of her lips upwards. It was quite funny to imagine that he wasn't able to sleep on anything less than an expensive mattress.

"You're acting like it's my fault that they haven't got the Ritz out in the middle of nowhere."

James scowled at her comment before returning to the menu.

After ordering and waiting for their food, Helena waited patiently for the comment that was surely going to come in regard to how much food she had just ordered. James had been silent as Helena had listed off the many items that she knew she wouldn't be able to consume completely. She'd always had eyes bigger than her stomach, and the realization that she didn't have to be frugal with what she bought was just too good to be true.

CHAPTER 8

They ate in an appreciative silence. Both of them breathed out in relief at the feeling of having a full stomach once again. Helena was at the point where she would burst if she even tried to shovel another mouthful of food into her, but she was still going to try.

"I don't think you've come up for air yet." hH said with a chuckle as Helena ignored him. "And I guess that you're picking up the bill?"

His comment caused her eyes to flicker over to his as he smirked down at her. Helena then rolled her eyes as she realized that he was playing her. He was trying to wind her up and be as annoying as though she was on this journey with a toddler.

"Whatever, you know that wouldn't happen." She muttered rather shamefully. "Thank you, for this."

"Don't think about it." James brushed it off.

She hated the fact that she wasn't able to contribute at all in terms of the finances of the situation, but Helena just didn't have money to waste. She didn't want to rely on their money, but at that moment, she didn't have much of a choice.

"So, do you think we'll find her today?" He continued to ask.

"I hope so." Helena nodded. "I really hope so. It just depends on what time we set off, but we should reach the house before the end of the day."

James sat back in his seat and stared out of the grubby diner window. His lips were pursed and Helena frowned as she tried to work out what she was thinking.

"Is it time to let me drive the Jag yet?" She asked with a smirk.

"Absolutely not." He shook his head but continued to stare out the dirty glass.

"What if you total it? Doesn't it make more sense for you to take the risk of letting me drive? Only for a few hours to give you a break?"

"I've had a break, I've slept and I've eaten. I'm feeling refreshed and ready to get back on the road." James said, as he tried to sound rather casual about it.

"You're not fooling me."

Helena was trying to make the large amount of food still on her plate look a lot smaller so that it didn't seem as though she was wasting so much. However, she couldn't get the grimace off of her face at the idea of wasting food.

In their household, they had always grown up with the idea of food waste being a pretty big sin. It showed that you had no regard for those in the world who went hungry. Helena winced at the thought as the waitress finally came over to take her plate. James was still staring out of the window as she returned her attention to him, although she couldn't understand why.

"What's wrong?" She asked with a frown as she turned in her seat.

"Just stay here for a moment." He muttered, as he quickly placed the right amount of bills and then some on the table.

Helena watched with a frown as he moved over to the door of the diner and quickly walked out toward a couple. They were standing by a car and appeared to be in the middle of some kind of heated discussion. Helena quickly got up and followed James out of the diner so that she was only a couple of paces behind him.

"You don't get to talk to me like that!" The man shouted at the much younger woman.

Helena continued walking until she watched in horror as his hand came down across her face. She suddenly stiffened as though someone had slammed on her emergency brakes, Helena sucked in a deep breath as the memories of a similar thing happening to her started to flood through her.

She knew the exact kind of pain that would sting the woman's cheek at that moment. It was like a kiss of pain; one that would tingle through the skin before diffusing out into a throbbing sensation. Helena closed her eyes for a moment as she tried to block the memories from triggering any kind of panic within her. It wasn't just the memories of herself, but also the memories of what her mother had gone through. Jane had been far too young to understand what was going on, and Helena had always brushed it off as not that big of a deal. But she remembered the nights when she would find her mother crying while clutching her cheek.

"Hey!"

Her eyes snapped open at the sound of James's voice. She realized in shock what he was going to do as he marched over to the large man who had just hit his partner. "What do you think you're doing hitting girls?"

His voice was a little deeper than usual, and Helena noticed just how tense his body was. She couldn't move still and watched as James continued walking until he was dangerously close to the man.

"Stay out of things that aren't your business!" The man shouted, as he pushed at James' chest.

"Oh no." Helena whispered, as she realized what would happen next.

James swung his fist back and quickly found purchase with it on the side of the man's face. He caused the man to grunt as he stumbled back slightly, but he regained his balance rather quickly.

"James, no!" Helena shouted.

She knew that the man deserved it, there was no doubt in her mind about that. But she could also clearly see that the man was much bigger than him, and much more powerful too. The two women watched on in horror as James tackled the man to the ground. Helena suddenly stirred into action and went first for the woman. She grabbed her arm, causing the woman to flinch.

"I'm sorry." She whispered, as she led the woman away from the car. "You're safe now, alright, we won't let him hurt you again."

"L-look," The woman raised a shaking hand up to point at the two scuffling men.

James was still on top of the man and delivering blow and blow while showing no signs of stopping.

"James!" Helena shouted at him as she quickly rushed over to him. Behind her, she could hear the woman shouting for her to not get too close, but Helena knew that she would have to do something to stop him. "He's done, James, stop it, you're going to kill him!"

"He deserves it!"

"James, I can't bail you out of jail and save my sister!" Helena shouted, as she tried to reason with him. "Come on, it's over. He's not getting up any time soon."

James finally stopped his movements and sat back. He hadn't come out of the fight completely unscathed; there were cuts across his eyebrow and his lip was bleeding. Helena shook her head as she looked at him, slightly unable to believe that he had really just thrown himself into such a dangerous situation.

"Call the police and say that he was abusing you." Helena urged the shaking woman in the same way that she had urged her own mother so many years beforehand. "They'll believe you, and they will protect you, I promise."

"O-okay." She nodded.

"I think you should go and wait in the diner while the ambulance arrives, take this." Helena said as she dipped her hand into James' pocket before quickly handing her a couple of notes. She wasn't sure how much she'd given the woman, but she didn't care. All she wanted was for her to be safe. "You're going to need to eat something, you've been through quite a lot."

"Thank you." She whispered, as Helena led her over to the empty diner.

She had a quick word with their waitress, who had seen everything, before returning to James.

"That wasn't exactly how I was expecting our morning to begin." She admitted with a slight chuckle.

"I didn't know you'd be so good under pressure." James muttered, as she gestured toward their motel room.

"There's a lot that you don't know about me."

She led him into their room before quickly turning on the cold water tap. Helena knew how to clean cuts and to help patch up small wounds, but her first aid knowledge was rather limited.

"There must be a first aid kit in here somewhere." She muttered, as she searched through the room. Sure enough, there was a kit at the bottom of one of the cabinets.

"How do you know all of this?" James asked with a frown as she motioned for him to sit on the bed.

"Like I told you before with the tire. You get resourceful when you don't have a lot of money. You would just go to a hospital, pay whatever bill they demand, and then you'd be on your way. We never had that luxury; if you hurt yourself, then you fixed yourself."

"What if you broke a bone or something?" James said with narrowed eyes.

"Well, you would get the luxury of a state hospital, but there would be no dinner waiting for you when you returned."

Helena knew that it must have sounded like an awful way to live, but it had made her careful. It made her think twice about everything that she did, since being ill was always so expensive.

"I'm sorry that you grew up like that."

"I don't want your pity." She said, as she quickly dabbed at his eye and lip with a wet cloth. She could tell that he was trying not to wince too much, but it was proving difficult for him.

"Alright." James said with a sigh. "Well, you have my respect. If that means anything to you."

Helena didn't respond, she simply continued to dab at the cuts on his face until the bleeding stopped. She sat down next to him to get a better angle, ignoring how close they were. It wasn't anything other than her trying to help him, and she really hoped that he would understand this.

"Does anywhere else hurt?" She asked while sitting back.

"No, I managed to block most of his punches."

Helena glanced down at his swollen knuckles and knew that James was probably lying.

"They look like they hurt." She commented, as he followed her gaze. He then placed his hands over one another so that she couldn't get such a good look at them.

"It's nothing."

"It could be something if you don't put some ice on them." She suggested. But James only rolled his eyes in response. "It was a really brave thing that you did back there." Helena was aware of how much softer her voice sounded than normal. She bit her lip and glanced down at the first aid kit to get the right antiseptic cream out.

"It's what anyone would have done." He said with a shrug.

"That's exactly what a modest hero would say." She chuckled.

"Was that…" James blinked in disbelief as he paused. "Was that some form of a weird compliment?"

Helena couldn't help but chuckle at the mocking tone that he was using; his voice was much softer than usual, and she couldn't help but think that perhaps they really were sharing a moment.

"I wouldn't go that far." She said, as she scrunched up her face.

"I'll take it." James laughed.

They were silent for a while as she prepared the cream by diluting it slightly.

"I'm not going to lie." She warned, as she moved slightly closer to him. "This is going to sting a little bit."

"How much? Ouch!"

James hissed in pain and jerked away from her hand as she dabbed the cloth against his open wounds.

"I did warn you." Helena said with a small and rather apologetic smile. "Look, we need to keep them clean or they're going to get infected, and then you're going to wish that you just let me help you a little."

James huffed but moved back to his original position. She could see that one of his hands was holding onto the duvet and gripping extra tightly whenever she pressed the cloth into his skin.

"God, that's not nice." hH muttered. "I'd take another punch over that any day."

"Stop being such a baby." Helena chuckled.

James grumbled something under his breath as she finished up with cleaning the cuts.

"There's not really much that I can do about the bruising that's going to come up, but you can put some ice on it for the time being."

"I suppose." James nodded.

"Unless you want a black eye." Helena said with a mere shrug.

"No thanks, I'm not trying to do an impression of you."

Helena froze at his words. They had come out much harsher than she had imagined, and even James looked slightly shocked at his words.

"I'm sorry, that-"

"It's fine, I know exactly how you feel about me now. I'm just the riff raff, right? Not your kind of people." Helena shook her head as she closed up the medical kit.

There was more that she could have done for him, but she was no longer in the mood to want to help him.

"Helena, I'm sorry, I really didn't mean that I just-"

"You just what? You think that you're better than me because you don't have to work every day to just try and keep a roof over your head? Well here's a little information for you, we were doing fine. My whole family was doing the best that it could before your stupid family came into our lives and ruined everything."

"Oh, so that's what this is about." He shook his head as he stood up.

"It's the truth! You people decided that my mother's life wasn't a financially viable thing for you, and so you let her die. You've decided that it's financially viable to have your cousin try and buy my sister in an attempt for you guys to get more money. When will you be done with us?"

247

James blinked at her outburst as Helena put the medical kit back where she had found it. All she wanted to do was get on the road and continue their search for her sister, but instead, she was playing nurse in a sketchy motel with another Bentley idiot.

"Helena, I'm sorry." He said in a small voice.

"I'm sorry too." She said with a sigh. "I'm sorry that I ever thought that you could be the good Bentley out of your family. I'm sorry that I thought you were different from them." James opened his mouth to say something, but Helena was done with talking about this. "I'll meet you in the car."

CHAPTER 9

James walked over to the car feeling an immense shame at the way that he had spoken to her. Helena had only been trying to help him, but he'd let their stupid feud get in the way of showing her that he actually did appreciate her.

Although he hadn't said it to her, he really did value her and respected the way that she had gotten through life by learning all sorts of tricks and skills to keep her and her sister alive. Helena was already sitting in the car as he approached after giving back the room key. James dreaded the idea of them having to spend any longer within the confines of the car. It could have been the most beautiful and expensive vehicle in the world, but he still wouldn't have enjoyed himself.

"Alright, let's get going." He muttered to himself as he sat down in the driver's seat. He wasn't exactly surprised that Helena made no attempt to respond to him, he wasn't expecting her to say another word to him for the rest of the trip.

They pulled out of the motel parking lot and were back on the main road within minutes. James winced as he stared at the satnav, it was saying that they were still a couple of hours away from it. He couldn't understand why they had moved so far away from their original house, but he didn't feel that it was the time to be asking questions about that.

"Helena?" He spoke up after a while.

Since there had been good silences and bad silences during their trip, this was definitely feeling like a bad silence. The kind that made him shift in his seat just to generate some kind of noise, but Helena just continued to stare straight ahead.

"I just wanted to apologize again. I want us to get along, I really do. I know that my family has wronged you, and I will never be able to say that I'm sorry on their behalf enough to make anything better. But I just want you to know that I really am sorry."

Silence cushioned his words once more. He sighed and settled back into his seat as he stared ahead.

"I don't forgive you, but I also don't like when we don't talk." She said eventually.

James let his eyes close for a moment in slight relief. It wasn't as reassuring as he had hoped for, but it also wasn't exactly the kind of answer that severed anything that they had left with one another.

"Thank you." He muttered. "I also want to understand better."

"Understand what?"

"I know that it's not my place to pry, but - when you're ready, of course - I would like to hear about what you and your sister have had to go through in life. From what I've heard already, it sounds like an awful lot. I respect you and Jane a lot, you're fighters and it can't have been easy."

He could see that she was now looking at him out of the corner of his eye. He knew that she would be searching his expression for any kind of hint that he was messing with her. But he wasn't. James was genuinely interested in finding out about her past because he wanted to sympathize with her better. He also just wanted to get to know her.

He was trying so hard to ignore the part of him that found her attractive. It scared him a little that there was a part of him that had marveled so much even when she had changed the tyre on his car. He found her resourcefulness attractive, her beauty of course only made this easier, and her hard exterior intrigued him.

"I don't know what to say." She said with a shrug. "Jane and I grew up with both of our parents for a while. So I guess we were lucky during our childhood. We weren't exactly rich, but we also weren't as poor as we would become. I barely remember it myself, and I know that Jane was far too young to remember any of it either. But then as we got older, I started to notice things that weren't quite right between my parents; my mother was often limping, and I would hear her crying when she was in another room. I was too young to properly put two and two together back then, but I accidentally walked in once to see my dad hitting her."

"I'm sorry." James muttered.

He could feel something pang in his heart, no child should ever have to see that.

"Don't be, I've been to therapy about it and I'm pretty much over it. It's just sometimes when you see others who are going through a similar thing…"

"Like that woman?"

"Exactly." Helena nodded. "It's just difficult because it brings up a lot of old memories and traumas that I had mostly forgotten about."

James wanted to ask about the black eye that she'd had before the dinner the other week, but he wasn't sure how to slip it into the conversation.

"Anyway, my mother managed to get us away from him. We went a long way from our family home, and we arrived here, well…back where we were. But we never really had too much money after that. My mom was a single mom trying to make a living for herself and provide for her kids, it was tough on all of us."

James nodded as she spoke. It sounded like a tough life that had been filled with a lot of stress, he couldn't imagine what his life would have been like if money was something that he had to worry about.

"I remember the day that I came home from school and my mother was looking at me with so much pain in her eyes. As the oldest, it was always my job to stay strong and be the one who would help keep Jane safe. My mom became too sick to work, she was diagnosed with cancer and put on many different kinds of treatments to try and save her, but nothing worked."

"I'm so sorry, Helena."

"I've told you many times." She said with a weary sigh. "I've never wanted your pity."

"I know but-"

"So I was forced to drop out of college and work. I worked my ass off so that the three of us could stay in our apartment and so that my mom wouldn't worry about trying to feed us while also paying medical bills. I never really let Jane know just how bad the situation was, at least, not until the rejection letter came. I scrunched that stupid piece of paper up and burnt it out of anger, but I now wish I'd kept it. It was the evidence that I had against the insurance company. They weren't going to pay for her life saving operation, they were going to let her die." Helena stopped for a moment, her voice wobbled from the weight of the emotions that were clearly running through her.

"That must have been awful." James gave her a look that he hoped she would see really was genuine. It broke his heart to think about the circumstances that had surrounded her as she'd grown up. "You're both so strong.'

"We didn't have a choice to be anything else." Helena said with a shrug. "If I'd have had it my way and gone through life the way I wanted to, I like to think that I would have been rather girly and sensitive. But instead, I had to be tough. I had to learn to be good at lots of things like mechanics, sewing, cooking, cleaning. There was no money to be anything less than resourceful because we didn't have enough funds to pay anyone else to do it for us."

"That really is admirable." James said, as he flashed her a small smile. "You have no idea how much I respect you for that."

He caught her eye, and for a moment, it felt as though the world around them had slowed down. He felt something flutter up within him and he knew at that moment that he had messed up. He'd let his feelings in and he'd let himself be controlled by them. James realized that he was softening up to the idea of getting closer to Helena, and that was a very dangerous thought indeed.

"Why are you looking at me like that?" She whispered, as James slowed the car down.

"I'm just admiring you."

He saw the way that she blinked a couple of times at his comment. He could tell that she didn't believe that he'd just said that, but she didn't respond in any way other than to stare down at her lap.

"And so you started work at the strip club?" He quickly tried to change the subject.

"Yes, well, I've always been working there behind the bar." Helena nodded. "It was dangerous, and there would be people waiting outside sometimes."

"What do you mean?" He asked with a frown.

James could feel his grip on the steering wheel tightening as she spoke. The idea of people out there trying to hurt her wasn't exactly one that he welcomed.

"Well, sometimes I would refuse to serve them because they would already be too drunk, and other times they would just be trying their luck with me." Helena said with a shrug.

"And they would hurt you?" He could feel the anger shaking his voice, but he didn't care.

"Well, they would try to, but they weren't always successful."

"Some of them were successful?"

"You saw my black eye." Helena said.

He hated that he'd just assumed she was the one getting into trouble. James hated that he'd made that comment to her about the fact that she had a black eye. He hated a lot of the things that he'd said to her, but this was something so inexcusable that it made him feel sick to his stomach.

"I'm sorry." He sighed eventually. "I mean it, Helena, I really am so sorry. I can't believe that I thought it was your fault and that you were just trouble, I was being an idiot."

"Don't worry about it. I get why people assume those things about me, but I just do what I have to do to survive on this rock." She sounded rather nonchalant about it all. James realized that she was probably in denial about how dangerous the situations were and how awful it was.

"I wish that there was something I could do." He sighed.

"I can point out each of the men if you want, I'll stand by with a first aid kit." She chuckled.

"Do it." He nodded eagerly. "I'd take them all out and then drag them home to their wives to show them what cheating pieces of shit they've married."

"Woah, steady there." Helena said, as she glanced up at him.

*****

Helena couldn't believe that he was actually taking her so seriously for once. It didn't feel real for a moment that he was being so tender with her, he was actually showing her that he cared for her. She had a moment where she wondered if this was real, or if she was actually dreaming that it had happened.

James could be nice and caring when he wanted to be, but she had never seen him like this before. He was being so...protective. It was as though there was something more behind his actions. Helena was also slightly thrown by the look that he was giving her, it was one that she hadn't seen before and she really wasn't sure how to read into it.

"So there you go, a brief history of Helena Miller." She said with a small smile. "I suppose it could be classed as some kind of tragic story. You know, the kind where she doesn't get a happy ending, but I haven't gotten that far yet."

"I hope for your sake that it is a happy ending." James nodded to her.

Helena smiled to herself as she turned to look out of the window. She thought about how good of a friendship they could have if they actually spoke to one another like that instead of bickering.

"I can't believe it." She said with a chuckle as she shook her head.

"What?" He frowned, as he glanced over at her.

"We actually managed to get through an entire serious conversation without any slight digs at one another." She said as though in disbelief.

"Don't ruin it now then." He said with a slight frown.

"Oh, I don't plan on it. I quite like this James. He seems much more understanding."

"And I quite like this Helena. She's not pretending to be so...tough."

CHAPTER 10

Charles was pacing. It seemed that within the space of the last forty-eight hours, he had taken it up as his new hobby. He wasn't proud of the way that he was handling it, and he knew that he must have looked like an absolute mess.

"Any news?"

"I'll tell you when I get news." He said in a much snappier tone than he had meant to towards his housekeeper.

Anna was gone by the time that he looked up to apologize. He knew that there was no point in taking it out on his staff, not when it was technically his own family's fault that she had run off anyway. Charles scowled as he thought about how all of this could have been avoided.

He quickly found out that Anna hadn't only appeared to ask if he had received any news from James and Helena, but she was also coming to announce that he had a guest. Charles' comment had stopped her in her tracks, and he assumed that this was her revenge of some kind. He turned at the sound of footsteps and quickly stopped a groan of annoyance in his throat before it could leave his lips.

"Charles!" His Aunt Rosalyn exclaimed as she saw him. "My goodness, you look so...tired."

He quickly pushed back his disheveled hair and rose from where he had been lounging on the sofa all morning.

"Aunt Rosalyn." He managed a smile as he moved to embrace her quickly. "To what do I owe this pleasure?"

"Well, I had some free time this morning and just thought that I would pop over." She smiled and glanced around the dark room. "Such a shame, it's such a lovely day outside and you have the curtains drawn. Are you sick?"

She took a step back slightly after asking the question but relaxed somewhat at the sight of Charles shaking his head.

"No, only lovesick." He said, as he thought on his feet.

"What do you mean?" She asked, with a sickeningly sweet smile.

"Please, do take a seat." He gestured to one of the couches in the room. "Anna, will you bring a tray of tea and coffee? And do open these curtains."

The housekeeper nodded as she kept her gaze to the floor, but she quickly carried out his requests. Charles tried his best not to wince as he turned his back to his aunt as Anna opened the curtains rather suddenly.Light flooded the room instantly, it hurt his head as he blinked a few times in an attempt to get his eyes to adjust to the sudden intensity of light in the room. He didn't like the way that the daylight would illuminate just how rough he looked, but there was no going back on it now.

"I'm just missing my fiance." He explained, as he sat down on the couch opposite Rosalyn.

She was searching his face for some kind of sign that he was lying, but he made sure that she found none. His stony expression wasn't going to be burnt down under her fiery gaze, not if he could help it.

He hadn't slept too well last night upon hearing the news that James and Helena were staying the night in a motel. He wished that he could have gotten a few more details from his cousin before he had hung up the phone, all he wanted to know was if Jane was really at the house.

"Ah yes." Rosalyn nodded, as Anna entered with a tray of refreshments. "Jack was telling me about this trip to Europe that the Miller sisters have embarked on. He said that they've gone to Austria, was it?"

"That's correct." Charles nodded.

"I do love it there." Rosalyn smiled fondly. "Do you know what hotel they're staying in? They have some absolutely beautiful places there, I really do recommend it for your...honeymoon." The word seemed to pain her in a way that caused Charles to smirk.

He knew that it was no coincidence that Rosalyn had come over to grill him on the matter only a day after his uncle. They were breathing down his neck and trying to squeeze as many details out of him as they could.

"I don't know the name of it off the top of my head." He said, as he narrowed his eyes. "Let me text Jane and I'll find out for you." He said quickly.

"That would be wonderful, if you give me her number, I could always call her to give her some good tips for traveling around. They have some great food markets in Saltzburg, but I suppose it depends on how long they're there for, doesn't it?"

"They should be back by the weekend," Charles said, as he noted how sneakily she was putting questions into her sentences.

"I see." Rosalyn said and pursed her lips. She always looked as though she had eaten something sour and was trying to cover it up. Charles normally found it quite an amusing look, but it was getting on his nerves at that moment.

Charles swirled a small teaspoon around in his cup as he let the hot handle of his cup scold his hand slightly. It felt as though it was the only thing tethering him to the conversation that was actually a silent battle for his aunt. She was trying to investigate where his fiance was without actually letting him know that was what she was doing. He narrowed his eyes and shook his head at the thought of her getting to him, he wouldn't let that happen.

"Have you spoken with Tucker lately?"

"He came over for dinner last night." Rosalyn said with a shrug.

Charles had no doubt that his marriage was surely one of the main conversation topics of that dinner, although he simply nodded in response to her answer. Tanner had been scheming all day, and he was going to have to try and investigate if he had come to any conclusion.

"Shall I let you in on a little secret?" She asked with a smirk.

Charles knew that his aunt wasn't exactly on his side, and so anything that she was going to tell him was going to be in her interest only. It wasn't ever going to be a secret that would actually benefit him.

"As long as it isn't going to put me in a difficult situation." He said while nodding.

"I suppose that depends on what you mean by difficult."

"It's not going to leave me with some big moral dilemma." He elaborated slightly. "For example, I don't really want to know if Uncle Jack has been making those illegal deals with the Colombian folks again."

He suppressed his smile as Rosalyn turned an unhealthy shade of pink, it completely overwhelmed whatever shade of blush she had already been wearing on her cheeks until she looked like a tomato.

"No, it's nothing like that." She muttered after taking a moment to gather her composure. "I was speaking last night with Tucker, and he seems to be under the impression that it's all fake."

"What's all fake?" Charles said, although he was having a hard time fending off the panic that rose up in his throat and closed it up. He tried to keep his breathing regulated and simply focused on the stirring motion of his teaspoon.

"The engagement." Rosalyn said, as though it was the most obvious thing in the world. "He doesn't believe that you're both in love, and he thinks that perhaps you should think about it a little more clearly."

"How do you suggest that I could think about this in a clearer way?" He asked with narrowed eyes.

"Well, the two of you haven't known one another for that long, I would just reconsider what you're signing up for."

"I'm ready for marriage." He fired back quickly.

"Is she?"

"Yes, she wouldn't have said yes if she wasn't. Why else would she have said yes?" He was quick to talk, but Charles was only focusing on whether or not he sounded believable.

"Charles, if I were you, I would just be careful. You don't want her marrying you for the wrong reasons."

"These would be?"

"She knows that you have money."

Charles swallowed thickly at her comment, of course, his aunt was right, but he wasn't going to let her find that out. He nodded slowly and knew exactly how he was going to be able to turn her entire argument on its head.

"And could you tell me something, Aunt Rosalyn?" He asked while leaning forward slightly. "Why was it again that you married my Uncle?"

He could see the internal battle that was happening with her expression. She was struggling to control the muscles in her face as she tried her hardest not to react to his question.

"You're just a stupid boy." She scowled at him. "You could never understand why I married your Uncle, and I don't think that it would be wise of you to even try to."

Charles merely shrugged at her comment, she was clearly trying to lash out at him, but it was clear that her comments weren't working.

"Of course." He nodded his head as he looked down at his lap and smiled.

"I suppose I should leave you to it then." She said, as she tried looking down her nose at him. However, Rosalyn only made herself look even more ridiculous, which Charles hadn't thought was possible.

"I suppose you should be." He nodded. "Do send my Uncle my regards."

She scowled at him as Charles didn't even bother to get up. He didn't think that such a vulture of a woman deserved his manners. He waited until the front door closed behind her before he could relax properly. He pressed a hand to his face and rubbed his tired eyes slowly; he was having a difficult time keeping up the lie, and an even harder time in facing the reality that Jane may not be back by the weekend.

"You should have told me that she was here." He muttered to Anna as she entered the room to clear away the tray of tea. "I would have told you to send her away."

"I know." She said, "That's why I didn't."

"You need to watch it." Charles groaned. He knew that he didn't mean it, he would never get rid of his loyal housekeeper, even if she did act out at times. Anna had always been good to him, and he wouldn't dare to throw it all back in her face.

"And you should learn to not snap at your staff." Anna responded, as she walked out of the room with the tray.

Charles was left on his own with just his thoughts to keep him company. He couldn't quite believe that she had just spoken to him like that, but there were much more important things for him to worry about.

"James?" He quickly jumped up as he saw that his phone was buzzing.

"Hey." He said through the phone. The rushing sound of the vehicle was evident in the background and Charles' heart dropped at the thought of them still being on the road.

"Please tell me you've found her."

"Not exactly..." James' voice trailed off and Charles felt a sudden urge to throw his phone across the room. If it wasn't his only way to contact his cousin, he would have done it in an instant.

"What do you mean not exactly? You've been driving for so long!"

"I know, but we stopped for a rest Charles. I'm not a machine, I can't just drive for hours on end without taking a break." James was quick to fire back at him through the phone speaker. "We're going as fast as we humanly can."

"Alright, alright." Charles said, with a sigh as he sank back onto the sofa. "I'm sorry, things just aren't good here."

"What's going on?"

"My delightful Uncle and Aunt are quite literally breathing down my neck. They want to know where Jane is."

"What did you tell them?"

Charles winced at the question, he didn't want to have to admit his elaborate lie to any more people.

"Charles?"

"Yeah, I'm here." He groaned. "Look, I was put on the spot and I didn't know what to say that would stop them from trying to reach out and contact Jane."

"What did you say, Charles?" There was no longer any humor in James' tone as he asked the question.

"I told them that she has gone to Europe with her sister to search for some long lost grandparents or something." He sighed, as he finally came out with it.

"You did what?" The sudden screech of Helena's voice filled the speaker, causing Charles to move the phone away from his ear for a moment.

"Look, I didn't know what else to do. I didn't know how long you would be, so I just...improvised."

"That isn't improvising, that's just making a difficult situation even harder." Helena snapped at him. "What are you going to do when she comes back?"

"I'll brief her on what I told my Uncle, Rosalyn, and Tucker, and do the same with you, and then-"

"Don't you get why she's gone in the first place?" Helena cut him off through the phone.

"I...I do. Of course, I do, but this is important too." Charles fired back with a glare on his face, even though she couldn't see it.

"You Bentleys really don't think about anything other than yourselves." Her voice came out as a laugh of disbelief.

"Look, just because you don't understand our world, doesn't mean that-"

"She's right Charles, you can't expect them to help you get out of this one when we find her. Jane is probably just going to want to recover and try to process the news that she received about our involvement in their mother's death."

If there was one thing that Charles hadn't expected to have to deal with that day, it was having Helena and James gang up on him on the phone. He couldn't quite believe that his own cousin was taking their side, Charles had thought that he hated Helena. He had certainly acted like it.

Charles waited for a while. The pause was quite long, but he eventually spoke up. "Whatever, just make sure that you find her and bring her back."

With that, he hung up, not wanting to hear another word of what they had to say. His eyebrows furrowed as he thought about how James had changed in the space of such a short time.

"What is going on on that car journey?" He chuckled to himself as he shook his head.

"Sir, may I make a suggestion?" Anna asked, as he walked out into the hallway.

"No, Anna, I'm not going to the police with this. It's too much of a risk. James and Helena are almost at the house and I'm sure-"

"That wasn't what I was going to say." She cut him off.

Charles felt his fists clenched as he breathed in deeply. He was sick of people cutting him off as he stared at her.

"Then pray tell." He knew that his tone wasn't at all too friendly toward her.

"I was just going to suggest that while you wait for news on her whereabouts, you should perhaps take the time to have a shower?"

CHAPTER 11

Helena was still in shock at the way that James had stuck up for her. She hadn't expected it at all, and it was only confusing her thoughts the more that she thought about it. She wanted to ask him about why he'd done it, but Helena was also quite content with the comfortable silence that had settled around them within the car.

The leather seat was beginning to annoy her since Helena wasn't used to sitting down for such an extended length of time, and the aircon was giving her a headache. She wished that they could take another break, but she was all too aware of how he would take that news.

"Thank you for doing that." She spoke quietly.

"Hm?"

"Thank you for defending me." Helena said, again as she turned to look at him. "You really didn't have to and I didn't expect-"

"Don't think about it, Charles is in the wrong a lot of the time, that was just one of the first times that I had really called him out on it." He explained.

Helena nodded as she thought about the bond that the two of them had. Charles and James acted more as though they were brothers than cousins; they had a close relationship and James seemed to always be around his house, yet Helena couldn't help but wonder if they really did get along that well, or if they just tolerated one another.

"Is there a reason that you don't normally call him out?" She dared to ask.

"I don't know." James said, with an honest shrug. "I suppose that we just normally avoid that kind of conflict between us.

We share enough of it with our uncle, and I don't think that there's any point in dividing up our family further."

Helena thought about the dynamics that the three Bentley men had. It definitely seemed as though James was the most diplomatic and the most tolerating out of the three of them. He was willing to talk with both sides about their conflicts and was always trying to reason with either Jack or Charles.

Helena couldn't help but wonder about James's own life. He didn't speak about his parents at all. At first, she had thought that Jack was his father, but that clearly wasn't the case since he often referred to him as his uncle.

"So." She decided to speak up. "Since I gave you my brief history, are you willing to do the same thing?"

"I suppose it's only fair."

Helena sat back and waited patiently for him to begin with his story, but James simply continued to stare straight ahead. His eyes were slightly narrowed, but his expression wasn't readable.

"I guess I should start back when I was a kid." He said with a sigh.

"You don't have-"

"I want to." He cut her off. "I grew up with my father and mother for the first few years of my life, but my dad was old already and he wasn't up to the challenge of bringing a son into the world after all. It was mainly Charles' father who raised me, he was a much better man than his brother and he was more of a father figure to me than my actual dad. My dad died only a few years later, heart attack, nothing that even the best doctors in the country could do to save him."

"I'm sorry to hear that." Helena said, as she glanced up at him. His expression was rather stoic, but there wasn't any sign of him being upset.

266

"Don't be, he really wasn't that great of a guy." James said with a shrug. "He was just another Bentley, siphoning money off of the family estate. A bit of a liability really."

Helena could see the sudden pang of pain that spread across his face, and she hoped more than anything that he didn't see himself as a liability too.

"And your mother?"

"She was about twenty years my dad's junior, and the epitome of a gold digger." James chuckled. "I think she has a lot in common with Rosalyn actually."

Helena could only imagine what that was like; she was sure that her parents had loved each other at some points in their lives, but the love was certainly gone by the time that she and her sister arrived.

"As soon as she could, she left him. It was just before he died as well, my father had full custody of me, but after he died, it was Charles's father who was there for me."

"I've never really heard much about Charles' mother." Helena said with a slight frown.

"I think it's a similar story. She was out of the picture before my father died, and so it's always just been us Bentley men sticking together."

"Or not sticking together so much, quite like your Uncle?"

"I suppose you're right there. Since the death of Charles' father, everything has just seemed to get worse. All of the nasty stuff got nastier and uglier, now all we look like is money hungry instead of the figureheads of a strong family estate."

Helena wanted to make a sarcastic comment about how she wished that she could empathize with him, but it didn't feel appropriate. She hadn't realized that he and Charles had experienced so much loss in their lifetimes. It was enough for her to feel sort of sorry for them.

267

"I suppose from the outside, your family always looked so ruthless that nobody could have even guessed what was going on within." Helena decided on phrasing it that way.

"I remember a few years ago, Forbes did an article on us and followed us around for the day. I'd thought that it was going to be a really good idea; it was going to show the world that we were also just people and that we weren't any better than others. The reporter was scathing though."

"I think I remember seeing that." Helena said, as she nodded. "I remember the media attention it brought to your family."

"It was awful." James said with a sigh. "We had people trying to dig up old family dirt, while others were trying to sell lies to the tabloids. A real PR nightmare, that's why these days we try to stay out of the press."

Helena remembered when the family had had a much bigger presence in the public eye. She had hated them for it, as though they were capitalizing on all of the hurt and chaos that they had caused. But now, she could see that at least one member of the family had hated every minute of it. She could imagine that Rosalyn had very much enjoyed the attention, and she was sure that Jack had too. But when she thought about James and Charles, it seemed that they were very much just victims of this family.

"It's an awful thing to say, but sometimes I quite like the idea of my family losing it all. I think it would be incredibly interesting to see who would sink and who would float without the money that Charles' father had mainly made."

"He was the main provider?" Helena asked.

"Yes, he was the one who had invested in the right places. That really was all there is to it; know where to put your money, pay people to put it in places where it will grow like good seeds. That way, it's a never ending cycle and you'll never have to lift a finger again."

"I feel that you may have just oversimplified the very existence of life for a lot of people." She said with a light chuckle.

"That may be true, but you only have to be a little bit financially literate to know that I'm right."

Helena thought about what he'd said for a while and frowned in confusion. If it was as easy as that, why weren't more people rich?

"But you need a lot of money to start with, right?"

"That's true." James nodded. "I think Charles' father had some inheritance that he used to take out a large loan with the bank."

"That was really all he had to do?"

Helena tried to ignore the sinking feeling in her chest as she thought about how she didn't even need that much money to solve a lot of her problems. She grimaced at all of the times that she had claimed to hate money, she had claimed that it would be their downfall and that they would be alright without a large sum in the bank. It was all of those times that she should have been embracing it, she should have been learning about how to make it grow, as James had said.

"But surely it gives your life little purpose if you don't have to lift a finger?" She circled back to his previous comment.

"I suppose you're right." He nodded. "But I'd rather be bored than suffer."

They continued to drive for another half an hour or so without saying much between them. Helena was still trying to process the fact that James had stuck up for her against his own blood. Especially after learning how close they were and the reasons behind that, she found that she had a newfound respect for him.

"How's your eye?"

"It's fine." James said, as he tried to brush off her question.

"It's not."

"It is."

"I'm not going to argue with you after we've had such a progressive day." She said with a chuckle. "But the next time we stop, I'm going to take a look at it and you're not going to stop me."

James didn't say anything to her comment, he simply let out a sigh. Helena glanced at his hands on the steering wheel, the knuckles of his right hand were blooming into a dark purple color. She was sure that he must be hurting, but he was just trying to act strong in front of her.

"Here, I think I have some painkillers in my bag if you want to take some?"

"I said I'm fine." James said.

"It will just help with the pain a little." She said, while putting her hands up in defense. "Maybe they will stop you from being so grumpy as well."

He didn't even bother responding to her, and so she knew that he must have been rather annoyed, or just in a lot of pain. Helena stared out the window for another few minutes until she noticed that the car was starting to slow down. For a moment, she thought that there was something wrong with the expensive vehicle again, and she was ready to start ranting about how such a flashy car sure was incredibly faulty. However, she then noticed that it was James doing it manually. They slowed to a stop as he pulled off of the main road. She glanced at him in confusion as he finally put the handbrake on and exhaled deeply.

"What's wrong?" She asked carefully.

"I'll take those painkillers now." He responded but continued to stare straight ahead.

Helena tried to hide the triumphant smile on her face at his comment, but it was hopeless. She quickly reached into her purse and handed him the pack of tablets.

"Thanks." He muttered quietly as he took two.

"They should kick in rather quickly, but I told you that you should have put some ice on your knuckles."

"You were right." He nodded, as she noticed the way that his jaw clenched. It was almost as though it pained him to have to admit that she was right after all. "I'm sorry."

"Don't mention it." Helena said, with a smile as she reclined further in her seat.

They set back off on the road, and she decided to put her feet up on the dashboard in an attempt to stretch out her legs.

"Feet off the dash." He grumbled.

Helena huffed in an exaggerated manner before doing as he said. She just wanted to get out of the car and walk around for a few minutes, but she also didn't want to test James's patience. They may have managed to move past their initial bond of just bickering to one another, but she wasn't sure where they were at during that turbulent few hours.

*****

"You seem angry." She said after a while. James wanted to growl in response to her remark since he wished that she would just leave it. What she didn't know was that he was just angry at himself, not at her.

He was frustrated with her, but he wasn't angry. He didn't want to ever give her the impression that he was angry at her again. His mind continued to drift back to what she had told him earlier in the car about her job. Knowing that there were people out there who had hurt her was causing him to clench his jaw and grip harder onto the steering wheel.

271

James hated that she had actually been attacked by men, and he hated that he couldn't get to those men while the adrenaline from his previous fight was still accessible. He wanted nothing more than to teach them a lesson, or they would simply go and do it to another poor woman.

"I'm not angry." He said, slowly as he tried to sound a lot calmer than he felt.

"Are you sure?"

"Positive."

James continued to stare ahead. He knew that if he were to turn and see her wide eyes staring back at him, it would put him in serious danger of melting and admitting how he really felt. He was concerned for her, and he no longer wanted to fight with her, he just wanted to make sure that she was going to be okay.

After telling one another about their pasts, James realized that perhaps they had a lot more in common than he had first thought. Sure, they may have come from two different worlds, two different classes that sat between them like a thick divider. But they also both came from similarly broken homes, and they had both had someone there to lean on throughout it. James hoped that Charles and Jane would also work out that they weren't too different in the end and that their marriage would work out. He knew that they just had to talk it out.

"Do you think that your sister will marry Charles in the end?" He asked hesitantly.

"I don't know, I think that it depends on what state we find her in. I just hope she's all right," Helena said while running a hand through her hair. "If we find her safe and sound, I'll talk to her about it."

"You'd do that?"

"Well, it's not like we have another income source." She admitted with a rather sheepish shrug. "I know that I said I'd go back to working at the strip club, but-"

"No." James quickly interjected.

"I...what?"

"You can't do that." He said, as he shook his head. "I won't let you put yourself in danger for money again, not when our family has more than enough and can help you."

"If I've learned one thing, it's that I'm not going to be taking out any more loans." Helena said with a chuckle. "I can't force my sister to go through with this marriage to Charles. If she doesn't want to do it, then I'm going to have to go back to work and so will she."

"It wouldn't be a loan." James continued. "It would be a grant. Just something to get you on your feet until you get a much safer job."

Helena glanced at him with narrowed eyes. He knew that she was questioning why he would do such a thing for her, but James wasn't about to admit to her that it was all because he actually did care about her.

"I don't get it, what's the catch?"

"No catch." He smiled at the thought of her thinking up all sorts of situations. "You just have to marry me." He jested.

Helena scoffed and rolled her eyes at this.

"Alright, I'm only joking." James laughed it off. "I didn't think I was that unbearable."

"I don't think you want me to respond to that." She murmured.

"Oh come on, you don't really mean that, I've seen the way that you've been looking at me. We're not just sworn enemies anymore, we've bonded on this trip."

"That doesn't make us friends."

He was hoping that she was only joking because he genuinely did feel as though they had bonded in a way that he couldn't have ever imagined two days ago.

"If you say so." He smirked, as he threw her a sideways glance.

The car descended into silence once more as James thought about all he'd learn about his companion. There was much more to Helena than met the eye, and he started to wonder what Charles or his uncle would make of her if they knew what she had admitted to him. He wondered if it would finally show them that they can't just judge people based on how much money they had in their bank account.

CHAPTER 12

Charles winced as his phone rang. It was the landline, the one that only a few people had the number for, and so he knew that it couldn't be good.

"The Bentley Residence, who's speaking?" Anna said, as she answered the phone.

Her features quickly jumped from calm to panicked within half a second as she turned around to stare at Charles.

"Who is it?" He whispered.

"Tucker." She mouthed.

Charles swallowed thickly and shook his head quickly at her. To someone who didn't know the context of what was going on, he could have looked like he was enduring a stroke. But Anna was loyal, and she knew what to do in an instant.

"He's not home at the moment, can I take a message?"

He paused and waited for her to hang up the phone.

"What did he want?"

"He didn't say." She breathed out. "He just said that you need to call him as soon as you're home, he said that it's very urgent."

Charles felt as though he had just jumped off of a tall diving board and had been plunged into a sea of confusion. His features were dragged down into the kind of frown that was sure to leave wrinkles if he didn't stop doing it so soon. He couldn't understand why his father's lawyer would need to speak with him so urgently. It left a sick feeling in his gut as he wondered what on earth it could mean.

"Should I call him back?"

"That depends on if you want to hear it, I suppose." Anna said with a shrug.

"It will be news about the inheritance, I'm sure of it." He knew that his housekeeper had little sympathy for him in terms of his intentions of getting his inheritance in any way that he could. But he also knew that Anna wasn't stupid. If he wasn't going to get his inheritance, then he was going to start losing a lot of things, her employment would probably be one of them. She may not like the situation, but she was still a big part of it.

"Do you think they've found a way to get it out from under you?"

"That would be impossible, I'm not thirty five yet, so they shouldn't be able to do anything." He said in a low voice.

He didn't know what to think, but his heart was starting to pound quickly in his chest.

"Can you pour me a scotch, and I'll answer the phone."

"Of course, Sir." She said rather pointedly.

Charles ignored the look as he took a seat next to the phone. He hated that Tucker could make him feel as nervous as he did at that moment, and he knew that it was no mistake on Tucker's side to make the situation sound so serious. The lawyer had a flair for the dramatics, and it was starting to come out in how he was handling this.

"All right." He sighed, as he took a sip from the scotch that Anna gave him. "Let's see what he has to say."

Charles ignored the way that his hand shook, he dismissed it as he called Tucker's number and listened to the hollow dialing tones as he was connected.

"Charles!" Tucker sounded too cheerful through the phone. "Your housekeeper said you weren't in?"

"I wasn't." He said, but gave no further indication or clarification.

"All right, well I suppose we shall sacrifice pleasantries on this occasion and just go straight to the main reason that I called."

"That works for me." Charles nodded.

He held his breath and waited quietly for the lawyer, like some kind of evil villain, to reveal his grand plan to him.

"So, as you know it states in your father's letter about the inheritance that you are the sole heir of this." Tucker started slowly.

"That's not exactly new information." Charles said rather dryly.

"I know, I know, I'm just using it as context to justify what has happened."

"And what exactly *has* happened?" He urged the lawyer to get to the point.

"The money, the estate, and all of your father's other assets have been transferred to your uncle already."

"What!" Charles shouted, as he pushed out of his chair and stood up. He was furious and felt as though someone had just let a grenade go off inside of him.

"See, you would have let me explain the context first, then we could have avoided this unnecessary anger."

"Keep talking Tucker! What have you done?"

"Well, you weren't going to really marry that woman for love. It was obvious that it was a marriage of convenience that you were entering into, and that just wouldn't meet the criteria of the stipulation, I'm afraid. So I've taken some liberties to have the title deeds and everything changed in advance."

Charles was speechless. He'd known something was wrong, he could feel it in the air when he was trying to work out what Tucker had been thinking about over lunch. Now he knew. Fire boiled his blood as his fists started to shake in anger. He was rather pleased that the conversation was happening over the phone since it meant that Tucker wasn't there in the flesh for him to throttle. Anna was peeking at him from a doorway nearby, but he didn't care if she saw his outburst. It wouldn't exactly be the first time it would happen.

"You can't be serious. There is nothing in the stipulation about the marriage having to be for love!"

"There technically is, and since I can prove that the marriage contract won't be valid in time anyway, I'm afraid it's just another win for the law."

"Don't act all high and mighty!" Charles raged at him down the speaker.

"Now, there's no need for this to get so heated. Why don't you go and calm down and we'll speak-"

Charles hung up before he could listen to another word that the weasel had to say. He could only see red and needed some kind of way to take his anger out. He grabbed the glass of scotch and gulped it down in one, allowing the liquid to burn his throat. It felt as though it did nothing to calm the flames within him. If anything, it was just fuel for his fire. In a rather sudden movement, he hurled the glass at the wall opposite him. He reveled in the sound of it shattering as Anna yelped from where she was standing.

"What did he say?"

"My Uncle has taken the money from me." He said, as he slumped down in his chair and let his hand rest over his eyes. "It's over, they finally won."

Defeat felt heavy as it started to settle into his muscles. It seemed to work in the same way that sand absorbed water; the sensation of defeat was eating at the last of his adrenaline and rendering him useless as he lay on the couch.

Charles realized that he was still partially in shock at what had happened. He just couldn't believe that they'd really managed to do it, even before the deadline too. He knew that he should have gotten married sooner, even if it was just to some random woman in Vegas, he should have done something sooner.

"Are you all right?" Anna asked, as she reappeared with a broom.

"What are we going to do?" He breathed out, his voice sounding incredibly weak.

"Well, for one thing, you can get up and help me sweep the floor. Otherwise, the only thing to be done will be getting the glass out of your feet." Anna spoke up rather bravely. "Come on, you look pathetic laying there having a tantrum."

Charles was in half a mind to snap at her at that moment, but Anna had always been loyal to him, and he realized that what he needed at that moment was a little bit of tough love.

He slowly got off of the couch, feeling slightly better to be doing something rather than just wallowing.

"Thank you." He muttered to her as she shrugged.

"Don't mention it." She smiled lightly at him. "I don't believe for a second that your Uncle will get away with this, and so I think you're going to have to have a few conversations with your own lawyers. But you can't do that if you're just going to sit and mope on the sofa now, can you?"

"I guess not." He spoke in a small voice as though he was being scalded by his own mother.

"Exactly, so let's get on with the task of cleaning, and then you go and call your people. There must be something that we can do."

CHAPTER 13

"All right, just...take it easy." James sighed, as he spoke into the phone. He couldn't quite believe that his uncle had managed it, but he really had found a way to take the inheritance.

"What's going on?" Helena asked, as she paced around the car.

They had stopped for a quick toilet break and so that she could stretch her legs when he'd gotten the call from Charles.

"Tucker called Charles, I still don't understand how, but he's managed to get the inheritance already."

"What?" Helena shouted, as she stopped walking and moved closer to James.

"I know, it's insane and I still don't fully understand how he's done it, but he has."

"What does that mean for all of us?" She asked.

"I still don't know." He shrugged again. "But I can't imagine that it will bring us any good."

James bit the inside of his mouth as he tried to think of how else he could be of use to Charles at that moment. However, he knew that the only thing he could do was to continue with what they had started. "Come on." He said, as he started walking back to the car.

"But, can't we just wait a minute?"

"We haven't got any more minutes to waste." He admitted to her as he climbed in. Helena was hot on his tail, but he could tell that she wasn't happy about this. "We've got to find your sister and get back as quickly as possible."

He ignored the way that Helena sighed heavily. The situation seemed to only be getting more and more dire with each moment that passed, and no bickering was going to help them.

They drove in almost complete silence aside for a couple of comments here and there for the next two hours, until finally, the satnav said the words that he had been waiting to hear.

"You have reached your destination."

"Is this it?" He questioned, as he glanced around. "Because I don't see a house. In fact, I don't exactly see much of anything."

"It's around a bend." Helena said, while rolling her eyes as she got out of the car. "It's only a short walk."

"The last time you said it's only a short...anything, I ended up on this long journey with you."

"Don't act like you didn't enjoy it." She muttered, as she quickly walked ahead of him.

James scowled but jogged slightly to catch up with her. The grass on the land around them was incredibly long, and the entire place seemed as though it was in dire need of some landscaping. James and Helena walked in silence as they approached the brow of the short hill and turned the corner. He stopped for a moment at the sight of the crumbling house in front of them.

"Like I said." Helena said, with a small smile while turning back to face him. "She's a little bit of a fixer-upper."

"I can see tha.," He chuckled. "Is this really where she would have come?"

"I suppose in a lot of ways, it's home," Helena shrugged. "It's more about the sentimental values, the memories in the walls, not the crumbling walls themselves."

"I thought that you said your parents..."

"Jane was too young to properly understand, and so she often spoke of how she missed this big house. I've caught her planning trips to come up here and visit on more than one occasion."

James felt another pang of guilt as he thought about how awful things must have been for Helena. She had chosen to process her trauma, while Jane had forgotten about it. He knew that there were only two years between the sisters, and so Jane must have understood something. He tried not to think about the two different ways that they had dealt with the same events, but it was a rather interesting topic.

"Is it even safe to go inside?" James asked, as he saw the way that some of the roof had fallen away and into the building.

"I don't know, but we have to go in to see if Jane is here."

"And what if she's not and we get hurt?"

"You can wait out here if you're scared." She fired back at him.

He didn't like the way that she was using the situation to try and get one up on him, but he let it slide for the moment. He followed her around the edge of the building, trying to ignore the places where there were empty beer bottles and graffiti on some of the walls.

"And you say that it's owned by the bank?"

"They repossessed it after we stopped paying the monthly mortgage payments." She explained. James nodded slowly as he glanced around the plot of land. He tried not to think about it in terms of an investment, this was their home, it was where they had grown up, but he couldn't deny that the place definitely had potential.

"Jane!" She called into the open front door. A brisk chill caused Helena to wrap her arms around her chest, and James winced at the sudden increase in the volume of her voice. "Jane!"

"Jane!" He called out too.

"Better if I do it, I don't know how she'll react to you being here in all honesty." Helena explained.

He wanted to protest that he hadn't come all of that way just to wait at the entrance, but he knew that she was right. If she was going to convince Jane to come back to the situation with his family, he was willing to do whatever it took.

*****

"Jane? Are you inside?" Helena shouted while trying to stop her voice from wobbling. The memories that the house in front of her threw up in her mind weren't welcomed. She shuddered at the sight of the front door and the number of times that she had seen her father storm out of it. Yet she was still saddened to see that the first home she had ever grown up in was now lying in ruins. Although, it did feel rather fitting for her house to be in such a way, especially when she thought about the ruins that her family was in too.

"Helena?"

The voice was small and carried along the gentle breeze of the wind. Helena blinked for a moment as she didn't quite trust what she had actually heard. She breathed out for a moment and waited to see if it would come again. Nothing.

"Jane?"

"Helena!"

Without giving it a second thought, she darted through the open front door and into the house that was half-exposed to the elements.

"Helena, no!" James called after her, but she quickly whirled around and shook her head.

"Don't follow me." She warned him in a whisper.

Written on his face was the moral conflict of whether he should listen to her or not. Helena didn't wait to see what he decided, she simply turned back around and walked deeper into the house.

"Jane, where are you?"

"I'm up here!"

She stared at the uneven staircase, a few of the pieces of wood had given out and snapped down the middle. Helena grimaced at the idea of going up onto the first floor, it wasn't as though the building was structurally sound anymore.

But Helena knew that she didn't have a choice. She was going to have to be there for her sister and show her that she can live in acceptance with what had happened. It was what Helena had done for years, she just had to show Jane how to do it.

"Are you hurt at all?" Helena called out as she placed one of her feet on the first step. Slowly, she tested the weight of it, wincing at the way that the wood was groaning.

"Not physically. "

Helena knew exactly what she meant, but she was also terrified to see how Jane had been living for the last day or two. There had been no sign of her moped outside, and Helena started to wonder how her sister could have traveled all that way on her own.

"I'm coming up." Helena announced as she started to climb the stairs rather slowly. A pang of panic ran through her every time that she heard the sound of creaking beneath her. Each step felt like it could be her last if her foot went through the wood, it would certainly mean a trip to the hospital. Finally, after what felt like an age of climbing stairs that she had once taken two at a time, Helena arrived on the landing of the first floor. She still didn't trust the ground beneath her feet and found that quite an unsettling feat.

"Jane?"

No response.

But Helena knew what room she would be in; her old room. It made the most sense, and she saw her sister curled up in a ball as soon as she entered the room.

"Hey." She whispered to her as her legs bent until she was crouched beside her. "Hey, come here."

There were fresh tears rolling down her cheeks as Jane quietly sobbed. She shook her head and tried to speak, but it was clear that she was far too upset.

"Shh." Helena spoke softly, as she held her sister as tight as she could. "I'm here and there's nothing for you to worry about."

"I just can't believe that this has happened to us." Jane finally whispered. "I can't believe that I almost went against mom like that."

"I know." Helena whispered, as she rocked her. "You didn't go against her though, you told that asshole of a billionaire exactly what he deserved to hear."

"I did, didn't I?" Jane managed a small smile as she looked up at her with a frown. "How did you get here?"

"I drove, I just thought that this was the only other place that you would come." She shrugged it off. Helena knew that there was no point in mentioning James yet, although she just hoped that he didn't decide to come into the house. It would only make things worse. "Do you want to come home with me?"

"Will I ever have to see any of the Bentley's ever again?" Jane sighed, as she started to sit up.

"Look, it's a lot more complicated than that." Helena sighed.

"What do you mean?" Jane narrowed her eyes as she stared at her sister. "You were the one telling me to abandon it all, you told me that we'd find another way and that we'd be fine."

"I know, but I just don't think we should rule everything out. Especially when there's so much to gain from them."

"I don't think I could use a single cent of their money again." Jane muttered.

"Is that really why you came to live in this shell of a house?" Helena chuckled as she looked at her sister. She could tell that Jane hadn't been sleeping while she was there, and she hadn't had much to eat judging by the small number of belongings around her. "How do you think I could get here to find you?"

Jane's eyes met hers in an instant, and she knew exactly what she was talking about.

"He's not actually here is he?"

Helena could hear the panic in her sister's voice, she suddenly seemed terrified, as though her words had put the fear of god into her.

"Who?"

"Charles."

"He's not here." Helena said. She wasn't lying when she said that, after all, there was another of the Bentley boys waiting outside for them both.

"Then how…"

"I was so worried about where you were when you didn't come home." Helena said, as she closed her eyes for a moment. "I genuinely had no clue where you'd gone or what you'd done. It was so stupid of you to run off like that."

"I know." She sighed and looked down. "I'm sorry for not telling you."

"I thought you promised in the past that you wouldn't do that to me again? Do you know how sick I was with worry?"

"So you went to Charles?" Jane winced, as she looked up at her sister.

"What else was I supposed to do, I figured that you were still there. But when I went to shout at him, he'd told me that you had been and gone. I was so panicked and terrified that you were driving while upset and had gotten into some kind of terrible accident. Then when I would try and ring you, your phone stopped ringing. I thought for sure that you had gotten yourself into some awful situation, oh the things I was thinking, Jane. It really wasn't fair of you to do that."

"I'm sorry, alright? I was just so upset and I didn't want to speak to anyone. I wanted to be on my own to think about this."

"Well, James offered to help me look for you." Helena continued. "We drove around town for a while, and even went back to the apartment to see if you were there. But as I started to realize and accept where you would have gone, I knew in an instant that it was going to take a seriously fast car to reach you as fast as possible. I had to use his help, even if it was unbearable."

"You spent all that time in a car with James Bentley?" Jane managed a smile as she asked the question.

"I know, and do you want to know the worst thing?" Helena smiled and spoke as they did in the old days when they were super close and would gossip together.

"I'm not sure I do."

"We even managed to bond." Helena said, as she scrunched up her nose.

"Ew."

"Not like that, we just went from being constantly annoyed at one another to only slightly annoyed at one another. But believe me, even that was a big step."

Jane was clearly thinking about what her sister was saying to her, but her eyes were searching the ground in front of her as though she was lost for words.

"I'm sorry that I put you through that." She said eventually. "I mean both the worry and having to interact with James for so long."

"It's fine, I'll get over it." Helena brushed it off. "I'm just so glad that you're safe. We were going to have to call the police if we arrived here and you weren't around."

"I'm sorry." Jane closed her eyes, causing fresh tears to snake down her face.

"It's fine, but we really do have to get going. And I need to talk with you properly about this business with the Bentleys."

"You still think that I should go through with the marriage?"

"I don't think that we should rule anything out just yet." Helena said rather diplomatically.

CHAPTER 14

James tapped his foot as he waited patiently outside. He felt like a dog that had been told by his owner to stay while they went about important matters. He then hated that analogy because it made him seem rather weak and inferior in comparison to Helena. But he didn't like the way that she had told him to just wait outside.

They had been traveling for so long and all he got to see of their derelict family home was the shadowed hallways from the holes in the walls. He still couldn't believe that the bank had let the place fall into ruin like that, it didn't make much sense, but neither did a lot of things when it came to the Miller family apparently. Finally, he could hear sounds from inside. Footsteps were approaching him just as he was ready to go charging in, just in case either of them had found themselves in danger.

"Are you alright?" James called, as he peered through the doorway.

"We're fine!" Helena said over the sound of snapping wood. The house sounded as though it was hollow even as they spoke, their voices bounced off of the walls and echoed for a while. James made a face as he glanced inside the hallway at the many broken bottles on the floor. He was sure that the vandalism to the place hadn't been caused by the Miller girls before they had fled the property.

"Here you go, watch your step." Helena said, as she held onto both of Jane's hands and led her out into the sunlight.

"Hello Jane." He said while nodding to her. He was glad that he was looking at her, otherwise, he would have missed her response completely. Jane only glared in his direction in response to his greeting.

"We've got some snacks in the car if you're hungry, which I guess you are." Helena carried on as she urged James to get out of the way.

She slowly led Jane down the path. He could tell that the younger of the two was incredibly weak, and it appeared almost as if Helena was having to hold her up.

"Are you sure that she doesn't need to go to a hospital or something?"

"She'll be fine, she just needs to get home." Helena said.

James followed them back down the small hill to where the car was parked. He quickly pressed the keys to unlock it so that there would be no delay in getting into the vehicle. James remained on hand to help Helena get her sister into the backseat, but she shrugged off his help until he eventually gave up and went to wait in the driver's seat.

He knew that Jane wasn't exactly going to be happy to see him, but he didn't like the way that her sister had suddenly turned so sharply on him like that.

"Alright." He said, as Helena got back into the passenger seat. "Ready to go?"

"Ready as we'll ever be."

He dared to glance into his rear view mirror to see that Jane was already falling asleep as the car engine purred into life.

"Here you go." Helena said, as she passed a packet of crisps and a granola bar back for her sister. "Here's some water too."

James continued to look at the road ahead for a while as he glanced back in his mirror every so often to make sure that Jane was all right. He had no bad feelings for the girl, he knew that he would have reacted in a similar way if someone had revealed such awful news to him too.

"Have you let Charles know?" Helena asked finally as she turned to him.

Her voice was a lot softer now than it had been when they'd first found Jane. He realized that she had just been so tense about making sure that Jane would get in the car willingly. He let go of any animosity he felt and shook his head slowly.

"No, not yet." James said. "He's probably on the phone with his lawyers at the moment, he'll be trying to sort out the mess that his Uncle and that awful lawyer have caused for him."

"Is there a way that we can still save the situation?" Helena asked, out of concern as she glanced up at him.

"I hope so, I really do."

He wanted to talk to Helena about what happened back there, but he could tell that she really wasn't in the mood to speak about it, and so he just left her to rest. It seemed like it had been a draining time for all of them, and so he wasn't going to press her too much. After a while, he realized that he should probably call Charles and let him know that they had finally succeeded in finding her.

"Please tell me it's good news."

"It is, we've got her here." James nodded, as he glanced back in his rear view mirror to see that Jane was still sound asleep. He found it rather sad that she had barely said two words while being in the car, but he didn't say anything about it.

"Oh thank god." He breathed out. "Is she alright? She wasn't hurt at all?"

"No, not that we could see. I think she's just a bit drained." He explained, as he realized that Helena was now awake and listening to the conversation.

"How about the two of you, everyone okay?"

"Yeah, I think we're all just looking forward to getting out of this car." He admitted with a shrug. James sent a small smile over in Helena's direction, and he wasn't expecting her to return it in the way that she did.

"Alright, keep me posted. Do you think you'll be back by tomorrow?"

"I...I'm not sure, to be honest. We'll try and get back as quickly as possible though." James winced, as he thought about spending another day in that same car.

He needed a shower in the morning if he was going to keep on like this. He was all too aware of the fact that wearing the same clothes for days on end was rather disgusting, but it wasn't as though he had another option.

"Okay, keep in touch"

"Of course."

Charles hung up and James stepped on the gas slightly. He knew that he was starting to push the boundaries of the speed limit, but he was suddenly so eager to get back home and out of that car.

"He sounded like he genuinely cared about her." Helena remarked.

"He's not as heartless as you might think." James said with a shrug. "I think he's also recently learned that from Jane."

"That's something at least." Helena said with a slight chuckle. "I never thought I'd see the day when my opinion of a Bentley was changed so much."

"He cares more about her than just because of the wedding, and I don't think he even wants to admit that to himself."

*****

Charles sat back in relief on the terrace after hanging up on his mobile. He breathed heavily as at least half of the battle was over. However, his lawyers were still working on the other part, the main fight where he would have to win back his inheritance somehow.

"Anna!" Charles called, as he rose from his chair and walked into the house. "Anna, I have some news!"

"What's happened?" She asked, as she quickly rushed into the corridor from one of the rooms on the first floor.

"They've got her, she's safe."

He could see the same relief spreading across her face as to how he was feeling and he smiled at her. However, Anna then did something that he hadn't been prepared for. She breathed out in relief and rushed into his arms. They embraced for a moment as relieved in how good it felt that Jane was safe.

"Sorry Sir, I was just so happy that she's alright."

"It's fine, I understand completely." He nodded to her.

"Do you know where she is?"

"She's in the car with James and Helena. They should arrive back by tomorrow hopefully." He explained.

"What does this mean about the wedding and the inheritance?" She asked with a frown.

"I'm not sure yet, I'm waiting for my main lawyer to call me back. But if he's found a loophole, then the wedding is back on."

Anna smiled at this as though she was genuinely pleased for him. Charles was still in shock that the wedding could still be going ahead, it seemed like such a foreign idea at that moment, but he knew there was still a lot of work to be done. For starters, he was still going to have to convince the bride to join him in this venture, and that was going to be a large task in itself.

"I suppose that you better get planning then."

Charles thought about having to plan a wedding mainly on his own. It wasn't the ideal outcome of the situation, but he wasn't sure what other choice he had. He frowned as he thought about the many things that came with planning a wedding.

"Oh god, it's going to be a lot of work, isn't it?" He winced ,as he looked back at Anna.

"I mean, I would get started if I were you." She chuckled and shook her head.

"Do you know of any good wedding planners in the area? Or could you perhaps find out their contact details?"

"I don't mean to be rude." Anna said, as she shook her head. "But I'm your housekeeper, not your assistant."

Charles remembered the time when he had tried to have an assistant. It hadn't ended well for either of them since she had called him far too demanding, and he had called her incapable of carrying out basic tasks.

"All right, I'll do it myself." He muttered, as Anna left him on his own in the hallway. He knew that there was no way he was going to be able to get it all organized on his own, and so he thought that there was no harm in getting a little extra help.

However, as he thought about having to explain to the wedding planner that nobody involved in the marriage actually wanted to get married and so the details didn't have to be too sentimental, he realized what a bad idea that would be. Charles grimaced and scratched his head in confusion.

"Right." He mumbled to himself. "It's time to plan a wedding."

Just as he was about to log onto his computer and start with what would be many hours of research that lay ahead of him. His phone started to buzz. Charles could feel his anger returning at an alarming rate at the sight of his uncle's name as it flashed up on the screen. He knew that his uncle was calling to gloat, but Charles was still determined that they would find some kind of loophole out of this mess. He sighed and quickly pushed his own feelings and anger to the side, he was going to remind his uncle that despite everything, he still had a wedding to attend.

"Charles!"

"Uncle." He spoke into the phone as though nothing was wrong. "To what do I owe this phone call?"

"Well, I heard that you spoke to Tucker earlier, is that correct?"

"Yes, he called" Charles nodded and focused on keeping his voice steady. The last thing that he wanted to do was give his uncle any kind of satisfaction in this situation.

"Ah, good. I just wanted to make sure that the news had filtered down to you, that's all."

"Yes, I heard loud and clear, thank you." Charles said.

"And?" Jack spoke after a long silence. "Don't you have anything to say about it?"

"Not really." Charles shrugged.

He couldn't help the way that a small smirk worked its way onto his face. He was quite enjoying the way that he wasn't giving anything to his uncle, he gave him nothing that he could use against him.

"Oh…" Jack said after another awkward hesitation.

"I know that you said you've got quite a busy month coming up, but you're still going to be around for the wedding, aren't you?" Charles smiled at himself in a mirror as he spoke into the phone.

He could practically feel his uncle's anger radiating through the phone speaker.

"I...what?" Jack's tone was of complete confusion. "You can give up the farce now Charles, the money is mine and that's not going to change. You don't have to marry her after all."

"Uncle, I wasn't joking when I told you that I'm in love with her."

"Then you're a bigger fool than I took you for." Jack snapped back at him.

He had gone in the direction that Charles had hoped for, and it was almost too easy to deliver the final blow.

"And you think your wife married you for love?" He asked into the phone. It felt good to finally be able to say it. "Then you're also a fool and it must run in the family."

His uncle put the phone down before Charles could say anything else, but he already felt as though he had said enough. He may not have the money yet, but Charles took that conversation as just another victory under his belt. Yet another battle won in this war against his father's inheritance that was rightly his.

CHAPTER 15

The afternoon was creeping dangerously into the evening, and the sun was already starting to set. James grimaced at the thought of spending another night in a cheap motel, but he knew that they really didn't have a choice. It was either that, or they would all have to try and sleep in the car.

"All right, we'll stop at the next exit?" James announced to the two women as he started to see signs for rooms available further down the road.

"If we set off early, we could be back by tomorrow afternoon." Helena nodded to him.

"Sounds like a good plan." He smiled at her.

She smiled back at him, and James felt something inside of him flutter. He knew that he shouldn't feel such a way, but he really couldn't help it. He was letting his feelings rule his actions again, and he knew that was a rather dangerous way to go about his life.

"I'll get two rooms tonight?" He said, as Helena nodded slowly.

"Are you sure that you don't mind?"

"Of course not, it makes more sense anyway."

He found that he liked being on the good side of Helena. It comforted him to know that they didn't have as much to argue about this way.

"Okay." She nodded, as he started to turn off of the main road. "I really hope you're right about Charles and his lawyers, otherwise there's no point in us even coming back."

"Don't say that." James sighed, as he looked at her. "He's going to sort it out, trust me."

Her eyes were narrowed, but she didn't say another word about it. They turned into the parking lot of the motel, it was a different one to the one that they'd stayed in the night before, and James cut the engine in relief. His hands and legs were aching, as was his head, from the constant concentration. He groaned and stretched in his seat as he thought about the prospect of finally getting out of the car.

"We should have taken a helicopter or something." He muttered, as they got out of the car.

"Funnily enough, the thought didn't even cross my mind." Helena said dryly.

He knew that it wasn't exactly a common mode of transport to have, and he started to regret what he'd suggested slightly. James rolled his eyes but continued onwards toward the front desk. He was just hoping that they would have two rooms available instead of only one, that way he would be able to get a good night of sleep without worrying about two other people in his room. Thankfully, he returned out to the two women with two keys in hand and a large smile of relief on his face.

"Two rooms that are conveniently next door to one another." He said with a grin.

"Great." Helena returned the smile.

They both then turned to look at Jane, who had perked up a bit since first getting into the car. She already looked to have some color back in her cheeks, and she was trying to smile. James could see that her eyes were incredibly red and knew that it was from the amount of crying she had been doing while at their family's house. His own smile faded slightly as he thought about how responsible his family was for the hurt that they had caused the two girls.

He tried not to think about it too much, afraid that the guilt would start to eat at him if he did. Jane looked so small and fragile compared with the last time that he had seen her, and

James felt as though he should at least try to take some accountability for the things that his family had done to them.

"Why don't you go and scope out if there's anywhere to eat around here, and we'll go up to the rooms?" He suggested to Helena.

She frowned at him as she looked between the two of them. He could tell that she was suspicious and that she wanted to say something, but Helena held her tongue and slowly nodded instead.

"Alright, but I'll only be a few minutes."

"No problem." He said, as he watched her walk off to the other side of the building.

"How are you feeling, Jane?" He decided to ask as the two of them made their way along the main building of the motel. He was checking the door numbers as he waited for her response.

"A little better, I guess." She said with a shrug finally.

"That's good to hear." He smiled back at her. "Listen." He said, as he stopped walking. His eyes were narrowed as he looked at her, but she was looking down at the floor. "I just want to say how sorry I am. I could tell you that it wasn't directly me that has hurt you, but it's my family, and by extension that does include me, unfortunately. But I want to help you."

"What makes you think that I could trust someone like you?" She asked with a frown.

"Absolutely nothing." He said with a slight chuckle. "I know that it's going to be difficult to trust any of us again, but I promise you I'm not lying. On the way here, Helena was telling me about a non-profit that you want to set up? It sounds pretty cool and something that I, as an independent investor, would like to help you with."

At his words, he watched as she finally looked up at him with wide eyes. The dark circles under her eyes told him all he needed to know about just how tired she really was.

"Really?"

"Yeah, I want to help you, and I know that it really is the least that I could do after everything."

Jane looked ready to nod in agreement at this but then stopped short as her eyes narrowed only slightly.

"You still want me to marry your cousin, don't you?"

"Well…" His voice trailed off as he realized that there was no point in lying anymore. "I've known Charles my whole life, and putting the whole financial side of it to the side, I really like the person that he was becoming when you were around."

"I didn't think that I really did that much."She said with a shrug.

"Well, you did." He nodded with a small smile of encouragement. "It was just something in his mannerisms that had changed, he was actually thinking about other people for the first time in a very long time. Jane Miller, I think it's very safe to say that you were making Charles a much better person."

"Don't you think he's going to hate me for trying to bail on him?" She asked with a wince.

"I hope not, and I really don't think that you'd have anything to worry about in that regard."

"What happened while I was away?" She asked, with a frown still etched into her features.

"It's a bit complicated." James said, as he finally found the two door numbers that correlated with their keys.

"How can it be complicated?" She asked. "Tell me what happened."

"Well, his Uncle and Tucker might have found a way to rob him out of the inheritance early. I still don't know the details of how they managed to do it, but they successfully managed to make sure that Charles won't be getting anything on his birthday this year."

"I don't understand." Jane frowned. "How did they manage to do it before he ran out of time? I was sure that he would be able to think of another way out of this.

"I don't know either, but it's already done. I think it was something to do with Tucker working out that the marriage was false."

He could see the way that she was processing the news as she bit her bottom lip and walked into the now open motel room.

"Is he angry with me?"

"No, he's genuinely concerned for your safety." James wasn't telling the complete truth as he could imagine that Charles had called her almost every name under the sun as he waited for news on her whereabouts.

"And if I go through with this, will you leave me alone with enough money to go and live my life quietly?" Jane asked slowly.

"You have my word."

"Alright." She nodded quickly. He was taken aback by just how sudden her decision was, but he nodded in response as she glanced at him with narrowed eyes.

"Thank you." He smiled at her. "Could you just do me one favor though?" James asked from the doorway as he glanced back down the hall to make sure that Helena wasn't coming.

"What is it?" She asked with a frown.

"I don't want Helena knowing about the fact that I want to help you fund your non profit?"

"Why not?"

"I can help you, all right? I have the right connections and the funds to make this a real success, but your sister will think I'm just another rich man who's throwing his money around."

"Isn't that what you are?" Jane seemed incredibly confused about the conversation that she was having with him.

"I know, I know." James said with a frustrated sigh. "But it's just another piece of information that I really don't need her knowing in all honesty."

"Right." Jane nodded slowly.

He could tell that she wasn't convinced, but the sound of footsteps approaching meant that all he could do was trust in her confused acceptance to his request.

"Alright." He said a bit louder as he stepped back away from the doorway. "I'll leave you two to it."

Helena narrowed her eyes as she looked between the two of them, but James merely smiled nonchalantly.

"I'll just be in this room next door if you need anything. If not, I plan to get some sleep."

"Don't you want something for dinner?" Helena asked.

"No, I'm not hungry anymore, I just want to sleep and get back on the road. Knock yourselves out though, here's some cash."

*****

Jane watched her sister finger the few notes of money that James had quickly handed to her before he dipped back into his room. She narrowed her eyes as Helena walked into the motel room and closed the door behind her.

"He didn't say anything weird to you, did he?" Helena was looking at her with a face filled with inquisitive suspicion.

"What would be classified as weird?"

303

"Don't be keeping any more secrets from me." Her sister warned as she walked over to one of the two twin beds and lay back on it.

"I'm not, believe me." Jane laughed.

She thought about what James had told her and what a strange request it was. Although she was starting to suspect that something was going on between Helena and James. It was in the way that they looked at one another, it was the kind of tension that she would only see when at the movies. She started to wonder if he didn't want her to tell her sister about his financial help because he didn't want to ruin his image and unimpress her. Jane smiled at the notion. She still couldn't believe that she was seeing the day where Helena was talking and interacting with two members of the Bentley family with little trouble.

"How was the drive with just him?" Jane asked after a while.

"It was long, but I do feel as though I got to know James a whole lot better than before." She admitted.

"That's good." Jane said with a chuckle. She found it quite nice that there was at least one positive that had come from the situation.

"Are you really not going to tell me what the two of you were talking about?"

"It wasn't anything like that." Jane said while shrugging it off. "He was just asking me how I was and if I was feeling any better."

"He's not like Charles in a lot of ways I feel." Helena said.

From Jane's point of view, that was the only sentence that she needed to know that Helena was facing her own kind of conflict in her head. Jane didn't feel as though it was the right moment to bring it up, but she smiled to herself at the thought of her sister actually having feelings for someone.

Of course, she would have much preferred that someone to have not been a Bentley, but she couldn't help her feelings. Jane's smile disappeared as she thought about her own situation and how she would have to face Charles as soon as they got back. It was something that filled her with dread, and Jane tried not to think about it.

"Come on, shall we get some food?"

CHAPTER 16

Charles awoke the next morning in rather good spirits. For the most part, a large section of his dilemma had been solved; Jane was on her way back to him. However, he still had to check in with his lawyer to see if there was any way around what his uncle and Tucker had done.

"Good morning, Sir." Anna said in surprise. It was clear that she hadn't been expecting him quite so early.

"Good morning." He smiled at her as he walked out onto the terrace and breathed in the fresh air of the day. The sun was only just up, but Charles wanted to be up and ready for the day as he realized that he was going to have to start planning a wedding.

"Did you want some breakfast?" Anna asked from the doorway.

"Anna, I believe that you're rather good at your job, but sometimes you do ask silly questions." He chuckled.

She smiled at him before shaking her head and returning inside. Charles turned back to the lawn and thought about the possibility of having the wedding out there; it would be a much cheaper option in terms of the cost of the wedding, and he wouldn't have to make sure that the venue was available since it was literally his house. He would hire extra staff for the event and make sure that top quality caterers were brought in.

Charles took a large gulp of water from his glass as he could feel a headache coming on. It was all the stress of knowing what to do and who to book for a wedding, especially when it was such short notice.

"Anna." He called to her as she placed down a tray of tea and coffee. "Did you plan your wedding?"

She paused for a moment before speaking. "Sir, I told you the other day, I'm your housekeeper, that's it."

"I know that, but did you plan your own wedding?"

"I did, yes." She nodded with a sigh.

"Say I were to pay you double for the next two months?"

He could see the conflict that arose on her face at his request. It was a rather sweet deal for her, but it still was probably cheaper for him than if he had hired an external planner.

"I'm sure there are professional planners that would be much better at the job than I am." She said while looking down at her hands.

"Yes, well it's not as though it has to be the best wedding in the world, just enough to pass off as a nice day all around." Charles brushed off her concerns. "I just don't want to deal with a planner for the next few weeks because they will find out that I really couldn't care less if the flowers are blue or yellow."

Anna continued to think about it for a moment before he saw her head slowly move into a nod.

"Alright, fine." She said with a huff. "As though I don't have enough to do around here already."

"Thank you, Anna, you're an absolute life saver."

"Don't mention it, Sir."

The pointed look was back, but Charles could only smile in response as he lifted his teacup to her in thanks. He turned back to the lawn before him as he heard her walking off into the house. It was going to be a lot of work, but he would be fair and balance it out with her.

His phone rang shortly after, and he was relieved to see that it was one of his lawyers. Charles always winced when he looked at the bill of what he paid those men, but he was hoping that all of that money was about to get rid of his concerns.

"Talk to me, Jones," Charles said, as he answered the phone. "Jane's on her way back and the wedding is back on, I've done all I can on my end."

"Right, then you're going to like this." His lawyer said through the phone.

The words were like music to his ears, and Charles couldn't help but smile widely as Jones continued on with what he had found. He knew that he was going to have to play this rather coolly if it was going to work against Tucker, but Charles was confident that he could do that.

"Tucker is here again." Anna said, as she quickly stepped out onto the terrace.

Charles had only just hung up on the phone with his lawyer as he stared at his housekeeper turned wedding planner.

"What do you mean he's here?" Charles asked.

He wasn't exactly dressed for visitors; he was wearing casual jeans and a cricket jumper with sneakers, but it wasn't exactly the kind of attire that he would wear for a brunch or anything.

"I mean that he's at the door and demanding that he talk with you."

"All right, I'll go down."

Charles straightened up and pushed his hair out of his face as he took a moment to steady his breathing. He was still reeling from the rather good news that his own lawyer had just given him. It was something, a slight loophole that they could easily use to their advantage when in a court of law.

"Tucker, twice in one week? I'm starting to think that you secretly *do* like me," Charles chuckled, as he walked down the stairs.

"I wouldn't be getting any ideas." The lawyer clearly wasn't very amused. "I came on behalf of your Uncle. He was wondering if you wanted to go and play a round of golf?"

"It's not even a weekend." Charles chuckled as he glanced at where his watch was, only to discover that he hadn't gotten as far as putting it on his wrist that morning.

"I know, but he figured that since you're missing your fiance so dearly, we would make an effort to get you out of the house."

Charles knew it was a trap. In their eyes, they had already won, or so Charles thought. He couldn't understand why they would go to all this effort if that was the case. Then he remembered when Jones had said on the phone, and he realized that perhaps their request hadn't been as successful as he'd first thought.

"All right." Charles nodded slowly. "I have an awful lot of planning that I need to get done though." He admitted, which wasn't technically a lie. "But a few hours out on the course won't do any harm."

"Perfect." Tucker smiled.

"Just let me go change into more suitable attire. I'll only be about five minutes."

Tucker went back to the car to wait with his uncle, and Charles quickly grabbed his golfing kit.

"Sir, if it's not too bold of me to say." Anna started from the other side of his closet.

"Go for it, Anna."

"Don't you think you're making a mistake in going?"

"It would be a mistake to not go. Fighting in secret against these men is like a dance, and you have to respond to each of their steps with very cautiously choreographed movements." Charles said, as he finally laced up his shoes.

"But what if it's some kind of trap? What if they have some information that you don't know about that could throw you off."

"Have a little more faith in me, Anna." He said, with a rather coy smile. "It's just a few rounds of golf, it will be fine."

Charles remembered the last time that he had played with them, his outburst was still fresh in his mind, and Charles didn't want a repeat of the last time. But he was just going to have to remain headstrong.

*****

Charles drove in his own car to the golf course, following his Uncle Jack and Tucker as they rode separately to him. It had been his own suggestion since it would make it a lot easier for him to have an easy escape if things did go wrong.

He couldn't deny that he was slightly nervous about the entire thing. He was terrified that they were going to corner him in some way and Charles was going to be left defenseless. He started to wonder if Anna had been right in advising him not to go, but at that moment, it was too late.

The two vehicles pulled into the parking lot of the golf course, and instantly the memory of the last time that they were there came flooding back. He was just thankful that this time, there weren't any wives or fiance's up on the terrace as spectators of whatever was going to happen.

"Good to be back, eh?" Charles said, as he flashed his Uncle a knowing smile.

Jack did nothing but roll his eyes as he muttered something that only Tucker could hear. Charles already didn't like the way that the two of them were already trying to gang up on him. He realized that if he had made a mistake in coming, it was now too late to get out of it without them knowing that he had caught on.

"So Tucker." Charles said, as the three of them walked through the lobby. "You've taken on a new role?"

"I don't think so." The lawyer frowned as they took their clubs through and onto the green. Charles had thought this would be a rather spontaneous outing, but three caddies were waiting for them as soon as they emerged from the building.

"I thought you were my Uncle's new flying monkey?" He asked, with a slight smirk.

"I don't know what you're talking about?" Tucker tried to regain his composure.

"Oh you know, you've been doing all his dirty work, and now you're even handing out face-to-face invitations to golf while my good Uncle here waits in the car." Charles was quick to point out.

The slight tinge of pink in Tucker's cheeks was celebrated by Charles. Although it was a very small and petty victory in the grand scheme of things, it was still a victory.

"That's an interesting take on it." Tucker nodded. "The two of us have just simply become a lot closer since I was also his brother's lawyer. I just want to see justice served."

"Of course." Charles nodded.

He had promised himself that he wasn't going to say a word about the inheritance, and so far, he had kept that with himself.

"Have you heard from Jane?" His Uncle asked, as he clearly ignored the bickering that was going on between the other two.

"Yes, she's having a wonderful time with her sister." Charles nodded with a small smile. He tried to imagine James, Jane, and Helena in a car together and 'wonderful' definitely wasn't the word that he was going to use to describe how they were all coping no doubt. But again, he kept that little nugget of information to himself.

"That's good to hear, it's so nice to get out of this country every now and again."

"Of course, a good bout of traveling is always in order." Charles smiled.

He himself actually couldn't wait to get away once the whole ordeal with the wedding was behind him. He had no plans to travel anywhere with Jane, as he was positive that he was the last person on Earth that she would even want to spend two more seconds with, let alone a vacation.

"And you say that they're going to be back soon?"

"Awfully kind of you to fund that." Tucker chipped in.

Although it wasn't explicitly said, Charles knew in an instant that his comment was a slight dig at the fact that Charles wasn't going to be receiving any more money from the family estate.

"Well, it would have been cruel of me to not help them out when it comes to potentially finding members of one's family. I was so excited to hear that they may have other relatives and so were they. It would have been so harsh to not help them go over and visit."

"At such a busy time as well." His Uncle continued, as they started to walk toward the first hole. "I mean, you are trying to plan a wedding when your fiance is on the other side of the world, right?"

"Yes, the time zones have been a challenge." Charles nodded.

He was chuckling to himself inwardly because he felt as though he was handling the sudden bombardment of questions rather well.

"Do you think that these grandparents will want to come all this way to attend the wedding?"

"I'm not sure." He responded to his Uncle. "They are very old and settled over there. I'm not sure that they're fit to fly for such a long distance. It will be a shame, but that's just life isn't it? Sometimes it doesn't go to plan."

"Indeed." Tucker said. His eyes looked like they were blazing at Charles' words and the way that he was looking so smug at the two of them.

"I can't lie to you, Son, I'm slightly shocked that you're going through with this wedding in the first place."

"Well, I love her. We've been getting excited about this for the last few weeks, and I just feel that it would be a really big waste of excitement if we don't take advantage of the situation." The two men were nodding as he spoke, but neither gave any kind of indication as to whether or not they believed him.

"In an ideal world, I would want to wait to make sure that we can have the big white wedding that I think she deserves. She really is an amazing girl, but Jane says that she just can't wait to get married and that's why we're going to be doing it a little more lowkey."

"I see." His Uncle nodded, although he had since narrowed his eyes.

"I know what was said over the phone, Uncle, and I truly meant no offense with my words. But I really do love this girl, and that's not a lie."

"You know that it's not going to change anything, right?"

Charles frowned at his Uncle's words as Tucker fired the first ball. It was miles off, but the intensity of their conversation left nobody in the mood to comment on the lawyer's awful aim.

"Change anything about what?"

"Don't play dumb with me, boy." Jack said, as he lined up his own swing. "About the stipulation." He fired the ball and it was a lot more on target than Tucker's, but that wasn't a difficult feat. "It doesn't change anything regarding the paperwork that has already gone through."

Charles knew that it would have been too easy for him to have just given up the information that his own lawyer had informed him about that morning. But he kept his cards close to his chest. The last thing that Charles wanted to do was to give his uncle any kind of advantage or even just an inclination into what he knew.

"All right, well I'm over it." Charles said with a shrug.

"Like hell you are." Tucker laughed and shook his head. "You really aren't fooling either of us, so I think you should just drop this act that you're in love with this girl."

"What act?"

Both of the men were glaring at him, but Charles maintained his point. He thought to himself that he should have been an actor in another life because he was trying his best to maintain that he didn't understand why they were so persistent on him. In reality, he knew that they were trying to crack him like a nut, they were just trying to apply as much pressure onto him as possible.

"Look, we've had the press snooping around as to who is going to be the inheritor of the Bentley Estate." His Uncle spoke to him.

Charles knew then that this sentence was the same as the tripwire appearing too late for him to dodge it; he had fallen into their trap.

"What's that to me?" He asked rather defensively.

"Well, I'm going to have to talk about the whole situation, and that's going to drag the Miller's into this too."

"It doesn't have to." Charles pointed out.

"Exactly, it doesn't have to." Jack spoke with a sickeningly sweet smile on his face. Charles assumed that he must have learned the diabolical look from his wife. "But if you don't stop with this farce, then I'm going to have no choice but to release my first draft about the family that are marrying into this esteemed world."

"Uncle, your classism is showing again." Charles whispered, although it was loud enough for both of the men to hear him.

"I'll send you the draft so that you can read it yourself, and I like to think of it as....not holding back too much. I thought that it would get a lot of clicks if I included a few well known buzzwords. You know strip club, poverty, gold-digger...I could go on if you want, or you can read it yours-"

"You will do no such thing in publishing that." Charles spoke, as he took a step closer to his uncle. All of his own advice in terms of not letting himself be too emotional had gone out the metaphorical window. Charles was feeling the pressure as the two men smirked at him, and he was starting to crack.

"Well then call off the wedding."

"Don't threaten me." Charles spoke in a growl.

"Then step back." Tucker interjected, as he got even closer to Charles.

He could feel the heat coming off of the man as he clenched his fists. They were away from the main golf club, but the caddies were dawdling around. Charles didn't want things to turn violent, and so he quickly checked himself. He knew better than to throw the first punch at least.

"Don't lose your cool on the golf course, Charles." His Uncle said with a smirk.

"I think that you should listen to your own advice." He said, while glaring at the lawyer who stood in his way. "I don't understand why you're doing this, you've got nothing to gain from tearing them down."

"Well, it might make things a little harder for them to get jobs," Jack said with a shrug.

"You wouldn't dare."

"Then call it off."

Charles felt as though he was trapped. It felt like he was in the corner of a dead end with no way out other than to succumb to the predator before him. He didn't want the vultures to win, he didn't want to keel over and let them pick at him until there was nothing left. He was starting to feel as though Jane was actually one of the only good things in her life; he'd almost lost her once, but this would be enough to lose her forever. She would never forgive him if he let an article like that be published about her. He shuddered at the thought of how much she would hate him if he didn't yield.

"I'm going to need to talk to Jane about this." He muttered.

"Then call her and tell her now."

"This is a conversation to be had in person." Charles said.

"No, you're just stalling." Tucker said.

"I wasn't talking to you." Charles returned his gaze to glare at the man in front of him.

"What are you going to do about it?"

"Why do I get the feeling that you're trying to rile me up just so I'll rise to your bait?" Charles asked him plainly.

He'd got him. The lawyer's face dropped slightly as he realized that Charles wasn't going to play ball, but it quickly morphed into an expression of anger as he glared at the younger man in front of him.Without Charles having to say anything else, it ended up being Wyatt Tucker who threw the first punch.

CHAPTER 17

"You idiot!" Charles could hear his Uncle shouting at the lawyer as he quickly got to his feet. Charles could see the regret on the man's face, but all he really saw in front of that was red. Charles wasted no time in letting his own fist clash with Tucker's cheek. The force sent the man sprawling back.

He collided with Jack, and the two of them were on the floor in an instant. Charles worked quickly to deliver one more punch to the stunned lawyer as he spat blood beside him. His cheek was throbbing and Charles had no doubt that there would be a lovely dark bruise there in the morning to remind him what a mistake it had been to come to the golf course again.

"If you touch me again, it will be the last thing that you ever do." He seethed, as he looked down at the cowering man. He noticed how much thinner Tucker was than he had ever properly observed, it made him look even more vulnerable at that moment as Charles stood away from the man. "How's that for a threat?"

He wiped the cut on his cheek before grabbing his own clubs off of one of the shocked caddies and made his way back to the main building. It was at that moment, that Charles knew the only good decision he'd made of the day was in driving himself there, otherwise, he would have been stuck dealing with the consequences of his actions.

*****

"If I said that I told you so, would you fire me?" Anna asked, with a heavy sigh as she stared at him. Charles walked in through the door while clutching his cheek. He wasn't in the mood to hear her taunting, but he knew that there was no way that he could avoid it.

"I'll accept it if it could perhaps come accompanied with a piece of frozen meat." He managed a smile while pointing to the bruise that was already forming.

Anna nodded quickly and darted off to the kitchen. Charles placed down his golfing clubs, relieved to no longer have to carry the weight on his shoulders. He wondered how real his uncle's threat had been though, and what the fight with Tucker would mean in terms of them releasing that article. He could imagine his Uncle releasing it in a fit of anger at that very moment, but Charles had no way of knowing if Jack had even been contacted by a reporter at Forbes.

"Here you go." Anna said, as she reappeared with a slab of frozen steak.

"Thanks." Charles nodded to her as he quickly placed it over his throbbing cheek area where the punch had made the most impact.

"I told you so." She muttered.

He noticed the slightly smug smile on Anna's face in knowing that she had actually gotten away with saying it, but he was far too shocked by the situation that he let it slide.

"So it was a trap?"

"Of course it was a trap." He nodded, as he walked through the house until he got to the library. He was thankful to see that there was already a fire lit as he lay down on one of the sofas and breathed out heavily.

"What was the trap?"

"It was blackmail." Charles said before pulling a face. He hated that word; how it sounded, how it tasted as he said it. He hated that he had let someone get the advantage on him like that. It didn't feel right that his uncle was still in a better position walking away from the altercation. "He has a scathing article

318

that he's threatening to release to the press if I don't call off the wedding."

"What the..." Anna muttered, as she sat down on the sofa opposite him. "Is this all right?" She hesitated as she had clearly realized that she'd forgotten her place. But Charles didn't care, he simply nodded and waved it off.

"The article will be about Jane and Helena. He said that it's going to paint them out as the worst kind of people."

"Why would he do such a thing?" Anna asked, as she shook her head.

"Because he's power and money hungry. Those things always go hand in hand in this world with blackmail, and he's played this game rather well." Charles said, although it really did pain him to admit that.

"Have you warned them?"

"I've just walked through the door!" He fired back with a groan.

"No Charles, this is where you are proactive and warn them about what they are coming back into."

"I will, but I haven't even spoken to Jane yet about everything. I'm making plans for the wedding, but I don't even know if the bride will be in attendance!" He fired back.

"Alright." She sighed and shook her head. "Call James, tell him not to put you on speaker and let him know about what has happened. He can speak to Helena about it and then-"

"And then the two women will hate us even more than they already do." Charles finished her sentence off for her.

"You don't know that, you're all on the same side now, and it will do you no good to be so divided. It's what your Uncle wants."

"Yeah, well tell that to Helena, I'm sure she'd be thrilled to hear that news." Charles scoffed.

Anna shook her head at him, but he didn't care if she was just going to sit there and pass judgment. He knew that he probably did deserve it, but it still annoyed him that she thought she could act all high and mighty.

He realized that it was probably a good thing that he didn't know much about his housekeeper since he had nothing to fire back at her in terms of mistakes that she could have made in her past. He narrowed his eyes as he thought about how he would even know if the article was going to be published.

"Call James." She urged him again as he finally sat up. Charles nodded slowly as he bit his lip, he knew that there was no arguing with her on that subject.

*****

"This had better be good." James said with a sigh of annoyance. "I was making really good time before you asked me to pull over and answer the phone." He had walked away from the car so that neither of the sisters could overhear what he was saying.

"How far out are you now?"

James noticed the worry in his cousin's tone, whatever he was calling for, it certainly wasn't good news.

"I don't know, a couple of hours maybe? I *was* aiming to get home before dark, but someone is stopping me from making any progress." James reiterated how frustrating it was to be stopped when he was on such a roll.

"If you're making such good time, why aren't you already home? And I don't want you to even think about speeding while in that car, because you'll be paying the speeding fine if you get given a ticket."

"Sure." James groaned. "Anyway, what is it?"

"I'm afraid we may have another situation back here?"

"When you say *situation*, do you mean that the stipulation can still go ahead, the wedding is all organized and all I need to do when I get home is show my face?"

"I wish it were that easy, James." Charles sighed heavily through the phone. He didn't sound good at all. "I went golfing with Tucker and Uncle Jack today."

"Why the hell would you put yourself in a dangerous spot like that?" James wanted to throw his phone out of frustration. "You couldn't have just laid low for another day or so? We're so close to home and this is going to need all of your attention."

"Right." He said. "You're going to have to rethink that strategy I think." Charles sighed. "Jack seems to think that he still has all of the inheritance at his fingertips and that he's already won this...whatever this is."

"This is war, Charles, that's what it is." James snapped.

"I know, it just sounds kind of corny sometimes so I thought I wouldn't....anyway that's not the point." Charles continued. "He's been contacted by Forbes, or at least he's alleging that he has. He says that he's written some kind of scathing article about all of this that doesn't exactly paint Helena or Jane in a good light."

James felt himself tense up at the idea of that kind of scrutiny going onto them. He knew exactly what it was like to have random strangers hurling abuse at you online, and he swallowed thickly at even the thought of it.

"Is he blackmailing you with that?" James breathed out.

"He is." Charles said. "He wants me to call off the wedding or he says that he will release the article."

"Do you believe him?"

"Do you want to take that risk?"

321

"That's true." James said, and pressed his lips into such a tight line that his teeth started to dig into the skin. He flinched at the mild pain, but he was so deep in thought that he didn't care too much about it. "Our options aren't looking good, are they?"

"Not at all, and now I don't know what to do."

James glanced back at the car for a moment. Despite the tinted windows, he had a feeling that both of the sisters were looking at him through the glass and waiting for him to inform them of what was going on.

"Do you want me to tell them?"

"Do you think that would help?" Charles asked.

"I could tell Helena in private somehow?" James tried to think of what else he could do. "I'll be honest, I don't think that Jane is in the right frame of mind to hear this news right now."

"All right, then I trust your judgement."

James wasn't even sure that he trusted his own judgement, but it was now clear that he didn't really have a choice. He was going to have to brief at least one of the sisters on the news, and it just so happened to be the one that he was starting to feel strangely attached to.

"She's going to hate us all over again, isn't she?" James asked, with a groan as he thought about all of the progress that he had made with Helena. It was all about to be wiped away in an instant.

"I really hope that she can see past it." Charles said, although his voice sounded quite weak through the phone.

"Don't worry, we'll find a way through this." James tried to reassure his cousin, although he wasn't even convincing himself with his words.

"Do you think so?"

"We can only hope so."

After hanging up, James stood and took a deep breath. The last thing that he wanted to do was go back in that car and break the news to Helena, but he knew that there really wasn't any other way that they were going to get around this. He knew that it would be worse for either of the sisters to find out about the article from someone else and then find out that he had been keeping this information from them. With a heavy sigh and an even heavier heart, James opened the car door and quickly moved to sit down inside.

CHAPTER 18

Helena was in shock at what she had just heard. She blinked slowly and tried to come to terms with what James had just told her. Jane was asleep in the back of the car again, and she was incredibly thankful that her younger sister hadn't heard what had just been said.

"I think I'm going to be sick." She muttered, as she rested her head back against the seat and closed her eyes.

"Wait really? Because Charles will kill me if I get…"

"No, it's fine. I just feel a little nauseous, but definitely not enough to be sick." She said and shrugged it off.

"Oh, are you alright?"

"Obviously not." Helena scowled at him. "Do you know how hard it's going to be to get a credible job if he goes ahead with this slander piece?"

Helena groaned at the fact that their uncle was in such a powerful position. She winced at the thought of future employers having to read about what she did in a strip club when she was thirty. Helena shook her head and glanced over at James.

"If it's that difficult to get a job if this piece is published, then I can always…"

"Don't say it, I really don't want your help." She shook her head.

Taking money from Charles already left her with a bad taste in her mouth, but she couldn't imagine what it was going to be like if she was in both of their debts. She understood that she technically was in James's debt anyway because of how far he had driven to help her find her sister.

"The offer is always there if you need it." He said again. Helena shook her head and glanced back to see that her sister was still fast asleep.

"Thank you, it really is kind of you, but I don't want to be any more in your debt." Helena managed a smile as she nodded to him.

"But I wouldn't expect it b-"

"I don't want to be in your debt, and if I take money from you of any kind, then I will be." She reinforced to him.

James quickly got the message and shut his mouth. Helena turned to look out of the window as she tried to think about what they were going to do to get out of this. She could help to save a billionaire's inheritance, or she could save her own reputation. If she had asked herself that question a month ago, Helena knew that she wouldn't have even hesitated to have said the latter. But now she wasn't so sure. With no source of income, Helena reluctantly had to admit to herself that she really was at the mercy of Charles Bentley, and what a grim place it was to be.

"What are we going to do in terms of calling off the wedding?" She asked, and turned back to look at James.

"I...I don't know. It's going to be a very difficult decision to make, I'm afraid."

"I know." Helena nodded in agreement. She could see that the calm and controlled way that she was trying to process the news was starting to freak out James, as he continued to look at her in complete disbelief. "Stop looking at me like that."

"Oh I'm...I'm sorry. I just thought that you would be a lot less reasonable with this news." James muttered, as he turned his attention back to the road.

"What do you mean a lot less reasonable? I'm just trying not to freak out too much because I don't want to wake up my sister and I certainly don't want to just go around in circles with this. This is serious, and it's going to matter what we do next. The last thing that I want to happen is to have my personal life published in a large magazine like that, and so I'm just trying to come up with solutions in my head."

"All right, it was just freaking me out for a moment." He muttered.

Helena returned to staring out the window as the world passed her by. She couldn't believe that there were people in this world like Charles' uncle. He was beyond evil and would clearly stop at nothing, no matter who was in his path if it meant that he could get money at the end of it.

She shuddered at the idea of Jane seeing the article, she knew that it would break her and she wouldn't be able to marry Charles anyway. The only thing they could do was do as Jack said and call off the wedding. But Helena didn't want to just roll over and accept their defeat. She knew that there had to be another way.

"This doesn't change anything between us, does it?" James asked after a while. His question caused them both to frown at one another. Helena had felt as though he was being much softer as of late, but she had just put it down to the fact that they had found Jane and now things were going to be alright. She hadn't really thought too much more into it.

"I guess there's nothing for it to change." She said with a shrug. Although Helena still wasn't too sure what he meant by his phrase.

"I just mean that we have been managing to get over the way we were fighting in the beginning and, well, I think I prefer this to our bickering."

"Oh, right." Helena nodded, as she thought about this for a moment. "I suppose that it is a lot less exhausting to interact with you like this instead." She said with a small smirk on her face.

James nodded and smiled to himself as he faced the road once more.

"I think that Jane should talk to Charles before we tell her about what's happened with his Uncle." Helena nodded.

"You're right, it would be so much easier if she gets over that before we put yet another hurdle in her path." Charles nodded in agreement.

"Alright." She smiled and thought about how they were going to bridge the subject with her.

First thing's first, they still had another hour or so before they got back to Charles where there were already some difficult conversations to be had. Helena wasn't looking forward to it one bit, and she was hoping that they would simply agree to continue on with the wedding as was planned.

*****

Jane woke up as the car trudged over gravel. The sudden change in surface jolted her back to reality, and she realized that they were now driving up the road to the mansion at the end of it. Dread and panic suddenly decided to merge into one within her gut as she shot up and stared out of the window as she tried to work out how much time she had.

"Turn around." She said quickly.

"What?" Helena asked, with a frown as she whirled around in her seat.

"You heard me, turn the damned car around, I want to go home. I don't want to see him yet, not like this." Jane said, as she felt the car coming to a slower pace.

She shuddered at the thought of having to go in and see Charles when she looked like she was trying to resemble someone homeless. Jane just also didn't feel ready to talk to him yet, coming up the drive had brought the memory of the last time she'd seen him fresh to the surface. She winced at the sound of her screaming back at him that he would never see her again, she had told him that she refused to marry him, and yet there she was back at the house.

She couldn't believe that this had been her sister's plan all along.

"I want to go back to the apartment." She tried to plead with Helena as she stared at her intently. "Don't tell me that your new boyfriend here has made you soft and now you want to use them for their money!"

Jane knew that it was a rather harsh blow, but she wanted to show them that she was still too angry to talk to Charles.

"Look, it will be much nicer if you clean up here instead." Helena argued against her. "Just please try this for me, Jane, I know it's hard."

She could see the way that both of them had blushed at her comment, and Jane was almost certain that if something hadn't happened between them yet, it was bound to happen in the future.

"You want me to go and get clean in the very place that I left." She scoffed and shook her head.

"Please Jane, I'll take you in and we can go get you some clean clothes. You can take a shower and you won't have to talk to him until you're ready. But this is a much cleaner and safer option than going back to the apartment."

"When has that ever stopped us before?" Jane quickly fired back.

"Because we haven't had an option like this before. Look, there are still things that have happened that I need to get you up to speed on, so can you just trust me that this is the right way to go about this?"

Jane knew that there was no point in arguing against them. She wasn't the one that was controlling the car, and the option of getting out and walking would take far too long. Jane knew that Helena wouldn't let her do that, and so her only real option was to let them take her into the house to get cleaned up.

"All right." She breathed out and stared between them. "But I really don't want to have to interact with him until I'm ready to."

"That's fine, you won't have to." Helena said, as she shot James a pointed look that Jane didn't miss. He then nodded and continued to drive down the driveway at a slightly faster pace than he had been going beforehand. She figured that he was doing that so that Jane didn't get any ideas about getting out of the car while it was still moving, it was too dangerous at that speed.

Finally, they arrived outside of the large mansion, and Jane hunkered down in her seat while James quickly got out of the car.

"It's going to be alright." Helena smiled back at her as she held out her hand for her to take.

"Do you really think so?"

"I know so." Her sister nodded. "We just...have to do some things that we don't like for a short amount of time, but it will pay off in the end."

Jane thought about her non profit and how James was going to help her with his connections as well as fund it. She couldn't believe that something that had always been just a dream of hers had slowly managed to turn into a goal, and was now in reach. She genuinely couldn't believe that he was willing to help her and it made her realize that perhaps they weren't as bad as she had thought.

It was, after all, their fathers who had made all of the decisions about which companies to invest in. Healthcare insurance had been a profitable game when Charles' father was alive, but that still didn't make the blow any easier to bear in Jane's mind. She wanted to tell Helena about the fact that her non profit was going to happen, but she didn't want to go against James's word. Especially when there was clearly something going on there. James gave a thumb's up from the door, and Helena quickly undid her belt.

"You'll be fine, I promise we'll just go straight upstairs and we won't talk to him just yet."

"You promise?"

"I swear on Mom." Helena spoke seriously.

If Jane had previously had any doubts about her sister's word, they disappeared as soon as the words left her mouth. She didn't want to dishonor their mother, and so she slowly took off her belt and got out of the car with her sister.

"Are you sure about this?" Jane asked for clarification just one more time as she smoothed down her hair and approached the front door cautiously. She hated that she was even wondering if Helena was lying, she knew that it wouldn't be possible if she was bringing their mother into this. But Jane didn't hold James to the same regard, and she knew that he could have easily been lying when he gave her sister the signal that everything was clear.

"Just up here." Helena muttered, as she quickly led her sister up the large staircase.

"Welcome back, Miss Miller." Anna smiled warmly at her. "Would you like me to run a bath for you?"

Before Jane could answer for herself, Helena cut over her. "That would be great, thank you."

The housekeeper sent her another small smile of sympathy before Jane was whisked away and into the bedroom that she had stayed in for a while. She couldn't deny that the idea of a warm bath at that moment did sound magical.

"See, everything is just as you left it."

Jane looked around, but she still felt like a stranger, like an outcast. This wasn't their world, and it still felt as though they had regressed back to their childhood where they would play pretend.

"Are you alright?" Helena asked, as she quickly pulled her sister in for a hug.

Jane melted into the embrace. She hadn't realized just how badly she'd actually just needed a hug from her sister after sitting in a car all day. Jane could feel fresh tears forming in her eyes as she thought about what to do next.

"Why don't you get ready for your bath and we can talk while you're getting changed?" Helena suggested, as she pointed to the screen in the corner.

"I don't know what to say, Helena." Jane said, as she grabbed a robe and quickly walked behind the screen. It was only once she was in the clean world of the Bentleys did she realize just how badly she smelled after spending days in the same clothes.

"I'm just glad that you're back and safe."

"I don't understand how you've changed your tune so much when it comes to James?" Jane cut straight to the point as she realized that it was bothering her quite a bit.

"What do you mean?"

"Well, before I left, you were determined to bring the family down and make sure that they didn't benefit from us in any other way possible. Now that you've brought me back, it's like you're trying to play happy families or something."

Jane's statement was followed by an uncomfortably long silence. She waited patiently behind the screen as she started to peel off her pants.

"I know how it looks." Helena started finally after a heavy sigh. "I know that it shows I'm being a hypocrite, and I really don't mean to be. But during my search for you, I got talking to James, and they aren't the perfect family by any means. They've dealt with more losses than most, and we realized that aside from our financial situations, we actually do have a lot in common."

Jane listened intently, but she wasn't sure what to believe anymore. She felt as though everything she thought she knew or even just thought she knew had been turned on its head.

"Did you hear me?"

"I did." Jane answered slowly. "I'm just trying to piece it all together, sorry that I'm a little slow."

"Don't apologize." Helena said, with a friendly chuckle. "Can I ask something though?"

"Sure."

"What did you mean about James being my boyfriend in the car? It felt like a weird blow."

Jane chuckled and shook her head as she removed her top and quickly reached for the robe that was hanging up for her.

"You really are still clueless when it comes to all of that kind of stuff, aren't you?" Jane smiled, as she thought about how to explain this. "I don't know, you may have only taken away that you have more respect for him from this small trip, but I think he may have taken something else."

"I don't get it."

"You don't have to, but you can't be that blind to it, right?" Jane asked with a frown. "You must have caught on to the way that he looks at you?"

"I suppose so." Helena said slowly. "Anyway, back to you, you're going to have to talk to Charles at some point. I'm sure he's downstairs right now and really eager to talk to you."

"I'll have my bath and then when I'm in a clean change of clothes, I'll talk to him." Jane nodded.

This was going to be like a bandaid, whichever way she decided to do it, it would be painful. So Jane decided that there was no better time than now to rip it off.

CHAPTER 19

Her bath felt like it was a welcome balm to her. Jane closed her eyes and let the water soothe her as she lay back in the water and let it heal her. She sighed out in relief and even let her hair get wet. She wasn't usually a fan of letting her hair get wet when she had baths, but when Jane thought about it, she rarely got the luxury of bathing like that.

Back at the cramped apartment, they had a small shower that you had to let the water run for a little while because it would otherwise come out a strange orange and brown color. Jane turned her nose up at the memory and quickly shook it off as she focused on relaxing. Her next task wasn't going to be quite so nice for her, and so she reveled in the good feeling provided by the warm water around her.

She was trying to place the scent that the housekeeper had added to the bath. Jane was sure that it was in the bubbles, but she had never been too good at identifying what scents were which. She could hazard a guess that this was lavender and that it was the kind of scent that was used mainly for women when they were trying to relax. It was working.

Jane let all of the horrid memories of her past trauma go as she sunk deeper into the water. The bath was much bigger than she had been anticipating, some may have called it a small swimming pool.

She breathed heavily and thought about nothing other than the warmth around her and the bubbles that fizzled against her skin. Jane did something for the first time that she hadn't done for the past few days; she smiled.

Her peace was short-lived. Jane winced as the water temperature slowly cooled. It felt that with each minute that she sat within the waters, it was another minute that brought her closer to her conversation with Charles.

"Are you ready to get out yet?" Helena's prompt from the other side of the door told her that she had been in the bath for long enough.

"I suppose so." Jane sighed, as she lay back one last time. She glanced up at the ornate ceiling of the bathroom and dreamed of a better life; one where she wouldn't compromise her morals so that she could make sure she had enough to live off of.

Slowly, and rather reluctantly, Jane got out of the large bath and quickly wrapped a towel around herself. She didn't care much for her modesty around her sister, for they had lived in an apartment on top of one another for many years and she had really seen it all.

"Are you alright?" Helena asked, as she looked at her sister.

Jane quickly glanced at herself in the mirror and was pleased to see that the color had returned to her cheeks due to the heat of the bath. She smiled in sweet relief as she felt a lot more like herself again.

"I'm great." Jane nodded, as she let out a breath that she hadn't even known she'd been holding. "I don't think I properly thanked you for coming all that way to get me."

"You don't need to." Helena shrugged it off. "I know that you would have done the same for me if I'd needed you."

"I suppose that there's just one more than that I need to do for the two of us, isn't there?" Jane asked, as she winced at the thought of facing Charles.

"Believe me, if you weren't in so deep, I would change places with you in a heartbeat."

"But then you wouldn't be happy." Jane said with a frown.

"Better me than you, little sis."

Jane realized at that moment all of the times that she really had taken her sister for granted. She still couldn't believe at times that Helena was so strong and still so caring towards her, she proved that she really would do anything for her sister.

Jane embraced her sister, not caring about the way that she was still dripping wet from her bath. Helena chuckled, but she didn't complain about the wetness, they were both just so happy to have one another safe once again.

"I picked out an outfit for you, I'm not sure if you're going to like it and I know that there are many to choose from around here, so don't feel obliged to-"

"I'm sure it's perfect." Jane cut off her sister's babbling as she nodded to her reassuringly.

"All right, I'll leave you to get changed."

*****

Helena stepped out of the room and breathed out a sigh of relief. She could tell that her sister was finally coming around to the idea of marrying Charles. There was a moment of slight peace, but Helena knew that she was still going to have to explain to her about the article, and she knew that would only throw them into more turmoil.

But that wasn't an issue for that afternoon. In fact, she quickly decided that it wouldn't be an issue for another day or so. She wanted to give Jane as much time as she needed to recover from the shocking things that she had learned over the past few days.

"Is she alright?" James asked, as he quickly jumped up at the sight of Helena coming down the stairs.

"She's fine." She nodded. "She's just changing now."

"Well, she certainly knows how to keep a man waiting." Charles grumbled, as he walked after his cousin.

"Just don't be too harsh on her, she's still really fragile."

"I'll do my best." Charles said with a sigh.

Helena forgot for a moment that she was going to have to deal with him and not James, who appeared like an angel in comparison to his cousin.

"Well, you're going to need to do better than your best if it's going to still upset her."

"All right." James held his hands up in an attempt to diffuse the situation. "It will all be fine, let's go into one of the front rooms while we wait? I suppose it would be better if we don't all bombard her at the bottom of the staircase."

Ever since her sister had made the comment about how James looked at her, Helena couldn't stop herself from catching the small glances that he made in her direction. Now that it had been pointed out to her, it was more obvious than anything in the world.

"Promise me that he'll be good?" She muttered to James as they walked ahead of Charles.

"I can't make any promises, but I've told him for the last hour or so that he's not to put the blame on her for any of this." James responded in a low voice.

"All right, I trust you." She whispered.

Even her words caught her off guard, and the two of them stared at one another, unable to believe that Helena had really just said that.

"O-okay." He stammered, as they entered the front room with Charles hot on their tail.

"I'll go and get her in a moment if she takes too long." Helena spoke up as a tense silence broke out around them. She didn't like the awkwardness that was settling in, but there was nothing that she could do about it.

Finally, at the sound of footsteps on the stairs, the three of them quickly jumped to attention as though they were in the military. Helena and James quickly stepped out of the room and into the hallway, but Charles waited patiently in the front room. She realized swiftly that this was the room he'd chosen as his stage.

Helena smiled widely at her sister and gave her another hug as Jane appeared much more like her old self. She was wearing a pair of comfortable linen trousers and a white t-shirt. It was casual and appeared to be the perfect kind of outfit to wear fresh out of a bath. Her hair was still wet, but it really didn't matter. All that mattered at that moment was that Jane was going to talk with Charles and it wouldn't end in an argument again.

CHAPTER 20

Charles sucked in a breath as she was finally before him. It felt like an age since the two of them had been in a room alone together, and yet it had only been the best part of a few days.

"You look...good." He muttered awkwardly, causing Jane to flush as she shut the door behind her.

"Thanks." She muttered.

Neither of them made a move to sit down, and neither of them smiled as an air of awkwardness settled between them incredibly quickly.

"Shall we?" He finally made the move to gesture toward the sofa.

"Sure."

Jane sat on one, and he sat on the other so that there was a good amount of space between each other but they were still facing one another.

"So." He started, as he cleared his throat. "How have you been?"

"Peachy." Jane's dry response radiated sarcasm and was only reinforced by the fact that she didn't move her expression at all. It remained stony and unreadable.

"Look, I'm just going to come out and say it. I'm sorry for the part that I played with my family's money being tied up in that medical insurance company. It's awful what happened, and although it may not have been directly me who was involved in that case, it's my name on that paperwork. It's my surname that caused you all of this pain, and so I apologize from the depths of my heart."

He waited to see what she was going to say. He had forgotten just how radiant she was, and fresh from bathing, she seemed to almost glow in the heat of the room.

"I can't forgive you yet." She started with a heavy sigh. Her voice was a lot more hollow than he remembered. "But I do appreciate your apology. I will keep it in mind and I will be able to move past this, I just won't be able to forget so easily."

"I understand." He nodded to her and smiled. "I'm just so glad that you're home and safe, I really am."

"I thought that all you cared about was your family's money?"

"Well then, you thought wrong." Charles said as he shook his head. "When Helena came by and said that you hadn't come home yet, I felt this...worry inside of me that I haven't felt for a long time. I just hated to think that something awful had happened to you, it really would have affected me in a way that I hadn't even realized myself until I was in that situation."

He could see that his words were working. Her eyebrows raised slightly out of curiosity, and Jane shifted in her seat slightly.

"Do you really mean that?"

"Of course I do, you were going to marry me. Whether either of us liked it, you were going to be part of this family that seems to grow smaller every year. I've lost a lot of people in my life, Jane, and I know that's not something that I've been too open about with you, but it's because it still haunts me to this day."

"I'm sorry." She muttered, as she looked down at her lap.

"Don't be, I just want you to know that you are important to me."

Another silence hung around them for a while as he could tell that Jane wasn't going to speak up.

"I also have some news." He said while moving to get more comfortable. "My Uncle has the inheritance already, he's gone against the stipulation and I think that my lawyer has found a way out of it. I can't let him win, and I certainly can't let him have all of this."

He realized that Jane hadn't said anything about the bruise on his cheek, but he didn't know if it was worth bringing up at that moment.

"Oh, does that mean the marriage is still on?"

She continued to stare down at her lap.

"Have you thought about reconsidering? The last time that I saw you, you said that you wouldn't go through with this marriage. I was wondering if you are having other thoughts?" Charles asked her slowly.

She looked up at him and stared deadly into his eyes for a moment. He was slightly taken back by the intensity of her stare and held his breath as he waited for her to respond.

"Yes."

It was a simple affirmation, and her voice sounded rather small as she spoke. But the singular word elicited such a wave of relief from Charles that he physically slumped back in his chair as he breathed out heavily for a few moments.

"Thank you." He smiled at her genuinely. "Thank you so much, I know how hard this is for you, but I promise-"

"I have some conditions though."

He pursed his lips upon hearing her words. That was something that he hadn't expected, but he felt like a bit of a fool for not taking it into account.

"Of course." He nodded and gestured for her to proceed.

"I will see you at the wedding." Jane said, as she held his gaze. "But that's it."

Charles wanted to interject that he was going to need her help with the planning and she was going to have to show her face in front of his Uncle in order for him to stop breathing down his neck about the marriage. He hadn't even told her about the article, but he knew that was another conversation for another day. This was still a rather big hill to get up. He sucked in another breath as he let her continue with her conditions.

"The second is that I won't have to see you after the wedding."

"Done." He nodded quickly.

Although, something within him panged at the thought of never seeing her again. He wasn't sure what it was, but it was somewhere between him being sentimental and also feeling a pang of immense guilt for the trouble that his family had caused hers.

"And the last thing is that after a year, we will get divorced and move on with our lives."

Charles wasn't sure if he could just agree to that one so quickly, and he wasn't sure why. There was nothing in the stipulation that stated he had to stay married, but there was also nothing on the subject of divorce.

"I'll get back to you on that." He muttered.

"If it's a yes, then I'll do it. I'll marry you." Jane said with a deep breath following her words.

"All right, I'll see what I can do." Charles nodded. "It should all be fine though, I don't see why we shouldn't be able to divorce. Although, it may get in the way of your second condition since I would probably have to see you in court."

"Sure." Jane shrugged, as she glanced around the room.

"I think that's it then, I just really wanted to tell you how sorry I was about what happened and-"

"Thanks." Jane said, as she managed a weak smile.

The two of them slowly rose up from the couches. Charles wasn't sure why he did it, but he held his arms open for her to walk into. Jane hesitated, as though she was waiting to see whether or not it was a trap. But after waiting a moment, she decided that there was no harm in it clearly.

He held onto her for a moment, breathing in the scent of lavender and fresh linen. He found it rather calming, although he could feel her thumping heart pounding against his chest.

"Thank you, Jane, and I really am glad that you're back here and safe."

"Thank you for the apology, Charles." Jane said, as she smiled for a moment longer before she turned toward the doorway.

He watched her go and felt a heaviness settle into his heart. For a moment, a pang of panic ran through him as he waited to see if the sensation would intensify. Ever since the death of his father, Charles had always suffered with the rather irrational fear that one day his heart would just stop working and he would drop dead.

But this wasn't the kind of pain that came from cardiac arrest. This wasn't something physical, this was the feeling that you got when you realized that you were the one who had caused someone else pain. Someone that you cared so deeply for that you didn't even understand it yourself was in pain because of you.

Charles grimaced as he was left in the room on his own. He swallowed thickly and stood up a little straighter. It felt as though the walls around him were closing in as he squeezed his eyes shut for a moment. Although he may have fixed one thing, there were still many issues in his situation that were nowhere near being made complete.

"You alright, cousin?" James asked, from the doorway as he peered into the room.

Charles nodded slowly as he tried to pull himself from his thoughts. He'd zoned out while standing up and swayed slightly, he held onto the sofa for a moment to balance himself. He wished that James hadn't seen that, but there was nothing he could do about it.

"I'm fine." Charles nodded, as James moved further into the room to help him.

"Did it go all right?"

"She agreed to the marriage." Charles said, as a smile of relief arrived on his face.

"I knew she would." James beamed back as he chuckled out of relief. It was such a sweet feeling that took over one's body like a storm would dominate an entire landscape. It rendered someone unable to control how they would react, and people would often mistake their laughter as rather rude. In reality, it was just a natural reaction to a situation that was incredibly high in tension.

Charles waited for the sound of the two sisters going back up the stairs before he emerged with his cousin from the room. He took a second to exhale deeply as he looked around his house. It was a small but positive start to the end of his problems, he just knew that he had to hang in there and everything would work itself out eventually. Charles glanced over at James, and the two of them laughed.

We hope you Enjoyed Book Two of the Accidental Engagement Series. Now Continue Reading the Story by Reading the Book Three.

Make sure you signed up to Bridget Taylor's mailing to receive FREE BONUS CONTENT which compliment this book. Just go to https://bit.ly/aebonuscontent to Sign Up and Get Notified of New Releases.

THE ACCIDENTAL ENGAGEMENT

SERIES BOOK THREE

DESCRIPTION

With the wedding preparations fully underway, Jane is feeling rather overwhelmed by it all. She has no choice but to help with certain parts of the organization, and she has to do the one thing that she never had anticipated she would do; try on wedding dresses. What some might have perceived as one of their greatest days out, Jane was dreading it as though it were a dark day for her. Charles can't wait to get through the day and get it over and done with. He wants the money more than anything, but as the wedding draws nearer, will he have a change of heart? He can't help but think about all of the unhappiness that his greed had caused up until that moment. This forces him to beg the question - is it all worth it?

CHAPTER 1

Before you start reading book three on the next page please make you get notified for the release of next series. Go to

https://bit.ly/aebonuscontent to sign up to get notified of Bridget Taylor's new series coming out and to receive free bonus content and take part in giveaways. If you like this series you will love the next one :-).

Join Bridget Taylor's Exclusive Mailing List for FREE BONUS CONTENT and Discount Coupons

☆ Click below to receive free bonus content, discount coupons, take part in giveaways and get notified of Bridget Taylor's new releases.

☆ A new series is about to be launched. You will be one of the first to be notified with a discount coupon.

CLICK HERE TO SIGN UP

Just go to https://bit.ly/aebonuscontent to follow Bridget Taylor

START OF CHAPTER ONE

Jane sighed out heavily as her leg bounced anxiously. She still couldn't believe that she'd actually agreed to this, but there she was; sitting in a ridiculously big house, planning a ridiculously lavish wedding for two people who could barely stand one another.

"So." The woman in front of her snapped her away from her thoughts. "Coffee cream, Frosting Cream, or Cannoli Cream?"

The perfectly made-up woman who sat opposite her in the parlor was talking about what color the serviettes were going to be on the tables at the reception. Jane was still having a hard time accepting that there was more than one shade of cream, let alone ready to make any kind of decision on the subject. Charles had left her about half an hour ago, he claimed that he could hear the phone ringing, but Jane hadn't heard it. She knew that he just wanted out of this room and out of the clutches of the wedding planner. Darcy was far too bubbly and loud about her job, Jane was hating every moment of this.

"Uh…" She glanced between the three different shades. Although Jane could have sworn that two of them were quite literally the same shade. "That one?"

"You don't sound convinced." Darcy said, with a frown as she sat back.

Jane wasn't convinced of anything anymore. She wanted to snap at the woman, but she knew that it would do her no good to take out all of her frustrations on someone when it wasn't even her fault.

"Well, I am." Jane shrugged. "Sorry, I'm just a bit tired and this is all very overwhelming."

Darcy looked at her for a moment out of curiosity, but Jane wasn't too bothered if she was being judged at that moment. "It's just the color of the serviettes."

Jane couldn't believe that the woman was making it out to be nothing. She was the one who had made her narrow down the color scheme from what felt like a hundred different shades of cream to just three. Jane hadn't even known that it was possible to have so many variations of the same colors.

"I'm sorry, you're right." She said after breathing heavily. She knew that admitting defeat in this situation would be her only way to appease the overzealous wedding planner before her.

"I get it." Darcy said with a shrug. "When you first take on the task of planning a wedding, I don't think a lot of couples realize just how detailed you have to be. There's so much to do and it's going to feel like there's not enough time to do it all, but I'm here to make this all easier for you both. You're just going to have to give me something back."

Jane felt as though this was the kind of conversation that she should have been having with Charles since he was the absent one. He was the one who had hired Darcy in the beginning, and Jane had realized upon doing some research of her own that she was one of the most in demand wedding planners in the country. She had TV shows and book tours, and Jane started to realize that Charles must have used some serious cash to convince her to come out to them and help.

"Of course,." Jane said. She forced a friendly smile onto her face in an effort to show the wedding planner that she actually did want to be there. In contrast, she had never wanted the comfort of her dingy flat more in her life.

"So how long have the two of you been together?"

"Well, we were on and off for a couple of months." Jane started, although she knew that it wasn't the best way to begin that kind of story. "So it really hasn't been too long, but you know when you just...know."

"I sure do, honey." Darcy said with a beaming smile.

Jane was confused for a moment as she thought about how the woman before her hadn't seen a single ounce of chemistry between the pair. She was clearly being paid enough to sit there and agree to anything that Jane was going to say. She thought about having some fun with this, but Jane couldn't be bothered at that moment in time. The session felt as though it had been going on for an age, and she wanted nothing more than for it all to be done.

"Alright, Cannoli Cream." Jane nodded finally.

"I knew you would go for that one, I just knew it." Darcy gushed, as she quickly made a note in one of the many folders that she had brought with her. "Now onto the-"

"Darcy, do you think we could take a quick break? I just need to go and find Charles to make sure that everything is alright."

"Oh, of course."

Jane didn't wait a moment longer with the expected pleasantries, she was up and out of her seat before Darcy had finished responding to her. She quickly made her way out of the room and deeper into the house in search of the man who had ditched her.

"There you are." Jane sighed in frustration as she saw him standing out on the ground floor patio. Charles was doing what Charles apparently did best; he was staring out over his domain like some kind of all-powerful emperor. Except all of his power depended on whether or not he was going to pull his finger out and actually help Jane with planning the wedding.

"Are you coming back inside?" She asked from the doorway. There wasn't any warmth in her voice as she spoke to him, but Jane also didn't expect him to have any when he spoke to her.

"Do you know that I can't stand that woman's voice?" Charles said, as he extinguished his cigarette.

"I know what you mean." Jane nodded, as she walked over to stand next to him. "But I'm not going to be able to handle her on my own."

"I can't do it." He mumbled.

"Then I'm going to send her home for the day because I can't do this either." Jane said while shaking her head.

"What do you mean you can't do this?" He turned to look at her properly.

"I'm not the one who wants all of this...fuss. She's going on about the different colors as though she has access to an entire rainbow that's only reserved for the rich." Jane knew that she was exaggerating slightly, but she didn't care. "I told you that I didn't want to see you until the wedding."

"I know, but-"

"It's only because my sister and James convinced me to come over and help you out that I'm even here. I should have just ignored their requests and left you to do all of this by yourself, but...I felt sorry for you."

"Thanks?" Charles said with a slight frown on his face.

"I'm not taking pity on you anymore though, not if you're just going to leave me in there on my own like that. Darcy might grate on you, but she does the same to me too. I don't even live here, I don't want to be here."

"Can't you just go and finish up picking all of the colors and then I promise you that I'll handle the next session on my own." Charles said with a grown.

"Honestly, you sound like a petulant child." Jane tutted and shook her head. "And no because apparently it's not as simple as that; if I take too quick a time in picking, she assumes that I

351

haven't properly thought my options through, and if I take too long, then she doesn't think I'm sure enough to have made a decisive decision. I can't win!"

"What do you want me to do about it?" Charles asked, while scrunching up his nose slightly.

"I'm done for today."

"No-"

"I can't sit in that room anymore, it's making me nauseous." Jane said, while holding up a hand. "I've had my wedding quota for the day, I simply can't make another decision about this damned event."

"All right, but you're going to have to go in there and tell her that we can't do any more today."

"Why can't you go in there and do it? You were the one who hired her, I just want to go and sign the piece of paper that legally states we're married. That way it's all over and done with."

"You know that we can't do that." Charles said with a frustrated groan. "My uncle has already managed to sucker me out of this money once, and the only way I'm going to be able to get it back is by pretending that you and I, honey, are in love."

Jane glared at him as Charles gave her a rather pointed look. Neither of them wanted to spend as much time together as they had been, and Jane was simply looking forward to the time when they would be able to go their separate ways. She couldn't wait for that final day, the day when she wouldn't have to see him again. The only time she would ever encounter him would be in court to settle their divorce proceedings.

"Alright, but I'm sending the wedding planner home for the day, *honey*." Jane said while continuing to glare at him. She liked to think, if looks could kill, she would have just started

352

the far more exciting story of how she had been a gold digger all along and was only after his money. But Charles was still before her and trying his best not to look too affected by her angry looks.

"Fine, as long as everything is done for the date, I don't care what happens." Charles said with a shrug.

"Fine." Jane nodded as she turned toward the back door. "I'm going to go and tell her now that it's you who's calling this off though. Pretend you have stomach cramps or something."

She caught the way that he was rolling his eyes at her as she stepped back into the house. Jane hated that he was treating her in the same way that he treated the other people who worked for him; they were just there to pick up the pieces of his life and solve his problems for him. They would be the ones to have the difficult conversations so that he could just lounge in his garden and smoke himself into an early grave.

CHAPTER 2

Charles waited for the click of the door before relaxing his posture. He couldn't believe her sometimes and found it difficult that Jane was going to be around a lot more. He knew that he wouldn't be able to pull this off without her, but that didn't make her any easier to bear at certain times. He could tolerate her almost as little as the wedding planner. He thought back to when nobody had known where she was and how much they had all worried about her. Judging by her attitude upon her return, Charles felt like a fool for ever caring about her. She could at least pretend to be happy about what was going on since he was going to be paying her a lot of money for the trouble. He didn't understand how she could be so rude to him when there was a life changing amount of money on the table for her.

But then he thought of the reason that she had run off in the first place. It still left a bad taste in his mouth that his father had done business with such a sleazy medical insurance company. It didn't make sense to him even when he looked at the yields of the company as to why he would have even thought it was that impressive of a business model to invest in. Since then, he'd made sure to pull their stake out of the company. It hadn't exactly been a popular decision within the investor world, but Charles knew that it was better to appease the woman that he was due to marry than some old men in gray suits. Business had become about picking his battles very carefully. Charles had decided not to test the limits of Jane, and he figured that if he revealed this fact to her, that it would help her to come around slightly.

"Has she gone?" Charles called at the sound of the door clicking behind him. He didn't turn around as he awaited the voice to reveal who they were, although he assumed it would be Jane.

"Who do you mean?" Anna's voice came. "Jane's left and so has the wedding planner."

"Ah." Charles muttered, as he tried to stop himself from shaking his head.

That girl was going to be the death of him. She knew exactly how to infuriate him without even trying too hard. He found it quite a clever skill, but just not when it was aimed at him.

"I was just coming to ask when you would like dinner."

"I don't know, I'm not hungry yet."

Charles was aware that he still sounded like an annoyed child, and he really didn't mean to take it out on his housekeeper, but Jane was just able to get under his skin.

"You should try and tolerate her a little more, you know?"

"Who do you mean?" Charles asked, as he turned around. "Jane or the wedding planner?"

"Very funny, Sir," Anna responded dryly. "I mean Jane. Although you should probably be a bit nicer to the wedding planner too."

"Have I been coming across that rudely?"

"Well, you have been rather dismissive of Jane when she's been talking to you."

"Talking at me." Charles corrected his housekeeper. "All she does is complain."

"That's all you do, Sir." Charles shot her a look, but Anna didn't apologize. Instead, she merely sighed and shrugged.

"I don't know how you want me to be, Jane just gets on my nerves so easily." Charles said, as he glanced back out at his surroundings. "I know that the wedding planner is annoying, that's why I'm out here. You would think with the amount that I'm paying her that she could stomach a few more hours of it."

"If I'm being too plain with my words, do tell me." Anna started. Charles was in half of a mind to remind her that she was always too plain with her words. "But I do think that you should be a little more sympathetic to her position. She doesn't even want the big wedding, so it doesn't seem fair for her to have to plan it on her own."

"I've been helping."

Although, judging by the look that Anna was throwing at him, he knew that he wasn't fooling anyone.

"No offense, but I've been around when that woman is here. You've not been of too much help now, have you?"

He didn't say anything, but he didn't have to. She had found him out and there was no denying the truth any longer. Charles pursed his lips and shook his head. Anna was talking to him as though she was his mother, and he was starting to regret confiding in her so much. But she was the only one that was able to keep him in check most of the time. He would tell James something, but his cousin would merely 'advise' him on the best thing to do without really enforcing it.

"When's the next wedding session."

"Tomorrow." Charles grumbled.

"You need to make more of an effort with this." Anna told him straight. "Otherwise, you're going to have a runaway bride, the sequel, on your hands."

Charles groaned at her comment, but he knew that she was right. If he continued to push Jane away again, she would only do something rash and jeopardize his entire plan once more.

"Fine, I'll try and make more of an effort tomorrow." He nodded to her. "But I'm not sure that I can make any promises on that front."

"It's better than nothing, I suppose." Anna said with a light chuckle. "You really can be difficult sometimes, did you know that?"

"I've been told a few times." Charles said. He kept his tone monotonous as he sat down in a chair on the patio. The weather was rather overcast that day, but he felt that it matched his brooding mood. "God, I just don't know if we're really going to be able to pull this off."

"I've got faith in you, Sir if that's any consolation."

"Thanks, Anna." Charles nodded. "I know that you're looking for a pay rise though, so I'm not sure about how much it's going to really help me."

"You did say that I would be able to help plan your wedding."

"Do you really think that we would have got anything done together?" Charles asked with an amused smirk playing on his lips. "You know as well as I do that we would have spent about ninety percent of the time just arguing about childish things. I don't think we would have ever been able to plan something on this scale."

Anna chuckled but nodded in agreement.

"It would have been a lot of work, but it would have been a real feat to see it come to life in the end." She said with a small smile. "I also wouldn't have made you pick the color of every small detail."

"I swear that this woman is just wasting our time on those small things. They really don't need to be that complicated do they?"

Anna thought about his comment for a moment before speaking, and Charles was slightly scared to hear what she had to say.

"With all due respect." She started. "You're Charles Bentley. When people think of your wedding, they don't think of an event that has just been thrown together in a matter of weeks.

They think of the kind of event that holds a bit of prestige to it, the kind that will show those sorts of attention to details. I know that it may be a lot to deal with, but if you really want this to work, then I suppose this Darcy woman is your best bet."

He didn't like the fact that Anna was right on this occasion. Darcy really was going to be their best bet when it came to convincing people like Tucker and his uncle that they really were in love and cared deeply about the wedding. Charles thought about how his uncle was planning to throw him off.

"What do you think my Uncle will do?" He asked out loud with narrowed eyes. He was simply curious as to what Anna would say in response to this.

"On the day of the wedding?" Anna asked with narrowed eyes.

"He's not going to let me enjoy it and then take the inheritance from his account without putting up some kind of fight." Charles was aware that he was simply thinking out loud.

"Ah, I see." Anna nodded. "I think you're wise to be preparing for some kind of attack already. It's quite a sad truth that he is going to do something, but I don't think I'm evil enough to anticipate what he will do."

"He really could do anything." Charles breathed out. "He really could go to the most extreme lengths to ruin this entire event. We're just going to have to keep watch over him."

"Overwhelm him with the details." Anna offered.

"What?"

"Have all of these details at your wedding that Darcy is offering you. I know you may have turned some of them down already. But just make it look like you've really put your heart and soul into this, and it will be much more difficult for him to unravel it."

Charles blinked a few times in surprise. He really couldn't believe that his housekeeper was offering him such useful advice.

"I suppose that would work." He nodded slowly as he thought it over in his mind. "But that would mean explaining to Jane that she has to spend even more time here with me, I don't think that's the kind of idea that she's going to warm too without any protest."

"I'm sure that if you put it in the way that I've just said, she'll be a little more understanding. At the end of the day, this is all about you getting the money. You both just have to be willing to do whatever it takes. Now if you would excuse me, I'm getting behind on my duties."

"Anna." He stopped her before she could quickly turn around to enter the house.

"Yes, Sir?"

"Have you ever thought about changing places with James?" He asked with a small smile on his face.

"I'm sorry?"

"Well, you just give so much better advice than he does. I figured that you would potentially make better company than him. I also just want to see James using a mop for the day." Charles said with a chuckle.

"I see." Anna smiled at the thought. "That would be an interesting switch, although I'm not sure what I would do all day. I only ever see James lounging on the sofas when he's here."

"I'll tell him you said that." Charles chuckled, as he mockingly warned her.

"Then dinner will be late!" She called back with a smile as she disappeared into the house.

He turned back to the lawn before him with a small smile resting on his lips. He felt slightly better about the entire situation, although he wasn't sure that he was in the mood to reach out to Jane yet after she left so suddenly again.

CHAPTER 3

"You're back early." Helena commented with narrowed eyes as Jane stepped through the door. She was in a sour mood and had been ever since she'd left Charles' house. A light drizzle of rain had started as she drove down the driveway on her moped, but it had graduated to a full on storm by the time she was in the center of town.

Jane arrived home drenched completely, and that hadn't even been the reason that she was in a bad mood.

"Don't." Jane warned her sister as she held up her hand.

"Alright." Helena said while looking at her with wide eyes.

"I don't want to talk about it, I just want to forget about the stupid wedding for the rest of the night."

"Well, on a totally and unfortunately related note, I was just going to tell you about some dates for your diary." Helena said while watching her sister flop down on the couch with a groan.

"What did I just say?"

"We have a very important appointment for wedding dress shopping coming up, and it's the kind of experience that neither of us are realistically going to enjoy again." Helena tried to reason with her sister. "So I think we should just go in there and savor every moment of it."

"Helena, I'm just going to tell you now so that you're not disappointed. I'm not going to enjoy a moment of it, especially because of who's coming with us."

Jane remembered when Charles had told her that Rosalyn wanted to come with her to get her wedding dress. She had laughed at first as she had thought that it was some kind of sick joke, but Charles hadn't laughed at all.

"Think of it this way." Helena sighed, as she moved to sit closer to Jane. "It's going to be you and me, you could even bring some of your old friends as well if you wanted to? I know you haven't been able to see them for a while, so it could be a nice thing to do?"

"I suppose." Jane sighed. "But I just wish Rosalyn wouldn't come."

"We're going to outnumber her." Helena continued. "She's going to be the weak link in this situation, and I'm not going to let her drain the energy out of this event. We're going wedding dress shopping, you're going to spend thousands on a dress with Mr. Bentley's credit card and you're not going to regret it for a second."

Jane couldn't even get excited about it when her sister said it like that. She scrunched up her nose when she thought about all of the other things that she could spend money like that on. It really upset her to think that she was going to be wasting money on a dress that she was only going to end up wearing for one day.

"Don't you think this is all getting a little ridiculous?" Jane asked with a sigh. "We could just go to the registry office and sign the paper at the end of the day. Nothing more to it than that."

"You know that's not the case, and Charles has already told you this on multiple occasions."

"Helena." Jane said, a little harsher than she had planned to. "I don't think you understand how painful this is going to be for me."

"I understand completely, it's going to be the same for me. I'm going to be by your side all the way through it, I'm your maid of honor after all. I'll even start coming to some of the planning sessions to help if you need."

That was exactly what Jane needed to hear. She let her eyes close for a moment as Helena's offer felt like a slight weight off of her shoulders.

"Thank you." She muttered and nodded in her direction.

"It's all right, but I don't understand how planning the wedding can really be that bad."

Jane smirked as she realized that Helena was yet to properly meet Darcy and take part in one of her grueling meetings. It was that thought alone that put a new spring in Jane's step at the thought of Helena attending the next meeting with her.

*****

Helena suddenly regretted ever telling Jane that this was all going to be a walk in the park in terms of dealing with the wedding planner. She could suddenly understand why both Jane and Charles had been so reluctant to work with the poor woman. Darcy was the kind of person that wouldn't stop until every single detail had been so meticulously planned that there really wasn't anything else that could be done.

Helena sat in her first meeting with the bubbly woman only the next day after she had told Jane to relax about it all. Darcy was stressing her out with only her tone of voice, let alone the many options that she was giving her in regard to the flower arrangements.

"Do you know how many bridesmaids there's going to be?"

"No." Helena said, as she turned back into the conversation.

The meeting had started off with both Jane and Charles present, but they had both managed to wriggle out of it with various excuses a little earlier on. Helena had felt overwhelmed before, but now that it was just her left to do everything, it suddenly didn't feel as fun as she had been expecting. Helena thought about when they were younger; they had watched wedding shows on TV and spoken about it with their mom, Helena

363

remembered how excited she'd been at the thought of walking down the aisle in a white dress. It was a dream that had slowly fizzled out over the years. Nowadays, she dreamed of merely having a stable and safe job to keep a roof over her head. The big white wedding felt as far off to her as that of a coronation; the kind of event that all little girls dream of, becoming a princess and a bride were both visions that Helena couldn't exactly see herself ascending to.

This was the closest that she thought she would ever get to having a wedding of her own, and it was for her sister - who didn't even want to go to her own wedding. Helena tried to keep her expression in a friendly smile as the woman before her continued to speak.

"Alright, well Jane told me that it's going to be a relatively small wedding, right? So we're going to need the dresses and flowers that the bridesmaids have to pop. If there's not going to be that many of you, then the color is going to have to be perfect."

"I don't think I really want to stand out that much," Helena said with a small shrug. "It's Jane's big day, isn't she the one who-"

"Nonsense! She's going to have her beautiful, big, white dress that's going to do all of the talking for her. That's going to be her big statement that this is her wedding, you're the next best thing to stand out."

Helena wasn't sure if she was meant to take that as a compliment as she nodded slowly. However, she kept her eyes narrowed as she thought about the color of the dress that she'd like to wear.

"Now to make sure that you're going to compliment the decor around you, I don't think that you should try and go for a dress in a store." Darcy continued.

Helena was slightly distracted for a moment by the bright red lipstick on the woman's lips that seemed to exaggerate that feature. It was evident enough without the lipstick that Darcy liked to talk, but the bright red color felt so out of place and rather dramatic.

"Not from a store?" Helena frowned, as she tried to think of what the alternative would be. "I don't understand."

"So, I took the liberty of finding some different fabrics from this really nice fabric store in town." Darcy said, as she dipped a hand into her handbag. Helena was reminded of that scene from Mary Poppins where she would have an outrageous amount of things in her bag. Just when she thought that there wasn't anything else that they could possibly talk about during the meeting; Darcy seemed prepared with a whole new subject of decisions.

"I think that these colors would just look so good with the flowers that will be around the aisle," She gushed, as she showed the small samples of different fabrics.

Helena did have to give credit to the woman, she knew what she was talking about. Each of the colors was a pastel shade of purple or blue, but they all appeared as though they would compliment her dark hair and skin tone well. Helena smiled at the five different colors in front of her at the thought of how they would indeed look good on her.

"I was thinking that this blue would work, but of course, it's completely up to the maid of honor." She beamed up at Helena.

"What will be done with the fabric when I choose what color?"

"Well, depending on how many bridesmaids you have, I'll send the fabric to a designer who will mock up some different styles of dresses. I think it would look rather good if you all had the same color with a slightly different cut of dress."

Helena was slightly overwhelmed by the number of things that Darcy had 'thought about' as though it had just been an idea she'd had on a whim. The kinds of ideas that she was having sounded like the type that would take place at a royal wedding or something similar to that. She thought back to how drained Jane had looked when she'd walked through the door the day before. All of a sudden, Helena could understand why her sister had looked the way that she did because it was exactly how Helena was feeling at that moment.

"Alright." Darcy announced, as she sat back for a moment. "So there's just a few things for you to think about and obviously feedback to the pride. Have you spoken much to the best man? I want the two of you to coordinate in any way that you can."

Helena was incredibly grateful that she had managed to fix the fake smile onto her face for a long time without letting it drop. She was sure if she hadn't spent the past few hours practicing such a look, her expression would have dropped at this. She knew that it was wrong of her, but she really had been avoiding James since they'd got back from their little trip to find her sister. Helena bit her lip as she thought about how strange things had been with him, but she continued to deny that she didn't feel anything for him. She was sure that he didn't feel anything for her either and that it had all just been symptoms of cabin fever after spending so much time in a car with him.

"Uh...no, I haven't spoken to him that much." Helena shook her head, as she looked down at her lap for a moment.

"All right, well I would suggest that the two of you get better acquainted." Darcy recommended. Helena wanted to scoff if only she knew. "It always pleases the bride and groom a lot more when the best man and the maid of honor get along well. Did you...James already?"

"Uh..." Helena wasn't sure what to say for a moment. "Yes...well, kind of. I've seen him around here and I've spent some time with him..."

"Alright, well then there's some homework for you. I think that the two of you should try and spend some time together and get to know one another." Darcy said with a small smile on her face. "Perhaps he could come to the next meeting as well and take a bit of the load off of you, I know that all of this stuff can be a lot to take on."

"It's not too bad." Helena tried to brush it off, although she was absolutely exhausted.

She couldn't help but feel slightly amused at the idea of James having to sit through one of those meetings too. It would be like sitting next to him in the car all over again, except she was now going to have to act as though they had become great friends in front of Darcy. Helena felt her amusement wane at that rather grim realization. She shuddered at the thought but kept her expression rather neutral. All she focused on was how she was going to kill her sister when she could finally get out of that room to do so.

CHAPTER 4

She smirked as James arrived for the day of wedding planning while appearing none the wiser about what he was about to enter into. Helena couldn't help but chuckle as he nodded to her with a small smile.

"You don't speak to me for ages and then laugh at me when we're finally forced to sit in a room together for hours?" He asked, while cocking his eyebrow up at her.

"I'm sorry." She said while biting her lip. "I really am, but I don't think that you know what you've actually signed up for here."

"What's that supposed to mean?" He asked with narrowed eyes.

"I don't suppose you've spoken to Charles recently?"

"Not in the last few days, I actually have a life outside of this house. Why? Where is he?"

"He's just through there." She gestured deeper within the grand mansion. "Just you wait until you meet with the wedding planner?"

"She can't be that bad, can she?" He asked with narrowed eyes.

Helena was pleased that she could bridge the awkwardness of the fact that she hadn't been in contact with him much since their trip by deflecting the subject onto their current situation. Although, she was more than sure that he was going to want to sit down and talk about it at some point. Helena didn't feel as though there was much that needed to be said, and she knew that she was going to hold her ground on that.

"She's not bad." Helena said, as she shook her head. "She's just...a lot."

"Is that why neither the bride or groom are here today?" James asked with a small smile.

"Believe me, I think they've both had their fill of Darcy for the rest of the month."

James was frowning at her, but Helena simply shrugged in response. She knew that he would understand in due course, it was just going to be a matter of when he finally met her.

"What if she's actually all right and you're just doing this to avoid talking to me properly?" He asked with narrowed eyes.

"What are you talking about?" Helena asked in shock. "I am talking to you properly right now, how is this not talking properly?"

"You know what I mean." He said, as he shot her a look.

"Alright." Another voice entered the hallway as Darcy appeared in the wake of her clicking heels against the stone floor. "Ready to do this?"

"Anna." Helena said, as she quickly caught the housekeeper. "Could you grab us some refreshments for this meeting?"

"Of course." She nodded before scurrying off.

Helena knew that if she was going to get through this meeting in one piece, she was going to have to keep herself occupied. She wasn't sure if James would sit through the entire thing with her or if he'd dip out in the same way that Charles had done to Jane, but she was going to need snacks to get through it either way.

"Let's do this." James muttered, as he walked first into the room.

Helena didn't want to miss a moment of the realization dawning on him that he was in over his head.

"I hope you don't mind, but I brought two assistants today so that we could get through even more things before the end of the meeting." Darcy waved it off as though it were nothing. However, Helena could feel her heart sinking already when she saw the number of folders that were waiting for their turn on the coffee table. It was already mid-morning, but she knew that there was a long day ahead of them.

"Now, normally a lot of this is spread out over other days, but we don't have too much time with this particular event." Darcy explained, as she started to rearrange some of the folders. Helena could see just how much paperwork was in some of them and she tried to stop herself from wincing at the thought of having to do all of this work.

She wasn't being paid to be there like Darcy was, and so she felt as though she was being held captive by the world's most detail-orientated wedding planner.

"I'm sure we can get through it." James smiled from his seat beside her.

"That's the spirit, James!" She beamed at him.

Helena had to stop herself from rolling her eyes. Of course, he was going to get on well with the wedding planner too. He was always acting like he was the perfect child, and this was only reinforcing that in her mind.

"Now then, first thing first. James, this is going to be the color of Helena's dress, so we're going to have a tie made for you in the same material. Is that all right?"

She could see the smile slightly falter on his face as he glanced down at the small sample of the fabric that she had passed him. It wasn't an awful color on him, but Helena knew that he wasn't really thinking about the tie.

He was clearly having the same realization that she'd had the day before. It was the realization that just when you thought there couldn't possibly be a detail that was too small for her to pick at, Darcy would find it.

"Uh...yeah, that's fine."

As the hours continued on, Helena had noticed that there was a lot less enthusiasm in James' voice. The questions just kept coming no matter what, and Helena was praying to anyone that was willing to listen that each one would be the last. It seemed that her prayers were only answered by the chiming of the large grandfather clock in the corner of the room.

"I say that we should stop for some lunch." Helena suddenly announced. She sat up a little straighter at her own idea as it would give her the perfect reprieve from all of the concentration on things that really shouldn't matter.

"You weren't joking." James muttered to her almost as soon as the two of them were alone.

"Do you really think that this would be the kind of thing that I'd joke about?" Helena asked. She couldn't quite manage to wipe the slight look of amusement on her face at his reaction. She knew that it would be too good to be true that he would tolerate Darcy and her hundreds of questions.

"The woman is so anal about *everything*." He said with a groan. "Down to every single detail."

"She really has thought of it all." Helena nodded.

"How long do you think we'll get away with saying we're on a break for lunch?" He asked slowly while glancing around.

James had directed Helena into the library before she could join Charles out on the patio, and she hadn't complained at the opportunity to hear his thoughts.

"Not long enough."

"This is insane." James said, as he ran a hand through his hair. "I knew that Charles wanted everything to be perfect, but I didn't think that he would actually find someone who embodies perfection like that."

"I know, it's quite insane, isn't it?" Helena spoke in a low voice.

She was terrified that the poor woman would hear them talking about her. She couldn't think of anything worse than upsetting the only person who actually cared for the wedding.

"I mean, it's definitely going to have my uncle and aunt very shocked. I don't think they'll expect this much effort."

"I don't think anyone will." Helena said while shaking her head. "I don't think even Jane or Charles thought that it was going to involve so much."

She knew that he couldn't deny that. Jane and Charles clearly didn't like one another, and the excessive planning was doing nothing but putting more strain on their already very strained relationship.

"What do we do if this doesn't go to plan? It's going to be a lot of wasted time from a lot of people."

"We're just going to have to hope that the plan works." Helena said with a mere shrug. "I don't know what more we can do."

James was silent for a moment as he nodded slowly. Helena could practically hear the cogs turning in his mind as he thought about the very thing that she didn't want him to bring up.

"So, are we going to talk about our own friendship?"

Helena scrunched up her nose at the way he'd phrased the question.

"No." She muttered. "There's nothing to say. I still don't like you or your family that much, but I have to tolerate you. I'm grateful for how you helped me find my sister, but I don't think there's anything that I can say beyond that."

James pursed his lips upon hearing her say this as he nodded slowly. It clearly hadn't been the blunt answer that he was expecting, but Helena wasn't sorry for what she'd said. She wanted to establish a clear boundary with the unusually attractive man in front of her. It was clear that something had changed between them, they'd grown closer after spending such an extended period of time together, but Helena had enough on her plate with worrying about her sister's wedding. She didn't feel the need to complicate things any further.

"Oh." Was all he could say in response.

"I'm sorry, but I really don't know what else you expected me to say." Helena said.

"I thought we were on the way to becoming better friends than this." James shrugged.

"We are, but I still don't like your family."

"Understandable." He mumbled while looking down.

He moved away from her slowly to give her some more space. Helena had barely realized just how close they had gotten while talking in quieter voices. She bit her lip and tried to think of something to say that would break through the awkward tension that now stood between them.

"I'm going to go and get some lunch?" She gestured to the door.

"Good plan." James nodded.

Helena walked in front as she started out the back door to where Charles was waiting. Darcy was sitting at the glass table and clearly enjoying the view of the lawn.

"I just think it's going to be such a magical day out here in a couple of weeks." She gushed, as she stared out.

Helena turned to the lawn in front of her and tried to imagine the large marques that Darcy had told her about. It was incredibly useful that Charles had a good amount of land for them to use, it made escaping into the familiarity of his house from the wedding much easier.

One glance in James' direction told Helena all that she needed to know about how much he wished that he wasn't listening to Darcy droning on about the wedding again.

"It should be a lovely day out here." She agreed while managing a small smile.

Helena made sure to take a seat at the table that would mean she wasn't directly next to the wedding planner. The last thing that she wanted while on a break from all of the decision making was to talk more about the event that had consumed her morning.

She could feel James glaring at her as he slowly sat down in the seat on Darcy's left. Even from across the table, Helena could see the reluctance in his actions to do so. But he didn't really have a choice as there were only two other seats; it was either sit on her left, or on her right.

CHAPTER 5

"I don't know how much longer I can go on like this." Charles groaned, as he lay sprawled on the sofa in the library. He held a glass of scotch in his hand as he tried not to think about the pressing deadline of the wedding that was approaching much quicker than he had anticipated.

"At least you have someone very dedicated to the case." James responded from the other sofa with a light chuckle.

"I don't even know how you're able to joke about it after enduring most of the day in that room with her." Charles said with a heavy sigh.

"Are you talking about the wedding planner or Helena? Both were rather grueling."

"Don't act like you didn't enjoy the big sister's company." Charles said with a small smirk as he glanced over at his cousin.

He wasn't sure if it was the scotch that James was drinking, the heat from the fire, or the mention of Helen Miller, but James' cheeks were tinted a sudden and rather obvious scarlet.

"I can't stand her." James muttered, but Charles didn't believe him for a second.

"That's how you managed a whole day of it, isn't it?" Charles asked with a coy chuckle. "You were only there because it meant that you could flirt with Helena."

"I didn't...I don't know what you're talking about." He mumbled while glancing into the fire.

"I'm talking about the woman that you find incredibly attractive, even if you won't admit it." Charles continued to smirk over at him.

James opened his mouth to say something, but quickly closed it and looked down at his glass.

"I'm right, aren't I?"

James didn't answer him verbally at first. Instead, he rose from his chair and walked over to one of the shelves. Charles hadn't seen his cousin like this before, and it intrigued him to think that he really was intrigued by someone like Helena.

"Is it that obvious?" James asked, as he dragged a finger along the bottom of one of the shelves. He then inspected the dust that had accumulated on the pad of his finger before brushing it off and turning back to Charles. "Is it?"

"I wouldn't say so."

"But do you think that she suspects something?" James asked again.

"I... she may." Charles said slowly.

"Oh god." James said, as he put a hand up to his face.

"But I don't think that's necessarily a bad thing." Charles tried to save the situation.

"It is a bad thing, Charles, it's a really bad thing." James returned to his seat and held his head in his hands properly after putting down his drink. "She hates our family, just like Jane does. I mean, I understand their reasoning and all, but she would never like someone like me."

Charles frowned as he looked at his cousin. He knew that part of the reason that James was admitting this to him was because of the scotch in his veins, but Charles knew that some of what he was saying must have been true if he was saying it.

"I've not seen you like this before for a girl." Charles remarked. He didn't know what else to say to comfort the man. James was right; both of the women weren't exactly the biggest fans of their family name.

"I know, and I don't think I've ever felt like this before." James admitted as he looked back up at his cousin. "I really don't know what to do about it either."

"Is there anything that can be done?" Charles asked rather carefully. "I mean, we've both seen what she's like when she gets angry. I don't know if you want to be on the brunt end of that."

"Believe me, I've been there before." James sighed sadly. "I don't want to be there again, I really don't. But if that's the worst that will happen to me, maybe I should just tell her how I feel?"

Charles considered this for a moment before a rather selfish thought came into his head. He knew that it was the kind of thought that made him a bad person. He was thinking about number one again, and he knew that sooner or later, karma was going to get him for doing so. But he just had one more request for his cousin.

"Perhaps you should do it a little closer to the wedding? Or perhaps even once it's done? That way things may be a little less tense." Charles asked while wincing slightly.

However, James slowly nodded in response to him. It wasn't exactly the response that Charles had been anticipating, and so he was slightly cautious about it.

"I think that's a good idea." James said while continuing to nod. He reminded Charles of one of those bobble head dolls, but he kept that thought to himself. "Weddings are always happy times, right? Even weird ones like this one. There will still be a moment when Helena will be happy to see her sister in a wedding dress, I'm sure of it. I'll try and catch her during that moment."

Charles wasn't sure that was the best move, it could put her in a pretty bad mood if she really didn't feel the same. However,

Charles didn't want to crush the man in front of him any more than he already seemed to be.

"Alright, that's sorted then." James nodded, as he smiled to himself. "I'm going to do it. I'm going to tell her, and then I'll ask her out."

*****

James felt good about himself as he went to bed that evening. It had been a long and tiring day, but he wanted to put the awkward tension of the wedding planning behind him. He hadn't been able to stop thinking about Helena since their long car trip together. It was a strange sensation within him; one that made him realize that he really did have strong feelings for her.

Dread filled him at the thought of even having to admit that to her. He knew that Helena wouldn't like it, she would make all sorts of comments about how she never thought a guy like him could feel that way for someone like her. He hurt at the idea of her being upset with him over the way that he felt.

It wasn't like he could help it. These were his feelings, ones that he'd been trying to ignore for the longest time, but it seemed that nothing worked. Helena was the only girl that he could think about, even when he wanted to think about others.

James knew that his name and his wealth could get him a lot of places, but it could also get him a lot of girls if he wanted that sort of thing. He thought about all of the women that would jump at such an opportunity and how he'd developed feelings for the one woman who simply didn't want him. Helena didn't like him, that was a truth that James had thought he'd managed to accept. But being out on the road with her, he'd thought that in some way they had managed to move past that somewhat. She had been kinder to him, and the two of them had got on better than either of them could have expected.

He knew that the scotch within him had worked its magic in unraveling his sober thoughts. It had turned them into words that Charles had aided in coaxing out of him. James wasn't sure how he felt about his cousin knowing about this. It was a subject that he'd kept to himself for the past few weeks, and it was now slightly more out in the open than he had originally intended.

James rolled over in his bed as he realized that he was going to have an incredibly difficult time getting to sleep that night. Coming to terms with the thoughts out loud had been a much bigger step than he'd initially realized.

He was still hesitant and terrified about the thought of telling Helena. He wondered if the right moment really did exist, or if he was just going to have to come out and say it one day without properly preparing himself. James shuddered at the thought. He closed his eyes and felt as though he could picture her reaction within his mind. Helena would screw up her face and stare at him in disgust at what he was telling her, he just knew that she wouldn't feel the same way back.

CHAPTER 6

With the sound of her alarm blaring through her speaker alerting her to the doomed reality of the day that lay ahead of her; Jane winced and rolled over slowly. However, she knew that her sister wouldn't let her sleep in that morning, not when such an important task lay ahead of them. But Jane wasn't at all interested in making the decision of what wedding dress she'd wear while walking down the makeshift aisle on Charles's lawn.

"You know what day it is." Helena called from the doorway only a couple of moments later.

"No." Jane groaned, as she turned away from her sister.

"Come on, this is the kind of place where you need an appointment months in advance if you want to even get a look at the dresses." Helena said, as though it was an impressive thing.

"I don't care." Jane groaned. "If it takes months, then how did Charles..."

"Do you really need me to answer that?" Helena sighed from the door.

They both knew that the answer was something that they were both lacking; money.

"I'm not moving from this spot until you show me that you're actually going to make an effort to get up." Helena persisted from the doorway.

"Fine." Jane sighed, as she pushed back her covers. She instantly regretted her rather dramatic move due to the cold that quickly took hold of her body.

"Jane!"

"I'm coming!" She quickly responded to her sister by sitting up too quickly.

"Hurry then, we don't want to be late for this kind of appointment."

Jane didn't care what dress she wore, and she still didn't feel comfortable with spending too much money on it. However, she could tell that her sister was of the complete opposite opinion. Helena seemed surprisingly on board with the idea of throwing money at some white material that Jane was only going to wear once.

"I still can't get as excited about this as you are." Jane said with a huff as she finally emerged from her room ready to go.

"I know, but it's not like we'll get to do this again any time soon, so we should try and enjoy it, right?"

"What if I just found a second hand thing that I could wear." She suggested, as the two of them walked out of the apartment.

"Do you really think that anyone will let you walk down the aisle in something anything less than extravagant?" Helena asked with a chuckle. "Besides, think about how beautiful you'll look."

No matter how hard she tried, Jane just couldn't see herself in some custom dress that would no doubt cost thousands of dollars.

"I really don't know about this." She muttered while shaking her head.

"You'll be fine." Helena reassured her. "I'll be here for the whole day, and I'm sure that whatever you pick will be great."

Jane wished that she had prepared herself a little earlier for the fact that they were going to be meeting Rosalyn in the morning. The sour-faced woman seemed to have a distinct dislike for the early hour, but then again, Jane realized that her expression could have just been her resting face. She was waiting for them outside of the prestigious-looking bridal building that Jane realized she'd driven past countless times. It was the kind of place that looked from the exterior to be like some kind of exclusive club. Knowing that Charles must have bribed his appointment into the books only reaffirmed to Jane that this was some kind of club.

"Good morning, girls." The older woman said while looking down at them both.

Jane could tell that the woman in front of her had dressed up for the event, and she suddenly felt rather underdressed in her sweats. But she then realized that if she was going to be spending her day getting in and out of countless wedding dresses, then this was surely the best outfit choice that she could have made.

"Good morning." Helena's smile looked genuine, but Jane didn't feel up to it.

Rosalyn hadn't exactly smiled at them either, and so Jane didn't waste her energy on trying to please the woman who was soon to be her aunt-in-law.

"Are you both excited?" Jane managed to strike up some form of conversation to clear the awkward tension that had arisen between them.

"Very." Helena nodded, as Jane finally managed to put a small smile on her face.

"It's where I was fitted for my dress." Rosalyn said, as she brushed it off. "They are the best of the best here. I don't know many other places that can do what they do."

Jane couldn't understand how they could possibly be better than the usual bridal store, but she supposed that she was about to find out.

They walked towards the grand entrance that looked like it should have been part of the walkway towards a five star hotel instead of a wedding dress shop. Jane was glancing around in awe at the marble fixtures on the building and just the overall grandeur as a security guard opened the door for them. She tried to keep her expression neutral as she stepped inside and passed the large glass front door, but it was proving a difficult task.

The room was busy with various people waiting for their appointments, but Jane was far too busy to notice their judgmental stares because she was taken back by how clean and sleek everything looked. She felt even intimidated by the way that the building stood before her; the architecture lent itself to that of the interior of a church, and Jane felt as though the building was being robbed with its current purpose.

The floors were marble or white carpet, and she was terrified to walk on either one out of a fear that she might slip over, or dirty the carpet with her sneakers. Jane wished that she'd done a little more research into the place before deciding on what she would wear, but she wasn't about to admit that to anyone.

"Ah, it feels good to be back here." Rosalyn said with a smirk.

She was holding herself suddenly as though she was part of the royal family. Jane let the woman walk a little ahead out of amusement. Rosalyn had puffed out her chest slightly while walking as though she were some kind of peacock. Her sleek outfit suddenly made sense as Jane realized that other women were looking at her with approval. She knew what she was doing, and so far it was clearly Rosalyn that was winning whatever game she was playing.

"Good morning, do you ladies have an appointment?" The woman at the front desk asked as she smiled up at Rosalyn.

Jane caught the way that the woman's smile waned as she glanced at the attire that she and her sister had chosen for such a place.

"Yes, in fact, we do." Rosalyn nodded. Jane noted the way that she had added a tone to her voice that made her sound as though she was from a much higher class. "For Charles Bentely's bride."

"Oh!" The woman exclaimed as she quickly returned her gaze to Jane in slight confusion. "Of course, we were expecting you. If you could just come this way, Coco will be with you shortly."

Jane was suddenly whisked over to a much quieter area of the room that was slightly elevated from the other part of the room. She couldn't help but smile at the way that the other women in the room were glaring, she knew that the only reason she was getting special treatment was because of that damned Bentley name.

She had suddenly ascended to some sort of level of being better than the women around her, a level that was completely foreign to Jane. Staff were offering if she wanted tea, coffee, or perhaps something a little stronger. She was still reeling from the woman's sudden change in treatment from barely acknowledging her to acting as though a famous celebrity had just walked in.

*****

Helena watched her sister in anticipation. She could tell that this was all completely out of her comfort zone, but she simply hoped that Jane would learn to enjoy what was going on and try to at least find some good in the moment. Instead, Jane looked as though she was being forced against her will to be there - which in a way, she technically was.

She wanted to shake some sense into her younger sister, although she didn't want to cause a scene. Helena was even more unnerved by the way that Rosalyn wasn't giving much away. Since they had entered the building, the older woman had been incredibly cold and closed off. She spoke to the staff only if she had to, and she didn't use manners as one of the staff

384

handed her the mimosa that she asked for. Helena stuck to a coffee.

"Right then." The woman who had been on the reception desk said as she walked back over to the three women. "I'll take you through to Coco since I'm sure that you ladies would like a private room to yourselves?"

Helena was still unable to believe the special treatment that they were getting. All they had to do was mention the Bentley name, and they were suddenly being waited on hand and foot. She led the trio down a corridor and after a few turns, they emerged in a beautiful white room. Helena still couldn't quite get over the building; she felt like a kid in a candy shop, while Jane was starting to look like a bull in a china shop. The last thing that they needed was for her to ruin the day. Helena could only imagine if that information was to get back to Jack from Rosalyn. It would be the perfect ammunition that they would use against Charles to rile him up.

"I already have a few designers in mind." Rosalyn was speaking with the receptionist as Helena decided to sit down on the plush couch while they waited.

"Oh that's just great!" The receptionist gushed as she smiled widely at Jane.

"You need to act a little better than that." Helena whispered to Jane through gritted teeth.

She felt as though the two of them had walked into the rich people's lion's den. If they were going to survive an experience like that, then they were going to have to suck up to them in any way that they could.

Helena looked up at the sound of a much more flamboyant voice coming from down one of the hallways. She frowned for a moment until a man burst into the room surrounded by a flurry of assistants.

"Ladies." He said, as he gasped and looked between the three women. "It is an honor to meet you three."

"Coco! It's been too long!" Rosalyn smiled, as she walked over to him and greeted him with a kiss to either cheek. Helena wanted to make a comment about how Rosalyn missed out on the chance to kiss his ass physically as she was clearly going to do it with her words anyway.

"I know, my dear." He chuckled, as he turned to the two sisters.

Helena suddenly felt rather tense under his inquisitive gaze, but she felt her faith in Jane dwindle slightly at the sight of her. She looked as though she was trying to hide within herself from the situation at hand. Helena knew at that moment that there was a long day ahead of them.

CHAPTER 7

Jane stepped up onto the small podium, her entrance was greeted like the other three had been; with a chorus of ooh's.

"It does look good on you." Helena said, as she flashed her sister a reassuring thumbs up. Jane wasn't sure what she would have done if she'd had to go through that experience without her sister. She was sure that she wouldn't have been able to survive trying another one on if she hadn't been there for her.

"I'm not sure about the sleeves." Rosalyn said before turning and whispering something to Coco.

Jane was starting to get fed up with the way that Rosalyn was trying to take over the day. She was coming up with all sorts of designers that sent Coco's assistant's off in a flurry to go and retrieve certain dresses and collections.

She could feel her chest tightening at the thought of having to try on any more and being the center of attention in a room filled with people for a moment more. It seemed that everyone around her was just looking to pick apart another area of her appearance that she hadn't thought about before.

"What about Vera Wang?" Rosalyn asked slightly louder.

"Is that an expensive option?" Jane dared to pipe up.

Her question was met with a few chuckles. Jane figured that they were enough to answer her question. She had already managed to glance at a few of the price tags on the dresses that she'd tried on, and she felt about ready to faint. It really was baffling to her as to why anyone would want to spend so much money on a dress for one day.

"My dear." Coco smiled, as he walked over to her. "I don't think that's something for you to worry about, alright?"

Jane nodded slowly, she knew that Coco was aware of the Bentley's wealth. Rosalyn had clearly come to the best of the best when she'd married into the family too, but Jane wasn't the same kind of person. Sure, she was getting married to Charles so that he could help her financially, but she wasn't lying to him. They both knew where they stood with one another, and that meant that she didn't have to pretend to be affectionate with him or profess to him that she was marrying him for just love.

"I just don't know." Jane sighed, as she glanced at the dress in the mirror. It was rather plain apart from the lace details on the sleeves that Rosalyn hadn't been too sure about. She just wanted a dress that did the job of telling everyone that she was the bride. She didn't feel as though she needed all of the pomp and flair that came with a show stopping gown. Jane certainly didn't want the kind that stuck out and made her look like some kind of cupcake.

"What don't you know about, sweet?" Rosalyn asked with a sudden frown.

Jane remembered what Helena had told her about staying strong and not giving the awful couple anything that would be considered ammunition against them.

"I'm just not sure about the shape of this one." Jane said.

What she really didn't know about was whether or not she'd be able to live with the fact that she was going to have to accept spending so much on a dress that she didn't even care about.

"Alright, well we'll have you try on some Vera Wang ones." Rosalyn brushed it off. "They're much more...dramatic than these traditional shapes."

That wasn't at all of any comfort to her, but Jane nodded so that she simply didn't have to talk to the woman anymore.

"What about one of the second hand ones?" Jane spoke up rather innocently.

"What?" Rosalyn asked with a chuckle.

"Well, they aren't as expensive, are they?" Jane offered.

She could see her sister shaking her head from the couch, but Jane couldn't hold back anymore.

"I don't think it would look too good if Charles Bentley's wife was in a second hand dress." Rosalyn chuckled, as she looked Jane up and down. "But I suppose that if the shoe fits."

Jane found herself fighting hard to not react to the bait. She glared at the woman in front of her but didn't say another word. She could feel that her nostrils were flared, but Helena was quickly at her side and squeezing her arm gently.

"Let's just try on a few more." She muttered. "Alright?"

"I told you." Jane spoke in a low voice to her sister as Rosalyn moved away from them. "I really don't want to do this anymore."

"Jane." Helena's tone was much harsher. "Just try on the damned dresses."

She could feel panic welling up inside of her as she tried to breathe normally, but it was proving to be a challenge for her. Jane wasn't sure if it was the tight dress that was pushing against her ribs or if it was just worry, but suddenly, breathing felt incredibly difficult.

Jane tried to get off of the podium as quickly as she could, but it was proving to be a lot harder than she had initially thought.

"Jane, honey." Rosalyn called to her. "The Vera Wang one will be here in a minute, and then we'll look at other options."

The older woman then went back to talking with the assistant. Jane cringed as she heard some of the figures that were being thrown around; she wasn't just talking about the thousands, she was now talking about pushing into the tens of thousands for a damned dress.

"I can't do this." Jane muttered, as she quickly rushed back behind the curtain.

"Jane!" She could hear people calling for her.

"I'll just be a minute!" She managed to say as her voice wobbled.

She winced at the way that the panic was starting to sting within her. Jane used to have panic attacks when she had been growing up, but it was one of those things that she hadn't had for a very long time. The closest that she had been to having one recently was when Helena had told her about the Bentley's involvement with her mother's death.

"Come on." She whispered to herself as she put her hands on her hips and tried to breathe normally.

"Are you alright in here, Sweetie?" One of the women asked, as she poked her head around the curtain.

"I'm fine." Jane said, a little harshly. She felt as though it were an invasion of her privacy to be coming in without asking. She knew that it was only a matter of time before her sister would be coming in to try and help her, but Jane just didn't want Rosalyn to see her like this. Tears were blurring her vision as she tried to process what was happening.

"You're going to be okay." She whispered to herself as she ran her fingers through her hair.

It seemed that no matter what she did, it didn't help the way that she was feeling.

"Jane?"

"In here." She called weakly.

Helena's frown melted away as she saw her sister hugging her arms to her chest and crying silently.

"Hey." She spoke in a much softer voice. "It's all right, you're going to be alright."

"I can't do this, Helena." Jane cried into her shoulder. "I've tried, I really have, but I can't do this. I'm not used to all of...this kind of stuff, and I can't spend that much money on a dress."

"I know that it seems like a lot, and I know that it must be very overwhelming for you right now. You're just going to have to breathe through this and try to find a way to cope."

Helena had always been good at giving the kind of advice that was both comforting and useful; she wasn't overly sappy with her just to try and get her to feel better, she was productive in the way that she comforted her sister.

"I just need you to play along for a couple more hours. You've been so good up until this point, and I know that you've got it in you."

Jane thought about the idea of going back out there and trying on, even more, dresses after this. There was nothing that she wanted to do more than to simply go home and curl up in a ball in her bed.

"I don't think I can." Jane shook her head. "I won't be able to wear a dress that is this expensive on the day, I know I won't. What if I get it dirty? Could you imagine the bill to have it dry cleaned?"

"Hey, hey." Helena took hold of her hands and squeezed them gently. "Stop worrying about things like that. It's in the future yet, you don't have to worry at the moment about it. Just worry about keeping a brave face on like you have been all morning."

"Can you try and find some second hand ones?" Jane sniffled, as she glanced down at the expensive dress she was wearing. She was terrified of getting a mark on any of them and then having to buy them anyway. "I just can't stand the idea of wasting money on material like this."

"You're marrying into the wrong family if that's your worry." Helena said with a small smile. "I'm sorry, I know this is difficult. It's not exactly the easiest thing to watch either."

"I just want to be in a comfortable dress that has more sentimental value than anything else."

"I know, I'll see what I can do. You dry your eyes and then wait here. I know that Rosalyn still has a few dresses that she would like for you to try on if that's alright?"

Jane was in half a mind to say no, but she knew that it would cause the least amount of trouble if she were to just go along with it.

"Alright." She nodded with a weary sigh. "But I'm not sure I'm going to be good at being enthusiastic about any of them."

"Don't worry about that, let's just get through the day in any way that we can."

*****

Helena held her breath as she stepped back through the curtain and walked back into the room.

"Is she alright?" Rosalyn asked with a rather judgmental frown.

"She's fine." Helena nodded. "She just sometimes gets in her own head about things. I think Jane's just overwhelmed about how expensive some of the dresses are."

"She should just get over it." Rosalyn waved her hand as she laughed with one of the assistants. "It's not like the girl is paying a penny for the wedding, is it?"

Helena clenched her fists as she looked at the woman in front of her. She wondered what would be the worst thing that would happen if she let rip about how she really felt about Rosalyn. But Helena managed to keep her anger in check this time; she had just told Jane to tolerate this day, and so she couldn't go and be a hypocrite about it.

"I was wondering." Helena spoke in a quieter voice to Coco. "Do you have any second hand dresses around here?"

Coco and the assistant closest to him looked as though Helena had just asked one of the most offensive things in the world. His eyes bulged as he stared at her as though she had just sprouted another head.

"I'm sorry?" He asked, with a slight chuckle of disbelief.

"Well, it's just that my sister and I are always very cautious about the environment." Helena said, as she thought quickly about an excuse. She knew that it was quite a feeble way to excuse her question, but she was hoping that it would work. "We know the amount of material and energy that goes into making these fine gowns. Jane has always had this idea of making a more...vintage statement with her wedding dress."

Helena was trying to think back to the wedding TV shows that she caught the end of whenever she flicked through the channels. She wasn't exactly the kind of person who was clued up on her knowledge of the fashion world, but she was hoping that she had done enough. Helena had learned over the last few weeks that if you sounded entitled enough, people tended to listen to you more.

"I see..." Coco said, slowly as he narrowed his eyes. He was clearly thinking about this and the smile had slipped off of his expression. "That would be rather iconic."

"I mean, I know that there will be members of the press there on the day." Helena continued. She could see out of her peripheral vision that Rosalyn's head had snapped in her direction very suddenly. "I think it would just be the perfect message to show that we're an environmentally conscious family and we have a strong link with our past."

"Oh, I really love that." Coco nodded as his smile returned. "Yes, yes, that would be perfect!"

Helena realized that all they had needed to do was replace the word secondhand with vintage and she had all of the assistants in the room buzzing.

"Great." Helena smiled. "I'll let you have a think about that idea."

She turned around to see that the older woman was glaring at her. Helena placed a smile on her face in response. It constantly felt as though she was battling against Rosalyn in a silent war of expressions and snide remarks, but Helena felt as though in this situation, she had the upper hand. However, she didn't let herself get too cocky; she knew that she had merely won one of the battles, but the war of the wedding was still very much ongoing.

"Vintage?" Rosalyn commented with a slight smirk as Helena sat back down on the sofa near her. "I suppose you want to go for the cheaper option because that will save money. If Charles isn't getting the inheritance, then I suppose a Vera Wang would technically be out of his price range."

"We never said that." Helena said with a small smile.

She wasn't sure what Charles had planned in terms of getting his money back from his uncle, but all she could do was hope that he really did have a plan to get it back.

After that comment, Helena made a point of ignoring the small comments that the sour woman was saying from next to her. She didn't like the way that Rosalyn was getting under her skin, but she wasn't going to let her succeed with her plan. Helena sucked in a deep breath and glanced at the clock. Their appointment was still for a couple more hours, all she could do was hope that her and her sister would get out of this in one piece.

CHAPTER 8

"How was it?" Charles asked with a welcoming smile as the Miller sisters walked in. Jane shook her head and went straight upstairs as Helena walked over to where he stood with James. "Was it really that bad?"

"It was...eventful." Helena said with a slight shrug.

He narrowed his eyes at her comment, not fully understanding what she was going on about.

"I thought that it would be a good day out for you girls? Isn't it supposed to be the part that the bride enjoys the most?" Charles asked in confusion as he looked between James and Helena.

"I suppose it is, if your bride actually wants to get married." James said in an attempt to reason with him.

Charles sometimes had to remind himself that Jane really was against the idea of marrying him, despite the fact that there was so much in it for her.

"Ah." He nodded slowly. "I suppose that would make some sense."

"Did you agree on a dress?" James asked, as he turned to Helena.

Charles tried not to roll his eyes at his excuse to talk to Helena. It was becoming more and more obvious to him that he had feelings for her, but Charles simply hoped that he would bide his time in telling her.

"I think so." Helena nodded slowly. "I'll warn you though, Charles, it's nothing flashy."

"What's that supposed to mean?"

"She went for something...vintage, it's not one of the newest in season...or whatever you call it."

It seemed that Helena was just as clueless about the business of wedding dresses as he was. Charles wasn't sure if her statement was supposed to make him worried or not, and as he turned to James, he had a similar look on his face.

"I suppose it shouldn't matter as long as she's wearing a white dress?" He asked with a slight frown.

"That's the same attitude that Jane had." Helena nodded.

"Then what was the issue?"

"Rosalyn."

That was the only word that Helena had to say for Charles to understand perfectly how the day could have turned so sour. His aunt wasn't exactly known for being friendly, especially not to the two girls. It had been her request to accompany them, and Charles knew that there was no point in refusing her something like that. He'd thought that she would have behaved since they were around other people too, but it seemed that wasn't the case.

"Was she really that awful?" He asked with a wince.

"She knew everything about wedding dresses, I think she should seriously consider a professional career in it." Helena said while rolling her eyes. "She was pressuring Jane to try on all sorts and throwing around fancy names as though they meant anything to either of us."

"I see." Charles said, as he pursed his lips.

"She was just really rude for the entire day, but I didn't bite to her comments." Helena said with a proud smile on her face.

"Good, I think we're all going to have to take a page out of your book when it comes to the rehearsal dinner and all of the various events leading up to the big day."

"About that." Helena continued. "Rosalyn told me to let you know that she'll be coming around for lunch tomorrow. She said that she wants to speak with you."

"No doubt that I'll get the other side of the story then." Charles muttered. He knew that his expression mirrored that of someone who had just eaten something foul. But he couldn't help it, that was simply the way that his face automatically reacted at even the mention of his aunt.

"I think I'm busy tomorrow." James muttered, earning a glare from his cousin.

"Great, then I shall host my aunt on my own." He said with a heavy sigh. "How is Jane?"

"I think she's just tired from the long day, it really was quite grueling for her to be scrutinized in front of so many people. Also, those wedding dresses are heavy."

"Is it worth trying to speak to her now?"

"I don't think so." Helena said, as she shook her head. "I'll take her home and let you prepare for your special guest tomorrow."

"Great." Charles let out a groan at the thought of having to spend a long amount of time alone with Rosalyn. He could think of a million things that he would rather do instead, some of them were quite unappealing, but almost anything was better than spending time with his aunt.

*****

Charles wasn't even hungry for lunch the next day, he was too busy preparing himself to have the most amount of patience that he had ever possessed. He promised himself that no matter what, he wasn't going to lose it at the woman and ruin the wedding preparations.

"Charles." She smiled sweetly while stepping through the door.

"Always a pleasure, Aunt Rosalyn." He smiled and kissed her cheek.

He felt like he was already doing some sort of dance with a venomous serpent, doing whatever was necessary to stop her from attacking him. Charles led her through to the terrace out the back of the house to where a table was prepared for their lunch.

"How lovely." She smiled, as her heels clicked against the stone floors.

His aunt had always reminded him of some kind of slender monster; she was slightly taller than his uncle and her height only heightened itself to the way that she liked to try and intimidate everyone.

"How have you been?" Charles asked, as he took a seat opposite her.

Normally there would be other people present at such an event, and so he was slightly thrown off by the way that all of her attention was on him. It would remain that way for the entirety of the lunch, and he suddenly felt as though there was a lot more pressure on him. Charles then realized that this was exactly how she wanted him to feel. He sat up a little taller and sniffed as he looked at her.

"I've been very well, although tired after spending all day shopping yesterday."

"Ah, yes." Charles forced a smile onto his face. "And how was that?"

"Have you not spoken to your bride or her sister about it?" Rosalyn asked, as she peered at him.

"I have, but only briefly, they were very tired when they came back yesterday."

"I see." Rosalyn said, as she sat back in her seat slightly. "Well, it was certainly eventful. I see why they must have been tired, it takes a lot out of you when you cause a scene like that."

There it was. She was already trying to get to him with information that he hadn't known before. Charles tilted his head to one side slightly, but he chose not to say anything. They were suddenly locked in a strange impasse; whoever spoke first would lose.

He busied himself by taking a sip of his tea, but Rosalyn continued to stare at him out. He cocked an eyebrow at her, gesturing for her to continue with what she had been saying. Charles wasn't going to give her the satisfaction of reacting just yet.

"I'm assuming that you heard about the scene that she caused?" Rosalyn said finally after rolling her eyes.

"Yes."

No. Helena had failed to mention that part. He had been able to tell when they'd come in that it hadn't been completely smooth sailing throughout the day, but he hadn't known that this was the reason why.

"I don't know why she got so upset." Rosalyn sniffed, as she glanced at her own tea. "She was acting as though she was going to have to wear one of those expensive dresses as though it were a burden instead of a treat."

He hated the bitter chuckle that followed her words. Charles could feel something tugging at his heart as he thought about Jane being upset.

"She comes from a different background." Charles tried to defend her in a nonchalant manner. "These things can be overwhelming for her. I'm sure some of those dresses were probably costing the same as what she used to make in an entire year."

"Yes, well I thought that was something that she would have thought about when she agreed to marry you." Rosalyn shot back at him.

"I don't know, I suppose she's still just going to have to get used to it." He said with another shrug.

"I never had any trouble adjusting to this kind of life."

"Well, I think it's safe to say that you and Jane aren't quite the same person." He said with a slight chuckle. Charles felt as though within their verbal battle, his comment had landed a solid blow to Rosalyn. She glared at him from across the table, but she refrained from saying anything for the moment.

"What's that supposed to mean?" Rosalyn asked with a small smile returning to her face.

Getting Charles to have to explain his remark was clever, it would make him out as the bad guy in this situation. He knew that he had to think quickly.

"Well, you were aware of my Uncle's wealth and the two of you dated for a lot longer than Jane and I did before getting married. You had longer to get used to this."

"Hm."

He couldn't tell from her response what she was thinking, but he was just glad to have wormed his way out of that one. Charles sat back and drank some more of his tea as Anna returned to the terrace with a platter of fresh sandwiches.

"Thank you." He smiled up at her. Rosalyn simply ignored the housekeeper and stared at the layered platter. Charles wasn't sure how she managed it, or how she found it comfortable, but the woman seemed to constantly have a sour expression. Even when looking at the kind of mouthwatering food that his cook had prepared for them both, she still managed to look disappointed.

"So, you enjoyed the experience anyway?" Charles continued, as he picked up a cheese and cucumber slice. The crusts had been cut off and the sandwich was shaped into a long rectangle, perfect for a couple of bites.

"I did." Rosalyn smiled. "I love going to see Coco, he's made a few dresses for me, not just my wedding dress. I just wish that your bride had had more fun."

"Jane told me that it had been alright." Charles lied with a slight shrug.

"Really?" Rosalyn laughed, as she shook her head. "The poor girl looked like someone was holding a gun to her head at all times."

Charles let his face drop slightly as he quickly distracted himself by taking a bite of his sandwich. He couldn't believe that Rosalyn was being so blunt with him about this.

"Is the dress nice?" He asked in the end.

"I suppose so." She nodded slowly. "It's quite plain and simple. Helena was going on about her making a vintage statement, but it looks like she just went for the cheapest second hand deal."

"It doesn't have to cost a lot to look beautiful." Charles tried to defend her again.

"I know, but it certainly helps at times."

He grimaced at the way that Rosalyn really did only seem to care about how much everything cost. It didn't matter whether it really looked good or not, it just mattered that it raised some eyebrows whenever she mentioned the price tag.

"Honestly Charles." She said while taking another sip of her tea. "She caused such a scene that it was rather embarrassing. Her sister was trying to defend her by saying that she sometimes gets panic attacks, I mean can you imagine such a thing happening in front of Coco?"

She was laughing in disbelief again, and Charles could feel his jaw clenching as he listened to her mock Jane.

"I didn't realize that it had been a panic attack." He managed to mutter while keeping his voice steady.

His heart was aching again for Jane as he realized that she really was in pain throughout this entire experience.

"Well, it was all a tad dramatic for my liking." Rosalyn continued. "She seems quite unstable, you know? But I suppose that's what you get when you choose to marry an unstable girl from an unstable background. Did you know about her parents?"

"I did." Charles nodded curtly.

His mind was reeling as he thought about all of the awful things that his aunt was saying. He didn't find it too fair that she was getting to say such things about Jane and her sister. He knew what kind of life that they came from, and it put a lot of differences in their path, but he was still trying to overlook that. It wasn't helping that Rosalyn was now trying to come in and dig it all back up.

"Well, I thought you should just know what Jack and I think about it." She persisted.

"It really doesn't matter what kind of background she comes from." Charles said, as he kept his voice level. The last thing that he wanted was to show her that her words were affecting him.

"Oh? Do you not think so? If she was from a respectable family, I doubt that yesterday would have turned out the way that it did."

"It doesn't matter, Rosalyn, you're not exactly from a respectable family either, are you? I sort of agree with you then, because if my memory does serve me correctly, you do love to cause scenes too, right?"

His words quickly shut her up. His tone had been a lot more harsh than he had been anticipating, but Charles was done with trying to be diplomatic about everything.

All he wanted to do was put the entitled woman opposite him back in her box. Rosalyn was far too selfish and thought that she was much more important than she really was.

She glared at him from across the table as Charles took the moment to finish off his sandwich.

"Well, I suppose even people from respectable families can cause scenes." She muttered, as she tried to throw it back around on him.

"Of course." He agreed with a small smirk. Charles knew from experience that the fastest way to dismantle any of her insults would be to simply accept those parts of himself and embrace them. "I think that the rich like to cause more scenes than normal folk." He declared rather controversially. "After all, we have nothing else to do all day. Causing a scene is the only way that I can sometimes inject some entertainment into my day."

"Like right now?"

"Well, there's nobody to cause a scene in front of, is there?" He smiled at her.

It was the kind of sweet smile that Rosalyn would plaster onto her face whenever she greeted people. It was a false pretense that hid her true nature underneath it. Rosalyn was glaring at him and shaking her head.

"I don't know why I entertain you sometimes, Charles." She sighed heavily, as though lunch was a sudden burden that she had to bear.

"If I'm not mistaken, it was you who invited yourself around here for lunch." He frowned.

"I know, but I thought that I would use the time to bond with you. You're my nephew after all."

"Not by blood, and definitely not by choice."

"But now I see that you're impossible." She scowled at him as she rose from her seat.

"You and my Uncle have this in common." Charles remarked, as she let the legs of the chair screech horrendously against his stone terrace. "Whenever the conversation is turned around on you, it seems that it's time for you to take flight and get out of here. It's almost as though you can't defend yourselves."

"Stop it, you horrid man." She sneered at him.

Charles smiled. He knew that was the reaction that she'd hoped to get out of him, but he'd managed to turn it around and get her to do it instead. He slowly shook his head as he went in for another sandwich. If there was one thing that he wasn't going to do, it was to show Rosalyn that she could affect him.

"Anna will show you out." Charles said. "Unless you'd like to take your share of sandwiches to go?"

His offer was answered only by the sound of the slender woman's heels clicking against the stone floor. She walked away and left him out on the terrace with a smug smile on his face. However, as soon as she was out of sight, his face dropped slightly as his thoughts returned to Jane. Charles hadn't realized that she'd really had such a hard time yesterday. He wanted to talk to her about it. He considered that it could be a good way for the two of them to get to know one another and get closer.

CHAPTER 9

"Ready for another day of planning?" Charles asked, with a small smile as Jane walked in the door. She rolled her eyes almost instantly, but pursed her lips and nodded slowly.

"I guess I don't really have a choice." She mumbled.

"It's alright, I promise that I won't bail on you today." He tried to reassure her.

Charles could see that his comment had caused some confusion within her. She was trying to work out why he was being so nice to her. The truth was that he was feeling rather pitiful of her, especially after what Rosalyn had said about the way she'd been so upset when dress shopping.

"I don't understand, surely there must be some kind of catch to that?" She chuckled lightly.

"No catch." Charles shook his head. Although, he knew that in a few hour's time, he was bound to regret offering such a thing.

"Are you drunk?"

"What?" He frowned at her. "No, it's the morning."

She shot him a look and he knew that it meant he wasn't passed being drunk in the morning. Charles rolled his eyes and walked with her into the parlor. Darcy hadn't arrived yet, and so he took the opportunity to speak with her properly.

"Thank you for all of this." He spoke in a soft tone.

"What do you mean?" She frowned while looking up at him.

"Thank you for tolerating this, I know that it can't be easy for you. I just wanted to say that I really do appreciate that you're making an effort."

"It's...alright." Jane said slowly. "What do you want?"

"What?"

"You must have something in mind, something more that you're going to ask of me."

"No." Charles frowned at her. "I just wanted to say thanks, that's all."

Jane still looked rather wary of him as she nodded slowly.

"Helena told me that you had lunch yesterday with Rosalyn." Jane said while looking back up at him. "How was that?"

"It was tolerable." He lied. "She tried to say some things about you, but I thwarted her attempts to get a rise out of me."

"Thanks, you really don't have to. I can handle someone like her talking about me." Jane shrugged it off.

"She did say something about what happened while dress shopping though. I just wanted to make sure that you're alright after that experience."

"I'm fine." Jane said so quickly that Charles really didn't believe her.

"Are you sure, because you can talk to me if you're not-"

"I'm fine, Charles, and I wouldn't come to you anyway." She said again in a rather harsh tone.

"Alright, I was just concerned because it sounded like you were rather upset when choosing a dress."

"Yes, I was." Jane snapped at him. He could tell that she was being incredibly defensive about this, but he knew that he couldn't exactly blame her. "Not everyone comes from the kind of well off families where you can just throw that much money away on a simple white dress. I'm not that kind of entitled."

"Alright." He said while holding his hands up in defeat. "Forget that I ever asked then."

Jane sighed and shook her head as she glanced away from him. The room was plunged into an awkward silence, it was the kind that weighed down on Charles and it felt as though it was trying to push him from the room.

He was in half a mind to leave Jane to Darcy on her own for the day after the way that she had just spoken to him. But he was determined to try and get through to her and show her that they could get along in time for the buildup to the wedding. He knew that things would be slightly easier if they were able to communicate with one another without arguing.

"I'm sorry for bringing it up." Charles tried, as Jane only moved further away from him.

"I really don't want to talk about it, alright?" She said again.

"We're going to have to act like we're in love as soon as Darcy walks through that door, so I suggest that we at least try and make up now."

Jane hesitated for a moment before turning back to look at him. She let out a heavy exhale and closed her eyes as her head hung slightly low.

"Fine." She muttered and nodded.

"Thank you." Charles managed a smile. "I know it's going to be difficult, but-"

"Please stop patronizing me like that."

"Sure thing."

*****

Jane couldn't believe how time could betray her like this. The hours seemed to pass by at the same time as a small age. She felt as though she had spent all of her time in that one room with Charles at her side and Darcy sitting opposite them.

If she could have had it her way, she would have had more space between the two of them as they sat on the same sofa. But

Charles had insisted on staying close to her in an attempt to show that they really were in love.

Jane found it quite an amusing thought, although she was sure that Charles wouldn't be laughing if she gave anything away. It felt like quite a powerful position that she was in; if she were just to open her mouth and tell Darcy that they actually weren't together and didn't even like one another. This was all just an elaborate plan for Charles to get more money.

While Darcy was rambling on about table placements, Jane started to reflect back on when she had first stood on his doorstep and knocked on the door. It felt like an age ago, and she couldn't believe that it had been that simple action of wanting to get a good tip that had steered her onto this path. It baffled her as she remembered the first time she'd seen his address pop up on the order screen. That had been the first of many offers that would be far too good to refuse, even if it meant that she was going to go against everything that she stood for.

"All right, so who do you want on the main table?" Darcy asked, snapping Jane back to reality.

"Not my Uncle or Aunt." Charles said quickly.

"Ah, family feuds?" Darcy asked with a chuckle as she quickly made a note of that. "Don't worry, I've seen some things in my time as a planner."

Jane tried to imagine some of the stories that she must have had. It sounded like a very stressful job, and she was slightly excited at the thought of Darcy meeting Rosalyn. She could see it going either really well, or the two of them would clash instantly.

"Trust me, the last thing that we'll need on our table will be those two." Charles said again.

"Alright, any other exceptions."

"Wyatt Tucker." Charles said, as they watched Darcy consult with the guest list.

"Any reason? Sorry, I'm just being nosy."

"He was my father's lawyer and he's known the family for a very long time. He's never liked me that much and I can't say that I like him, it's more of an obligation to have him here. I also don't want him to sit at the same table as my Uncle and Aunt."

Jane glanced at Charles hesitantly as she wondered whether that was a good idea. It would give them a reason to be slightly more vexed than usual, and Jane wasn't sure if that was a smart move.

"Alright." Darcy nodded, as she scribbled down some more notes. "Believe me, some of the seating charts I've put together have looked like battle plans to avoid any clashes in family conflicts."

Jane let Charles do the talking when it came to organizing the rest of his family. It turned out that he had distant relatives in a lot of places too, but the rest were rather normal in comparison to his bitter uncle.

"Shall we take a break?" Jane asked, before Darcy could open her mouth to say anything else when Charles was finished speaking.

"Good idea." Charles nodded, as the two of them moved to stand up.

"Alright, be back here in about twenty?"

"Do you really think it's a good idea to separate Tucker from your Uncle and Rosalyn?" Jane muttered, as they walked through the house without Darcy.

"I don't know." Charles said, as he made a face. "But I do know that the thought of having them together and scheming at one table sounds rather dangerous."

"You don't want to poke the bear though, right?"

"I know." Charles said while running a hand through his hair.

"Ah, Charles." James was sitting out in the garden and smiled as the two of them walked into the fresh air. "How's the planning going?"

"Just great." Charles grumbled while taking a seat next to his cousin.

"I've had Jack on the phone this morning. He was complaining to me about what a bad host you were to Rosalyn."

"Whatever." Charles shrugged it off. Jane frowned at the way that he was being so dismissive of the subject. From what he'd told her, it had sounded as though he really had defended her against her nasty words. She regretted the way that she'd snapped at him before Darcy had arrived, but it had been nothing more than a defense mechanism against him. She wasn't sure why he was trying to be so nice to her all of a sudden, but Jane was still incredibly wary of him and his family.

"He said that you were saying all sorts of horrible things to her and that she left rather early." James was speaking with a slight smile on his face, and it was clear to the three of them that nobody was too bothered that the woman had been upset.

"She came in here and was trying to insult my fiance. I just turned all of her insults around on herself. It was funny, because a lot of the ways that she was trying to get to me through Jane were also applicable to her."

"I sort of wish that I'd come along now." James said with a chuckle.

However, Jane could only frown at his comment. She hadn't thought that Charles cared about her enough to have stuck up for her in such an obvious way. She couldn't help but smile to herself lightly at the thought of him rushing to her defense.

Earlier that morning, she had been so sure that he was after another favor from her, and she had been very ready to say no. But it seemed that his intentions had been a lot purer after all.

"I'm not having them on the main table of the wedding either." Charles announced to his cousin.

"Wow, that's going to raise some eyebrows." James said with a chuckle.

"It will just show everyone what I think about the two of them. I really can't stand them sometimes, James. Especially since this whole inheritance business has ramped up, they seem to have found a way to become even more unbearable."

"I can't argue with you there." James said with a chuckle. "Are you both done for the day with the planning?"

"I wish." Charles said, as he pinched the bridge of his nose and shook his head. "She's still finding things that haven't been done, and I didn't even know that was possible."

Jane smiled at his words, it did seem that she had a never ending list of things that needed to be done. The amount of detail that was going into the event had long ago crossed the line of unnecessary.

"Can we start telling her that we don't need some of these things?" Jane chimed in, causing both of the men to look at her.

"What do you mean?"

"It's not really going to matter if the tents aren't perfectly in line with one another, or if the canope's match the flower arrangements. They're extra details that might impress one or two people, but they aren't the kind of things that someone might look at if they were skeptical of how genuine our marriage is."

She could see that Charles was thinking about this for a moment.

"I think it will be a fine line." He nodded slowly. "We don't want the event to look thrown together, but I suppose you're right, we don't want it to look too planned."

"And you're going to tell this to Darcy?" James cocked an eyebrow as he laughed at his cousin.

"I don't know how I'll phrase it, but I'll come up with something." Charles muttered with a slight groan.

Jane could tell that he really didn't want to do this, just as much as she didn't, but she felt as though she had at least lessened their workload a little bit.

"Don't forget that we've got the rehearsal dinner coming up next week." James warned them both.

"Why did you have to remind me?" Charles groaned.

"Oh come on, it will be the perfect time for the two of you to practice pretending to be in love."

"I think we've got that mastered." Charles said with a slight shrug.

"Oh trust me, if you think you've gotten it mastered, you're going to need to think again."

Charles could only huff in response to that.

CHAPTER 10

Helena woke up a week later with an awful knot in her stomach. It was the day of the rehearsal dinner and she was terrified that everything was going to fall apart. People like Charles' uncle would be there, but there would also be Bentley family members there that she hadn't met before. She shuddered at the thought of any of them doubting how genuine the wedding was.

It was an awful thought to have, but she could easily imagine Charles and Jane not playing along well enough for people to truly believe that they were in love.

She thought about being labeled as the maid of honor all day, it was going to mean that she would have to spend a lot of time with James, and that was also something that she wasn't looking forward to. She could just imagine the way that he would look at her constantly, she didn't understand why he did it, but she wasn't in the mood to deal with him that day.

There were much more important things at stake than just worrying about the strange relationship that she had formed with the groom's cousin. Helena knew that it could wait for another time when the pressure wasn't on them to perform as though they were in some messed up circus.

"Come on, Jane." Helena called from the lounge. "We've got to get over to Charles' to get you ready."

Since it was only the rehearsal, they weren't wearing their actual outfits. Helena was glad about this since she still hadn't tried on her dress; it had only arrived a couple of days ago, and Darcy had given it to her as though she was handing over one of the most precious treasures in the world.

"I can't believe it's already time for this." Jane mumbled, as she appeared from her room.

"You're going to be fine." Helena smiled at her reassuringly.

"A whole day with Charles, it's not like I've not been spending time with him recently, I suppose."

"That's the spirit." She said while trying to laugh at the situation. However, it was proving almost impossible to find any part of what was to come enjoyable. Helena knew that she was going to have to try incredibly hard to not lose her patience with her sister, but even that was going to be a challenge.

Only an hour later Helena stood in Jane's room at Charles' manson as she waited for her sister to get into her dress. It was a simple but elegant item, one that fitted Jane's petite figure well and accented her curves. However, it didn't seem to help put a smile on her face as she started to do her makeup. Helena herself got dressed, the deep blue of her dress was a color that she rarely wore. Yet she herself wasn't feeling too excited about the idea of having to spend the day with a lot of people from the Bentley family.

The more that she thought about it, the more that she winced at the idea. Especially spending time with James, although they became closer, Helena was still wary of him because of his family.

"Charles said that we should be ready as soon as possible." Helena said, as she finished applying a modest layer of lipstick.

"I'll be there when I'm there." Jane shrugged it off.

"Look, I know that this isn't what you want to do, but you're just going to have to suck it up and try to look like you're having a good time. I know that you just want to get this whole wedding over and done with, but it's not going to go any faster if you continue complaining. You might as well try and enjoy yourself."

"Are you going to give Charles a similar speech?" Jane asked with a slight smile of amusement playing on her lips.

414

"I'll leave that up to the best man I think." Helena chuckled.

*****

Jane put a smile on her face as she walked down to the ground floor. She was feeling rather reluctant at the idea of having to pretend to be happy for the entire day. It was going to put a strain on her, but she was going to try her best to make this work.

She knew that she hadn't been making things easy for anyone, and so she quickly tried to adjust her attitude to seem much happier and willing to go through with the wedding. Her sister's words had struck a nerve with her. Helena was right; there wasn't going to be any way that the process would speed up, and she was only going to make things more difficult for herself if she continued with her sour attitude.

"You look nice." James nodded to her as Jane thanked him in the form of a small nod. She still didn't quite know how to react around either of the Bentley men; she didn't feel as though they trusted her, and she certainly didn't trust them. "How are you feeling about all of this?"

"I just want to get it over and done with, in all honesty." She sighed.

"Good, I think that makes two of us." James smiled. It was the kind of smile that was fueled by sympathy, and Jane wasn't sure how she felt about that.

"Are you both ready to get through this thing?" Charles sighed, as he walked over to them.

"That would make three of us." James muttered under his breath. "All ready to get on with it." James said a little louder.

"Good." Charles said. "I hope that things will run smoothly and we'll have nothing to worry about."

"Me too." Jane said with a small nod. "Are the guests arriving soon?"

415

Some of the core members of their family were coming, but Jane had only invited a handful of her friends from her side. Originally she hadn't wanted to invite anyone, but Charles had convinced her that they had to make the wedding look convincing.

"Soon." Charles said, as he closed his eyes for a moment. "Let's just enjoy a few more minutes of peace before we have to deal with my insufferable family."

James chuckled at this and shook his head, but Jane could feel herself filling with dread. She was going to be the center of attention throughout a lot of various introductions, and she wasn't looking forward to it at all.

"Alright, let's get this party started." Helena's sarcastic voice came from behind her. Jane turned to see her sister in a beautiful blue gown; it was a color that suited Helena well, and she couldn't help but stare in awe at her sister. Jane glanced back just in time to catch the way that James was looking at her.

She couldn't help but smile discreetly at the way that he was trying to not ogle at her too obviously. His eyes had widened for a moment and he pursed his lips as he glanced from the floor to her dress, and then back to the floor.

"You look gorgeous." Jane smiled, as she walked over to Helena.

"Thanks, but I'm not sure I like how this dress is trying to squeeze me into oblivion." Helena said, as she gestured to her torso. "Well, you have an admirer anyway."

Helena frowned at her sister's comment for a moment, but Jane watched as the realization spread across her face.

"Don't say things like that." She said in a mutter. "I want as little to do with him as possible."

"Sure." Jane smirked at her.

She wouldn't be surprised if something did blossom there. The two of them had grown close on the drive out to their old family home, and Jane could see that there was definitely some kind of tension that sat firmly between them. The only problem was that Helena couldn't stand his family; it was the same issue that Jane had with being friendly with them, and whenever they had a moment where someone would crack a joke, she felt almost guilty for finding them amusing. These were people from the family that had been partially responsible for her mother's premature death, Jane let that thought sit in her mind. It was a constant reminder of why she never wanted to be in a room with them for too long.

Over the course of the following hour, people started to arrive at Charles' mansion. They were shown directly into the main marque that had been erected on the rear lawn, complete with tables and places for all to sit at. Jane still didn't fully understand the need for there to be a rehearsal like this, all they were going to practice were things that she considered should come naturally anyway. Jane tried to push the thoughts of doubt from her mind about whether or not she would be able to do this.

"Are you ready?" Charles asked from her side.

It was time to enter the tent and start with the introductions that she had been dreading so much.

"I suppose." Jane said.

She just wanted to get it all over with, and so she rolled her shoulders back while her arm was entwined with Charles'. Jane was trying to exude a level of confidence that she knew she didn't possess, however, nobody else in that tent knew that.

"Come on, you need to sound better than that." He turned to her slightly before they started to walk toward the large tent.

"I'm trying my best." Her voice was low but still curt.

"Then try harder." He grumbled.

Jane knew that he was stressed about this, but she also didn't like the way that he was now trying to take out his frustrations on her. It was those kinds of small comments that she knew she wasn't going to stand for. She sighed and shook her head as she thought about how she was going to be able to tolerate him if he was in that kind of mood.

"You need to make an effort too." Jane spoke up.

"Then laugh as though I just said something funny." Charles muttered, as they approached the entrance to the marque.

Jane hesitated for a moment, confused by his request until she realized that it would be a good way for her to act a little more natural. She let her expression crack into a smile as she laughed lightly and hit her arm playfully against his. Charles was now smiling too as the two of them stepped inside of the temporary venue.

Instantly, most pairs of eyes were on them as they walked up the main walkway and toward the head table. Charles was nodding to a few people, but Jane was failing to notice anyone that she knew too well. Finally, she managed to catch sight of the table where some of her friends from high school were beaming at her. Some of them were people that she hadn't properly spoken to in a very long time, but she'd had to make up the numbers on her side of the guest list.

"Charles." An old man said as he was the first to approach them. "So good to see you."

"And you." Charles said while clasping the man's hand in his own. "Rubert, this is my fiance Jane. Jane, this is Rubert, a distant cousin."

"Still present enough to turn up to these events though." Rubert said, as he held onto Jane's hand for slightly longer than she had been expecting.

Jane smiled politely and nodded to the man. She started to wonder how many Bentley relatives were looking at her at that moment, and she could feel a heavy sense of dread sinking into her at the thought of how many of them were wondering if she was a gold digger. The thought was enough to cause her to hold onto Charles tighter as she moved closer to him.

She was going to act as though she was hopelessly in love with the man, and she wasn't about to give anyone in the room a reason to doubt that fact.

She felt as though she were the main act in some twisted circus as Charles led her around the room. Jane glanced up at the head table to see that Helena and James were sitting waiting for the actual rehearsal to begin. Neither of them looked as though they were enjoying the other's company, but it wasn't as though there was any pressure on them to look as though they were having fun. Jane, on the other hand, could feel her cheeks hurting from having to constantly smile at the various people that Charles was introducing her to.

She'd lost track a long time ago as to who she was meeting and what relation to the family they had. Some people were only friends or business partners that Charles had worked with over the years, Jane didn't think it was quite as important to make a good impression with them. She could soon start to tell who was of the prestigious family in the room. Jane was sure that it was in the way that they held themselves; as though someone had planted a straight piece of wood against their back and a sour grape in their mouth.

Although there were a few of the Bentleys from the younger generations that were a lot more tolerable. Jane could tell that they weren't as interested in coming across as stuck up, in a similar way to how James behaved.

Finally, they took a seat at their table and watched as the people in the room did the same. Jane hadn't thought that so many of the guests would have wanted to come to a mere rehearsal

419

dinner. However, this wasn't just any rehearsal dinner, and it wasn't just any family that she was marrying into. Jane had been forgetting that from time to time, and she knew better than to ever underestimate the Bentley family.

"Do you think it's going alright?" Jane asked, nervously as she glanced at Charles.

"I think so." He shrugged nonchalantly.

She wanted to tell him that it would be no good if he continued to be so dismissive toward her, but she didn't want to anger him. She could feel her own annoyance building as she glanced at him out of the corner of her eye.

If people were to even suspect that they were marrying for anything less than love, then it would be a huge misstep in helping Charles get his inheritance.

"I think we should talk to each other more." Jane suggested in a very quiet voice.

"Why?"

"Because right now it looks like we've both been forced to sit next to one another when we'd both clearly be elsewhere." Jane said. "Look, I'm only trying to make an effort like you said I should."

"I don't care anymore." He sighed. "I just want to get through this dinner."

She could tell that his patience was thinning and he was starting to go into the kind of shut down mode that always got on her nerves. Just like when they would be in a meeting with Darcy and he would suddenly stop contributing to the conversation, he would then leave the room shortly after and leave Jane to deal with the meeting herself.

"That's not how it's going to work." She scolded him.

Jane glanced across the room to the table where his aunt, uncle, and lawyer had been banished. Even from where they sat, Jane could see the glares on their faces. They weren't happy about being cast to the back of the room. She knew that it was a very bold move, but it was one that was only going to pay off if they were exuding the sense that they were in love.

Thus far, Jane thought that his side of the family had taken to her quite well. At least to her face, there had been a lot of warm smiles and pleasantries exchanged. She couldn't understand what could have triggered Charles's annoyance at that moment, but Helena and James were also starting to notice it.

"Is everything alright?" Her older sister asked in a whisper.

"I think so." Jane nodded.

"You're doing great." Helena praised her.

"Thanks, but Charles has stopped talking to me." She said, "I don't know what to do."

"You're just going to have to brush it off as nothing and really hope that he doesn't get angry at your persistence." Helena said with a sigh.

"I hope you're right." Jane shuddered at the thought of getting on his bad side at that moment. The last thing that either of them needed was an argument, but she could feel one brewing.

"I never knew you had so many cousins." She remarked, as she smiled across the room.

"Yeah, there's a lot." He responded in a gruff voice.

Jane bit down on her anger as she shook her head and pushed at his arm. She was acting as though he had just said something else hilarious, but he still couldn't even manage a smile.

"Come on." She said while continuing to smile. "At least give me something here."

"I don't know what you expect me to do."

She could see the way that he was glancing over at the table with his uncle and aunt constantly, even just their presence was rattling him. But Jane couldn't believe that he was really the one ruining the dinner after he'd told her to be on her best behavior.

"Act like you love me." Jane spoke in a harsh tone. Her voice was quiet, but she still managed to achieve a tone that made her words incredibly cutting.

"I can't." He muttered.

She wasn't sure what it was that stirred within her. A mixture of disappointment and anger was swirling around in her gut, and Jane knew that if she stayed there any longer, she was going to do something that she would regret.

"I can't believe this." She muttered, as she quickly rose from her seat and started for the exit.

CHAPTER 11

Charles was up and out of his seat in an instant. His anger had been simmering slowly, but her sudden action caused it to bubble over as he followed her out of the tent. He couldn't believe that she was running away from the situation again.

"Stop!" He called after her as she walked into the house.

Charles quickly ran up the stairs in pursuit of her, he couldn't believe that they had just left a tent filled with people.

"Jane, what the hell?" He snapped, as he followed her into the room that he'd let her have.

"You don't get to say that to me after how you've just acted." She spoke back with just as much anger in her tone.

"What?" Charles said. He was livid with her, and he couldn't believe that she was spinning this on him.

"People were looking at us, including your Uncle and Tucker, they were looking at us and what would they have seen? A couple that looks like they've been forced to sit with one another despite how much they dislike each other." Jane said.

"Look, I'm sorry but I just got angry at the sight of my Uncle. I was thinking about the inheritance and-"

"Of course." She said, with a sarcastic chuckle. "Because that's all you people think about, isn't it? If it's not money, then you really don't want to know. You don't have to lie to me about that, it's as clear as day that you're all the same really."

"I don't understand where this has come from!" He snapped back at her.

"It's come from the fact that you think you can tell me one way to act, and then do the exact opposite. We didn't look like we loved each other in that tent, and if people get wind that there's trouble in paradise, you might as well kiss your inheritance goodbye."

"And what do you think they'll say now?" Charles raised his voice again. "You just stormed out of your own wedding rehearsal. I had no choice but to follow you, and now we're going to have to explain ourselves."

"I wouldn't have done it if you had just managed to keep up the act, that we're happily engaged for a few more hours. If I can manage it, then you could certainly have been able to do so."

"I..." Charles was slightly stumped by her words.

He'd let his uncle get in his head, he'd been thinking about the reality that he wouldn't get the inheritance and what he'd have to do for a living instead. It was the kind of thought that haunted him in the night, but it was also the kind of thought that he was normally able to keep at bay.

"Come on, we need to do better than this."

"I can't believe you just stormed out though." He said while shaking his head in disbelief. "People are going to be talking about this. They're going to wonder what's wrong with you and-"

"What's wrong with me?" Jane scoffed. "What is wrong with you and your people? Why do you all have to be so judgmental about everything?"

"I-"

"No, you will listen to me, Charles Bentley. I told you that I don't want to see you until the wedding, but I'm trying to make this work by coming to all of your stupid pre-wedding events. I've been judged at every step of the way for not making enough of an effort when you are barely making an effort either."

Charles was silent as she glared at him. He could feel his own anger building up within him, but he didn't want to say anything that he may regret later.

"I'm sorry you feel this way, but-"

"You're not sorry." She chuckled darkly. "You're sorry that you've made me this distressed, and you're sorry that you're going to have to send me back out there with those people. But I won't go."

"No you can't say that!" He said in a much louder voice.

"I can and I just did, I'm not going back in that tent until the wedding day."

"What am I supposed to tell all of those people?"

"That's not my problem." Jane waved a hand through the air. "I'll see them all in a week's time when it's the real day."

"If you're not going back down there, then neither am I."

*****

Helena listened at the door. Her heart plummeted as they both bowed out of the dinner in their own ways. She couldn't believe that the pair of them couldn't even hold it together for a few hours. She hoped that the wedding would be different, but Helena wasn't exactly holding out hope.

"What's going on?" James whispered, as he stood by her side.

She put a finger to her lips quickly and gave him a look that told him not to speak again. James in turn made an action with one hand as though he had zipped his mouth shut, earning nothing but an eye roll from the maid of honor. Finally, she sighed and pulled him further down the corridor and away from the closed door.

"I just heard them both say that they aren't going back down there."

"What!"

"Shh." Helena lurched forward and covered his mouth with her hand.

She then quickly retreated from the sudden close proximity. It was too much for her and she wasn't sure how she felt about being so close to him.

"What?" James said in a quieter voice. "What are we going to do?"

"I don't know." Helena said while running a hand through her hair. "I suppose we could just call it off, or we could try and convince the two of them that they have to come back out?"

"I mean, I'll let you do the honors with that one." James said with a chuckle. "You know how stubborn they both are, they won't want to do anything that they don't want to do."

"I know." Helena groaned. "But I don't see what other option we have."

"We could just cover for them." James said while shrugging. "Just say that Jane is sick and that's why she left so suddenly."

"Do you really think that people will buy that?"

Helena scrunched up her nose at the thought of continuing on the dinner without the bride and groom. She and James would have far too much attention on themselves for her liking, but it would be the best way to appease the people that were waiting for them back in the tent.

"Let's just go and talk to them, we'll tell them they have to come out."

"And when they say no?" Helena asked.

"Then we'll tell them our plan to cover for them."

Helena didn't like either of their options, but she didn't know what else to do that would help to rectify the situation. She let out a groan as he walked over to the door.

"Charles? It's Helena and James, can we come in?"

"Just a second." He called.

A few moments later, the door opened, revealing a rather angry-looking Charles.

"Is everything alright?" Helena asked, as she walked into the room and spotted her sister on the other side of the large space.

"No, she won't come back downstairs." Charles glared at her.

"Because he's not even living up to the very things he's been telling me to do." Jane fired back.

Helena suddenly felt as though she were a mother and was telling off two quarreling children.

"You both need to come back down." She said, "People are going to start thinking things, and this really isn't a good look if you want to try and portray that you're both together for love, not money."

Her words were received by groans from them both, and she quickly turned to James for some backup.

"She's right." He nodded. "You both need to come back down."

"I'm not doing that." Jane shook her head.

"If she's not, then I'm not." Charles said.

"What do we do then? Do you want us to send everyone home?" James asked.

"I don't know." Charles shrugged.

Helena glanced between the unhappy couple with narrowed eyes. She had heard the argument and knew that her sister was slightly in the right in terms of what she was arguing about.

Although Helena thought that Jane had a better resolve than to just walk out of a place like that.

"Can you cover for us?" Jane chimed in.

"What? This is your wedding, I'm not covering." Helena shook her head. "You're coming back down and you're just going to say that you were ill or something."

"Can't you just say that I was too sick to come back down?" Jane asked with a wince.

"But that would be a lie." Helena fired back.

"I don't care, I'll face the family on the wedding day, but that's it."

Helena couldn't believe that this was happening. She glanced over at James to see that he was also shaking his head in dismay. It just didn't make any sense that they were going to bail out of the very event that the two of them had organized.

"Look, can't we all just return to the dinner and we'll talk about this later." He suggested, as he gestured to the four of them.

"No, I'm not going back down." Charles said, as he kept his gaze on Jane.

Helena wasn't sure what kind of game he was playing, but it was one that clearly rattled her sister.

"You know that this is only going to give your Aunt and Uncle more ammunition against you." Helena spoke up in a much harsher tone than she had been previously using.

"I know." Charles said with a shrug. "As long as we're there for the wedding day, it doesn't matter."

Helena wanted to say all sorts to the man. She wanted to wave her fists at him and curse him out for being so annoying, but she knew that wouldn't get her anywhere.

"Fine, if this is what you really want." She muttered. Helena ignored the look of bewilderment that James was giving her as she started for the door. "I'll cover for you both this time, but it's never happening again, all right?"

CHAPTER 12

James followed Helena out of the door in a cloud of confusion. He couldn't believe that his cousin and her sister weren't coming back down with them, and he wasn't sure how he felt about having to make an announcement in front of his family.

"Are you sure about this?"

"Absolutely not." Helena said. "But I don't see what choice we have."

"We could just stay here." James suggested, although he knew that it wasn't really an option. "We could just stay in the house until all of the guests get bored of waiting and leave."

"You know that we can't do that." She said with a sigh.

It was true. James had thought that they would perhaps be able to wait out the storm in a similar way to Charles and Jane. However, the truth was that they would only be making the situation even worse if they did that.

"I guess we just go back in there and tell them all that Jane is sick?"

"It's the only plan we've got." Helena nodded slowly. "I'm not sure how many people are going to buy it though."

"And then what do we do?"

"We continue the dinner and serve the first course as quickly as possible." Helena muttered, as she took his arm and walked toward the tent.

James would have been lying if he'd said that her action hadn't stirred something within him. He smiled at the way that she held onto him and wished that he could have enjoyed the moment for a little longer. However, the circumstances around them dictated that he wouldn't get this option.

"Are you sure about this?" He whispered, as they walked into the tent.

"Not at all." Helena muttered back.

*****

Helena bit her lip as she looked around the room. People were talking amongst themselves in the wake of her announcement. She had waited until the two of them had sat down before speaking up, but she was now wishing she'd done it while she still had the support of James' arm. Helena quickly took her seat next to James, now at the centre of the main table.

It all felt very wrong, but she knew that there really wasn't anything else that she could do about it. She wanted to get up from the table and go to be with her sister, but she couldn't leave James all on his own.

She thought about Jane and Charles and whether or not they were still arguing in her room. She wouldn't have been surprised if they were, but she also hoped that they were giving one another space.

The announcement consisted of her explaining that Jane wasn't feeling too good and her kind and caring fiance was by her side to make her feel better. She could see the frowns on some people's faces, and for a long time, she dreaded even looking over at the table with Rosalyn and Jack on it. They were talking in hushed tones, but every now and again would glance over in the direction of James and Helena. She swallowed thickly and wished that this nightmare would end soon.

"Seems to have been received better than I had anticipated." James whispered to her.

"Do you think?"

"I don't know anymore." He said with a shrug.

"Neither do I, but I'm sure that if people were accepting of it, there wouldn't be so much talking."

Helena was trying her hardest to catch any words that people were saying, but it became slightly easier as the servers came in with the first course. Her eyes widened as she saw that one table was mentioning a baby and morning sickness being at all times of the day. She knew that it was a plausible topic to suspect, especially after how Jane had left so abruptly. It would make sense, but she couldn't help but feel even more dread rising up within her. Jane wasn't pregnant, she couldn't even stay in a room with the man for longer than was necessary. She hated the idea that they were going to have to explain themselves in one way or another.

The first course was only a small dish of soup. Helena picked at it as she thought about how many more courses lay ahead of them. If it were a normal wedding, she knew that there would only be the normal three courses, and that would suit people well. However, this meant that their stay in the tent was going to be extended to much longer than she wanted it to be. Helena grimaced as she remembered the many courses that had been talked about during the planning of the day. Jane had agreed to so many in the hope that it would stall her for time in terms of having to dance in front of everyone. Helena was now cursing herself since she remembered how she had been in support of that idea.

"Are you alright?"

"I'm fine." Helena said without even looking over at James. She could tell that he was looking at her, and so she quickly took a mouthful of soup.

"Are you sure? Because you've been picking at a dish that could quite literally be gone in five bites."

"I said I'm fine, I was just thinking."

"Well, I think it's our turn to act as though we get along." James suggested, as he gestured to the people who glanced their way every few minutes.

"I thought we got along anyway?"

His face lit up at her question, but James turned back to his own soup for a moment.

"I suppose we do." He mumbled.

The two of them finished their soup in silence, but James had been right, the soup was gone in a matter of moments.

"How much longer are we going to have to endure this?" Helena groaned, as she tried to make it seem as though she was having a good time.

"Who knows?" James said. "I think we're doing an alright job though?"

"You would say that." Helena shook her head. "Once the meal is done, people are going to be milling about and you can bet anything that they're going to want to talk about Charles and Jane's disappearing act."

"We'll just tell them that she got sick, some of it got on her dress and she wasn't feeling up to coming back out. We could blame it on her nerves as well or something, saying that she just doesn't want to make a bad impression."

"I think it's too late for that." Helena said dryly.

"Look, it's all going to be fine." James said, as he touched her arm lightly.

Normally, Helena would have jerked away from an action like that. She would have glared right at him and scolded him for such a thing. However, they were the center stage, and she knew that she could do no such thing without bringing the wrong kind of attention to herself.

They continued on as course after course came and went through the main entrance of the marquee. Helena was still in shock that they were having to cover for the couple again, and she knew that they were both going to owe them big time when it was over. She thought about what she would request of them both as she sat there, but it was difficult for her to think of many things.

"I don't think I can handle another course." Helena spoke under her breath, earning a chuckle from James on her left.

"I'm not sure that you're going to get much of a choice." James said, as she tried not to show her disappointment in response to his words.

"I wonder what Jane and Charles are up to." She muttered.

"I can imagine that they aren't spending much time together." He said with a light chuckle.

Helena managed a smile as she knew that it would look like a good image if people could see them getting along.

"I hate that there's so much focus on us." She sighed.

"I know, but it will be over soon. We're almost at dessert." James reasoned.

Helena smiled at some people and winced at the thought of having to introduce herself to any more Bentleys that day. But she knew that it would be coming, she wanted nothing more than to retreat in the same way that Charles and Jane had already done.

"How nice to see you both here." James smiled at Charles' Uncle and Aunt once the dinner was over. People were milling about, but Helena got the impression that lots of people were wanting to talk with them.

"Indeed." Jack said, as he looked down his nose at them. "Although, I can't help but notice that we're missing the bride and groom."

"Yes, well Jane has been rather sick and it wasn't a good idea for her to come back out here." Helena explained. "I tried to get

Charles to come back down, but he wanted to stay with her and make sure that she's alright."

"How...good of him." Rosalyn said, as she forced a smile onto her face.

Helena could tell that they weren't convinced, although out of everyone there, she hadn't expected those two to be the ones to accept this as the truth.

"Will he be coming back out at all?" Jack chimed in.

"I don't think so." James said. Helena felt relief run through her that James had chosen to help her in answering this. "I think he wants to stay with Jane."

"She didn't look too ill when she first came in." Rosalyn said.

"Well, I think it just came over her suddenly." Helena said, as she plastered a smile onto her face.

"How bizarre." Rosalyn mumbled. "I have a few friends who would have strange and abrupt spells of sickness like that. Nine months later and they had a little more than they expected to show for it."

All of them knew what she was talking about, Helena flinched slightly as she knew that Rosalyn was trying to twist things. There was certainly no hope that they were going to be expecting any time soon, but she knew that she couldn't just shut down that option so quickly.

"I'm sure we'll find out when they're ready for people to know." Helena brushed it off. "It could have just been the result of a gone off meal last night."

"I suppose so." Jack said slowly. "I just think it's strange that the bride and groom miss their own rehearsal dinner."

"Well, we aren't exactly conventional in this family, Jack." James said, as he tried to reason with him. "I wouldn't expect things to be completely smooth sailing in this family."

"I guess you're right."

"Don't you remember your wedding? We had cousin Dickie drunk at every pre-wedding event." James said with a chuckle.

Helena was slightly shocked at how well he was handling the situation, but she still wasn't sure that it was going to be enough.

"Ah yes...I suppose you're right." Jack grumbled. He glanced down at the floor and could no longer meet either of their eyes. "I suppose he's still hoping that he'll get his inheritance if he marries this girl, right?"

"I don't know, he hasn't really spoken about that recently." James said.

"Of course he hasn't." Jack chuckled. "James, you know I really thought better of you. I thought that you weren't the kind of man who would cover for a guy like Charles."

James hesitated for a moment as he looked at his uncle. Helena held her breath as she waited for him to say something.

"I don't know what you're talking about, Jack." He said, with a small smile on his face.

Jack's cheeks were flushed and it was clear that he didn't know what to do or say in response to this. Instead, he seethed quietly as James turned to look at Helena.

"I think we should go and talk with a few more people." He suggested, as she nodded in response. "See you both around."

"That doesn't bode well, does it?" Helena said, once they were out of earshot.

"No, not at all." James admitted while exhaling deeply.

They started around the room and smiled at the various relatives of the Bentley family that had made the effort to come to the event. Helena had thought that there would have been a lot fewer people at the rehearsal, but it seemed that everyone had come with keen eyes to get a look at the 'happy couple.'

CHAPTER 13

James and Helena remained at the dinner until the guests slowly started to filter home. He was incredibly thankful that not too many of them wanted to outstay their welcome. He had thought about what to do if some of the guests wanted to continue drinking in the house. James figured that it would be a good way to flush out Charles and at least get him to show his face once again.

He sighed and shook his head, unable to believe that this was really happening. Helene had handled the situation well at his side, but James was still tentative that the sudden disappearance of the bride and groom would only prompt a lot of suspicion to arise. He felt rather annoyed at how his cousin had left it up to him to get the message across that Charles and Jane wouldn't be returning to the dinner.

"Well, I think that this certainly could have gone much worse." James remarked, as they finally arrived back in the house.

"I guess, although Charles' Uncle and Aunt went in with their teeth bared during that conversation." She said while shaking her head. "Honestly, I've never met anyone so determined to bring down a family."

"I know, it's quite a scary thing to come up against. But a greedy man will stop at nothing to be the one on top. Jack just seems to prove that time and time again."

"I'm sorry that you're related to him." Helena said with a chuckle.

"I suppose through this marriage, you will be soon as well." James shook off her comment. "They really are the worst of us, and Charles' father's death only amplified that."

"Do you think that you would have a different relationship with him if money wasn't so much of an issue for the man?"

"Of course." James nodded. "But that would mean changing most of his personality. Jack seems to only care about money, and so I couldn't see him being himself and uncaring for something that normally takes up so much of his thoughts."

They walked through the house and into the library, James assumed that Charles was upstairs in his room and sulking like a child. He couldn't believe that the man really had left him to deal with the guests, but that was going to be a conversation for another time.

"I wonder how Jane is doing." Helena muttered, as she sat down opposite James. "I should probably go and check on her."

"Wait." James said, as he stopped her before she could rise from her chair. "Why not stay for a while and just take a load off of your feet? I mean, we've both been putting in a lot of effort to appear as though there's nothing wrong in this god damn family."

Helena frowned as she slowly nodded and sat back in her seat.

James had decided that he was going to tell her. He hadn't given her any clues as to what he was going to reveal so far, but he remembered Charles's words well. He had wanted him to wait until closer to the wedding, or even after the wedding. However, James felt as though if he kept his feelings to himself any longer, he might burst.

He was sure that she wouldn't mind hearing what he had to say, especially since they had successfully managed to spend so much time with one another without killing each other. He smiled at the thought of how well they had got on at the end of their trip, and part of him found himself longing for those hours spent together in the car.

"Actually." He started as he sat up slightly. "I was wondering if I could ask you something?"

"Alright." Helena nodded.

He could see the wariness in her expression, but she made no move to question him further. Instead, Helena waited patiently with her arms folded across her chest and an eyebrow cocked up in curiosity.

"Okay." James said, as he took a deep breath. "I know that you're really busy at the moment with all this wedding planning and making sure that your sister is all right. But I was wondering if at some point you would want to...go out?"

The words hung in the air for far longer than he felt was a comfortable amount of time, but James made no move to say anymore. It suddenly felt as though they were locked in some kind of stalemate where they were both seeing who would speak first because they would be the loser.

"I...what?" Helena blinked finally.

*****

She had known that his feelings for her were starting to show, but never in her wildest imagination had Helena thought that he would have been bold enough to ask her such a thing. Her thoughts were reeling as she tried to think of something that she could say that would lessen the blow.

Part of her, a much larger part than she cared to admit, wanted to say yes. She wanted to break out into a smile and embrace him, but there was still another part of her that held her back. It was the part that reminded her about why she hated his family and the kinds of things that they had done over the years to make her feel that way.

James wasn't like his family, but they would still be around him, and that was something that she didn't want to deal with. She knew that he could be one of the good guys, and it hurt her heart at the thought of upsetting him, but Helena knew that she wouldn't be able to say yes.

"James." She began with a sigh.

He looked down at his lap as he seemed to sense that her answer wasn't going to be a positive one.

"I can't." Helena said, in barely a whisper.

"Why?" He asked, while looking up at her.

Both of them held a level of hurt in their expression as they stared at one another. But Helena couldn't do it, she couldn't fall for someone from his family.

"There are so many reasons that I want to say yes, but there are also so many that I can think of that make me think no is the better choice here." She explained.

"I don't believe you."

"What do you mean?" She frowned. "I can't be with someone like you, we are so different and have such different ways of doing things. It just...it wouldn't make sense."

"I think that it makes perfect sense." He fired back. "I like you, and you like me - don't even try to deny that."

Helena pursed her lips as she stared at him. She knew that he was right to some degree, but she wasn't ready to admit that to herself. It wasn't an easy decision that she was making, and she hoped that he understood that. But Helena felt as though it was the right decision.

"I don't think I could do this...us." She said, while gesturing between the two of them.

"Why not?"

"Because we just have so many ways that we're different and it wouldn't work. We would be like Jane and Charles where we fight over things that couples shouldn't fight over. That's because I'm happy with just the bare necessities, I don't need all of this. I don't want that to be something that we argue about all of the time."

441

"Alright, well I can change." James said, while holding his arms out.

"You're not supposed to change though." She sighed. "You're supposed to be who you are and not have to worry about changing for someone else."

"I don't care about all of that." He brushed it off while shaking his head. "I care more about trying to give this a go."

Helena shook her head at his words, she just knew that it would cause too much upset. She thought about what her sister would say if she heard this. Jane would think she was the biggest hypocrite in the world after the way that she had told Jane not to marry Charles for so long.

"I can't." She said while shaking her head.

She thought about her parents and how unhappy they had been. Of course, it was a rather extreme example, but that was the only example that she'd had of how love truly unfolded. Helena had always told herself that she would protect herself from such a thing, that she would never let herself get to the position where she would be hurt by a man.

By saying no to James, she was just ensuring that this was the case.

*****

James couldn't quite believe that she was turning him down in the way that she was. He blinked a few times and tried to push away the hurt feeling that was sinking inside of him. His pride had been bruised, but it felt like nothing compared to how his feelings hurt. He was sure that she was holding something back, although he just couldn't put his finger on it.

Helena was acting as though she wasn't able to completely tell him everything that was wrong. He wished more than anything that he knew what she was thinking and that he was able to help her.

"You're just going to give up without even trying?" He asked.

"Don't say it like that." She shook her head and sighed.

"No, that's exactly what you're doing. You're showing me that you don't care at all about me, and that the last few weeks meant nothing to you. I know that's a lie, and I also know that you're lying about why you're saying no."

"Can we just drop this?" Helena asked, while pinching the bridge of her nose. "I don't want to talk about it, and there's nothing that you can say that will prompt me to talk."

"I don't believe you."

"Well, then that's on you." Helena snapped at him. "I'm not talking, and you're just going to have to respect that. Although it's pretty clear that you have no respect for me either."

"That's not..."

James couldn't be bothered to argue his case any longer. It was evident that she wasn't going to give him a chance, but he was far too angered by the way that she was going about it than the initial issue.

"I'm out of here." He sighed, as he quickly left Helena sitting on her own.

He could feel his anger boiling over as he walked toward the door and decided that it was time to go home. James had considered staying behind to talk with Charles, but after that, he wanted nothing more than to be left on his own. He wanted to mull over what had happened and what had been said. But it was much more than that; he also wanted to focus on what hadn't been said between them, Helena hadn't denied her feelings for him, only that she couldn't do anything about them. James knew that he was being hopeless, but he didn't care, it still gave him some newfound hope.

CHAPTER 14

"Come on." Helena said, as she opened the door to her sister's room. "We're going home."

"Haven't you ever heard of knocking?" Jane groaned, as she looked up at her sister.

"Haven't you ever heard of just sucking something up and getting on with it?"

"There's no need to be like that." Jane said with a heavy sigh.

She wasn't in the mood for whatever reason her sister was angry. Jane knew that it had been foolish of her to walk out of the dinner, but Charles was making her so angry that she hadn't wanted to do something that would have put the marriage in even more jeopardy.

She thought that her decision had been the most sensible one, even if her sister didn't see it from that angle.

"I'm sorry for leaving you with James, I didn't think it would be that bad."

"I don't want to talk about it." Helena said, as she picked up her bag from the bedroom floor. "Now will you come with me back home?"

"I guess." Jane said with a shrug.

She had been lying on the plush double bed that felt as though she were resting on a cloud. It made even the thought of her hard mattress at home sound like a nightmare. But she didn't care, it hadn't been bought by anyone under the name of Bentley.

"What happened between you and James?" Jane asked, only when they were in the car. They were having one of Charles' chauffeurs drive them back to the apartment, but Jane wasn't worried about him hearing their conversations, he never spoke.

"Nothing." Helena shook her head.

"Are you sure, because you seem-"

"I'm fine, I'm just tired and want to go to bed." Helena shook it off.

Jane decided that it was best not to press it any further. She wanted to ask about the dinner and how Jack and Rosalyn had been after they disappeared, but Helena's tone wasn't the kind that invited conversation.

Jane held her tongue and decided that she would wait for the morning before daring to ask anything like that. She couldn't believe that the dinner had collapsed in the way that it did, but she was blaming Charles for the way that he had been acting. It wasn't at all as they had talked about and made Jane look foolish and as though she cared more than he did. She had thought that he would have been on board with not promoting any kind of wrong message to others. But it seemed that she was wrong.

By the time that they arrived back to the apartment, Jane wondered if her sister's anger had simmered somewhat. She was scared to ask anything too much that would have annoyed her more, but Jane had to know.

"So do you want anything to eat, or-"

Helena's answer came in the form of her bedroom door slamming shut behind her, followed by a tap on the ceiling above them from their neighbor. Jane closed her eyes for a moment as she sighed heavily and thought about how differently the day should have gone.

*****

James arrived early at Charles' the next morning, he wanted to talk to his cousin and confide in him about what had happened. He was still incredibly wary that Helena or Jane would be around, and so he entered the house rather cautiously.

445

To his surprise, Charles was already up and sitting in the garden with his breakfast. He sat alone at his glass table and sipped at a cup of morning tea.

"Ah, there you are." Charles said, as James stepped out into the fresh morning air. "I thought you would have joined me for a drink after dinner last night."

"I know, I just...wasn't feeling up to it."

"Was everything all right?" Charles asked.

James thought that it was a bit rich coming from him to ask if it all went all right. He could have been there to find out for himself.

"Yes, I think it went all right in the end." James nodded. "A few people were asking us what was wrong with Jane, and Rosalyn even asked if this was because she was pregnant."

James hadn't been expecting his comment to make his cousin laugh so much, but Charles held onto his stomach as he laughed at the thought.

"That is amusing." He smiled to himself as he finally calmed down. "Was Helena alright?"

"Yes." James said, although he didn't give any more details. He could see the inquisitive look on Charles's face that his sudden curtness had caused, but James didn't care. He didn't know how to tell him about what had happened.

"So you're telling me that things are all good between the two of you?"

"Have you spoken to Jane?" James asked, as he glanced back at the house.

"They both went home last night." Charles stated. "Anyway, you're deflecting from my question."

"Things are...fine, or at least they will be...I think." He said.

"James..."

"Fine." He sighed. "We got into an argument at the end of the evening because...I asked her out."

He saw the way that his cousin's eyebrow raised at this. James shook his head and turned to look out at the lawn before them, the marque was still up and would be from now until the wedding. He winced at the thought of having to spend time with the maid of honor after what had happened.

"Oh god." Charles said while looking down. "And you really thought that last night would be the best time to tell her that? I told you to wait until-"

"Wait until closer to the wedding, the day is almost upon us now, and so I figured that it was an alright time. I got it completely wrong though and she said no."

He could see Charles frowning at this, although he wasn't sure if Charles was curious or angry at him.

"I'm sorry to hear that, but maybe it would have been better if you'd waited until after the wedding like I said." He suggested.

"It had just felt like the right moment, since we had been getting on well for the evening, I thought...it doesn't matter now I suppose."

"How have you left it?"

"I stormed out of the library." James answered honestly. "I don't think there will be much talking between us after this."

"Don't say that." Charles groaned, as he rubbed his eyes.

"Oh, because things are going great between you and Jane?" James fired back.

"That's a completely separate issue since there are no real feelings between us." Charles said.

"Whatever, I just wish that it had gone differently because I know that she feels a similar way. She didn't deny it, Charles, when I told her how I felt, and I said that I think she knows the feeling, Helena didn't deny it."

"Do you hear yourself?" Charles asked, with a chuckle. "All of our lives, we have never had to worry about getting the girl. Maybe that's something that other guys have to worry about, but never us. Now all of a sudden, I need Jane in order to get this money, and you're falling for her sister who just rejected you. James, when I tell you that there are plenty of girls out there who would happily take her place, I'm not joking."

James wanted to tell him that he didn't want other girls, and he knew that other girls would only want him for his money anyway. He shook his head and looked down at his lap. The hurt that he felt was more than he could properly tell Charles. He felt like a fool for falling for someone that wasn't willing to admit that she felt a similar way back, especially when he thought that Charles was right.

It wasn't a nice fact, and James knew that it wasn't completely for him, but for his money. He could have had a lot of other girls, but there was only one that he wanted.

"Do you really think that she feels that way about you?" Charles asked.

"I know she does, I've seen the way that she looks at me from time to time." James said ,as he nodded. "I'm not sure what it is that is holding her back, but there's definitely something that she isn't telling me."

"If you're sure about that, then I would just give it some time." Charles said.

"But we don't have time. The wedding is soon, and it's going to be a disaster if even the best man and the maid of honor aren't speaking to one another."

448

James knew that there wasn't much either of them could do but hope that Helena and Jane would come around in time for the wedding. Things were beginning to look pretty bleak, and he knew that they were going to be in a lot of trouble if they couldn't just get along for one day.

"I think we should have some kind of meeting between the four of us before the wedding. It would be the best way to have them understand that we're going to have to be much more willing to cooperate on the actual day."

James thought about how Helena wouldn't receive such a meeting well. She was strong willed and feisty, and he was sure that she wouldn't take to being talked to in such a way by someone like Charles.

"I can't believe we've just let things fall apart like this." Charles sighed. "I thought that it would all run smoothly and we would be able to have the inheritance to dish out at the end of it. Now it doesn't even feel like we're all going to get to the end of this without killing one another."

"Don't be so dramatic." James chuckled. "I'm sure that when the actual day arrives, things will be much more relaxed. They understand the importance of being good on the actual day, and I don't think that they would jeopardize such a large sum of money like that."

"I hope you're right, James."

CHAPTER 15

Jane awoke the next morning feeling rather awful about herself. Upon reflection, she knew that she could have tried harder to at least not let Charles get to her with his bad attitude. But she had still done what she thought was the right thing to do, and she was going to stand by that.

She shook her head and tried to think about how she was going to apologize to Charles in a way that would also prompt him to apologize too. She didn't feel as though what had happened the day before was entirely her fault, but she did know that Charles was going to be reluctant in taking any accountability.

It was the same as he always was, although Jane was hoping that he wouldn't be like that in this case. She hoped that he would at least be able to see the errors of his ways and realize that his attitude had prompted her to get up and leave the rehearsal.

"Are you alright?" Jane asked, as she walked out into the kitchen area of their small flat. The apartment stunk of eggs from breakfast, but Helena was lying out on the couch.

She had the kind of expression and body language of a sad teenager, and she reluctantly sat up to let her sister have some space on the sofa.

"I'm fine." She grumbled.

"Are you sure? Because you left me rather abruptly last night, I just want to make sure that you're alright, Helena." Jane said, as she looked at her sister with worry.

She hadn't said a word to her since they had got in the car that had taken them back to the apartment. Jane was worried that something really bad had happened, and she couldn't stop her mind from gravitating to some of the worst case scenarios.

450

"Was it Rosalyn or Jack?"

"It was nothing." Helena said, as she turned away from her sister.

"Come on, Helena. You can tell me, I'm your sister and I won't judge you for anything. I don't think there's anything that you could do that would have put you in the wrong. I know for a fact that I shouldn't have walked off, and I'm sorry for leaving you with James, but I was so angry at Charles. I would have said something wrong or blown the entire thing if I'd have had to stay in that tent yesterday."

"I understand why you had to leave." Helena said with a heavy sigh. "I don't blame you for that, but something else happened between James and I."

"I knew it." Jane nodded, as she sat up a little more on the couch. "I promise that I won't tell a soul."

"Good, because this is the kind of thing that I don't want Charles to know. Although I'm sure that James must have already told him his side of the story."

Again, Jane tried not to let her mind wonder as to what she was talking about, but she was finding it quite the challenge.

"We went into the library once the guests had left, and we were just talking and decompressing after the stress of being the centre of attention. I really was exhausted after that event, but James thought that it was a good time to talk about his feelings."

Jane's eyes widened at her sister's words. She had always had a suspicion and Charles had even made a few comments from time to time, but she never thought that he would go through with anything and say something to Helena.

"What did he say?"

"He just asked if I'd like to go out with him some time." Helena said in a rather nonchalant tone.

"Helena!" Jane exclaimed, as she held onto her sister's shoulder while sitting up even further on the couch.

"I know." She said, "I couldn't believe it either."

"What did you say to him?"

"I told him that I couldn't do it." She said, while looking off at a blank space on the wall. "I told him that it just wouldn't work."

Jane could feel the smile falling from her face as she thought about her sister's words. She could feel something tugging at her own heart after hearing how Helena had handled the situation.

"And I'm guessing that James wasn't exactly pleased to hear that?"

"Something like that." Helena managed a weak smile.

"Why couldn't you have done it?"

"Because, after everything, if I was to get with a man from a family that I'm supposed to hate, then I would be the biggest hypocrite alive." Helena said.

Jane thought about this for a moment. She didn't think her sister was a hypocrite, she was only human after all. She had seen how well they had gotten on when they spent so long together in the car, and so she found that she actually wasn't too surprised that James had expressed such feelings. She wished that Helena hadn't turned him down, because all Jane wanted was for her to find someone who would make her happy.

"What did James say exactly when you told him no?"

"He was just disappointed." Helena said, with a shrug.

"And are you on speaking terms now?"

"Not...exactly." She muttered.

"Oh god." Jane sighed. "So now we have the bride, groom, best man, *and* the maid of honor all not speaking to each other."

She couldn't help but chuckle in disbelief at how ridiculous the situation sounded.

"What are we going to do?" Helena asked, as she ran a hand through her hair.

"I think we're going to have to go and speak to them about this before the wedding." Jane announced.

"Since when were you so level headed?" Helena said, with an amused smile.

"Since I want us to get this money so that we never have to see Charles again." Jane said with a shrug.

"What about James?"

"Well, I suppose that's up to you and what you really want."

She let her sister think about this for a moment as she got up and walked over to the kitchen. Jane couldn't lie that she wasn't feeling anxious as to whether or not Helena was going to sort things with James. She really hoped that the two of them would at least be able to be civil for the wedding day.

*****

Later on that day, Helena didn't feel like going out or doing anything. She was still reeling from the way that James had revealed his feelings to her the night before, and how much it had caught her off guard.

She swallowed thickly as she thought about going out on a date with James. Part of her really wanted to do it. Helena couldn't ignore that a large part of her had thought that it would have been really easy to just say yes to him. But she wasn't sure if she would have been able to live with herself.

"Are you still thinking about it?" Jane asked, as she came back into the apartment. She hadn't been too long at the store, but

Helena felt slightly bad that she hadn't moved from her position since she'd left.

"No." She lied.

"Come on." Jane sighed, as she moved to grab her arms and pull her up. "I'm not going to let you sit around and mope all day, especially about a guy. And a Bentley guy at that."

"Fine." Helena groaned, as she finally rose from the couch. "What do you want to do?"

"I don't know, but let's just go out and forget for a few hours about everything that we've been having to deal with."

Helena liked the idea of just forgetting herself for a few hours. It would be a good way for her to take her mind off of everything.

CHAPTER 16

"This is quite literally the last thing that I want to be doing right now." Charles grumbled, as he put his clubs in the car and groaned.

"Come on, you're going to have to show your face at some point. You know that they will just be loving every second of this if you hide away until the wedding, it's exactly what playing into your uncle's hands will look like."

Charles wanted nothing more than to sit at home and read in the library, or perhaps just lay low on his terrace. He wanted to enjoy the simple pleasures instead of the ones that certainly weren't found while out on a golf course.

"I'm sure that it will be a good course today anyway." James said with a shrug.

"You're in good spirits." Charles said with narrowed eyes. "Did Helena change her mind?"

"Not exactly." James said while glancing down at the floor. "But I just figured that there isn't much point in wallowing."

"Good." Charles nodded to him. "Especially going to see Jack and Tucker, we're going to need our wits about us and we can't be distracted."

When Charles had awoken earlier that morning, the last thing that he ever wanted to do was go and play golf with his uncle and his father's former lawyer. The two men were going to flaunt the fact that they still had his inheritance money, and he was going to have to explain his absence from the rehearsal dinner. The entire day just felt like one big culmination of events that he didn't want to do, but he didn't have a choice.

He knew that his cousin was right; things would only be worse if he didn't show his face until the wedding, and all he could think about were his own lawyer's words. If he was to have his inheritance, then he was going to need to make the marriage believable.

They arrived at the golf club promptly on time, although they hadn't spoken much on the car journey over there. Charles was sure that Helena was still occupying James's thoughts, and that he wasn't being fully truthful with him. He couldn't blame his cousin, but he didn't want James to be too distracted when they would inevitably come face to face with his uncle and Tucker.

"Are you alright?" Charles asked, as he sat in the car for a moment.

"I will be." James nodded. "I'm trying not to think about it, but I think that I'm also much more shocked at just how upset the whole thing has made me."

"Really?"

"Yeah." He let out a shaky breath. "I think I care a lot more than I would like to comfortably admit."

"We'll talk about this later, because I really do think that you should contact her and try to talk to her about this. But for now, we've got another issue to face."

"You're right." James said, as he sucked in a breath. "We can do this though, I'm sure of it."

"Good to see you, Charles." Jack said, as the four of them convened in the parking lot. "I thought that you would have run away again."

"Don't speak too soon." Tucker said from his side. "There's still time."

Charles managed to keep his smile on his face as he stared at the pair of them. He could tell that they were clearly very pleased with themselves and the jokes that they had made. He wanted to just roll his eyes and get on with the day, but Charles

456

was still trying to not give them anything that could be used as ammunition against him.

"Good morning, Uncle, Tucker." He nodded to the two of them. "Good to see you."

"How's your fiance doing?"

"She's a lot better today." Charles said. "I think it was some kind of food poisoning."

"It did come on very quickly." Tucker said with narrowed eyes.

"Well, I suppose you can't really control when you're sick." Charles responded in a rather cutting tone.

"Shall we go and get out on the course?" James asked.

It felt as though the only reason Charles came to the golf course was to have talks with his uncle about things that weren't even his business. He remembered the fight that he'd had with Tucker and grimaced at the thought of things ever getting violent with them again. Charles knew that he was incredibly lucky that the man hadn't pressed charges, but he had also been the one that had started the fight in the first place.

"Do send Jane my best wishes, I hope she recovers quickly. It's never nice to get food poisoning." Jack continued, as they walked into the golf club. "I told you that you should get better cooks, or is this all part of your cost cutting since the loss of money?"

Charles increased his pace as he walked ahead of his uncle. He wasn't going to let himself get drawn into things like that again, especially not when it was exactly what his uncle was intending.

The first few holes went by with no more comments, which Charles was incredibly thankful about. The last thing that he wanted was to have to use his patience on something like ignoring his uncle's remarks at him. He kept his head down

457

and played a few more holes before he felt as though he would be able to talk to his uncle without getting into an argument.

"Did you enjoy the dinner?" Charles asked, while turning to Jack.

"I did, although it would have been good to see more of the happy bride and groom."

Charles didn't like the way that his uncle put a little more emphasis on the word happy, but he chose not to react to it.

"Yes, well she's on the mend now and will be fine for the big day." Charles said while forcing a smile onto his face.

"Oh good." Jack nodded. "Wouldn't want a runaway bride on our hands, would we?"

Charles merely shrugged off the comment, he wasn't in the mood to try and combat his uncle's words with much harsher things. He knew that he could take it there, but it wouldn't have been worth it.

James was talking with Tucker, although Charles could tell from the small snippets of conversation that he could hear that it was a rather labored back and fourth of questions.

"I still have to pinch myself that the big womanizer Charles Bentley is settling down." Wyatt said, with a slight chuckle. Charles hadn't been as discreet as he had previously thought in his glances towards his cousin.

"I know, it's quite a change." Charles smiled, as he held out his arms. "But what can I say? It happens to the best of us. You find the right girl, and the rest really is history."

"Of course." Tucker smiled.

Charles hated the way that the man always looked like he was trying to calculate something, but he especially hated it when his attention was solely on him. He didn't want to show Wyatt

Tucker that his stares were intimidating him, but Charles would have given a little more than a penny for his thoughts.

"Rosalyn has had her dress designed by the same man who was showing your fiance some of the finest wedding dresses in the country." Jack said while changing the subject to ease some of the tension out of the conversation. Charles knew that his uncle's go-to subject would of course be something related to money. He chose not to say anything about the sudden change but instead nodded.

"Is that the man by the name of Coco?" Charles asked, as he dug deep into his memory to remember something that had never seemed too relevant to him.

"It is indeed." Jack said. "I was surprised to hear that you managed to get her booked in there at such short notice, but then again, I suppose you just used the name, right?"

"Exactly." Charles nodded, as he glanced at James. "But Jane wanted to have a dress that told a little more of her story. She wanted something modest and something that would show her as an advocate for sustainable fashion."

"I see." Jack nodded. "Well, I just wanted to tell you that Jane has nothing to worry about in terms of my wife outshining her. Rosalyn knows her place, although I did really have to reel her in this time in terms of her not going all out."

"That would have been a real shame for her to outdo the bride, but I suppose she's polite enough to not want to rob another girl's day."

"Of course she is." Jack nodded quickly.

Charles was more than used to the games that his uncle was playing with him. He understood perfectly just how it worked and he wasn't afraid to stand his ground anymore.

"That still meant that the dress cost a pretty penny though." Jack chuckled. Charles knew that the older man wouldn't have been able to resist having a conversation without talking about how much something cost him.

"Oh really?"

"Yes, well, Coco isn't a cheap man to go to. He wanted to do a lot more with the design that Rosalyn gave him, but we had to compromise on a few things. He's one of the best, and so I really didn't mind paying so much in the end."

"How much?" Charles asked the question finally.

He had been wanting to hold out and not give into his curiosity because it was exactly what his uncle would have wanted of him. However, he also knew that Jack would stop bringing it up if he were to ask the question.

"It was somewhere in the region of twenty something, I believe." Jack said with narrowed eyes. Although Charles didn't believe for a moment that his uncle hadn't known what the price was. He knew that the way he was acting so nonchalant about not being able to remember the price was a very old trick that was used to show just how wealthy he was. He also understood that when Charles was talking about twenty something, he was referring to the thousands.

CHAPTER 17

"Well that was a lot quicker and less drama-filled than I thought it would be." James chuckled, as they made it back to the house.

"I don't get it." Charles said more to himself than anyone else.

"What do you mean?"

"I don't understand why they would have invited us if all they wanted to do was make their usual remarks." Charles said while scratching the back of his head. "I mean, in the past, they've used the golf course to corner me. They thought that I wouldn't be willing to show my true reaction in public, but–"

"But they had been very wrong about that." James said with a slight chuckle.

"Exactly." Charles brushed off the comment. "So I don't understand why they didn't try something else today, it was the perfect opportunity for an ambush."

Charles hated more than anything that it didn't make sense. He wanted to understand what they were up to in their schemes and he wanted to try and stay one step ahead of them. However, that seemed impossible at that moment in time.

"Maybe they're just bluffing." James shrugged.

"What do you mean by that?" Charles asked with a frown. "How could they be bluffing at this point when they're the ones with the money."

"Think about it; they want you to believe that they have this money and that no matter what you do, you aren't going to get your hands on it."

"Right…" Charles said slowly.

"But really, they must know that you have some kind of plan to rightfully inherit the money in a week's time when you officially marry Jane. Either that or they think that you're bluffing."

Charles walked through the house and quickly took a seat on one of his sofas as he thought about the complexity of the situation. He didn't like that they didn't know what Jack's plan was, but James was right, he could narrow it down at least.

"I don't know what to do with this information still." Charles admitted with a chuckle. "We're just going to have to hope that they don't pull anything at the wedding in some kind of last attempt at making sure the inheritance goes to Jack and Rosalyn."

"Have you thought about what you'll do if it does end up going to them?"

Charles heard the hesitation in his cousin's voice as he spoke because he knew that it was clearly a very sensitive subject.

"I don't know." He said with a mere shrug. "I don't plan to be in that position, but we'll just have to cross that bridge when we come to it."

Anna appeared in the doorway some moments later, causing Charles to frown since he hadn't summoned her for anything.

"What is it?" He asked with a frown.

"Helena and Jane are here to see you both." She said rather tentatively.

Charles quickly glanced over at his cousin to see that his eyes were trying to bulge out of his skull. If it were any other situation, he would have found the reaction slightly amusing, but there was nothing funny about this. He grimaced at the thought of getting on the wrong side of Jane again, but he knew that they were all going to have to talk at some point.

Slowly, he straightened up and quickly nodded to his housekeeper. Charles made sure to make no sense of worry appeared on his face as he glanced over at James.

"Good, I was going to ask if they could come over anyway so that we could all have a chat." Charles even managed a smile as he spoke. However, James merely grimaced as he stared down at the floor.

*****

James could feel his heart pounding as Charles sent his housekeeper away to bring in the two women. He had thought that he wouldn't have to deal with Helena until at least the wedding day. He'd thought that the time apart from her would allow the situation to cool down and they could have spoken about it in private.

But the current circumstances were dictating a different path to him. James hated the idea of having to talk about it in front of Jane and Charles. He hoped that the meeting would be about nothing more than the issues between the bride and groom.

The sounds of footsteps on the hallway floor grew louder, and James continued to keep his gaze down as the two women entered the room. He swallowed thickly, but he was unable to look up and meet Helena's gaze.

The heavy weight of shame was still building up inside of him after he had been so coldly rejected by her. However, he still wasn't sure where he even stood with her. He hoped that after Jane and Charles had spoken, they would be able to go somewhere and talk more privately.

"This is a pleasant surprise." Charles said, as they sat on the sofa across from him. James was standing behind Charles, although he moved forward slightly so that he looked as though he was more involved with the conversation.

"I just felt that we should talk after what happened the other night." Jane spoke up, much to his surprise. Her posture was rather rigid as she sat with her hands in her lap. James could see that she looked tired, as though she hadn't been sleeping well. He cast his mind back to the dingy apartment that the sisters called home, and he couldn't imagine ever getting a good night of rest in a place like that.

"Yes, I figured that we should probably talk about what happened there." Charles responded in a rather dry tone.

"Do you still think that it was just my fault?" Jane asked with a light scoff. "Because I can assure you, it's not just my fault, I wouldn't have done something like that if I wasn't provoked."

"And you're saying that I provoked you?" Charles asked.

James decided to step forward and take a seat next to his cousin, he knew that he was going to have to play a mediator of sorts.

"You were dismissing me and going into that shut down mode where you barely react to anything that's going on around you." Jane fired back. "I knew that there was no way we would have looked like a convincing couple if you were going to do that all night."

"And so you thought that the best thing to do would just be to get up and leave me there on my own?" Charles asked with a scoff.

"You had James and Helena." Jane said. "I can see now in hindsight that it really hadn't been the best idea on my behalf, but I had only been doing what I thought was right. I didn't want us to look unconvincing and so I figured that it was better if I just left."

"That's ridiculous!" Charles said, as his voice rose in volume slightly.

"What's ridiculous is that you told me to be on my best behavior and told me that I shouldn't show that I'm unhappy about the situation, then you went and did the complete opposite of your words!"

"All right." James cut in between the two of them with his hands outstretched. He didn't want the conversation to merge into an argument as it had done so many times beforehand. "Are you both done?"

"No, I don't think that she should try and shift the blame onto me like that." Charles shook his head.

"It doesn't matter who's to blame anymore." James cut in before Jane could even open her mouth to respond to him. "All that matters is that we pull off the main event next week. After that, it really doesn't matter, does it?"

His words were met with a heavy wall of silence. James quite liked how he'd managed to quell such an argument from brewing with just his words. But he was tired of listening to the ongoing conflict between Jane and Charles.

"You both sound like a broken record, and you argue the same points every time. Neither of you are clearly going to get anywhere with it, and so I propose a ceasefire so that we can just get on with the final wedding plans."

James knew that a ceasefire wouldn't mean that they were both happy with the situation, but it would mean that they were at least civil with one another for the time being.

"Do you really think that we're going to be able to pull this off?" Jane asked, in a quieter voice. "The bride and groom are fighting, so are the maid of honor and the best man."

James couldn't help the way that his eyes met with Helena's properly for the first time since she had entered the room. He quickly looked away and felt his cheeks heating up at her sister's comment. He had known that Helena would have told Jane, but he really didn't want to talk about it at that moment in time.

"We're all going to forget about our conflicts for the wedding day." He said after managing to keep his voice steady. "We're going to have just one day where we all get along as though we really are about to become one big happy family."

"Yes." Charles nodded at his side. "Just one day stands between us and this inheritance now."

"Just when I think that either of you care about anything more than money, you come out with comments like that." Jane said with a weary exhale.

"Whatever." Charles shrugged off her comment. "We've come so far, we're not going to fall at the last hurdle, we're going to stride over the finishing line."

"You know, if you don't get your inheritance out of this in the end, you should totally look into a career as a motivational speaker." Helena said.

Her tone sounded so dry that it was almost difficult to tell if she was joking or not. James glanced at her, but she was no longer looking in his direction. He knew that he'd messed up with her and that she wasn't going to be happy with him for a long while, but he was also upset at how she had reacted to the news so badly.

"Very funny." Charles responded in a tone that was just as dry as hers had been. "But we need to be serious now. I don't know what's going on between the two of you, but you need to bury it for the actual day."

James couldn't believe that his cousin was technically covering for him. Charles knew exactly what was going on, but he was playing a very smart game.

Helena looked down at her lap in the wake of his words, James knew that she still wasn't over their argument. He swallowed thickly at the thought of talking to her about it, but he knew that it would have to be done at some point. Biting the bullet was always going to be a difficult task, especially with a woman as feisty as Helena, but James knew that it was better to get it out of the way sooner rather than later.

Jane and Charles both stood up as though they knew that the conversation was over. But James glanced over at Helena to see that she was still looking down.

"We'll be out on the terrace." Charles said, as he quickly prompted a reluctant Jane to step out of the room. She was glaring at him but followed suit.

*****

"What are you doing?" Jane asked, in a hushed tone as soon as they were out in the hallway.

"They need to talk about what happened, and I don't think they would properly open up with both of us in the room like that."

"What makes you think that?" Jane frowned, as she spoke. "I thought that they would be fine talking about it in a similar way to how we just did?"

"I know, but their feelings are real. It's not like we actually feel that way."

Charles' words were followed by a rather strange and awkward silence. Jane couldn't quite place what it was about his words that had made her stop and think, but she wasn't sure how to feel about it. She was so conflicted that she almost didn't notice that he was walking down the hall and heading for the rear stairs that led straight up to his terrace.

"Do you really think that they will be able to have a conversation without shouting at one another?"

"Well, we managed it." Charles shrugged off her question.

"But we had them as mediators." Jane reiterated.

"James isn't as argumentative as me."

Jane knew that she couldn't say the same about her sister, and so she simply pursed her lips in response. She thought about what was going on downstairs, and her concern continued to rise for her sister.

CHAPTER 18

Helena shifted in her seat as she looked up at James as soon as the door clicked shut. She hadn't wanted to come back to the house so soon, and she had regretted it almost as soon as she had stepped through the grand front door. Through the window, she could see that the marque was still up. It was a reminder of the night that had been so strange in the end. The last thing that she had expected was for James to talk to her like that and actually ask her out.

"I suppose I should start by apologizing for my reaction." Helena said with a sigh.

James's reaction came in the form of blinking profusely. She waited a moment, but he still didn't say anything.

"Look, I'm sorry for the way that I was that night. It was stupid of me to be so harsh for no reason." Helena tried again. "I hope that I didn't hurt your feelings too much."

"It's fine." James's words were curt. "I just wish that you were honest with me and yourself."

"I have been." Helena said with a frown. "I don't get what you mean by that, because I've only been honest with myself *and* you."

"I'm not sure about that last part."

Helena knew what he was talking about, but she didn't want to come clean about the way that he made her feel. Giving James the satisfaction of knowing that he had such an effect on her just didn't sit well with her.

"Well I am." She stood her ground. "I know what you want me to say, and believe me, I've thought about this for a lot longer than you would think. But as I said last time, I just...can't."

"Is that supposed to be a good enough excuse?" He asked while shaking his head. "You just can't?"

"I can't, and I really am sorry about that, but I can't see you in that way."

She could see his mind working to try and understand why she was saying such things, but it was proving to be no use. James simply sighed and nodded as he looked down.

"I really thought that you felt a similar way to me. I thought that you would have been willing to overlook our different situations and would have just given it a go."

Helena knew that it would be no good to entertain something with him. It would result in a lot of hurt, and she wasn't about to let herself go through with that.

"I'm just here because Charles is going to help pay for our lives." She said in a much harsher tone than intended.

"I know you're not that shallow. You care too much about things to really mean that." He said with narrowed eyes. Although Helena had seen the hurt flash through his eyes at her words.

"I mean it, James, and I'm sorry that I led you to think that I wanted anything more. That was wrong of me, I just want to put this really weird chapter of my life behind me."

She watched as he nodded slowly at her words, even Helena wasn't sure that she believed herself. Helena could feel a large part of her yearning to at least try, but she couldn't hurt herself like that. She wasn't going to let herself get hurt if she already had suspicions that it was on the cards.

"So you just want to go through with the wedding and then what? Never see us again?" He asked with narrowed eyes.

"James, you know the association that this family has with the cause of my mother's death. It was that very event that put me on the course that led me to this very moment. It has brought me so much pain and hardship that I'm more than ready to have to suck up a pretend wedding for a day to end it."

"And then we'll never see each other again?" His voice sounded a lot smaller than before.

"I don't know." Helena said as she rubbed her eyes for a moment. "I really don't know."

*****

James knew that there was something else going on, he tried to consider what it may have been, but nothing came to mind. He couldn't believe that she was able to sound so harsh with her words. He shook his head and tried to ignore the fact that Helena had openly admitted to him that she was just there for the money.

Her words felt as though they had stung, and he winced at the thought of not seeing her again after the wedding. Although, James couldn't quite face even imagining a world where he wouldn't see her again, yet he would have to live with the burden of knowing her.

Even as he looked at her, the warmth had gone from her face. Helena's stare was cold and distant, but it all felt rather deliberate. It felt as though she had put those walls out to purposefully keep him out.

"I know that you haven't had it easy in your life." James said. "And I respect you and your sister so much after hearing about what you've been through. I know that my family has played a large role in that, but don't you think I'm different? I'm not like my family at all."

"I know." Helena said, but she shook her head. "I know that you aren't the same kind of people as your father or Charles' father. But it's still the same money, and you have the same family name. That's just not something that I can overlook so quickly."

471

James knew that there would be no reasoning with someone that was as headstrong as Helena was. Once she had made up her mind, there would be no changing it. He swallowed thickly since the reality that he now faced was a rather bitter pill to swallow. James felt slightly better that there wasn't so much animosity as there was awkwardness between them now. He felt like a fool for even asking her out in the first place.

"Let's just try to forget about this?" Helena offered with a slight wince.

"Sure." He nodded.

James wasn't sure how he was going to pretend to have a good time on the actual day of the wedding. He knew that it was customary for the maid of honor and best man to do a lot of things together on the day, and he was dreading even the thought of it.

"Alright." He said, while standing up from his seat. "I suppose we should go and join the others."

"James." Helena spoke, as she remained where she was.

James had already started for the door as she spoke, but he quickly stopped and turned around at the sound of his name on her lips.

"I really am sorry." Helena said, while slowly looking up at him.

"I know." James said. "So am I, forget I ever said anything. You clearly don't want to be honest with yourself."

With that, he left the room.

*****

Charles glanced between the pair as they arrived up on the terrace one at a time. He knew that meant that they hadn't come to an agreement that meant they were as friendly as they had been in the past.

He still couldn't quite believe that James had taken the leap and told Helena exactly how he felt. Charles found it slightly amusing but judging the look on his cousin's face, he could tell that it wasn't something that was a laughing matter yet.

"Not long to go." Charles spoke up as Helena sat down at the table. If the two of them had managed to resolve anything, there was nothing in their expressions or body language to show this. "In a week's time I'll have my money, transfer it, and we can all go and get on with our lives."

He hadn't known what to expect in response to his words, but absolute silence wasn't the reaction that he had first thought he would achieve.

CHAPTER 19

Jane hadn't spoken to Charles for a couple of days, and she would have been lying if she said that she hadn't enjoyed the peace and quiet. Helena, on the other hand, was acting as though she was going through a breakup.

"I'm telling you, this will pass." Jane said with a sigh. "You just have to see him for one day and then that's it."

"I know." Helena huffed, as she stared aimlessly at the wall from her position on the couch.

"I never thought that I would be the one telling you this, I thought that it would be you trying to convince me to actually go through with this." Jane chuckled, as she shook her head. "I can't believe that in two days I'm going to be having a wedding with Charles."

"It does sound rather crazy when you say it like that. My little sister is getting married before me."

"It's not a real marriage, don't feel too bad about it." Jane chuckled, as she started to clean up some of the clutter that was starting to suffocate the kitchen area of their small flat. She was finding that they were bringing more and more of the clothes that Charles had let her have back to their apartment. They didn't have enough wardrobe space for much, let alone the kind of clothing that cost a couple of month's rent when added up all together.

"I know it's not a real marriage, but you're still gaining something from it; a lot of money." Helena said, while turning until she was lying on her back and staring up at the ceiling.

"A lot of money that we're both going to be able to use to kickstart what we want to do with our lives." Jane was trying to reason with her.

But Jane could tell that her sister wasn't in a reasoning mood. She was in the kind of mood that Jane would sometimes get into and she would call the hopeless lamenting period. It was the kind of mood where it felt as though nothing was going to go right and she was going to be stuck in this constant cycle for the rest of her life. She knew that it sounded a tad dramatic, but Jane had been there many times herself.

Seeing Helena in that same position was the kind of thing that Jane felt as though she wasn't supposed to see. Helena was the one who looked out for the both of them, and it didn't feel right to see her in such a vulnerable state. It was like seeing a parent cry, and Jane didn't like the uneasiness that it left within her at all.

She knew that her sister would push through this, but she just wished that Helena would hurry up with that.

"I was hoping that we could maybe go out and do some shopping. Maybe grab a bite to eat or something before the big day?" Jane suggested. She wasn't expecting Helena to say yes to her proposal, but she was hoping that her older sister would at least want to spend some time with her outside of the apartment.

"I'm not sure." Helena grunted. "I was going to say that we'll have to look at our finances for this month, but after what you're about to do, I'm not sure that we'll ever have to do that again."

Jane still struggled to comprehend just how much money the billions of dollars really was. In her mind, it was a number that she just couldn't quite fathom, although Jane hoped that she was going to be able to handle her share of the money without just blowing it all.

She remembered the many lessons that both Helena and her mother had taught her before she died about being frugal. It was one of the most valuable skills that Jane had ever learned, and she knew that she owed it to the women in her family for bringing her up in such a modest way. She had learned to have respect for material things, but she didn't have a burning need for so many unnecessary things as lots of other children had been brought up to believe.

"How are you honestly feeling about the wedding?" Helena asked.

The question caught Jane off guard since she had tried to not think about it. The date had felt like some curse that had been placed on her family, one that she would only be able to lift if she were to sign away her soul.

"I don't know in all honesty." Jane sighed. "Sometimes I think that it will be the best thing that I can do for the two of us. It will be something that will end the main stress in our lives and it will sort out our troubles. But then I think about Mom and how much I miss her. It hurts to think that her death could have been avoided and that these people couldn't really care less about what they did. But I'm trying to be positive about the experience and I'm trying to project good thoughts about the actual day."

"Mm." Helena said in response as she continued to look up at the ceiling. "Nothing is going to be the same after this, is it?"

"I think nothing was ever the same once I had said yes to his original proposal."

Jane thought back to when she had first said yes to the rich man in response to such an outrageous idea. She wanted nothing more than to be rid of the weight of her college debt, and this felt like too good of an offer to refuse. Jane smiled to herself if only she had known back then.

But now there was more on the cards; a substantial amount of money that Jane could never have even dreamed of obtaining, as well as James's promise that he would help her with her nonprofit organization. She felt guilty that Helena still didn't know about that, but Jane knew that Helena wouldn't like the idea of James poking around in places that he wasn't supposed to.

*****

Charles was pacing again. He knew that it was the kind of thing that he did when he was stressed, and he was sure that the past week would go down in his personal history as one of the most stressful weeks of his life.

"You're making me stressed." James said from the couch as he lay staring up at the ceiling. His words were slurred slightly, and Charles made a mental note to not let his cousin have any more scotch that evening.

James seemed to be on some kind of warpath to remain perpetually drunk until it was time to get through the wedding. Charles was even sure that his cousin would probably enjoy a lot of drink on the actual day too.

"Well, I'm stressed." Charles admitted while running a hand through his hair. "The wedding is only a couple of days away and I don't know if I should talk to Jane or not."

"Why would you talk to her?"

"What if she has backed out without telling me? She might be leaving me at the altar in one final stunt of humiliation." Charles voiced something that was a genuine concern for him. He knew that it sounded rather stupid to be worked up over it, but he wasn't sure that he could trust in Jane's actions enough.

"She wouldn't jeopardize the wedding like that." James chuckled, as he continued to slur his words. "She has too much to gain from this, and I don't think that after getting a taste of this life that either of them will want to go back to working long hours and barely getting by."

Even through his drunken haze, Charles was surprised that his cousin was making sense. James looked incredibly relaxed on the couch, although he knew that all of this was because of the conversation he'd had with Helena.

When Charles had asked him about what was said, James had been vague and he clearly hadn't wanted to talk about it. Charles wished that he had potentially pressed the subject a little harder, although he didn't want to upset James any more than he already was.

CHAPTER 20

Jane lay in her bed listening to the stuck ticking of a clock that she had long ago forgotten to change the batteries of. From the window outside, she could hear the world waking up and it filled her with dread. She swallowed thickly and breathed heavily at the thought of the day that lay ahead of her.

It was finally time. After the many weeks of planning and organizing, the different dinners and events that Charles had made her go to. Everything had been leading up to the day that lay ahead of her. She hated how much importance was being placed on a few hours, but Jane was determined more than anything to get through this without any kind of incident.

She lay there and thought about the day that she had decided to go out to the wealthy address in search of a good tip. Never in a million years would she have thought that it would lead her down the path that she had found herself on. It had completely changed her life, and she still hadn't decided if it had been for better or for worse.

Finally, Jane could hear Helena getting up from the room next door. She knew that her sister wouldn't let her sleep in on such an important day, but Jane didn't want to go back to sleep anyway. She was content in getting up and starting her day because she just wanted it all over and done with.

Slowly, she swung her legs over her small bed and let her bare feet make contact with the cool wooden floor. Jane shuddered as she crossed the room and started to get ready for the day. Her nerves had reached an all time high, and she felt slightly sick about the day that lay ahead of her.

This wasn't going to be like the other times when she would be able to run away. This was the event. This was the only time that it was going to count.

"I can do this." She muttered to herself as she glanced at the bags that were packed by her door. She had enough clothes and makeup for a small army of women, but she was still terrified that it wouldn't be enough. Jane sighed and thought about how different her life would be the next day. She wouldn't have to worry about finances if this really worked, since Charles had promised her a sum of money that was much larger than the original amount that he'd offered. Jane was glad that he had upped the amount, although part of her still felt terrible in marrying for money.

It was going to sort out so many of their problems, that she was willing to do this and do whatever it took to get the money.

"Are you ready to go?" Helena called from the kitchen. "You better not still be in bed or there will be-"

"I'm up." Jane said, as Helena opened her door anyway.

She could see the surprise on her sister's face that she really was up and not causing any unnecessary problems.

"Oh." Helena muttered. "Well, it's good to see you up."

"Thanks." Jane said with a slight frown.

"How are you feeling?"

"I'm scared, Helena." Jane admitted.

"You have nothing to be scared about, you're going to be fine." She smiled reassuringly.

"I don't know, what if something goes wrong and this is all for nothing? What if his uncle-"

"We're just going to have to have positive thoughts today, none of this unnecessary worrying, all right?" Helena said, with a small smile on her face. "Just play your part right, and that's all you can do."

Jane nodded slowly and bit her lip, she was stressed even just thinking about all of the last minute preparations that were going on over at Charles' house. But she found that more than anything, Jane was dreading having to see Darcy all day too.

The woman was going to be in her element, but she could also imagine her running around as though she were a headless chicken.

It didn't take long before a car was waiting outside to take them to Charles' mansion. Jane walked behind her sister as some of their neighbors stared in confusion. Jane thought that they must have been used to the sleek black cars that were often waiting outside of the building every now and again, but it seemed not.

She didn't like being the center of their curiosity, and she knew that as soon as they got the money, they were getting out of that apartment for good. Jane and Helena sat in silence during the car journey, she stared out of the window and tried to think of something that would put her in better spirits. It was, after all, her wedding day, even if it was a fake one.

*****

"You're going to be fine today." Helena said, as the car pulled down the long driveway.

"I hope you're right." Jane said, as she let out a shaky breath. It seemed that no matter what she did, she couldn't get rid of her nerves. She was squeezing her hands together and trying all sorts of unorthodox things to get rid of the nerves, but nothing was working.

"There she is!" Darcy gushed, as Jane finally stepped through the door to Charles' place. She had forced a smile onto her face after getting out of the car, and she was determined to do what her sister had told her and play her part right. "How is the bride today?"

"I'm good." Jane smiled, as she took Darcy's outstretched hand.

The woman had even brighter lipstick on than normal, which Jane simply hadn't thought was possible. She breathed out and glanced around to see that the groom was nowhere in sight.

"Where's Charles?" Jane asked with a frown as Darcy started to lead her up the stairs.

"It's bad luck for the bride to see the groom before the ceremony." She chuckled, as Jane was followed by a small cohort of people.

She felt as though she had her own personal army of stylists and hairdressers. Jane thought that it was a bit much as she was whisked away into a chair and told that she was going to be getting her hair and makeup done by the many people around her.

Darcy was rambling on about a wide array of things, but Jane was barely listening. She simply focused on the fact that there were far more people touching her than she was comfortable with, but she let it happen to not cause a fuss. She breathed out deeply as the stylists talked amongst themselves and were addressing the color scheme.

"Do you have any preferences?"

"Not really." Jane brushed it off. She knew that this wasn't the kind of answer that was going to fly with Darcy, nothing would get past her.

"Oh come on, Jane." Darcy said with a sigh. "It's your big day, what colors are you thinking of for your eyes?"

Jane thought about this for a moment, she laughed lightly as though to suddenly play the role of the ditsy bride who didn't know what she wanted.

"I'm not usually a big fan of makeup, so maybe just something a little more neutral?" Jane asked.

She could see some of the makeup artists and hair stylists around her sending each other looks. She didn't know if she'd said something wrong, but Jane had no choice but to simply ignore their judgment.

Helena was sitting in the room with her, but it felt as though she was going to be there for hours as the many stylists teased and curled at her hair. People were applying things to her face that Jane probably would never have thought of on her own. She kept her expression blank as they worked on her face, and she knew that there was going to be a big reveal at the end. There was no mirror in front of her, and Jane was anxious to see what they were doing.

Helena had been on her phone for a while and only paid attention when Darcy would ask her a question. It seemed that with each moment that passed, Jane could feel her nerves reaching a new all time high. Just when she thought that she had reached the peak of her nerves, they seemed to skyrocket even more and send her limbs tingling. She was glad to have gotten past the nauseous phase of being nervous, but Jane was still terrified that she wouldn't be able to go through with this.

"Alright." Darcy said with a wide grin. She clasped her hands together as she looked at Jane. "Are you ready for the big reveal?"

Jane had guessed that they were going to go for this kind of dramatic reveal at the end. But she really was looking forward to seeing how she looked. She nodded quickly and eagerly as two of the stylists uncovered a mirror in front of her.

Jane took a moment to look at the woman who stared back at her with wide eyes. She couldn't quite believe that she was looking at herself. It almost didn't feel real that she was staring at a made up version of her. Her mouth hung open slightly as she stared at the woman who looked slightly like her, but then when she turned her head slightly, it was almost as though she was a completely different person.

Helena was also looking at her in shock. Jane's hair was styled half up, and the rest was curled and sitting about her shoulders. She seriously couldn't believe that she was looking at the same woman who had woken up that morning.

"You look beautiful." Helena breathed out.

"Thanks." Jane managed a smile through her shock. "I...I can't believe it."

"I don't suppose you could work that magic on me too." Helena chuckled.

"Oh as the maid of honor, it's expected."

Jane laughed as she saw the way that her sister's eyes lit up upon hearing Darcy's words. She had never seen Helena move so quickly as she got into the chair and sat waiting for the same to happen to her.

*****

Charles took a sip of scotch as James smoothed down the back of his suit. He hadn't anticipated that he would actually be so nervous when the day finally came around. He grimaced and stared at himself in the mirror as though he was trying to psych himself out.

"I can practically hear your nerves, they're radiating off of you, Charles." James chuckled and shook his head. "You're just going to have to relax. Darcy said that Jane is here and getting ready as we speak. Everything is going to go perfectly."

Charles nodded slowly, although he wasn't sure that he would be able to believe that.

"I hope you're right, James." Charles said. "I really do."

"Come on, you just have to relax a little." James said, while smiling at him from the mirror. "Everything is going to be fine, you just have to say it out loud."

"Everything will be fine." Charles muttered.

He'd never been a fan of projecting things like that, but he knew that he didn't exactly have a better plan at that moment.

"Everything will be fine." Charles said again while taking a deep breath.

"See, you've just got to believe it."

Charles wasn't sure that he did believe it, but he certainly was going to try.

"Do you really think that Jane is going to go through with this?"

"I've told you already that I know she will." James nodded with a small smile.

CHAPTER 21

It was time. Jane held her breath as she stared at herself in the full length mirror. She was pleased with the gown that she had picked, but she was also happy at how her hair and makeup complimented it so well. She couldn't believe that the day was finally upon them and that the hour had arrived.

"Most of the guests are already downstairs." Darcy said, as she fussed around Jane for the final few moments.

"Are Jack and Rosalyn here?" Jane asked with a slight wince.

"They are." Darcy nodded. "Don't worry though, they're near the back."

Jane sighed in relief at the thought of not having to see them anywhere near the front of the ceremony.

"You really do look amazing." Helena said, from her side as Jane started to get ready to make her way out to the tent.

"Thanks." Jane smiled, as she pulled her sister in for a hug. "So do you."

The blue dress that Helena wore hugged her figure perfectly, the color complimented her hair and complexion, and Jane couldn't believe that the two of them could really scrub up so well. She then reminded herself that almost anything was possible with the right amount of money.

"I just wish that mom was here to see us looking like this." Helena said with a sigh.

"I know." Jane nodded in agreement. "She would have loved it."

Jane was going to be walking down the aisle with James. She knew that it was rather unconventional to be with the best man as she walked down the sacred walkway, but she didn't want to do it with anyone else, and Jane really didn't want to do it alone. She sighed and tried not to think about the pressure of having so many people watching her on the day.

"You're going to be great!" Darcy was encouraging her as she continued her walk down to the ground floor. "Everyone has been seated, and Charles is standing by at the end of the aisle."

Jane nodded slowly, she was breathing deeply in an attempt to calm herself down. Her hands were shaking slightly, but she figured that there were worse things that could be happening at that moment.

She felt slightly thankful that Charles was letting his best man walk her down the aisle. She was sure that he may have needed James's support too, but she was happy that he'd thought of somebody other than himself for once.

"You're going to do great." Helena whispered to her as she walked toward the door to the rear of the house. They could hear the faint hum of chatter over the sound of delicate music being played within the large tent. Jane sucked in a breath and started down toward the entrance of the marquee, where James was waiting for her.

*****

Charles was starting to regret the fact that he had allowed James to help Helena instead of being at his side. It was the moment that everything had been building up to, the moment that would allow him to transfer the inheritance from his uncle's account to his. Charles swallowed thickly as he thought about being able to finally breathe and relax about his financial situation. It wasn't as though things had been too tough on him, he knew that there were lots of people that went through a lot worse in terms of financial hardships. But Charles had just hated the uncertainty of not knowing whether or not things were going to work out in his favor.

He waited at the end of the aisle and tried not to look as terrified as he felt on the inside. The room was filled with people, and he knew that he couldn't let himself break at that final hurdle.

The bustle of people started to quieten down from the back to the front of the marquee, and Charles caught sight of Darcy through the slight gap in the opening. He bit his lip and watched as the guests were prompted to stand from their seats. Moments later, the door was opened fully, revealing Jane and James standing at the other end of the aisle.

Charles felt struck for a moment as he stared at her. He couldn't believe that she was really in front of him and that she looked as good as she did. It was finally time to get this over with, but he slightly shocked himself by how taken he was with Jane.

Her dress was simple, and yet still beautiful. Charles could see a few reporters around the room taking the chance to photograph her as the music started to play. It was a soft classical piece that accompanied her walk down the aisle. Jane had a light smile on her face, while James looked slightly terrified to be walking down the aisle.

The sea of familiar faces around them was framed with faux foliage and fairy lights that illuminated the marquee in a way that Charles had never anticipated for his wedding. He had wanted a much more sleek display, but that hadn't been possible since Jane had suggested a few images that looked similar to the scenery around them. Since it was more for Darcy to plan, she had agreed with the idea in a display of gushing emotion. Charles had known from that moment on that not too many of his ideas would become a reality for the wedding. But he didn't care too much, he knew that he was going to have the money soon, and that was all that mattered.

But as he looked at Jane walking down the aisle in all of her beauty, he started to question whether that was really what he wanted. Charles frowned and stared hard at Jane as she approached him, the music was still playing in the background and the people around him were beaming at him as he waited for her to reach the same part of the front as he stood.

He could feel a slight awkwardness between them that he tried to quell with a small smile on his face, but he wasn't sure who he was fooling with that. Jane was also slightly smiling as she stared up at him and let her eyes do the talking.

Although they were wide, they were also filled with a certain amount of distance that told him not to push his luck. Charles sighed since he knew that he would never get through to her about how happy they could be together. It was a thought that caught him off guard, but it was also a thought that stemmed from him thinking about not seeing Anna again. He grimaced at the idea of being without her and to never see her again.

Charles realized just as she was about to approach him in front of a room of people that he didn't want to have to say goodbye to Jane, that he had grown a certain fondness towards her.

She kept her gaze down at the ground as she finally stood opposite him. Charles thought about the many times that he had imagined making it to that moment, it felt like a feat in itself, but it also was starting to feel like a huge disappointment.

He wasn't sure what it was, but suddenly the money no longer felt too important. The look on Jane's face showed him that she wasn't enjoying herself and that he had put her through so much. Charles could see that she was trying her best to remain happy as she stood opposite him, but it was clear that her resolve was failing.

Charles held onto her hands and stared at her intently. He nodded as though to reassure her slightly that everything would be all right, but even Charles didn't believe himself. They were going to be fine once the money was in his account, but he still felt the deep sense that he didn't even want it at that point. What he realized was important to him was that he could have had a great wedding with someone that he really loved, and it would have been the happiest day of his life. Instead, Charles found himself surrounded by forced smiles and empty words.

"You look beautiful." He whispered to her.

Jane smiled for a moment, but it quickly faded as the man before them started to speak.

"Dearly beloved…"

*****

Jane wasn't sure what was wrong with Charles. There was a look in his eyes that she hadn't expected to see when she reached the end of the aisle. It was the kind of look that was sad while trying to be happy at the same time.

She knew that her own expression was probably no better, but Jane was still trying to make this work. His words had thrown her off slightly; Jane hadn't expected Charles to give her any compliments, and the way he'd said it in such a small voice made her question his intentions. She would have understood if he'd spoken up a bit louder so that other guests would have heard, but this had felt much more private and intimate than Jane had thought he was capable of.

She wasn't listening to the vicar beside them as he read out the ceremonial words. Jane just wanted to get this over with so that she could go about her life as relatively normal as possible. She thought about James's promise to her that he would give her help with her nonprofit and use his contacts to make it a success. Jane really hoped that she could count on him for that. He stood by Charles's side with a smile on his face as he looked at the couple in front of him. Jane wished that she could have shared in his happiness on that day, but no matter how hard she tried, it just didn't feel right.

She had thought that she would have been relieved to get to that day, but Jane felt nothing as she looked at Charles. She suddenly felt very numb to the situation around them.

"Jane, do you take this man to be your lawfully wedded husband?"

They were words that Jane had never thought she'd get to hear. She glanced up into Charles' expecting eyes and took a deep breath.

"I do." Her voice was a lot quieter than she had anticipated, but Jane still managed to get the words out.

"And do you, Charles, take this woman to be your lawfully wedded wife?"

Jane glanced up at him nervously. They had had a rather strenuous relationship during the past few weeks, and Jane wasn't sure if he was going to go through with it after all.

"I do." Charles said while nodding.

She closed her eyes for a moment as she breathed through the relief that ran through her. It was done. Of course, they were still going to have to sign some of the documents to show that it was all legal, but those were just the legalities of it.

"You may kiss the bride."

They had managed to make it through the actual wedding ceremony without any incident, all that stood in front of them now was the kiss.

Jane pursed her lips before leaning in. Charles did the same, although she could see the hesitance in his actions. She knew that they couldn't afford to look anything less than in love, and while it was a detail that they both had avoided speaking about during the planning of the event.

Their lips met with a tentative amount of pressure. Jane felt her eyebrows furrow slightly as she pressed her lips against his.

The action tingled slightly, as though she had received an electric shock from it, but Jane continued to kiss for a long enough amount of time to make the act look convincing. The crowd had erupted into a roar of applause and cheers for the happy couple, and Jane smiled slightly sheepishly at Charles. She couldn't place the look on his face; it appeared as though Charles was deep in thought with narrowed eyes and his lips pressed into a tight line, although Jane couldn't be sure what was going on in his head.

*****

The wedding was a blur. Nobody could deny that they hadn't looked completely in love when they had kissed, but Charles still wasn't sure what he had felt. He swallowed thickly and tried to gather his thoughts into a more cohesive order, but it was no use.

He went about his day being congratulated by everyone around him, but he continuously was having to force the smile on his face to stay put.

"Congratulations, Cousin." James said, with a smirk as he nudged him. "Just the reception dinner and then the money is yours."

Charles was trying his best to put a smile on his face, but he just couldn't quite manage it. Despite the flourish of decorations around him, many of the guests had commented on the detail that must have gone into the planning of them. He wanted to say that they should go and speak with the wedding planner Darcy, it will be the ultimate test of their patience.

"This isn't what I'd thought it was going to be, James." Charles kept his voice low.

"What do you mean?"

492

"Well, just look at all of the unhappiness that we have caused in pursuing this. Think about Jane and Helena and all that they have been through, this just doesn't feel...worth it anymore."

"Not even getting the money?" James asked with a slight frown.

"It feels wrong that all we've proven from this is that there is nothing stronger than my greed."

Charles felt a wave of shame running through him at the thought of this. He wanted nothing more than to take back his actions and reassure the two sisters that everything would be all right.

"I don't understand." James said. "What do you want to do now then?"

"I want to get through this party with a glass of scotch in my hand that is never empty."

"I mean with the money? I spoke to Wyatt before and they're being forced to make the transaction by the end of tomorrow." James reiterated.

"I don't know yet." He breathed out. "I think I'll put it into a trust until we know what to do with it."

James nodded slowly at this, although Charles could see that he wasn't convinced.

"I'm sorry, James, I just feel far too guilty about so many things. Maybe if I just sit on this for a while, I'll find the right thing to do."

"Alright." James said while holding up his hands. "I'll put my trust in you on this."

"And this time, I promise that I'll try my best to make the right decision."

We hope you Enjoyed Book Three of the Accidental Engagement Series. Now Continue Reading the Story by Reading the Book Four.

Make sure you signed up to Bridget Taylor's mailing to receive FREE BONUS CONTENT which compliment this book. Just go to https://bit.ly/aebonuscontent to Sign Up and Get Notified of New Releases.

The Accidental Engagement

Series Book Four

Description

Charles and Jane have finally said I do and are off on their honeymoon. However, neither is looking forward to spending time with the other. Jane has plans to spend as much time away from Charles as possible on this trip. All of her hopes and dreams come crashing to a halt when a blizzard hits, stranding her and Charles at the airport. But will spending the night alone in a hotel room together be too much temptation for the sexual tension that has slowly been building since their fated kiss?

Anna, who is accompanying the newlyweds for their honeymoon, runs into the one man she never thought she would see again. Her ex-husband Evan, who is also stranded with her at the airport. With Helena and James trapped together at Charles' mansion, Anna, Evan, Jane and Charles trapped within the airport will they all survive? Or will they give into their temptations?

CHAPTER 1

Before you start reading book four on the next page please make you get notified for the release of next series. Go to **https://bit.ly/aebonuscontent** to sign up to get notified of Bridget Taylor's new series coming out and to receive free bonus content and take part in giveaways. If you like this series you will love the next one :-).

Join Bridget Taylor's Exclusive Mailing List for FREE BONUS CONTENT and Discount Coupons

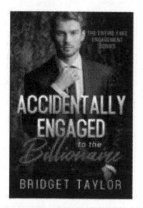

☆ Click below to receive free bonus content, discount coupons, take part in giveaways and get notified of Bridget Taylor's new releases.

☆ A new series is about to be launched. You will be one of the first to be notified with a discount coupon.

CLICK HERE TO SIGN UP

Just go to https://bit.ly/aebonuscontent to follow Bridget Taylor

START OF CHAPTER ONE

"Cape Town, really? You are now married to a millionaire, someone who could take you anywhere in the world and you pick South Africa?" Helena said, still shocked that she was helping her sister pack for her honeymoon.

"What are you talking about? It's going to be awesome. This is the best part of this whole experience. I couldn't believe he said I could pick anywhere in the world for our honeymoon. I thought for sure he was just going to tell me where we were going."

When Charles had told Jane she could decide on their honeymoon the night of their wedding, she was shocked. A good shocked, but shocked. She had known right away where she wanted them to go and once again she was surprised when he simply said he would book the tickets and the resort for them. She was expecting him to complain about going to South Africa, but not a single complaint left his lips. Jane had noticed a change in Charles, it was subtle, but it was there. After their ceremony, during the reception he seemed subdued, sad almost. She wasn't sure what was going on with him, but at the same time it wasn't her business. This was purely a business transaction, a year contract, that she would uphold on her end. That didn't mean she had to be a loving and doting wife. They were going to live separate lives and it would be best to keep their emotions out of it,

"I can't believe he agreed. Why the hell would you want to be going to Cape Town?" Helena asked, as she helped to fold Jane's clothes for her suitcase.

"Why wouldn't I? There's surfing, zip lining, penguins, paragliding, and you can go cage diving with great white sharks." Jane said with a huge smile.

"None of that sounds fun to me. But we are two different people." Helena said with a warm shake of her head.

"They also have cruises, beaches and wine tasting so you would not be left unentertained."

That was the one thing that greatly differed between the two sisters. Helena liked calm and relaxing, especially after working in a bar. She liked going on boats and spending all day lazing around on the sand. Jane though, she was a beer and whiskey girl. She wanted to play sports and not just sit and watch. She loved adventure, she loved being active and helping people. She had no problem getting dirty and working with her hands.

"He's going to kill you." Helena said with a smile, referring to Charles.

"He said I could pick and I never said he had to come with me everywhere. He's going to be spending his honeymoon in the resort and I will be spending it out of it. I'm even going to a nearby village to help them with building some houses. It's going to be awesome. This might be the only chance I have to go on my dream vacation and I am going to jam as much as I can into it."

Jane had no idea what was going to happen within the next year or what came after, but what she did know was that she was only going to take what she needed to pay off her debts. She was going to work and make a living like a normal human being. This was her and Helena's chance to get out from under the weight of their debt and start a new life. She wasn't going to have it connected to Charles and his money. She would discuss with James about him investing into her non-profit, but that will be strictly as a donor and she would make sure legally everyone was covered. If there was one thing Jane had learned it was that she didn't want to be classed anywhere within the realm of Aunt Rosalyn. She was not going to be a woman that settled for less than love because the man had money. She wasn't a gold digger and she would not lower herself to that level. She enjoyed working and she was going to keep doing it. Once she returned from her honeymoon she would turn her full attention to her schooling and start looking for a decent job.

"I don't blame you there. Now can we talk about how weird it is going to be that Anna is joining you? I mean, who brings their housekeeper with them on their honeymoon?" Helena asked, confused by the notion completely.

"Ya that one I don't get." Jane agreed, as she finished packing.

When Charles had informed her that Anna would be escorting them, she thought he was joking. They were supposed to be newlyweds, so why would they bring Anna on their honeymoon? It seemed so weird and Jane could tell that Anna wasn't impressed by the idea either. It had clearly been Charles who wanted her there, but why Jane had no idea. It was all very weird to her, but it wouldn't affect her from having the time of her life. If Charles wanted some company while he sat on the beach, then good for him.

"Maybe he has a crush." Helena teased.

"Oh my god." Jane laughed as she tossed a pillow at her sister.

Helena laughed as she caught the pillow and spoke. "What? Stranger things have happened."

"I'm fairly certain Anna has more standards and taste than that."

"Says the girl that married him." Helena countered with a smirk.

Jane responded by throwing another pillow at her, one Helena wasn't able to catch or dodge, resulting in it hitting her in the face. Jane couldn't contain her belly laugh at the shocked look on Helena's face.

"I'm going to kill you." Helena said with a calm edge to her voice.

"Serves you right." Jane responded, as she headed over to where her coats were. She wasn't sure on how well the weather would hold up so she was going to bring a couple different ones.

"Are we ever going to talk about that kiss?" Helena asked, as she sat down on the edge of the bed facing her sister.

"You mean the kiss we had to have to make our marriage official?"

The kiss was the last thing Jane wanted to talk about. It wasn't because she felt dirty or that it was terrible. She wished that was how she felt. Instead she could still feel the ghostly imprint of Charles' lips against hers. Just a single kiss had her whole body coming alive with electricity under her skin. She had kissed a few different guys in her life, but none had ever felt like that and she was not ready to start processing what all of that could mean. She couldn't be attracted to Charles. He was everything she hated and she was not going to let whatever chemistry there might be buried underneath be unearthed.

"That wasn't exactly a peck Honey. You leaned into it. You must have felt something."

"Nope, nothing."

Jane tried to say it completely calmly, but Helena could pick up the lie to her voice. She knew better than to push though so for now she would let it go and see how it all played out. It would appear that this honeymoon was going to be interesting on many different levels.

*****

"Cape Town? You let her pick Cape Town?" James asked, completely shocked and confused.

"I said she could pick any place she wanted to go. That's what she picked." Charles said, as he continued to pack. They were set to leave for the airport within the hour and he didn't want

500

to be late. He knew the weather was only going to get worse and he didn't want to be stuck driving through heavy snow.

"Ok, but South Africa? Why didn't you say no?"

"I don't know."

"Oh come on, you've been off ever since you said I do. Including not being sure you want your father's money. I mean the whole point in all of this was so you would inherit it over your uncle and aunt."

Charles knew that was why he had started this whole mess. Why he asked a complete stranger to marry him in exchange for paying off her student loans. It sounded like a simple business transaction, something that stayed that way all the way up until that kiss. He didn't even think about it beforehand. It never once crossed his mind that they would have to kiss. He knew she wasn't interested in him in any sexual manner. It was that moment that he realised how much this arrangement would hurt her, was hurting her. To him, he was a guy, he could kiss any girl without it being a big deal. Whether he was attracted to them or not, to him a kiss was a kiss, no big deal. However, Charles wasn't as much of a caveman as people suspected. He knew that for women it was different. A kiss wasn't just a kiss, it was something that was to be shared with another person they were attracted to. He knew Jane wasn't attracted to him and he hated that she had to kiss him, that she was forced to do it. Yes, she would be getting out of debt, but that didn't make it any less dirty, any less wrong.

Charles let out a sigh, as he looked up from his suitcase and gave James his full attention. "I did all of this so I could get my father's money, but it never occurred to me the cost I would be paying. The cost Jane would be paying. I took a normal woman and dragged her into our world, a world of lies and deception, mistrust and stuck up rich people that love nothing more than to judge anyone who is different. And to make it worse, I haven't defended her to them. I haven't supported her and protected her from them. Yes, she is getting something out of this arrangement, but her life has been completely altered. And if Jack and Wyatt do in fact have an article about her and Helena, their lives will be destroyed and it was all for money. For greed from this family. My father would be ashamed."

James could hear the pain within Charles' voice. He loved his father, he had always looked up to him and it was hurting him a great deal to know that his role model would be turning in his grave at this. Charles' father had good intentions when he put the stipulation of him having to have a wife by the age of thirty-five. He didn't want his son to die an early death from drinking and partying. He didn't want him to have multiple children with different women, women he didn't even know their names. He wanted to tame his wild son so he could take over the family businesses and not lose the empire his father had put his blood, sweat and tears into. It was Charles' fear of disappointing people that made him not want to get married. He didn't want to have to be responsible for someone, because then he could disappoint and hurt them. The millionaire playboy with the self-confidence of a servant.

"So then you change it. If you don't want to hurt her, then don't. I know it's not that simple and it's going to be a lot of hard work, but you are capable of working hard. You used to talk all the time growing up about what you wanted to do with your family's company when it was your turn. You had all of these dreams and plans for how you could help people, how you could start charities so people who were sick could get the treatments they needed. You're a good person Charles, you just got a little lost along the way. Take this chance to find yourself again."

"Trust me, I already planned on doing some soul searching on this trip. I can't keep doing this and I need to figure out what I am going to do with the company. Their mom could have lived and she is just one person out of thousands that have died because the company said no. People shouldn't have to know what it feels like to need a treatment to save their life, only to receive a piece of paper that says their life isn't worth the investment."

"I couldn't agree more. I didn't know treatments like that were being denied. It's not right and the only one that can do something about it, is you. I think it's good that you want to. Assuming you survive South Africa." James said with a playful smirk.

"I booked us a resort. As long as we stay on it, then we'll be fine. Besides, it's a beach at least." Charles said with a small shrug as he closed his suitcase.

"Ya I'm sure Anna is going to look very nice in a two piece."

Charles groaned at that. "I know she shouldn't be coming, but I need her. She's the only one that will tell me what she honestly thinks. I'm going to be trying to work through some stuff for the company and I need that honesty. Plus, I need to try and make things right with Jane. Hopefully Anna will be able to help me with that as well."

"So it's a working honeymoon, very romantic." James said sarcastically.

"It's not a real honeymoon. Jane isn't attracted to me and the last thing I want to do is make her feel uncomfortable. Plus with Anna there, she'll have a female she can hang out with and go to the spa with or whatever. I'm hoping it will make her feel more comfortable. We even have separate rooms."

"Wow you have thought of everything. Alright, that's good. I'm sure Jane will appreciate it."

"I hope so. Come on, let's see if they are ready so we can hit the road." Charles said, as he grabbed his suitcase.

"Do you think the flights will be grounded?" James asked, as they headed out.

"No, it's just snowing right now. I can't imagine it will get much worse. Soon enough we;ll be out of the snow clouds and off to South Africa."

"At least it'll be hot there."

Charles was hoping that nothing horrible happened on this honeymoon. He was also hoping that maybe this was what they both needed to be able to face the next year of marriage ahead of them.

CHAPTER 2

"Ladies and gentlemen, we do apologize for the delay. Due to the weather and blizzard making its way into our area, all flights have been grounded until the weather has cleared and it is safe to fly."

A collective groan could be heard all across the airport as thousands of passengers were now left stranded in the airport. *Just perfect* Jane thought to herself. When they had left the Bentley Estate the snow was getting thicker and heavier, but they were hoping that it wouldn't be too bad for the planes. She understood the need for the pilots to be able to see in order to fly safely, but she figured they had flown in worse. Turns out, a blizzard was set to hit them head on and they wouldn't be out of the area in time. The result was grounded planes until the storm blew over, which could be anywhere from an hour to a full day. It was a nightmare and reflected their honeymoon perfectly.

"Well, I need a drink." Anna commented before she headed off.

"Now she has the right idea." Jane stated, as she watched Anna make her way through the growing crowd.

"And she will not be alone. It won't take long before every place that serves here is packed with people. I hope there was nothing in your checked suitcase that you needed."

"No, I kept it all in my carry on. Maybe it will blow over soon and we can get out of here. What about our rooms at the resort, will they hold if we miss check in?"

This was a disaster and the last thing Jane wanted to deal with was missing out on their rooms because of a blizzard. She was also worried that Charles would call it all off and have them go to some other location. This could very well be her only chance at seeing Cape Town and she really didn't want to miss it.

"I'll call them and inform them of what is going on. It will be fine. We won't lose the rooms."

Charles couldn't have cared less if they didn't go to Cape Town, but he also wasn't an unintelligent man. Jane could have picked anywhere in the world and she picked South Africa. She picked it because it was the one place in the world she wanted to see. Charles was sure of it because it was human nature to pick the one place you always wanted to travel to when given the opportunity. For whatever reason Cape Town was her dream vacation and he was not about to take that from her. Even if he didn't understand why.

"Good. I should call Helena and see if she made it home ok."

"Of course. If your apartment isn't safe for her to be there, she can always stay at the house. There's no generator, but if the power goes out we have a fireplace for heat. James was going to stay at the house until the storm passed."

"Thanks, I'll let her know." Jane said with a small smile before she headed off to speak with Helena in privacy.

She didn't know why, but she was surprised that Charles had offered his home to Helena. She knew that Charles didn't care too much for either of them, they were too headstrong and didn't play by his social circles' rules. Still, he had offered his home as a safety net should their apartment not be suited for Helena during the storm and Jane couldn't help but wonder if maybe, just maybe, there was more to Chalres then he showed the world. Jane made her way over to a quiet corner of the airport as she pulled out her phone and called her sister.

"Let me guess, grounded?" Helena said once she answered.

"Yup. Every single flight is grounded until the blizzard clears up. Did you make it home ok?"

"Didn't even get to leave. I was about to when the weather warning came up on my phone. James got one too and he all

506

but barricaded the front door. I'm not saying I would have driven in it, but I'm annoyed that he went all caveman on me and didn't give me the choice in the matter." Helena said and Jane could tell she was still pissed off by it all.

"It seems to run in the family. But Charles did offer to let you stay at the house during the blizzard. He said they have a fireplace if the power goes out. Maybe send your caveman out to collect some wood before it gets real bad."

"He's already doing it. What's your caveman doing?"

Jane rolled her eyes as she spoke. "He's calling the resort to update them on our current situation. Afterwards, no idea, probably going to get a drink."

"He is really good at that part."

"Which part, telling people what to do or drinking?" Jane said, only half joking.

"Both I guess. I meant the drinking part though. I have never seen one house have so much alcohol in it."

"Look at the bright side, at least you have an open bar. That's one way to get through a blizzard." Jane said with a warm smile.

"Damn, you're right. Why the hell am I complaining about it?" Helena said and Jane could hear her moving. She suspected over where the liquor was stored to see which victim she was going to pick.

Jane gave a warm laugh before she spoke. "See, things are looking up. And if the power goes out, you and James could get naked and curl up to stay warm."

"Fuck you."

That only made Jane laugh harder. Helena was a mixture of someone who loved wine and wanted the finer things in life, but also a loudmouth, cursing trucker. She was the best of both worlds, but unfortunately those worlds didn't often collide. And when they do, it usually results in some horrific accident that makes the six o'clock news. Jane didn't know who she felt bad for more, Helena or James at this moment.

"He seems like a nice guy. Well, as nice as a guy in their world can be I guess. Maybe he's got layers." Jane commented.

"I doubt he's an onion." Helena grumbled.

"Ok, but maybe he's a parfait, you know just a couple of layers. You don't really know him. You've been judging him from the moment you heard his name. Maybe now is the perfect time for you to see past his name and focus on the man that he is. You never know, he might surprise you."

"Oh and are you going to be taking your own advice?" Helena challenged.

"No, Charles is very much one-dimentional. I'm fairly certain if you look at his sideways he disappears."

"Yes, I am sure all of his muscles just disappear." Helena countered as she rolled her eyes.

"His ability to fill out a suit is not impressive."

"You might not think that way if you ever saw him without a shirt on. Come on, he's good looking, are you really telling me you don't feel any attraction to him?" Helena challenged.

"Nope, not a drop." Jane said stubbornly.

She was not about to admit to Helena or to herself that she may be attracted to Charles. Looks weren't everything and she refused to allow herself to feel anything towards him because the outside looked good. There was no point in being attracted to a pretty face if everything that was important was hideous.

"Fine, keep living in your world of denial."

"My world or denial? You are the one that openly admitted to liking James, but you won't do anything with him because of your messed up beliefs." Jane countered.

"Fine, then I'll make you a deal. I will try to let my guard down and try to see James as just himself. If you do the same for Charles." Helena offered.

"Deal."

Jane knew that she wasn't about to do that, but as far as Helena was concerned, that was exactly what she was going to do. She also knew her sister, she wasn't about to drop her shields either. It would be a broken deal all across the board, but neither of them would call the other out on it.

*****

Charles made his way through the airport as he spoke to the receptionist at the resort. He was able to get them to hold their rooms for them without a single problem. Charles suspected it wouldn't be a big deal. He was paying for three luxury rooms for the next week. The resort wasn't going to risk losing his money by not holding onto their rooms due to the blizzard. Still, it was a call that needed to be made and now that he had finished it, he dialed James to see how he was doing.

"Ya?" James answered with a slightly out of breath.

"Hello to you too." Charles said with a smirk.

"Sorry, I was outside getting firewood. Figured I would get a fire started now just in case we lose power here. I don't want to be trying to start one in the pitch black."

"We?" Charles asked, picking up on the word.

"Helena is here. She didn't get to leave before the alert went out on the blizzard. I can't decide if I am in Heaven or Hell."

"I'm stuck in an airport, I'm in hell. You are stuck in a mansion with a beautiful woman, you're in heaven." Charles clarified.

509

"Yes, but said beautiful woman appears to hate me. I think I would take the uncomfortable plastic chairs at the airport."

"I'm heading now to try and see if I can get a hotel room. I don't see this storm passing over us within the next hour. As for Helena, maybe she hates you or maybe that is just a cover. You said you clicked during your road trip."

"And we did, at least I thought we did. But ever since she's been adamant about not doing anything, I don't even think she wants to be friends."

"Well now is your perfect chance. You're stuck in the house together, talk to her. Get her to know the real you and not the image she has made of you in her mind."

"I thought I was supposed to be the wise one?" James said in a warm voice.

"You are, but every now and then I get to be. It's not like she can hate you more." Charles reasoned.

"This is true. Fine, I'll try and see if I can get through her walls. But it's your fault if it ends in a blood bath."

"It better not, I can't ask Anna to clean up your blood and I am certainly not doing it."

"I like how you assume it would be me that gets killed." James said, annoyed.

"Even if you hit women, which you don't, my money will always be on Helena. That woman is a firecracker that worked in a strip club. She is the type of woman that you don't want to piss off or meet in a back alley."

"She does keep pepper spray in her purse." James commented.

"See."

Charles was not afraid of strong women, he liked them. It was a nice and refreshing change to the women he normally associated with. But he also knew that James would not be prepared for a woman like Helena. Just like he wasn't prepared for Jane.

"I will be on my best behavior. Let me know when you get on the plane finally."

"I will. Be safe and don't get any blood on my rugs."

"I can really feel the love coming through the phone Cousin." James joked.

Chalres gave a small chuckle to that. "Have fun."

Charles ended the call just as he arrived at the now very busy hotel lobby. He was hoping he would be able to secure a hotel room or hopefully two if possible for him and Jane. He had a feeling that they would be stuck here overnight and he didn't want them to be stuck trying to sleep on the ground or in an airport chair. With any luck they would be able to get boarded soon so they could start their honeymoon. He was determined to make sure it was a great vacation for her. It was the least he could do.

CHAPTER 3

Charles was grateful that he had been able to secure a room for both him and Jane. They did not have another room that he could get for Anna. However, he did see Evan Cooper getting off of the hotel elevator and heading out. He knew that Anna would most likely run into her ex-husband and they could also share together. If nothing else, he would make sure that Anna had a place to be so she was comfortable for tonight. Charles didn't bother with heading up the elevator to check out the room, it didn't really matter what it looked like as it would be better than the plastic airport seats. As he made his way through the hotel lobby he saw the one person he had been trying to avoid for months now. Kristy.

There had been many women in Charles' life, a good majority of them he did not regret. Kristy on the other hand, he regretted, he regretted her so very much. What had started off as a fling six months ago became a casual sexual relationship, at least to him it was. He always made a point in letting any woman that he has been with that he didn't want anything serious. That he didn't date or have any intentions of getting married. He didn't want to be responsible for someone. To him that wasn't a marriage. If you had to take care of your wife like you would a toddler, then that wasn't anything he wanted to spend his time or money on. If he wanted something with that level of responsibility attached to it, then he would have gotten a dog.

"Charles, oh my gosh is that you?" Kristy asked, in her fake voice that Charles absolutely hated.

She always got this high pitched girly tone to her voice whenever she spoke and Charles knew it was fake. Her real voice couldn't have sounded like that because it wasn't that sound when she was moaning. Charles let out a sigh and had no choice, but to turn slightly to see her. She had always been beautiful, but Charles quickly learnt that was a trap. Kristy was what Charles envisioned his Aunt Rosalyn looked like back in the day. Kristy was pure gold digger at heart and her only goal in life was to secure a rich husband. She wasn't poor, but she was not within the one percent of the one percenters within society.

"Kristy." Charles simply said.

He didn't want to be polite with her, being polite would tell her mind that he still wanted to sleep with her. They had only shared a casual relationship for approximately three months and in Charles' opinion that was three months too long. Kristy had become obsessed with him and very jealous. She would constantly call or text him, send him emails when he didn't answer or respond fast enough. It got to the point where he had to block her completely and even then she's had the habit of showing up at events to try and get back with him. Stalker probably wasn't the right word, but he wasn't sure what else to call her.

"How funny is it that we are both trapped here? Were you able to get a room?"

"I have, yes. I need to get going though." Charles said, as he started to head for the airport elevator that would take him back down to where the gates were. He needed to find Jane and inform her that he secured a hotel room for them.

"You're lucky, they are all sold out now. What room are you in, we could make it a memorable night." Kristy said, as she followed Charles over to the elevator.

"I'll be working all night. I'm sure there is another guest that would love to host you for the evening."

"Host me, you make it sound like I'm some type of escort." Kristy said, slightly offended.

Charles hadn't meant it that way, but at the same time she was dressed for it. He would never understand why women wanted to travel in cocktail dresses and six inch stiletto heels. It seemed very uncomfortable. He himself was stuck wearing dress pants and he wished he wasn't. Jane had been the only smart one and wore yoga pants so she would be comfortable on the long flight. Charles truly wished he could have worn sweatpants without hearing his father's disapproving voice in his head.

"That was not my intention." Charles instantly said, as they both got onto the elevator.

"Where are you off to once the weather clears up?" Kristy asked, as she stood right next to Charles despite the fact that the elevator was empty.

"Cape Town."

"Oh is that in Italy?" Kristy asked, with an excited smile.

"South Africa." Charles corrected.

"South Africa? God, why would you want to go to a miserable country?"

Kristy's disgust was not surprising at all to Charles. He knew that people within his social circle would have the same opinion. To them Africa was a disgusting place that had no business being spoken of. For someone to willingly go there, you had to be insane. Still, it was where Jane wanted to go so Charles was going. That didn't mean he was going to be telling Kristy that he was honeymooning there. That would not end well and Charles just wanted to get away from her. He didn't want added drama from her or for her to feel the need to crash his honeymoon.

"Business. Where are you going?" Charles asked, trying to get the focus back on her.

"Rome. It was a present from my sweet Sugar Daddy. He wanted me to go and have some fun while he had to work. He's so sweet."

And most likely married. Charles thought to himself. He knew Kristy had a few Sugar Daddies. It was the only way she was able to uphold her lifestyle. Her newest Sugar Daddy most likely had to send her off on a vacation so he could spend time with his wife without the threat of Kristy showing up.

"Good for you." Charles said, as he got off the elevator.

Kristy threaded her arm around Charles' as they headed off down the hallway.

"We should get a drink." Kristy suggested.

"I have a business meeting I have to get to. I am sure though you will find someone to chat with in one of the bars." Charles said, as he pulled his arm away from her hold.

"But I want to spend time with you. We've barely spoken within the past few months." Kristy said with a pout.

That was by design. Charles thought to himself.

"I don't have time. I have a business to run, you know that. I have to get going. Enjoy your vacation Kristy." Charles said with a final tone before he walked faster and pulled out his cell phone.

He had no one he needed to call, but it was the best way to get Kristy away from him. He couldn't believe she was here out of all people and places. He was hoping she would find someone else to harass for the night. Charles let out a sigh, he had to find Jane so they could hide away in the hotel room for the night. The last thing he needed was for Kristy to discover he was married. She would lose it and he was not looking to deal with that level of nuclear drama that would rain down.

CHAPTER 4

Anna couldn't believe that they were all stranded here at an airport. It wasn't bad enough that she was going on her boss' honeymoon, but now she was stuck here at an airport with a bunch of strangers. When Charles had stated, stated and not asked, that she would be going with them on their honeymoon she thought he was insane. It was a honeymoon, fake marriage or not, it was meant for the happy newlywed couple to enjoy by themselves. You didn't bring a staff member with you on it. She knew she wasn't going to be the chaperone, but instead his personal assistant. That was not her job, she was the housekeeper, it was on her to keep the house clean and in order. It was not her job to play babysitter and yet here she was playing babysitter to a thirty-five year old man.

Anna truly believed that there was a good man, a good soul within Charles, he just needed someone to smack it out of him. That was one of the reasons why she liked Jane. Not only was the sweet girl down to earth and humble, but she also was brave and strong willed. She was not going to allow Charles to push her around, especially now that the wedding business was taken care of. Charles had always focused all of his efforts and energy into money. He didn't truly work for anything and his father, god rest his soul, always gave whatever Charles wanted. The man was spoiled and there was no denying that. However, she had seen a softer side to him. She knew he did care, but it was buried underneath his armour that he wore. She couldn't blame him though, if she had to deal with his uncle and his aunt as often as he did, she would be wearing armour as well. She wouldn't want to show any weakness around them. They were like great white sharks that swarmed the second they smelt a single drop of blood in the water. Having to live like that made a person cold and afraid to show any human qualities.

It was why she liked Jane. She was starting to bring out different sides to Charles, not all of them were bad. Her hope was that Jane would help Charles to finally embrace who he was and his family be damned. She could never understand why he was trying so hard to please the likes of his uncle and aunt. They were certainly not worth the aggravation, and his father would agree. There's a reason that man didn't want his brother to inherit his fortune.

"Anna?"

At the sound of her name being called, she looked up and started to scan the area around her. She couldn't see anyone that she recognised right away, but after a moment her eyes landed on a man that she thought she would never see again. Evan Cooper, her ex-husband that disappeared on her ten years ago. They were high school sweethearts and despite everyone saying they would never last, they got married. Anna couldn't have been happier and she knew their marriage had been a bit rocky, but she believed they would be able to get through anything together. She had been working as the new housekeeper to the Bentley's at the time when she came home one night to discover he had left. All of his clothes and personal items were gone and in their place was a simple note stating that he was sorry, but couldn't do this anymore. She had been left devastated that the man that she was madly in love with, the man that she expected to spend the rest of her life with was gone.

It had come out of nowhere and still to this day she was confused about what had happened, what had gone so wrong. She thought they were happy, that they were working together to build a life for themselves. She knew they were going through rough patches. Evan had some family drama going on around his senior year in high school and he had to drop out to work to help support his mother. Not having a high school diploma was hard on Evan and it made it impossible for him to get a decent job. She had been working extra hours for the

Bentley's to be able to cover the household while his money mostly went to his mother's needs. They were often exhausted and feeling stressed, but she thought they could handle it together. That they would pull through it all. She had been so horribly wrong.

Anna had to do her best to push down the unresolved feelings she had for Evan. She told herself that she didn't notice how handsome he looked in his black suit. That the slight grey tone to his black hair didn't make him distinguished or even more attractive. The fact that he was wearing a suit greatly confused her. She had seen this man attend a funeral in black jeans and a black t-shirt. He wasn't a man that wore suits and ties, at least he wasn't when she knew him. Putting on a brace smile she spoke.

"Evan, fancy meeting you here."

"In all of the airports in all of the towns right? What are you doing here? Going on vacation I hope."

His rich and warm voice filled Anna with many pleasant memories of their time together. She always loved the sound of his voice and even his age hadn't changed the effect it had on her.

"In a way. I am accompanying my boss on his honeymoon. He has requested that I come along should they need something. And what about you? As I recall you held zero desire to have your feet leave the ground."

Evan was not a man that liked to travel or to fly. It was an issue they often shared, but one they didn't see the need to talk to death. They didn't have the money to go on vacations so Anna's desire to see the world was pointless when they couldn't afford the taxi ride to the airport, much less get on a plane.

Evan gave a warm chuckle before he spoke. "I still would love to keep my feet firmly planted on the ground and I am man enough to admit I never sit next to the window. But, at times I do have to fly for business. I was set to head to Paris for some meetings, but the blizzard has put a hold on that."

"Paris? Wow." Anna said, trying her best to not sound bitter.

Paris, France, the one place in the world that she wanted to see before she died and it was looking like it would never happen. She never got vacation times, she barely got sick days and if she was sick he had better be dying from it. The Bentley's needed her available at all times and that meant that she lived with them and was constantly on call. There were no hours in the day that she could take for herself. She thought it would get easier after Charles' father passed; however, that ended up not being the case. It appeared Charles was making up for his father's absence. The result was long hours and very little time to herself. It was a job that she willingly took on knowing that it would be hard at many points in her life, but she took it with the belief that her husband would be there for her to go home to. And now he was traveling to the one city she wanted to see more than anything. The bitterness burned her tongue as she felt the pang of jealousy hit her.

"Have you been yet? I know it was always your dream to see it."

He had the decency to sound slightly ashamed that he was getting to go to her dream town. It didn't help make Anna feel any better at all, but at least he knew he was stealing something special from her.

"No, working for the Bentley's doesn't leave much time for leisure travels. It's a shame the weather isn't cooperating today." Anna said, desperate to change the subject.

"I had expected it wouldn't. When I booked these meetings I made the unfortunate mistake in not looking at the weather forecast first. Though, one can never predict when a true blizzard will hit. Hopefully it clears soon and today will not be a total write off for everyone. I am sure the happy couple are desperate to get started on their honeymoon. Where are they going?" Evan asked with a warm smile, he was not looking to end their conversation just yet.

Oh yes, a very happy couple. Anna thought to herself as she remembered the disaster of these past few weeks. The fact that the wedding didn't end in a blood bath was impressive all in itself. Thankfully, that would be one mess she wouldn't have to clean up.

"Cape Town, South Africa."

"Really? That's different." Evan said, with a surprised look across his face.

"Charles' wife, Jane, is very down to earth and more of a free spirit type. She wanted more than white sandy beaches and a swim up bar. It will be fun for them and certainly allow them to bring back memories." Anna said with a warm smile, but internally she was actually worried about the trip. Charles held a love for leisure and drinking where Jane wanted more out of life. She wanted adventure and to help people, it would be a very interesting two weeks.

"It sounds like he caught himself a fabulous woman then. I remember this absolutely gorgeous and spectcaular woman that loved spontaneity and adventure. You could always find her up for a good time whether that was hiking down a rocky cliff or spending the night in a haunted house just to prove it wasn't haunted." Evan said with a fond smile.

"That house was not haunted." Anna instantly insisted and it caused Evan to give a rich chuckle.

"You were adamant about proving everyone wrong. Even when all of our friends said we would be killed in the middle of the night. I was terrified and you distracted me in the best possible way."

Anna had to contain a warm moan at the memories that this was bringing up. They used to have so much fun together, so much adventure and life they shared. All of the good times always outweighed the bad, the petty arguments that they had shared over their years together. That night was a rather fun night together.

"It was a good night and now we have grown too old for adventures."

"No such thing my Dear. Come grab some coffee with me. I would love to properly catch up."

Anna would be lying if she said that her whole body was screaming yes at her. She hadn't forgotten about Evan, not for a single moment over the past decade. She was still in love with him, she knew that. However, she also knew that he was clearly not in love with her. You don't leave the woman you love without even saying a proper goodbye. Without giving any form of an explanation. He had fallen out of love with her, probably for another woman. Getting coffee with him could lead to being the biggest mistake of her life. Knowing that though, she still wanted to. She still wanted to talk with him and feel all of the good memories that she locked away in a box within her mind. A box that she swore she would never open again. But perhaps just once, she could indulge herself and allow herself to pretend that they were both going to Paris and trapped here together due to the blizzard. Afterall, what could a little pretending hurt?

"That would be lovely." She said with a warm smile.

"Shall we?" Evan asked, as he held his arm out for her, which Anna gladly took before they headed off to find a cafe.

CHAPTER 5

"Thank-you." Anna said to the waitress that brought her coffee over.

She couldn't believe that she had met Evan, out of all people, here in the airport. She never expected to ever see him again. She figured he was long gone, off having a whole new life with a new wife. Probably someone younger that liked to wear makeup and get her nails done. Anna was never the girly type, too busy working with her hands or playing touch football with the boys in the neighborhood. She was more of a tomboy, but she knew how to dress up and make a man turn his head.

"You look as beautiful as ever." Evan started.

"Oh stop, I look like I am getting old." Anna said, as she waved her hand to dismiss the notion.

"You have only gotten more beautiful over the years my Dear." Evan said with a warm smile and a heat to his eyes.

The look he was giving Anna made her feel a bit nervous, as if they were going on a first date. It was ridiculous because they had been married for crying out loud. She didn't need to be nervous or feel awkward about having a coffee with him. They have had plenty of conversations over coffee together, she could do this. He was the same man that she fell in love with, just a bit older. But perhaps that was why she was feeling nervous, because he was the man she fell madly in love with and still was the man she loved.

"You said you were going to Paris for meetings. Are these meetings for work?" Anna asked, changing the subject away from her.

"They are, yes. I started my own company roughly eight years back."

"Really?" Anna said, completely surprised.

Evan had always talked about not being capable of running a business. After he had dropped out of high school his self-confidence was shattered. He always believed he wasn't smart enough to run a business or try to get his GED. It was one of the few arguments that we would repeatedly have. I always told him he was capable of anything, but hearing me saying it and him believing it were two very different things.

"For the last three years of our marriage I always felt like a burden to you. You had to work all of these hours to carry the household while I worked minimum wage jobs and gave half of my paycheque to help my mother out. I hated seeing you coming home exhausted and with blisters on your feet. I wanted more for you than that life. I didn't want to be a burden to you any longer."

"Oh for pity's sake, you were never a burden to me. We were a team, I thought we were a team. We both worked hard to make a good life for ourselves. I never held any of it against you. I loved you."

"And I loved you, with everything in me. I couldn't keep putting you through that pain, that exhaustion. I had to leave, I had to be a better man and allow you to have the chance at a better life. Leaving you was the hardest thing I have ever had to do in my life, but I didn't do it because I didn't love you. I had to be a better man."

"I didn't need you to be a better man, I just needed you there Evan. If you wanted to improve yourself, then fine, but you could have done it with me. We could have done it together. You let your self-consciousness ruin our marriage. I thought we were happy, I thought we were both in love. So imagine my shock when I go home after a long day, thinking I was at least going to be able to see my husband and sleep in bed together, only to discover a note. You couldn't even give me the respect and decency to leave me in person. A flipping note Evan, as if we were in high school for crying out loud."

Evan had felt terrible for how he left, but he just didn't know how else to do it. If he saw her face, if he had to look at her and say the words, he knew he never would have been able to do it. He had to take the coward's way out, it was the only way he could leave. He truly believed that it was what was best for her. For her life. If she didn't have to worry about having to care for him. If she didn't have to worry about anyone but herself she could have a better life. She could live more stress free and that was what he wanted for her. He loved her so much, he had to leave her.

"I can't tell you how sorry I am for leaving a note, but I couldn't leave you face to face. I couldn't see the hurt in your eyes. It would have broken me. I know my leaving has hurt you, but I also know you Anna, I knew you would survive and become stronger and ever. You would thrive without me and that brought a bit of comfort to me. I know it wouldn't have brought any to you."

"Yes, I am a strong woman, but I also shouldn't have to be all the time. I shouldn't have to be the strong one. I should be able to go to my husband and cry on his shoulders when I need to. I should have been able to lean on a man and know that he would be able to carry the weight when I couldn't. I thought I had that with you. I thought I didn't have to be the strong one all the time, that my loving husband would be there to be strong for the both of us. I loved you just how you were, all I asked of you was to be there and you couldn't even do that for me." Anna countered, not at all impressed by how Evan was trying to justify his actions.

"I know, I failed you. I completely take responsibility for it. But I didn't do it because I didn't love you. I did it because I loved you with everything in me. After I left, I went and got my GED. I got a loan from a bank and started investing with it. Now I have my own company that helps hotels and air B&Bs all around the world to improve their rooms and business to generate more revenue. I still invest as well. Between it all I have made billions. I bettered myself, made myself the type of man that is worthy of you."

Anna was happy for him. He went and got his GED and has been able to build himself an empire. They had always talked about doing just that. Opening a business where they could help hotels and B&Bs to generate more revenue by upgrading their rooms and the services that they offered. It was everything they had dreamed about and he had gone off and done it himself. She was happy for him, but she was also bitter, because he went and created their dream all alone. They should have done it together. They could have done it together, but Evan chose to cut her out and that was a hard pill to swallow.

"You say it as if you did all of this for me. And yet, you haven't called. You never tried to find me. You went and made our dream a reality, but you left me behind. How am I supposed to take this Evan?" Anna asked with a slight edge to her voice. She was trying to mask the hurt she was feeling, but she knew Evan would still pick it up.

"Words can't even begin to describe how sorry I am. I've wanted to call you. I can't tell you how many times I've dialed your number but didn't have the courage to hit send. Or the number of times I've seen you out and about in town. I wanted to go up to you and tell you how sorry I am. That I am still madly in love with you Anna Cooper. But I was terrified that you had moved on to a better man. I hated doing all of this without you and you deserved to be a part of it. It's why I made you my sole beneficiary in my will. So you would get to have your dream as well, even if I couldn't share it with you. The biggest regret of my life was leaving you; followed very closely by not reaching out to you since that night ten years ago." Evan said with complete sincerity to his voice.

Anna was shocked by his confession. She never expected for him to still care for her, certainly not love her. And to the level that he was leaving his entire company worth billions over to

525

her should he pass. It was massive, it was out of this world unreal and yet she could hear the truth and sincerity to his voice loud and clear. She didn't know what to say. What could she say to something like that?

"I don't... I don't even know what to say Evan. I have thought about you over the years, but I assumed you had left me for another woman. That you had gone off and got married and had children with someone else. It's all just a tremendous shock."

"I know this is a shock. I wrote a very long letter explaining my actions and why I picked you to benefit everything. I never expected to be able to speak with you face to face again. But Anna, how could you ever think that another woman would ever hold a candle to you? You are my first love and you will always be held within my heart. No woman could ever replace you." Evan said with complete devotion to his voice.

A warmth washed over Anna's entire body. She never expected for any of this to be happening. She thought she would never see Evan again, much less hear any of what he was currently saying to her. To hear that even after all of these years he was still in love with her, it was a dream come true. Anna knew better though than to believe in dreams. You always woke up at the best part, but for now she was going to enjoy the ride. She could always chalk it up to the blizzard outside, plus the chances of them ever seeing each other again were astronomical, what could one day hurt?

"I haven't remarried either, no serious relationships. And it's not just because I have been so busy with work. I still love and care for you. I've often wondered how you were doing." Anna admitted.

Evan gave her the biggest warm smile, a smile that had always put butterflies in her stomach. He was very happy to hear that she still cared for him, that maybe he still had a chance to repair their relationship, to potentially restore it and give them a second chance.

"Tell me, what have you been doing?" Evan asked, as he picked up coffee. He wanted to know everything about Anna, about the woman she had become.

"Oh no mister. I want to hear all about your company first. How did you get started, what are these meetings you are going to?"

Evan gave Anna a warm smile. It made him feel good to know that she wanted to hear about the company and the meetings. He had no doubt that she would have some insights and opinions on certain matters. That didn't bother him at all though. He always loved how alive she became when she was talking about something passionately. This blizzard was looking to be the best thing to ever happen to him.

CHAPTER 6

Helena had been hoping that she would be able to leave the Bentley Estate before the roads got too bad. However, luck was not on her side as the roads started to get pretty bad once Jane and Charles had left. Still, she was debating on if she should leave and take the risk.

"You shouldn't be driving." James commented, as he came back in with some wood for the fireplace.

James was both pleased and displeased with having Helena here in the house with him. He was pleased for obvious reasons, he would be able to spend more time with her. He was displeased though for the exact same reason. He liked her and it hurt more than he cared to admit that she was refusing to even give them a try. She had more walls up around her than Fort Knox and he had no idea how he was ever going to get through them.

"The roads might not be that bad." Helena argued.

She really didn't want to be driving, but it seemed like a better idea than being stuck in this house with James. She knew her apartment wouldn't be well suited if the power went out. Their heat was electric, so without power she would be without heat. Not ideal in a blizzard. Not to mention her building was old and drafty and was normally pretty chilly in winter to begin with. It would be smarter to stay here and wait out the storm, but that didn't mean she wanted to do that.

Being alone with James was just as dangerous as facing a blizzard on her own. The more time you spend alone with someone you like, the greater the chances of you doing something stupid and acting on it. Helena didn't want to make that mistake, no matter how much her body might be screaming at her to.

"Even if you could drive to your apartment, it wouldn't be safe for you to stay there. What would you do if the power went out? At least here we'll have a fire going." James said, as he started to get the fire ready.

"Do you even know how to start a fire?" Helena challenged, as she moved over and leaned against the doorway into the living room.

"I've done it before. This isn't the first blizzard that I've spent in this house. My place doesn't have a fireplace so whenever the power goes out in winter, I always come over here. If we close both doors it will trap the heat in here with us."

Helena had to give it to him for that. At least they would be warm and safe here in the house. Still, her mind was telling her to get into her crappy car and to get as far away from him as possible. Just as James was able to get the fire going the lights flickered for a moment.

"You think they'll go out?" Helena asked.

"I don't think so. Not every blizzard knocks the power out. Normally it's a bad rain storm that will do it." Just as James answered the lights flickered once again before going completely out.

James didn't need to turn around to see the annoyed look that would be all over Helena's face right now. *Someone up there hates me.* James thought to himself. He let out a sigh before he got up and turned around to see Helena not looking impressed, but also there was a hint of an I told you so glint in her eyes.

"Where are the flashlights?" Helena asked.

"I don't know. I don't even know if there are any." James answered honestly.

"Candles?" Helena asked next.

"Not sure." James said again.

It was taking everything in Helena not to roll her eyes, though the only light in the room was from the fire, she doubted James would even see if she did roll her eyes. Helena couldn't for the life of her figure out how someone could not know what was in their house. She knew this wasn't James' actual home, but from what she had been told he was here most of the time. He should know where things were kept.

"How can you live this way?" Helena asked.

James was instantly offended and had his guard up. He didn't appreciate the judgment within Helena's voice. This wasn't his house. It wasn't his responsibility to know where every little thing was kept. He knew where they were in his home, but they weren't at his home.

"I don't live here Helena. The staff know where everything is, but Charles had them leave before they were caught in the storm as well. I know where they are in my own home."

Helena could tell by his tone of voice that he was offended by what she had said. That wasn't her intention at all. She genuinely didn't understand how he could live his life this way. Yes, he didn't live here so it made sense that he wouldn't know where the candles or flashlights were. Still, he didn't appear to be living. He was spending his time going from his home to over here. He was here so often then he should have seen a flashlight in the kitchen or something. They always kept them in a junk drawer in their kitchen. It seemed like the most normal things in the world that James was lacking. Still, she didn't mean to offend him, that wasn't her intent.

"I'm sorry I didn't mean to offend you with my question. I meant you are living a life, but you aren't really living. From the time we've spent together, and I know it has only been weeks, but within that time you've never relaxed. You never wear jeans or sweatpants. You are always dressed for an event. You are either at your place or here with Charles. Did you ever get your clothes dirty growing up? Have a snowball fight?"

James let out a sigh. He had jumped to conclusions about Helena's question and that wasn't fair to her. Still, it was a sore spot for him. He hated it when people judged him. When people made assumptions about who he was or what he had been through because he was a Bentley. People really didn't understand how hard it was to be a Bentley. How much it sucked on numerous occasions.

CHAPTER 7

James let out a soft sigh as he went and sat down on the arm of the couch before he finally spoke.

"People always think that being rich, living within this society is easy. They focus on how great it would be to live in a big house and drive fancy cars. To get anything they ever wanted. It sounds great, but what they don't know is what else comes with it. Parents who are strict and emotionally detached. They would rather give you cash than their time or affection."

"I'm sorry." Helena said.

She could hear the hurt within his voice and she hated that she had been the one to help put it there. James clearly didn't like reliving his childhood and from the sounds of it Helena couldn't blame him.

"There's nothing for you to apologise for." James responded with a small sad smile before he continued. "To answer your question, there were no snowball fights. We were to always look presentable and act appropriately. We were taught manners and social etiquette from the moment we were old enough to sit at the table. You didn't get dirty, you didn't talk back, hell most of the time you didn't talk at all unless addressed by an adult. My parents firmly believed that children should be seen and never heard from. If they could help it, they didn't want me to be seen unless absolutely necessary."

It was not easy for James to talk about his childhood. He hadn't been abused. His parents never raised a single hand to him. There was no violence, no swearing, no yelling, the house was always quiet. James also felt like he was an inconvenience to his parents. As if his mother got pregnant and it was too late to abort the pregnancy. They weren't loving, they didn't go out of their way to make him feel loved. Whenever he was sick, they treated it as a burden they would have to deal with. He wasn't wanted and he wasn't loved.

"That's insane. I'm sorry you had to go through that, no child should. I'll never understand why people have children if they don't really want one. There is such a thing as birth control. I'm guessing they were very strict."

"Very much so. You were not to get dirty or to make a mess. You never wore jeans and rarely you could wear shorts if it was for swimming or golfing. Other than that it was either a school uniform or dress pants and a polo shirt. When I wasn't in school I was to be in my room studying or outside where I wouldn't disturb them. There wasn't really anything that was fun. The most fun I had growing up was with Charles and his grandfather Henry. I spent a lot of time over there with them. After Henry passed away when we were ten. Charles and I would avoid going home for as long as possible."

Helena couldn't believe this. She would never understand why anyone would have a child if they truly didn't want to be a parent. They might not have had much growing up, but what they always had was the love of their mother. They knew that when they were sick, she would be there for them with soup and a cold damp cloth. She always made sure to hug them and kiss them goodnight. There was never a point in their lives that they couldn't crawl into their mom's bed if they had a nightmare. She gave them all the love that they could ever need and more.

It hurt for Helena to hear that James didn't get to have that experience. Every child should be able to know what the love of a parent felt like. James didn't deserve to be treated like an inconvenience for the majority of his life. He deserved better than that.

"But they aren't alive anymore. You aren't living under their roof. A huge part of living is having fun, experiencing different things. Otherwise, you aren't really living. Don't you ever get tired of having to be perfect and presentable all the time? Don't you ever want to leave your house in sweatpants and sneakers?"

That was the thing with Helena. She could never handle having to be presentable from the moment she woke up until she went to bed. If she wanted to run to the grocery store in yoga pants, then she would. She couldn't imagine having to get dressed, put on makeup and wear heels just to grab some eggs and milk. It was overkill to her. At the same time though, it had to be exhausting. For James to constantly feel like he had to present himself in a specific manner all the time. He could never let his hair down, metaphorically speaking, and have fun. How was that living?

"Of course I do. I hate having to conform to what this society dictates in regards to my appearance and lifestyle. When I was sixteen I rebelled, my big rebellion, was going out and buying some black jeans, a black leather jacket and I got a tattoo of a wolf on my right shoulder blade."

"Shut up, you have a tattoo?" Helena asked, shocked. She was also doing her best to ignore the image of James in jeans and a black leather jacket. That seemed very sexy to her.

James held his hand up slightly as he spoke. "I had a tattoo. It tasted six months before my father caught me with my shirt off and saw it. He lost his mind over it and dragged me down to get it lasered off, something that was extremely painful. He also tore through my room and removed any contraband. That summer I had to live with Jack, which ended up being a completely different level of hell. That was the end of my rebellious streak."

James really didn't want to think about that summer he had to live with Jack. Jack had always made a point of informing James that he was not his family. James' mother, Catherine was sisters with Charles' mother. James' mother had ended up marrying another Bentley cousin. Charles' father had been his uncle through marriage and Jack held no interest in playing family with him. James never understood it though, because his father was second cousins with Jack, making them third cousins. They were still within the realm of blood relatives, but apparently it wasn't good enough. James suspected it had something to do with who his mother was.

"Ok so screw them. Your parents are gone, no offense, all the family that you really have is Jack, his gold digging wife and Charles. Who cares what any of them think? You can't let a bunch of stuffy judgment old rich people dictate how you live your life or who you should be. And who cares what they think of you? The only reason they deal with you is because of your last name. Life isn't about living your life for other people. It's about you living it for yourself. The only people you should care about; the only people whose opinions matter, are the ones that will be crying at your funeral and not the people who won't even care enough to show up."

Helena knew it wasn't her place to speak up, but that had never stopped her before. She couldn't let James keep living his life like this. He couldn't be living in fear or stuck in some stereotypical box because he didn't want to upset a bunch of old backwards thinking men. That wasn't living, not to Helena anyways. She was a firm believer in living your life for yourself and not for someone else. James had been living his life for other people, even following those rules when his parents were dead.

"You make a valid point." James softly agreed.

He had never thought of it like that before. He was living his life still based on the rules of his parents. Based on the rules within the society. He shouldn't have, he knew that, but it wasn't that simple. He had grown up this way and even though he hated it, changing and going against those rules was rather difficult. Him and Charles had spoken about it before when they had been drinking. They both wanted to break free from their prison, but they didn't know how. Both had said they would if the other did first, but neither made the first move. They were playing a game of chicken and neither wanted to blink first. The result was them continuing to do the exact same thing day after day.

"Charles and I have talked a few times about wanting to do something crazy and seize our lives for ourselves. We never did though, but maybe it is time I stopped caring so much about what strangers think. Maybe once the blizzard clears up you could go with me to buy some jeans." James said with a warm smile.

"Oh hell ya. I have to see you in jeans." Helena said with a flirty smile as she thought about how great his ass would look in tight jeans. She quickly pushed that thought away and picked up her phone. "We should check around for some candles or something."

James gave a nod in agreement before he stood. He tossed a couple of pieces of wood onto the fire before they headed out. He would also grab some wood as well before the snow got so bad that it became too hard to walk through. James wasn't sure how well this night would go over, but he was hoping it wouldn't be too bad and maybe, just maybe, he would be able to convince Helena to give them a try.

CHAPTER 8

Charles was finally able to find Jane sitting down at one of the bars within the airport. She had a glass of whiskey in front of her, something that surprised him. He hadn't known of any woman that enjoyed drinking whiskey. That was always his go-to drink and the women he had been with in the past only drank wine or a cocktail. They had never drank whiskey straight up.

"I've never met a woman that can drink whiskey." Charles commented, as he sat down next to Jane at the bar.

"Further proof that you have been hanging around the wrong type of women." Jane commented with a smirk.

Charles gave a deep chuckle before he spoke. "Their drink choice was the least of their offenses, trust me there. I was able to get us a hotel room. However, there was only one left so we will need to share."

Charles wasn't sure how Jane would feel about sharing a hotel room with him. He wasn't too happy about it either, he liked having his own space and he wasn't thrilled with the idea of being trapped in a small room with Jane. He wanted to give her space, to give her the freedom to be herself without having him around. He also liked his own space so he could decompress and relax. He wasn't used to having people around him. He wasn't used to having a woman around him outside of sex. He had no idea how he was going to handle having Jane around him at the house for the next year. He knew she didn't want to live with him, but it would be too hard to explain away why she was often not at the house.

"What about Anna?" Jane asked.

"I saw her with her ex-husband looking very cozy together. He's already got a room, I am sure she will be joining him."

"She has an ex-husband?" Jane asked, shocked.

She had only known Anna for a few weeks, but she didn't know that she had been married previously.

"Technically they are still married. He left her ten years ago roughly now. They were high school sweethearts, got married and were planning a whole life together. Only for her to come home one night after work to a note that he left."

He had only been twenty-four at the time, but even then he could see how devastated Anna was when she came into work that next day. It took months before she ever smiled again. He hated that. He had come to care for Anna and he wanted her to be happy and to live her life. He knew he didn't make her life any easier, but Anna was really the only family he had outside of James. He relied on her for not just her skills, but her opinions and wisdom.

"Jerk. Who breaks off a relationship like that through a note. It's not like they had only been together for a few months."

"It was a coward's way out. And it left her decestated for a long time. I don't know why she is talking to him, but hopefully she will be able to get some closure from it."

"Do you believe in closure?" Jane asked, before she took a drink from her glass.

"I don't know. I've never had to seek it. Any relationship I have been in has never been serious and I've always been the one to end things. I don't know if closure is universal, I think it just depends on the person and their situation. What about you?"

"I think people use their need for closure as an excuse to keep being hung up on someone. To justify seeing someone that hurt you. If someone breaks up with you, then you should move on and chasing your need for closure just feels like an excuse to not move on."

Jane knew that some people swear that closure was the only way to properly move on from a failed relationship. To her though she believed closure came from within and it didn't matter if you get the truth from your ex. People are your ex for a reason and there's nothing you need from them for you to move on.

"I would agree with that. Do you want to go back to the hotel room? We can see what food there is to order if you're hungry."

Charles didn't want to spend much time in the bar. He was trying to not drink as much, he knew it would be hard, but he needed to start to be somewhat responsible. He would be running his father's companies soon enough and he needed to be ready for it. It was time he started to get serious with his professional life. It was time he stopped being a disappointment and time he started to act like a man. One that his father would respect.

"Ya, I could eat." Jane answered, as she downed the rest of her drink.

They both made their way out of the bar and headed for the elevators that would take them up to the hotel lobby. They both kept quiet as they weaved their way through the crowds. Jane took notice of how busy it was within the hotel lobby and she suspected everyone was trying to get a room for the night. She had been hoping the blizzard wouldn't go on that long, but it was looking like it was going to be an all night thing.

"Did you get a hold of the resort?" Jane asked, once they were within the elevator going up to their hotel room.

"I did. It was no problem."

Jane just simply gave a nod as there was no need to keep talking about it. Once they arrived on their floor, Jane followed Charles down the hallway until they reached their hotel room. The second they walked inside they were both disappointed to see that there was only a single king size bed within the room. The room itself looked like a normal hotel room and would be nice if it wasn't for the fact that there was only one bed. If they were a proper newlywed couple that wouldn't be a problem. Only they weren't a normal newlywed couple, they didn't have any love between them. They had only shared one kiss and that was at the altar. Sharing a bed for the night was going to be awkward.

"Sorry, I didn't know it would only be one bed. This was the last room they had." Charles said with regret within his voice.

"It's ok. We might not even be grounded all night. And if we are, we'll make it work."

Jane knew that Charles hadn't done this on purpose. They were lucky they could even get a room. She wasn't going to be upset by a single bed. A king size bed was more than big enough for the both of them to sleep in it without touching the other. Jane went over and pulled out the menu for the hotel kitchen. Charles put their order in and once he ended the call his phone rang and he saw it was his lawyer.

"Excuse me, I have to take this." Charles said, before he headed out into the hallway so he could talk in private.

"Hello." Charles started.

"Good afternoon Charles. I hope you are faring well with this weather."

"I am at the airport in a hotel room currently. The plane was grounded before we could even board. It's looking like we won't be flying out until tomorrow morning. Were you able to find something for me?"

Charles still didn't know what he wanted to do with the money, but he did know he couldn't roll over and let his uncle and aunt get their greedy hands on it.

"I have gone over your father's will and nowhere does it specify what type of marriage you are in. Due to it not specifying then you don't have to prove that you are in love. You just need to be legally married. That won't stop your uncle and his lawyer from trying to argue that the words love didn't have to be written, that it's implied. They can drag this out in court for years if they wanted to."

"Of course. Were the funds ever transferred over into my uncle's name?"

Charles knew that his uncle would be doing just that. He was a greedy man and he was not going to tolerate not inheriting his brother's money. It didn't matter that he didn't work for it or contribute to it really, to him it belonged to him because he was the next born within the family. He should rightfully be the head of the family.

"Nothing was. It would be a complete breach of your father's will. They could face charges for transferring the company and funds over to them without a court order. They are still set to be transferred over to you once you provide the marriage license. Do you have that?"

"Yes, it's at the house. Once the storm clears I can have James send it over to you. I'd like to have a new bank account set up for the funds to be transferred to."

"I can do that for you, that's no problem. May I ask why?"

"I don't want my uncle or my aunt to have any connection to it or know where it is. After this is over, I also would like for you to start looking for a legal way to get them out of the family business."

"You want full control. I can see what I can do. I'll go through all of the legal documents connected to the company. I will get the new bank account created and once I have your marriage license I will file it and get the money released to you. Afterwards, I will get started on finding a legal way to set you as a sole proprietor."

"Thank-you, I appreciate everything you've done for me."

"It's no problem. I hope you have a good honeymoon."

"Thanks."

Charles ended the call and let out a sigh. He was really hoping that his uncle would go quietly into the night, but he knew that wasn't going to happen. They would be getting dragged in and out of courts for years before they would eventually give up. It was a mess, this whole situation was a mess and it all could have been prevented if his father hadn't made that stipulation within his will. He understood why he did, but that wasn't helping him right now.

Charles headed back into the room and instantly Jane was able to tell he was annoyed by the call. She wasn't sure who was on the phone, but she knew it could only be a few people that would upset him like this.

"Who was that?" Jane asked.

"My lawyer."

Jane felt worried over that. The conversation clearly didn't go well and she was worried that maybe his father's fortune was being transferred over to his uncle. Something they were all trying to avoid for their own reasons. Jane knew that she should be washing her hands of it all and letting herself be free from this drama and mess, but they were already married and a deal was a deal. She wasn't about to break it and despite not liking Charles, it wouldn't be fair for them to get divorced that quickly.

"What did he have to say?" Jane asked.

"It's nothing for you to concern yourself with." Charles said dismissively.

Hearing that tone within his voice had only resulted in angering Jane. She hated being dismissed and here Charles was, acting like she was the help. It was ridiculous. She had barely tolerated it before they were married, but she was not going to tolerate it any longer. They were married, like it or not they were, and she refused to be treated like the little woman who was to look good and keep her mouth shut. They were equals and he was damn well going to treat her as one.

CHAPTER 9

"I am not your help nor do I appreciate being treated as such." Jane snapped, as she got out of her chair and went and stood. If they were going to have this discussion she was going to make sure he understood that they were on equal grounds. She wasn't about to talk to him while sitting down and have him looking down upon her.

"What?" Charles asked, very confused by the sudden outburst.

"We are supposed to be married, even if it is all a shame. That doesn' change that I am a person, a living, breathing human being. I am not less than you. I am your equal. This is the twenty-first century, women have the right to an opinion."

It was high time someone told him. Jane thought to herself. She was confident he was used to women just nodding their heads and smiling at him. Allowing him to do whatever he wanted and bowing down to him. She was not going to tolerate it, even if it was for a year. She was not going to be dealing with him if he was going to dismiss her like she was nothing.

"I'm sorry, I'm confused. I have no idea what you mean or what brought this on." Charles said, trying to catch up but he was completely lost.

"Me being a woman doesn't change that I am your equal. I know that might be hard for you with your backwards old traditional thinking that you and your whole family have. A woman doesn't have to be barefoot in the kitchen. And she can wear pants. What is with the obsession of you wanting to put me in dresses or skirts. I hate skirts and I barely tolerate dresses. I can wear pants and still be a woman. I have equal rights, the same rights as you. You don't get to talk down to me or dismiss me like I'm your servant. I'm supposed to be your wife. You don't get to put me in the corner with your aunt while you go off and golf or have a drink with your uncle. I'm not your little woman. And for the record, I like to golf and I could probably golf circles around you."

Charles was both shocked and impressed by Jane's words. The only woman that had ever stood up to him was Anna. Normally all of the other girls he had brought home or dated very shortly were all submissive. They did whatever he wanted and were happy to go to the spa or go shopping, hang with his aunt and learn more about being a gold digger. Yet, Jane didn't seem to want any of it. He had no idea she had been feeling this way, that was not his intention. She was so different to every woman he had ever known and that was what intrigued him.

"I'm sorry, I didn't realise you have felt this way. I didn't know it bothered you. The women that I have always been around were always submissive. They grew up in this world. They were raised to know that women were to find a husband and allow him to take care of them. In return they were to look good and act appropriate. It's normal to me. I foolishly assumed you would be like them. That you wouldn't want to do anything physically active and you would enjoy shopping or going to the spa."

"I hate the spa and I don't mind shopping, but not when the items are thousands of dollars. Even if I woke up tomorrow with a billion dollars in my bank account, I still wouldn't shop at any of the high-end boutiques. I would still shop around based on the weekly flyers for groceries and use coupons. That's who I am."

"And I respect that. I'm sorry I didn't mean to make you feel like I was belittling you or treating you as if you were less than me. I am just not used to women wanting to know personal things about me. Wanting to know more about my life and what is going on with it. Normally they only care about what money they can get from me."

"That's not me. I'm not a gold digger. And I know that sounds hilarious given our current situation, but I'm not looking to take money from you. When we divorce, I don't want anything from you. No spousal payments, nothing. This is purely a business transaction, but that doesn't mean I am going to tolerate you treating me as anything less than an equal."

Jane knew that Charles had grown up in a world where women were to be seen and not heard essentially. They were to look good and weren't expected to uphold an intelligent conversation. However, that wasn't her and if that was what he wanted then he should have asked anyone else to marry him. He asked her, despite the fact that they were complete strangers. She suspected that was what interested him. It was a lot easier to keep things professional and not allow the lines to blur if it was two complete strangers. After their divorce, he would never have to see her or be around her again at any function. It would be a clean break and that was what she wanted as well. But they were here now and they needed to find a way to coexist with each other for the next year.

"I'm truly sorry that you have been feeling this way. That was not my attention at all. I don't view you as the help or a servant. I honestly didn't know you wanted something more." Charles said with regret in his voice.

"I don't need to be wrapped up in the business end of things, but you can't dismiss me either. We're supposed to be married, and whether it's real or not that doesn't change we will have to be around each other for celebrations and family gatherings. It would be easier if we could be friends. It certainly would make things more bearable."

Charles had to agree with her on that. It would make the occasions that they needed to both be present for easier. If they could get along and be able to interact and appear to be a happily married couple, it would make the next year exceedingly easier.

"You are right, it would be easier for the both of us if we were at least friendly with each other. We are set to be together for a year, there's no reason for it to be hostile between us or for it to be more difficult than it needs to be."

Charles went and leaned against the desk within the room as he continued. "The lawyer wanted to inform me that my father's estate hasn't been allocated to my uncle, despite what they have said."

"That's good though. That means they were bluffing."

"They were. He looked into my father's will and there is nothing that specifically states that I have to be in love at the time of the marriage. It's implied, but because it is never officially stated my uncle and Wyatt can't use our marriage against me. Once the storm passes James will send over our marriage license and my lawyer will file it within the court and have the money transferred over to me."

"Sounds like it was a good phone call, so why the issue?"

Jane couldn't see the problem in anything that Charles had to say. It was sounding like they had won.

"The issue is there is nothing stopping my uncle from filing in court to have it changed. The funds can be within my bank account by the time we get back, but if my uncle wanted to he could have me tied up in court for years. He'll slander anyone to try and get the money. He is also involved with the companies and he could try and throw a non-confidence vote to have me removed from ownership with the board of directors. And that is before you factor in the article he may or may not have about you and your sister. An article that could make it impossible for you both to find respectable jobs."

"Ok, we work it one problem at a time. You can't control what your uncle will do with filing in court. That's out of our hands. However, you can control what he releases to the press and the company." Jane said, trying to work it out like a normal problem. She was an expert when it came to problem solving from the life she's had.

"I don't see how. He has the right to release whatever he wants to the press."

"We can't control what he says to the press, but we can control the narrative by beating him to the punch. What if we released an article and spun it in our favor. Yes, Helena and me come from nothing but everyone loves a rags to riches story. We make it sound like a whirlwind romance that swept us both up."

Jane didn't like the idea of her story being out in the public, but she also knew if her and Helena were ever going to stand a chance at getting a decent job again, they had to get ahead of this. If they could control the narrative then it would look like his uncle was being petty and would reflect badly on him and not them.

Charles thought about what Jane suggested for a moment. He had been hoping to avoid the article all together, but he also knew that his uncle and Wyatt would not go quietly into the night. If they couldn't attack him or his marriage, they would turn their attention to Jane and Helena. Regardless how he felt about either woman, he was not going to allow them to be dragged through the mud. If they could produce an article quickly and spin their past in their favor, it could work.

"That's a good idea. The company has a public relation specialist, I'll reach out to her and have her start drafting an article. We'll need to have it written within the week."

"How do we go about doing that?"

"She will have a professional write the article. We'll need to provide a guide of what we would like to have discussed within the article and the writer will only use that information. We could work on it tonight or on the plane so it can be done before we land."

"Ok, ya I can work on that tonight. I have a notebook in my carry on."

Jane was more than happy to get started on it so it could be passed along to the right person. She could also write Helena's part so they wouldn't have to drag her into this.

"I have a laptop with me, you can use it to type up your parts then I can forward it over to Melanie." Charles offered.

"I appreciate that." Jane said with a small smile.

She had no idea how well this would go over. She was hoping they would be able to make it through the next year without any blood spilt, but she was also being realistic. Yes, her and Charles were starting to come to an agreement, an understanding of the other, but it was a small drop in a very large bucket. This really was not how she expected to be spending her honeymoon. Jane thought when she got married it would be to a man that she was madly in love with and couldn't keep her hands off of him. Charles was attractive, and she was honest with herself enough to admit that she was attracted to him. She would never admit it to anyone else. Jane was truly hoping that this was the start of a civil relationship between her and Charles.

CHAPTER 10

"Attention all passengers due to the weather all planes have been grounded until morning at the earliest. We apologize for the delay. Hotel rooms are available within the airport should you wish. Thank-you." The female voice said over the speakers.

Anna let out a groan at the reality that she would be sleeping on a hard airport seat tonight. There were rooms available within the hotel, but based on the thousands of people now stranded here, those rooms will be all booked up within thirty minutes. When Charles had booked this trip they never expected for a blizzard to hit. Yes, the weather hadn't been perfect, but it didn't have a blizzard warning to it. The weather app simply said it was going to snow, apparently that was the understatement of the year.

"I had a feeling the planes would all be grounded for the night. That is why I booked a hotel suite hours ago. Would you care to join me up in my suite?" Evan offered.

Well, there is a loaded question. Anna thought to herself. She would be kidding herself if she said she held zero desire to go up to his hotel suite. They had been sitting here for hours drinking coffee and talking. It had been the best hours of her life in a decade. It felt like old times, as if they hadn't missed a single day with each other. The conversation flowed perfectly, they didn't miss a single beat. It was only natural that the old connection they shared was still alive. They didn't get divorced because they didn't love each other, technically they didn't get divorced. It was hard to file for divorce when you couldn't find the other person.

Still, did Anna want to go up to his hotel suite? And if she did, what was she hoping for? She knew it would be silly for her to think that two grown adults, who were legally married, could be alone in a hotel suite together without anything happening. But was that what she wanted? Did she want to feel him against her again? There were so many uncertainties and she honestly had no idea how she felt about any of them. It was a leap of faith that she would have to take, she just hoped it wouldn't bite her in the ass when it was all said and done.

"That sounds lovely, thank-you." Anna replied with a warm smile.

"Wonderful, shall we?" Evan said, as he rose and offered his arm once again.

Anna gave him a bright smile, as she stood and intertwined their arms once again. Anna allowed herself to be guided through the now bustling airport to the elevators where they would take it up to the hotel lobby. From there they would need to switch to the hotel elevators to reach Evan's hotel suite.

"Oh my goodness." Anna said, as they arrived at the crowded hotel lobby.

Everyone was trying to obtain a hotel room and it seemed like complete strangers were even going in on a hotel room with two beds for themselves or their families. Anything that would ensure their children wouldn't have to sleep on the cold and hard ground for the evening. It warmed Anna's heart to see the care that everyone had for each other and not just selfishly for themselves. At the same time, it saddened her to know that some of those children would indeed have to suffer through the night thanks to Mother Nature. Anna may work for a wealthy family, but she herself was not wealthy. She knew all too well how hard it was to stretch a dollar when you only had a handful of them. She knew that Charles and his family had no earthly idea just how cold and cruel the world could be. It was one of the reasons why she liked Jane so much. She would hopefully show Charles all of the misfortunes in this world so his eyes would start to open. If he in fact did inherit his father's fortune, it could do a great deal of good within the world, he just needed to see it.

"I feel bad for the workers here today. They were not expecting a flood like this. Not to mention the poor workers that were supposed to be off already will need to pull a double shift." Evan commented, as they worked their way through the thick crowd.

"I didn't even think of that." Anna responded, as she tightened her grip on Evan's arm to ensure she wouldn't get pulled free.

She had been so focused on the stranded passengers, she didn't think about the workers who must already be exhausted and now they were trapped having to work a double shift to cover the other workers that couldn't make it in due to the weather. It was not going to be a pleasant night for anyone involved, workers and passengers alike.

They were finally able to get onto one of the three elevators up to the hotel room floors. Anna took notice that Evan had hit the penthouse floor and instantly her interests peaked. She had never been in a penthouse hotel suite before. She had certainly cleaned a good number of them, but she never got to enjoy them for herself. She couldn't help but wonder what the bathtub would look like. A long soak in a hot bath sounded positively to die for right at this moment.

Once at their floor Evan guided them both down the hallway to his hotel suite. The second the door opened, Anna's breath caught in her throat. It was stunning, absolutely stunning. The second she walked through the door she could see a full wall of floor to ceiling windows. All she could see was white from the blizzard, but it was gorgeous. On a clear night it would have been remarkable and she knew you would have been able to enjoy the sight of planes coming and going. The suite was divided up into a few areas, but it was all an open concept. In front of the stunning windows was a sitting area with leather couches, a coffee table and a flat screen television mounted to the one wall to the right. To the left of the seating area was a dining table and a computer desk. Just off of that was an

552

impressive kitchen for a hotel suite. It wasn't just some kitchenette with a small bar fridge, a tiny sink and a counter. It actually held a stove, a full apartment size fridge and a double stainless sink, it was even complete with a dishwasher. This hotel suite was designed for CEOs. It was a place where you worked and lived for a week or more at a time.

"This room is gorgeous." Anna commented, as she walked over to the windows.

" You should see the bedroom and bathroom. I am fairly certain five people could fit in that bathtub." Evan said with a warm smile, as he went to join Anna at the windows.

"I would imagine there have been five people in that bathtub at some point. A place like this has seen some things." Anna said confidently.

Evan gave a rich chuckle to that. "I would imagine you yourself have seen some things in hotel suites. I remember the stories you used to tell me when you cleaned for the Four Seasons."

"Some people hold no shame. I still don't understand how so many women can leave a hotel room without their panties. Surely that is the first thing you notice is missing." Anna said with a small shake of her head.

"Well, if I had to leave a hotel suite without a piece of clothing, I guess not having any underwear is the piece you want to miss. It would certainly be better than no pants." Evan countered.

"I suppose you are right. Have you stayed here before?"

"I have not. Though, I have stayed at my fair share of airport hotels. I seem to have bad luck when it comes to weather it seems." Evan said, before he gave Anna his full attention. "Though, this time around I am glad that Mother Nature threw a wrench in my travel plans."

"You always were a smooth talker." Anna said, fighting against a blush that was threatening to overtake her cheeks.

"Only you my Dear. Are you hungry? Shall we order some room service?"

"I suppose I could eat." Anna agreed.

Evan went over to the kitchen and picked up the hotel kitchen menu. He spoke as he walked back. "I suppose it would be best to place our order now before the hoard of people in their new rooms begin to order."

"Oh that poor kitchen staff."

"The good news is that a lot of workers will be getting tips today." Evan commented, as he handed over the menu to Anna.

They took a couple of minutes to go through the menu and decide what they wanted to eat. Once Evan placed the order in, he returned to the window to stand next to Anna.

"Do you travel often?" Anna asked, after a moment of silence.

"I do, yes. I have been to many places I never thought I would go. India was an interesting experience. I have certainly learned which countries I enjoy and which ones I would prefer to avoid since starting my company. What about yourself? Any travels?"

"None for pleasure. I don't tend to travel anywhere unless it is absolutely necessary. Charles seems to believe I am more than a housekeeper compared to his father. I often have to remind him that I am not his personal assistant." Anna said it with a slightly annoyed tone, but Evan could pick up the care underneath. She cared for Charles and wanted to see him do well.

"A difference of generations. I am sure you will set him straight. At least you get a vacation this time around, even if you have to be around him."

"I may accidentally forget my phone in the hotel room." Anna said with a sly smile that caused Evan to laugh.

554

"Now that sounds like the Anna I know and love. Please tell me you are still painting at least."

A warmth flooded through Anna's chest at just the mention of painting. She loved to paint, had ever since she was a little girl. She swore up and down to anyone who asked that she was going to be a famous painter one day when you grew up. It was her dream, one that quickly dissolved when reality set in and she had to make money. Painting hadn't paid the bills and over the years her free time dwindled down to nothing. Now she didn't even possess a single paint brush, it was a sad thought when she allowed herself to think about it.

"I haven't had the time to paint. I don't even have supplies for it anymore." Anna admitted.

"Now that is a true crime. You always came alive when you painted. You have real talent, a gift, you shouldn't give that up for anything my Dear."

"It's not that simple. I haven't had the time and over the years it was placed on the back burner in place of making a living. The Bentley's require a great deal of my time and any free time that I get to myself I use to take care of my own needs. I simply don't have the time to focus on a painting."

"You have been robbed of a gift my Dear. I hate hearing that you have not been painting still. That was your dream, you shouldn't allow it to wither away and die. We are not getting any younger."

"Oh don't remind me." Anna was all too aware that she was getting older.

She knew what Even was saying was true, but she also knew that it just wasn't that simple. She had responsibilities that she needed to ensure were fulfilled. She couldn't simply quit her job and start to paint for a living. She didn't even know if her paintings would be any good with how rusty she would be. Not everyone gets to live their dreams, Anna had accepted a long time ago that she was one of those people.

"I am merely saying that you shouldn't give up something that you love, something that makes you happy, for anything my Dear."

"I will think about it." Anna relented.

She knew it wasn't going to be easy, but maybe, just maybe, she could find the time to paint, even if they were just for herself and no one ever saw them.

CHAPTER 11

"You truly have thought of everything." Anna stated as Evan turned some classical music on, her favorite.

"Your taste in music has grown on me over the years we were married." Evan replied, as he handed her a glass of red wine.

"I remember in high school you loved head banging music. You used to blare it from your car. It was god awful." Anna said with a delighted smile at the memory.

"I won't lie, I do still love a good death metal song when the day calls for it. Some days are so frustrating and tedious the only way to get through it is by cranking up some old tunes and jumping around like a teenager again."

"Oh to be young and dumb." Anna said with a giggle as she held her glass up. Evan easily clicked his against hers.

"If you ignore the horrid weather, I must say this day has been a dream come true for me." Evan stated.

"How so?"

"I got to spend it with you. As cheesy as it may sound, all I've wanted was another chance, one more day with you, and now my wish has come true."

"You are right, that does sound cheesy." Anna countered with a playful smile.

She had to admit though, she was having a good time as well. She couldn't help but wonder if Charles was as well, considering he had yet to call her for something. She was hoping that meant he was able to get a room for him and hopefully Jane. Knowing him though he would have forgotten that he was supposed to make sure Jane was taken care of as well. She had no faith in him, but they were both adults and more than capable of taking care of themselves. Tonight, she was going to enjoy every single second that she could before the bubble burst and she would be back to her day job.

Evan took a drink from his glas before he set it down on the table and rose. He held his hand out as he spoke. "Will you dance with me, Anna Cooper?"

"I suppose I could allow one dance." Anna agreed, as she set her glass down as well and placed her hand within the offered one.

Evan guided them over to a free space in between the seating area and the dinning room. He placed his right hand on the small of Anna's back and pulled her close to him. At their closeness Anna was able to smell his intoxicating aroma. He still wore the same cologne that she always loved. She had purchased it for him when he was sixteen for their one year anniversary present. She made a point of purchasing a small bottle of it every year on their anniversary. It warmed her heart to know that he was still using it.

"I still love that smell." Anna commented, as they began to dance to the slow music.

"A few years after I left I went into a store looking for some cologne. I smelled all of these different samples, but I couldn't bring myself to purchase any of them. Seeing the bottle for the cologne always reminds me of you, it's the best part of my day. Wearing it makes me feel like you are still here with me."

"If you had never left, I would have still been there with you." Anna pointed out.

She was doing her best to not allow her emotions and hurt from his past actions affect their night. Seeing him, feeling these feelings, it didn't change that she was still upset about his leaving. It was a wound that had yet to scar over and seeing Evan today, it was only poking at that opened wound.

"A regret that I will take with me to my grave and beyond my Dear. But we are here now, together again. I can't express how happy I am that our paths crossed today. It was as if it was a sign from the Heavens. I know a lot has happened, a lot of hurt has been done and it's all from my doing, I'm not arguing that. Perhaps though, just for one night, we pretend that hurt isn't there. We pretend that we are both on our way to Paris when a blizzard struck, forcing us to spend the night here in this hotel suite. Let's have fun, like we used to when we went on an adventure together."

Anna had to admit, it did sound amazing. They had often dreamt about going away on vacation to Paris. They would book a hotel right by the Eiffel Tower and they would spend their days traveling all over the city and seeing the rich culture and art that it had to offer. At night they would be wrapped up in each other's bodies that they barely stopped to come up for air. It would be magical and an experience they would never forget.

But could she really put it all behind her and pretend that they were married and madly in love still? Sure, for the night it would be amazing, but come morning would she really feel the same? Anna knew it was ridiculous, that she should be putting a stop to all of this, but at the same time, she didn't want to. It had been a decade since she had felt like this. Since she had felt alive and beautiful. She didn't want the night to end. What could pretending for one night truly hurt?

"Well Mr. Cooper, I do hope you are not tired." Anna said with a playful smile.

"I'm never too tired for you Mrs. Cooper."

Evan closed the small gap between them and he pulled Anna in for a deep and passionate kiss. Anna hungerly kissed back, devouring Evan's tongue that was instantly within her mouth. The sexual chemistry between them was sparking with electricity. Evan didn't hold much patience, he wanted to feel

Anna's body against his now. He immediately deepened the kiss as his hands made quick work of removing Anna of her clothes. Once she was in nothing but her lace panties he placed his hands on the bottom of her butt and lifted her up. Anna instantly wrapped her arms around Evan's hips as he walked them over to the bed.

He gently laid Anna down onto the bed and then his mouth was on her breast and she was moaning and arching up into him. His mouth was spectacular, it made her whole body feel like it was on fire. Evan worked Anna's other breast as he moved his hands down to her panties. He quickly removed them as he kissed his way down further. Anna willingly opened her legs for him and she could feel herself getting wet just by thinking of what he was about to do. Evan kissed his way down to her folds and then with a small lick his tongue was on her. Anna gave a small moan at Evan's light teasing before he finally gave her what she desperately wanted, a long and deep lick. Anna knew it wouldn't take long before she was cumming. She was too worked up, too turned on and when his tongue slid inside of her Anna felt her insides clench and the heat in her belly was exploding.

"Evan." Anna moaned as she came. The only time she had ever came this fast was with Evan. He knew her body better than any other man ever could.

When he didn't stop, even after Anna had stopped pulsing she found a whole new level of pleasure. He continued to lick her folds and rubbed his finger over her clit. The sensation was almost too much for Anna. She felt like she was going to lose her mind if he didn't bury himself inside of her.

"Evan, it's too sensitive." Anna was withering beneath him, completely at his mercy and she was loving it.

Evan pulled back and just gave her a warm smile. "I'm not done with you yet."

Evan quickly removed the rest of his clothing and then shuffled Anna back up the bed. Anna's body was tingling with anticipation. She had missed feeling Evan inside of her and she knew he was going to make her scream and feel amazing. She wanted to feel all of him inside of her. Anna moved her hand and gave his dick a stroke. His skin was so soft, and it felt much better than the hard plastic ones that she had resorted to using over the past decade. Evan gave a deep moan at the contact and Anna wanted to hear him do that more. Evan pulled back so he could grab a condom, but stopped when Anna spoke.

"I'm negative."

Anna would never have unprotected sex with anyone, but Evan. He was the only man that she trusted on that level, even after all of this time apart, she knew she could trust him.

"Me too. You on the pill still?"

"I am."

"Thank God."

They both wanted to feel the heat of skin on skin. Evan placed himself between Anna's legs and slowly pushed his hips forward, pushing his dick inside of her inch by inch. The second his tips broke through Anna's walls she was a goner. It felt amazing. To be able to feel real skin, there was nothing better. When Evan was balls deep inside of meher he gave Anna a moment to adjust to his size. Evan began to kiss her neck and just allowed Anna to catch her breath. Evan waited until he felt her relax before he pulled out and slammed back into her, causing them both to moan deeply. Anna wrapped her legs around his waist and the new angle made Evan hit her g-spot once again.

"Don't be gentle." Anna moaned.

She wanted to feel everything Evan had for her. Anna had missed this feeling. She had missed feeling Evan's body against her, inside of her. They had always shared amazing chemistry within the bedroom and that chemistry was alive and well.

Evan gave Anna the sexiest sound she had ever heard, a growl and then his hips were pistoling in and out of her. Hitting Anna's sweet spot dead on each and every single time. Anna was no longer moaning but giving off small screams from the pleasure that rocked her entire body. Evan's thrusts were fast and deep, and Anna loved every second of it. She could have done this for days without a single complaint. Evan felt absolutely out of this world. It wasn't long before she was cumming again and after a moment Evan slammed into her and came hard and deep inside of her. His cum burned Anna's insides in a way that she couldn't even begin to explain. Everything felt so amazing, so unbelievable that her body was shaking from the pleasure.

When Evan stopped pulsing he didn't pull out right away. He bent forward and gave Anna some of the sweetest and softest kisses she had ever had and he didn't stop until they were both breathing normally again.

"The first round is always hard and fast. The second round though." Evan said, as she started to slowly pull out and push back in.

Anna gave a deep moan. She arched her back as Evan began to move once again. She could fall in love with this man all over again tonight.

CHAPTER 12

Helena walked back into the living room and saw that James had some candles lit that he had found. She had struck out on candles, but she did find some very dusty board games in a crawl space under the stairs.

"Oh good you found candles." Helena said, as she placed the games down.

"I did in Anna's room. I'm really hoping she doesn't mind me invading her privacy." James said with a small awkward smile.

"I'm sure the extenuating circumstances clears your guilty conscience. I didn't find candles or flashlights, but I did find some board games." Helena said with a warm smile.

She went and grabbed a cloth from the kitchen so she could wipe the boxes down. There was so much dust on the lids that Helena couldn't even see what the games were.

"To burn?" James asked, confused. He wasn't too sure why Helena would dig out the board games. They had clearly seen better days. He wasn't even sure where she found them. Charles' parents were even stricter than his own had been.

"No, not to burn. What crazy person burns board games? I figured we could play them. Beats sitting around waiting for the snow to stop."

It took everything within James not to point out that they could have sex to pass the time. He had a strong feeling that Helena wasn't going to go for that option.

"I've never in my life played a board game. I don't see me starting now." James commented and Helena's head snapped up at his words.

"I'm sorry, you've what?"

That wasn't possible. There was no way that James had never played a board game before. You play them in school, during rainy days with your friends. Everyone has played at least one board game in their life.

"I've never played. My parents didn't believe in fun and neither did Charles' for that matter. They must have been from Henry sneaking them in. He used to do a lot of things that Charles' father didn't approve of. After Henry died no one must have found them, otherwise they would have been thrown out."

"No, come on, you're joking with me right now. Everyone has played a board game in their life. Are you seriously telling me not once have you ever played a board game in school or over at a friend's place?" Helena asked skeptically.

"I went to private schools, so games were completely out of the equation. As for friends none of them played games either that weren't a video game. They didn't even have a deck of cards." James said with a small shrug.

"Ok, ya we are changing that." Helena picked up Monopoly as she continued. "This is a classic and you should like it, it involves money and buying properties."

James gave a small snot to that, but he couldn't help the smile that spread across his face. Helena moved the coffee table over and got the board all set up. She then sat down on the floor with a pillow under her butt as she explained the game. It seemed pretty straight forward to James, but he couldn't see how it would be fun. He was taking it though, because it allowed some of the walls that were surrounding Helena to come down just slightly.

"I have a question for you, if talking during game play is allowed." James started

"Of course it is. This isn't the library James." Helena said with a playful smirk.

"What do you want to do with your life? If you could do anything with money not being an option, what would you do?"

James knew questions like that would be irrelevant to Helena. She didn't have an endless supply of money where she could do anything, but James was curious. He wanted to know more about her and that included her dreams. He was really hoping that she would answer him.

"You mean in some magical make believe world where money doesn't exist and everyone pays their bills with gumdrops?" Helena said skeptically.

She knew James was just trying to talk, but she really didn't see the point in answering questions like that. She was never going to be able to fulfill her wildest dreams. She was going to have to find some type of job. She knew that Jane had said Charles would be able to provide money to her as well, but that also made her feel uncomfortable. She would only be taking what she needed to pay off her debt and then she would be figuring out what type of job she could do that would pay the bills. She had been flip flopping back and forth on taking any money from Charles. She wasn't comfortable with taking money from him. It made her feel like a gold digger. She never wanted to be like that. She was an independent woman that could stand on her own two feet. She would take only what she needed for her debts to give her a blank slate and then she would handle life on her own once again.

"No, but you are allowed to have dreams. Plus, you will be getting some money from Charles, you could put it towards your dreams."

James didn't know from personal experiences, but he could understand that it would be hard for someone to go from having nothing to having money. It could feel overwhelming and leave a person feeling uncertainty.

"I will only be accepting the amount that I need to pay off my debt. No more. I will be working for my money, just like I have always done. I'm not a gold digger and I will not lower myself to that level. I'm not afraid of hard work."

"I never said you were a gold digger. Trust me, I have seen a lot of gold diggers in my life and you are the exact opposite of one. The fact that you aren't afraid of hard work is what makes you attractive. You aren't afraid of doing things the hard way. Your worth ethic is inspiring. I was just curious what your dream was."

Helena let out a slow breath as she thought about it. She had dreams growing up sure, but she never really thought about it in her adult life. Once her mother passed away she put all of her focus into helping to pay the bills and to keep her and Jane in an apartment and not out on the streets.

"Before my mother was sick I had been going to college for business. I didn't get to finish it before she got too sick. I had to quit to help take care of her and to work to pay for the bills. We also had medical bills we had to pay for and medications."

"I'm sorry that she got sick. And I'm sorry that my family didn't approve of her surgery." James said with a heavy heart.

It pissed Helena off still, but she wasn't blinded by her rage anymore. She cou;d see the difference between his family's company and him. James wasn't the one that stamped the denial on her paperwork. It hurt, it hurt a great deal, but it was a hurt she had to live with.

"It's not your fault. You weren't the one to personally deny her."

"No, I wasn't. I only do some administrative work in the company. Jack refuses to allow me to do anything else." James said, as he rolled his eyes. "How much longer did you have for your degree?"

"I was a year away when I dropped out. It was a hard decision, but easy at the same time. My mom needed help and it was better for me to drop out and work then Jane. I always told myself I would go back, but I've never been able to yet."

It hurt Helena to know that she was a year away from her degree in business. She had worked really hard to get where she was and she had been looking forward to walking across that stage. To be the first person in their family to graduate from college, to hold a degree. It was going to be a huge accomplishment and hopefully be the change that their family needed. She had so many plans for her future. Plans that had been ripped away from her.

"Maybe you should. With your debt paid off, you could go back for your last year and finish what you started." James said supportingly.

James would have offered to pay for it, but he knew that Helena would take offense to the offer. Even if he suggested it as a loan without interest. They weren't at that level and he had to respect that.

"I don't know, maybe. The plan though was to start a real estate business where I would purchase rundown properties and flip them. I had taken some extra courses in construction so I could do a good chunk of the work myself. I wanted to be able to provide more affordable homes to people who couldn't afford a million dollar house for their family."

Helena and Jane used to talk all the time about how they would work to change their neighborhood. How they wanted to help those like them who grew up with nothing. They wanted to be the change that they wished was in their lives when they were younger. The best way to do that would be to become the heroes they wished they had. To give back to a community that was fighting tooth and nail to survive each and every single day.

"I love that idea. You like working with your hands?"

James was surprised that Helena enjoyed working with her hands. He was so used to women refusing to touch anything that was even slightly dirty. You would never catch any of them dead on a construction site. He loved that Helena was more of a hands on person. She was unique, and not just in his world. James knew for a fact that she would be special even within her social circle. She was a strong, independent woman who could get her hands dirty. She couldn't have been any sexier to him. James had no idea what his ideal woman was before he had met Helena. Now he knew without a doubt she was his. If he couldn't convince her to give them a real try, he was going to be heart broken quite possibly for the rest of his life.

"I do. I always have ever since I was little. I was that girl who loved building birdhouses and as I got older I would take old furniture and flip it. We couldn't afford much, normally if we needed a dresser or table it would come from a second hand store. I would sand it down and repaint or stain it to make it look brand new."

"That's amazing. I love that. I bet you had some pretty wonderful ideas about your old house."

"I did, ya. I wanted to redo it all and add some fencing all around the property and turn it into a real home. I wanted to be able to keep it within the family. To have our own little family estate so each generation would always have a place to call home. Jane and me, we were supposed to be the start of a new generation for the Miller family. Turns out it was harder than either of us could have imagined." Helena said with a small sad shrug.

"You got lots of time to make that dream into a reality though Helena. Don't count yourself out just yet, you have a lot of life left in you. You can still achieve your dreams." James said in a serious voice. The last thing he wanted was for Helena to think that she would never accomplish her life goals. She had a lot of years left in her, she could easily get their old house back and turn it into something remarkable.

"Maybe, we'll see. What about you? What was your dream?" Helena asked, looking to get the conversation away from her. It hurt her a lot still when she thought about losing their home. She always dreamt of keeping it in the family and the reminder that she failed always shot pain throughout her chest. It was a constant reminder of failure, her failure, and it was still a bitter pill to swallow.

CHAPTER 13

"My dream?" James asked.

"Yes, your dream. What would you do if you didn't have to follow all of these ridiculous social rules?" Helena asked with a warm smile.

James was taken back in surprise by the question. It seemed like a simple question, he had just asked her the exact same one. Yet, he was surprised because no one had ever asked him what he wanted to do with his life. He was told at a very young age that he would be working within the family business. He knew he wouldn't hold an important position, Jack had made that very clear. He never had the chance to dream or to find his own way in the world. Before he was even born his life had been mapped out without any thought that he might not want it. Even after his parents were killed in a car crash by a drunk driver, he never allowed himself to think about doing something different. By that point it was too late. He was already working for the family business and he had long accepted that was his life and it would never change.

James thought about it for a moment. Him and Helena were a lot alike, because he also has always loved real estate. He used to always watch the home renovation shows and he would take notes on what he liked, any of the codes they mentioned, any pointers from the experts and real estate agents. He would spend hours watching them and he used to have notebooks full of notes in his room. Even at his age he still loved to watch the shows and he often found himself imagining what he could do on an empty piece of land.

"Growing up I was always told what I would be doing. That I would be working for the family business. Dreaming of doing something else, it wasn't forbidden, but I never did it. There wasn't a point when I knew it would never be allowed. Even after they both passed, I still continued to work for the company. I became complacent. When I was younger though I used to love watching the home improvement channel. I used to fill notebooks with notes and tips from the experts. If I had gotten to choose what I wanted to do with my life, I would most likely have chosen land development."

Helena couldn't help but be shocked. She had no idea that James would be interested in that stuff. She had been obsessed, still was, with the home improvement network. She was always watching it, especially after a bad day at work. She would put it on and allow her mind to imagine what it would be like to be one of the people working on the homes. How amazing it would feel to take an old rundown house and watch as it transformed into a work of art. A piece of art that would provide a home for a family that was in desperate need for one. She would imagine how the walls would be filled with the echo of laughter from the children. How you would hear the pitter patter of little bare feet on the floor. It would go from an eyesore to a beautiful family home.

Helena never expected for James to also be interested in restoring homes. He didn't come across as the type of guy that would enjoy working with his hands and doing manual labour. It was surprising and really told Helena that she didn't actually know this man that was sitting across from her. Helena could feel her heart beating faster at the realisation. She couldn't care about him. They could only be cousin in-laws, friends even, nothing more. She couldn't allow herself to be a hypocrite, to go against everything she believed in where his kind came from. The problem she was having though was placing him within the stuck up and entitled rich box that she had locked him down in. He was banging against the lid and for the first time, Helena wasn't sure it would stay on.

"I used to watch those shows all the time. I still do when I want to relax or after a really bad night at work. I'm surprised. You don't come across as the type of guy that would like to do any manual labour. I mean, your nails are nicer than mine."

"I'm not afraid of getting my hands dirty. I do my own landscaping at my place. I don't have a housekeeper that lives with me. I do hire a cleaning service that comes in once a week, but I clean up as I go. I cook my own food, I even change my own oil in my car. I can work with my hands and I do enjoy it. And there is nothing wrong with having healthy nails." James said that last part slightly offended. Yes, he got mani pedis, but he believed that health was from the top down.

"I never said there was." Helena said with her hands up slightly in a mock surrender before she continued. "I was just saying they are nicer than mine."

"Looks like you need to go to a new nail salon." James countered.

"Ha, jokes on you, I've never been to one." Helena said with a smirk.

"We should change that then. We could go together, as friends of course."

"Of course." Helena agreed with a playful smile.

She had no idea what she was doing. Going anywhere with James had the potential for danger and not in a fun way. The more time she spends with him the more she was going to want him. The more he was going to surprise her and that was not a good thing. Normally it would be, but with him being a Bentley, with his family being responsible for her mother's death essentially, it would be devastating. She was sure her own mother was rolling in her grave right now. Both her and Jane were playing a dangerous game. They were allowing themselves to be close to a man that their own family denied their mother the surgery she needed to save her life. The very last thing Helena wanted to do was dishonor and disrespect her mother.

"So you don't have any help at your house?" Helena asked, after a moment.

"I don't. We used to growing up, but after my parents were killed, I didn't want everyone around. I wanted to be alone and live my life without eyes always on me."

"Your parents were killed?" Helena asked, shocked. She had no idea how his parents had died, but she figured it would have been old age or an illness maybe.

"They were, yes. A drunk driver when I was twenty. The driver also died on impact."

"I'm sorry, I had no idea." Helena said with sympathy to her voice.

"It's ok. It was fifteen years ago. It was hard at first and I had a lot of unresolved feelings towards them. It took about a year before I broke and went to speak with a therapist to get the feelings out and deal with the loss. It helped me to move on."

Helena offered him a warm and supportive smile. She knew from personal experience that most people, especially men, didn't want to go and speak to a professional about their thoughts or feelings. It took a great deal of courage to go and to freely speak about it.

"I'm glad you were able to heal from it and move on. It's good that you spoke to someone that could help you cope with the death of your parents and the emotions attached to it. Why not go crazy though once they were gone? Why continue to follow their rules? Because of Jack?" Helena asked, slightly confused as to why at twenty he would still follow the old rules. He essentially was free, so why not take advantage of that?

"The rules had been told to me since I could remember. When I did rebel at sixteen, that summer with Jack was horrible. He was always yelling and he got violence with me a few times a week. It was a long eight weeks, but it did the trick. My father knew it would, it's why he sent me there. When I got to come back home after the summer, I was too afraid to do anything against them."

James didn't like thinking about his summer with Jack, but it was the only way for Helena to truly understand why he was the way he was. Why he didn't break all of the rules when he was an adult. He knew though that in order for Helena to see him as more than a Bentley man, as more than a rich man, he would have to talk about the pieces of his life that made him human.

*****

Helena couldn't stop the hurt that filled her chest at just the thought of someone hitting James as a child. To think that he had been punished to that level before he wanted to wear jeans or get a tattoo. God, she had four of them and piercings. It hurt to hear and she couldn't help but picture a scared teenage James being hurt by someone that was supposed to be his family member. He didn't deserve it. She could tell deep down he had a good heart, he just needed to let it out more.

"I'm sorry you had to go through all of that. But doesn't surviving it mean you owe it to yourself to live your life how you want to live it. Not how your family has dictated you should? I know it's easier said than done, really I do. But you have to live your life for you and in a way that will leave you with the least amount of regrets. You only get one life, do you really want to waste it by conforming to beliefs that you don't share?" Helena tried to reason.

James knew what Helena was saying made sense. He knew he didn't have to conform any longer to what his parents or Jack had expected for him to be. It wasn't easy though. It wasn't easy to get the voice in his mind to stop. He wanted it to stop though. He wanted to be able to wear a pair of jeans without feeling like he was going against the rules or he was going to be looked down upon and ridiculed. He had considered going back to speak with his previous therapist to work through the issues, but he never had the courage to make the call. James was thinking that maybe he really should make that call. Maybe now was the time to work through these issues so he could live his life how he wanted to. So he could wear a pair of jeans without feeling Jack's fist against his skin. So he could date a real woman and have children one day without inflicting his family's beliefs onto them. That was what scared him the most. Having children and for them to grow up like he had to. He didn't want that and he would never wish it upon his worst enemy. If James wanted something real, he would have to make that call and put the work in.

"I don't, no. I want to be able to be free from it all and not feel guilty when I don't follow the rules. I've thought about it over the years, but I've never had the courage to break through that wall. I'm not getting any younger and if I ever want to have children, I need to break through the wall. It might be time I start putting the work in and fighting back against them." James said with a small smile.

"Well, as your new cousin in-law, I will always be there for you to help should you need it." Helena offered with a loving smile.

Knowing that Helena would be by his side filled James with courage and strength. He would be the one having to fight, but he wouldn't have to do it alone and that made it all a lot less terrifying.

CHAPTER 14

Jane let out a sigh as she finished typing up the information for the article in regards to her and Helena's story. She was hoping it would go over well and that they wouldn't be portrayed in a negative light. She slid the laptop over to Charles where they were sitting at the table. Their food had arrived about twenty minutes ago and they had spent their time eating in silence as Jane worked on the article.

"What do you think?" Jane asked.

Charles turned his full attention to his laptop. He hadn't said anything while Jane was typing away because he didn't know what to say. He didn't want to interrupt her or distract her. He knew from his father that people don't tend to like being interrupted when they are working. He could remember clearly how annoyed his father was when he would interrupt him when he was younger. It often resulted in his father either yelling, kicking him out and slamming the door in his face or giving him a look of pure annoyance that always made him wish his father had just yelled. He hated it when his father would look at him like that or when he had a disappointed look on his face. He had seen that a few times growing up when his report card came home. It wasn't that Charles wasn't smart or bad in school, it was that he didn't get straight A's. If he came home with a B, his father was disappointed. It was always a great deal of pressure and the only way he knew how to handle that pressure was to party, drink and be irresponsible. If he was the irresponsible son, then he couldn't disappoint his father. He was the problem child and no one ever expected something great from a problem child.

"This sounds good. I'll send it off to Melanie and she will get started on it. We should be able to have it released within a few days."

Charles was happy with the spin on their history and it would reflect well on both Jane and Helena so they would not be labelled as a gold digger. They would be able to still get a decent job and have a normal life when this was all over and done with. Charles sent off the email before he closed his laptop. He then turned his full attention to Jane and finally asked the question that he had been wondering for a week now.

"Why Cape Town? You had a completely free pass to pick anywhere in the world, I was expecting a beach resort or Italy, Paris even, but South Africa?" Charles asked, confused.

"It's the one place I've always wanted to go. I know it's not traditional or a place where most people would want to go, but there are a lot of great things to do over there." Jane said with a warm smile.

Charles couldn't help but notice the slight warmth that began to fill his heart at seeing a true smile on Jane's face. He wasn't certain he had ever seen a real smile on her face before now, a thought that was sad all in of itself. He was her husband and he had never seen her truly happy.

"What kind of things?" Charles asked, as he sat back.

"There's a lot of cool things you can do in Cape Town. There's obviously the beaches, but you can go ziplining, there's hiking trails, you can go up to Table Mountain. There is one beach where there are penguins that you can go up to and see. There are museums and botanical gardens. What I can't wait for though is to go cage diving with great white sharks." Jane said with a huge smile.

Charles couldn't believe this. He expected that Jane would be spending all of her time in the resort. He had no idea that she would want to go on different adventures and be that active. It was a huge difference to the women he had been around in his life. They all wanted to be in a spa and go shopping, they would be caught dead if you suggested they got their hands dirty. And here Jane was excited to go cage diving with great white sharks. It was insane and amazing. Charles had always wanted to go out on adventures, but he had to live up to his father's expectations and image of what a wealthy man in their social circle was to act like. It was fine if you wanted to golf or go boating, but you weren't supposed to do anything more adventurous. You had to uphold the image of a wealthy man and a wealthy man does not get dirty. They don't wear jeans and t-shirts, no leather jackets or sneakers. It was a life he was used to, but that didn't mean he didn't want something different.

"You are going to go cage diving?" Charles asked, shocked.

"I am. I've always wanted to do it."

"I'm just surprised. I had no idea you would be adventurous, or that adventurous. I just assumed you would be spending the days at the resort going to the beach and the spa. I didn't think you would want to leave it and travel around. I didn't know Cape Town offered any of that stuff."

"It's a great place to be. There's lots of history and tourist attractions. It's not like a lot of other African cities where it's dangerous. You can leave and be perfectly safe just like you could in Paris or Rome. I've always loved to be active and live life to the fullest. I don't believe in leaving this world with regrets of things left undone. I'm going to a nearby village on the fourth day to help them build homes for an area that was destroyed by rebels. It's a very poor village that barely has drinking water, but they are trying to rebuild and make it a village again."

"You really care about people." Charles stated.

"I do, yes. I think it's important for people to help those that are below the poverty line. To help in our developing countries to give them a better life. The children in the village that I am going to visit, they all deserve to have a normal life. They

578

deserve the opportunity to go to school and learn. They deserve to go to bed at night and not have to be afraid of what could happen while they are sleeping. One child that is in the village that I'll be visiting, she's eight, she used to go to sleep counting the seconds between the gun fire." Jane said sadly.

"That's terrible. I couldn't imagine." Charles said.

He knew the majority of the world didn't live like he did. Despite what people believed, he did know that he was very lucky to have had the life he did have. He knew money didn't grow on trees and that most people struggled with their finances and lived well below their means. He wasn't blind to the world. He wanted to help, but he didn't know how and he wasn't in a position to help. It wasn't his actual money, but his father's and to his father and uncle for that matter, they would see it as a waste of money. Any money they've donated to charities were always for a tax write off and they were always charities for medical advances and never for children, not even a sports team.

"It's hard. Children are the ones that are destroyed the most by poverty. It's why I want to start my own non-profit to try and help as many families as I can."

"What would the non-profit do?"

"It would provide a space where people who are under the poverty line or just above it could go to gain more education. I would like to offer workshops on different programs from computer ones like Microsoft Excel, to how to write a resume, do interviews, and provide them with training. I'd like to partner with other businesses who would hire the clients of the non-profit. I want to create a place that is filled with resources to help people take their life and make it better. It's one thing to say for them to go out and get an education to find a better job, but it doesn't work that easy. Most of the time people who are working a minimum wage job can't afford to go to College. It's an endless loop that they are forever stuck in and often their children get trapped in it as well. I want to help break the cycle and the only way to do that is by giving them the opportunities that they need to grow."

Charles could see how much passion she had for helping people. What she described sounded like a wonderful place for the right people. He could also see the business benefits for a business to partner with her. He knew from his father's company that people who are underqualified, but given the proper training, tended to be a harder worker. They appreciated their job more and were willing to work harder to ensure they kept it. Compared to someone that was overqualified and always looking for something better. It was a win/win, the company got better employees and the employees were able to make a decent living for themselves and their family.

"I think that is a great idea. I'd be willing to help you with it in any way that I can. I have a great deal of business contacts that would be willing to sit down with you and discuss partnering with you." Charles offered.

"Really?" Jane asked, surprised.

She knew that James had offered to help her as well with investing within the company to get it started, but she didn't expect for Charles to wish to help as well. She thought he would dismiss the idea and call her foolish for believing in trying to change the world. Yet here he was surprising her. *Maybe he's not so bad afterall.* Jane thought to herself.

"Absolutely. It sounds like it will be a beneficial partnership on both parties' behalf. I know a good number of CEOs that would be willing to work with you for them to have employees that are willing to work hard and be loyal to the company. You have a great idea, one that I believe will do well in the city." Charles said warmly.

"I think so too. And that would be great. I'd be more than happy to meet with them." Jane said with a friendly smile back.

"I'll set something up for when we return. I'd like to go with you to the village if that is alright. I'd like to help out."

"You want to get your hands dirty?" Jane asked, surprised that Charles would be willing to leave the safety of the resort.

"I have no problem working with my hands. I've always wanted to do more, to go on adventures and experience life. That was never allowed growing up. You had to keep a specific appearance about yourself and a lot didn't fit into that category. I would love to go skydiving, learn how to surf. Hell, I would go cage diving with great white sharks. My uncle might have a heart attack if he saw a picture of it." Charles said with a small laugh.

"You should come with me then. And I don't just mean to the village. Come with me cage diving, I'm also going zip lining, you are more than welcome to come with me. Though, it would require you to wear jeans." Jane said with a smirk.

"I will have you know that I own a pair of jeans and packed them." Charles said with a proud smile.

"Contraband?" Jane teased.

Charles gave a rich laugh to that as he sat back. "Not this time. Though when I was a teenager I used to have a pair of jeans hidden in my room. We were never allowed to wear them growing up, my father believed it made you look cheap. It didn't matter if you spent three thousand dollars on a single pair of jeans, to him just wearing denim meant you were poor. I used to sneak them out when I went out with my friends and would get changed in my car or behind a bush when I didn't have one."

"Wow, that is really sad. You know you're not a teenager anymore and he is dead. No offense at all, but he's gone he can't tell you what to do or how to live. You have the chance to be your own man, to be who you have always wanted to be. This is your time to live your life and be your own person, you should be embracing that. Screw what your uncle or aunt says or thinks. You're gonna be thirty-five within two weeks, be who you want to be. Wear what you want, do what you want. It's your life, not theirs and you have to live your life with the least amount of regrets."

Jane knew it wasn't her place to try and change Charles. But if they were going to be friends, then that meant having open and honest conversations. She wasn't telling him anything she wouldn't be telling a friend. He couldn't live his life for his dead father, he had to live it for himself. He was the one that was still alive and it was his life, he needed to embrace that.

She's right. Charles thought to himself. He had been living his life to his father's expectations even after his death. He had grown so accustomed to living a specific way that he didn't even think about the possibility of changing it. He didn't have to be the problem child, the disappointment any more, because there was no one to disappoint but himself. He could wear jeans without having to feel the need to hide them. He could go out and play basketball if he wanted to. He was his own man, for the first time in his life he had full control over what he wanted to do.

"You're right. I've never thought about it like that before. I've gotten so used to living my life a certain way, being a certain way, that it didn't even cross my mind that I was free to just be myself. Thank-you for pointing that out to me." Charles said with a rich smile.

"What are friends for." Jane said with her own smile in return.

They had a long road ahead of them, but for the first time since meeting him, Jane was starting to feel like maybe this next year wouldn't be so horrible after all.

CHAPTER 15

It had been a couple of hours since Jane and Charles had arrived at their hotel room. After they had finished eating and their conversation they had started to do their own thing. Charles was currently working away at his laptop. He was trying to determine what he wanted the company's future to be. He had made the decision to mold it in his own view. Currently it was what his father had wanted it to be and now it was his turn to mold it into his own vision. One where mothers like Jane's didn't have to receive a letter informing them that their life wasn't worth the investment in saving. It sickened Charles to know that Jane and Helena's mother could still be alive to this day if it hadn't been for his family's company. It was a deep stab to the gut and he was not about to make the same mistake as his father. He was going to find ways where they could continue to make money, but not at the expense of another person's life. That wasn't a decision he could live with.

Charles looked up once he heard the bathroom door opening. Jane had retreated to take a shower and get changed into something more comfortable. The weather forecast that was currently playing on mute on the television had the blizzard going all night. They both knew that they would not be going anywhere tonight and there was no point in pretending. Charles wasn't sure what type of reaction he would have seeing her like this, but he wasn't expecting what hit him. Her hair was just slightly damp and was in small waves from being towel dried. She had on a simple black tank top and short blue jean shorts. It wasn't anything fancy and it shouldn't have been sexy. He had seen gorgeous models dressed in lingerie in front of him, all for him to enjoy. And yet none of them had turned him on as strongly as seeing Jane in a pair of short distressed denim shorts. He could see clearly from where he sat that she obviously painted in them. He could see speckles of different colors where the paint had splashed onto the shorts. Even a few streaks that he imagined she had wiped from her hand onto her shorts. She was beautiful, absolutely beautiful.

"How was the shower?" Charles managed to force out. He couldn't stop looking at Jane, but he knew he had to say something before it got weird and creepy.

"It was good. I thought maybe the hot water wouldn't last with the hotel being so full and the blizzard, but it never ran out." Jane commented, as she went and sat down on the bed against the headboard.

"Hotels like this are built and designed for full capacity and any type of weather. I'm glad you enjoyed it though."

Charles tried to force his eye back onto his laptop so he could continue working. The problem was though, they kept peeking up at Jane. She was looking at her phone and Charles suspected that Helena must have texted with how fast her fingers were flying over the keys.

"James and Helena have lost power. They found some candles though and James was able to get a fire going before it went out."

"The fire will keep them warm. I've wanted to get a generator for the house, but it's such a large house it would take a rather large generator and a great deal of gas to run it. If they stay in the living room and close the surrounding doors the room will stay warm with the fire going. James knows that."

Charles wasn't worried about James. The man had been through enough storms in his life to know how to survive in the house. However, he could tell from Jane's tone that she was slightly worried about Helena being in the house during a storm like this. He wanted to offer her what comfort that he could.

"They'll be fine. It's not like it's the first blizzard to hit the city. Helena even said she found some old dusty board games when they went looking for the candles. She was going to try and rope James into playing them." Jane said with a small smirk,

Charles gave a soft chuckle at the image that it created in his mind. James grew up much like himself being told how to act within society. Board games were not one of them. He didn't even know they were still in the house.

"I don't think James has played a board game in his life."

"Seriously? How is that possible? You play them in school all the time, especially when it was raining outside and you had an indoor recess."

Jane couldn't believe that James would have never played a single board game in his life. It just wasn't possible. You played them in school, with friends, on family game nights, every single person has played Monopoly at least once in their life.

"The schools we attended never believed in playing games and if you didn't get a recess due to the weather, you continued to be taught right through it. As for growing up, James grew up like myself. There were never family game nights, you sometimes would go days without speaking to your parents. Conversation at the dinner table was about work or school, nothing personal, or light. If you didn't have anything intelligent to contribute to the conversation you were to eat and be quiet. Games were never allowed nor played in either home." Charles informed her.

"But then how did the games get there?" Jane asked.

She couldn't believe that Charles and James had never experienced the true joys of being a child. It was starting to make a lot more sense to her why they were both the way they were. They were never allowed to be children and make messes, play games and be happy. They always had to be presented in a specific light, putting a huge amount of pressure on children. It was wrong and it made Jane a bit sad.

"My grandfather, on my father's side, was very strict with my father growing up, but I always suspected that he regretted it. He died when I was ten, but all of my memories of him are of a loving and fun old man. The stricter my father got with me, the more fun he got. It was opposite extremes. He got the board games and he would hide them away in a servant's cubby and when we were alone he would bring them out and we would play them while eating candy and chocolate. My father never wanted me to have sugar, because he believed it would make me unruly so whenever my grandfather would come by he always snuck candy or chocolate in for me. I used to hide the wrappers under my bed." Charles said with a warm smile at the memory.

"Really? You had to hide sugar?" Jane couldn't imagine growing up like that. Their mother always treated them to sweets, whether that was candy, chocolate, ice cream, donuts or cookies, they were always allowed to have a treat after dinner or in their school lunch pals.

"I did. After my grandfather passed, I continued to sneak them in. When Anna started working for us I thought she would tell my father, because she knew there was never to be sugar in the house. Instead though so used to hide candy and chocolates underneath my pillow. Usually when she could tell I needed the cheering up. It became our secret."

"Anna, she is truly a wonderful woman." Jane said with a bright smile.

"She is remarkable and I wouldn't have made it through some days without her. It's why I invited her along on this trip. If anyone deserves a week in the sun and in a spa, it would be her."

"Ah, and here I thought it was a buffer between us." Jane said with a smirk.

"There is that, yes. And I may have assumed you would want a friend to go to the spa with. However, I can acknowledge I made some judgments of you that are unwarranted."

"Oh god, I would never go to a spa. Helena would, but that's not my style. She's rough around the edges, but she has a girly spirit. I'm more tomboy." Jane said with a shrug.

"There's nothing wrong with that." Charles said and Jane could have sworn there was a heat to his eyes.

She looked down for a moment before she cleared her throat and spoke. "So tell me, what was the craziest thing your grandfather did?"

Jane wasn't sure what was happening with her. She shouldn't be attracted to him, and yet she was finding herself falling for his magic. Maybe it was this hotel room and being trapped here from a storm, but he didn't seem as unattractive as he did just days ago.

Charles gave a deep laugh and it only fueled the warmth starting to spread throughout Jane's chest.

"I was eight when one day my grandfather drove up to the house in this old beat up pickup truck. I thought my father was going to have an aneurysm when he discovered that my grandfather bought it. My father had a pretty strong belief that people who own pickup trucks are lower in society. It didn't matter how many CEOs owned one, to him you only own a pickup truck because you need to haul things for work, so you must work with your hands and that makes you lower in society. Combine that with his belief that a rich man never drives himself, his head almost exploded."

"Why did he buy one?" Jane asked with a big smile across her face. She was liking his grandfather, it was a shame he died when Charles was so young.

"Mostly to piss my father off. They had been arguing about my grandfather's state of mind. My father was trying to get power of attorney over him to get him away from the company and the money. He didn't like how free spirited he had become and therefore must be going senile. Whenever we had the chance he would pick me up and take me off roading and mudding. Still to this day it was the most fun I have ever had."

Charles couldn't help the pang of sadness go through him at the memories. He loved them very much and he would cherish them forever, but it also hurt because he had lost his grandfather. Once he died, all of the fun stopped and he started to get swallowed whole by the expectations and pressure that his father dropped onto his shoulders. Charles had often wondered what he would have been like if his grandfather hadn't died when he did. If he had been able to keep having that love and freedom that his grandfather had given to him.

"I would love to go mudding. It always looks like so much fun in the movies that I've seen it in."

"It was a lot of fun. We used to go for hours and when we came back to the house the truck would be covered in mud. He would only be able to see out of part of the windshield from it all. Afterwards he used to grab the garden hose and we'd spray it down, which always ended up in a water fight. Whenever we could, we used to sneak James along with us."

"He sounds like he was a great man. I'm sorry you lost him." Jane said with a great deal of sympathy to her voice.

"Losing him hurt, but I was able to get ten years with him and that is more than what some people get." Charles offered with a small sad smile.

Charles wasn't sure why he was talking about this. He normally never mentioned his grandfather to anyone, not even James. It was a sore topic for him, because he missed him greatly and wished to this day he still could feel his hugs or hear his laugh. It was even getting harder for him to remember the sound of his voice. It hurt a great deal, but he found himself wanting to open up more to Jane. Maybe she would be able to understand why he was the way that he was. Maybe, just maybe, they would be able to become real friends and build something between them even after the year was up. For the first time since he had opened the door to her, Charles didn't want her gone from his life and that realisation scared him more than he cared to admit.

CHAPTER 16

"What are you working on?" Jane asked, sensing his need to change the subject.

She herself was having a hard time with the current topic, only because it was hard to see him hurting. She was surprised with how much it hurt her to see him upset like this. Jane could tell that he felt joy with the memories, but much like herself with her mother, she could also see that they still hurt. Even though the wound was twenty-five years old, they hadn't fully healed. She couldn't hold that against him though, from the sounds of it, his grandfather was the only piece of a true childhood he had. It would be hard for anyone that had grown up in a strict environment with only one person that offered you the chance at freedom from all of the rules and expectations.

"Trying to come up with ideas and a strategy for the company."

"It's insurance right?" Jane asked, not fully aware of what his family's company does exactly.

"It is technically yes. We offer insurance for medical purposes. That could be people for health insurance or it could be a company or a doctor. Every practicing medical professional needs to have liability coverage, which is something we offer. The company generates revenue from the interest rate on the packages, along with any deductibles that clients have to pay out. We also offer corporate rates to large corporations. The company also invests to ensure the profits also generate passive income."

"And it's strictly medical?"

"Right now it is. I am just trying to figure out a way to maybe change that. I've never gotten involved with the business before. I held zero interest in it, I still don't, but I am the one that will be running it along with my uncle. We now both have a fifty/fifty split in control. I can't make changes without his approval or the Board of Director's approval."

"And what kind of changes do you want to make?"

Jane wasn't all that surprised that he didn't find the family business interesting. She could never find insurance an interesting topic. If she had come across a guy that wanted to date her and he worked in insurance, that would be a hard no. Jane had to give Charles credit though, because he seemed to be trying to get involved instead of sitting back and letting his uncle have full control.

"I've never been involved with the business, I had no idea that surgeries were being denied. I could understand if it was cosmetic and there was no need for it outside of vanity. However, hearing about your mother dying because she was denied a surgery that would have saved her life, that's not something I can accept or live with. I can't risk that happening again and in order for me to change the policies I need to get the Board of Directors on my side."

"Why not your uncle?"

The last thing Jane wanted to think about right now was the fact that her mother could have lived had it not been for Charles' family business.

"Jack and my father share the same beliefs. They don't care if it's a person's life that is on the line, all they care about is the bottom line. He won't agree to make any changes to the policy, it's why I have to go around him to get the Board of Directors on my side. We can all out vote him."

"Ok, so how do you get the Board on your side?"

"The Board cares about the bottom line just as much, however, they are also human beings and know that every life matters. If I can come up with a solution that makes them money, they will be more willing to agree to changing the policies so everyone that needs life saving surgery would automatically be approved."

"So as long as they aren't losing money, they don't care." Jane said with understanding to her voice.

"Exactly. It's cold, but I can work with it. We're an insurance company, but there's no reason why we are only medical. We could open ourselves up to other insurance packages that are relatable to medical, such as life insurance and personal insurance. People are more likely to purchase their insurance needs with one company versus multiple ones. If we open ourselves up to other avenues, we could double our annual revenue from the clients we already have. The added money would allow us to say yes to more people that need life saving treatments."

Charles knew it wasn't going to be that simple. He would have to draft a bullet proof plan that he would then need to present to the Board of Directors, including his uncle. He would have to go through a fire range of questions, not to mention his uncle will try to kabash the whole idea just because he didn't come up with it. It would be a heated debate, but if he was successful in getting the Board on his side, they could be saving a lot of lives. Charles knew the Board would be happy if it meant more money, the better the company does, the more they make each year. His father designed it that way to ensure the Board would always be motivated to better the company and to sell it to their connections. It helped to grow the company and Charles knew if he could get the members of the Board in agreement with him, they would take it to the next level.

"It also opens you up to new clients that get medical insurance through work, but don't get life insurance." Jane said fully understanding the business ramifications of expanding.

"Exactly. I just need to draft a plan that will appeal to the Board and then deal with my uncle. Ideally, I would like to buy him out, but I have a feeling he is not going to relinquish his shares easily."

"He doesn't really come across as the, go quietly into the night, kind of guy. Most businesses as large as yours though have bi-laws that everyone has to follow. Isn't there a legal way you can pressure him out?"

"What do you know about bi-laws?" Charles asked with a warm smile and Jane didn't take offense to it this time. He wasn't asking in a malicious way, but one out of pure surprise.

"I am going to College for a business degree. Helena went as well for business, but she had to drop out once mom got sick and couldn't work anymore."

It was at that moment that Charles realised he had never even asked about her post secondary education. He knew she was going to College, but he never asked for what or how long she had been in.

"I'm sorry, I just realised that I've never asked you about your schooling. How many years do you have left?"

"I have two left and then I'll have my bachelor's degree in business. I've been balancing it between working."

"Good for you. That's a hard program and you've had to balance it with working a lot of hours throughout the week. It's too bad that Helena had to drop out, perhaps she will go back."

"She might, I don't know. I'm not sure what she wants to do."

"I am sure she will figure it out and discover what she wishes to do with her life. You both are amazing women."

"I'm not too sure about that part, at least for me anyways." Jane said with a small shrug.

"It's true. You are truly a beautiful and extraordinary woman. The smartest decision I have ever made was asking a delivery driver to marry me." Charles said affectionately.

Jane couldn't help but look down as she felt a rush of heat flooding her cheeks. She didn't want to blush, she didn't want to show him how much his words had affected her, but looking down gave her away all the same. The depth of affection that he spoke with told her he meant every single word he said. It was a lot to take in for her though, because she didn't want to be attracted to him. She didn't want to like him, even as a friend. She risked getting attached and she knew she would never be able to keep him. Her and Charles were too different, they lived in polar opposite worlds, it would never work out. Yet, she couldn't help but feel her attraction building.

"Even a judgmental one?" Jane countered, as she tried to lock her emotions down.

"Some of those judgments were correct for you to make. You have made me a better man though and for that I am thankful for. It's been a long time since I've allowed myself to start being the man I want to be instead of the man I made myself to be. You've given me a sense of freedom and courage to be myself and not the image I've been portraying for so long to the world."

"Why the false image?"

Charles let out a soft sigh before he answered her honestly. "My father was always hard to please and very easy to disappoint. I learnt after my grandfather's death it was easier to be a problem child than the golden son. If my father always knew he couldn't expect anything from me or count on me to be responsible, then I couldn't disappoint him. Sometimes I could actually surprise him. It was easier to handle him that way. But then that became my image and once you are portrayed a certain way, it's hard to get anyone to see you as any different. Also, you start to only see yourself as that person. You've helped to remind me that I used to be different and that it is time to be myself again."

Jane didn't know what to say to that. It warmed her heart to hear that Charles was going to try and better himself, to show the world who he is at his core. Things between them were getting a lot more deeper than she was expecting them to though and that brought on her own uncertainties. She still didn't understand why he picked her out of all the people he could have asked to marry. She didn't belong in his world, she didn't fit at all in what he was raised to believe. So why her? A question Jane wasn't certain she would be brave enough to ask.

"I am glad that I could help. And you have helped me too. I grew up poor, which you know, but for the first time in my life I haven't had to worry and stress over money. I haven't had to try and figure out if we could afford real coffee and not instant coffee and still pay the electric bill that month. Trying to calculate how many hours in the week I need to work to cover my part of the bills. Even growing up when letters went home about a field trip, I was stressed over how my mom would be able to afford it. We've always counted pennies and since being with you, I haven't had to go to bed with an endless calculator going in my mind."

Charles was instantly hurt by her words. He wasn't insulted, he was upset for her. He felt her pain of having to grow up like that. He couldn't imagine what it would feel like to not know if you could buy food or pay for heat. They were basic needs that everyone should have available to them without having to forfeit one for the other. What made it worse was knowing that Jane wasn't the only one. Thousands of families in his own city were having to make that choice every single day while he wore ten thousand dollar suits. When he thought about it like that, Charles was disgusted.

Charles moved over to the bed and placed his warm hand over Jane's as he spoke. "I'm so sorry you had to go through that. No one ever should have to, least of all a child. I couldn't even imagine how you felt."

"It was hard at times, but my mom knew how to make it fun. She always did her best to stay positive and never let her stress or frustrations trickle down to us. You appreciate what you have more and take very good care of your personal items."

Jane turned her hand over so their fingers could intertwine. She had no idea what drove her to do it, but the need to feel his skin against her own became too great.

CHAPTER 17

The heat that started to creep up her hand and up to her chest was surprising to Jane. She had no idea what it was about Charles, but he seemed to ignite a fire within her that she didn't even know she had. It was insane, because she shouldn't want him. She shouldn't be attracted to someone like him. She knew she had judgments about him, a great deal of them were wrong. Charles had built up walls around himself in order to protect himself from a poor childhood. Jane couldn't help but wonder what Charles would have been like had his grandfather not passed away at the age he did. Maybe Charles could have had the chance to embrace who he was without the expectations and pressures from his father and the society he was born into.

"You are truly remarkable Jane. I've made a log of terrible decisions in my life, but the best decision I have ever made was asking a delivery driver to marry me. You make me want to be a better man. You make me want to be the man that my grandfather would be proud of. I can't thank-you enough for that." Charles said with a deep and heartfelt smile.

"The best decision I've ever made was saying yes, even though the idea was completely insane. Because of you Helena is no longer having to work in a dangerous strip club and we don't have to try and figure out if we can buy food that week and pay the electric bill. I'm sorry for judging you, that wasn't fair."

"I judged you. I'm sorry as well." Charles said, as he put his hand on Jane's leg, that was bent up with how she was sitting.

Jane leaned in so they were closer to each other. She couldn't stop thinking about how amazing it felt to have his lips against hers. They had only kissed once and yet she could still feel the ghostly imprint of his lips against her own. Maybe it was the weather and being trapped in a hotel room together or maybe their conversations had cleared the air, but Jane was truly hoping that Charles would close the rest of the gap between them.

Charles felt like there was a magnet attached to the two of them and it was pulling him towards Jane. Their kiss from the wedding was quick and simple, and yet it had been haunting his dreams ever since. Charles had kissed a lot of women, more than he could possibly count, but none of them had ever lingered like Jane's kiss had done to him. His body was craving her touch. His body was craving to feel her skin against his own. His hand was tingling from her own hand in his and it was nowhere near enough. Charles could see Jane's eyes travelling down to his lips a few times since they started talking and he was hoping that meant she wanted to kiss him. He decided that he would have to be the one to take the risk.

Charles leaned in and very slowly closed the gap between them. He wanted to give her the chance to pull back should she wish. He was relieved when Jane started to close the gap as well. The second their lips touched a wave of electricity washed over the both of them, causing them both to moan. Charles brought his hand up to the back of Jane's neck and pulled her in for a deeper kiss. Jane's hands went to the side of his face and when she felt Charles' tongue against her lips, seeking permission, which she quickly gave. The second his tongue touched hers she was giving a deep moan as the pleasure spiked within her.

Jane needed more; she needed to feel him. She moved her hands to his shirt and started to pull the hem free from his pants. That was all encouragement that Charles needed. His hands were instantly going to Jane's t-shirt and they both quickly removed the other of their shirt. Charles moved towards Jane, forcing her to lay back on the bed. She opened her legs and Charles was instantly placing himself between them.He began to trail kisses down Jane's neck. She couldn't help but moan as he hit her sweet spot along her neck. Jane had decided they were both wearing far too many clothes. She made quick work of grabbing ahold of his belt and opening his trousers. Charles didn't need any further encouragement as he went and started to open up Jane's demins horts. They worked together and rmeoved the other of the rest of their clothing. The second they were both naked Charles moved back so he could look down at Jane and take in her form.

He instantly noticed that her belly button was peirced and she had a red lilly tattooed onher her right hip. He had never been with a woman who had a piercing and a tattoo before, but he found it absolutely sexy on her.

"You are beautiful." He said, as he started to kiss his way down her body. Jane squirmed as sge felt his lips against her skin. He himself was quite the picture to look at. He had his own muscles and a six pack of abs to compliment his soft facial features. He clearly had been working out in the gym and took pride in his appearance. At the feel of Charles' tongue on her heat, Jane gave a deeo moan that filled the room. She spread her legs further apart to give him better access. Charles moaned at the sweet taste of her, sending vibrations all the way up Jane's spine.

"You taste so sweet."

"Hod don't stop." Jane moaned.

She wiggled her hips slightly to get more friction from his tongue, which was all the encouragement that Charles needed. He easily licked all the way up to her clit before he sucked on it, sending a bolt of pleasure throughout Jane's body. Charles used the distraction to slide one of his fingers inside of her and Jane was not surprised at all with how wet she already was. The sexual tension between the two of them had been growing ever since the day of their wedding and now it was about to erupt. Jane was a moaning mess by the time Charles added a second finger and began to stretch her. Stars danced across her eyes when he hit her sweet spot. Jane couldn't hold back the loud moan that echoed off of the walls in the room. Charles' tongue and fingers moved even faster within her. He could feel that Jane was close and he was determined to get a full taste of her. The was rewarded just a moment later when he hit her g-spot dead on once again.

*****

"Charlie!" Jane called out as she felt a deep heat work its way up her body.

Pulse after pulse her body gave him and he moaned as he licked every drop that Jane had for him. Even after her body had long finished pulsing, he continued to lick at her sensitive clit. It was all too much for Jane though; her body was too sensitive for his magical tongue right now. Her need to feel him inside of her was far too great.

"Stop, I need you inside of me." Jane breathed.

Charles was instantly moving back and reaching for his forgotten pants on the floor. He pulled out his wallet and grabbed one of the condoms he kept within it. With a condom in hand he turned his attention back to Jane and began to kiss all along her breasts.

"You taste so sweet, so good. I could lick you all night and never get tired of it."

"I'd let you." Jane easily agreed with a big goofy smile.

Right at this moment Jane could very well let this man do whatever he wanted with her. She was very confident that he would make anything feel amazing. Charles kissed his way over to her left breast, taking her nipple into his mouth. Jane hissed at the level of sensitivity her nipples were currently in. They were sensitive to touch, let alone to be sucked on and played with. Charles only kept it in his mouth for a few moments before he kissed his way across her chest to give her right nipple the same treatment. Jane could feel her inner walls pulsing already with need. Charles was keeping her on fire and it seemed like the flames were not going to be extinguished anytime soon. And that was more than fine with Jane. Charles' journey of kisses took him back up her neck before finally settling on her mouth. Jane's hands were instantly going through his hair, completely messing it up. Charles' hands were otherwise engaged with the condom. He was trying to get it open and on without breaking away from the kiss.

Jane knew Charles had managed to get it on when his hands were on her inner thighs. She easily spread her legs wider to make room for Charles and his hips. The second she felt his tip at her entrance she knew it was going to sting slightly. He was very large and she was not nearly stretched enough. Had they not been so entrapped within their desire they would have taken more time to play with each other. Jane would have loved to have felt his dick along her tongue. To be able to taste him and hear his deep moans as she pushed him over the edge. Giving a man oral was one of Jane's favorite parts within sex. To her it was empowering. Having the ability to take a man, an alpha male, and reduce him to a moaning and pleading mess of a man underneath her. She would have loved to see Charles that deep into pleasure where all of his walls crumbled down.

Jane moaned as his tip breached her heat and slowly, inch by glorious inch, Charles pushed his way inside of her. She could see the effects of her tightness all over his face. Once he was fully bottomed out inside of Jane they were both in need of a minute and breathing heavily. For her, she had to adjust to his size, but to Charles, he needed to calm his body down as Jane's hot walls were squeezing his dick. Charles placed his forehead against Jane's and she could see him fighting the urge to move. She understood it, he was in a tight, wet and hot place and all he wanted was to keep chasing that amazing sensation.

"Fuck, you're so tight." He said in a breathy voice.

"You're so big. You can move, just go slow."

Whether Jane was ready or not, she needed him to move. She wanted to feel him moving within her slick heat. She wanted to feel his tip hitting her sweet spot. She wanted a night that she would never forget, a night with pure and raw pleasure that could potentially ruin her for every other man that came after him. Thankfully, Charles didn't need to be told twice. He was instantly slowly pulling out of her all the way to his tip before he was pushing back in. Jane wrapped her legs around his hips as he started to build up a pace. No words were spoken between them, the only sounds in the room were our heavy breathing, their moans and the sound of skin slapping against skin. Jane's legs were trembling from the pleasure and her need once again rapidly building. Her whole body was tingling from the sheer amount of panting she was doing. Charles' grip on her hips was bruising and Jane couldn't help but wonder if tomorrow she would see actual bruises on them. Surprisingly enough, that only brought a deeper pleasure to shoot through her body.

They were both nearing their climax. Jane could feel Charles getting harder inside of her. His thrusts were becoming more erratic and she was right there with him. After another dead on hit to her sweet spot, she wasn't tumbling off the cliff, she was swan diving and landing in a sea of ecstasy. Jane was fairly confident that their next door neighbors could hear her scream as she came hard and fast. The tighten of her walls was enough to push Charles over the edge who came with a deep growl as he spoke.

"Jane."

She couldn't suppress the moan at feeling him pulsing inside of her. That was one of her favorite things about sex. This moment right here where she could feel the man pulse. It always sent a shockwave of pleasure throughout her body and caused her to pulse right along with him. Charles bent forward and placed his forehead against Jane's once again. She wanted to kiss him, but she honestly didn't have the energy or strength to close the small gap between them. Charles seemed to be in the same boat as Jane. So they both settled for focusing on their breathing and enjoying the ride on the pleasure train for a little bit longer. What Jane did know though, this was not going to be the last round they shared tonight. She needed more and she didn't want to stop until the sun came up.

CHAPTER 18

"You were right, this was a brilliant idea." Anna said, as she leaned against Evan's chest in the hot bath water.

"I told you this was exactly what you needed." Evan replied, as he placed a kiss to the top of her head.

"When you're right, you're right. It's a shame we can't do this again."

Anna had been expecting that the night would be a night she would never forget and so far it was just that. She knew it was early in the morning and shortly, assuming the weather permitted it, they would both be boarding a plane and going their separate ways. This night was supposed to be fun, nothing more, nothing less; and yet her heart was feeling heavy. It was harder than she had expected to be leaving him soon. The last few hours, they had felt like a dream. The way their bodies connected, their chemistry was just as strong as it had been when they first met as teenagers. Their bodies knew the other, they knew every place to touch, every place to kiss, to make their eyes roll back in pleasure. It was as if no time had come between them.

The night was extraordinary and now with the clock ticking down, Anna was starting to feel regret. Not because she hated the past eighteen hours roughly, but because she was going to lose the man that she loved all over again. They both lived in different worlds now. He was a billionaire and she was a housekeeper, there was no place in his world for her.

"Who says we can't?" Evan countered.

"Be real Evan, we come from two different worlds now. You are the billionaire CEO and I am the help. Two worlds that don't collide, unless there's some type of a scandal and the boss is found diddling with his secretary or nanny. No one ever diddles the housekeeper."

Anna tried to make light of it, but it was hard. They used to be on the same level, they used to be equals, and now she was the help. For the first time in a long time she felt self-conscious. It was hard, because they used to be in love and she never expected for Evan to become the man that he had. And if he did, she expected to be standing right there beside him when it happened. Now she was standing behind him, way in the back with everyone else that you would ignore in the day. She was no one and just like that the bubble popped.

"You are not the help. You are not the housekeeper, not to me. To me you are still that gorgeous, funny, sassy, intelligent, and creative woman whom I fell madly in love with. Who still keeps a tight hold of my heart and entire being. You are Anna Cooper and I am madly in love with you still to this day." Evan stated with a deep love and passion within his voice.

Oh my. Anna thought to herself. That was not what she had been expecting to hear from him. She figured he would laugh it off and switch topics, it was the reasonable thing to do. She didn't expect for him to hold so much love and passion for her still, even after a decade of being apart. She believed every single word he said. He didn't see her as unworthy or the housekeeper that you need to hide when company comes over. He saw her as his equal and still the woman he fell in love with and married. All of these emotions flooded Anna's body, so many that she couldn't distinguish one from another.

She had been in love with this man her whole life practically. Even when he left with a mere note. Even when she suspected he had another woman and children by now; she still loved him. It was crazy and something that she would normally read about in some cheesy romance novel, heck, she would even laugh and poke fun at the silly girl for falling for the sweet words. Yet here she was, falling for his words and allowing herself to imagine what their life could be like together. How it would feel to travel and explore the world together just as they had always dreamed of doing. Only they couldn't really, she had her own life, she had a job and responsibilities, just as he has his own now as well. Life wasn't as simple and clean as this hotel suite was leading them to believe. Still, she was far from foolish enough to allow a once in a lifetime love slip through her fingers, and certainly not twice.

"What are you proposing exactly?" Anna asked after a moment.

"That would depend on how open you are."

"Meaning?" Anna asked, slightly confused.

"I'm assuming you wouldn't be willing to quit your job and travel around the world with me."

"Surely you have gone mad." Anna instantly said. As if she could just up and quit her job, for a man no less. She might not love her job, but she refused to leave Charles high and dry.

"Love makes everyone crazy my Dear. However, I had a feeling you were not at the stage to leave your job. I know you take it very seriously and you would not want Mr. Bentley to be without proper services. I am willing to settle for dating."

"Dating, like what we did back in high school. How would that even be possible?"

Anna wasn't opposed to it. She just wasn't sure how it would all work. He was often traveling for business and she almost never got a night off. Although she wasn't counting it out, it just seemed to her like a logistical nightmare.

"We would go out on dates, spend time together, call each other when we are not able to see each other. It is possible to date someone nowadays my Dear. I know you don't have much control over your schedule, but I have full control over mine. We can set dates aside for us to see each other. If it is something we both truly want, then we can make it happen."

"I would like to try. I am uncertain how well it will work with my work schedule; however, I do care for you and I do not wish to miss out on a second chance." Anna said, as she turned her head slightly so she could look at Evan.

He gave her a rich smile before he closed the small gap between them and pressed his lips against hers. Anna was instantly kissing him back and she could feel the heat creeping up her body once again. This man was fire and her body was responding to him like it was made of gasoline. All too soon Evan was pulling back just enough so he could speak.

"Come with me to Paris."

"What?" Anna asked, fighting through the fog in her mind from the kiss.

"Come with me to Paris. Your boss is going on his honeymoon, he doesn't need you to go with him. He can manage to survive without having you around. This is Paris we are talking about my Dear, come with me."

"I can't, I'm working. Besides, what would I do while you are off in meetings?" Anna said, surprised that Evan would offer for her to go with him.

"I can do the meetings virtually at the hotel or you can come with me for them. I only have three, but I booked the hotel for a week, giving us plenty of time to explore the city. We can go see all of the tourist hot spots, take in some art, we could even go to Disneyland Paris and ride the roller coasters like we used to do back in high school."

"You can't be serious. I am going for work, not as a vacation with Mr. Bentley."

As tempting as it would be to go and explore Paris with Evan, she was supposed to be going with Charles to Cape Town. She had no idea what she was supposed to be doing for him, he was going on his honeymoon and certainly wouldn't need a housekeeper, but she was going for work. She couldn't just abandon him and go off to Paris with Evan. No matter how badly she wished she could.

"He's going on a honeymoon. He should be holded up in his hotel suite with his new wife. They won't even come up for air if they are doing things right. They have their own housekeeping at the resort, they don't need you there for it. Be selfish, for once in your life Anna, be selfish and do what you want to do and not what someone else wants."

That was the problem though, Anna had been working her whole life to take care of someone else. She was always volunteering growing up when she wasn't in school or working part-time. Then after she graduated, she got to work so she could make a living. She had been going for decades without much of a break, but Anna never complained, at least not too much. The other issue was exactly what Evan had said. Newlyweds didn't bring staff with them to a high-end resort. They spent the time together in the hotel room or out on the beach. It wasn't going to look good for them to have a chaperone.

"I don't know." Anna said, after a moment. She didn't know what to do.

"What do you want to do? If you could pick which plane to get on, what one is your heart telling you to board?"

Well that is easy Anna thought. If she could pick, she would be going to Paris and not Cape Town. Not that there was anything wrong with Cape Town, but it wasn't a destination that she thought she would ever be going to. Her dream had always been to see Paris, she wanted to explore many cities, but Paris was where her heart and soul lived. But could she really throw caution to the wind and go to Paris? Would Charles allow her to without being upset? It wasn't that she feared the man, but she also couldn't risk being fired either. She doubted that Charles would terminate her employment, she doubted he

608

could function without her, but that didn't mean he wouldn't fire her if she blatantly went against him like this.

"Paris, I would go to Paris. But life is not that simple Evan."

"I know it isn't, but I also know that life is far too short for you to not live it to the fullest. I highly doubt your boss will fire you if you go to Paris with me instead of on his honeymoon. And even if he does, you can come and work with me with the business. We can be co-owners and live the dream together."

Anna wanted to keep her head firmly on the ground and not in the clouds, but Evan painted a picture that she was falling in love with. She couldn't help but wonder what it would be like to run a company with Evan. How it would feel to travel all over the world with him and help other businesses. She would be lying if she said that didn't sound perfect. She couldn't do that, but perhaps she could roll the dice and be a little selfish for the first time in her life.

"I'm not going to quit my job, but I will get on that plane with you." Anna said with a warm smile.

A smile instantly spread across Evan's face and he was once again bringing Anna in for a kiss. He could not believe that he would be able to take her to Paris. He had wished he could have given her more when they were together and now he was finally getting his second chance. This time around he was not going to screw this up.

CHAPTER 19

It had been a couple of hours since the power had gone out. Both James and Helena had spent the time playing different games to try and pass the time. It hadn;t been anywhere near as bad as James was expecting, he did find that they could be fun if they were played with the right person. Though James suspected that he would find anything fun if Helena was doing it with him. He had thrown more wood onto the fire to keep it going. The room was getting warm enough for them to no longer need their sweaters. James was enjoying the sight of Helena in a tank top that had a deep scoop neckline. With her breasts being larger he had a great view of the top of them and it was getting to be distracting while they played the different games.

After they had finished playing the games they were both feeling a bit hungry so they invaded Charles' kitchen. Helena had found a pint of cookie dough ice cream and instantly she was picking it up. It wasn't even open yet, she opened it as James spoke.

"Let me guess, that's your favorite flavor."

"It is. But I will eat mint chip in a pinch."

"It's Charles' guilty pleasure, he'll eat it when he's stressed." James had also joined him in eating it a few times when they were both annoyed or frustrated with their parents or Jack.

"It'd be a shame to let it melt." Helena said, as she picked up two spoons, holding them out to James.

"It would be a waste for it to melt." James easily agreed as he took one of the offered spoons.

They both headed back into the living room and sat down on the couch. They sat down facing each other, close enough that they would both be able to eat the ice cream. Helena held onto the pint for them and James allowed her to take the first bite.

610

She gave a soft moan as the delicious taste hit her tongue and James thought he was going to explode. *Maybe ice cream was a bad idea.* He thought to himself as he took his own bite.

"I've never eaten ice cream out of the container before." James commented.

"Oh you poor sheltered man." Helena said, completely serious.

The tone to her voice caused James to give a deep laugh. He couldn't help it. The serious look on Helena's face was too much. As if he had just said he killed a puppy. James thought she was absolutely remarkable. Once he got through her touch exterior walls she was a warm and funny woman.

"Alright, dog or cat person?" James asked.

"Oh god dogs always. Cats are jerks." Helena easily stated.

"My aunt had a hairless cat when I was younger. The thing was pure evil. It didn't like anyone."

"Ya no, those cats are freaky. I am definitely a dog person, but a big dog. One that likes to swim and go for runs but can also scare the hell out of someone should they try to break in."

"Exactly. One that will be able to go on trips and not bark at every single person that walks by." James agreed. He had been with girls that had small little yappy dogs and it drove him mad. He couldn't stand hearing their barks all day and night long, not to mention they had to pee every two hours it seemed.

"It always looks so weird to me to see a big guy walking this tiny dog. I always want to ask them if their ex-girlfriend left it behind." Helena said with a bright smile.

"See you can do that, but if I do, I'll get hit."

"True. Have you ever been in a fight?" Helena asked next. She was enjoying getting to know James more. She was pleasantly surprised by what she had learnt about him today.

"I have, but only in a controlled setting. I've taken classes in different martial arts, boxing and kickboxing. I've done sparring essentially, but not a real fight in the streets. How many have you been in?"

James was still upset that Helena had been attacked at her previous job and no one had done anything about it. No woman should ever have to be afraid of the place they worked in. They should always be protected and the owners should have made sure their workers were as safe as possible.

"I have been in ten fights. Four were from being attacked at a job and six were from high school mostly. All but one were with girls though."

"I guess that is a good thing, but ten fights is a lot. Let me guess, in high school you didn't play well with others." James asked without any judgment to his voice.

"I didn't play well with bullies. My school was pretty rough and a lot of the kids felt that they could bully someone. Whenever it got bad I would stick up for the poor kid and teach the bullies a lesson. I never lost." Helena said with a proud smile.

"I bet you didn't. You're one badass lady. How was your mom with it?"

James didn't doubt for a second that Helena had won her fights in school. She was not a delicate flower and he was confident she could give any man a good run for their money. A woman who carries around pepper spray was a woman ready to rumble at any given moment. James didn't know why, but it made her very sexy.

"Oh she was great about it all. She knew why I was getting into the fights and she raised Jane and me to always stand up for the little guy. To never take crap from anyone. To her it wasn't an out of control teenager like my principal believed. I was simply growing into a decent young lady." Helena said with a fond smile. She felt the slight pang of loss in her heart whenever she spoke of her mom, but it was easing up as time went on.

"She sounds like she was a remarkable woman who raised two beautiful and inspiring women." James said with a deep loving smile that instantly brought butterflies to Helena's stomach.

"That she was." Helena said warmly before she spoke. "And get that look off your face Mister. We're just friends."

It was getting hard for Helena to remember that they were just supposed to be friends. The way James looked at her sometimes and the words he spoke made it very difficult for Helena to keep him on the outside of her walls. He was creeping his way in and she wasn't certain she would be able to hold him off for much longer.

"I know we are, but you still haven't given me a real reason why we couldn't be more."

James didn't want to push her, but he suspected that if he didn't they would never get anywhere. Helena would stay hidden in her fortress and he would forever regret not getting the chance to be with her. She was too unique and special to let slip through his fingers.

Helena knew James wasn't going to let this go, he had made that perfectly clear to her on previous occasions. She was hoping he would have lost interest in her. She had been planning on using Jane's honeymoon as an excuse to not come around and see James. Only she didn't expect to be trapped in a house with him. It was a dangerous position to be in and it was sucking the strength right out of her. Every time he looked at her with his caring and loving eyes, it did something to her. It made her want to throw caution to the wind and just kiss him. She couldn't lie and tell him she didn't see him that way. That she didn't feel an attraction to him, he would have been able to clearly see it in her own eyes. She had to tell him something, but when she thought about why she couldn't cross that line, it seemed so ridiculous. Far too ridiculous to say it outloud.

Still, she owed him the truth no matter how silly it may sound. Helena let out a soft sigh before she finally spoke. "It's not you personally. Honestly, you seem like a really great guy. You're not what I was expecting at all."

"But that's a good thing and all the more reason to see where this goes between us." James countered.

"It's not that simple." Helena started, but James calmly cut her off.

"Then explain it to me, please. I can handle complicated."

James was desperate to know the true reason why Helena didn't want to try being something more than friends. He couldn't try to correct the problem if he didn't even know what it was. He needed to know so they could talk it out and maybe come to an agreement of some sort.

"My mom worked for a high end hotel as a hotel clerk. She only made minimum wage, but she had decent medical insurance, at least we thought it was decent. I used to go and visit her at work and I would always see a guest at the hotel treating her like crap. It didn't matter if they were male or female, they were rich and talked down to her. Treated her like she worked for them and she didn't deserve to be treated like a human being. I grew up hating rich snobs. That only got worse when she got sick and was denied life saving surgery. I swore I would never, ever, date someone within that social circle."

James could understand why she was hesitant to try anything with him. He knew it was complicated because his family's business had denied her mother the surgery she needed to keep her alive. He wasn't minimizing that at all. Still though, he didn't sign that form. He held no control over who was approved and who wasn't. Just like Charles held no control over it. Jack ran the company practically. He wouldn't even tell

Charles when the board meetings were. Helena was denying herself the possibility of something amazing all because he was in a different tax bracket as her.

"I can't even begin to express how sorry I am about your mother and what my family's company has done to you and Jane. But I didn't have anything personally to do with the decision. I do administration work, I have no say in who gets approval and for what."

"I know, I know that. But being with you would make me a hypocrite and that's something I can't be." Helena said with strength.

James had expected a lot of different reasons why Helena wouldn't date him. He didn't expect the reason to be hypocrisy. He wasn't minimizing her concerns, but it seemed a bit ludicrous that she was refusing to be with him because of a stereotype that she created in her mind about his social circle. Yes, there were plenty that he would be the first to tell you were terrible human beings. However, there were a lot of great people within his social bracket. She was judging them, because of a handful of bad eggs, it wasn't fair and he truly thought they were past this.

"Or it would make you someone that was able to grow past their judgmental stereotype of an entire social bracket. You don't have to like everyone, but I thought we were past you judging me all because I have more zeros in my bank account." James said, slightly hurt that they hadn't appeared to make any progress.

"We are. I'm not judging you. I don't care about the zeros in your bank account. If you were poor tomorrow morning, it wouldn't change how I feel towards you. I just don't know how I could be with you and not disrespect my mother or myself." Helena said, sounding genuinely confused as to what to do.

"I never met your mother, obviously, but from what you have told me of her, she wouldn't want you to miss out on what could be a great love. You are worried about how you could live with yourself if we date, but Helena, how are you going to be able to live with yourself with the regret of not even trying?" James patiently said.

CHAPTER 20

James' words rang true within Helena's mind. She had no idea what to do, because she could very well be missing out on a great love. She doubted James would be her one and only, but she also knew great loves didn't always end in a happily ever after, but you never regret it. She had yet to have a love like that. To be with someone that left her feeling on top of the world. She wanted that experience. She wanted a love that consumed her and left her feeling connected to the other person. A love that people wrote about. Helena wanted that more than anything.

But could I really take that leap? Helena thought to herself. She had believed that she was saying no to James because of her beliefs and stance against the elite within society. She thought it was because of what happened to her mother, but now she wasn't too sure. She wasn't sure if she was using her mother as an excuse to not risk being hurt. *Am I hiding behind my hypocrisy?* Helena asked herself. She was confused and she had no idea what to do about any of this. If she listened to her body, it was screaming at her to allow James to touch her, to kiss him and take everything he had for her. However, her heart was telling her to run. That she could be hurt, that the same that sat in front of her could be the one to destroy her heart. She didn't want to be heart broken, she didn't want to be hurt, she didn't want to let someone get close. But by keeping her walls up, by keeping people at arm's length, she was denying herself the joys and comfort of having a man in her life.

Helena had to make a decision, she knew that. It was a now or never moment. She had to decide if she was going to listen to her heart or her body. She looked at James and quickly lost herself within his eyes. There was nothing but patience within them, but Helena could also see the spark of desire. He wanted her, out of all of the women in the world that he could have, he wanted her. It blew her mind that a man like James would want to be with her. Would hold an interest in her. She was as far from high society as you could get and yet he never treated her like she didn't belong right next to him.

Screw it. Helena thought. She went and placed the ice cream down on the coffee table as she spoke.

"You make a very valid point." Helena said with a flirtatious smile as she leaned in closer to him.

James gave her a big deadly smile right back as he started to close the gap between them. He was not about to miss his chance to finally get his taste of Helena. He placed his hand on the side of her face and around to the back of her neck. The second his lips touched hers Helena was giving a soft moan at the glorious sensation. The heat within them burned hot and fast as this moment had been building for weeks now. James was instantly deepening the kiss. He licked at Helena's lips, seeking permission. Helena quickly granted him entrance and met his tongue with her own. The feel of her tongue sliding against his own caused James to give a small groan as the pleasure shot through him.

James was the first one to move his hands to the hem of Helena's shirt. They broke apart the kiss long enough for each other to remove the other's shirt. James then turned his attention to Helena's black lace bra. He easily removed it and pulled back from the kiss when he felt something brush against his thumbs. He looked down and saw not only a glorious set of breasts, but each nipple had a silver hoop earring. At the sight of the nipple piercings his dick got rock hard. His eyes traveled further and saw that she also had her belly button pierced as well as both of her sides were covered in tattoos. She was the sexiest woman he had ever laid eyes on and he needed her desperately.

"God, you are breathtaking." James said, as he moved his hands to each breast.

Helena moaned as she reached over and started to undo James' pants. She wanted him naked. She wanted to see everything he had for her. James, picking up on Helena's urgency, reluctantly he removed his hands from her breasts and down to Helena's pants. They made quick work of ridding the other of the rest of their clothing. The second they were both naked Helena was moving.

Helena pushed James back slightly so she could get at his hard member. She gave his tip a quick lick to get the taste of him on her tongue. She then sucked his tip and started to take him in her mouth. James gave a long moan as Helena worked her way down his shaft to the base of his dick. She loved the feel of him in her mouth and she couldn't wait to feel him deep inside of her. She wanted to know what it felt like to feel him pulsing inside of her core.

"Helena." James moaned, as he placed his hand within her hair.

Helena moaned, sending a wave of pleasure down his dick as she continued to suck on him for a few minutes. She could tell he was getting too turned on by the hardness within her mouth. James was getting too close and he didn't want to cum this way. He needed to be in her. He gently pulled Helena back and then captured her mouth once again. He pushed her back so she was laying down on the couch now. Helena easily spread her legs to give James enough room to cover her body with his own. He began to trail kisses down her neck and over to each nipples.

James didn't even hesitate to take each nipple into his mouth and sucked on each of them. Helena couldn't contain the moan at the sensation of it all. And when James pulled ever so slightly on her nipple ring with his teeth, she was arching up into him with a deep moan. Her whole body felt like it was going to melt. She could feel his hard dick against her folds and she couldn't wait until she could feel him buried deep inside of her. James slowly kissed his way down Helena's stomach and to her wet folds.

"Oh fuck." She couldn't help but moan as his tongue took a long lick between her folds.

James moaned as the taste of Helena hit his tongue. It was intoxicating and he was already becoming addicted to it. He continued to lick and suck on Helena's clit, getting her wetter than she had ever been. She easily opened her legs more for him and allowed him to go to town on her core. Helena couldn't believe how phenomenal his tongue was. He had true talent and Helena could easily spend all day and night laying right here. Her whole body was tingling and she hadn't even came yet. Helena couldn't stop moaning and the more she moaned the more it turned James on.

"You are so sexy and you taste so sweet. I could do this all night." James said as he looked right at Helena.

"Fuck, I want you inside of me." Helena moaned. She almost couldn't take anymore and she hadn't even came yet. She desperately needed to feel him inside of her. Helena felt like she would go insane if he didn't soon.

James ignored her request and continued to lick as he slowly inserted his index finger inside of her. This wasn't the first time she had been fingered, so she knew what to expect. James slowly started to stretch Helena as he sucked at her clit. After a moment he added a second and then a third. James then ran his fingers over Helena's g-spot and she was seeing stars. She let out a loud moan as she was pushed over the edge.

"James." Helena moaned.

"So tasty, frig you're perfect." He moaned as he continued to lick and suck everything that Helena had for him.

"God it feels so good." Helena said with a shaky breath.

"If you think that felt amazing, just wait until my dick hits it. You'll be squirting your juices all over the place."

James removed his fingers and reached down for his pants. He pulled out his wallet and quickly grabbed the condom and rolled it on himself. Once he was ready he went and lined his tip up with her entrance. He looked at Helena and she gave an encouraging nod before he started to slowly push inside of her. Helena groaned as his tip breached her entrance. She was not fully stretched, but she didn't mind the slight sting of pain. She knew soon enough it would feel amazing. James was very well endowed and Helena was loving the thickness inside of her. James slowly pushed inside of her inch by inch until he was all the way buried inside of her. Once he bottomed out he stopped and they both let out a shaky breath. He placed his forehead against mine and we were both breathing heavily.

Helena couldn't believe how full she felt with James inside of her. She had never felt more complete and connected with someone before in her life. She never wanted him to leave. If she could live her life exactly like this, then she would have. James leaned down and kissed Helena for a few minutes to allow her to adjust to his size and to allow him to calm down. James was very tempted to let loose and go all out, but that would end everything too quickly. He wanted to enjoy this moment, this experience for everything that he could get out of it. Going too fast and it would be over way too quickly. After a moment they were both ready for him to move. James slowly pulled all the way out to his tip before he pushed back in. Helena moaned at the sensation and she couldn't wait for him to do it again. He continued going slow at first, but eventually, James picked up his pace.

As Helena loosened up she was finding herself enjoying it more than she could have ever imagined. She wrapped her legs around his waist as he was now pounding into her at a rapid pace.

"Oh god yes. Don't stop." Helena moaned.

"Oh baby, you are so tight, so warm. I could do this all night." James couldn't believe how remarkable this was feeling. He had slept with plenty of women in his past, but none of them could hold a candle to Helena. The way their bodies fit together, it was as if they were made for the other.

"Hell yes, do it. Fuck me till the sun comes up. I never want this to stop." Helena had never said no truer words in her life. She could have died at this very moment and she would have died happy.

When the tip of James' dick slid across her g-spot she saw actual stars as she screamed in pleasure. Helena couldn't believe that something inside of her could bring her that much pleasure. It felt unbelievable and she was already addicted to James and his body. James continued to hit her g-spot each and every time. She could feel her climax reaching once again and she knew she wouldn't last much longer. She was a moaning and writhing mess on the couch and Helena could feel her legs tingling from the pleasure.

James pushed up on his elbow and looked down at Helena. Their eyes locked and neither of them could look away. It felt like they had entered a trance of some sorts where the other couldn't look away. They had only met weeks ago, but Helena couldn't help but feel like she had known him her whole life. As if they had been together in a past life and they were finally reconnecting. Helena placed her hand on the back of his neck and pulled him down for a scorching kiss. She moaned at the taste of herself and he was all too happy to kiss Helena back.

James picked up his pace and started to thrust faster into Helena. He was getting close himself. He was teetering on the edge and he had every intention of taking Helena over that edge with him. She angled her hips even more, so James would have even better access to her sweet spot. His thrusts became erratic and it was becoming harder for them to continue to kiss with his thrusts being so strong, but they didn't care. They continued to kiss and cling on to each other as their orgasms were quickly approaching. As a true gentleman, he held on long enough for Helena to cum once again.

"James!" Helena screamed as she broke apart from the kiss.

"Helena!" James groaned as he snapped his hips and buried himself deep inside of Helena.

They were both breathing heavily as they continued to pulse around the other. Helena had no idea what was going to happen in the future, but she knew one thing. This couldn't just be a one-time thing with him. She needed more, so much more. James pulsed for what felt like ten minutes before he began to place soft kisses to Helena's cheeks and her lips. They were both breathing very heavily and their bodies were trembling from all of the pleasure.

"How many condoms do you have in your wallet?" Helena asked after a moment with a playful smile.

"Charles has a whole box of them in his room." James said back with his own smile that was filled with a promise.

They were going to be using a lot of those condoms before the storm cleared and Helena was perfectly happy about that.

CHAPTER 21

Jane collapsed down onto the bed for a final time. Both her and Charles were breathing heavily and the sound filled the room. Jane couldn't seem to shake the big smile from her face. Her whole body was tingling and she was very happy that she didn't have to move, because she seriously doubted she could if she had to.

"That was more than worth the wait." Charles said, as he fought to catch his breathing.

"You were waiting?" Jane asked, slightly surprised.

"You'd have to be blind not to notice how beautiful you are Kitten." Charles commented as he stood up and made his way over to the mini bar fridge within the room.

Jane wasn't sure how she felt about that. She had no idea that Charles had been attracted to her before this. He hadn't actually shown any signs that he saw her as anything more than an annoyance. Though, she had to admit to herself she never saw an attraction to him before this either. Ever since she felt his lips against hers at the wedding, she couldn't stop thinking about it. Their conversation today had only increased her attraction to Charles. Charles grabbed a water from the fridge and opened it before handing it over to Jane. He then grabbed one for himself.

"I gotta hydrate."

"Does that mean you're done?" Jane asked, with a flirty smile.

She couldn't seem to take her eyes off of him. He was standing there leaning against the dresser completely nude without a single care in the world. His body was sculpted in all the right ways. Jane had always been a sucker for muscles on a man, normally they came from hard labour and not working out in a gym, but she had to give it to Charles, he took pride in his appearance. Jane was currently taking a great interest in his body as well.

"Hell no, just in between rounds." Charles said with complete confidence in his voice.

Hearing it made Jane's body tingle all the more. They had already been going for a few hours now and Jane had already been impressed with Charles' stamina. She had never been with a guy before that could go more than once and Charles seemed to have no problem going all night. Jane took a drink from the cold water before she placed the bottle down on the bedside table. Charles finished his water and then he was instantly getting back onto the bed. He pulled the sheet off from Jane's body and placed his hands on her thighs and pulled her down to him. Jane laughed as Charles covered her body with his and began to kiss her once again. Jane was instantly wrapping her legs around Charles' hips to pull him closer to her. Charles couldn't believe how amazing it felt to have her against him. He had been with plenty of women, to the point where he almost couldn't count, but none of them had ever left him feeling this way. He never wanted to leave this room. He wasn't expecting to feel this way. He never thought being with a woman could feel this amazing. It was on a whole other level, one that he didn't know existed. Charles would have been perfectly happy to spend the rest of the week right here in this room.

"You feel so good Kitten." Charles said, as he broke a part from the kiss.

"So do you. Think you can make me purr?" Jane said with a playful smile.

"Oh definitely." Charles said with pure confidence.

Jane laughed as she put her hands around his neck and pulled him down to her. Once again their lips met and they both got lost in the other's body. They had been so lost in their own bubble that neither of them noticed the hotel room door was opened and closed.

"What the hell are you doing?"

At the sound of a new voice, both Jane and Charles startled and turned their attention to the new person in the room. Charles was instantly grabbing the sheet and covering Jane as he spoke.

"Kristy? How did you get in here?"

Charles had no idea what she was doing here. He thought he made it very clear that he held no interest in being with her. He knew that they were going to have an open marriage, that either of them could sleep with whoever they wanted, but Charles didn't want anything to do with Kristy. And after the past few hours, he didn't want to be having sex with any other woman that wasn't Jane.

"My key card." Kristy answered, as she held up the card.

Jane was instantly moving and grabbing her clothes while she kept the sheet covering herself. She couldn't believe this was happening. She had no idea that Charles had plans to have another woman up here with him. Hell, for all she knew this Kristy was supposed to be flying with them. She needed to get out of this room and she needed it now.

"I can't believe you Charles, you brought a hooker up into our room." Kristy said with disgust.

"She's not a hooker." Charles said with an edge.

He didn't know why Kristy was here, or why she seemed to still think she had a say in anything he did. But he was not going to tolerate her calling Jane a hooker.

"Oh please, she's clearly a hooker. I can't believe you would lower yourself and slum it with an airport hooker. For christ sake, she has a belly button ring and a tattoo. You just had to find the trashiest hooker in the whole airport."

Jane had enough of this and with the last of her clothing back on she was heading for the door and getting away from them.

"Jane, wait." Charles called after her.

"God Jane, really? Just when I thought she couldn't get trashier." Kristy commented, just as Jane headed out of the room.

Hearing the sound of the door closing sank Charles' heart. He didn't want Jane to leave, he wanted Kristy to leave. They were having a good time. Tonight had actually been amazing. They had talked, found common ground, they were even going to spend time together on their honeymoon. Not to mention the sex was unbelievable. For the first time since this whole ordeal started, they were getting along and having fun. Now Charles feared that everything he had gained with Jane was long gone.

"What the hell is wrong with you?" Charles snapped, as he got off the bed and grabbed his boxers.

"Me? I come up here to find you with a trashy hooker. God tell me you wore a condom or better yet I got here just in time to stop you from catching some horrible disease." Kristy said with pure disgust on her face.

"She's not a hooker, she's my wife. Who now thinks I'm cheating on her."

"A wife, please you and I both know you would never marry someone like her. She is clearly low class."

It was angering Charles to hear Kristy talking about Jane this way. She didn't know Jane and she couldn't hold a candle to the woman that Jane was. What was bothering Charles the most though, was knowing he would have believed the same thing that Kristy was. Before, he wouldn't have gotten to know Jane. He wouldn't have spent any time with her or even wanted to share a conversation with Jane. He would have seen her as lower class, she wouldn't have been worth the energy to up hold a conversation, even small talk. Charles hated knowing that he would have looked down on her. Except now he cared for her. He was finding himself wanting to see her smile, wanting to hear her laugh and make sure she felt safe. He had never felt that way about someone before and he wasn't sure what it was about Jane, but she was special and he couldn't ignore it.

"She is the most remarkable woman I have ever met. She's not low class, you are Kristy. I don't know how you even got a room key, but you are not welcome here. I am married to Jane. She is the woman that I want to be with. We are going on our honeymoon and I now have to explain to my wife that you are insane. I ended things between us months ago and I made it very clear that nothing would ever happen between us. You need to move on Kristy."

"You actually married that woman? How could you lower yourself to that level? You married the help god, what will everyone think? Do you have any idea how poorly this will reflect on me?"

It was taking everything within Charles to not yell at Kristy. He knew it wouldn't do any good, she would never understand how self-centered she was. He also hated that he had been a lot like her and that was sickening when he thought about it. Jane had allowed himself the safety and freedom to explore more of who he truly was and not the image that he believed he needed to portray. He had a lot he needed to apologise for and to make up for, but Charles was willing to put in the work to become the man that he was supposed to be.

"Jane is a remarkable woman who is strong and confident. She doesn't believe in materialistic ideals. She's down to earth, smart and compassionate. All she wishes to do is to help people and make this world better. If that reflects poorly on you, then I strongly suggest you do your own self-reflection on why you feel that way. I didn't lower myself to her level, she lowered herself to mine. Leave the key card here and get out. I don't want to see you again Kristy. If you can't respect that, then I will file a restraining order against you. I will not have you interfering with my marriage." Charles said with complete authority to his voice.

He knew Kristy wasn't going to be happy about any of this. She had an obsession with him and he should have shut it down a long time ago, but he didn't think anything serious would come from it. Now it was time for tough love and he was going to make sure her and her obsession could not come between him and Jane ever again. If that meant he would have to file within court to keep her away from them, then he would. He knew his uncle wouldn't be happy about it, filing for a restraining order against anyone, much less a womanw ithin their social circle, would be scandalous and reflect poorly on their family name. But Charles didn't care. He wasn't going to risk losing Jane over Kristy and her actions. Jane was too special for that.

"Fine, but you're going to regret this." Kristy said, as she tossed the room key at Charles before she turned and stormed out.

Charles let out a soft sigh into the empty room. He needed to calm himself down for a moment before he would go and look for Jane. He was hoping she hadn't gotten far and that she would be willing to hear him out. He knew how bad it looked and he couldn't blame her for being angry with him. He just needed to find her and explain himself to her. That Kristy was not a woman he wanted to be with and had been trying to keep her away from him for months now. Charles grabbed his clothes and quickly got dressed before he grabbed the room key and headed out. He had an amazing woman to try and find and he was not going to rest until he could get Jane to hear him out. Charles just hoped that she would be willing to let him explain.

CHAPTER 22

Jane rushed out of the hotel room and made her way down the hallway. She had to fight to hold back the tears that were threatening to build within her eyes. She was not going to give Charles Bentley the satisfaction of making her cry, not like this. Jane was kicking herself for not knowing better. She had thought maybe they could be friends, maybe there was something more underneath his shallow exterior and like a fool she had fallen for it. She had fallen for the man that he allowed her to believe hid within him. Of course he would have another woman here. Of course he found someone to spend the night with and instead of telling her, he tried to have the best of both worlds. Jane couldn't help but wonder if Charles thought they both would be ok with a threesome tonight, if that was his goal all along. It sickened her to the point that her body was trembling. Just moments before she was trembling from pleasure and that pleasure had quickly morphed into pain and horror.

Jane pulled her cell phone out with a shaky hand and saw that it was just after eleven at night. She had no idea if Helena would be awake, but she was hoping she would answer her phone. She needed to talk to someone. She had to talk out what she was feeling before she did something stuid like not getting on the plane tomorrow morning. Jane listened as the phone continued to ring and just when she thought it was going to kick her over to her sister's voicemail, she finally heard Helena's voice.

"Jane, are you ok?"

"I'm such an idiot." Jane said, as she blinked back some tears.

"No, you're not. What happened?"

"Charles was able to get us a hotel room. We spent a couple hours talking and getting on the same page. I thought we could

630

be friends to make the next year easier. He agreed and we were really connecting. He even wants to go with me to the village to help rebuild it. Things were going so well."

"That's good though. Shocking on his part, but it's good that you both were finding a common ground and learning more about the other. What's got you upset?"

Jane knew that Helena was going to brag about knowing that she was attracted to Charles. She really didn't want to hear an I told you so from her sister, but she had to talk about what had just happened and the only way she could do that was admitting to having sex with Charles.

"I kissed him and one thing led to another." Jane started, but Helena cut her off.

"I knew it! I told you that you liked him. Was the sex terrible? Is that why you're upset?"

"No, it wasn't terrible. It was amazing, the best sex of my life. We've been going for hours and would still be going if it wasn't for what happened."

"Oh you lucky bitch." Helena said with a sigh before she continued. "What did he do?"

"We were about to go for another round when this woman walked into our hotel room."

"Shut up. Who was she?" Helena asked, shocked.

"Some girl named Kristy. She showed up with a room key and very surprised that I was there. You should have seen her. She had long blonde hair, very thin with clearly fake boobs. She was dressed in this cocktail dress almost with high heels. She looked like a high level escort, I swear."

"Maybe she was."

"I wish, but no. She actually called me a hooker. Called me trashy because I have my belly button pierced and a tattoo on my hip."

"Piercings and tattoos make you a hooker, jeeze, I guess we're both hookers then. What did Charles have to say?" Helena asked, annoyed.

"He said I wasn't a hooker, but he didn't tell her I was his wife. And I know that we both agreed to an open marriage. I don't expect him to be celibate for the next year. I could do it sure, but that man likes to sleep with multiple women a day, there's no way he's going to make it. I just didn't expect for him to get a hotel room and tell me it was for us and then have some woman meet him there."

That was what hurt the most out of this. The fact that Charles didn't come out and say they were married. Even if it was under false pretenses, they were married and she deserved that level of respect to be called his wife. Especially when he was going to be hooking up with another woman. Not that Jane doubted the woman would have higher morals and not sleep with a married man. She didn't expect much from her or any other woman that Charles had been with. She knew enough to know that the women he had been with only liked him because of his wealth.

"No, you have every right to be angry with him. To be hurt. He had no right to do any of that to you. He should have corrected her and told her you were his wife. What did he have to say for himself?"

"I don't know, I ran out of there once I got dressed. I haven't seen him."

"Sweetie, you have to talk to him. You don't know what the situation is. I know it looks bad, but I can't imagine he would get a hotel room for the two of you and then invite another woman. Maybe he wasn't expecting for her to show up or maybe she had canceled on him or something. I don't know. I just know you need to talk to him and see what his side of the story is." Helena calmly explained.

Jane hated that she knew that Helena was right. She didn't want to talk to Charles about this. She wanted the blizzard to magically go away so she could get away from here, away from him. She felt like a fool for falling for his tricks. For allowing her body to give in to her basic needs.

"What could he possibly say? She had a key to the room Helena." Jane countered.

"And normally that would look bad, but the hotel is slammed with the blizzard, someone could have easily given her a room key without verifying with him first. If she was pushy and causing problems, any worker could have easily given her a room key to make her go away. I know he's not the most amazing man in the world, but I can't imagine he's that stupid to give a room key to another woman and then have sex with you."

Jane let out a sigh. She hated it when her sister calmed her down with perfectly logical reasoning. She wanted Helena to be outraged with her and for them to start plotting his murder. Instead she had convinced her to talk to Charles, the one man she didn't want to speak with.

"Fine, you're right. I won't run away from him if he shows up. But based on how Kristy was looking, I doubt he's going to be kicking her out and coming to find me."

"If he doesn't then you have my full support and approval to get him eaten by a lion or something in Africa."

"A tragic safari accident. I like it." Jane said with a warm smile.

"It'll make the news and be a great loss to the world of playboys. Talk to him preferably before you get trapped on a plane with him."

"I know, I know, I will. Is everything ok with you?"

"Oh ya we're good. The fire is still going and now we are just trying not to lose our minds. Don't worry, you focus on what you have going on with you. Let me know what happens."

"Always. I'll call you in the morning if we can board."

"Ok, be safe and I love you."

"You too." Jane said, as she ended the call.

Jane put her phone back into her pocket and tried to get her racing thoughts to calm down. She had no idea how she felt about any of this. She knew what Helena said made sense, it would be insane for Charles to have invited another woman to the hotel knowing that she would be in the room, but maybe he was expecting for her to say no. Maybe Charles figured she wouldn't want to share a hotel room with him so he was finding someone to spend the night with. That thought didn't sit well with Jane though. She found herself surprisingly jealous, something she wasn't expecting to feel where Charles was concerned.

"Jane."

Jane let out a slow breath before she turned around and saw Charles walking towards her. She had only made it down to the hotel lobby, which had calmed down considerably and Jane figured there must have been an announcement about no more rooms available. She could easily pick up on the staff's faces that they were relieved for the rush to be over.

"Shouldn't you be with Kristy?" Jane asked with a harsh tone.

"I didn't know she was going to show up, I swear. It's not what you think at all."

It was only because of the tone to Charles' voice that had Jane calm down slightly. He wasn't coming across as a man that had gotten caught trying to slip in a threesome. He seemed genuinely surprised that Kristy had shown up.

"Fine, then what was she doing with a key card?"

Charles placed his hand on Janes' forearm and guided her over to a small section of the lobby so they could speak without anyone overhearing them.

"Kristy must have gotten the card from the front desk. She either badgered someone into giving her one or bribed her way to a room key. She and I used to casually date roughly six months ago. We were never anything serious and she knew that going in. We only lasted three months when I called it quits. She became obsessed with me. She got jealous whenever another woman was around me for whatever reason. She was even jealous of Anna. After I ended things she would still come around to the house or she would show up at events I was having to attend."

"What like a stalker?" Jane asked, confused.

"Not to that level, but essentially yes. I've blocked her phone number and email so she can't reach me a couple months back and I thought that would be the end of it. I saw her earlier today before I got us a room. She wanted to hook up and I told her no that I wasn't interested. Apparently she took that to mean something else. I made her leave her room key and I informed her that I would be getting a restraining order if she continued this. I also informed her very clearly that you are my wife and in no way, shape or form a hooker."

That made Jane feel a bit better but it was still hurtful to hear how Kristy had spoken to her. She had already been feeling self-conscious about the differences between them, especially within the social hierarchy of the world. She knew she would normally be out of his league. Just like she would never be interested in Charles. Jane knew she had her own style, but she was a long way away from how Kristy looked. That was the type of woman that Charles was normally interested in. Jane was nowhere near that type of woman. She was the thrift store shopper who didn't care if she got dirt or paint on her clothes.

Kristy looked like she would never eat ribs or wings because it would make her fingers dirty. They were vastly different and it was easy to feel self-conscious around women that were that beautiful.

"I'm sorry I got mad. I shouldn't have jumped to conclusions, that wasn't fair to you."

Charles placed his hands on her hips and pulled Jane closer to him. "You had every right to jump to conclusions. I would have jumped to the exact some ones if the situation had been reversed. I'm sorry that she upset you and I am sorry for what she said to you. She's a stuck up priss that only wants to marry a rich man. She had no right talking to you that way. And for the record, I love the tattoo and piercing." Charles said with a warm smile.

Jane hated it, but just like that all of her worries and self-consciousness disappeared. To know that Charles had found her attractive, that he didn't see her differences as a flaw, it warmed her heart.

"I don't suppose you have the energy for another round?" Jane asked with a sexy smile.

"Oh Kitten, I have enough energy for at least another six."

"Careful, don't write cheques your ass can't cash Charlie."

Charles gave her a rich smile as he spoke. "You can always cash those ones, that is if you can keep up."

"Challenge accepted." Jane said, as she closed the gap between them and pressed her lips to his.

Charles pulled Jane's body closer to his as he deepened the kiss. He couldn't believe how amazing it felt to kiss her still. He was beginning to think it was never going to get old. He had no idea what the next year was going to be like, but he was hoping that tonight wasn't just a one-time deal between them. He wanted more of Jane and he was truly hoping he would be able to have it.

CHAPTER 23

Helena gave a soft moan as James' mouth worked its way over her neck and slowly down her body. She had no idea if this was a smart thing to be doing, but at the moment, it was the best way to get through a blizzard. They had already had sex twice and James still wanted more. Which worked out very nicely for Helena because she loved going multiple rounds. She was still in a state of shock that they had done this. She had been pretty adamant about not crossing that line with him, despite the fact that James wanted to. Helena was glad it did happen though, that she pushed through her hesitation and doubts and kissed him back. Her phone ringing snapped Helena out of her thoughts. She reached over to the table as James spoke.

"Ignore it."

"I will once I see who it is."

Helena looked at her phone as James' mouth continued to kiss his way down her stomach.

"It's Jane." Helena said, slightly annoyed that they were being interrupted right now, but she had to answer just in case something was wrong.

"I'm not stopping." James said and Helena could feel his smile against her skin.

"Something could be wrong." Helena countered.

"It could be, you should answer then."

Helena would normally move or hit the guy on the head to get him to stop, but James' mouth against her skin felt way too good and right now he was just kissing her stomach.

"Jane, are you ok?" Helena asked, finally giving in and answering.

"I'm such an idiot."

"No, you're not. What happened?"

Helena had been hoping that Jane was only calling her because she was bored. Now it was looking like an actual problem. All of that escaped her mind the second she felt James' tongue lick up her core. She had to slap a hand over her mouth to keep herself from making a sound.

"Charles was able to get us a hotel room. We spent a couple hours talking and getting on the same page. I thought we could be friends to make the next year easier. He agreed and we were really connecting. He even wants to go with me to the village to help rebuild it. Things were going so well."

"That's good though. Shocking on his part, but it's good that you both were finding a common ground and learning more about the other. What's got you upset?"

Helena looked down at James, who had looked up at her. She mouthed the word stop, but he just smirked before he went back to licking her.

"I kissed him and one thing led to another." Jane started, but Helena cut her off.

"I knew it! I told you that you liked him. Was the sex terrible? Is that why you're upset?"

Helena felt James give a chuckle and she knew he was thinking about the prospect of Charles being terrible in bed.

"No, it wasn't terrible. It was amazing, the best sex of my life. We've been going for hours and would still be going if it wasn't for what happened."

"Oh you lucky bitch." Helena said with a sigh before she continued. "What did he do?"

"We were about to go for another round when this woman walked into our hotel room."

"Shut up. Who was she?" Helena asked, shocked.

"Some girl named Kristy. She showed up with a room key and very surprised that I was there. You should have seen her. She had long blonde hair, very thin with clearly fake boobs. She was dressed in this cocktail dress almost with high heels. She looked like a high level escort, I swear."

"Maybe she was."

"I wish, but no. She actually called me a hooker. Called me trashy because I have my belly button pierced and a tattoo on my hip."

"Piercings and tattoos make you a hooker, jeeze, I guess we're both hookers then. What did Charles have to say?" Helena asked, annoyed.

"You are far from a hooker." James whispered, softly so only Helena would hear him.

"He said I wasn't a hooker, but he didn't tell her I was his wife. And I know that we both agreed to an open marriage. I don't expect him to be celibate for the next year. I could do it sure, but that man likes to sleep with multiple women a day, there's no way he's going to make it. I just didn't expect for him to get a hotel room and tell me it was for us and then have some woman meet him there."

"No, you have every right to be angry with him. To be hurt. He had no right to do any of that to you. He should have corrected her and told her you were his wife. What did he have to say for himself?"

"I don't know, I ran out of there once I got dressed. I haven't seen him."

"Who was she?" James whispered once again.

"Kristy." Helena very faintly answered, as she turned the phone away from her mouth. James instantly rolled his eyes and moved his hand up to his head and twirled his finger around to signal crazy.

"Sweetie, you have to talk to him. You don't know what the situation is. I know it looks bad, but I can't imagine he would get a hotel room for the two of you and then invite another woman. Maybe he wasn't expecting for her to show up or maybe she had canceled on him or something. I don't know. I just know you need to talk to him and see what his side of the story is." Helena calmly explained.

"What could he possibly say? She had a key to the room Helena." Jane countered.

"And normally that would look bad, but the hotel is slammed with the blizzard, someone could have easily given her a room key without verifying with him first. If she was pushy and causing problems, any worker could have easily given her a room key to make her go away. I know he's not the most amazing man in the world, but I can't imagine he's that stupid to give a room key to another woman and then have sex with you."

James shrugged his shoulders in agreement before he resumed his actions against Helena's body.

"Fine, you're right. I won't run away from him if he shows up. But based on how Kristy was looking, I doubt he's going to be kicking her out and coming to find me."

"If he doesn't then you have my full support and approval to get him eaten by a lion or something in Africa." Helena had to bite her bottom lip to keep herself from moaning as she felt James' tongue picking up its pace.

"A tragic safari accident. I like it." Jane said with a warm smile.

"It'll make the news and be a great loss to the world of playboys. Talk to him preferably before you get trapped on a plane with him."

"I know, I know, I will. Is everything ok with you?"

"Oh ya we're good. The fire is still going and now we are just trying not to lose our minds. Don't worry, you focus on what you have going on with you. Let me know what happens." Helena answered, as she gripped James' hair and wiggled her hips against him, causing James to moan.

"Always. I'll call you in the morning if we can board."

"Ok, be safe and I love you."

"You too." Jane said, as she ended the call.

Helena let her phone drop from her hand and down to the floor. She no longer fought to contain the moans from escaping her body. She gave a deep moan and arched her back off the couch as James' tongue worked its magic on her body. It wasn't long before Helena was reaching her climax.

"James." She moaned deeply as she felt her body pulse against his tongue.

James moaned as the taste of her hit his tongue once again and he greedily licked everything she had for him. After Helena finished pulsing James kissed his way back up her body as Helena fought to catch her breath.

"You are very good at that." Helena said with a heavy voice.

"It's a very important life skill." James responded with a smile against her neck.

"So what's the deal with Kristy?"

James pulled back and looked down at Helena and spoke in a warm voice. "That's what you want to talk about right now?"

"I need a five minute breather before the next round. Might as well get my curiosity out of the way."

James gave a nod and relented, but didn't pull back from Helena. "She was a girl that he had a casual thing with about six months ago. He broke it off with her when she got crazy."

"Crazy how?" Helena asked, now very interested in this story.

"Obsessive. She got jealous and possessive whenever another woman was around him. One time she even demanded that he fire Anna because she stood too close to him. Got it in her head that Anna must want Charles. After he ended things, she would call him and text him sometimes two hundred times a day. She would show up to different events he went to or the golf course. She basically became a stalker."

That was surprising to Helena, because to her Charles didn't seem worth all of that effort. It wasn't like he was a celebrity or anything special. He was an almost thirty-five year old play boy that didn't seem to want any responsibilities and just wanted to drink and party. Why fight so hard to keep him?

"No offense, but he doesn't really seem worth all of that."

"No offense taken, we didn't get it either. Best we could figure out she's a gold digger with some type of mental illness that she isn't being treated for. There are plenty of other rich single guys within our social circle she could be chasing after. Plenty that would die for her to chase after them. He had been hoping that she would let it go and for a while we thought so. He blocked her phone number and email and she stopped popping up to events. Somehow she must have met him at the airport and did what she does best."

"She walked in while they were in bed and called Jane a hooker. Somehow she got a room key."

"Probably bribed someone. And you and Jane are far from hookers. Although I get to tease the hell out of Charles for sleeping with Jane. I said it might happen, but he called me crazy."

"I said the same thing." Helena said with a big smile. She was really looking forward to teasing Jane once they returned from their honeymoon. "Jane said he's not who she thought he was. That he even asked to go with her on some of her adventures in

Cape Town, including going over to a nearby village to help build houses."

"I know it might seem surprising, but Charles likes adventures and going against what this society has labelled as appropriate behavior. He has no problem getting his hands dirty, but just like me, he was never allowed. Jane will be really good for him in that sense. She seems like the type that doesn't shy away from some adventure."

"She loves it. She's going cage diving with great white sharks." Helena said with a small shake of her head.

"Ya, I wouldn't do that." James said with a small chuckle.

"I wouldn't be doing it either. I think she's nuts, but she will get a person out of their shell and out of their comfort zone, that is for sure."

"Charles needs that. It should be very interesting to see how they are when they get back."

Helena had to agree with him on that. It would be interesting to see how they interacted, if anything had changed. Maybe they wouldn't be together, it could easily be just for a single night. Only time would tell. For now Helena was going to keep her focus on her own life and that included the very attractive and naked man above her.

"Ready for round three?" Helena asked with a flirty smile.

"Hell ya." James said, as he closed the gap between their mouths. He was more than ready for the next round.

CHAPTER 24

It was roughly six in the morning when both of their phones beeped, signally a text message. They had been awake all night rotating between talking and having sex. Jane currently found herself laying on Charles' chest with their legs intertwined together. Charles reached over and picked up his phone to see a text message from the airport.

"The blizzard has passed, and the flights are going to be resumed. Ours will begin to board in two hours."

"That's good. Are you going to text Anna?"

Jane was looking forward to getting to Cape Town, but for the first time since this whole mess started, she was almost disappointed that they would have to leave the bed.

"The airport sends out a text message to every passenger, but I will just in case."

"I guess that means we have to put clothes on." Jane said with a slight pout.

"Only if we want to leave the room, yes. But before you know it we will be at the resort in Cape Town and there is a very nice room at the resort."

Jane went up on her elbow so she could look at Charles as she spoke. "Maybe this is just the after-glow of a night of great sex, but what if we don't play pretend?"

"What do you mean?"

"We're married for at least a year, maybe we don't pretend to like each other. We both had judgments of the other and within the past twenty-four hours we now know that we were wrong on a lot of our assumptions of the other. And we obviously have chemistry in the bedroom. Maybe we should give this a real try."

Jane knew it was crazy. They were essentially strangers, but people used to be married to complete strangers all the time. Marriages where you didn't even see your future husband or wife until you arrived at the altar to say I do. They wouldn't be the first people to get married without truly knowing or caring for the other. They were married though and maybe they shouldn't be willing to throw it away or make a mockery of it.

"Is that what you want?"

Charles was a bit surprised that Jane would want to give their marriage a real go. He figured that the magic they shared between them would disappear once they left the hotel room. He wasn't bothered by the idea of trying for real with her. They were stuck with each other for a year anyways, why not make it more enjoyable. Even if they didn't get along, they would at least have great make up sex.

"I'd be willing if you are. I mean, we're stuck together for the next year anyways. We could grin and bear it or we could try for real. When the year is up we can evaluate if it's working or not. If we don't work out, then at least we can say we gave it our all and tried our best to make it work. I mean, chances are in three months I'll be strategically plotting your murder that I'll make look like an accident."

"I'm sleeping with one eye open." Charles interrupted, but Jane continued as if he didn't speak.

"At least we could both say at the end of the year that we both gave it our all and tried."

"I agree. I think it would be better to give this marriage a real effort compared to waiting our sentence out to walk away. I would rather regret being married than regret divorcing without ever knowing if things could have worked out."

Charles knew this was a crazy idea, but it was no crazier than asking a complete stranger to marry him so he can secure his late father's fortune. Jane was right though, they were going to be together, why not give it a real try. He would rather know he failed giving something his all compared to not even trying. If they got divorced in a year after he had tried his best, that was something he could live with.

"Exactly. You think you are up for it?" Jane asked, happy that Charles was in agreement.

"Don't suppose we could just spend a year in bed." Charles offered.

"Oh tempting." Jane said, as she leaned in and kissed Charles.

Charles placed his hand on the back of her neck to deepen the kiss. He could have happily spent the rest of his life right here in this room with her. He had never felt like this before. Normally he couldn't wait until the girl he took home that night left. He wasn't used to wanting to spend the night curled up with a woman or the interest in even sharing breakfast with her. Charles pulled back after a moment and spoke.

"As much as I would love to spend the rest of the week in this room, we can't. We have cage diving and ziplining to do."

Jane gave a groan before she spoke. "You have a valid point. Though, I think it's safe to say we only need two hotel rooms."

"Oh definitely." Charles easily agreed with a flirtatious smirk, causing Jane to laugh. "You shower first, I will order us some breakfast. Anything you'd like?"

"I'm a sucker for waffles."

"Makes two of us." Charles easily agreed.

Jane got up and headed off to the bathroom to get ready for the day while Charles went to work on getting them breakfast. He was hoping he would be able to get in their order before everyone else was up and moving. Within two hours they would be on the plane and heading to their honeymoon.

*****

Jane and Charles were making their way towards their gate. They had roughly thirty minutes left before they would start boarding, but they wanted to make sure they got there without having to deal with an enormous crowd for the elevators. Charles had called the resort letting them know that they would be there today and they no longer needed the third room. He was looking forward to spending the week with Jane now. They would go on some adventures and then spend the night wrapped up in each other's bodies.

"That's Evan." Charles said to Jane as they arrived at the gate and saw Anna with another man.

"They look cozy." Jane commented back.

"Anna, I see you found someone to spend the night with." Charles said with a smirk once they were close enough.

"Well I see the same could be said for you. You two look cozy." Anna said right back, as she took the two of them in. Charles currently had his arm around Jane's hips.

"Evan, this is my wife Jane. Jane, this is Evan Cooper, Anna's ex-husband." Charles said.

"It's lovely to meet you Jane." Evan said, as he held his hand out.

Jane easily took it as she spoke. "You as well. Did you both have a good night?"

"We had a great night in Evan's suite. There is actually something I wanted to talk to you about. Evan is going to Paris and he has invited me to go with him." Anna started and both Charles and Jane could tell she was a bit anxious about this conversation.

Jane looked over at Charles and she could see it all over his face. He knew what she was trying to get at.

"Go." Charles simply said.

"Are you sure?" Anna asked, surprised at how easy it was to get Charles to agree. Apparently his night with Jane was very good for him.

"I know I've never said this, but I do love you Anna. You have been like a second mother to me. I appreciate everything you have done for me. Paris is the one place within this world that you have always wanted to visit. This is your chance. Go, have a good time and explore the city of your dreams. Take all the time you need. It's time you got to experience living for yourself." Charles said warmly.

Anna gave him a bright smile as she went over and wrapped him into a hug. Jane moved away so Charles could have both of his arms. He easily wrapped them around Anna and he could feel the love that she had for him. They almost never hugged or touched, but Anna always knew when he needed one. When he needed a bit of comfort. That was mostly when he was younger, but it was Anna who had hugged him when his father passed. It was Anna who had helped me to work through his emotions on his father and what had transpired between them.

"I love you." Anna said softly.

"I love you too." Charles instantly said back.

After a moment Anna pulled back and then gave Jane a quick hug. Jane easily hugged her back before they all said their goodbyes to each other and Evan guided Anna to their own gate.

"I have to admit, I'm a bit surprised you let her go and gave her basically a complete blank slate to return whenever she wanted to. She could be gone for weeks or more for all you know." Jane commented once they were alone.

She had only known Charles for a few weeks, but in the time she had known him, it seemed like Anna was an important person in his life. Like he couldn't function without her almost.

She never thought she would see the day where Charles was willingly sending Anna off on her own without a single clue as to when she would return.

"I know but I think it's time I figured out how to stand on my own two feet for a change. She's done so much for me, more than I could ever repay her for. She deserves this opportunity to see Paris and to spend time with a man she is still madly in love with. I've seen her grieve the loss of him over the past decade. Now she has a second chance and I can't take that from her."

"You've really grown over the time that I've known you. I'm proud of you Charlie. Ana does deserve this second chance and it's really great that you are letting her have it. And for her to be able to have it without feeling guilty. I have a feeling she will be back before we know it and with a bunch of her own stories she can share." Jane said with a warm smile.

"I hope so." Charles said with a smile back.

"Passengers for flight 189A is now boarding for First Class." The overhead intercom system announced.

"That's us, are you ready for our first adventure Mrs. Bentley?" Charles asked.

If he had asked Jane that yesterday when they were set to board before the blizzard, she would have told him to shut up and walked off. She most likely would have ignored him all together and suffered in silence as they flew next to each other. Today though, it was a completely different day with a whole new mindset. She was looking forward to spending the flight with him. They could talk or watch a movie together. Hell, maybe they would join the mile high club. She was fairly confident that Charles would have already been a member, most likely many times over, but she knew he would be more than happy to welcome her to the club.

"Hell ya Mr. Bently."

They headed for the gate and once they handed their tickets over, Charles' phone began to ring as they walked down the long tunnel to reach the plane. He pulled it out and saw that Wyatt's name was across his screen. He hit decline before putting it back into his pant's pocket.

"You're not going to get it?" Jane asked, surprised that he would be ignoring a call from his family's lawyer.

"There's nothing I have to talk to him about and there is nothing he has to say to me. There's no problem going on with the company and the money will be in my new bank account before noon today. Whatever he wants, he can wait until we get home and then tell my lawyer all about it." Charles said with a proud smile.

"Good for you." Jane agreed.

Charles was not going to let Wyatt or his uncle ruin their honeymoon. They were going to make memories and get to know each other better. Any problem either of them had could wait until they returned. Charles was done with being a doormat to his uncle and Wyatt. If they wanted to keep playing, if they wanted to take him through the courts to try and steal his rightful inheritance, then they were more than welcome to. He wasn't going to stand around and let it happen. The both of them were in for a rude awakening once they came back and it was something that Charles was actually looking forward to.

CHAPTER 25

That little bastard. Wyatt thought to himself. He couldn't believe Charles had the nerve to reject his call. He was supposed to be the family's lawyer, for all he knew there could have been a problem with the company. He was proving once again why he was irresponsible and the wrong heir to the Bentley's fortune.

"You thought he would answer?" Jack commented from his seat on the couch.

"I don't care if he's in the middle of having sex, when I call he should always answer. There could have been a problem with the company. There could have been a health scare in the family. He doesn't know. My calls are to never be declined." Wyatt said with an edge to his voice as he went over to the bar and poured himself a scotch.

"He's leaving on his honeymoon remember; if he answers he's at a risk of saying something that proves he doesn't love that trashy woman."

"He didn't marry her for love and I will prove it." Wyatt promised.

"But does it matter? You said so yourself you're not certain that it matters. You said the will didn't specifically state in love for the marriage."

Jack was not happy at all about how things were progressing. It was bad enough that he had to wait around until Charles was thirty-five before he got to take what was rightfully his. Now Charles went and decided to get married just to be selfish and deny him what was rightfully his. Jack was the one that had to put up with Jacob growing up. He was the one that had to constantly be in Jacob's shadows. Everything should have automatically been left to him as the next head of the Bentley family. Not Charles, some irresponsible party boy that couldn't go a day without getting drunk. It was a slap to the face and disgusting.

"Love is implied when you speak of marriage. I don't care how long it takes or what I have to do, I will get him removed from the family's fortune. Jacob never wanted him to have it, certainly not the way that he was. His putting the stipulation of marriage was his last attempt to try and straighten Charles out and he is rolling in his grave at this mockery."

"Jacob changed the will within the last few weeks of his life, can't we claim insanity and get it revoked back to what it was?"

Wyatt knew it wouldn't be that simple though. Originally Jacob had it where Jack would inherit everything, effectively cutting off Charles completely. With Charles being cut off, he would have to find a job, plus he would be kicked out of the main house where Jack and Rosalyn would then get to move in. Charles would also lose his father's shares within the company and they would be transferred over to Jack's name. Everything in total came out to billions of dollars now and in the future. It was why Jack had been fighting so hard for it. Jack had also promised that Wyatt would be able to move into his mansion and he would get a large settlement portion of upward of a hundred million dollars for securing his inheritance. There was a lot on the line for the both of them.

"If we go to court and claim that Jacob wasn't mentally sound enough to make those changes that will open a deadly can of worms." Wyatt warned.

"I don't see how. The man died of a heart attack, we have the coroner's report proving that." Jack countered.

"A coroner we paid off to state that was the cause of death. If we file to have the old will reinstated basing it off of mental stability any lawyer that Charles hires will push to look into it."

"He might not hire a lawyer. He's too lazy for that." Jack argued.

653

"No one is too lazy when you are talking about billions of dollars Jack. He has money coming in from his shares within the company. He can afford a team of lawyers that will fight against us. All it would take is one lawyer to demand more testing done to verify cause of death. One lawyer to demand to see his medical file, which would be permitted given we are questioning his mental health. They get ahold of Jacob's medical file they will see he was perfectly healthy up until three months before his death. Then the sudden headaches, nausea, tiredness and weakness in his muscles will come to light. Charles is legally Jacob's next of kin, he could have his body exhumed and tests done on it."

"Who cares? Let him dig him up."

Jack really didn't see the bi gdeal about it. So Charles dug up his dead father, that wouldn't change what the cause of death was. That wouldn't change that any coroner would see it was a heart attack and nothing more. It would a;l be pointless and only help to prove them right.

"Poison lives in a person's body even after death. We're not in the clear yet and won't be for years before his organs have turned to mush. If they discover that Jacob was poisoned not only will we both be at risk of going to jail, but you will automatically trigger the forfeiture clause in your father's will."

Henry Bentley had been a man that you feared back in his prime. He was strict and always demanded the best out of his sons. All of that changed the moment he got his first and only grandchild. When Charles was born a flip had been switched in Henry and all of a sudden he became loving and carefree. Both Jacob and Jack saw Henry as a disgrace to the family and they were not upset when he died. However, Henry had gone and changed his will with a lawyer before Wyatt's time with the Bentleys. Originally it was to be a fifty/fifty split between Jacob and Jack, something the brothers had been prepared for and had already worked out who would get what. When the will came in for Henry it had forever changed the dynamic within the family.

Henry had left everything to Jacob, only allowing Jack to keep his shares within the company as a partner. Jack didn't get a single cent of the money. There were only two clauses, the first, if Jacob passed away before Charles turned eighteen then Jack would take over the company until Charles was legally allowed to. The second, should Jack ever try to overthrow Jacob, then he will trigger the forfeiture clause and lose every single cent to his name and his shares within the company. He will no longer be a Bentley and cut off from the business and fortune. Killing his brother through poisoning would trigger that clause.

"You said it couldn't be traced, that's why we did it with poison." Jack said with an edge to his voice.

He had been tired of waiting around for Jacob to finally get sick or die. He had been wrongfully cut out of his father's will, all because Charles was born. He was done with waiting around. When Wyatt had suggested the idea a year prior it sounded perfect, and undetectable. That was before they discovered the change in Jacob's will, something he did through a different lawyer. For the past year they both had been waiting for Charles to turn thirty-five so they could finally get their hands on what they believed they deserved.

"It is undetectable until you go looking for it. Coroner's don't run your blood for poison when you die unless there is a reason for it. All it will take is one lawyer to suggest a medical professional overlook Jacob's medical file for them to suspect something more was going on with him."

"Then what do you suggest? I am not going to sit around and lose everything again." Jack demanded, as he stood and started to pace around.

"We get him for the marriage. If we can prove that he went into their marriage with fraudulent intentions then we can get

655

everything taken from him. We could even have him charged and thrown in jail for it. We didn't come this far just to lose to that worthless excuse of a man."

Wyatt was not going to lose now, not when they were so close to finally getting their fortune. He was going to destroy Charles, even if it was the last thing he did.

We hope you Enjoyed Book Four of the Accidental Engagement Series. Now Continue Reading the Story by Reading the Book Five.

Make sure you signed up to Bridget Taylor's mailing to receive FREE BONUS CONTENT which compliment this book. Just go to https://bit.ly/aebonuscontent to Sign Up and Get Notified of New Releases.

The Accidental Engagement

Series Book Five

Description

With their one year deadline quickly approaching Jane and Charles have to decide if they are going to stay married or get divorced. However, when Jane becomes pregnant their simple arrangement becomes very complicated. Jane had always been told she could never get pregnant, making this baby a miracle to her. Charles had always been adamant about not having children. With his own childhood, he always believed he would make a terrible father, just like his own. Will their marriage survive a baby or will it finally be what forces Jane and Charles to face reality; that their marriage was doomed long before it even started.

Helena and James are in wedding bell bliss. They are engaged and set to walk down the aisle in a small and intimate wedding. What could possibly go wrong? Jack has now turned his attention to James' fortune. He couldn't get his hands on Charles' money and now he was trying to take James'. James is forced to deal with Jack and a DNA test that could rock their family to the core. Will Helena and James make it down the aisle or will it all fall apart before they ever have the chance to say I do?

Chapter 1

Before you start reading book five on the next page please make you get notified for the release of next series. Go to **https://bit.ly/aebonuscontent** to sign up to get notified of Bridget Taylor's new series coming out and to receive free bonus content and take part in giveaways. If you like this series you will love the next one :-).

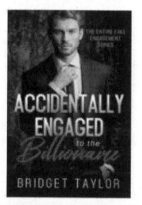

START OF CHAPTER ONE

"You would not believe what just happened." Helena said, as she walked into Jane and Charles' bedroom.

It had been almost a year since their honeymoon and they were still living together. When Jane had suggested they take their marriage seriously for the next year she wasn't certain it would go over well. She wanted to be able to say that she did everything she could to make her marriage work before getting a divorce. She knew it wouldn't change the outcome, but she would at least feel better about it. She would be able to tell the next man she wanted to marry that she gave her first marriage her all and it just didn't work out. There was no harm in it. What she didn't expect was to be in this weird limbo area. She didn't hate Charles, but she didn't know if she loved him either. She had never felt this conflicted about someone before. Normally it was straightforward and easy for her to know what she was feeling about a man. Yet with Charles she was left feeling a lot of different emotions and not all of them she could pinpoint.

Charles himself had been changing over the year. He no longer had her sitting out when he was playing golf with the men. He also had no problem whatsoever on their honeymoon doing anty of the adventurous activities that Jane had planned for herself. He loved cage diving with the Great White sharks and he didn't complain at all when they helped to build homes in a nearby village. In fact Charles donated money every six months to their organization to help them build more suitable housing and to have clean water. He had talked about them going back there and bringing them supplies. He had truly started to grow into the man he was always born to be. He was even wearing t-shirts and jeans when he didn't need to be in the office.

Jane had been spending the year working on her education and getting her not-for-profit up and running. James had been helping her with the start up funds and Charles had introduced her to a lot of great businessmen that were very interested in her non-profit. She had been working hard over this past year to get everything up and running and so far everything was going well. Jane had no idea if she was going to continue on in their marriage, but things were going well with everything considering. Even Jack and Wyatt had left them alone, but that was also nerve wracking. They didn't know what they were planning, but Charles was confident that they were planning something.

"Where are you?" Helena asked, confused. She didn't see Jane in the bedroom at all.

"The bathroom genius." Jane said, as she sat on the side of the tub.

"Well hurry up, I have to tell you something." Helena said impatiently.

Jane couldn't help but roll her eyes. She had no idea what was so important that Helena had to tell her. She was currently having her own issues. She hadn't been feeling well for the past few weeks. She had been really nauseous and exhausted all the time. It didn't matter how much she slept, she couldn't keep her eyes open. She felt like she was being dragged through the mud and she had no way of being able to stand up. At first Jane figured it was just the flu that she couldn't seem to shake, but then she started to notice that her bra was hurting her breasts. They were sensitive to the touch and that sent up a red flag.

"This is stupid." Jane softly whispered to herself. She made sure it was quiet enough so Helena wouldn't hear her.

She had finally given in yesterday and purchased a pregnancy test. She had kept it hidden under the bathroom sink. She didn't want Charles to know about it, because she was certain it was nothing. That she was overthinking things. She had barely gotten any sleep last night, because she knew the best time to take a pregnancy test was first thing in the morning. Trying to sleep last night though made her feel like a little kid on Christmas Eve. She was tossing and turning all night as her mind refused to shut off. Jane knew the possibility of her being pregnant was astronomical. She had been told she couldn't get pregnant when she was twenty and after ten years she had yet to get pregnant. Not to mention she was taking birth control to help keep her hormones in line. Her and Charles hadn't been using condoms for the past year, they had no need to with her being on the pill. She couldn't be pregnant, there was just no way.

"Seriously, what are you doing in there?" Helena asked, and Jane could tell she was getting fed up.

"I'll be out in a minute." Jane said.

Jane let out a sigh before she reached over and picked up the pregnancy test. She was fully prepared to laugh it off. That she would see a negative line and all of this worrying would have been for nothing. She would laugh it off as being silly and she would move forward. She would have to make an appointment with her doctor to see if something else was going on with her. Perhaps her birth control was making her sick. The second she saw the small pink plus sign the room spun. She was pregnant, there was just no way she was pregnant, and yet here she was holding this stick that was telling her she was. It was unbelievable and Jane had no idea how she felt about it.

With shaky legs, Jane stood and made her way out of the bathroom. The second she opened the door Helena knew something was wrong. Jane looked shell shocked. Like she had been hit by devastating news while she was in the bathroom. This was not what she was expecting to see when she came over here to give her sister some amazing news.

"What happened? You look like you got hit by a bus."

Jane didn't say anything, she just held up the pregnancy test and Helena was instantly taking it. Jane made her way over to the bed and sat down on it as Helena looked at the test.

"Holy shit, you're pregnant." Helena said, with a mixture of shock and excitement.

She could clearly remember how devastated Jane was when she was told she couldn't have children. That her body would never be able to get pregnant from her uterus. She had watched her to fight to accept it and move on from the loss. Jane had always loved kids and wanted at least three herself. It was a huge loss to her when she was told it would never happen. That her dream would never happen. This was huge.

"This is huge Jane. Why are you not excited?" Helena asked, as she moved over and sat down next to Jane on the bed.

"I'm not supposed to be able to get pregnant." Jane started.

"Well according to this, you're six weeks pregnant. So obviously you can get pregnant. This is huge, you should be elated right now. We should be jumping up and down screaming."

"We hate that type of girl." Jane pointed out.

"Not the point. Why are you not excited about this?" Helena pressed.

Helena couldn't understand why Jane wasn't more elated over this news. She was beyond excited at the fact that her little sister was pregnant. She was going to be an aunt, something they didn't think would be possible. Jane should be over the moon with excitement and yet she looked like she had just found out her puppy was killed.

"You know what the doctor said. It would be impossible for me to be pregnant." Jane instantly argued.

"Ok, but obviously that quack was wrong because hello, you're pregnant."

"For how long? How long will I be pregnant until my body isn't able to carry it? You heard what the doctor said, there is no room for a baby in my uterus, not with the fibroids. There's no point in being happy and excited Helena. I'm not gonna have a baby at the end of this." Jane said with a great deal of pain.

It wasn't that Jane didn't want a baby, she did, she wanted one desperately. It was the fact that science wasn't on her side. She had made peace with the fact that she would never be able to carry a child. That if she wanted one of her own she would have to use a surrogate or adopt to make a family. She made peace with it, after many nights of crying herself to sleep and drinking far too much whiskey. Still, she was able to accept it and move on. Now the world was throwing her a giant slap to the face and she didn't know how to process it. Helena went and placed her hand into Jane's as she spoke.

"We don't know what will happen. And until you speak with a professional, you shouldn't be assuming the worst case scenario right now. Allow yourself to feel happy over this. Don't stress, it will only make you sick. Try not to worry about it until there is even a reason to worry."

Helena knew that this wasn't going to be easy for Jane, but she didn't want her to worry herself sick. They had no idea what would happen with her pregnancy and it wouldn't do her any good to already think that she was going to lose the baby. Jane knew what Helena was saying was true, but she couldn't get her mind to stop thinking about all of the worst case scenarios. Chances were she was going to lose this baby and she would have to carry that loss with her for the rest of her life. She didn't even know what she would do about Charles. She couldn't imagine he was going to react well. He didn't even know about her uterine fibroids. She hadn't seen a point in disclosing the medical condition to him, because they wouldn't be together all that long. It wasn't really any of his business what her medical history was, just like it wasn't any of her business what his was.

They didn't have that type of marriage and Jane doubted they ever would.

"Is that an engagement ring?" Jane asked, as she noticed the new ring on Helena's finger.

"That's what I came here to tell you. James proposed to me last night." Helena said, as she fought not to smile.

She still couldn't believe that James had proposed to her. They had been dating for a year now and things had been rocky at times, but overall they had been amazing. Halena had been surprised on more than one occasion with how far James had come since she had met him. She was truly in love with him and she couldn't imagine spending the rest of her life without him.

"What? Why didn't you tell me?" Jane asked, shocked.

"That's what I was trying to tell you and then you one upped me with being pregnant." Helena said with a smirk.

Jane rolled her eyes playfully before she spoke. "How did he do it?"

"He rented this cottage on the beach for us and we had a romantic dinner on the beach and at sunset he proposed to me. I wasn't certain I would be really into the whole sappy romance of it all, but it was perfect." Helena said with a warm smile at the fresh memory.

"Aw, I'm happy for you. And I know a great wedding planner." Jane teased.

"Oh fuck no. I am not using that psycho. We are having a small and intimate wedding. We're not putting on a circus."

"I don't blame you. It was very pretty when it was all over and done with though. But the process to get there was just too much. I'm really happy for you." Jane offered a small warm smile.

She was very happy for Helena and James and she wanted them to have a great marriage and life together. She had always wanted for Helena to be happy and to have her own family and now she was on the road to making it happen. It was hard though to be fully happy though because of what she was currently going through. Helena leaned over and bumped her shoulder against Jane's as she spoke.

"Come on, let's get out of here and do some retail shopping therapy. There's a new vintage thrift store that opened up that I have been dying to check out."

Jane didn't really feel like going out, but the idea of talking to Charles about her newly discovered pregnancy was even more unappealing. She gave a nod and got up to get dressed. She was hoping that maybe this would be a good enough distraction for her to forget about what was happening to her body, at least for a couple of hours.

CHAPTER 2

To say that Jane was nervous would be the understatement of the year. She had no idea how Charles was going to react to her news. They had never talked about having children, they never talked about wanting kids or not wanting kids. She had no idea how he felt about them or if he ever wanted them one day. What made all of this even more confusing was the fact she wasn't sure she had wanted to stay with Charles. Their one year was coming up within the next couple of weeks and she would need to decide if she wanted to divorce him or not. Jane thought it was her only major decision and now she was pregnant with his child. A baby she never expected to be able to have. She had been told when she was a teenager that she might never be able to have a baby. She was upset by it, but had grown to accept that a biological child wasn't in the cards for her. If she wanted to have a family one day she would need to adopt and she had made peace with it. Now she was pregnant and she had no idea if she was pregnant by the man she loved or not.

Jane was very confused about her feelings towards Charles. She had been in love before, but it seemed so simple back then. She could easily tell that she was in love with the man, yet with Charles she couldn't quite put her finger on it. She thought she was in love with him, but she couldn't help but think if she was in love with him, then she wouldn't have this hard of a time trying to determine if she was or not. It shouldn't be this messy, which made her think she didn't love him. However, whenever she thought about leaving him, about divorcing him, she felt sad. It was all confusing and now she had a baby to add into the mixture. How could she get a divorce while she was pregnant? Could she really break up her family? Could she raise a baby on her own? She knew Helena would help, but she was starting her own family with James. She was set to marry him, they were living together, they didn't need her and an infant in their home as well. Everything was a mess and she needed to speak with Charles to see how he felt about the situation.

The problem was though, she had no idea how she even felt about any of this. She had always wanted kids, but had to accept she couldn't have any of her own. Now she was pregnant, something that should be a joyous time and she was feeling uncertain. She was worried that she wouldn't be able to make it to term, or that she would miscarry before the first trimester was even through. In which case, telling Charles would be pointless and if he did want to have kids, it could be devastating to him should she lose it. All of this was causing her added stress that she knew wasn't good for the baby. She had to tell Charles and then go from there. She just hoped he would be ok with this.

Jane made her way into the parlour where Charles was currently sitting down reading the newspaper. Jane was trying not to be nervous, but she truly had no idea how he was going to react to the news. Jane went and sat down on the couch as Charles put his newspaper down and gave Jane his full attention.

"Good morning Kitten." Charles said warmly.

"Morning."

"Are you ok? You were up awfully early." Charles asked, concerned.

Things between them had been rocky and Charles was trying his best to make Jane feel comfortable. They had been dating each other for close to a year now and he still wasn't sure how she felt towards him. He was madly in love with her, but he was afraid to show it too much. He was still waiting for her to turn tail and run on him.

"Oh Helena wanted to talk about the wedding. She is refusing to use our wedding planner." Jane said with a small smile.

"I don't blame her." Charles said with a chuckle. "You look tired, maybe you should lie down for a bit." Charles said concerned. Jane had been busy with her non-profit and still finishing school. He was worried it was taking too much out of her.

"There's something I have to tell you." Jane started, but she really wasn't sure how to tell him this. She had never expected to have to tell a man this.

"You can tell me anything Jane, always." Charles said, but he was preparing his hear for the words, I want a divroce, to come out of her mouth.

"I'm pregnant." Jane simply stated.

"I'm sorry, what?" Charles asked, confused. He was not expecting for Jane to tell him that.

"I'm pregnant. I just took a test this morning."

"A home pregnancy test?" Charles asked, still trying to get his mind wrapped around this.

"Yes. It says I'm four to six weeks pregnant."

"Ok, but you haven't gone to get a test done by a doctor. Those things can give you false positives. We should get a proper test done by a doctor." Charles said, as he was trying to process the news.

"You're right, we should get a proper one done. I'll call the doctor and get an appointment." Jane agreed, as she pulled out her phone.

She wasn't sure how she was feeling about the way Charles was reacting. He wasn't mad, but he didn't seem very happy either. He was more shocked than anything and it was good that he wanted confirmation. She didn't even think about the chances of a false positive. She should have made an appointment and gotten the official test done first before telling Charles.

"Good morning, Dr. Heath's office, how may I assist you today?" The receptionist asked after three rings.

"Hello, yes this is Mrs. Bentley, I'd like to make an appointment with Dr. Heath for a pregnancy test."

"Absolutely. I can squeeze you in tomorrow morning at nine if that works for you?"

"Yes, that'll be fine." Jane answered. She was a bit disappointed that she would have to wait until tomorrow. She really wanted to know either way, but there was nothing she could do about it now.

"Perfect, we will see you tomorrow morning."

"Thank-you." Jane ended the call. "Tomorrow morning at nine." Jane said to Charles.

"Alright. We'll find out for sure tomorrow then." Charles said with a small nod.

Jane really wished she could have asked how he was feeling about any of this, but she was too afraid to. She would save that for tomorrow if the test comes back that she was indeed pregnant. The next twenty-two hours were going to be the longest ones of her life.

*****

Jane couldn't stop her fingers from tapping her knee as she sat there on the doctor's examination table. Charles was currently pacing back and forth in the very small room as they were both left there waiting for the urine results. When Jane woke up this morning, she was expecting to go and see Dr. Heath alone, but Charles was already awake and ready to go. He seemed to be supportive and was coming around to the idea that he might be a father. Ever since they had been trapped within this room though Jane couldn't but be nervous. She had no idea what Charles was thinking or feeling. He seemed to be more nervous and anxious then she was.

"You are going to worry a hole into the floor." Jane said, as Charles didn't seem to be stopping his pacing anytime soon.

Charles stopped pacing and went and sat down in the chair as he spoke. "Sorry."

"It's ok. We're waiting on pretty big news. What are you thinking about all of this?" Jane asked for the first time. As badly as she didn't want to know, she had to know.

"There's no point until we know for certain that you are pregnant. You're on the pill I thought." Charles said. He still wasn't sure how this happened.

"I am, but it's not always effective. Women get pregnant all the time while on it." Jane answered with a small shrug.

Before Charles could comment on that the door opened and Dr. Heath walked into the room with her file. He gave them both a warm smile before he spoke.

"Well, congratulations are in order. You are indeed pregnant Jane."

Jane felt her heart go into her throat once again. She was confident that she was. There was no reason for it to be a false positive. Hearing an official doctor tell her though, it was a lot. She had no idea what to think or feel about any of this. It was hard to get excited when she knew there was a good chance her baby would never make it to term.

"Sorry, it's just." Jane started, but Dr. Heath cut her off.

"A lot. I completely understand. I take it this was not a planned pregnancy."

"No, no it wasn't. I um… I have uterine fibroids. I've always been told I could never get pregnant." Jane said, as she tried to get her mind to work.

"What is that?" Charles asked, as this was the first time he had heard of Jane having a medical condition.

"Fibroids are essentially a benign mass that takes blood from a person. It makes it very difficult for women to become pregnant and to carry to term. I was not aware that you have them. Do you know how bad they are?" Dr. Heath asked, and both Jane and Charles could pick up the concern in his voice.

"No, it's been close to ten years since I've had a scan done. It was bad enough though that at twenty my doctor said I would probably never have a child. That even if I did get pregnant my body would eventually reject it."

"It does make this a high risk pregnancy. However, women can carry to term even with the fibroids. It would really depend on how big they are and how many. I am going to refer you to an OBGYN that specialises in high risk pregnancies. I am also going to have you go and do a detailed ultrasound to see how bad the fibroids are." Dr. Heath said.

"And if they are bad? Is there something we can do?" Charles asked, as he tried to get his mind wrapped around this.

"If they are bad, your OBGYN might recommend that you terminate the pregnancy to prevent any complications to Jane. However, if the fibroids are manageable, we could do a non-invasive surgery where the surgeon would cut off the blood flow to the fibroids and kill them. That would give more room for the baby to grow and you could carry to full-term. It all depends on the fibroids and if something can be done to them."

It was a lot to take in for both Jane and Charles. Jane was still trying to process the fact that she was pregnant. She had spent the past decade believing that she would never be able to have children and now she was pregnant and there was a chance she could lose the baby. There was a chance she might have to terminate the pregnancy or risk the baby miscarrying along the way. It was a lot to take in and Jane had no idea how to process any of this. She couldn't even imagine how Charles was handling all of this.

"Is there a risk to Jane or the baby if she tries to carry to term?" Charles asked, with a distant sounding voice.

"If the fibroids can't be minimized and if you wish to continue with the pregnancy there is a chance that you could miscarry at any point within the pregnancy. You could go into early labour. There is also a chance that as the baby grows it can burst a fibroid and it could cause Jane to bleed out internally. It is something that you will need to discuss with the OBGYN and come to a decision together. I don't want you to worry about that just yet. Let's get the ultrasound done and see what it comes back with before we start to worry about what comes next." Dr. Heath advised.

"Thank-you." Jane simply said.

She had no idea what to do about any of this. It was all confusing and she wasn't sure what she wanted to do. She knew she would need to wait for more answers from the ultrasound and the OBGYN, but once again it was more waiting. She would have to wait once again for the test and then the results. She would also have to wait and be a nervous ball of energy with not knowing if today was going to be the day she had a miscarriage. It was stressful and she wasn't sure she wanted to go through it. It couldn't be good for the baby for her to be worried all day long either.

"When will she be able to have the ultrasound done?" Charles asked.

"I'll put the request in today and it will normally take a couple of days. I will also send off the request to the OBGYN and you should have an appointment within two weeks to speak with them. For now, the best thing you both can do is try and not worry. There is a chance Jane could carry to full-term and give birth to a perfectly healthy baby." Dr. Heath said with an encouraging smile.

Jane knew the chances though weren't in her favor. She had no idea what she was going to do, but she needed time to think about it all. She had to talk to Helena and see what her thoughts were on this matter. She knew she should be talking to Charles about this, the baby was half his, but she couldn't handle that right now. She needed time to process what she had just heard. She needed time to get her own thoughts and feelings in order. She had to work this out before she could handle any conversation with Charles. She still had no idea what he wanted to do or if he was even happy with her being pregnant. It was too much for her to handle.

"Thank-you Dr. Heath. I appreciate you taking the time to speak with us." Jane said, as she stood from the exam table.

"You are welcome. If you have any further questions please don't hesitate to ask." Dr. Heath said, as he shook both of their hands.

"Thank-you Dr. Heath." Charles said, before he placed his hand on the small of Jane's back and they headed out.

Jane pulled out her phone and asked Helena if she could meet up for a chat. She really needed to talk to Helena and hopefully get her thoughts sorted out, because right now, she was drowning and she had no idea how she was ever going to reach the surface.

CHAPTER 3

The room was silent with the exception of the drumming of Wyatt's fingers against the arm of the couch. He had told Jack that they needed to meet and the man had the audacity to leave him here waiting for him. Wyatt had been annoyed before he arrived at Jacks' home, now he was past that. For the past year his frustrations had been mounting. He had been annoyed when he discovered that Charles was going to get married. His annoyance slowly turned into frustrations and now after a year he was in full blown aggravation. Wyatt had been expecting the take over of Jacob's fortune would be easy. He suspected that Charles would never get married and when he did, he believed wholeheartedly that they would be able to prove fraud. Yet, it had been a year and Charles was still up holding the farce.

Wyatt had tried to get the decision overturned, but Charles had hired a lawyer that was more than prepared to go to the mat for him. As badly as Wyatt wanted to fight in court over the funds, he knew that they risked being exposed. Regardless of what Jack wanted, he was not going to potentially expose himself as being an accomplice to murder. It infuriated Wyatt when he thought about how close they had been, not once, but twice, to Jacob's fortune. They were mere seconds away from billions of dollars when it was ripped away from them twice. When Jack and Wyatt had decided to poison Jacob to remove him from the family, allowing Jack to inherit every cent the family had. Jack was set to inherit everything. He was the last standing male of the head family and it was rightfully his. With Jack getting billions, he was going to be giving a good chunk over to Wyatt and giving him his own mansion. They both would be getting what they had always wanted. Only for Jacob to screw them over once again.

Wyatt wasn't sure why Jacob felt the need to change his will within the last couple weeks of his life. He also didn't know why Jacob went behind his back and used a different lawyer to do it. Wyatt couldn't help but wonder if maybe Jacob suspected something more was going on with him. That he suspected that Wyatt couldn't be trusted. It was a moot point though, because Jacob was dead and their secret went with him. Receiving the will and discovering that everything had been left to Charles was an insult. The only bit of salvation they had was knowing that Charles had to be married within the year in order to receive any money. Wyatt had no idea why Jacob had placed that stipulation on his will, but he was glad that he did. Charles was a party boy, he held zero interest in settling down. Wyatt and Jack had relented into having to wait another year to receive their fortune.

Now a year later, Charles was still married and they were still being denied what was rightfully theirs. Wyatt had been having a private investigator following Jane and Charles around, but so far they had not received any intel that they could use as proof that they had committed fraud. Jane had even been living at the house and they were always going out to events together. They had never gone out on a date with another person. No conversations about faking their marriage. They were playing this perfectly and Wyatt was sick and tired of having to wait around for Charles or Jane to make a mistake. Wyatt was going to force their hand, one way or another.

Wyatt's head snapped up when he heard the front door opening. He didn't bother with hiding his annoyance when Jack strolled into the formal living room without a care in the world.

"Wyatt." Jack simply said.

"You have left me here waiting for thirty minutes and that is all you have to say to me?. I don't appreciate my time being wasted, especially when I am not on the clock." Wyatt replied with an edge to his voice.

"I was at lunch. I have to keep up appearances. Not to mention it was with a few members of the Board. Charles is trying to get them to agree to changing the policies on who gets treatment approval and who doesn't. He is potentially going to cost the company millions by approving expensive life saving surgeries."

Jack couldn't believe that a year ago he walked into a board meeting to discover Charles was already there. It had been a week after his fake honeymoon and the first time Charles had even been at a board meeting. He had inherited Jacob's shares, giving him fifty percent control of the company, but he had never held an interest in being involved. He almost fell over when he heard what Charles wanted to do. It was absurd and not something Jacob would have wanted. Jack knew that Charles was allowing Jane to whisper into his ear and that trailer trash of a wife was going to cost their family everything. Jack was not about to make less money every year just so some low life peasant wouldn't die. No one was above his love for money, absolutely no one.

"He's still trying to get it approved?" Wyatt asked.

Jack had informed him of what Charles had been looking to do. He didn't think it would get approved, but a year later and they were still battling it. Half of the board was interested in Charles' plan to expand into other insurance areas. They liked the idea of making more money. However, the other half of the board were against it because they knew Jack was. They were loyal to him and they were not about to help Charles with making major changes to the company. They were still battling it out apparently.

"He won't let it go. I have spoken to him about it multiple times now, but he is being stubborn and digging his heels in. It's Jane, that trailer trash of a wife is influencing him. He was wearing jeans and a t-shirt the other day. Not just in his home, but out in public. He's been helping Jane with her non-profit, meeting with CEOS within our social circle to get them to work with her. It's disgusting. He is ruining my name, my family's name and now he wants to try and change the company that his father, my brother built. I won't allow it. I won't let him tarnish my name any longer." Jack said, as he went over to the bar and poured himself a drink.

Wyatt could feel his hatred radiating off of him. The last time Jack had been like this was when they were speaking about Jacob. Wyatt could appreciate the irony in the situation. Roughly two years ago they were having the same conversation about Jacob. At the time Jacob had been slowly trying to cut Jack out of the company and take it into a different direction. Funny enough, Jacob himself wanted to expand into other insurance areas, but he hadn't moved past the research stage before he became too sick. Wyatt couldn't help but wonder if Jack was about to ask him if he could get his hands on the poison that killed Jacob again. This time around though it wouldn't be that simple. Charles wasn't older, doctors would run a lot more tests to find out what was wrong with him. Most would suspect cancer, requiring his blood to be tested for any number of inconsistencies. All of which could point them in the direction of poison. They also didn't know who would inherit the company and fortune. They would need to get their hands on Charles' will for that. Wyatt would guess though that James was Charles' beneficiary.

"He inherited his shares and fifty percent control of the company. In order to make the change he needs a majority vote for the Board. You have half of them on your side. You need to start working on the other half and get them to switch their votes to your side, then you can squash this abomination of an idea once and for all." Wyatt stated.

"Only it was his proposal and he can choose when to call the vote. He can wait as long as he wants to call it. I need him taken out of the equation."

677

"We can't kill him Jack." Wyatt said with strength to his voice as his eyes followed Jack's moving body around the room.

"That's what you said about Jacob, but you figured out a way. Why can we not do the same for him?"

Jack didn't understand why it would work for Jacob, but not Charles. He was a heavy drinker, no one would think twice about him dying from liver failure or any other complications associated with excessive alcohol consumption.

"Because poisoning a young and healthy thirty-six year old will not be the same as an older fifty year old. Doctors won't pass it off as old age or bad genes. They will run tests and those tests could lead them in the direction of poisoning. It's too risky."

"I want him out. Out of the company, out of the family. He stole my rightful inheritance. It was me having to deal with Jacob and his crap my whole life. I had to put up with my father and his quirks. I paid my dues and I want what is rightfully mine." Jack said through clenched teeth.

"I want him gone too. Do not forget that you are not the only one that has lost a fortune. We can get him out, we just need to prove fraud."

"And how the hell are we going to do that? You haven't been able to accomplish that within the past year." Jack snapped.

"Charles and his whore of a wife are not geniuses. They are morons who will slip up. We just need to give them a little push. Cause strain between them. If we can get Jane to admit to the fraud then we can use it against Charles. Could even offer Jane some money for her cooperation. If Charles is proven to have committed fraud he will lose everything and it will automatically be passed on to you."

Wyatt knew that Jane was simply an opportunistic gold digger, her and her sister. They simply needed to give her the chance to come to their side. It wouldn't be as simple as a conversation.

Where she stood she had a lot to gain by playing this game with Charles. However, if they could get proof that she was a willing participant they could use that to twist her arm. She would save herself and throw Charles under the bus in a heartbeat for that Wyatt was sure of.

"And how the hell are we going to do that?" Jack demanded.

"The marriage is a fraud, we both know that. Jane is the weak link, we get her to admit to what she has done, then we use that to get Charles. We find a man, one that will fit with her type. We use him to get the truth out of her."

"Can the private detective find someone to work undercover?" Jack asked, not opposed to the idea.

He could agree that Jane was the weak link and if they could break her, they would be able to break Charles. Women were morons and they always talked to any man that showed them a little bit of attention. If they could find a guy that interested her, he could get the truth from her. Then they could use that to ruin Charles once and for all.

"I'll reach out. He probably has someone that he could put in. It'll be worth the price to finally get Charles out of the picture. With Charles gone you will be able to have the fortune and full control of the company. However, that still leaves James in the mix."

Jack scoffed at that. "James is a nobody. He stays at the bottom of the company and does what he is told. James is no threat to me."

Jack was disgusted by James. He was a supposed cousin of his, but Jack seriously doubted it. His mother was a whore and he knew for a fact that she liked to cheat on his cousin. It wouldn't surprise Jack if James was the gardener's son.

"Maybe not, but with you having no children when you die it all goes to him. You either need to get rid of him as well or find a way to have a child. Otherwise Jack and his soon to be stripper wife, Helena, will be left with the empire." Wyatt pointed out.

This was the issue, they were running low on Bentley's. All that was left of the Bentley name was Jack, Charles and James. It all goes to James if Jack and Charles are out of the picture. Wyatt knew though that Jack didn't want a child. He hated children, thought they were worthless and a waste of time, energy and most importantly money. Wyatt was hoping to use that to his advantage. He wanted to get Jack to leave him everything, then once Charles was out of the way, he could take Jack out and be a billionaire before the year was up.

"I would never allow that to happen. They won't get a single cent of the money. And I refuse to lower myself to having a child. I'll make sure my will is very detailed about who gets what and who takes over. As for James, I doubt he's even a Bentley. I want his DNA ran. I want proof that his whore of a mother didn't lie to my cousin."

"That's easy enough to do; however, getting his consent to run it might be a bit difficult. He's not under eighteen, he's not legally obligated to provide proof. You will have to get him to agree to it willingly."

"He'll agree. He will do whatever it is I tell him to do. Including not marrying that stripper, I'll speak with him tomorrow about it. He will not keep disrespecting our family name. A name he stole. I tolerated this crap when my cousin and his whore were alive, but I am done placating the dead. Both James and Charkes need to be removed from the family and kicked out onto the streets where they belong. Them and their gutter mistresses."

Jack was not going to rest until he had what was rightfully his. What his father and older brother had stolen from him. He was not going to tolerate Charles having all of the fortune and power. He was the oldest, he was the head of the family and it was time he got everything that he wanted. He didn't care who he had to trample on in his path. He was going to get what he wanted, no matter what.

CHAPTER 4

"Are you sure you don't want me to stay?" Helena asked James, as she grabbed her coat.

James wanted to tell her to stay. To not leave him alone with Jack, but he couldn't do that. Jane needed her big sister right now and James was not about to take that away from her. He knew from Charles that she had a bomb dropped on her yesterday and she really needed the sister time.

"Don't be silly. Jane needs you right now." James said warmly, as he went and took the coat from Helena and helped her to get it on.

"I know, but when you are alone with Jack it changes you." Helena countered, worried about leaving James alone with Jack.

Over the past year Helena could see a difference in James. He was starting to come out of his shell and be his own man. A man that he was born to be. He was helping Jane with her non-profit and he was even starting to build his own business in land development. He was becoming the man he had always wanted to be and Helena couldn't be prouder of him. However, whenever he had to be alone with Jack, he faded away. That was the best way Helena could think to describe it. She suspected that something had happened between Jack and James when he was younger. When he had to spend the summer at Jack's house at the age of sixteen. Helena had tried to get James to open up to her about it, but he never would. He didn't flat out dismiss her, but he would give a vague answer and quickly change the conversation. Helena didn't push. She didn't want to force him to talk about something that was potentially painful when he wasn't ready. She was hoping though that he would tell her soon. That he would trust her with the most vulnerable side of him.

"You don't have to worry about me, I'll be just fine. If he gets unruly I can kick him out. Go and enjoy lunch with your sister. She could use some support and cheering up right now." James offered with a warm smile.

He didn't want Helena to worry about him. He was a grown ass man and he would be just fine with Jack. He had been growing this past year and he was very happy with the man that he had become. He had to get a grip on himself where Jack was concerned.

"Alright, but call me if you need me." Helena relented.

"I won't need you, but yes, I promise I will call." James easily agreed.

Helena leaned up and placed a quick kiss to James' lips before she turned and headed out. She was set to be meeting up with Jane at their favorite restaurant to discuss the baby. The second the door closed James let out a slow breath. Jack would be here soon and he needed to get mentally ready for it. Normally he would be going around making sure everything was in order and nothing was out of place or messy. He would be making sure his clothes were ironed and on point. Today though, he was trying to loosen up a bit. His home was still clean and organized, but it wasn't surgically clean. He was also wearing a t-shirt and blue jeans today. He was trying to convince himself to not get changed.

The summer he spent trapped with Jack had been the worst time of his life. Still to this day, it was the worst thing that ever happened to him. Most would assume the worst day of his life was when he lost both of his parents to a drunk driver, but that was nothing compared to the horror of living with Jack. James was still suffering through nightmares from those two months with him. Those two months had changed him for years to come and he was just starting to get back to being the man he had always wanted to be. And it was all thanks to Helena. She had been incredibly supportive of him. She was his strength when he wasn't sure he would be able to do something. She had gone with him to purchase his first pair of jeans in close to twenty years. A fact that was sad all in of itself. Helena had been incredible and James still couldn't believe they had been together for a year now, that they were engaged.

James never expected to find a woman that he loved and wanted to marry; to spend the rest of his life with. He certainly never thought that woman would be a woman like Helena. He had grown up around a certain type and he had been expected to marry within the society. Helena was the exact opposite of any woman he was expected to be with and it was one of the reasons why he loved her. She was unique and special and she was not afraid to tell you what she thought. James loved how strong and independent she was. She didn't need a man to take care of her, but she could be vulnerable around the right one. When he couldn't be strong, she would be and when she couldn't be, he was right there for her. They were partners and James wouldn't have it any other way.

Letting out a sigh, James made his way into his kitchen. He was going to crap himself a cup of coffee, though he would have preferred a glass of whiskey for this meeting. Jack hadn't specified why he wanted to meet, but James wasn't an idiot. He knew that Jack would have heard by now that him and Helena were getting married. They weren't broadcasting it, both wanted it to be small and intimate, but that didn't mean word wouldn't travel to him. He knew Jack wouldn't approve of Helena and with him being the head of the family, as he likes to call himself, he believes it was up to him what everyone else did. James knew it was going to be aggravating, but he was hoping to shut it all down with Jack today. He didn't want it to be a fight the whole time. They simply wanted to get married and start their life together.

James was relieved that Helena wanted a small and intimate wedding. James himself didn't want to have to put on a show for people like Charles and Jane had to do. Their wedding was beautiful, but they didn't want to have to go through that whole experience.

James was hoping that Jack wasn't going to try and insert himself into their wedding plans or try and derail them. James was brought out of his thoughts at the sound of his front door opening. He couldn't contain the annoyed eye roll by the fact that Jack never knocked. He figured that because the house belonged to his first cousin that meant that he could come and go whenever he pleased. As if it was his house and not James'. It annoyed the hell out of him and something he was planning on correcting today. This wasn't Jack's house, this wasn't James' father's house, it was his house and if Jack wanted to be here, he was going to have to respect that.

James made his way towards his front door with his coffee in hand. He could see the instant disapproval on Jack's face at his appearance. James had to steel himself though to not shrink under the eye scolding he was receiving. He was a grown man in his own home, he could wear whatever he wanted.

"Polite people knock and wait to be allowed in." James said, with more strength to his voice than he actually felt.

"I don't have to knock to enter my own home." Jack said dismissively, as he went into the formal living room.

"It is not your home. My parents left everything to me, not to you. I will not tolerate you walking in here whenever you feel like. From now on you will knock. The door will be locked and I will have the locks changed so your key doesn't work." James said, as he went and sat down in one of the chairs. Normally Jack sat in the chair, forcing James to sit on the couch to feel like a school boy being scolded. James was making a point today. When Jack was in his house, James was the head of the household.

"I am the head of this family. Everything belongs to me." Jack said with an edge to his voice, as he sat down on the couch.

Jack could not believe that James was trying this crap with him. Helena was changing him for the worst. Before she came into the picture James was always doing what he was told. He was submissive and didn't ever stand up against him. Now he wanted to try and be a man, Jack was not going to tolerate it and he was going to make sure James knew his place.

"Nothing I own belongs to you. Nothing Charles owns belongs to you. You only have a small percentage of things that belong to you. Neither one of us are going to tolerate you trying to control our lives. We're grown men, if you don't like who we are you are welcome to not come around us."

James knew this wasn't going to go over well and he knew he couldn't technically speak for Charles. However, he did know that Charles had already started to put boundaries in place and was doing his best to keep Jack away from him, Jane and their life together. They were also going to be having a child and neither of them wanted Jack anywhere around the baby. They needed to get Jack out of the family and James was trying to help Charles to make that happen. It was more complicated with Jack having fifty percent control of the company. They would have to try and figure out a way to get him out of the company so all Jack would own would be his home and the money in his bank account. They just needed a way to get him legally out of the company, because they both knew that Jack would never agree to a payout.

"You both are bringing disgrace to the Bentley name. You are marrying a stripper for God's sake." Jack said disgusted.

"Helena's not a stripper. She worked as a bartender and now she is a College graduate and building her own real estate business. We are going into business together. She is a good woman and I love her. Just as Charles loves Jane. You married a gold digger who you were not in love with nor her to you. You are the last person that gets to throw stones at someone's relationship."

James knew for a fact that Jack and Rosalyn were not in love with each other, they never had been. He also knew for a fact that they both slept with other people. He had seen it himself during those months he lived with them. Their marriage was strictly a business transaction. Jack was able to do whatever he wanted with her in the bedroom and Rosalyn had access to his money. She was essentially a very well paid escort. Jack was the last person that got to judge someone's marriage.

"My wife is from this society. She belongs within the society and knows how to uphold our family's good name. Those sisters are trailer trash and have brought shame and mockery to the Bentley name. You are not marrying that woman and that is final." Jack said, with a deadly edge to his voice.

James couldn't help but smirk. "You seem to be confused Jack. I'm not your son, you have no say in whom I marry or don't. But don't worry, you aren't invited to the wedding."

"As long as your name is Bentley, I have every say in what you do and who you marry."

"I'm thirty-six years old. I don't need permission to live my life. If that is all you wanted to discuss, you know the way out." James said, as he stood.

He was done with this nonsense and he was not going to tolerate this any longer. Jack held no power over his life decisions and he was sick and tired of giving him that power. He was not going to sit here and listen to him judging and talking down about his soon to be wife.

"I have reached out to a lab, they are expecting your call." Jack simply said.

"A lab? For what?" James asked, completely confused.

"For a DNA test. I've always believed your whore of a mother cheated on my cousin. If you wish to keep living in my family's home, then you will need to provide proof that you have Bentley blood in you."

"You can't be serious." James said, shocked.

He knew that Jack never liked his mother, he had no idea why because his mother's sister was Jack's sister-in-law, apparently Charles didn't need a DNA test, but he did? It was a pathetic excuse to grasp at straws.

"I've already spoken with a lawyer."

"You mean Wyatt." James interrupted, but Jack continued nonetheless.

"If it comes back that you are not a Bentley, like I suspect, you will have to repay every cent of Bentley money that you have used since you turned eighteen. If you do not take the test and provide proof that you have taken it within the next two weeks, your accounts will be frozen and you will be evicted until you provide proof that you are a Bentley. You can consider this your two weeks notice." Jack said with a knowing smile.

"I'll go tomorrow and take the test. I have nothing to hide. I know who my father is. Once this test comes back that I am a Bentley, always have been, then you will be out of my life. There will be no reason for either of us to interact with the other."

James would go through with this test because he was going to shut Jack up once and for all. He was going to prove that his mother wasn't the whore he made her out to be. He knew who his father was and he had no problem shoving the proof right into Jack's face.

"I look forward to the results." Jack said smugly as he stood up.

James didn't say anything as Jack headed out. He would need to make sure that he spoke with the lab and had the results sent to him as well. He didn't trust that Jack wouldn't try and doctor the results somehow. He might even request that the results go to another lab to be verified. He was not going to allow Jack to play him. He would prove that he was a Bentley and then he would help Charles to get rid of Jack once and for all.

CHAPTER 5

After he had dropped off Jane at the cafe where she would be meeting with Helena, Charles had driven around for a little while to try and get his thoughts in order. He still couldn't believe that Jane was pregnant or that she had fibroids. He knew nothing about it and he felt like as her husband he should have known that she had a medical condition. It bothered him a great deal that Jane had never confided in him about it. That was something that married couples discuss. That was something that a husband should know about his wife. It bothered Charles a great deal that him and Jane didn't seem to be on the same page or at a married couple level. He thought they had been doing well, but apparently he was wrong.

Charles pulled up in front of James' home. He had to talk to someone about what had happened and the only person he could talk to was James. Charles knew that James had his own things going on with the wedding to Helena, but he was hoping they would be able to chat. Charles waited until he saw his Uncle Jack leaving before he got out and headed for the door. He had no idea what his Uncle Jack wanted with James, but he was assuming he had heard about the impending wedding. Charles knew that Jack would not be happy with James marrying Helena. To Jack, she was a stripper, it didn't matter that she was only a bartender at the club; to Jack it was all the same and she would only bring shame to the family.

Charles went over and headed inside. He walked into the formal living room and saw James' head snap up and immediately saw the annoyance in his eyes. It quickly faded when he saw that it was Charles and not Jack once again.

James let out a deep sigh, as he sat back in his chair and spoke. "You missed the show."

"It looks like it was a good one. What did he want?" Charles asked, as he sat down on the couch.

"He came by to inform me that I was not allowed to marry a stripper."

"Helena isn't a stripper." Charles instantly argued.

"He didn't care for that argument. According to Jack, he is the head of this family and he has a right to do whatever he wants and what he says is final. When he walked in without knocking, I told him to knock next time. That this was my home and he couldn't walk into it whenever he wanted. He informed me that this was his home, that everything belongs to him with him being the head of the family." James said, annoyed.

"Of course he believes that. He's been blocking me from adding new insurance avenues to the company. He doesn't care it will make the company more money, all he cares about is that it wasn't his idea. He needs to be handled and removed from the company and this family. What did you tell him?"

Charles knew that James was not shy from confrontation, but Jack was his kryptonite. Ever since he had spent those two months with Jack, James has always been fearful of him and he avoided any confrontation towards Jack as much as possible. Charles knew it would be on him to protect James from Jack and fight his battles where he was concerned. That didn't bother him though, because James was not only his cousin, but his best friend. He would do anything for James.

"I stood up to him. It was hard, but I told him that this was my home and not his. That I was going to marry Helena and he was in no position to tell me what a marriage was supposed to be like. I told him he married Rosalyn because she wanted money and he wanted a woman that didn't care what he did. He wasn't impressed that I wasn't going to back down."

"Good for you though James. You haven't stood up to him since you were sixteen. He's been stepping all over you your whole life. It's about time you stood up against him." Charles said proudly.

"He didn't take it very well. After I kicked him out, he demanded that I take a DNA test. He doesn't believe that my father is my biological father." James stated still hurt and not surprised by it.

"Fuck off. I know for a fact that my aunt never cheated on him. She was madly in love with him."

Charles knew that James' parents had their ups and downs, but there was one thing crystal clear between them, they were madly in love. There was no doubt in Charles' mind that James was his cousin. It wasn't just how his aunt and uncle interacted with each other. James was a spitting image of his uncle. He even looked a bit like Jack. There was no way James was someone else's son.

"He doesn't believe so. He thinks my mother, both of our mothers, were gold diggers. He stated I had two weeks to provide proof that I went to the lab to get the DNA test done. Failure to do so and my accounts will be frozen and I will be evicted until the DNA comes back that I am a Bentley. He also stated, according to Wyatt, that if I am not a Bentley I will have to pay back every cent that I have used since I turned eighteen."

"He's just doing this to try and stall your wedding. He wants you out of the family; he always has because when I die, everything goes to you. If you aren't a Bentley, then it would all go to him. He's still pissed that my father left everything to me instead of him, like he was supposed to. He picked the lab?"

Charles wasn't all that surprised that Jack had already spoken with Wyatt about it. He wanted James out, he needed James out. It was why Charles was worried about Jack or Wyatt discovering that Jane was pregnant. There was not telling what they would do if they discovered that Charles had a pending heir to take over the family. Currently, James was set as

Charles' beneficiary to take over everything should he die. Jack needed James out of the picture so he could claim what he believed was rightfully his. Charles didn't trust Jack at all and he wouldn't put it past him to falsify the lab results

"He did, but I am going to have an outside lab connected to the court system to run the DNA test. I want to make sure whoever runs it, can't tamper with it. I know Jack will want me to not be a Bentley and he's not above changing the results to get what he wants. If it's through the court, he can't touch the results or get to a lab tech to alter the results in his favor."

James was not taking any chances with Jack or Wyatt. He was going to make sure his ass was covered, because he knew they had no problem fighting dirty.

"Good, you can use my lawyer. She hates both Jack and Wyatt and she will make sure you are protected until the results come back. Take it through the court and force Jack and Wyatt to play by the rules. She will be able to keep you protected and the results will be given directly to the court and done by a court appointed official." Charles advised.

"Jack won't like that. He wants to make this as quiet as possible." James said and Charles could tell that he was a bit nervous about upsetting Jack. It was understandable given what he had been through.

"Jack is a bully and he wants to keep abusing and controlling you. The only way you are going to be rid of him, is by showing him you won't stand for it. Do it the proper way James. Call my lawyer and have it done through the courts, it's the only way to protect yourself and Helena. You have to think about the future. If you and Helena have a child one day, you need to protect that child. Do it through the courts and screw what Jack or Wyatt has to say about it. You don't have to make it easy for him and my lawyer will make it so that you can't have your bank account frozen or be kicked out of the house. Everything that belonged to you father was left to your mother and everything of your mother's was left to you. They both died in a car crash and it all went to you. Any lawyer could argue that it is rightfully yours because it was automatically transferred to your mother when your father died."

"You're right, I didn't think of that. My father did die five minutes before my mother and not the other way around. Ok, I'll go through the courts and call your lawyer today."

James had no idea what would happen, but he had to fight. He did want a future with Helena and that included children. He had to protect his future children and his future wife from Jack.

"You gotta protect yourself James, especially because everything can change in a single second." Charles said, and James could pick up the stress within his tone.

"Has something changed with you?" James asked, concerned that him and Jane were having problems.

For the past year they seemed to be doing good. James was surprised when they returned from their honeymoon and had decided to try and have a real marriage. It was a good surprise, but it was unexpected. For the past year things between them seemed to be doing well. They had a couple of downs, but they were able to work through them. James truly believed that Charles loved Jane and they made a good couple.

"Jane is pregnant." Charles stated, as he sat back onto the couch.

"Wow." James said, completely stunned.

"Ya." Charles agreed, just as equally stunned.

"Congratulations?" James said, confused.

They had never had a conversation about having children before. Neither of them were in the position to have a child. Up until Helena, James had never been in love with a woman and Charles had never dated anyone seriously until Jane. They always wore protection so they never had to worry about having a child. James knew he would be excited to have the chance to be a real father, but Charles and his father did not have any kind of healthy relationship. It was very toxic and abusive without any physical damage done.

"She told me yesterday, she did an at home pregnancy test. We went today to see the doctor and get a real one. She told Dr. Heath that she has uterine fibroids."

"What is that?" James asked, confused.

"Benign masses in her uterus that takes blood from her body. It makes it very difficult for her to get pregnant. Dr. Heath said they would have to do an ultrasound to see how many there are and how big they are. With them she is a high risk pregnancy, she could lose the baby. Worst case scenario, they both die."

Charles was still in shock over that. He had no idea something like uterine fibroids even existed and now that he knew about them, he was terrified of what it could mean for Jane. He was in love with her and he just now discovered she had something that could be a serious medical complication in her life. He had to imagine that her health was at risk even without being pregnant. She should have told him and it hurt a great deal to know that she didn't trust him enough to tell him something this important.

"Holy shit. And she never told you?" James asked, shocked that Jane had something like that inside of her. He immediately couldn't help but wonder if it was genetic and Helena suffered from the same thing.

"First I heard of it was in the doctor's office. She should have told me. Even if she wasn't pregnant, she should have told me. I'm her husband, I have a right to know that she has a serious medical issue. She's on the pill, but if I knew she had the fibroids, we could have made sure she didn't get pregnant. We could have taken extra precautions so her life wouldn't be at risk."

"She probably figured she wouldn't be able to get pregnant. Women take birth control to help keep their hormones in balance and to help with acne. She probably never figured she would get pregnant. How does she feel about all of this?"

"I don't know. Right after the doctor's appointment she sent a text to Helena to meet up for some food. We haven't had a chance to talk. Even yesterday after she told me, she kept to herself all day. I have no idea how she is feeling or what she is thinking."

"What do you feel or think about all of this?" James asked instead.

Charles let out a sigh as he rubbed his hand over his face. He had no idea what he was feeling or thinking. He never expected to be having children. He knew he was still young enough to have them, but he just figured he would never find a woman he wanted to have children with. That wasn't a goal he had in his life. After everything that happened to him growing up, he never expected to bring a child into this world. The love he received from his grandfather meant the world to him, but he didn't believe that he himself would possess that same capability to a child.

On top of finding out that Jane was pregnant, he discovered that she could die bringing their child into the world. It was a lot to take in and he had no idea how he felt about any of this. He knew he needed to figure it out though before he went home and talked to Jane. They would need to talk about this and decide what they wanted to do. The whole situation was a mess and Charles had no idea what to do about any of this.

"I don't know James. I thought I would never have children. I figured it was better for the world if the Bentley name died with us. I can't imagine I would ever be a good father. Not after my own. I didn't even get the chance to process Jane being pregnant when the risk of her dying was put on the table. I don't know what to think or what to feel. Part of me wants her to try and have the baby only because this might be her only chance to have a child of her own. At the same time, I don't want her to. I don't want her to die. I don't want her to go through a pregnancy only to potentially lose the baby on any given day. I don't want that hurt for her."

And that was what it came down to for Charles. He didn't want Jane to be destroyed by this. He didn't want her living in fear for nine months. To have to worry about feeling sick or something not feeling right. To constantly stress over what could happen to the baby. It wasn't like they had to only make it a month or two, nine months was a ridiculously long time to live in a state of constant worry and fear. It wouldn't be healthy for her or for the baby.

"It's hard, I know. And there really isn't a clear cut answer here. You have to talk to her and see what she wants to do. She has known she wouldn't be able to get pregnant for a good chunk of her life, maybe she made peace with it and doesn't even want kids. You have no idea what she wants and you won't until you talk. But you have to be honest with her too Charles. If she decides to keep the pregnancy, she deserves to know if you are one hundred percent in or out."

James wasn't sure if Charles would be in or out. He did know though that if Jane did want to keep the pregnancy that meant that Helena would be in one hundred percent. James would need to be supportive of the both of them and be there for whenever they needed someone. Even if that meant that Charles was out, he himself couldn't be. He wasn't going to turn his back on Helena. He was all in with her and he never wanted to let her go.

"I love her. I do. I just don't know if she loves me. I don't know if she wants this marriage and if she doesn't, would having a baby really be a good idea?" Charles asked, hurt that the woman he loves didn't truly feel the same way about him.

"That's a decision you both have to come to. She's got to be confused herself and uncertain what to do. You both have gotten closer since your wedding, but you still have a long way to go. You haven't connected fully, you both still have a bit of a wall up. It's like you both are waiting for the other to throw their hands up and call quits. You need to talk it out and decide if you both want to keep being married. Then figure out if you are going to have this baby or try to. You gotta talk to her, Charles. Only the two of you can decide what happens." James said with a great deal of patience to his voice. He knew this wasn't easy for Charles.

Charles knew what James was saying was right. He was just terrified to discover what Jane's answers would be. He loved her and he wasn't certain he would be able to survive losing both of them.

CHAPTER 6

Jane sat there at the patio table at the cafe and waited for when Helena would be here. She knew she would arrive first and that was fine with her. She needed some time to herself so she could try and get her thoughts in order. She never expected to be in this position and now that she was in it, she was uncertain what to do. It wasn't helping her that she had no idea what Charles was thinking about any of this. She knew she needed to talk to him, to have an open and honest conversation, but she wasn't ready for that yet. She needed some time to get her own thoughts in order so she knew what she wanted to do. There was no point in having a potential argument over something that could be pointless. Why argue over a pregnancy if she decides to not keep the baby?

"Well, don't you look happy." Helena commented, as she sat down.

Jane let out a sigh before she spoke. "I'm drinking decaf, who couldn't be happy about that?"

"Touche. Should I take it that the doctor's appointment went well?" Helena asked, confused as to what Jane was feeling.

She had known growing up that it would be next to impossible for Jane to get pregnant. She had offered to be a surrogate for Jane one day should she find a man to love and wish to have a child with. So far that hadn't been in the cards and now that Jane was pregnant Helena wasn't certain if she was supposed to be happy with her or if she was supposed to be the realistic sister.

"He did confirm that I was pregnant. I told Dr. Heath about the fibroids and he said it would make me a high risk pregnancy. He's going to refer me to an OBGYN that specializes in high risk pregnancies. He's also going to send me for an ultrasound to see what the fibroids are like." Jane started.

"Ok, but we figured they would make you high risk. I mean, we've always been told that you couldn't get pregnant. Did he say anything about what it would be like for you?" Helena asked, looking to get all of the information that she could.

"He said that there was a low chance that I could carry to term. That if the fibroids are too big they could kill the baby or my body could reject it. He even said that if one were to burst, I could bleed out and it could kill both of us."

"So not good." Helena said, shocked that Jane's situation was more dire than she had expected.

"If the fibroids are big, he said there could be a non-invasive way to kill the blood flow to them so it would kill the fibroids, giving the baby more room. He also said though that it might be recommended by the OBGYN to terminate the pregnancy. Either way, it's going to be hard to carry to term."

Jane had been doing her best to not think about the possible outcome of having a miscarriage. That wasn't a goal she had for her life, no woman did. She was so confused about what to do. She knew what the logical thing would be, to terminate and move on, but she wasn't sure that was what she wanted to do.

"Ok, but he didn't say it would be impossible. Plus, he's not a baby doctor, he's only going by what he's read or heard. You shouldn't make any decisions until you hear it from an OBGYN. You need the ultrasound to see how bad the fibroids are to decide if it would be impossible to carry. Your OB might tell you it's possible." Helena said, trying to stay positive.

It sounded bad, yes, but they didn't have all of the information that they needed to make a reasonable and logical decision. Jane needed to wait until the OBGYN told them that she should terminate or not. Until then they needed to wait before making any decisions.

"Not likely. I mean come on Helena, I've gone a decade knowing that I would never be able to carry a baby, am I really supposed to believe that I've been given a miracle?" Jane said, skeptically.

"Who's to say you haven't? Women who are in their fifties have gone their entire adult life not being able to get pregent despite all of the unprotected sex and IVF treatments, only to wake up pregnant one day. And they have given birth to perfectly healthy babies. Women who are going through cancer treatments and pregnant deliver healthy babies. It the fibroids in you can be reduced, who's to say you can't carry to term? As long as there is room for the baby you should be ok."

Jane wasn't too sure about that. She knew miracles happen all the time. She knew that women who could never conceive a baby were able to and they got to have a healthy baby by the end of it. She also knew though, that for every success story there were ten unsuccessful stories. Ten people that lost their baby and had to go through the pain of a miscarriage or a still birth. The odds were not in her favor and Jane wasn't certain she was strong enough to handle that type of loss.

"We don't know that though. I could easily lose the baby." Jane said, refusing to allow herself to have any hope. It would be easier when the OB told her to terminate.

"I know, but you can't think worse case scenario here. You don't have enough information to do that. What about Charles? How did he take the news of you being pregnant?" Helena asked, trying to determine what support Charles will be in this.

"He was shocked, rightfully so. It didn't help that at the doctor's office he had to find out about the fibroids."

"Wait, you never told him?" Helena asked, shocked.

"No, we've never had that conversation before. I didn't see the point. I figured we would be getting divorced in a year and there was no need to inform him of my medical history."

Jane did feel bad for not informing Charles about the fibroids before today. She honestly didn't think it would be relevant though to their situation. Even though they had agreed to give their marriage a real shot for the year, that didn't mean they would still be together by the end of it. Jane had been holding part of herself back for the past year, because she wasn't sure if they would be together after their first year. She didn't want to lose Charles. She didn't want to love him and then have to say goodbye. The result was her holding pieces of herself back and keeping Charles at arm's length.

"Jane, you should have told him. If nothing else you should have told him before you went to the doctors. That's not fair to ambush him like that. How did he handle it?"

"I don't know. We didn't talk about any of it yet. I asked him to drop me off here. I don't know how he feels about any of this, about the baby or what could happen. After I told him yesterday, I went into my room and stayed there."

"You need to talk to him Hun."

"I know, I know I have to. I just needed time to process all of this myself before I add in what his thoughts and feelings are. I don't even know if he wants to have a baby. He's thirty-five, almost thirty-six, and he doesn't have a baby yet. I have to think he doesn't want one. He certainly wasn't excited about it yesterday when I told him. What if he doesn't want this baby?" Jane asked as the tears built in her eyes.

Helena spoke as she reached over and placed her hand overtop of Jane's. "No matter what happens you will always have me in your life. If Charles doesn't want to have a baby you'll be ok. I will help you and be there for you at every step of the way. It has to be his choice if he wants to be involved. Just like it has to be your choice what you wish to do with your body. It's your choice if you want to have this baby or not. You can get his opinions, but at the end of the day it is your body and you have the final say."

Jane could feel the worry starting to reduce. Being around Helena had a way of making her feel better. Helena always knew what she needed to hear to make her feel better and this was exactly what she needed to hear.

"You're right, thank-you." Jane said with a warm smile.

"Anytime. You gotta talk to Charles and then don't make any decisions until you hear from your OB. There's no point in jumping off a cliff that might not even be on fire." Helena said with a wink.

"I'll talk to him when I get back. We need to hash this out. I can't keep letting it drag on, that isn't going to do either of us any good." Jane wiped at the few tears that ran down her cheeks before she spoke again. "Ah, stupid hormones. Ok tell me about your day."

Jane needed a change in conversation. She needed to get her mind off of everything baby related.

"When I left Jack was about to come over. I asked if James wanted me to stay, but he said he could handle him. I'm worried that I am going to get home to find James curled up into a ball on the couch." Helena said half-joking, but Jane could tell she was seriously worried about that possible outcome.

"God, what did that jackass want?"

Jack and Wyatt were a serious pain in her ass. Thankfully for the past year they had basically left her and Charles alone. They were surprisingly not fighting them in court over the money. Charles was relieved, but Jane suspected something else was going on. No one just let's billions of dollars slip through their fingers.

"I don't know. James suspected he heard about our wedding and I'm guessing he wasn't coming by to congratulate us. I'll get the full story from James when I get back. I'm just worried about him. He had a hard time with Jack when he was sixteen. He had to go and live with him for two months in the summer as a consequence of rebelling. Ever since then he's been afraid of him. I think Jack abused him, but James has never talked about it. I'm trying to respect his pace."

"I'm sorry to hear that, that's too bad. I haven't heard much about Jack from Charles, but I know Charles' father wasn't very loving himself. I don't think he was ever hit, but the mental and emotional abuse is still pretty evident in him. It's what makes me think he might not want a child. I don't know. All I know is these Bentley boys have got us running ragged."

"God, who would have thought that we would be here at any point in our lives? One of us married and knocked up by a rich socialite and the other about to marry the cousin. What the hell happened to us?" Helena said jokingly.

"You got attacked at a strip club and I said yes to marrying a stranger. We're either very stupid or very adventuerous, I'm not really sure which one it is right now."

"It's been one hell of a year though. Plus, there's been some epic sex." Helena said with a smirk.

"That does make up for a lot of it." Jane easily agreed, her own smile touching his face.

The sex was epic with Charles. The best she had ever had and that did not go away after the honeymoon. That was how she was currently in her predicament of being pregnant. Leave it to Charles Bentley to be the one man to get an infertal woman pregnant. Jane had no idea what she was going to do, but she did know what she had to do. She had to talk to Charles and see what his thoughts and feelings were on the matter. Afterwards she would take Helena's advice and wait to see what her OBGYN said about her odds. Only then would she be able to make an informed decision. Jane was just hoping she wouldn't allow herself to develop any hope between now and then.

CHAPTER 7

Jane let out a long breath as she walked into the house. *The house and not home, I really have to figure this out.* Jane thought to herself. She had to decide a lot in her life. She needed to decide if she was going to divorce her husband. She needed to decide if she was going to have this baby or not. Plus, she needed to decide if she was going to have this baby even if Charles didn't want one. It was a mess, her life was a mess and in between it all she had a non-profit to run, plus her last year of school. It would be insane to try and do it pregnant, but Jane wasn't certain she wanted to terminate even if the OBGYN said it was best. She needed time to get her thoughts in order, but she couldn't start to do that until she knew what Charles wanted.

Jane made her way through the house until she found Charles sitting outside on the bench overlooking the pond. She knew he went there when he needed time and space to think something through. Jane knew she caught him off guard with her fibroids, but she honestly never thought it would be an issue. She didn't expect for them to be married longer than a year. She never thought they would have to have a conversation like this. Jane went and sat down next to Charles on the bench and waited to see if he would speak first. When he didn't Jane broke first.

"I'm sorry."

"For getting pregnant or not telling me you have a serious medical condition?" Charles asked in a calm voice.

"I never thought it would be an issue. We went into this believing we would be together for a year. I didn't see the need to tell you something that personal when in a year we would be divorced and living our own lives." Jane calmly explained.

Charles turned to look at her as he spoke. "And I understand that for the first six months maybe. I thought what we have was real. It stopped being a countdown to me months ago. I thought we were two married people living our lives together. I didn't know there was still a clock on our marriage."

"You don't want a divorce?" Jane asked, surprised. She thought that Charles would have wanted a divroce. That he would have wanted to live his single bachelor life once again.

"Jane, I am madly in love with you. I know you don't feel the same, and that's ok. But the very last thing I want is a divorce."

Charles knew that Jane didn't love him. He knew that she was still uncertain about their marriage and if they should be together. He had been hoping that they would be able to keep being married and eventually Jane would loosen up enough to allow herself to love him. Now though, Charles wasn't so sure. Jane couldn't help but be surprised. She thought that Charles would want a divroce, but now she was discovering that he didn't. He had also never told her that he loved her before. It warmed her heart to hear, but at the same time it saddened her because he knew she wasn't at the love stage yet. She had been keeping herself closed off, afraid to let this marriage become real. She was afraid he didn't love her and wanted his old life back.

"I thought you would want to go back to your old life. To be a carefree bachelor again. I've been keeping myself closed off so I would be ready for it. I didn't know you felt differently."

"I don't miss my old lifestyle. You have opened my eyes to the world Jane. I don't want pointless one-night stands. I want to share a life with you. I don't regret marrying you. This year has been the best year of my life and I would love many more to come. I want honesty, I want to know the good parts and the bad parts. I want clean and I want the messy. I want you, one hundred percent, you. I'm all in Kitten."

It warmed Jane's heart to hear that Charles didn't want a divroce or to run away. That he wanted the real her, one hundred percent. It made her feel better and she could admit to herself that she lost a small piece of her heart to him at this moment. He wanted her, but she had no idea if he wanted her and a baby. There was one question she had on her mind first though.

"Why do you call me Kitten?"

Jane had been wondering that from the moment he first called her it in the airport hotel room. It was different. Most people called someone Baby or Sweetheart, they didn't tend to go with Kitten. Jane wasn't sure how she felt about it yet. She wasn't sure if he meant it as a possessive thing, like she was his pet.

"I've never officially dated a woman before, but the women I have been with I've called them Baby or Babe, mostly because I could never remember their names. You are special Jane, you shouldn't be called something that I would call a one-night stand that means nothing to me." Charles said with a warmth to his voice that made Jane's heart flutter.

She couldn't help the small smile that touched her lips at hearing Charles' explanation. It warmed her heart to hear that he was calling her Kitten because it was special, because she was special. It wasn't meant as a possessive term or label on her.

"I'm sorry I haven't been more open with you. I didn't know you were taking this that seriously or wanted for this to continue on after the year. I haven't been very fair to you. I've been keeping walls up and not allowing you to get close to me. That's not fair to you and I'm sorry." Jane said honestly.

"It's ok, I know our marriage was untraditional. There's no guide book on how to handle being married to a complete stranger. Neither one of us expected very much from this marriage when I proposed the idea of it. There's going to be bumps along the way and I'm ok with that. I want this to work, but it'll only work if we both wish for our marriage to continue. What do you want Jane?" Charles asked with complete patience to his voice.

That was the million dollar question to Jane. She wasn't sure if she wanted this marriage to work or not. It was no longer simple, she was pregnant and she might decide to try and have this baby. Charles wanted her, but did he really want a child to go with it? And if he did, could Jane give up her one shot at having a biological child for a man?

"It's not simple anymore. I'm pregnant, that makes everything complicated."

"I know it does. How are you feeling about it?"

"I don't know yet. I'm still processing it all I think. Helena suggested that I shouldn't make a decision until I've spoken with the OBGYN after getting the ultrasounds. That it would be best to wait to hear from a specialist what she believes would be best."

"I think that's a good idea. Only, it's not you. It's us, we will go and speak with her and we will decide what to do. You aren't in this alone Kitten and I am not about to let you be. We'll figure it all out. We don't have to make any decisions right now, we shouldn't. We should wait for all of the information first before making an informed decision."

Charles also needed time himself to still process and determine what he was feeling and wanting to do about the baby. He knew it was Jane's body, it was her ultimate decision, but he wanted to be able to give his thoughts on the matter. He wanted to be able to help her come to a final decision and in order for him to do that he needed to know exactly what he was feeling. He needed all of the information as well before he could help Jane decide what the right move would be for her and for them.

"What do we do now?" Jane asked, sounding lost.

Charles didn't have the answer she was looking for, it was impossible to give, so he decided to try and lighten up the mood.

"We could go and have sex." He said with a flirty smirk.

Jane's shocked face had Charles laughing and she playfully pushed him away.

"What? It's not like you could get more pregnant." Charles countered.

"Typical man." Jane said with a shake of her head, but Charles could see the smile on her face and it was all worth it.

He placed his arm around her shoulders and brought her in to him. Jane instantly curled against Charles' chest as he spoke.

"We will figure it all out Kitten, I promise."

Jane wasn't too sure how they would be figuring everything out, but she did feel a bit better knowing that Charles was serious about their marriage. Maybe they would be able to work it all out. Maybe a bit of hope wouldn't destroy her.

CHAPTER 8

James was currently in the kitchen working on making dinner for the both of them when the front odor opened and Helena walked in. She had been out with Jane for the majority of the afternoon. She wanted to make sure she felt better before she headed home to Charles. Helena was hoping that her and Charles were able to have a civil and decent conversation about all of this and not a screaming match or Jane ignoring him all night. Helena was hoping that the next time they spoke Jane would be feeling better about her current position.

"Hey Babe." James said, as Helena went over and placed a quick kiss to James' lips.

"Hey, what are you making?"

"I am going to grill up some chicken and vegetables. The grill is already heating up. How was Jane?"

Helena let out a puff of air, as she leaned her back against the kitchen counter. "Confused. Honestly, she was a hot mess."

"Can't say I blame her. It's one hell of a shock. I have to imagine it was more of a shock to her than normal with being told she was infertile practically." James grabbed the plate and headed out to place the food on the grill.

He didn't have a barbeque before. It was something that went against what he was raised into believing fit within the high society lifestyle. That first spring that him and Helena had been dating he purchased his first barbecue and they had been using it every other day. James was a huge fan of barbeque and he was very happy that Helena was as well. They used it more than they did the oven.

"It's a huge shock. We were always told it would never happen for her. When we did find out about it ten years ago, I had told her if she ever found a man and wanted to have a baby that I would be her surrogate. We never expected this."

"Do you have fibroids?" James asked, slightly worried for Helena's health.

"No, I don't. I could develop them later on in life, but currently I am cleared. I have no medical issues or I would have told you. I could not believe that Jane hadn't mentioned it to Charles. You don't have any medical conditions that I should know about?"

"I do not. I am perfectly healthy. And it's a relief to hear that you are as well. How is Jane handling the news?" James asked, as he grabbed them both a beer.

"She's trying not to spiral but I can tell she is getting close to it. I told her to wait until the ultrasound was completed and she heard from her OBGYN before making any decision. She doesn't think she'll be able to have the baby, but she might be able to."

"Could she?" James asked, confused. He wasn't sure how any of this worked, but he wasn't a doctor. He wouldn't want any woman to go through the traumatic experience of losing a baby, especially his soon to be sister in-law.

"I don't know. That's for the OB to decide. But, women have children all the time that are high risk. Women with fibroids have had children. She might be able to carry to term or close enough for the baby to be viable. We won't know until the OBGYN has a chance to review the ultrasound and see what her prognosis is."

"I would have to imagine Jane wouldn't be the only woman to have a baby in her position. I agree though, it would be best for her to wait until she hears from the specialist and then make an informed decision."

"How is Charles feeling about it?"

That was something James wasn't too sure about himself. He knew that Charles didn't have a good childhood, especially once his grandfather passed. Children weren't something that Charles had wanted and he wasn't sure how well he was going to handle all of this going on. James knew he would be there for the both of them, he just hoped that Charles could come around to the idea of them having a baby and being ok with it.

"I'm not sure Charles knows how he is feeling about the situation. You have to understand, Charles didn't have a loving childhood. His relationship with his father was toxic and emotionally abusive. He's always been worried about becoming his father and that fear had made him extra cautious with having children. It's not that he won't be happy about having a baby if it goes that way, it's just going to take him a bit to come around to being happy."

Helena couldn't be mad at Charles for that. She had suspected that things in Charles' childhood had been hard because she knew some of what James had told her about his own. She could understand how hard it might be for someone, for a man, to have a child after a hard childhood themselves. Men look up to their father's and use their own experiences to know how to be a man and a father themselves. That becomes extremely difficult if your own father was not someone to look up to. She was hoping that if Jane did decide to keep the baby that Charles would be able to come around and be supportive of it. Their marriage was still up in the air and they needed to figure out what they both wanted in order for it to all work out.

"Do you think he will be if they can keep the pregnancy?"

"I think with time he will be happy and I think he would make a great dad. He knows what makes a terrible father, he just has to do the opposite and he'll be great. He'll come around to the idea of it all once he has some time to process it and gets all of the information." James said confidently in Charles' defense.

"If you think so. I hope that is the case. I hope they can both have this baby and everything works out. I truly believe Jane loves him, she's just afraid to admit it to herself currently."

"He loves her. For the first time in his life he is in love with a woman. Charles isn't about to let her slip through his fingers. They'll be fine." James said confidently.

Helena truly hoped that would be the case. She didn't want Jane to have to raise a baby on her own or go through losing a baby on her own. She was truly hoping that their marriage would work and they could be parents. She decided to change the conversation's focus onto him.

"How was your meeting with Jack?"

James scoffed as he answered. "I hate that man."

Helena reached out and took James' hand in her own as she spoke. "What happened Babe?"

James let out a slow breath to calm his emotions before he spoke. "He heard that we were getting married. I knew he would eventually, but I didn't think it would be this soon. He came in here acting as if he owned our home. When I told him he had to knock, he told me he was the head of this family and could do whatever he wanted. He doesn't want me to marry you. He believes that you are not good enough and are only marrying me for my money."

"Pot meet kettle." Helena instantly said.

"That's basically what I told him. That his wife was a gold digger and only married him for his money. Just like he only married her because she always said yes in the bedroom. He didn't believe it was the same thing. I told him I was marrying you and there was nothing he could do about it. He wasn't too happy about it."

"Well, it's a good thing that he isn't invited to the wedding." Helena said with a warm smile.

When they had decided to get married they both agreed that they wanted it to be small and intimate. They didn't want a large group of people that didn't care for their marriage or even know Helena. They had seen what it was like for Jane and Charles and neither wanted that. The first people to be banned from their wedding was Jack and Rosalyn, followed very quickly by Wyatt.

"That's not all he wanted to talk about." James started and Helena cut him off with a deep worry to her voice.

"He didn't find out about the baby right?"

"No, no, he doesn't know anything about that and as long as we are all careful he never will until the baby is born." James knew eventually Jack and Wyatt would discover that Jane was pregnant or that she had a baby. James was going to make sure to prolong that for as long as possible for everyone's benefits. "He wants me to take a DNA test."

"Wait, what?" Helena asked, confused.

James was thirty-six years old, why in the world would he have to take a DNA test? It made no sense to Helena and it seemed like Jack was just looking to cause him harm. It pissed Helena off that Jack was pulling this crap now. If Jack doubted that James was his cousin, then he should have said something when James was younger. Not after James had been raised by his parents and was thirty-six years old. Helena knew that Jack was only doing this to hurt James.

"He doesn't believe that my mother was faithful to my father. He wants me to do a DNA test to prove that I am a Bentley."

"He doesn't have any right to demand that." Helena instantly said, as she crossed her arms and leaned against the counter.

"Legally he has every right to demand a DNA test for anyone that has inherited or set to inherit money from the family. Any family does and it is common practice within high society to have heirs tested to prove that they are rightfully entitled to the money. He already reached out to a lab and has dictated that if I do not get the test done within the next two weeks, and provide proof that I did the test, our bank accounts will be frozen and we will be evicted until the results come back."

James was upset about it, but he had time to calm down and think it all through. Talking to Charles had helped and he had called his lawyer and she was making it so the test would be done through the courts so Jack couldn't forge the results. He also knew that Jack was not going to be happy when he received the paperwork in the mail. He wanted to do this quietly and James had no obligation to do things how Jack wanted. He was well within his rights to go through the proper channels.

"Fuck off. He just wants the money. He doesn't care about you or about your father. He's just a money hungry piece of crap and thinks he can force you to do whatever he wants."

Helena was pissed. It wasn't bad enough that Jack had abused James when he was a teenager, but he wanted to humiliate James like this by forcing him to take a DNA test. He wasn't forcing Charles to take a test. It was as if Jack had given up on trying to get the fortune that Charles inherited and has now turned his attention towards James' money.

James went over and placed his hands on Helena's arms and ran them up and down as he spoke. "I know. I know he's after the money and not just our's but the money that I would inherit should Charles die. Right now it is set up for me to inherit everything from Charles, including his fifty percent controlling share within the company. He wants all of the money and the power and he will never get it if everything is left to me."

"Ok, but that doesn't even make sense. Jack is what, fifty-seven? He'll be in his seventies before Charles is even in his fifties. He'll be dead long before Charles. What's the point in any of this? Besides, even if Charles did die first, wouldn't everything just automatically go to Jane?"

Helena could understand if they were all close in age, but Jack would never outlive Charles. Charles would have to die in some accident or a terminal illness. Chances are Jack would be dead long before Charles was.

"Charles has a will and it still states that it all goes to me. He has stipulations within it though that Jane would get so much a year. He did it that way to protect her from Jack and Wyatt trying to go after the money. If it all goes to me, there's nothing they could do. If the baby is born, then he will change it so it reflects the baby. Should he die before the child is eighteen, it will go to me and then be transferred to the child."

"So they would still be taken care of?" Helena asked, looking for confirmation.

"Completely, yes. Charles loves Jane and he wants to make sure she is taken care of even after he dies. As for Jack, he wants money, power and control over everything. He was supposed to inherit half of what Henry, Charles' grandfather, possessed. However, when Charles was born he changed it and left everything to Jacob. Then within Jacob's will, everything was supposed to go to Jack, but Jacob changed it without anyone knowing so Charles would inherit everything. Jack has been trying to get his hands on his father's money for decades now. He believes he was robbed of what was rightfully his with him being the oldest and he has been chasing it ever since." James explained.

"Selfish prick. And now he is trying to steal from you. Isn't there something that we can do to stop him?" Helena was not about to let Jack try and take advantage of James, not while she was still breathing.

"I've spoken with Charles and he provided me with his lawyer's number. I have already reached out to her. I was originally going to do the test and Jack's lab as well as one of my own to ensure he didn't try and forge the results. However, Charles was able to get me to agree to doing it through the court. Our lawyer is already drawing up the paperwork to do the DNA test through the courts and it will ensure that Jack won't be able to do anything to our accounts or evict us while we wait for the results."

Helena couldn't help the very tiny smile. James always said ours and not mine. It was something he had always done with her once they were serious. James wanted to make sure that Helena knew what was his was hers and Helena made sure James knew that what she had also belonged to him.

"This is bullshit. He's almost sixty, shouldn't he be out playing golf and living in Florida?"

James couldn't help but chuckle at that image. He wrapped his arms around Helena as he spoke. "The day Jack moves to Florida to live out his retirement is the day I go into work completely nude."

"Ooh, now that is a sight I would like to see." Helena said with a big flirty smile.

"You could see that right now." James said, as his hands traveled down Helena's back to her butt.

"But dinner." Helena playfully argued.

"It cooks itself. We've got plenty of time to enjoy dessert first." James said, as he brought his lips closer to her's.

"I've always had a sweet tooth." Helena said, as she closed the gap between their lips.

Helena had no idea what the future was going to hold for any of this, but what she did know was that she could handle it with James by her side.

CHAPTER 9

It was ten days later when Jane and Charles found themselves sitting in another doctor's office. Today they were meeting with Dr. Heather Roberts to see what the prognosis of Jane's pregnancy would be. They had spent the past ten days both doing their best to not think about what the possible outcome could be for Jane's pregnancy. It was hard though, for the both of them. They were stuck in this limbo area where they had no idea if they should be preparing for parenting or if they need to be prepared for a loss. Charles had been trying his best to be supportive of Jane during this time, but he wasn't sure what to do exactly. He had no idea what it was like to be a good father. He had no idea what it was like to be a good parent, period. He didn't have any role models in his life that he could look up to. That he could use as an example of what a good parent was. He only had negative influences. All he knew was what didn't make a good parent. Charles knew what James had said made sense. If he knew what a bad parent was, then he could do the opposite, but it wasn't that simple. He knew what the opposite was, but he didn't know how to do it.

Charles knew after this they would be talking over the results and trying to determine what the best action plan would be. Charles honestly didn't know where Jane was standing with any of this and that wasn't helping. They needed to have a real and honest conversation, but he was afraid of what that conversation would lead to. He didn't want to lose Jane. He didn't want her to die. He didn't want her to leave him. He had told her that he loved her, he meant every word of it, but he also knew that she didn't say it back. He knew she didn't love him, he was't even certain she liked him outside of the sex. It was a hard place for him to be in, because he was also in limbo where his marriage was concerned. He wanted her to trust him. He wanted Jane to be all in with him and for them to truly try to make something together. He just wasn't certain that was what she wanted. They were going to be in for a very long conversation after this meeting and Charles wasn't too sure he was prepared for it.

The door to the room opened and Dr. Roberts walked in. She gave them both a warm friendly smile as she spoke. "Good morning. I am Dr. Roberts and I will be taking on your pregnancy with you. How are you feeling Mrs. Bentley?"

There's a loaded question. Jane thought to herself. Physically, she was exhausted, her boobs hurt and she was throwing up at least three times every single morning. She had been trying to focus on her non-profit business plus school, all the while she was having to fight an endless nausea that never seemed to go away fully. She was exhausted all the time and some days it had been a true effort for her to get out of bed at all. She had known friends that were pregnant and they experienced the same things, so Jane knew it was common and not something that she needed to be alarmed about. Still it was taking everything out of her and she didn't have the time to spend being sick in bed. She had a lot she needed to focus on. She had her last year of school to finish up and she was getting her non profit up and growing. She had been doing really well over the past year with getting her life started. For the first time in her adult life Jane had been able to focus on her schooling and her future without having to balance multiple jobs. Now, she was worried it would all be for nothing if she lost it because she was pregnant.

That wasn't even including how she was doing mentally and emotionally with this situation. She was constantly worried that something was going to go wrong. She was constantly afraid every minute of the day that she would miscarry. She was stressed about how Charles was feeling about the pregnancy. What she would do if she did decide to roll the dice on this pregnancy and Charles didn't want a baby. The unknown of everything was not helping her to feel any better about any of this. When a woman discovers she is pregnant, it's supposed to be the happiest time of her life and yet all Jane could do was worry and stress over it.

"Fine, thank-you." Jane answered automatically. She was far from fine, but that seemed to be the best answer she could give.

"She's been very tired and nauseous." Charles answered.

He had been very worried about Jane and he had ben keeping an extremely close eye on her. He had been working from the house for the past ten days just so he could be there for Jane. He knew she was trying her best and keeping to herself. He could tell that she didn't want to be perceived as weak or needing support from anyone. Her walls were making it even harder for him to get close to her and help her. It was something that would quickly grow from annoyance to frustration.

"That is very common for the first trimester. I know it's not fun, but it should pass once you are within the second trimester. Now, I say should, because some women experience morning sickness all throughout their pregnancy. It really depends on how your body handles it. There are some remedies that you can do though to help minimize it. We can go over that as well." Dr. Roberts said with a warm smile.

"Is there a point?" Jane couldn't help but ask.

Dr. Roberts was talking as if Jane could carry to term and Jane knew that wasn't likely. She was going to lose this baby and there was nothing she could do about it. She had been told that ten years ago, she had made peace with it.

"I have your medical file and I do see that approximately ten years ago you were told by a Dr. Arthur that you had uterine fibroids and you were infertile, or close to it. The problem with seeing a doctor at a free clinic, they see hundreds of people in a twelve hour day. When you have a specialist like myself, you can get the true picture." Dr. Roberts started.

721

"Are you saying she doesn't have fibroids?" Charles asked, confused as to why Dr. Roberts was saying these things.

"She has fibroids. There is a small one in Jane's uterus off to the left side, it is approximately two millimeters. It's very smal. You have fibroids though in both of your ovaries. And that is what Dr. Arthur failed to explain to you. The chances of you becoming pregnant are abysmal. This pregnancy is as close to a medical miracle as you can get. Your eggs can barely get through to your fallopian tubes because of the fibroids. However, your uterus is fine."

"Wait, are you saying I can have this baby?" Jane asked, shocked.

She had to be hearing the doctor wrong. There was no way she could be able to carry a baby to term. She had been told she would never be able to have children. For ten years she had made peace with the fact that she would have to adopt or use a surrogate to have a child. It hurt, she had cried herself to sleep plenty of nights as her heart tried to heal itself. Now another doctor was telling her she could actually have this baby. That this could be her own chance to have a child.

"I am telling you that your uterus is more than fit enough to carry the baby to term. I can't tell you what to do Jane. All I can do is provide you with the information so you can make an informed decision. Your ovaries are filled with fibroids, but your uterus only has a very small one. If you want a biological child, then in my medical opinion this is your only chance to carry the baby yourself. If you wish to have more children or now isn't the time, but you still want to have a baby down the road, we can take your eggs and freeze them. That is a conversation we can have as well."

"But she can have the baby without the risk of them dying?" Charles asked, shocked as well.

This wasn't the news that they had been expecting to hear. Charles was fully prepared to hear that Jane would need to terminate the pregnancy and he would be there for her. He was expect to have to take care of her and hold her while she grieved. He wasn't expecting that she would be able to have the baby. That there was a chance they could both live.

"Absolutely. Obviously, there are risks with every pregnancy and we all need to be careful. However, there aren't any added risks to Jane over your average woman. Jane's body is more than capable of carrying to term." Dr. Roberts said with a warm smile.

"What um... what happens now then?" Jane asked, as she tried to get her thoughts in order. This was a lot to take in and she was not expecting any of it.

"Well, you have a decision to make. Based on the ultrasound you are six weeks pregnant. You have six more weeks before your window closes for termination. If you decide to continue on with the pregnancy, I will keep you on my service instead of transferring you to another OBGYN. We will keep a close eye on you, but there is nothing within the ultrasound that gives me any cause for concern. Until you decide on what you would like to do, it would be best for you to take a prenatal vitamin just in case you do decide to continue with your pregnancy."

"So I can have this baby?" Jane asked, looking to hear it again.

Dr. Roberts went and took Jane's hand in her own as she spoke. "Jane, you can have a beautiful, healthy baby. You are not high risk. Your body can handle going through a pregnancy. If keeping this baby is what you wish to do, then we can make that happen. It's your decision and it is not a decision you need to make right this moment. You have some time to think about it."

Jane gave a distant nod and Dr. Roberts moved back as she spoke again. "I will set an appointment for you for six weeks from now. If I don't hear from you before then. Take all the time you need to think everything over. This is a major life decision and should not be taken lightly. Feel free to call me if you have any further questions or concerns."

"Thank-you Dr. Roberts." Charles said on their behalf.

"I'll see you both in six weeks." Dr. Roberts said with a warm smile before she opened the door and headed out.

Charles looked over at Jane and he could see she was trying to process everything that she had just learnt. It was a lot to take in for himself he couldn't imagine how hard it was for Jane currently. He knew she would need some time to process the new information before they would be able to have a conversation about this. He was hoping though that they could once they arrived home. Charles didn't want to draw this out. He couldn't handle another ten days wondering they they were going to try and have a baby. He needed to know what Jane wanted so he could prepare himself for it. Charles stood and went over and placed a hand on the small of Jane's back as he spoke.

"Come on Kitten, let's head home."

Jane wordlessly stood up and allowed herself to be guided out of the doctor's office and into the car.

CHAPTER 10

The whole car ride home Jane didn't say a single word. Charles had wanted to give her time for her mind to process the new and unexpected information they received from Dr. Roberts. Jane had appreciated the quiet. She was in a state of shock, she knew that. It was a lot for her to take in and she had not been expecting that. Jane had been mentally prepared to hear that she would need to terminate the pregnancy. She had not been expecting to be told that she could give birth to a healthy baby. She had gone ten years having been told that she could never have a child. That her uterus had too many fibroids. Only to discover that now her free clinic doctor hadn't read her ultrasound correctly, or he didn't care to even properly look at it. Her ovaries were filled with fibroids and that was what was causing her to be unable to have a child. Yet, here she was six weeks pregnant and Jane couldn't stop thinking about how this could be her one and only chance.

When they pulled up to the house Jane still wasn't ready for the inevitable conversation. She knew they had to have it. They couldn't keep putting this off. They had to be adults about this and have an open and honest conversation. Jane knew it was on her that they hadn't already had this conversation. She wasn't ready for it and she wasn't ready for what Charles could say. Jane wasn't certain that she loved him, but she did know that it hurt when she thought about losing him. She didn't want him to walk away and she was terrified that this would make him walk away. He had said he was all in, but that was when they both believed she would lose the baby. Now she could actually have it and Jane knew that could change everything.

They headed inside and Jane made her way into the kitchen. She wasn't hungry nor thirsty, but having this conversation in the parlour or formal living room didn't feel right. She didn't want this conversation to feel like a business meeting. She wanted it more personal and casual. Jane went and sat down on one of the bar stools at the island counter as Charles spoke.

"Are you hungry? Do you want something to drink?"

"No, I'm alright. We should talk."

Jane was dreading this conversation, had been since two little plus signs appeared on that stick. There was no going back now though, they had to be adults and have this conversation. Jane needed to know what Charles felt and thought so she could make her own plans.

"We should." Charles agreed, but he didn't sit down nor continue. He just stood there on the opposite side of the island counter looking at Jane.

Charles had no idea what he was going to do. He had a feeling he knew what Jane wanted. She had been told for ten years she couldn't have a child. Only to now be told that the one time she got pregnant it was a medical miracle and would be the only chance she had of having her own child. No woman would turn that down, Charles knew that. Still, he had no idea what to tell her. What to say to her when she asked what he wanted to do. It was her body, she had the final say, but that didn't mean that he was off the hook for it. Charles had to decide if he was going to be a father or walk away from the women he loves and their unborn child. It was not a position he ever thought he would be in. He had always been careful with the women he slept with. He made sure they would never get pregnant and with Jane he had gotten sloppy. He had gotten comfortable and now Jane was pregnant with his child.

Charles knew this should be a happy and joyous moment for them. They both just discovered that their unborn baby had a real chance of seeing this world. They should be celebrating and yet Charles was filled with uncertainty and fear. He knew he had to try and push his own fears and insecurities down though, because he wanted Jane to be happy and excited. This

726

was going to be her only chance of getting to be pregnant and he wanted to make sure she got to experience the full joy of the milestone.

"I know we haven't spoken about this that we wanted to wait until we had all of the information. I know this information was not what we were expecting. How do you feel about all of this?" Jane started.

"Surprised. I had been expecting her to inform us that it would be too dangerous. I was not expecting to discover that the fibroids were located in your ovaries. That had to come as a shock to you." Charles said, trying to get a read on Jane so he knew how to react. He wanted to be supportive, she was the woman he loved, but he also didn't want to talk about how he was feeling right now. He needed more time.

"It feels unreal. When I went to the free clinic when I was twenty it was because I was having a lot of pain across my lower abdomen. Dr. Arthur had me do an ultrasound and told me it was fibroids, that there was nothing they could do. That I would have to deal with the pain for the rest of my life. That I would never be able to have a baby. Helena had offered to be my surrogate should I wish to have a baby when I got older. It just became a part of my life."

"And now you know the truth. Do they still hurt you?" Charles had no idea that Jane had been in pain from the fibroids. He was now worried that she had been in pain for the past year and he never noticed.

"I'm used to it. I take a couple of over the counter pain pills once a day and it helps to make it better. If it's really bad I'll put some heat on my one side to help. I've gotten used to it. The only way to fix it would be to have surgery to remove my ovaries, but most doctors don't want to do that with someone my age. Not to mention it's expensive. I've just lived with it for the past decade." Jane said with a small shrug.

"I wish you had told me. We could have gone to a specialist and seen what we could have done to take the pain away. I know you have been used to only having a small amount of money. Of not being able to have extra set aside for emergencies. However, that's not the case anymore. We could have gotten you in to see a doctor, we could have gotten the surgery for you so you won't be in pain Kitten."

Charles hated that Jane didn't disclose this to him. They could have prevented her from being in pain. He knew that meant she wouldn't be pregnant, but they could have done something different. She didn't have to be in pain every day for the past year.

"I'm used to it. And if I had, then I wouldn't be pregnant right now." Jane said with a small shrug.

"That is true. How are you feeling about all of this?"

"I think I'm still in shock. This was not what I was expecting at all today. I think it's a good shock though. I know we've never spoken about children. We thought this would be a year and then we would be out. I don't know if you want kids or not and if you don't it's ok. I have to have this baby though. This could be my only shot, I have to take it."

Jane had no idea how Charles would feel about any of this. If he wanted to be a father or not, but she had to do this. She had to take her chance, because it was going to be the only chance she had. She couldn't let it slip through her fingers. Especially now that she knew she could have a healthy pregnancy. There was no way she could give this chance up, give this baby up. If Charles didn't want anything to do with her or the baby, she wasn't going to hold it against him. She would get her own two bedroom home and she would raise this baby. She was going to love her child and she was not going to allow this opportunity to pass her by.

"I know you do. I understand why you want to have this baby. I didn't expect anything less. My concern was losing you both, but now we know it is safe for you to be pregnant. I completely understand why you want to have the baby. And I will be here to support you through this."

Charles knew Jane was going to want to have this child. It wasn't surprising at all and this was her only chance to have her own child. He loved her and despite the fact that he held zero interest in having children, or that he thought he would make a terrible father, he also loved Jane. He didn't want to lose her so he would need to figure out how to handle this new life. He needed to figure out how to be a father, when he had no interest in being one. It was going to be difficult, but at least he had nine months to figure it all out.

"But do you want children?" Jane asked, noticing that Charles didn't seem excited for this.

"Children were never in my plans, no. However, I didn't have any plans to marry either and I am glad that I did. This will be an adjustment for myself, but I will get there. We have nine months to both be ready for a baby."

Jane knew this was unexpecting, but she couldn't help but feel like Charles didn't really want her to be pregnant. She suspected he didn't have plans for children in his life. He was thirty-six and up until a year ago he was sleeping with anything that had two legs practically. He wasn't looking to settle down with a wife and a few kids. She understood that going into the marriage. The problem was, she wasn't expecting to come out of it pregnant. Jane had always figured that when she got to have children it would be with a man that she loved and wanted to start a family with her. Not a man that she married for convenience, on both of their parts, and was planning to be divorced after a year. The situation was a mess, but she couldn't hold it against Charles for not being excited about a baby. Jane wasn't certain if they would stay together after this, but she could give him the chance to try and adjust to their new situation.

"I know this is a huge adjustment for you to make. It's not something either of us ever expected to happen. I want you to know though, at any point should you wish to not be involved, I'll understand. You don't owe me or the baby anything Charles. I'm not going to take you to court and sue for child support or anything like that. If you want off the hook at any point, all you have to do is tell me. I won't be upset or judge you. I'll get my own place and live my life and you will get to go back to living yours." Jane said with complete understanding to her voice.

Charles could appreciate Jane offering him a way out. Most women, especially within his social circle, would not have offered him an out. Or if they did it would be connected to a very large sum of money to make them go away. Jane was offering him a way out, a clean and full way out without having to worry about making payments or giving her hush money. She simply wanted to make sure that he wanted to have a child in his life. He loved her, he loved her deeply. Jane was the first woman that Charles had ever loved. He was worried though that he would let her down. That he would let her and the baby down. He didn't think he would be a good father. He didn't know if he could handle changing diapers and being up all night with a sick baby or a screaming baby. He knew Jane wouldn't tolerate the idea of having a live-in nanny. It would be on them and that made Charles very nervous.

He had nine months to wrap his head around things, but he wasn't too certain he would be ready in nine months. He had to try and figure out how own thoughts and feelings still. At the same time, he would need to be supportive of Jane and be there for whatever she needed. It would be hard to find the balance, along with everything else he had to handle during the day, but he would manage. Jane was worth it.

"I appreciate that. I'm not looking for an out. I don't know anything about children or parenting, but I'll try my best."

Jane offered Charles a warm smile. She knew this was completely out of his league, but she appreciated him trying. She was doubtful it would last, but when it did end they could both say they tried their best and there was nothing more they could do.

"The offer stands. For now, I am exhausted. I think I'm going to take a hot bath and then get some sleep." Jane could feel the exhaustion in her bones and she was looking forward to catching a quick nap to try and give herself some more energy.

"Of course. Do you need me to do anything for you? I can get some food for you if there is something in particular you'd like." Charles offered, just looking to help.

"No, I'm good right now, but thank-you." The last thing Jane wanted was food currently.

She gave Charles a quick kiss to his cheek before she headed up and made her way into their bathroom. She was hoping that after taking a hot bath and getting some sleep she wouldn't feel so rundown. She had a bunch of school work she needed to get completed and now she would be finishing her last year in College pregnant. Jane knew it was going to be a lot of work and it would leave her feeling more exhausted than she had ever been in her life, but she also knew it would all be worth it. The second she would be able to hold her baby in her arms, anything that happened before that moment would be completely worth it.

CHAPTER 11

Helena and James made their way into their lawyer's office that morning. They needed to meet with their lawyer to ensure that James' inheritance stayed with him and was kept far away from Jack. Helena had made a point of letting James know that he wasn't alone in this fight, that she would be there for him through it all. She didn't want James to feel like he had to handle his family on his own. She didn't care about the house or the money, to her it didn't make life worth living. However, she was damn well not going to allow Jack to bully his way into a fortune. She was not going to allow him to take what was rightfully his.

They made their way up, hand in hand, to the lawyer's office. Once there Helena removed her hand from James' so he could speak with the receptionist.

"Good morning, how may I help you?" The receptionist asked with a friendly smile.

"We have an appointment with Ms. Whistler." James answered.

"Your name please?"

"James Bentley."

"I will let Ms. Whistler know that you have arrived . You may have a seat in the waiting room."

James gave a nod and they both made their way over to the black leather couches that made up the waiting area. They both sat down and Helena placed her hand within James' once again to try and offer him some form of comfort and support. She knew it wouldn't be much, but it was all she could do for him right now. She would be his support pillar and make sure he knew that he wasn't going through this alone. That she would be strong for him when he couldn't be the strong one. Just like he had been her pillar of strength when she couldn't handle it.

"It'll be ok." Helena whispered.

"I just wish I didn't have to do this. That it didn't come down to all of this." James said with a great deal of regret to his voice.

James didn't want to have to go through all of this. He didn't want to have to get a DNA test just to prove that he was his father's son. It was ridiculous, especially because he died almost sixteen years ago. The time for DNA tests had long since passed. If Jack had doubts he should have addressed them when James was an infant, not when he was thirty-six years old. The other issue James was facing was the doubt. He couldn't help but wonder if maybe his own father doubted it as well. If maybe that was why he had been cold towards him. Maybe he always doubted if he was his son. Maybe Jack had influenced his father to make him question James' paternity. James wished he could have asked his father what he thought. To hear his father laugh and tell Jack that he was out of his mind and to leave it alone. Only that wasn't going to happen and all James could do was what was in his power to do. He was getting this test and working on a way to forever eliminate Jack from his life.

"I know, but this is the situation that we are in. All we can do is what is in our power to do. We go through this and make sure Jack has no place in our lives afterward."

"He will be out of our lives. I won't risk having Jack poison our family like he has tried to poison Charles and Jane's family. It's time we all stood up to him and make sure he has no power over us or the Bentley name." James said with a deep strength to his voice.

He was not going to risk having Jack pulling any crap with Charles and Jane's baby or his own one day. They needed to eliminate him from the family and the business. They deserved to be free from him and Wyatt's poison and it was time James and Charles took a stand to make it happen.

"Mr. Bentley, Ms. Whistler will see you now." The receptionist said with a warm smile.

James gave a nod and they both stood and followed the receptionist down the hallway to Ms. Whistler's office. Once inside the door was closed and James guided Helena over to the desk.

"Mr. Bentley, it's nice to meet you." Ms. Whistler said, as she held her hand out.

"Please call me James and it's nice to meet you. This is my fiance Helena." James said, as he took her hand.

"It's nice to meet you. And please call me Susan." Ms. Whistler said, as she took Helena's hand.

They all sat down and Ms. Whistler started the conversation. "Alright, from what I have gathered you James need to have a paternity test done to confirm that you were entitled to inherit your father's fortune. Correct?"

"That is correct, yes. My cousin, Jack Bentley, is making claims that I was not my father's biological child. He has demanded that I take a DNA test at a lab that he has picked. He told me I had two weeks to show him proof that I took the test otherwise he will freeze my bank accounts and evict us from our home. My cousin, Charles, told me to call you."

"As you should. It's not uncommon for wealthy families to demand a paternity test for them to inherit what is left to them. However, it should always be done through the courts to ensure the test is not tampered with and it is conducted in a proper testing facility. I will draw up the papers for you and have them filed within the court by the end of tomorrow. Your cousin, Jack, will receive a copy of them for his own knowledge. He can also give them to his lawyer should he wish to hire one.

Once the paperwork has been filed, he has no power to freeze any accounts or try and evict you from your home. He has to wait until the DNA results come in."

"I'm not worried about the results, I know my mother didn't cheat on my father. However, if that is not the case, I brought both of my parents' wills. They died together in a car crash from a drunk driver. My father died first and within ten minutes my mother died next. My father had his will set where everything would be left to my mother if she was still alive at the time of his death. My mother then made it so everything she had was left to me. Wouldn't that mean I inherited everything from my mother and not my father?"

James knew it was a complicated situation. His parents had died within minutes of each other. It wasn't like his father died years before his mother. It wasn't as black and white as a normal inheritance chain.

"I will need to review the wills, but the short answer would be yes. If the wills do state that everything from your father is given to your mother, even though she died ten minutes later, legally it still counts. Everything would have been her's the second your father's heart stopped beating. With that being said though, if it did come back that you are not biologically your father's son, it does complicate things. Your cousin could try and fight for the money still. He could go at it from a time of death standpoint. He could call into question who actually died first, especially because it was minutes and not days or hours even apart. Time of death is not an exact science like you see in the movies or on tv. A liver temp can only give you a rough estimate and most of the time doctors or paramedics just call time of death when they arrive on the scene or the body arrives at the hospital. Depending on how the paramedics treated each parent, your cousin could try and argue that your mother was dead first, but the paramedics got to her after your father."

That sounded like a complete mess to both James and Helena. They had no idea what happened at the scene of the accident, not even James knew. He was only twenty at the time of their deaths and it was a lot for him to handle. The drunk driver died at the scene, so James had no need to dig into the police reports. If Jack wanted to, he could make it a down and dirty fight to try and get the money.

"So it would be best that James was his father's biological son. Which we know he is." Helena said.

"Correct, the best outcome would be for James to be his father's biological son. At that point it won't matter who died first because it all would go to James. I understand that this isn't something you want to do, but it is best to do it through the courts. Too many times DNA results have been tampered with when no money was on the line. We are talking about an obscene amount of money. People don't tend to let that go, especially if they feel that they are entitled to it. You are doing the right thing here James, even if it doesn't feel like it."

And it didn't feel like it to James, not at all. He knew Jack was a selfish, greedy pig, but he didn't ever expect for him to go this low. To want to actually steal what his parents left to him, it was despicable and he would be lying if he said it didn't hurt.

"Is there anything I need to do for the paperwork?" James asked.

"You have a fax?" Ms. Whistler asked.

"I do at home, yes."

"I'll get the paperwork in order and fax it to you to sign. Once you fax it back I will file it within the court. Other than that you just have to wait until you are requested for the DNA swab. You don't have to be present for any of the court hearings I can represent you."

"Very well. Thank-you for taking the time to meet with us. I appreciate it." James said.

"It's my pleasure. I hope you both have a wonderful day." Ms. Whistler said, as she rose.

Both James and Helena shook her hand before they made their way out of the office and back to the car. Helena stayed quiet, she knew James needed some time to gather his thoughts and feelings on the matter. They drove home in complete silence and once there Helena made her way into the kitchen while James headed off to his office. Helena went to work on getting some coffee going and by the time that James got back it was ready. She was surprised to see that James had a land schematic with him.

"You got a new client?" Helena asked, as she placed the mug down in front of James.

"No. All of this with Jack has gotten me thinking about the future, our future. And not just mine and yours but Charles and Jane's as well. I wanted to have a piece of land that we could all turn into a vacation home or a summer home. A place where we can take our children and allow them the freedom of being outdoors to explore and make memories." James began to explain.

"It sounds wonderful. Did you find a place?"

Helena loved living in the city, but she also missed being further out in the country area. A place where you could have all of this land to run around and build on. A place where you could have a pool or a trampoline for the kids to enjoy. A place where you could have massive Easter egg hunts or birthday parties. It was an experience she would love for her child to have.

"I found the perfect place." James stated as he laid the schematic down. "Your childhood home."

"What?" Helena asked, shocked, as she looked down at the schematic.

She would know that house anywhere, even in a one dimensional drawing. She couldn't believe that James had purchased her childhood home. She had been heartbroken when she discovered the bank had taken it. She had considered purchasing it now that she had some money, but even though James always made a point of saying theirs or ours, she knew it was his. In her heart and mind she couldn't stop thinking about how it was his family money and not hers. She had been hoping that one day she would be able to buy it back from the bank, but she was nowhere near the asking price. The land itself was worth a lot more than the soon-to-be condemned house. The fact that James had purchased it and not just for them, but for Jane and Charles too, meant everything to her.

"I know the house won't be what it was when you grew up there, but we can try and keep as much of the structure as possible and add on to it so there is plenty of room for both families."

"I don't even know what to say. I loved that house growing up and it was devastating to lose it, to both me and Jane. I have always dreamt of fixing it back up, of making it into another generation. I love it and I can't wait to see what we come up with for it." Helena said with a huge smile as she went and tossed her arms around James.

"I can't either. It's going to be remarkable and it will be just ours."

James had no idea what the future would look like between him and Jack. What he did know though, his future was going to be bright with Helena by his side.

CHAPTER 12

It had been a month since Jane and Charles had discovered she was pregnant. She was now ten weeks along and so far things had been going well. Jane was surprised that there hadn't been any issues yet, but her doctor had said everything would be fine. That she could carry to term just like every other woman out there. It was a huge relief to her, but Jane was still constantly worried that something would go wrong. Jane was trying to not let that hold her back though from enjoying this time. She was only going to get to be pregnant once and she wanted to embrace it fully. Her and Helena had picked up a scrapbook and she was taking photos of her belly every week to track her pregnancy. She wanted to make sure she had something to remember all of this experience by. She also thought it would be nice for her child to see when they were older.

What had been different was Charles. He wasn't warming up to the idea like Jane had expected for him to. She knew he said he loved her, but she also knew he didn't say he wanted children either. He didn't seem excited to be a father. He didn't seem to be too interested. He was helping her when she wasn't feeling well. He would bring her some soup or he made sure she had water so she stayed hydrated. Still, he was doing that for her own welfare and not necessarily for the baby as well. He hadn't asked about the process or how it all worked. Jane knew it wasn't rocket science, but most guys had questions about how big the baby was getting, when it would move, when you could find out the sex, all of that. Charles hadn't mentioned it and there were no baby books laying around. Jane hadn't picked any up either, but she believed in knowing how to be a parent from your own childhood experiences. Plus no amount of reading was going to fully prepare her for childbirth or dirty diapers.

Jane was hoping that Charles was excited for the baby in his own way. She didn't know if he really showed that much emotion like this. She had seen him be happy of course, but she had never seen him be excited. She wasn't sure what that looked like on Charles' face or in his body language. Jane knew that eventually she would need to talk to Charles about it all, but she wanted to wait for now. There was no point in making him feel pressured into wanting this baby. She would wait it out and see how Charles dealt with it. If things didn't feel right when she was further along she could always leave. She refused to allow her child to grow up in a home where one parent didn't love or want them. She would rather be a divorce single mother than have her child feel unwanted or unloved by their father.

Jane made her way down the stairs and headed into the kitchen. Charles had left early for work and she was planning on spending the day working away on her school work to try and get ahead a bit. She was starting to feel a bit better as she approached her second trimester. She still had a few mornings a week where she felt pretty gross, but she was able to fight through it most mornings now. She was still feeling tired, but it wasn't as debilitating. Either that or Jane was getting used to being so exhausted all the time that her body thought it was normal.

Jane couldn't contain the large smile that touched her lips when she walked into the kitchen to see Anna there cooking waffles.

"Well aren't you a sight for sore eyes." Jane commented, forcing Anna to turn around.

She gave Jane a rich and warm smile as she went over to her and instantly wrapped her arms around her.

"There's my favorite girl. How are you feeling?"

Anna still couldn't believe that Jane was pregnant. She mostly couldn't believe that Charles was going to be a father. That was a milestone that she never expected for Charles to cross off in life. It wasn't that Charles hated children, he often donated money to charities and within the past year he had donated his time as well to help out. Charles just wasn't interested in having children close by him for long periods of time. The thought of Charles changing a dirty diaper was still good enough to make Anna laugh out loud. Charles had gotten better over the past year. He had been cooking and cleaning up after himself. He had terminated everyone, but herself that he had working around the house. It was good for him and Anna knew it made Jane feel better. She was a simple girl with down earth roots. She didn't like people waiting on her. The only reason Anna suspected they kept her on was because she was their family friend and the house truly was too big for one person to clean it. Jane would have to spend her days cleaning to keep the house in order. Something that wasn't possible with her being in school and running her own non-profit. They both needed the help to keep the house tidy and in order.

"I'm doing ok. The morning sickness is getting better. How was your trip?"

Anna guided Jane over to the stools at the island countertop before she went over to the waffles as she spoke.

"It was amazing. We traveled all over Europe working on different contracts. We had a lot of meetings, but it was a good trip. It is nice to be back here though. There's only so long you can live out of fancy hotel rooms before you start missing your well-worn comfy bed."

Jane gave her a warm smile. "I know what you mean. Whenever I've had to travel with Charles for work, as much as the fancy hotel rooms are fun, there's nothing better than your own bed."

"So true. How has it been with the baby?"

"Um, it's been ok. I mean it's not doing anything but making me feel sick and tired. But I guess this is the easier trimester because soon enough I'll be huge and unable to bend over to tie my shoes." Jane lightly joked.

Anna spoke, as she placed two plates down on the island countertop with waffles before she sat. "How are you doing with it all? It has to be a lot for you to take in considering you were told it would never happen."

"It's a lot, ya, but I am trying to make the most of it. I am trying to not be worried and stressed every second of the day. I even got a scrapbook and have been taking photos every week to track my growth. I'm trying to make the best out of the gift I have been given. My doctor said there was no way I was supposed to get pregnant, but I did. I won't get this miracle twice and I want to make sure I experience everything with it."

"And that is the best thing you can do. You need to allow yourself to embrace this experience fully so you won't have any regrets. I would completely recommend that you do everything to embrace this joyous experience. No matter how silly someone says it is. My good friend, when she was pregnant she went to this woman who makes a paper mache mold of your belly when you are eight or nine months pregnant. You can paint it if you want and she mounts it so you can hang it up." Anna said with a warm smile.

"That sounds beautiful. I'll have to do that when I am almost due. It sounds like a wonderful idea for a keepsake. Though the paper mache sounds a little cold." Jane said with a slight chuckle.

"Maybe just a little, but you would get used to it." Anna said with a dismissive wave before she continued. "How has Charles been handling things? I haven't asked him yet, I find those questions are always best left for in person."

742

Anna was worried about how Chalres was dealing with the shocking news. Not only did the man discover that the woman he loves has a medical condition that she had kept from him, not something that Charles would be happy about. But she was also pregnant, something Charles had never planned for. Anna knew deep down in her heart that Charles would make an amazing father. The problem was going to be convincing Charles of that fact. Charles had long given up on himself being a good man, they had his father to thank for that. Anna had been able to see the happy and go-lucky little boy that Charles used to be when his grandfather was alive. She had also been able to see when that little boy disappeared into an emotionally distant and self-absorbed man that didn't care about anything serious and neglected all responsibilities. She always believed that Charles had a massive amount of potential. That he could be anything he wanted to and that he could change this world for the better.

Ever since Jane had come into Charles' life she had started to see that good man that he had buried deep down inside of him. He was getting involved in the community, he was being more open with his emotions. He was even wearing jeans and having fun. It made Anna feel good to see it and she couldn't wait to see the man he would continue to grow into being. With that said though, she wasn't sure if he was ready for fatherhood, especially when his own father left everything to be desired.

"I don't know how he is. When I told him he was rightfully shocked. He knew I was on the pill so getting pregnant really wasn't something to be expected. Plus I had to tell him that I was told I had uterine fibroids and the most likely scenario was that I would lose the baby. It was a lot to take in and I knew it would be. But then we were told that I would be able to have this baby without those complications. I didn't expect much. I gave him an open out, but he said he didn't want it. Still, I thought maybe once the shock wore off that he would feel excited at least."

"Charles isn't used to showing emotions. He did when his grandfather was alive, but after his death he started to shut off his emotions. He has been that way for twenty-five years. It's only been since you have entered his life that he has started to open up more and come alive. He's still learning to allow himself to feel all of his emotions and to show them."

"That makes sense, I've never thought about that before."

Jane knew that Charles' childhood was hard, but she never thought about how it would have affected him emotionally. She could understand how it would be hard for Charles to show certain emotions when he was not used to feeling them.

"You have to keep in mind Dear that Charles did not grow up in a loving home, at least not for very long. He doesn't know what a father is, because his own was horrible. He is probably feeling very nervous and feels like he's not good enough to be a father. Give him some time, he'll come around."

"And if he doesn't?" Jane asked, almost too afraid to voice the words.

"He will. He's got a lot of months left for his mind to process and figure it all out. He'll make mistakes, but all new parents do. He might not know what makes a good parent, but he does know what makes a horrible one. And that my Dear, is so much more important." Anna offered with a warm knowing smile.

"I'll take your word for it."

Jane wasn't fully convinced, but if Anna believed it then she would trust in her gut. One thing Jane did know, she was happy to have Anna back. She knew with Anna by her side, she would be there to help her with her pregnancy and maybe with her around she might be able to get Charles to process things faster. At least, Jane hoped.

CHAPTER 13

It was a few days later when Jane was sitting outside one of her favorite cafes having lunch. Jane had been working hard to try and get her school work done while running her business. It was a lot of work before she had morning sickness and a heavy exhaustion plaguing her. She was currently feeling a lot better and she wanted to take advantage of it. She had fallen a bit behind in her work and she was going to get caught up today and tomorrow hopefully she would be able to get ahead so she could graduate this year. Jane did not want to lose out on her graduation or have to defer a year because of her pregnancy. She could finish her last school year and graduate, yes she would be eight months pregnant, but it was possible. She had worked too hard and for too long to achieve her dream and she was not about to lose it now.

After her talk with Anna she did feel a bit better about Charles, but at the same time she didn't. She kept hoping that each morning she would wake up to see Charles excited for the baby. And each morning she kept waking up to disappointment. It was hard and Jane was truly questioning how long she could do this for. How long she could live in this unknown realm of if she had Charles' support or not. If Charles wasn't going to be interested in providing true emotional love to their child, then she needed to know so she could move on with her life. She needed to find a suitable place for her and the baby. She needed to make sure she was financially stable so she could support her child on her own. She needed to get the divorce finalized, all before she gave birth because she didn't want any loose ends that could distract her from her child. There was only so long she could keep living this way and if Charles didn't start to show any signs that he wanted this baby, Jane was leaving.

Jane was not about to let a man dictate what her life was going to be like. She was a strong and independent woman, she didn't need Charles in her life for her to raise her baby. She could handle being a single mother. It might not be the choice she wanted. She would have preferred to have a two parent household, but she wasn't going to allow her child to be in an unloving and miserable home. If they couldn't live together, Jane would hope that they could co-parent and have his support, but she wasn't going to force it. Jane would prefer not to be a single parent, but she was strong enough to handle it. She wasn't willing to be unhappy just to make a family work. Jane knew that a child always suffered if their parents were miserable and she was not going to put her child through it.

Jane looked up when a shadow overtook her table. Jane saw there was a man standing there with a to-go cup of coffee in his hand. He had on black straight cut jeans, black combat style boots, a black t-shirt and a black leather jacket. The man had a built physique, but not overtly large. His shorter hair and his appearance had Jane thinking he was either currently within the military or he was ex-military. He was easy to look at, that was for sure. Jane had always loved a man that was rough around the edges. She liked a man that she could have passion with, a man that you could fight and make up with a great deal of passion. A man that you knew had lawyers and was deep and just slightly broken. That had been the type of man that Jane had always found attractive, because she could relate to them. She was a bit broken and didn't fit into any stereotype box. A man like that could keep her safe no matter what they came across.

"Good afternoon, you're Jane Bentley correct?" The man asked with a deep and slightly raspy voice.

"I am, yes. Can I help you?"

Jane wasn't sure who this man was or why he knew her name. She supposed he could have seen her within the press. She had been trying to stay out of the press and she was eternally grateful that Charles understood her desire to be kept as private as possible. It wasn't that she was ashamed of him or any of the work he was doing, it was just that she preferred to have a private life.

"I'm Carter Jones, I was actually just discussing with my hiring manager your non-profit. She informed me that you are looking to connect people with open positions within a company. I'd love to speak to you about it if you have the time."

"Of course, please join me." Jane said with a warm smile. She was always happy to speak to someone about utilizing their company for her clients.

Carter sat, as he spoke. "I appreciate you willing to talk with me. I don't normally do business this way, but when I saw you I figured it must be fate."

"It's no problem at all. I am always happy to meet with businessmen to discuss my business with them. Are you looking to hire from within my company?"

"I would be open to it, yes. It's my understanding that your non-profit focuses on helping those within the lower tax bracket to receive training for them to have a better job."

"That is correct, yes. I have found that people who are not overly qualified for a job position tend to stay longer, be loyal to the company and work harder. They appreciate the company more because they know what a chance and opportunity they have been given. I've never had a single complaint yet from any of the businesses that work with me."

"I believe it. I have worked with many different people from all walks of life and I know how hard people work when they have everything to lose. Some of the best workers I have been around have been those that were given a chance at a better life. My company is a security firm and we hire for security guards, sales associates, client representatives as well as personal assistants to help when we need to put on an event for our clients. I am always looking for new workers as I expand.

Would that be something your non-profit would be able to help us with?"

Jane was certain that they would be able to handle most of it. However, the security guard positions would be a trickier challenge. Security guards needed to undergo a specific training to ensure they understood the law and how to handle the physical aspects of the job. Not just anyone could carry a weapon or do a physical take down. It all required a certificate in a Government certified course. Jane wasn't sure where they were offered, how much it would be or how long the training would take. She would have to look into that more.

"Sales associates, client representatives and personal assistants I can definitely do for you, there's no problem there. However, and I am sure I don't need to inform you of this, but to be a security guard there is specified training. I'm not sure we my company is ready for that just yet. I would have to research it more to find the courses."

"My company works with a licensed school a runs the security course program. Doing the training is not a problem for us, my issue is finding decent workers. My hiring team seems to have a knack for hiring the worst employees possible. I have had to fire a great deal of them for lack of professionalism, not showing up, being reckless in the field, you name it. I am more than willing to train if the person will be dedicated to the job and take it seriously. Good employees are worth waiting for, I just need some help finding them." Carter said with a rich smile.

"Well, that is something I can definitely help you with. I have a few clients right now that are ex-military. They have been trying to get in with a few security firms, but without the certificate they have all been turned away without even a second look. As you are aware the security course is rather expensive and not something an employed person could afford. These men would love an opportunity to utilize their skills once again and if your company is willing to give them that chance, you'll have their loyalty and dedication for life."

"They sound perfect. I would love to meet with them and see what we can do. I'm glad I came here today for my coffee, it seems like we are going to have a great business relationship together." Carter said with a big smile.

"I look forward to it." Jane said with her own smile back.

Jane had no idea that she was being watched though by a man sitting in his car just across the street. Damon smirked as he took a photo of Carter and Jane smiling with each other. This job was all too easy for him. Wyatt had enlisted his services before and they were pretty run of the mill cases. Most of them were for him to try and get dirt on someone that was standing in Wyatt's way. He paid a high price and the work was easy. Damon didn't care whose marriage he was blowing up or what he had to do to get his full price, he always delivered and if he couldn't get real proof, he had no problems making it himself. He had been following Jane around for weeks and so far there was nothing interesting about her. That was until this morning when he overheard her talking on the phone. She was pregnant and Damon was willing to bet that Wyatt had no idea. He was going to be using it to get more money out of him, afterall, it was one hell of an information nugget. Damon sent the photo off to Wyatt and not even a minute later his phone was buzzing across the dash of his car.

Damon smirked as he answered. "Wyatt."

"The photo is good, but we need auto of her admitting to the fraud."

"She's not going to admit that on the first meeting. I'll get my guy to wear a wire next time. She seems to like him, you might get her on cheating. You could use that against her, assuming they have a prenup of some kind."

"Possible. Even if not, she's an idiot, I could get her to believe she would lose everything. It's a backup plan. Just get me what I need."

"I got something else for you." Damon started.

"What is it?"

"It's not a freebie. But trust me this tidbit of information is worth the price tag I'm going to put on it."

Damon didn't care, he knew Wyatt would pay up. He wouldn't be happy about it, but he would pay. There was no way Wyatt was going to let Damon not tell him and Damon knew it.

"Since when do you start changing the price?" Wyatt asked, completely annoyed.

He had worked with Damon for years and there had never been a single problem with him. Now he was looking to charge him more and Wyatt was not pleased by this, not at all.

"Since this new piece of information is very valuable. Trust me Wyatt, when have I ever not delivered for you?"

Damon didn't care what Wyatt said, he was paying him or he was not going to be getting this information.

Wyatt let out a deep huff before he spoke. "How much?"

"Five large." Damon said with a huge smirk as he watched Carter and Jane interact.

"If it's good enough, then fine. Otherwise you get nothing." Wyatt stated.

Damon gave a shrug, even though Wyatt couldn't see it, he wasn't worried about not getting paid. He knew how valuable this piece of intel was.

"Deal. Overheard a conversation, your target is pregnant."

"She's what?"

Wyatt couldn't believe this. Charles had slipped up and gotten a gold digger pregnant, not even Jack had been that stupid. Wyatt knew though that he could use this to his advantage. There was no way in hell that Charles would ever be willing to give up his money nor lifestyle for some brat. He would never raise a child and that meant Wyatt could use it to his advantage to get Jane to turn on him. Now she had a baby to support, it was one more thing that Wyatt could use to put a nail in Charles' coffin.

"He knocked her up. Can't see any bump, so she ain't that far along. Overheard her say it was a miracle, that she wasn't supposed to be able to get pregnant."

This was perfect to Wyatt. He could use this to get Jane to turn against Charles and if he couldn't, he could use the photos of her and Carter to get Charles to leave her. If he had Charles believing that Carter was the baby's father, he would kick Jane out. Then Jane would have no choice but to turn to Jack for help.

"That was worth every cent. Keep an eye on them."

"Got it." Damon said, as he ended the call.

He sat back with a smile on his face. He was going to enjoy this job a lot more than he had expected.

CHAPTER 14

"I still think it might be too early for this." Jane said, as she walked into the baby store with Helena.

She was now fourteen weeks pregnant and even though her doctor kept telling her that she would be ok, she was still paranoid. She was still worried that she would lose the baby. Going to look at nursery items and teenie tiny outfits seemed a bit premature to Jane. Still, Helena was insistent that they go and get a rough idea of what she liked and what she didn't. That way if they found any items that they wanted to order, they would have plenty of time for them to come in. Jane could understand her logic, but they still didn't know if they were having a boy or a girl yet.

"It's not too early. You are in your second trimester and your doctor said you would be carrying to term. There is no reason why you can't have some fun and get some ideas. We need to know what you want for the nursery so we can start getting things ready. You have about six months left, but they will go fast. We gotta get some ideas for the room and then we will need to start stockpiling clothes, wipes and diapers. Trust me, it's going to suck already having to be awake at two in the morning, the last thing you want is running out of diapers at that unholy hour."

"Because you would know with all those children you have running around." Jane said sarcastically.

Though if she was being honest, she had to give Helena points. She was right, it would suck to run out of diapers in the middle of the time. Jane could see the benefits of having a stockpile of diapers and wipes. Jane could also see her point in having a rough idea of what she wanted the nursery to look like. She knew that furniture pieces only came in neutral colors so she wouldn't need to know if she was having a boy or girl.

"It's common sense. Besides, some of the girls I used to work with have small children, remember? On more than one occasion I've had to listen to them complain about running out of diapers. There's no harm in looking."

I guess that's true. Jane thought to herself. She was constantly worried, but for right now she was going to enjoy this experience. She was going to enjoy allowing herself to dream and plan for what she could make her nursery look like.

"There is a lot of stuff in here." Jane said, as she tried to take it all in.

The baby store was divided up into two levels. On the main level there was clothing, toys, books and bedding. The upper floor was where all of the furniture was kept. Jane had been told by Anna that this place was a great one-stop shop for all baby items and they were reasonably priced. She knew how much Jane hated to waste money still and Anna had made a point in recommending places that she knew Jane would enjoy. Jane was really appreciating having Anna back.

"There is, but it's all very cute." Helena said, as she held up a tiny pink dress.

"Ok, that's adorable." Jane easily agreed.

"Do you care what you are having? Some people prefer one over the other."

Jane had never really thought about it. When she was younger she had obviously wanted to have a boy and a girl. She always thought it would be perfect to have one of each so her and her husband could have a mini me. Now that she was only going to be able to have one baby she wasn't sure what sex she wanted. All that mattered to her was that the baby was healthy.

"All I care about is a healthy baby. Other than that, it doesn't matter. The world is only giving me one chance to have a baby so if it's a boy or a girl, it's up to the world to decide. Whatever gender I have it will be because the universe believes they need to be in the world."

"Wow, that was very zen." Helena teased.

"Shut up." Jane countered, as she lightly pushed on Helena's shoulder, causing Helena to laugh.

"Ok, but I agree. As long as the baby is healthy then it doesn't matter if it's a boy or a girl. I bet Charles would want a boy though."

Jane spoke as they made their way through the store. "That would require for Charles to actually talk about the baby."

"You haven't spoken about it?" Helena asked, surprised.

She knew that Charles was shocked at first, but she would have figured that he would come around by now. That he would be able to get over the initial shock and process the news. They should have had a conversation about the baby by now. Lots of conversations. That was what expecting parents did. They talked about baby names and what they would like to have, what the nursery would look like. It was all very typical of happy expecting parents. It concerned Helena that Charles had yet to get over the initial shock, because then it wasn't initial shock and something more.

"Nope. I have been trying to give him time to process, but nothing. He doesn't ask me anything about the baby. He will ask how I'm feeling, but that's it. He doesn't even seem to be paying attention at the doctor appointments. And at the ultrasound the other day, our first ultrasound, he didn't even look at the screen. I don't know what I'm going to do."

Jane was reaching the point of no return with Charles. If he didn't change within the next few weeks, she was going to have to leave. She couldn't wait any longer for him to decide what he actually wanted out of their marriage.

"Well, what has he said about it?"

"I haven't asked him. We don't talk about it. We are two people living in a house right now. We don't even do anything sexually anymore. At first I was sick and tired, but even after the morning sickness wore off, nothing. We go to bed right next to each other and we barely touch. We used to sleep wrapped up in each other and now you could put a whole other person between us. I honestly don't know what to do." Jane said, feeling defeated.

"You have to talk to him. The man told you he loves you, but you never said it back. Maybe he doesn't know how he's supposed to act around you because he doesn't know where you stand. I mean I am in no way, shape or form taking his side in things. I'm just saying looking at it from his perspective. You have this woman who you love that is pregnant and you have no idea if she is even going to stick around. Maybe he's afraid to connect with your pregnancy because he thinks you won't stick around."

Jane could see where Helena was coming from and she had never truly tried to see how this whole situation looked to Charles. He had told her he loved her, but she had never been able to say it back. Jane was still feeling confused by everything. There were plenty of days where she hated the thought of leaving him and then there were days where she told herself that she could do it. Jane was confused and her pregnancy hormones weren't helping her any. Sometimes Jane thought maybe it would be best for her to up and leave. Maybe then she would finally know how she felt and how Charles did.

"Ok, that's fair. But it takes two to have a conversation. He could say something to me as well. He could act like he was interested in this baby. If he's so worried about me up and leaving, then why is he acting this way? If he doesn't want me to leave, then he's got a funny way of showing it. He should be trying to show me that he wants to be a father, that he wants our marriage to be something real."

"True, but you know men don't always think that way. You need to have a conversation with the man and see where you both stand. If you don't love him, the least you could do is put him out of his misery. "

Jane knew Helena was right. She had to talk to Charles and figure out their marriage once and for all. In order to do that she needed to determine how she felt about him. If she didn't love him and didn't think she ever would, then she needed to end it so Charles could move on with his life and find a new love.

"I will talk to him alright? We will figure it out. If he doesn't want to be a father then I'll find a place to live and figure out a job until my non-profit is able to handle me taking a salary."

"Or you could just live with me and James. You know you both will always have a room in our home." Helena easily offered.

"I know and I love you both for that. But if I do leave Charles, I need to stand on my own two feet. I have to have a place where me and my baby can build a family together. I'll talk to Charles and see where his head is at and what he honestly wishes to do about the baby. I'm not about to force anyone to be a father. If he doesn't have an interest in it, then that's fine. I need to know though before the baby comes. I'm not going to have a man coming and going out of this baby's life. That's not fair to a child. He's either all in or he's all out."

Jane would be sticking to it as well. She wasn't going to tolerate Charles bouncing in and out of their child's life. She was not going to put that level of disappointment within her child. It was something she was going to be making clear to Charles when they did finally speak. Helena wasn't too happy with Jane being willing to end things with Charles before even giving him much of a chance with the baby. She could understand where she was coming from, but at the same time she felt bad for Charles. He never expected to have children nor a wife. Now he was getting used to having a wife, and being a husband and he gets hit with a whole new shock of Jane's pregnancy. It had to be a lot for him to handle, to process. When women find out they are pregnant their minds can process it faster because they have to. They have a human being growing inside of them. The men tend to take a bit more time. They feel the weight of the responsibility more and that could come across as being distant or uninterested.

"I know that you feel strongly about this, but all I am saying is for you to give him a chance before you execute the man. Men and babies, it makes them go stupid. Even the smartest man in the world becomes a complete idiot the second that little plus sign shows up on the stick. You need to talk to him and be open to his feelings and be honest about yours."

"I will, ok, I promise." Jane agreed. "Now, can we please stop talking about it and focus on looking at baby things. Please?" Jane said with a warm smile.

She wanted to stop talking about Charles and her feelings. She wanted to focus ons something more enjoyable and right now that was looking at nursery ideas. She had no idea what was going to happen with Charles, but she knew that she was going to have this baby and she was going to enjoy every second of it. Starting with making a rough plan of what the nursery would look like.

CHAPTER 15

James handed Charles a cup of coffee before he sat down in his chair. Charles had come over when Jane went out with Helena to look at a baby store. James was all for the outing. It seemed exactly when Jane needed. He had seen Jane stressing and worrying over her pregnancy for weeks now and he knew it wouldn't be good for the baby. Helena had also been worried about Jane and when she had brought up the idea of taking Jane to the baby store, James had encouraged it. It seemed like the perfect way for Jane to see the big picture. For her to see that she was going to have a baby and she needed to build a nursery for the little one. James was hoping that Helena would be able to help Jane and he was hoping to be able to help Charles.

James had seen how Charles had been with Jane ever since he had discovered she was pregnant, and able to carry to term. He knew it was going to be a shock, but he had been hoping that Charles would have come around by now. James was worried that Charles was going to ruin his family before it even began. He didn't want that for Charles. He didn't want him to miss out on the opportunity to finally have a family of his own. To be a real dad to his child. James didn't want Charles to lose out on that, not when this was very possibly the only chance he was going to have.

"How is Jane doing?" James asked.

"She seems to be feeling better."

"How are you guys doing though?" James pressed.

Charles let out a sigh before he spoke. "I don't know. I'm trying to connect with the pregnancy, but I don't know if she loves me and wants to have a family together. She hasn't said anything and she seems to be distant recently. The intimacy we once had is gone and I don't know how to get it back. I don't know if she wants it back. We went for an ultrasound and I couldn't even bring myself to look at the screen."

"Why not?"

Charles had wanted to look at the screen; everything in his body had been screaming at him to look at it. But he couldn't. He couldn't because he couldn't get attached to a baby that he might never get to see. He wasn't fooling himself, he knew he was going to be a terrible father, but he did want the chance to try. He was madly in love with Jane, but he had no idea what she was feeling. He couldn't get attached to another human being and have to watch them leave.

"She's going to leave. I can feel it. She's distancing herself. She is constantly working on her school work or she is out meeting with employers for her non-profit. She isn't home barely anymore and when she is she's not present. She doesn't try to touch me, she doesn't kiss me. When I go and try to touch her, she moves away. Even in public, I can't even hold her hand anymore. I can't get attached to this little baby and then have to say goodbye to them. She doesn't want me, I have to respect that."

"Just tell her how you feel. Maybe she doesn't even notice that she has been pulling away from you. She's hormonal, she could be feeling any number of things. Besides, from what I have gathered from Helena, Jane doesn't know what you want to do. You both need to talk before it gets out of hand."

Charles wasn't so sure about that. He doubted that Jane was feeling uncertain about his stance, because he was still there. He didn't kick her out, he didn't tell her he wanted an abortion. He thought he had been supportive with helping her wherever she needed it and taking care of her while she didn't feel well. He thought he had been a very supportive husband.

"I'll speak with her later. I didn't come here to discuss Jane though, I came here to discuss the company's future."

"What about it?"

James knew that things at the company were getting very tense. He was only in a lower level position, but he had heard enough whispers about the tension on the Board. Jack was still trying to block Charles from expanding the company and offering more life saving surgeries and treatments. Jack was digging his heels in because it hadn't been his idea and to Jack the prestige of an insurance company came with your denial rate. The more money you had the better your company and if the Board agreed to Charles' proposal that mant the company would lose more money. Charles had determined a way for the company to make triple what they were making now while still paying out more. That was why half of the Board was all for Charles' plan. However, they needed a majority vote and so far they were dead center down the middle.

"I think it's time we talked about your position within the company. Right now you are just an administrator, but you should have a seat on the Board. Your last name gives you that right and Jack has been trying to take that right away from you since you were born practically. I think it's time we took it back."

Charles knew it would be a fight with Jack to get James on the Board. However, James was a Bentley and that gave him the right to have a seat on the Board. Jack wouldn't be happy about it, but he also couldn't fight what was biologically James' right. They may have to wait until the DNA test results came in, but they could start the process nonetheless.

"You know Jack won't be happy about it. He doesn't want me on the Board. He doesn't even want me in the family. I don't get why, because him and my father got along very well."

"He likes money, you know that. I overheard Wyatt and him talking a few years ago about how Jack was supposed to inherit everything from your father, but it was changed to you. He probably feels like your mother trapped your father and he lost out on millions of dollars. It's not personal, it's his greed."

"His greed has cost him a great deal where family is concerned. You would think he would have seen that by now." James said with a small shake of his head.

"You know Jack, he doesn't care about family. All he cares about is money and prestige. It's all about keeping his image in tack. He got married because it would make him look better. Not to mention his sexual desires are not typical. Jack only cares about himself and everyone else is expendable, especially if you stand in his way."

"How would I even get on the Board? Doesn't he have to approve?"

"Your last name gets you a seat. That's the rule, but Jack has always made sure you wouldn't request a seat."

"But with the court case, would I be able to have a seat?"

James wasn't sure he even wanted a seat on the Board. He knew his seat would push the vote in Charles' favor and he was all for it. He agreed with Charles' vision for the future of the company. He wouldn't have a problem helping him, but being an active member of the Board wasn't something he wanted to truly do. If he could do it as a part-time gig and still be able to focus on his own company then James would be fine with it. He had been slowly working his way out of the company so he could focus on his own business. It was something he wanted to talk to Charles about.

"You could, but we might have to wait until the DNA results come in. You took the test so we should know within six weeks. You don't have to accept a seat, but the offer is there."

"I don't have a problem with a seat on the Board, especially if it will help you to put the company in the right direction for the future. However, I wanted to talk to you about quitting my position within the company. As you know I have been working on my own land development company and I would like to focus on that full-time."

Charles had known that James was working on his own company and he couldn't have been prouder of him. He had known that James loved building ever since he was a young boy and he would have already been a developer had he been allowed. It was one of the rules within the Bentley family that all males were to work within the company, whether you liked it or not. Charles had no idea what he would be doing if he had been given the option to do something else. He did enjoy his work though and he knew that James wasn't happy with his position within the company. If James wanted to leave, he wasn't going to be trying to convince him to stay.

"The Board only meets once a month and you obviously don't have to work at the company to be on the Board. If you want to quit, you are more than welcome to. I'm not going to try and keep you there. I know you have a contract, but I can come up with some legal reason why you can be let out of it. I just want you to be happy James." Charles said with a warm smile.

"I would love to be let out of my contract. My company is starting to take off and I would like to put all of my focus into it. It would also give me some time to start working out what to do about the new vacation home."

Charles gave a nod. He had been more than happy when he heard that James had purchased Jane's and Helena's childhood home. They were all going to work on it and see what they would be able to come up with. They would make something that would work for the future and their expanding families. At least that was the plan, now Charles had no idea what was going to happen with the home. He would still help them with it, because he wanted to make sure Jane was taken care of and their baby even if she left. He was still going to love her and he doubted he would ever be able to love any other woman in his life. Jane was too special and he was going to make sure she was always taken care of and protected.

"Any idea what the plan is for the house?"

"Not yet. The house itself is pretty rundown and most of it will have to be rebuilt. We are going to try and keep as much original character of the home that we can. I was thinking we should expand the house to accommodate for two families. We don't really have anything drawn up officially, just some rough ideas. Helena said Jane was very enthused about the house and what we could do with it."

"Yes, she was happy to hear that it would get to stay in the family. It was a good idea and I am sure the children of the future will love it. I was thinking with the extra land, we should put in a pool."

"I like that idea. I also want to have a wooden fence all along the property as well. I really like the pool idea, there are some great companies that can build amazing and custom pools. We could meet with them and draw something up."

"Works for me. If we could have all of the construction going on at the same time it would be easier. How's the wedding planning going?"

"It's good. We're going to be getting married in six months. It's going to be simple and intimate."

The wedding planning had been going very well. James and Helena had decided to do it all themselves so they could make sure it was exactly what they wanted without anything extra added. It was a lot of work, but they both knew it would be worth it in the end.

"I'm happy for you two." Charles said with a warm smile.

He had no idea what was going to happen between him and Jane, but he knew that James and Helena would have a great marriage. Unlike him and Jane, they were marrying for love and they were a perfect match. Charles had no idea what was going to come from his talk with Jane, but he was hoping that maybe he would know one way or the other if their marriage was over or not. Charles was hoping he would be strong enough to handle that conversation.

CHAPTER 16

The second Jane walked into the house she was annoyed. There wasn't anything that had made her annoyed; it was more of the fact that she would have to once again walk on eggshells and tiptoe around Charles. She was getting sick of feeling uncomfortable in a place that was supposed to be her home. This had to end, she just didn't know how it would end, but it needed to. Jane walked through the house until she was able to locate Charles. He was in the study working away at his desk. When Jane walked into the room Charles didn't even look up and that only fueled Jane's annoyance.

"Hey." Jane said, as she leaned against the doorway.

She had no idea how she was going to even start this conversation but she knew it was time they had it. Helena was right, they couldn't keep tiptoeing around this. Jane had enjoyed her time at the baby store though. It was good for her to be able to get an idea for items that she wanted for her baby and what they could use. There were a lot of great items that she had never seen before or even knew existed. She was feeling more excited about the baby now that she had seen the store and gotten some ideas for the nursery.

"Hello." Charles said with his head still down as he focused on his work.

That was Jane's breaking point. The fact that Charles didn't even give her the decency to look up and acknowledge her presence just told Jane how much he doesn't respect her. She was done with this. She was done with him. She was done with their marriage. She was just completely done.

"Are you kidding me? You won't even acknowledge me and yet we're supposed to be married. You're supposed to be in love with me. Is that what love is to you?" Jane started in a harsh tone.

Charles was instantly looking up. He had been so focused on the paperwork in front of him that he hadn't even realised it was Jane speaking to him. He had only heard a voice and he automatically responded. He didn't mean to ignore her or make her feel like he was actively ignoring her.

"No, no that is not what love is. I'm sorry, I didn't even realise it was you. I have been working on this endless stack of paperwork for the office. I'm sorry Kitten."

"And what's your excuse for the past few months? You have been ignoring me from the moment I told you that I would be keeping this baby. You barely speak to me. You have slept on the couch four nights a week for weeks now. You don't kiss me, you don't hug me, you make sure to avoid any forms of contact with me when we are out in public. Like you are ashamed of me. You don't ask about the baby. You show no interest in anything having to do with the baby. You didn't even look at the ultrasound. Our first ultrasound of our baby and you can't even be bothered to look at the screen."

Jane could feel her whole body starting to shake. She knew she had to be careful, that she couldn't allow for her emotions to become out of control. It wouldn't be good for the baby. Still, she was finally getting the words out that she had been holding within her for months now. She was finally going to be able to tell Charles exactly what she was feeling.

"What the hell are we even doing here Charlie? You don't want to be a father, you don't want a baby. You have made that perfectly clear in your actions. So what the hell is the point in us being together? I told you months ago that if you didn't want this life to tell me, but you kept your mouth shut. And instead of being a man and saying you wanted out you have allowed me to be a sucker. To be dragged around waiting for you to finally step up or tell me to get out. Well, I am done waiting for you to decide to be a man. For you to decide that you actually want a real family with me. I'm done. We're over."

Jane didn't even wait for Charles to respond to her. She turned around and stormed down the stairs. Charles sat there shocked for a moment. He had no idea that Jane had felt that way at all. He thought she was feeling conflicted about their marriage and he wanted to wait and make sure she knew what she wanted. He thought she was the one trying to keep distance between them. He had no idea she felt like it was his doing. Charles could acknowledge that he had been keeping some distance between them because he had been waiting for Jane to leave him. He had been trying to prepare himself for when Jane left with his unborn child. He had no idea she felt this way. He was instantly getting up and chasing after Jane. He found her outside going to her car and he instantly panicked.

"Jane, wait please." He said, as he ran over to her.

"I'm leaving and there is nothing you could tell me right now to change my mind." Jane said, stubbornly.

"If you want to leave, I'm not going to stop you. But please you can't drive when you are like this. Please let me call you a car and they can take you anywhere you want. Jane please, think of the baby." Charles begged.

He didn't want to risk Jane driving right now. It wouldn't be safe for her being this emotional and with her body trembling to drive. He had to make sure she took a car so he knew she would at least be safe. The very last thing Jane wanted was anything from Charles, but she couldn't argue against him on this. She was too worked up to drive and she was not about to risk getting into an accident. Jane just gave a nod and Charles quickly called her a car. Once he put his phone away Jane spoke.

"Leave me alone."

Jane headed off to go to the end of the driveway. It was a long walk, but it was better than being around Charles at the moment. Charles had no choice but to stand there and watch as the woman he loved walked away from him. He didn't go inside, not even when he could see Jane at the very end of the driveway where she waited for her car. He wanted to make sure she got off ok and he wouldn't have been able to focus on anything else until he knew she was safe in the car. He knew she would be going over to James and Helena's place. That also brought comfort to him because he knew she would be safe and taken care of there. James would make sure she was settled in and he knew Helena would be able to speak with Jane and hopefully get her to calm down.

Charles knew he had a lot of work to do to make all of this up to Jane. He hadn't seen the signs that something more was going on between them. He thought he had to wait until Jane made a decision on their marriage. He failed to realise that he had a say as well. That she could have been waiting for him to do something to help her make that decision. Charles didn't know if he would be any good at being a father, but he had decided he wanted to try. He wanted to be there for Jane and for the baby. He wanted his family and a future with her. He had a lot of work he needed to do to prove to Jane that he was serious about his family. Charles was determined though to prove it to Jane. He was going to win her back even if it was the last thing he had to do.

*****

Jane found herself having to fight the tears back as she sat in the car. She was on her way to Helena and James' place and she was hoping they would be home. She knew she should have called, but she also knew that Helena wouldn't care if she showed up unannounced. It wouldn't be the first time they had just appeared at the other's place. Jane knew she was the one to walk away, but she didn't expect for it to hurt this much. She didn't expect for her to be crying and upset. She felt like a piece of her heart had just been destroyed and she would never be able to get it back. She never thought she loved Charles, but now she knew the truth. She did love him and now she had lost

768

him. It hurt so bad. Jane had no idea something could hurt so much. She thought she would be ready if she had to leave him. She thought she would be strong enough to get through it, but she was wrong. It hurt so bad, so much worse than she could ever imagine and she had no idea how to make it stop.

"Thank-you." Jane forced out once they pulled up to the house.

She was instantly getting out and heading for the door. She knocked and waited for someone to answer. She knew they had been keeping the door locked to keep Jack from entering the house whenever he wanted. After a moment the front door opened and Helena was standing on the other side. Jane could no longer hold the tears back and she let out a deep sob at the sight of her sister. Helena was instantly pulling Jane into her arms as she spoke.

"It's going to be ok."

Helena moved them both back into the house. She closed the door as she continued to hold onto Jane. After a moment Jane pulled back and tried to wipe at her cheeks to remove the tears. It was pointless though, because they kept going. Helena guided them over to the living room and sat them both down on the couch.

"Try and take a slow and deep breath." Helena advised.

Jane did her best to try and get herself back under control. It had been such a long time since she had cried like this. She almost never cried and when she did it was always when things had reached a breaking point. After a moment she was able to get her breathing back under control.

"It's over. My marriage is over and I didn't realise until it was over that I love him." Jane said with a great deal of hurt.

"What happened?" Helena asked, gently.

"I want to speak to him, but he didn' even acknowledge me when I said hello. I got upset and I told him everything I was feeling. That he was being distant and not wanting the baby."

"Ok, what did he say?"

"Nothing. I didn' even him the chance to say anything. I stormed out and he stopped me just before I got into my car. He called me a car and I went and waited for it alone. He didn't try to stop me from leaving. He didn't tell me I was crazy and that he was in love with me and the baby. He didn't say anything about what I said to him. He just told me to not drive. He really doesn't want the baby, he doesn't want us."

"But you don't know that. He didn't tell you that." Helena tried to reason.

"He didn't say it either Hel. He could have opened his mouth and screamed that he wanted us. That I was reading into everything when I shouldn't be. He could have tried to stop me from leaving. He didn't say anything. That right there tells me everything I need to know."

Helena knew it sounded bad, but she also knew that things could be said in the heat of the moment, things that people didn't mean. She also knew that sometimes in a fight the other person doesn't get the chance to argue back because their partner takes off before they could even process what was happening. Charles might not care about them, but from what Helena had seen he was in love with Jane, she couldn't imagine that Charles didn't want a family with her.

"Look, it's been a long day. I think the best thing you can do is to take the night off from him. Have a bit of space and allow yourself to process everything and give him time to think over what you said. You can go and speak with him tomorrow and see once and for all what he wants to do."

Jane knew their marriage was over, but she could see Helena's point. She had to take some time to calm down and think about what she wanted. Tomorrow she would go and see Charles and get what the truth is once and for all. Tomorrow she was either going to be a married woman or she was going to be a soon-to-be divrocee. Tomorrow would tell and that scared the hell out of Jane.

CHAPTER 17

It was the next morning and Jane was sitting outside of the cafe on her own. She had appreciated Helena and James last night. They didn't talk about what happened, they just allowed her to be hanging out on the back deck as she tried to get her own thoughts in order. When she woke up this morning she had decided that she would go and speak with Charles once more to finalize everything. If she was going to leave him, then today she would be packing up her things and leaving. She wasn't going to draw it out. If her marriage was over she wanted it to be a clean break. She was going to enjoy some breakfast alone and then she was planning on heading over.

Jane was dragged away from her book when Jack sat down in the chair across from her. Instantly her mood soured at the sight of the man. She hated him and had made a point of avoiding anything that had to do with him for the past fifteen months. And now it seemed like he had found her.

"What do you want Jack?" Jane asked, with a sharp voice.

"That's not a very polite way to say hello to someone Jane." Jack said in a condescending voice.

"That's because I don't like you." Jane simply said.

"The feeling is mutual. The good news is you will be out of my life soon enough."Jack said, as he tossed down the photos of Jane and Carter.

Jane looked down at the photos and two things happened. The first she was pissed off that she had been followed and the second Jack had clearly been the one to hire the person following her. She was disgusted by this man and the lows he would go to just to try and manipulate the people around him.

"You've had someone following me?" Jane asked with an edge to her voice.

"My investigator was able to snap these lovely photos of you and Carter. Carter works for my guy so I wouldn't expect his call anytime soon. I have to give it to you though Jane you are smarter than I thought you were. No matter what Carter said, you wouldn't give up the truth. You wouldn't finally admit that it was all a lie. That your marriage was a fake."

"My marriage isn't a fake. As for intelligence, you are the one trying to prove the same thing for over a year now with zero results. You are never going to be able to prove we committed fraud, because we didn't. The money is not yours, it belongs to Charles. Get the hell over it."

Jane was sick and tired of this man trying to get money that didn't belong to him. He was a bully, a lazy bully, that wanted to have everything that wasn't rightfully his. He tried to steal Charles' money and when that didn't work he was now trying to steal it from James. It was ridiculous and Jane was sick and tired of this man. There would be one good thing to come from her marriage being over, she would finally be free from Jack and his insanity.

"That money does belong to me. He was my brother and I was set to get it all from our father and then from him. Charles doesn't deserve it, I do. I don't care what I have to do, I will win. I will get my hands on what is mine. Now, you have two choices. You can either keep your mouth shut and foolishly stand by Charles. If you do that, then I will go to him and show him all of these photos. I'll tell him you have been cheating, that the bastard baby you are carrying isn't even his. He'll throw you out and you will lose everything. Or, you can tell me exactly what I want to hear and I'll make sure you get some compensation to cover you for the next few years. It's simple really, even for a small minded woman like yourself." Jack said with a smirk.

Jane couldn't believe that Jack thought he could try and threaten her. That she would just give in and tell him what he wanted so she could walk away with some money. It was the dumbest thing she had ever heard. Even if she hated Charles, she still wouldn't tell him anything about their marriage. She wasn't a gold digger and she didn't care about the money that Charles had. Jane had no idea if Charles would believe she had cheated on him or not. She had no idea if he would believe the baby wasn't his or not. That was something entirely different. But she had informed him of Carter and what his business was. Jane would hope that Charles wouldn't believe his uncle over her, but she couldn't say for certain.

"I am going to make this very clear to you Jack. My marriage, my family, with Charles is very much real. He would never believe that I cheated on him. He knows who Carter is, he knows that we have been working together for my business. Nothing you tell him or show him will change that. He's not going to believe you. He's not going to kick me out. And I will never tell you our marriage was fraudulent, because we love each other." Jane collected her things before she stood. "You are nothing more but a sad and pathetic old man Jack."

Jane headed off and got into her car. She couldn't believe that Jack had tried to convince her to go against Charles. Had offered her money like she was some prostitute that stood on the street corner. It pissed her off and she wanted to desperately see that smirk wiped off his face. She would love to be there the day he lost everything. Jane let out a huff before she turned her car on and started to make the drive back to the house. She had something she needed to get figured out with Charles first and then she would deal with Jack.

*****

Jane walked into the home that she shared with Charles. She wasn't sure if they were still going to be sharing it. It truly depended on how this next conversation went. She was going to take Helena's advice and talk calmly with Charles and see what they both wanted. If they both wanted different things

774

then the only logical decision they could make would be to walk away. Jane was expecting to find Charles in the living room or the kitchen with it being still early in the morning. However, Charles wasn't on the main floor at all. Jane made her way up to his study, but once again it was empty. Jane checked the bedroom, but it was also empty. Jane was starting to question if Charles was even here, but she saw his car in the garage when she parked her's. Unless he took a car, he had to be here.

Jane made her way down the hallway to see if Charles was anywhere else in the house. She was shocked to find him in what used to be a rather large reading room that was right next to their bedroom. The room normally had bookshelves all along the walls and a couple of old leather style chairs to read in. They never used the room and according to Charles, the room was more for show than actual use. That his father had never stepped foot into the room. Jane couldn't help but be shocked when she saw that the room was completely empty. Not only was it empty, but Charles was in it painting. The walls were almost complete and it was a smokey grey color. The exact same color that she had told Helena she loved for the nursery. He was actually painting the room and Jane couldn't help but hope that meant that Charles wanted to make this room the nursery.

"Charlie." Jane said, snapping Charles' attention away from the wall he was finishing up.

He turned to look at her and Jane couldn't stop her heart from skipping a beat. He was wearing blue jeans and there were paint speckles on them. He had a black t-shirt on and his biceps looked amazing in the shirt. I had to give it to him, he always looked sexy.

"Hello Kitten." Charles said, as he put the roller down into the tray.

"What are you doing?" Jane asked, softly as she moved further into the room.

"Helena told me that this was your favorite color for the nursery. That you liked how you could add accents in blue or pink, depending on what we're having." Charles moved closer to Jane as he continued to speak. "Jane, I'm sorry for coming across as distant. I love you, I am madly in love with you and I do want this baby. I wasn't sure at first. My father was horrible, you know that and I have no idea if I'll be any good, but I do want our family. I thought you were still uncertain about us and I was afraid to get attached to this baby only for you to leave me. It wasn't because I didn't want you, I was just scared of losing the both of you. I'm so sorry Kitten."

Jane couldn't help the tears that instantly built in her eyes. She never expected for Charles to tell her this and it was exactly what she needed to hear. She should have talked to him about it last night. She shouldn't have gotten so angry with him. Helena had been right, she had to look at things from Charles' point of view and he had felt exactly how Helena had guessed he did. Jane hated that she had made him feel like she was going to up and leave him. That wasn't what she wanted. She was upset with herself, because Charles had been waiting to see what she would do when all she had to do was talk to him. All of this could have been avoided if they had just communicated better. It was a mistake she was not about to make twice.

"I love you Charlie and I want our family. I want you."

Charles' chest flooded with a deep heat at hearing those words coming from Jane. To hear that she did in fact love him. That she wanted their family to work. It made him feel like he was on top of the world. Charles placed his hands on the side of Jane's face closer to the base of her neck and pulled her in for a passionate kiss. Jane instantly melted against Charles' lips. She had missed the feeling of his body against hers and it felt even sweeter today. She couldn't believe she had almost thrown it all away and it would have been over nothing. It would have been over her own foolish mistakes and stubbornness. To think that they could have avoided all of this if she had just opened her mouth and told him what was on her mind. Jane wasn't going to make that mistake again. She wasn't going to risk losing the man that she loved over something so silly and pointless.

After a moment when the need for breath became too great, Charles pulled back. He hated that he had to break their connection. He wanted to keep kissing Jane. He wanted to take her to bed and enjoy every square inch of her body. He had missed her so badly over the last few months and he wanted nothing more than to make up for the time they had missed.

"I love you Kitten." Charles said with a deep love to his voice.

"I love you too Charlie."

Jane took Charles' hand and started to pull him out of the room as she spoke once again. "I think after that level of a fight we are going to need at least a day of make up sex. Think you can handle it?"

Jane knew very well that Charles was more than capable of handling it and she was going to enjoy every single second of this day. Tomorrow she would burst their bubble and tell him about Jack. But today was all about them and she was not about to let that old man ruin it.

"We'll have to stop for breaks so you can eat and rehydrate." Charles said, as he placed his hand on Jane's belly for the first time before he continued. "You both are far too important to me for anything to go wrong."

"I have zero problem with eating in between rounds." Jane easily agreed as a warmth flooded her chest.

"Then you Mrs. Bentley, are all mine for the next twenty-four hours." Charles said, as he kissed Jane's neck.

"And every day afterwards." Jane promised.

CHAPTER 18

It wasn't until the next afternoon did Charles and Jane finally wake up. They had spent the entire day and most of the previous night reconnecting with each other. They had made breaks throughout the time to ensure Jane ate. When it was time for their dinner break and Jane was craving Chinese food desperately, Charles easily ordered everything her and the baby were craving on the menu. It was an amazing day and night and the both of them couldn't have been happier if they tried.

"How do you feel about leftovers?" Jane asked, as she looked in the fridge.

"Sure, I'm easy." Charles easily agreed.

"Oh I know." Jane said with a playful smile that caused Charles to laugh at.

"Only for you." Charles said, as he placed a kiss to the side of Jane's neck before he spoke again. "Now go sit. I'll get the food."

"I can help you know." Jane said, as she went and sat down on a stool at the island.

"I know, but you have enough going on and it's my job to take care of the both of you. I'm no chef, but I can certainly work a microwave." Charles said with a warm smile.

"You are a better cook than you give yourself credit for."

Jane sat there and enjoyed the view of Charles in just his boxers cooking them some food. This was something that they had been able to do a lot more often within the past year. Anna had been living here, but she had moved out to live with Cooper. She still came by twice a week to help keep the place clean. Jane and Charles cleaned up after themselves, but it was a rather large house and it needed a good professional clean a couple times a week. Jane also knew it was Charles' way of being able to still take care of Anna, but also giving her the freedom to enjoy her second chance with the man that she loved.

Charles placed the plates down on the countertop once they were ready. He then made sure to grab a glass of orange juice for Jane before he sat down next to her.

"Thank-you, this smells amazing." Jane said, as she started to grab some of the food.

"I know we haven't spoken much in the past few months. I know you are trying to get your last year of schooling completed and also running your non-profit, but do you need any help with any of it?"

Charles wanted to make sure that Jane knew he was going to be there for her no matter what. If she needed help with her non-profit he could handle it while she was pregnant and trying to finish school. He understood why Jane wanted to keep going and not have to defer her schooling for a year. It was her final year and it had been a long time coming. She deserved to graduate on time. She had worked extremely hard to get to where she was and Charles wanted to make sure she could graduate with her classmates.

"I'm ok for now. My school is going well and I have been able to work ahead in some of my courses. I might need some help with the non-profit later on, but right now we're doing good. I have to file for taxes though for the first time in two months." Jane said, a bit worried about that.

"I can help you with them. And by me, I mean my amazing accountant that handles taxes for the company." Charles said with a smile.

"As long as it's not me for the first year I am good. I have no idea how to file business taxes, much less not-for-profit taxes.

Everything in that retrospect though is going well. There is something we do need to talk about though."

Jane really didn't want to have this conversation with Charles, but she knew they had to. She couldn't keep this from him, because she knew for a fact that Jack was going to show Charles those photos. He didn't want Charles to be caught off guard, that wasn't fair to him.

"Of course, anything Kitten you know that."

"Yesterday morning before I came here I was at the cafe when Jack showed up." Jane started.

"What the hell did he want?" Charles asked with a slight edge to his voice.

He had been having to deal with Jack over the past few months more often that he would have liked. Charles had been trying to get Jack out of the company and he suspected that Jack knew it. Charles didn't care though, because he still had half of the Board on his side. He had also been making sure that Jack didn't discover that Jane was pregnant. He didn't want him to add any stress to Jane's life. He wanted this pregnancy to go well for her because it was the only one she was going to get. If that meant he had to deal with Jack more, then so be it.

"He showed me photos that he had of me. Apparently, he's been having me followed by a private detective. He had photos of me and Carter."

"He's been what?" Charles asked with a deadly edge.

He was furious, beyond furious, that Jack had been watching his wife. She didn't deserve this and he was pissed that he hadn't noticed it was going on. He knew Wyatt and Jack weren't going to let the money go, but he never expected for them to target Jane like this. He was going to be putting a stop to it.

781

"He told me he wanted me to confess that our marriage was based on fraudulent intentions. Otherwise he was going to show you the photos and tell you that I was having an affair and that the baby wasn't yours."

"He's a fucking idiot. I know you have never cheated on me. You told me about Carter and his security company. Though, we could probably assume that Carter doesn't have a security company and is just working for the private investigator. What else did Jack say?"

"That if I told him what he wanted to hear, that he would give me some money to get me through. I told him off and then came here. I don't know how he found out I was pregnant."

"He's had a private investigator following you for months now, he could have overheard a conversation or seen us leaving the doctor's office. He knows that if we have a child then he's place in the family goes further down. Think of it in terms of medieval times. We're the King and Queen and the only way that Jack could get the crown is if we have no children. Our child would make Jack even lower on the list for who could get the money. It's why once the baby is born I'll have to redo my will to ensure the baby is in it and place James and Helena as representatives of the baby should we both die before he or she is eighteen."

"That makes sense. So what do we do?"

Jane had never thought of it like that. It made sense why Jack would be trying to get Charles to believe the baby wasn't his. Only Charles knew Jane, he knew his wife better than anyone and he knew that she would never step out on him. All Jack was going to do was upset Charles even more, something that wouldn't end well for the man.

"You don't have to worry about Jack or Wyatt. I will handle them, same as our lawyer. If they become too problematic I will have them removed, one way or the other. I am already working on a way to get Jack out of the company. James is helping me with it. The only thing you need to worry about is that baby and keep him or her inside of you until it's time. That is the most important job you have Kitten."

"Ok, I don't like it, but I understand. After this baby is born though you and I are going to be a team again where Jack and Wyatt are concerned though."

Jane was not bing to allow Charles to have to handle all of this on his own. She was his wife, his partner and she would be there for him.

"You won't hear any arguments from me." Charles said warmly.

Jane gave a warm smile in return before she changed topics. "We have the ultrasound in two hours. We might be able to find out what sex we are having. Is there one you are rooting for?"

"It doesn't matter to me. As long as the baby is healthy, I will be happy either way."

"Me too. I have a catalogue from the baby store that Helena and I went to the other day. Maybe later you would like to look at it with me. There's some things in there that I liked." Jane offered, trying to get Charles more involved with the pregnancy.

"I would love nothing more." Charles said, before he leaned in for a kiss, one Jane willingly gave in return.

Jane felt relieved that Charles wasn't angry at her for everything that had been going on with Jack. She knew he wouldn't believe that she had stepped out on him, but it was still nice to hear that he did believe her. That not even for a split second did he doubt her. It only hit home to her how much he did love her and she knew they would be able to handle anything that came their way.

*****

Jane laid there on the exam table with her eyes locked on the monitor. Her left hand was in a tight grip of Charles' hand as they both waited to see if they would be able to discover what sex the baby was. Both of them were excited and anxious to find out because then it all started to become more real. They would know if they needed to purchase pink or blue items. If they needed to pick out a boy or a girl name. If they were going to have a prince or a princess. It was special and they couldn't wait until they would finally get to find out.

"Ok Mom and Dad, are you ready?" The ultrasound technician asked.

"God yes." Jane answered for the both of them.

"You are going to have a little boy." The technician informed them with a bright smile.

"Oh my God, we're having a boy." Jane said with a big smile to Charles.

"A son, I'm going to have a son." Charles said, amazed.

He didn't care if they were having a boy or a girl, but deep down he did want a son. He wanted the chance to play catch with him. To go off-roading and to teach him how to fish. He wanted to do everything with his son that his grandfather had taught him. It was a special bond and he desperately wanted to carry that bond on. He was going to get to have a son and show him the love that his grandfather had shown him. It was perfect and Charles couldn't have asked for anything better.

"You are going to be an amazing father." Jane said with a loving smile.

"I promise you, I promise him, that I won't be like my father. He is going to know what love is and what fun is. He's going to get to enjoy playing in the dirt and going on imaginary adventures. He's going to enjoy getting to be a child." Charles promised.

Jane went and placed her free hand against the side of Charles' face before she spoke. "I know you are. You are going to be amazing with him. And we are going to raise a brave and adventurous little boy that knows exactly what love is."

"I love you Kitten," Charles said with a deep love to his voice.

"I love you Charlie."

Jane couldn't have been happier than she was at this moment. They were going to have a son together and it was going to be amazing.

CHAPTER 19

"I feel like a beached whale." Jane commented, as she sat down in her Maid of Honor dress.

She was currently seven months pregnant and she felt every single minute of it. The last few months Jane had been able to graduate with the help of Charles. He had taken over running her non-profit for her when she was too exhausted and overworked to do it. Jane loved him for it even more because he cared about her business just as deeply as he would his own. He had been able to keep it going and running smoothly while she was needing to focus all of her energy on her schooling. As the weeks went by Jane was getting more tired from her pregnancy, but Charles never complained. He was always there for her. Cooking meals, running her a bath, giving her a massage, he even helped her get her shoes on when she could bend over that way anymore. He was the sweetest man Jane had ever met and she couldn't believe how far he had come since the moment she first met him.

She couldn't help but feel like they were both different people that night when Charles opened his door to her. She was there with his food and she thought he would just be another stuck up rich bastard that would at least tip well. She never expected to be madly in love with him and having their son just shy of two years later. It was surreal and yet Jane wouldn't change a single second of it. She wouldn't change any of their fights or memories because they all lead them to who they were today and that wasn't something Jane would ever wish to change.

"You look beautiful." Helena said with a warm smile.

Today was Helena and James' wedding day and they were having it at Jane and Charles' house. They had an arch set up in the backyard by the pond for the ceremony. They were only having a small gathering, twenty-five people, for the whole ceremony and the reception afterwards. Both James and Helena wanted a small and intimate wedding and having it at Jane and Charles' house was perfect. It was where they had started their relationship and developed deep feelings for the other. It felt perfect for them to have their wedding here. They had hired a caterer to handle all of the food and they had an event planner set up the backyard. The food was going to be buffet style and they would have tables set up outside for people to sit and mingle. They had even hired a DJ and set up an area outside for a dance floor. It was going to be beautiful, especially once the sun went down. The backyard was decorated with solar lights that would provide a very romantic feel to it tonight.

"You look gorgeous." Jane said, as she took in Helena in her wedding dress.

It was a mermaid gown that hugged all of her amazing curves. She looked like a princess and it fit Helena's body and personality completely. She was a gorgeous bride and Jane knew she was going to make an amazing wife and eventually mother.

"How are you feeling?" Helena asked, still worried about Jane being pregnant with it being warmer out today.

"I'm fine, you don't have to worry about me. Charles is going to be doing that enough for everyone, trust me on that. The closer I get to being full-term the more he worries."

"He wouldn't be a good man if he didn't worry. All guys worry when the woman they love is pregnant and could go into labor very soon. Don't worry he'll be fine once the baby comes."

"Did you decide where you wanted to go for your honeymoon?"

Helena and James had been going back and forth on where they wanted to go or what they wanted to do for their honeymoon. Jane wasn't sure what they had decided to go with just yet.

"We are going to Italy. We're going to visit a few different cities and spend a lot of time on the beach."

"And in the hotel." Jane said with a knowing smirk.

Jane knew for a fact that Helena and James were going to have an amazing honeymoon, but she also knew they would have a hard time leaving the hotel room. That was what Jane and Charles had a hard time with and they weren't even in love when they went on their honeymoon. Helena just chuckled and she had to agree with Jane, it was going to be hard for them to leave the hotel room, but she wanted to see Italy so she would make sure they came up for air so they could explore.

"It's going to be a lot of fun and I plan on picking up a bunch of baby stuff while I'm there."

"You are going to spoil this baby."

"That's an auntie's job." Helena said with a smirk.

Jane rolled her eyes playfully just as there was a knock on the door before it opened. Anna walked in and gave both Jane and Helena a bright warm smile.

"You both look beautiful."

"Thank-you, you look amazing." Helena responded with her own smile.

"Everyone is ready. Are you set to get hitched or do we need to run to the car?" Anna teased.

"I can't run, but I can waddle behind you." Jane added, which caused both Anna and Helena to light laugh.

"Both of you stop. I am not running, or waddling anywhere. I love James and I am going to marry that man today."

"Then let's get this show on the road. That man has waited long enough to marry you." Anna said warmly.

Jane pushed herself up and off the couch with a groan. She couldn't wait until she was no longer pregnant and would be able to enjoy the freedom of moving around again. Still, she was loving every second that she could experience being pregnant. Every minute that this little man stayed inside of her was another minute he would make it to full term and that was all Jane needed to keep going in the day.

*****

James stood there at the front of the aisle waiting for when Helena would be ready to start the ceremony. Charles was currently standing beside him as his best man and it was the only thing keeping James calm. He wasn't nervous, he wanted to marry Helena. He wanted to marry her more than anything in the world. But he was anxious for that very reason. He wanted to finally make her his wife so they could start their lives together. They were finally going to be married and they could start their own family soon. James wanted nothing more than to experience life as a husband and as a father one day.

"You good?" Charles asked.

"More than good. I've been waiting for the moment for so long, I can't believe it's finally here."

"I know. It's insane to think how far we have both come within the past two years. Who would have thought we would both be married to sisters? And not just any sisters, but two amazing and strong women that don't care if we have a single dollar in our bank account. It's unreal still to me when I think of it."

"It is unreal and I couldn't be happier to have them both in my life." James said with a warm smile.

He had never expected to be able to get married. He was a lot like Charles in the sense that he didn't want to marry a woman that only cared about money and what she could purchase with it. He wanted a partner. Someone that he could trust and rely on when he needed help. He didn't want to marry a woman that he would have to take care of like a child. Helena was everything he was told he wasn't allowed to have and she was perfect for him. James couldn't imagine going through life without Helena by his side and he was determined to make sure he never had to find out.

"Me too, cousin." Charles said with a smirk.

James couldn't help the soft snort at Charles' word choice. He had received his DNA results finally two months ago and James was indeed officially a Bentley. That didn't make Jack nor Wyatt happy at all. They had crawled into a hole and had disappeared for the past two months, but they both knew they would be back. There was no way that Jack and Wyatt were going to let all of this go. They wanted their money and when you were talking about the amount of money that both Charles and James had, you didn't give that up easily. James had accepted a seat on the Board now that he had legal proof that he had a right to a seat. That only pissed Jack off even more and with James on the Board, Charles' plan for the company was able to move forward. Ever since that Board meeting Jack hadn't been around.

James had been focusing on his own company, but he had helped Charles with his new plan to get it all set in motion. He was going to make millions off of his shares in the company so James was more than willing to help grow the company. He also knew how important it was to Charles to ensure that more life saving treatments were approved. He wasn't going to put any amount of money over someone else's life. Charles was refusing to make the same mistakes as his father. It was going to be a lot of work, but they both knew it would be worth it.

"Thankfully Jack isn't going to crash the wedding. That would be under him." James commented.

"He won't show, he would have to eat a huge slice of humble pie. He won't show up until he has another plan put in place. It's going to be an endless war with battle after battle until he finally dies, but we'll handle it. We don't need to talk about him today. Today is all about you and Helena. Jack has no place here in physical form or in conversation."

"I couldn't agree more." James easily agreed.

Anything else he had to say went right out the window when the music started and he watched as Jane started to walk down the aisle. James looked over at Charles and he could see the deep love in his eyes for Jane. They were both madly in love and James couldn't have been happier for the both of them. They made a perfect couple and he knew they would be amazing parents. Everything around James faded away as his eyes landed on Helena, the woman he loved. She was gorgeous, breathtaking in her wedding dress. James couldn't believe he was lucky enough to be able to marry her. To be loved by her. He never expected to be able to have a partner in his life and he never expected for his partner to be as amazing as Helena. She was perfect in his eyes and he was the luckiest man alive to be able to marry her.

Helena gave James the biggest teary eyes smile as she arrived at the front of the altar. Helena noticed that James looked very handsome in his suit. She loved when he dressed casual, but she also loved how sexy he could look all dressed up in a suit. And she loved that this sexy man was all her's.

"Dearly beloved, we are gathered here today to celebrate the love that James and Helena share for each other. They are two spirits that have finally found their soulmate within this world. They have prepared their own vows to share here today." The Officiant started.

With a nod to him, James spoke. "Helena, from the moment we met I knew you were different to any woman I had ever met. You fascinated me and then you surprised me. You were apprehensive at first, but I would have chased after you all over the world for the rest of my life. You are my everything. You are the light in my darkness. You are my strength when I don't

791

have any. You are the beauty within my world. I never want to go a day without you in my life. I promise to always support you. To always be your light when the darkness reaches you. I promise to love and cherish you, to never take you for granted. I love you more than anyone in this world and I am proud and honored to be your husband."

The tears that Helena had been trying to hold back lost the fight at James' words. They were perfect and it meant everything to Helena. She couldn't believe that she had been able to find a man like James. He was everything she ever wanted and Helena never wanted to go through this world without him.

"Now you got me crying." Helena said with a small smile. James gave her a warm smile as he reached up and wiped at her cheeks for her.

Helena cleared her throat before she spoke. "James, I couldn't stand you when we first met. I thought you would be everything I hated and I had no interest in giving you the chance to prove me wrong. But you wouldn't give up. You wormed your way under my skin and quickly stole my heart. You showed me what it felt like to be loved, to be cherished. You showed me that I didn't have to always be so hard and tough. That it was ok for me to be vulnerable around you. We've had ups and downs and I wouldn't change any of them for a single second. I love who we have grown into being and I can't wait to see how much more we grow together. I promise to always be by your side, to always defend you whether you need it or not. I promise to support you and love you. I promise to be your wife and your best friend in this life and in the next."

James wanted nothing more than to kiss Helena at this moment, but he knew he couldn't. He had to wait just a little bit longer before he could finally kiss her.

"James, if you would repeat after me please." The Officiant started. "I James, take you Helena to be my wife. I promise to be true to you in good times and in bad, in sickness and in health, I will love you and honor you all the days of my life."

"I James, take you Helena to be my wife. I promise to be true to you in good times and in bad, in sickness and in health, I will love you and honor you all the days of my life." James repeated as a flood of warmth filled his chest.

"Helena, if you would repeat after me please." The Officiant started. "I Helena, take you James to be my husband. I promise to be true to you in good times and in bad, in sickness and in health, I will love you and honor you all the days of my life."

"I Helena, take you James to be my husband. I promise to be true to you in good times and in bad, in sickness and in health, I will love you and honor you all the days of my life." Helena said with a bright smile.

"It is with my pleasure to announce to everyone for the first time, Mr. and Mrs. James Bentley. You may now kiss your bride." The Officiant completed.

That was all James needed to hear before his lips were pressed against Helena's. Everyone clapped and stood as James and Helena got lost in their kiss. They had been waiting so long for this moment and now that it was finally here, they couldn't believe how amazing it felt. They were finally married and now their life together could truly start.

EPILOGUE

Jane had no idea something could hurt this much. She had woken up around midnight to a deep pain all across her stomach and lower back. She had originally thought something was wrong, but then her water broke and she knew she was in labour. Charles had immediately gotten up and grabbed her hospital bag and helped her to get dressed and into the car. Jane had to give it to the man, he had been a lot calmer than she was expecting. They knew she could go into labor any day, but Jane still didn't believe it. She was thirty-eight weeks pregnant and the size of a baby elephant, at least she thought she was. Charles never missed an opportunity to tell her how beautiful she was, big and all. Jane had called Helena on the way to the hospital as well as Anna. both women had been vital to her getting through this pregnancy and she wanted them both there for the birth. Anna was family, and Jane always made sure she knew it. They always included Anna in every family event.

Her and Cooper had been doing amazing, they even adopted a dog that had a love for travel just as much as they did. Anna had already been spoiling the baby and he wasn't even here yet. She said it was what an auntie did and neither Jane nor Charles had the heart to try and stop her. Anna was too old to start having children, it was never in the cards for her, but she was planning on spending a lot of time with the baby. Anna had even offered to move back in for a little while to help them with the baby. Both Charles and Jane had taken her up on the offer. They were both a nervous wreck. They still knew nothing about babies and having the extra help would be a godsend. Anna had worked with babies before as a nanny, so she would be able to help get them started and teach them a few tricks.

"You're doing great Kitten." Charles said, as he stood right by Jane's hospital bed.

Charles knew that Jane was in pain, but she was refusing any pain medications. The doctors had assured them both that it would be ok for the baby, but Jane wasn't taking any chances. A completely natural birth was best for the baby so Jane was pushing through the pain. Charles had to respect her wishes, but he hated that he couldn't take the pain from her. He knew the pain would almost instantly stop once the baby was born, but it wasn't easy. It had been four hours since they had arrived at the hospital and the pain had only gotten worse. Helena had taken up a post on the other side of Jane and was holding her other hand. James and Cooper were currently waiting in the waiting room for when the baby would be delivered.

"Ok Jane, you are ten centimeters dilated. On the next contraction I want you to push down as hard as you can." Dr. Roberts said with a warm smile.

"Ok." Jane said with a very exhausted sounding voice.

She wanted this baby boy out of her so the pain would go away. She knew it would once the baby was born, but she also knew it would get worse before it would get better. She just needed this baby to be born and then she would be able to finally hold her own child in her arms. That was the only thought getting her through all of this. She needed to desperately hold her son in her arms. She never thought she would ever get that moment and now that she was this close to it, she wanted nothing more in this world. At the next contraction Jane moved so she was sitting up a bit more. Jane began to push and Dr. Roberts spoke.

"That's it Jane, push down for as long as you can."

"You are doing so good, Kitten." Charles encouraged.

Jane pushed for as long as her body could allow her before she had to stop. She was breathing heavily, but she knew she wouldn't get much of a relief from the pain before the next contraction would hit.

"If you push as best as you can on the next five contractions Jane, then this baby boy will be out."

That was all the encouragement that Jane needed. She spent the next fifteen minutes pushing off and on before finally their son was born. Instantly the pain was gone and the room was filled by the only sound of an infant's cry. It was the sweetest sound that either Jane or Charles had ever heard and instantly it brought tears to both of their eyes. Their son was really here, he was alive and here with them. Everyone kept their eyes on the baby as Dr. Roberts took him over to the infant table to clean him up and check him over.

"Is he ok?" Jane asked, as a nurse took over making sure she was ok after giving birth.

"He is doing just fine. I just have to do an exam to make sure everything is normal." Dr. Roberts advised.

"He's beautiful." Helena said with a proud smile.

"How much is he?" Anna asked, as Dr. Roberts put him on the scale.

"He is six pounds and eleven ounces. He's a good size."

Jane and Charles had no choice, but to wait until Dr. Roberts was finished with their son before they would be able to hold him. That moment came five minutes later when Dr. Roberts placed the baby in Jane's arms. Jane couldn't stop smiling as she looked down at her crying son. He was beautiful and absolutely perfect.

"He's our son." Jane said with a tearful smile to Charles.

"He's perfect. You did amazing Kitten." Charles said, before he kissed Jane on the forehead before kissing his son's forehead.

"You are all set here Jane. I am going to get you a private room set up. He is perfectly healthy and so are you." Dr. Roberts said.

"Thank-you so much." Jane said with a warm smile.

"You are most welcome. Would you like me to inform your friends in the waiting room that they can come in?"

"That would be great, thanks." Jane answered.

Dr. Roberts gave a nod and she headed out with her nurse. Once they were alone Jane looked over at Charles as she spoke.

"How about you hold your son Daddy."

Charles wanted nothing more than to hold his son. He gently took him from Jane and the second he held his son in his arms he felt this flood of warmth overtake his whole body. He was a father. This was his son and he was going to make sure that his son grew up knowing just how loved he was. He was going to follow in his grandfather's footsteps and raise him like his grandfather had raised him. He was going to make sure that the cycle was broken and there would be a new generation of Bentley men. Men that could be strong, but also have emotions and not be bound by the ridiculous notions that their society dictated. His son was going to embrace everything within him and live the life that he himself dedicated and not anyone else.

"Knock, knock." James said, as he opened the door.

"Hey, come on in." Jane said.

James and Cooper were instantly walking into the room. James went over to Charles' side and looked at his new baby cousin.

"He's adorable." James said with a proud smile.

"He is perfect. Absolutely perfect." Anna said with tears still building in her eyes.

The others all had to agree Jane and Charles had made a perfect little baby and now all they needed was his name.

"What's his name?" Helena asked.

Jane and Charles hadn't told anyone what their son's name was going to be. They wanted to keep it a secret until he was born. They wanted a bit of a surprise with it, especially because it was going to be a very special name for the family. Jane looked over at Charles and gave him a small nod to let him know that he could be the one to say it.

"Allow me to do the honors of introducing you all to our son, Henry James Bentley." Charles said with a great deal of love to his voice.

When Jane and Charles were trying to come up with a name for their son, they had bounced around different ideas. But the one they kept coming back to was Henry James. They wanted to honor Charles' grandfather, the man that was a true father to Charles. They wanted to make sure his name got to live on. They chose James as his middle name to represent James being their son's godfather.

"Oh it's perfect." Anna said with a rich smile.

"Ya man, it's perfect." James said, as he fought to talk around the lump in his throat. He had no idea they were going to give their son his name. It just showed James how much they both loved him and appreciated him in their lives and now their son's life. They were a family and now they had a new member to love and cherish.

*****

Jane stood there as she looked down at her son sleeping in his crib. They had just arrived home from the hospital and Jane was feeling tired, but she didn't want to leave her son just yet. He looked so cute when he was asleep. The past couple of days had been long ones, but they weren't as bad as Jane had been expecting. She had spent the past two days in the hospital. With her being a new mom it was regulations by the hospital to keep her and Henry for two days to ensure they were both ok. Jane was more than ok with that as the lovely nurses had taught her how to feed, change and bathe Henry safely. There was a learning curve, but she was more than determined to beat it. Charles had been amazing. He never left their side and he was always asking questions and making sure he was doing everything he was supposed to when helping to take care of Henry. He was being a very hands-on father and Jane loved him even more for it.

"You need rest too Kitten." Charles said softly, as he placed a kiss on Jane's shoulder.

"But he's so cute." Jane protested and Charles gave a soft chuckle to it.

"Yes he is. Come on, you need sleep, he'll be up before we know it."

Charles guided Jane out of the nursery and over to their bedroom. Jane had been getting up with Henry every time he cried and the result was her not getting enough solid sleep. Now that they were home he was going to make sure that Jane got proper sleep.

"I'll get him when he wakes up. You need to get more than two hours of sleep Kitten."

Jane wasn't too happy about not getting up with Henry, but she understood that she needed to get enough sleep so they don't have to worry about her developing postpartum. Charles helped to get Jane changed and into bed. He then picked up the baby monitor so he could take it with him.

"I love you." Jane said warmly.

"I love you too my beautiful wife."

Charles placed a soft kiss to Jane's lips before he moved back and headed out of the room. He went back to the nursery and looked down at his sleeping son. He still couldn't believe that he was a father. He had no idea if he was going to be a good one, but he was going to do everything he could to make sure he wasn't like his own father. His son was here, but the war was just beginning. He still had to fight with Jack for the company and Charles knew it wasn't going to be a fair and clean fight.

Jack wanted to take everything from him and he wasn't going to stop until he was dead or he had taken everything from Charles. Charles wasn't going to let that happen. He would protect his family and he would take Jack out once and for all, even if it was the last thing Charles did.

THE END

FREE BONUS CONTENT

Thanks for purchasing Books 1-5 of Bridget Taylor's new series "The Accidental Engagement Serics". <u>BEFORE YOU START READING THIS COLLECTION</u> I strongly recommend you sign up to my mailing list below. There is BONUS FREE CONTENT that compliments this book that you can ONLY get from my mailing list.

Just go to https://bit.ly/aebonuscontent to Sign Up to Get Notified of New Releases, Giveaways and Free Bonus Content

MAKE SURE YOU SIGN UP TO Bridget Taylor's VIP list FOR free below. YOU WILL GET LOTS OF

COOL STUFF FOR FREE AND GET NOTIFIED OF ALL THE NEW AND EARLY RELEASES!

Just go to https://bit.ly/aebonuscontent to sign up

*EXCLUSIVE UPDATES

*FREE BOOKS

*NEW REALEASE ANNOUCEMENTS BEFORE ANYONE ELSE GETS THEM

*DISCOUNTS

*GIVEAWAYS

*FREE BONUS CHAPTERS AND CONTENT

FOR NOTIFACTIONS OF MY _NEW RELEASES_:

The Sign-Up Page Will Look Like This:

Join Bridget Taylor's Exclusive Mailing List for FREE BONUS CONTENT and Discount Coupons

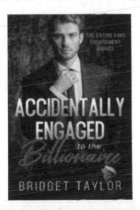

☆ Click below to receive free bonus content, discount coupons, take part in giveaways and get notified of Bridget Taylor's new releases.

☆ A new series is about to be launched. You will be one of the first to be notified with a discount coupon.

CLICK HERE TO SIGN UP

AUDIO BOOK

Make sure you get a copy of the audio book of The Accidental Engagement Series Books 1-5. You're going to want to listen to it as well as read it :-). It's a great compliment to reading and enhances the experience. I strongly recommend you listen as well as read. Especially, if this is something you haven't tried yet. Give it a try. You will LOVE it!

If you have an Audible Membership, go to https://bit.ly/aeboxedsetkindlebookaudioboxedsetpromo to get The Accidental Engagement Series Books 1-5 Audible Version

For those of you that do not already have one , you can try it for one month for FREE and you can continue after that with a small monthly fee if you wish. You can cancel at anytime. :-)

**Just go to
https://bit.ly/aebookonekindlebo
okaudiobook1promo to Try
Audible for One Month for
FREE and Read the Accidental
Engagement Series Books 1-5**

Made in the USA
Middletown, DE
29 November 2021